PENGUIN CLASSICS

THE EGOIST

GEORGE WOODCOCK was editor of *Canadian Literature*, which he founded in 1959, until 1977 when he retired. He has received many literary awards for his books and in 1973 was awarded the Molson Prize, the highest Canadian award for achievements in the arts and humanities. He received the UBC Medal for Popular Biography in 1973 and again in 1976 and was made a Fellow of the Royal Society of Canada in 1968. He has published some forty books – on travel, history, verse, literary criticism and biographical studies. His latest books include *Thomas Merton: Monk and Poet*, *The Canadians*, *Taking It to the Letter*, *Confederation Betrayed*, *The Benefactor*, *Letter to the Past* and *Collected Poems*.

•

GEORGE WOODCOCK has also edited William Cobbett's *Rural Rides*, Herman Meville's *Typee*, Charles Dickens' *A Tale of Two Cities* and Thomas Hardy's *The Return of the Native* for Penguins.

GEORGE MEREDITH

✕✕✕✕✕✕✕✕✕✕✕✕✕✕✕✕✕✕✕✕✕✕✕✕✕✕

The Egoist

EDITED WITH AN INTRODUCTION
BY GEORGE WOODCOCK

PENGUIN BOOKS

PENGUIN BOOKS

Published by the Penguin Group
Penguin Books Ltd, 27 Wrights Lane, London W8 5TZ, England
Viking Penguin, a division of Penguin Books USA Inc.
375 Hudson Street, New York, New York 10014, USA
Penguin Books Australia Ltd, Ringwood, Victoria, Australia
Penguin Books Canada Ltd, 2801 John Street, Markham, Ontario, Canada L3R 1B4
Penguin Books (NZ) Ltd, 182–190 Wairau Road, Auckland 10, New Zealand

Penguin Books Ltd, Registered Offices: Harmondsworth, Middlesex, England

First published in 1879
Published in Penguin Books 1968
9 10 8

Introduction and Notes copyright © George Woodcock, 1968
All rights reserved

Printed in England by Clays Ltd, St Ives plc
Set in Monotype Bembo

Contents

✠✠✠✠

George Meredith was born in 1828, the son of a Portsmouth tailor. He was educated in local schools and later at the Moravian School at Neuwied near Coblenz. In 1844 he was articled to a solicitor but turned instead to writing, publishing *Poems* in 1851 and his first work of fiction, *The Shaving of Shagpat*, in 1856. In 1849 he had married Mary Ellen Nicolls, Thomas Love Peacock's widowed daughter. After a few years the marriage foundered and, having left Meredith, Mary Ellen died in 1861. In 1864 he married Marie Vulliamy. From his first introduction to the literary world, Meredith became a hard-working man of letters, acting for many years as reader for Chapman Hall, and devoting much time to journalism. This, however, did not interrupt the flow of his novels. The best known were *The Ordeal of Richard Feverel* (1859), *Evan Harrington or He Would be a Gentleman* (1861), *Emilia in England* (1864) – later republished as *Sandra Belloni* (1886), *Rhoda Fleming* (1865), *The Adventures of Harry Richmond* (1871), *Beauchamp's Career* (1876), *The Egoist* (1879), *The Tragic Comedians* (1880), and *Diana of the Crossways* (1885). His most important works of non-fiction were his volume of poems, *Modern Love* (1862) and his *Essay on Comedy and the Uses of the Comic Spirit*, 1897. After a long period of relative neglect, Meredith became famous and respected in his old age, and in 1905 he received the Order of Merit. He died in 1909.

Introduction

I

The Egoist is George Meredith's most self-consistent and characteristic novel. It is the work in which he makes the least concession to the ways of Victorian novelists and to the pre-dilections of Victorian readers; in which he reveals most openly the tensions between his own nature and his philosophy of living; in which he exposes with the most accurate and merciless of laughter the distortions of feeling which a society of self-seekers imposes on its devotees.

The Egoist was not the most popular of Meredith's novels among his contemporaries; that distinction was reserved for *Diana of the Crossways*, a much weaker book, in which he compromised notably with the sentimentality he himself always denounced. It was not even Meredith's own favourite, perhaps because in writing it he had exposed too much of himself; he gave his preference to that heroic failure, *Beauchamp's Career*, a strange combination of probable politics and unlikely passion.

Yet *The Egoist* is the book for which Meredith is most re-garded at that crucial period in a writer's fame, the second half-century after his death; today it is probably more read and certainly more discussed than any of his other novels. Like Congreve's *The Way of the World*, which Meredith regarded highly, and Wilde's *Importance of Being Earnest*, which as far as I know he never even mentioned, it is among those *jeux d'esprit* in which art and intellect dance together in forms that are literature's nearest effective approach to abstraction. In Meredith's other works his mannerisms and artifices perplex and annoy; in *The Egoist*, for once, they are entirely appro-priate, entirely absorbed into a carefully integrated structure of speech and thought.

The thought is important, for Meredith's intent in writing
The Egoist was far from that of producing a work of art for
art's sake. Wilde's occasional propagandizing for a hedonistic
libertarianism may perhaps be dismissed as a lapse of aestheti-
cist consistency; Meredith never ceased to be – in his own way
– a self-consciously didactic writer, and even *The Egoist*
reflects his didacticism. He had definite and detailed views on
the need to live naturally. In his novels the physical exertions
in which he rather loudly indulged in daily life were transferred to the positive characters, and in such a context became
the symbols of a healthy attitude to existence. He had, moreover, strong opinions on that malignant sickness of Victorian
England, the class system, and the agonies of snobbery and
social pride which he suffered within himself were transformed into fiction so that they might be observed and
analysed with exemplary effect.

More tenuously, in the shadow of the Meredith concerned
with moral-social problems, there lived a political Meredith.
Though James Thomson called him 'the Browning of our
novelists', and Wilde slyly amended the definition into his
famous quip, 'Meredith is a prose Browning, and so is
Browning', the only attitude that Meredith and Browning
tangibly shared was a common political concern for the
Italian Risorgimento, which aroused Meredith's enthusiasm,
sent him to the front as a correspondent during the abortive
war between Italy and Austria in the summer of 1866, and
resulted in two romantic novels, *Sandra Belloni* and *Vittorio*.
At home Meredith professed himself a Radical, but a sure
instinct told him that writers are best outside political activity
and his one burst of electoral campaigning, when he can-
vassed for his friend F. A. Maxse at Southampton in 1867,
was most important for the literary use he made of it in
Beauchamp's Career.

At least one Marxist critic has devoted a lengthy book to
arguing Meredith's right to be considered a class-conscious
revolutionary novelist (Jack Lindsay, *George Meredith: His*

Life and Work, London, 1956). Yet, though the political scene figures in most of Meredith's novels, in part for the good reason that in that age of Reform by easy stages politics were the active concern of the kind of people he portrays, his principles were diluted in practice by the fact that he was a hard-working man of letters who did not always show very delicate scruples as to how his pen was used; for years, as an anonymous editorialist for the Tory *Ipswich Journal*, he wrote for money against his avowed political allies.

His concern with class was genuine and passionate – as it has been with so many English novelists of the past two centuries – but it was rarely expressed in direct political terms, mainly because he was less interested in the machinery of politics than he was in the more delicate mechanisms by which social conventions affected individual men and women, shaping their outlooks and perverting their feelings. Even in *Beauchamp's Career* the actual election is less important as a political event than as a symbol of Nevil Beauchamp's attempt to break free of the conventions of his own upbringing and of the effect of that attempt on his relationships with others of his class. In *The Egoist* politics echo hardly at all; there is merely Sir Willoughby's vague intention to enter Parliament in some unspecified future. But the novel would not exist at all if it were not for Meredith's passionate opinions about the effect of Victorian ruling-class conventions upon human feelings. The very first sentence confesses the fact:

Comedy is a game played to throw reflections upon social life, and it deals with human nature in the drawing-rooms of civilized men and women, where we have no dust of the struggling outer world, no mire, no violent crashes, to make the correctness of the representation convincing.

In other words, Meredith is seeking deliberately to rise above the political struggle, even to the extent that it figures in *Beauchamp's Career* and to illuminate the pretensions of the most powerful class within the very citadel of security which its members have built out of their social conventions. The paradox of the great Egoist, Sir Willoughby Patterne, is that he is dependent for his self-assurance on the good opinion of others, and to gain and keep that he must always make the appearance of being successful in terms of the prevailing fashion. He manipulates conventions for his personal ends, but in turn becomes their prisoner within the gaol of his own social prestige.

2

The peculiar flavour of *The Egoist* comes largely from this fact that it is a study of social pretensions within a stable situation. Its characters are limited deliberately to a group of people close enough in terms of class to come together naturally in an extended house party; no major character is socially insecure, ascending or descending the ladder of class.

Thus *The Egoist* in fact differs from the earlier novels not only in the elimination of the more flamboyantly heroic aspects of the struggle against social conventions, but also in abandoning, as fictional mechanisms, acute class differences and extreme snobbery; both exist in the world of *The Egoist*, but they seldom surface, to make a telling point, as in Sir Willoughby's treatment of his distant relative, Lieutenant Patterne.

By contrast, Meredith's first novel, *The Ordeal of Richard Feverel*, introduces class in a very direct way through Richard's marriage to a girl of lower status, which leads to his later troubles, and also contains one of Meredith's earliest disquisitions on the nature of snobbery.

I now see [says Adrian Harley Richard's cousin] that the national love of a lord is less subservience than a form of self-love; putting a gold-lace hat on one's image, as it were, to bow to it. I see, too, the admirable wisdom of our system: – could there be a finer balance of power than in a community where men intellectually nil, have lawful vantage and a gold-lace hat on? How soothing it is to Intellect – that noble rebel, as the Pilgrim has it – to stand, and bow, and know itself superior!

In fact, snobs are of two kinds, those who – as Adrian suggests – can look on others' social eminence with satisfaction, and those who wish to share that eminence. Proust was inclined to be a snob of the first kind, Meredith – outside his persona as a writer – of the second. But he was too intelligent for his attitude not to be ambivalent. In later years he elaborately attempted to conceal the fact that he came of a line of tailors, yet in *Evan Harrington* (1861), rather obviously subtitled *He Would Be a Gentleman*, he wrote daringly near the bone by telling the story of a tailor's son striving to ascend the social ladder. If Evan Harrington is a social climber, Richmond Roy, the father of the hero in *Harry Richmond* (1871), is the grossest kind of social impostor, and in others of Meredith's works the struggle of lower middle class men, stained by their involvement in trade, to rise above their origins by effort or fraud, is important and is always the subject of comedy, a comedy which doubtless gained piquancy in the writing from the fact that Meredith was exposing his own most sensitive nerve-ends.

The most curious of these studies in snobbery occurs in one of Meredith's least known works, *The House on the Beach*, a novella of unusual brevity (40,000 words) and almost Dickensian quaintness. Published in 1877, it became a kind of burlesque transition from the earlier novels to *The Egoist*, which appeared two years later.

The novel is set in a shabby little seaside resort, the minor Cinque port of Crikswich. Martin Tinman, the bailiff of Crikswich, is a retired tradesman who dreams that his position as a very minor royal official will eventually lead to his acceptance at Court. Gradually he builds up a life of fantasy centring upon hours of posturing secretly before a cheval-glass in the Court suit he has bought in preparation for the event. The summons in fact never comes, but it seems to Tinman that the achievement of his ambition may have been brought a stage nearer when Van Diemen Smith and his daughter Annette arrive in Crikswich.

Smith is a friend of the distant past, returning with a fortune from exile; long ago he deserted from the British army and fled to Australia, where he made good. Tinman knows the secret of Smith's desertion, which could still result in imprisonment, and, having been rejected as a possible spouse by all the wealthy and marriageable women of the district, he coldly proceeds to blackmail his old friend into allowing him to marry Annette. Smith resorts to parental prerogative in overruling Annette's growing unwillingness, until he quarrels with Tinman and refuses to allow the marriage to proceed. Tinman writes the letter of betrayal, but before he can post it, a great storm springs up in the Channel and his house on the beach is threatened by the mounting waves. Tinman is in the grip of his dream, posturing before his mirror and oblivious of the winds and waters raging outside. In the nick of time he is saved by a rescue party dispatched by Van Diemen Smith, and carried away from the collapsing house which, with all his possessions, is engulfed by the waves.

For a moment, after his rescue, Tinman stands on the sea wall in full view of his fellow citizens.

In this exposed position, the wind, whose pranks are endless when it is once up, seized and blew Martin Tinman's dressing-gown wide as two violently flapping wings on each side of him, and finally over his head. Van Diemen turned a pair of stupefied flat eyes on Herbert, who cast a shy look at the ladies. Tinman had sprung down. But not before the world, in one tempestuous glimpse, had caught sight of the Court suit.

The person whom this exposure of the pretensions of her former suitor affects most strongly is Annette, fully conscious now of liberation from the marital tyranny which had threatened her.

It ... seemed to her the most wonderful running together of opposite things ever known on this earth. The young lady was ashamed of her laughter, but she was deeply indebted to it, for never was mind made so clear by that beneficent exercise.

The 'opposite things' which Annette perceives are of course the natural impulses represented by the storm and the un-natural pretensions which, in destroying Tinman's house and so ludicrously exposing his pretensions, it defeats.

The House on the Beach was completed late in 1876 and published in the *New Quarterly Magazine* in January 1877. By that time Meredith was already preparing for his famous lecture at the London Institution on 'The Idea of Comedy and the Uses of the Comic Spirit'. The lecture was delivered on 1 February 1877 and published in the April issue of the *New Quarterly Magazine*, though it did not achieve book form for another twenty years, being finally published in 1897 as *An Essay on Comedy*. Before 1877 had ended, Meredith was already at work on *The Egoist*, which was finished in February 1879 and published in October that year. The fact that *The House on the Beach* was published, the lecture on Comedy delivered, and *The Egoist* commenced, all in the same year, signifies more than a temporal link between these works. It shows the extent to which, at a time when he was despairing of the wide popularity which came to him eight years later with *Diana of the Crossways*, Meredith for a brief period abandoned compromise with the tastes of his time, not only by writing the most dazzlingly intellectual of all his novels, but also by developing to their logical extremity the ideas on egoism, on sentimentality, and on the function of comedy, which had been part of his equipment almost from the beginning of his literary career. It may also be that Meredith, who completed *The Egoist* in his fifty-first year, had reached the height of his creative powers and wrote in consciousness of this fact; certainly nothing that he produced in his remaining twenty years of active writing showed a comparable sureness of touch.

On the most obvious level the link between *The House on the Beach* and *The Egoist* can be seen in the peculiar twisting of the

Meredithian sexual theme which dominates the plots of both novella and novel. The heroines, Annette and Clara, are both engaged to wealthy and egotistical men, who are the victims of their own overweening pretensions. In each case a father – for reasons of his own – seeks to force the heroine to keep her troth to a man she has grown to despise; in each case the egoist is exposed, so that his neighbours and friends see him at last for the empty being he is; by this exposure and by her own recognition of the freedom conferred by a comic view of her situation, the girl is liberated. Finally, there is in each novel a modest aspirant to the heroine's hand (in *The House on the Beach* an actual journalist and in *The Egoist* an aspiring journalist) who waits until the comedy of egoism is played out and his worthiness can triumph.

Both Martin Tinman and Sir Willoughby Patterne are emotional vampires; they seek to establish and sustain their pretensions by preying on the emotions of others, while all they have to offer are the mechanical responses of sham senti-ment. In each case their victims or potential victims include the whole of their immediate circle, but the prime victim is a woman. This pattern of the victimization of woman appears in most of Meredith's major novels; it was complemented, outside his fiction, by a genuine concern for the liberation of women from the social and legal discriminations which they suffered in the Victorian era. The New Women who accepted *Diana of the Crossways* as a fictional manifesto for the cause of feminism were not entirely wrong.

Yet they were only partially right, since the battle of the sexes was never neatly resolved in any of Meredith's books. It was still being fought out in his last novel, *The Amazing Marriage*, whose writing bridged a very long span, from its beginning in 1879 immediately after *The Egoist* was completed, to its final publication in 1895. Even in this last novel, some familiar types of *The Egoist* period are still present: the vain Fleetwood, who, like Sir Willoughby, has been jilted by one woman and regards the winning of the heroine mainly as a victory to re-establish his own superiority; the selfish and calculating guardian uncle (the parent-substitute) who forces the marriage of Carinthia and Fleetwood; Carinthia herself, originally as innocent in the ways of the world as Clara Middleton, but quick to develop in understanding when Fleetwood deserts her, and ready to reject him when he undergoes a sentimental revulsion and wishes to resume their relationship. Carinthia eventually shows her independence by going off with her brother to support the Carlist rebels in Spain; meanwhile Fleetwood dies in a monastery and Carinthia, returning from Spain, marries a Welsh mine-owner whose modest, unspectacular virtues provide the necessary contrast to the rather flamboyant villainy of Fleet-wood.

It is a sign of the growing importance in Meredith's imaginative vision of the liberation of women as the end of the sexual struggle that the emphatic male hero vanishes from his novels in 1876, when Nevil Beauchamp throws his stormy life away rescuing the child whom Meredith describes as an 'insignificant bit of mudbank life'. From that point the driving passion that characterized such relatively conventional heroes as Beauchamp and Richard Feverel is given only to the villains, who expend it in the service of their vanity; the quiet dependable men whom Clara, Diana and Carinthia eventually marry in recognition of their devotion are the precursors of the heroes and anti-heroes, men without passion and emphasis, who appear in so many twentieth century novels.

3

In Meredith's novels, sexual passion is never in fact so important as sexual domination, which may often be a matter of the coldest calculation. No censorial decision was more absurd than that which led Mudie's Library to kill the prospects of *The Ordeal of Richard Feverel* in consequence –

according to Meredith – 'of the urgent remonstrances of several respectable families who objected to it as dangerous and wicked and damnable . . .'. On the other hand, if *The Ordeal of Richard Feverel* or *Diana of the Crossways* or *The Egoist* could have been banned as a threat to the Victorian patriarchal family, there might have been logic in the act. Yet the outspoken feminism of Meredith's later years was a by-product rather than a cause of the sexual conflicts represented in his novels. A didactic writer, in that he recognized and sought to use the power of comedy in affecting the outlooks and hence the actions of men, Meredith was not a reforming propagandist. Here there was a sharp distinction between him and a writer like Bernard Shaw, who criticized him from the Fabian point of view. Shaw would use a play quite deliberately to discuss an immediate social problem and to implant in the minds of his audience the idea of a concrete remedy. The problems that concerned Meredith were not so easily solved; placed in an unavoidable social setting, they were essentially problems of personal awareness. The therapy of comedy was not expected to reform societies; it was expected to cure individuals of certain malformations of feeling.

None, Meredith recognized, was in greater need of therapy than himself. Sir Willoughby, he once told a young writer, 'is all of us', and there is no doubt that he exposed more of himself in his negative characters than in his positive ones, who were much more likely to take their characteristics from his friends, for example, F. A. Maxse, Leslie Stephen, Robert Louis Stevenson.

It is when we touch this sensitive problem of the materials out of which Meredith fabricated his novels, and particularly *The Egoist*, that we come near the roots of his view on the war of the sexes. His relationship with the Peacock family, in particular, is central to any consideration of his characteristic moral preoccupations, of the content of his novels, and even in his ways of writing.

The relationship began when Meredith, a lawyer's clerk of twenty and yet untried as a writer, met Edward Gryffydh Peacock, the son of the author of *Nightmare Abbey*. The two young men were members of a literary circle which gathered around the bohemian lawyer Richard Charnock, to whom Meredith was articled, and they contributed to a handwritten *Monthly Journal*, in which appeared Meredith's first works to receive even the limited publicity of a privately circulated magazine. Edward Peacock's widowed sister, Mary Ellen Nicolls, was also a contributor to the *Monthly Journal*. Soon, in 1849, she became Meredith's wife; he was twenty-one and she was seven years older.

Meredith's marriage brought him close to Thomas Love Peacock, particularly when the financial difficulties of the young couple made them accept his temporary hospitality. In human terms the experiment was almost disastrous. Peacock, a man who liked comfort, quiet and peace of mind, resented Meredith's exuberance and was distressed by the openness with which financial and emotional difficulties were aired by his daughter and son-in-law. The two men disagreed politically; as a crowning infliction, Meredith smoked incessantly and Peacock detested tobacco.

Yet, despite this temperamental incompatibility, Peacock's literary outlook impressed itself strongly on Meredith at this formative stage in his development as a writer. As late as 1872, almost a quarter of a century after their first meeting, he wrote for the *Graphic* a series of intensely Peacockian dialogues entitled *Up to Midnight*, and his predilection for developing his novels through scenes of dramatic conversation, to which the narrative was subordinated, became the mechanism for an intellectualization of the novel along lines which Peacock had prefigured. Nevertheless, he advanced on Peacock, in that his characters were never merely the mouthpieces of *idées fixes*; they projected clearly individualized temperaments; they learnt from experience, and if they did not always grow in the process, at least they gained in self-awareness, which can hardly be said of any of Peacock's totally static characters.

It is in *The Egoist* that the Peacockian dialogue is most effectively naturalized into an instrument of Meredithian analysis. Meredith's dialogue is not necessarily more realistic in its texture than Peacock's. One cannot imagine any two living creatures conversing as Sir Willoughby and Laetitia Dale do at their most sententious. But it does chart the emotional lives of those strange beings of Meredith's imagination in such a way that we are aware not of mere intellectual crotchets, but also of genuine feelings, of worthy and unworthy calculations, of cracks in the carapace of affectation through which we can feel a beating of human blood. In fact, it is one of Meredith's great originalities that he can give a highly poised and intellectualized dialogue such transparency that in the end it becomes more revealing of the inner motives of the speakers than a deliberately realistic conversation would be. Virginia Woolf, the daughter of Meredith's intimate friend Leslie Stephen, defined the effect of this achievement when she remarked that in *The Egoist*, 'Meredith pays us a supreme compliment to which as novel-readers we are little accustomed. . . . He imagines us capable of disinterested curiosity in the behaviour of our kind.'

But Peacock was not merely, for Meredith, a father-in-law turned into a literary parent. He also became the model for one of the principal characters of *The Egoist*. Dr Middleton, Clara's father, is a classical scholar who speaks and looks as Peacock did, who harbours his Tory prejudices, who shares his love of wine and food and ease, and who displays the same ruthlessness in his efforts to avoid any human complications that may disturb the calm he regards as essential for his scholarly work.

The formal elaboration of *The Egoist*, paralleling the elaboration of conventions within which the appropriately named Patterne dances his pompous minuet of life, is characterized by the triangular grouping of characters: Willoughby–Clara–

Laetitia; Willoughby–Clara–Vernon; Clara–Vernon–Horace; Willoughby–Mrs Jenkinson–Clara. The shifting relations within and between such triangles are the choreography of the work as a whole. Most interesting of all the triangles is that of Willoughby–Clara–Dr Middleton, the triad which provides the clues to the genesis of *The Egoist*.

In this key triad Dr Middleton alone is immediately recognizable as a character rather faithfully derived from a model in real life. Willoughby and Clara have gone through many rebirths before they are incarnated in *The Egoist*, but their beginnings are to be found in Meredith's own past, in the early triangle of Peacock–Mary Ellen–Meredith. Meredith's marriage with Mary Ellen foundered in the conflict of two proud intellects; in 1857, eight years after they had married, she left him for Henry Wallis, the pre-Raphaelite fellow-traveller whose livid painting of *The Death of Chatterton* is to be seen in the Tate Gallery. When Mary Ellen wished to return to him, Meredith proudly refused a reconciliation, and in 1861 she died, unhappy and alone.

Neither Mary Ellen's departure nor her death was for Meredith the end of the relationship. It dominated the rest of his life, haunting him with the images of her misery and his inflexibility, but as the years went on these twin spectres underwent curious transformations. The most literal rendering of the lost marriage was Meredith's long poem, *Modern Love*. The actual incidents described in that poem are already somewhat changed from those in Meredith's marriage, but we cannot doubt that the conclusion he expresses in analysing the failure of the imagined love relationship sprang from his own experience:

> Thus piteously Love closed what he begat:
> The union of this ever-diverse pair;
> These two were rapid falcons in a snare,
> Condemned to do the flitting of the bat.
> Lovers beneath the singing sky of May,
> They wandered once, clear as the dew on flowers,

But they fed not on the advancing hours:
Their hearts held cravings for the buried day.
Then each applied to each that fatal knife,
Deep questioning, which probes to endless dole.
Ah, what a dusty answer gets the soul
When hot for certainties in this our life!

Meredith suggests that he and Mary Ellen, proud and independent spirits, were diminished in the net of marriage until, using the mind to wound and dominate each other, they betrayed the heart. There is already much of *The Egoist* here. Sir Willoughby, seeking a certainty through conventions and sentiments, but incapable of real love, gets in the end the dusty answer of losing Clara and marrying the second-best lady, a fading Laetitia who no longer even adores him.

Even before *Modern Love* was written and before Mary Ellen was dead, Meredith had begun to develop another aspect of the great marital failure which in various forms dominated the rest of his life as a writer. *The Ordeal of Richard Feverel* appeared in 1859, the year after Mary Ellen's elopement with Henry Wallis, and the story of Sir Austin Feverel, Richard's father, parallels extraordinarily that of Meredith himself.

The outline of the Baronet's story was by no means new. He had a wife, and he had a friend. His marriage was for love; his wife was a beauty, his friend was a poet. Sir Austin Feverel did nothing by halves. His wife had his whole heart, and his friend all his confidence.

The poet lives in the household; he and the wife are thrown often together. 'In time he touched his guitar in her chamber, and they played Rizzio and Mary together.' Sir Austin learns of their faithlessness.

. . . He forgave the man; he put him aside as too poor for his wrath. The woman he could not forgive. She had sinned every way. Simple ingratitude to a benefactor was a pardonable transgression, for he was not one to recount, and crush the culprit under the heap of his good deeds. But her he had raised to be his equal, and he judged her as his equal. She had blackened the world's fair aspect for him.

The monstrosity of Sir Austin's self-love is evident. In terms of the novel his unfortunate marriage is mainly important as the motivation for the elaborate upbringing, designed to make him proof against the ravages of love, which is inflicted on his son Richard and which breeds its inevitable rebellion. The rejected wife appears in the latter part of the novel as a dim, veiled figure, but certainly a victim figure.

Apart from his temperamental egoism, Sir Austin bears no obvious resemblance to Meredith; it is mainly their situations that are similar. But it is significant of a division in Meredith between the private man and the writer (a division which recurs through his life), that he continued to exclude Mary Ellen from his life at the same time as he implied a condemnation of Sir Austin for similarly excluding the erring Lady Feverel.

The Ordeal of Richard Feverel in fact makes it clear that, if Meredith's pride would not allow him to admit publicly any blame for the failure of his marriage, his conscience nagged, and to that continually nagging conscience we owe the series of relationships between the sexes in successive novels in which the man more clearly becomes the unfeeling tyrant and the woman the potential victim. The main shift that takes place in the relationship – apart from the rather minor one of making Clara a yet unmarried girl, and therefore a jilt rather than an adulteress – is that the woman's defection ceases to be an act of betrayal or weakness, and becomes an act of liberation, the liberation of the feelings from the rule of convention and sterile sentiment.

Thus Meredith's view of the relationship of the sexes, as symbolic of the wider relationship between freedom and the tyranny of custom, led him far from the real-life origin of his preoccupations. Dr Middleton, an essentially minor character, could safely be modelled on Peacock. But Clara Middleton had grown as far from Mary Ellen Nicoll as Meredith's views on the fate of women had changed since the agony he exorcized in *Modern Love*.

The Egoist, in its construction, has the kind of economy which is more usual in drama than in fiction. It is true that like almost every book that Meredith wrote, its entrance is protected by a rather fearsome *chevaux-de-frise* in the form of a preface on comedy, heavy with elaborate parody, and an introductory chapter on Sir Willoughby's youth and his celebrated leg, which appears excessively precious until one realizes how surely it sets the artificial tone of the world in which Willoughby poses for the edification of his admirers, the formidable Mrs Mountstuart Jenkinson (surely a lineal ancestress of Wilde's dowagers) and the languid and brainy Laetitia, that personification of the feminine mind made sterile by enslavement to convention. But once the reader has undergone the preliminary tests which Meredith expects of him, the course is clear and the action follows in a brisk series of dramatic episodes, each fulfilling a triple purpose of enlightening us a shade more on Sir Willoughby's nature, of developing the resistance of the other characters to his insolent expectations, and of building the tension that rises steadily in this close circle of emotionally involved people like the heightening atmosphere before a thunderstorm. Apart from any of its other virtues, it is a fine work of suspense, paced on by witty conversation, economical in introspection and narrative, and, from the moment when Clara begins to detect the real and detestable Sir Willoughby, making the reader a fascinated observer of the shifts by which her feminine cunning surmounts the obstacles successively falling in her path. There are aspects of *The Egoist* which are madly improbable. Could Dr Middleton really betray his beloved daughter for a diet of old port? Was Willoughby's only way of living down his rejection by Clara really to marry a Laetitia who had learnt to despise him? Such an ending is indeed not consonant with realism but it is with poetic justice, and that is what Meredith seeks. For *The Egoist* is after all a comedy, and, just as Meredith observes the unity of place and – within reasonable limits – the unity of time, so he ensures that the good – Clara and Vernon – shall get their reward, and the villain shall live to digest his suitably dusty answer.

All this gains in meaning when we remember that *The Egoist* is the extreme expression of Meredith's recurrent drama of the defeat of Egoism by the power of Comedy. At the mid nineteenth century, when Meredith began to write, Egoism was much in the air. In 1843 Max Stirner had published his treatise advocating Egoism as a revolutionary force, *Der Einzige und sein Eigentum*, and it is possible that Meredith, with his interest in the German intellectual life of the time, was aware of it. 'Enlightened self-interest', even 'enlightened Egoism', was spoken of freely in England to justify the irresponsible relationship between industrialists and their employees, and it had been denounced by Carlyle, whom Meredith then respected. But these external circumstances are hardly sufficient to account for the way in which, from his first published work of prose, *The Shaving of Shagpat* (1856), he consistently identified Egoism as the great enemy of truth, feeling and progress, and associated it with artificiality and with sentiment, which is the artificiality of feeling. This preoccupation sprang from the agonies of self-analysis by which Meredith fed his art.

The great sin of the Egoist is that he values nothing for its own sake. Willoughby does not see in Clara a real girl whom he can love and cherish; he sees an ornament which will enhance his regard in the eyes of the world. Vernon Whitford is retained at Patterne Hall not from any sense of friendship on Willoughby's part, but because a resident writer adds lustre to his employer's public image. Thus everything is prized or rejected for a false reason and a whole structure of artificial relationships is built up and sealed by sentiment. Love can thus be simulated at will and Sir Willoughby woos Clara and Laetitia within a few hours of each other, with almost identical and equally meaningless phrases of conventional passion.

It is this world of artificial relations that we enter with Clara Middleton, aware that the never-encountered Constantia Durham had already fled from it in panic. We breathe its curious dry air as, through the eyes of Clara, and later of Colonel de Craye and even eventually of Laetitia, we observe Willoughby's conceit and callousness reveal themselves in full monstrosity.

Then, almost exactly half-way through the book, Clara reaches the point where she can endure no longer Sir Willoughby's attentions and the obtuseness of her father. She runs away, and as she does a great storm beats over the countryside. The storm clears the air and the flight clarifies the situation like the great cleansing sheets of rain. Everyone is suddenly aware, that, even though Clara returns, the relationship between her and Willoughby has irrevocably changed, and from this point Clara (her very name, used in earlier Meredith books, is significant) looks on her situation with the clear eye of comedy, so that slowly her fear of Willoughby vanishes and all that remain are the Egoist's wild and comic manoeuvres to find a solution that will fit the realities of the situation and at the same time save his face among the snobs who surround him.

Comedy is, for Meredith, the dissolving element of Egoism. *The Egoist* is described as 'A Comedy in Narrative', and its Prelude invokes the Comic Spirit. Meredith was not the first English novelist to attempt a definition of the comic spirit in literature. Fielding had preceded him a century before when he wrote the Author's Preface to *Joseph Andrews*. Fielding went part of the road which Meredith followed. Like Meredith he denied any intention of perpetrating Burlesque, and maintained that it was not the Monstrous, but the Ridiculous that fell into his province.

The only source of the true Ridiculous (as it appears to me) is affectation. ... Now, affectation proceeds from one of these two causes, vanity and hypocrisy: for as vanity puts us on affecting false characters, in order to purchase applause; so hypocrisy sets us on an endeavour to avoid censure, by concealing our vices under an appearance of their opposite virtues ...

From the discovery of this affectation arises the Ridiculous – which always strikes the reader with surprise and pleasure; and that in a higher and stronger degree when the affectation arises from hypocrisy, than when from vanity: for to discover anyone to be the exact reverse of what he affects, is more surprising, and consequently more ridiculous, than to find him a little deficient in the quality he desires the reputation of. I might observe that our Ben Jonson, who of all men understood the Ridiculous the best, has chiefly used the hypocritical affectation.

In Fielding's definition, Joseph Surface, the most consummate hypocrite of English literature, would also be its most comic character. He is not, nor does he or any of Fielding's own characters achieve a comic complexity approaching that of Sir Willoughby Patterne. Parson Adams is funnier than Sir Willoughby, but that is not quite the same thing; one is meant to provoke our laughter, the other to stir our thought as well. The difference in approach can be seen when we consider the most famous and most characteristic passage from the *Essay on the Idea of Comedy*:

If you believe that our civilisation is founded in common sense (and it is the first condition of sanity to believe it), you will, when contemplating men, discern a Spirit overhead; not more heavenly than the light flashed upward from glassy surfaces, but luminous and watchful; never shooting beyond them, nor lagging in the rear; so closely attached to them that it may be taken for a slavish reflex, until its features are studied. ... Its common aspect is one of unsolicitous observation, as if surveying a full field and having leisure to dart on its chosen morsels, without any fluttering eagerness. Men's future on earth does not attract it; their honesty and shapeliness in the present does; and whenever they wax out of proportion, overblown, affected, pretentious, bombastical, hypocritical, pedantic, fantastically delicate; whenever it sees them self-deceived or hoodwinked, given to run riot in idolatries, drifting into vanities, congregating in absurdities, planning short-sightedly, plotting dementedly; whenever they are at variance with their professions, and violate the unwritten but perceptible laws binding them in consideration one to another; whenever they offend sound reason, fair justice; are false in humility or mined with conceit, individually, or in the bulk – the Spirit overhead will look humanely malign and cast an oblique light on them, followed by volleys of silvery laughter. That is the Comic Spirit.

It is the sign of Sir Willoughby's complexity in comparison with the comic characters of Fielding, that he is not guilty of a single affectation, of one glaring manifestation of vanity or hypocrisy, but that all the sins against common sense which Meredith details can be brought against him. Nor does the complexity lie merely in the many-sidedness of his folly. It lies also in the method of representation. Fielding's characters, and even those of Congreve and Wilde, who seem nearest to Meredith among English comic writers, are at best three-dimensional; we see in clear action the divergence between deed and pretension, the evidence of deception or self-deception. But in the case of Sir Willoughby we have not merely the external witness; we see the process at work within him and realize, in the depth of his thoughts, the extent to which natural impulse has been replaced by artificial calculation, in the same way as the living substance of some perished animal is replaced by the fossil's hard stone. This probing complexity gives Meredith's comic art an analytic quality, which, before him, was almost unknown among the writers of comedy. Their approach tended to be the descriptive one of the old-fashioned natural historian; to observe, and represent, and wonder at man's folly. Meredith's is the diagnostic approach, seeking the pathology of vanity and its ultimate causes. Once we know those causes, he suggests, we may not suddenly cure a patient so chronic as Sir Willoughby, but we shall cease to become enslaved by his pretensions and, in ceasing to do so, we may – as Meredith suggests that Laetitia will do – begin his liberation.

But, though Meredith undoubtedly intended this lesson to

be understood by those who read *The Egoist*, to end on the didactic note would be to leave a wrong impression of his actual achievement. It is as a consummate portrait of vanity and egoism that *The Egoist* succeeds; Sir Willoughby reformed would be Sir Willoughby destroyed, and in the wisdom of his art Meredith did no more than hint at the possibility. Here his obedience to the rigid laws of classical drama stood him in good stead; no novel benefits more from its observance of the unities. This is the story of the exposure and the defeat of Egoism; the transformation of Egoism would be another story, and Meredith was too much Sir Willoughby and too sensible an artist, to attempt it.

A Note on the Text

✖ ✖ ✖ ✖

The text of *The Egoist* which I have used is Meredith's last, from the 1897 collected edition of his works. Meredith's revisions of many of his novels show great dissatisfaction with the earlier versions and, in such books as *The Ordeal of Richard Feverel*, involve major structural changes which do not always seem justified. In the case of *The Egoist*, however, Meredith seems to have recognized this for the *jeu d'esprit* it was, and to have realized that any great meddling would have destroyed it. In consequence the changes he made were minor – a few brief cuts, a few substitutions of more felicitous words and phrases – and they represent no more than a last polishing of a work nearer perfection than anything else he wrote. A very few misprints which found their way into the 1897 edition have been corrected by reference to the First Edition, and on a very few occasions I have reverted, for the sake of clarity, to earlier and to my mind better punctuation.

A FACSIMILE OF THE TITLE PAGE OF THE FIRST EDITION

THE EGOIST

A COMEDY IN NARRATIVE

BY

GEORGE MEREDITH

IN THREE VOLUMES

VOL. I.

LONDON

C. KEGAN PAUL & CO., 1, PATERNOSTER SQUARE

1879

PRELUDE

⚒ ⚒ ⚒

A Chapter of which the Last Page only
is of any Importance

COMEDY is a game played to throw reflections upon social life, and it deals with human nature in the drawing-room of civilized men and women, where we have no dust of the struggling outer world, no mire, no violent crashes, to make the correctness of the representation convincing. Credulity is not wooed through the impressionable senses; nor have we recourse to the small circular glow of the watchmaker's eye to raise in bright relief minutest grains of evidence for the routing of incredulity. The Comic Spirit conceives a definite situation for a number of characters, and rejects all accessories in the exclusive pursuit of them and their speech. For being a spirit, he hunts the spirit in men; vision and ardour constitute his merit; he has not a thought of persuading you to believe in him. Follow and you will see. But there is a question of the value of a run at his heels.

Now the world is possessed of a certain big book, the biggest book on earth; that might indeed be called the Book of Earth; whose title is the Book of Egoism, and it is a book full of the world's wisdom. So full of it, and of such dimensions is this book, in which the generations have written ever since they took to writing, that to be profitable to us the Book needs a powerful compression.

Who, says the notable humourist, in allusion to this Book, who can studiously travel through sheets of leaves, now capable of a stretch from the Lizard to the last few poor pulmonary snips and shreds of leagues dancing on their toes for cold, explorers tell us, and catching breath by good luck, like dogs at bones about a table, on the edge of the Pole? Inordinate unvaried length, sheer longinquity, staggers the heart, ages the very heart of us at a view. And how if we manage finally to print one of our pages on the crow-scalp of that solitary majestic outsider? We may get him into the Book; yet the knowledge we want will not be more present with us than it was when the chapters hung their end over the cliff you ken of at Dover, where sits our great lord and master contemplating the seas without upon the reflex of that within!

In other words, as I venture to translate him (humourists are difficult: it is a piece of their humour to puzzle our wits), the inward mirror, the embracing and condensing spirit, is required to give us those interminable milepost piles of matter (extending well-nigh to the very Pole) in essence, in chosen samples, digestibly. I conceive him to indicate that the realistic method of a conscientious transcription of all the visible, and a repetition of all the audible, is mainly accountable for our present branfulness, and that prolongation of the vasty and the noisy, out of which, as from an undrained fen, steams the malady of sameness, our modern malady. We have the malady, whatever may be the cure or the cause. We drove in a body to Science the other day for an antidote; which was as if tired pedestrians should mount the engine-box of headlong trains; and Science introduced us to our o'er-hoary ancestry – them in the Oriental posture; whereupon we set up a primeval chattering to rival the Amazon forest nigh nightfall, cured, we fancied. And before daybreak our disease was hanging on to us again, with the extension of a tail. We had it fore and aft. We were the same, and animals into the bargain. That is all we got from Science.

Art is the specific. We have little to learn of apes, and they may be left. The chief consideration for us is, what particular practice of Art in letters is the best for the perusal of the Book

of our common wisdom; so that with clearer minds and livelier manners we may escape, as it were, into daylight and song
from a land of fog-horns. Shall we read it by the watchmaker's
eye in luminous rings eruptive of the infinitesimal, or pointed
with examples and types under the broad Alpine survey of the
spirit born of our united social intelligence, which is the
Comic Spirit? Wise men say the latter. They tell us that there
is a constant tendency in the Book to accumulate excess of
substance, and such repleteness, obscuring the glass it holds to
mankind, renders us inexact in the recognition of our individual countenances; a perilous thing for civilization. And
these wise men are strong in their opinion that we should encourage the Comic Spirit, who is after all our own offspring,
to relieve the Book. Comedy, they say, is the true diversion, as
it is likewise the key of the great Book, the music of the Book.
They tell us how it condenses whole sections of the book in a
sentence, volumes in a character; so that a fair part of a book
outstripping thousands of leagues when unrolled may be compassed in one comic sitting.

For verily, say they, we must read what we can of it, at least
the page before us, if we would be men. One, with an index on
the Book, cries out, in a style pardonable to his fervency: The
remedy of your frightful affliction is here, through the stilla-
tory of Comedy, and not in Science, nor yet in Speed, whose
name is but another for voracity. Why, to be alive, to be quick
in the soul, there should be diversity in the companion throbs
of your pulses. Interrogate them. They lump along like the old
loblegs of Dobbin the horse; or do their business like cudgels
of carpet-thwackers expelling dust, or the cottage-clock pen-
dulum teaching the infant hour over midnight simple arith-
metic. This too in spite of Bacchus. And let them gallop; let
them gallop with the God bestriding them, gallop to Hymen,
gallop to Hades, they strike the same note. Monstrous monotonousness has enfolded us as with the arms of Amphitrite!
We hear a shout of war for a diversion. – Comedy he
pronounces to be our means of reading swiftly and

comprehensively. She it is who proposes the correcting of pretentiousness, of inflation, of dulness, and of the vestiges of rawness and grossness to be found among us. She is the ultimate civilizer, the polisher, a sweet cook. If, he says, she watches over sentimentalism with a birch rod, she is not opposed to romance. You may love, and warmly love, so long as you are honest. Do not offend reason. A lover pretending too much by one foot's length of pretence, will have that foot caught in her trap. In Comedy is the singular scene of charity issuing of disdain under the stroke of honourable laughter: an Ariel released by Prospero's wand from the fetters of the damned witch Sycorax. And this laughter of reason refreshed is floriferous, like the magical great gale of the shifty Spring deciding for Summer. You hear it giving the delicate spirit his liberty. Listen, for comparison, to an unleavened society: a low as of the udderful cow past milking hour! O for a titled ecclesiastic to curse to excommunication that unholy thing! – So far an enthusiast perhaps; but he should have a hearing.

Concerning pathos, no ship can now set sail without pathos; and we are not totally deficient of pathos; which is, I do not accurately know what, if not the ballast, reducible to moisture by patent process, on board our modern vessel; for it can hardly be the cargo, and the general water supply has other uses; and ships well charged with it seem to sail the stiffest – there is a touch of pathos. The Egoist surely inspires pity. He who would desire to clothe himself at everybody's expense, and is of that desire condemned to strip himself stark naked, he, if pathos ever had a form, might be taken for the actual person. Only he is not allowed to rush at you, roll you over and squeeze your body for the briny drops. There is the innovation.

You may as well know him out of hand, as a gentleman of our time and country, of wealth and station; a not flexile figure, do what we may with him; the humour of whom scarcely dimples the surfaces and is distinguishable but by very

penetrative, very wicked imps, whose fits of roaring below at
some generally imperceptible stroke of his quality have first
made the mild literary angels aware of something comic in
him, when they were one and all about to describe the gentleman on the heading of the records baldly (where brevity is
most complimentary) as a gentleman of family and property,
an idol of a decorous island that admires the concrete. Imps
have their freakish wickedness in them to kindle detective
vision; malignly do they love to uncover ridiculousness in
imposing figures. Wherever they catch sight of Egoism they
pitch their camps, they circle and squat, and forthwith they
trim their lanterns, confident of the ludicrous to come. So
confident that their grip of an English gentleman, in whom
they have spied their game, never relaxes until he begins insensibly to frolic and antic, unknown to himself, and comes
out in the native steam which is their scent of the chase. Instantly off they scour, Egoist and imps. They will, it is known
of them, dog a great House for centuries, and be at the birth of
all the new heirs in succession, diligently taking confirmatory
notes, to join hands and chime their chorus in one of their
merry rings round the tottering pillar of the House, when his
turn arrives; as if they had (possibly they had) smelt of old date
a doomed colossus of Egoism in that unborn, unconceived in-
heritor of the stuff of the family. They dare not be chuckling,
while Egoism is valiant, while sober, while socially valuable,
nationally serviceable. They wait.

Aforetime a grand old Egoism built the House. It would appear that ever finer essences of it are demanded to sustain the
structure; but especially would it appear that a reversion to
the gross original, beneath a mask and in a vein of fineness,
is an earthquake at the foundations of the House. Better that
it should not have consented to motion, and have held stub-
bornly to all ancestral ways, than have bred that anachronic
spectre. The sight, however, is one to make our squatting imps
in circle grow restless on their haunches, as they bend eyes
instantly, ears at full cock, for the commencement of the

comic drama of the suicide. If this line of verse be not yet in our literature,

> Through very love of self himself he slew;

let it be admitted for his epitaph.

CHAPTER I

✠✠✠✠

A Minor Incident Showing an Hereditary Aptitude in the Use of the Knife

THERE was an ominously anxious watch of eyes visible and invisible over the infancy of Willoughby, fifth in descent from Simon Patterne, of Patterne Hall, premier of this family, a lawyer, a man of solid acquirements and stout ambition, who well understood the foundation-work of a House, and was endowed with the power of saying No to those first agents of destruction, besieging relatives. He said it with the resonant emphasis of death to younger sons. For if the oak is to become a stately tree, we must provide against the crowding of timber. Also the tree beset with parasites prospers not. A great House in its beginning lives, we may truly say, by the knife. Soil is easily got, and so are bricks, and a wife, and children come of wishing for them, but the vigorous use of the knife is a natural gift and points to growth. Pauper Patternes were numerous when the fifth head of the race was the hope of his county. A Patterne was in the Marines.

The country and the chief of this family were simultaneously informed of the existence of one Lieutenant Crossjay Patterne, of the corps of the famous hard fighters, through an act of heroism of the unpretending cool sort which kindles British blood, on the part of the modest young officer, in the

storming of some eastern riverain stronghold, somewhere
about the coast of China. The officer's youth was assumed on
the strength of his rank, perhaps likewise from the tale of his
modesty: 'he had only done his duty'. Our Willoughby was
then at college, emulous of the generous enthusiasm of his
years, and strangely impressed by the report, and the printing
of his name in the newspapers. He thought over it for several
months, when, coming to his title and heritage, he sent Lieutenant Crossjay Patterne a cheque for a sum of money
amounting to the gallant fellow's pay per annum, at the same
time showing his acquaintance with the first, or chemical,
principles of generosity, in the remark to friends at home, that
'blood is thicker than water'. The man is a Marine, but he is a
Patterne. How any Patterne should have drifted into the
Marines, is of the order of questions which are senselessly
asked of the great dispensary. In the complimentary letter
accompanying his cheque, the lieutenant was invited to
present himself at the ancestral Hall, when convenient to
him, and he was assured that he had given his relative and
friend a taste for a soldier's life. Young Sir Willoughby was
fond of talking of his 'military namesake and distant cousin,
young Patterne – the Marine'. It was funny; and not less
laughable was the description of his namesake's deed of
valour; with the rescued British sailor inebriate, and the haul-
ing off to captivity of the three braves of the black dragon on
a yellow ground, and the tying of them together back to
back by their pigtails, and driving of them into our lines upon
a newly devised dying-top style of march that inclined to the
oblique, like the astonished six eyes of the celestial prisoners,
for straight they could not go. The humour of gentlemen at
home is always highly excited by such cool feats. We are a
small island, but you see what we do. The ladies at the Hall,
Sir Willoughby's mother, and his aunts Eleanor and Isabel,
were more affected than he by the circumstance of their
having a Patterne in the Marines. But how then! We English
have ducal blood in business: we have, genealogists tell us,

royal blood in common trades. For all our pride we are a queer people; and you may be ordering butcher's meat of a Tudor, sitting on the cane-bottom chairs of a Plantagenet. By and by you may ... but cherish your reverence. Young Willoughby made a kind of shock-head or football hero of his gallant distant cousin, and wondered occasionally that the fellow had been content to dispatch a letter of effusive thanks without availing himself of the invitation to partake of the hospitalities of Patterne.

He was one afternoon parading between showers on the stately garden terrace of the Hall, in company with his affianced, the beautiful and dashing Constantia Durham, followed by knots of ladies and gentlemen vowed to fresh air before dinner, while it was to be had. Chancing with his usual happy fortune (we call these things dealt to us out of the great hidden dispensary, chance) to glance up the avenue of limes, as he was in the act of turning on his heel at the end of the terrace, and, it should be added, discoursing with passion's privilege of the passion of love to Miss Durham, Sir Willoughby, who was anything but obtuse, experienced a presentiment upon espying a thick-set stumpy man crossing the gravel space from the avenue to the front steps of the Hall, decidedly *not* bearing the stamp of the gentleman 'on his hat, his coat, his feet, or anything that was his', Willoughby subsequently observed to the ladies of his family in the Scriptural style of gentlemen who do bear the stamp. His brief sketch of the creature was repulsive. The visitor carried a bag, and his coat-collar was up, his hat was melancholy; he had the appearance of a bankrupt tradesman absconding; no gloves, no umbrella.

As to the incident we have to note, it was very slight. The card of Lieutenant Patterne was handed to Sir Willoughby, who laid it on the salver, saying to the footman, 'Not at home.'

He had been disappointed in the age, grossly deceived in the appearance of the man claiming to be his relative in this unseasonable fashion; and his acute instinct advised him swiftly of the absurdity of introducing to his friends a heavy unpresentable senior as the celebrated gallant Lieutenant of Marines, and the same as a member of his family! He had talked of the man too much, too enthusiastically, to be able to do so. A young subaltern, even if passably vulgar in figure, can be shuffled through by the aid of the heroical story humourously exaggerated in apology for his aspect. Nothing can be done with a mature and stumpy Marine of that rank. Considerateness dismisses him on the spot, without parley. It was performed by a gentleman supremely advanced at a very early age in the art of cutting.

Young Sir Willoughby spoke a word of the rejected visitor to Miss Durham, in response to her startled look: 'I shall drop him a cheque,' he said, for she seemed personally wounded, and had a face of crimson.

The young lady did not reply.

Dating from the humble departure of Lieutenant Crossjay Patterne up the limes-avenue under a gathering rain-cloud, the ring of imps in attendance on Sir Willoughby maintained their station with strict observation of his movements at all hours; and were comparisons in quest, the sympathetic eagerness of the eyes of caged monkeys for the hand about to feed them, would supply one. They perceived in him a fresh development and very subtle manifestation of the very old thing from which he had sprung.

CHAPTER 2

�खखख

The Young Sir Willoughby

THESE little scoundrel imps, who have attained to some re-
spectability as the dogs and pets of the Comic Spirit, had been
curiously attentive three years earlier, long before the public
announcement of his engagement to the beautiful Miss Durham, on the day of Sir Willoughby's majority, when Mrs
Mountstuart Jenkinson said her word of him. Mrs Mountstuart was a lady certain to say the remembered, if not the
right, thing. Again and again was it confirmed on days of high
celebration, days of birth or bridal, how sure she was to hit the
mark that rang the bell; and away her word went over the
county: and had she been an uncharitable woman she could
have ruled the county with an iron rod of caricature, so sharp
was her touch. A grain of malice would have sent county
faces and characters awry into the currency. She was wealthy
and kindly, and resembled our mother Nature in her reasonable antipathies to one or two things which none can defend,
and her decided preference of persons that shone in the sun.
Her word sprang out of her. She looked at you, and forth it
came: and it stuck to you, as nothing laboured or literary
could have adhered. Her saying of Laetitia Dale: 'Here she
comes with a romantic tale on her eyelashes,' was a portrait
of Laetitia. And that of Vernon Whitford: 'He is a Phoebus
Apollo turned fasting friar,' painted the sunken brilliancy of
the lean long-walker and scholar at a stroke.

Of the young Sir Willoughby, her word was brief; and
there was the merit of it on a day when he was hearing from
sunrise to the setting of the moon salutes in his honour, songs
of praise and Ciceronian eulogy. Rich, handsome, courteous,
generous, lord of the Hall, the feast and the dance, he excited

his guests of both sexes to a holiday of flattery. And, says Mrs
Mountstuart, while grand phrases were mouthing round
about him, '*You see he has a leg.*'

That you saw, of course. But after she had spoken you saw
much more. Mrs Mountstuart said it just as others utter
empty nothings, with never a hint of a stress. Her word was
taken up, and very soon, from the extreme end of the long
drawing-room, the circulation of something of Mrs Mountstuart's was distinctly perceptible. Lady Patterne sent a little
Hebe down, skirting the dancers, for an accurate report of it;
and even the inappreciative lips of a very young lady trans-
mitting the word could not damp the impression of its
weighty truthfulness. It was perfect! Adulation of the young
Sir Willoughby's beauty and wit, and aristocratic bearing
and mien, and of his moral virtues, was common; welcome if
you like, as a form of homage; but common, almost vulgar,
beside Mrs Mountstuart's quiet little touch of nature. In seeming to say infinitely less than others, as Miss Isabel Patterne
pointed out to Lady Busshe, Mrs Mountstuart comprised all
that the others had said, by showing the needlessness of
allusions to the saliently evident. She was the aristocrat reproving the provincial. 'He is everything you have had the
goodness to remark, ladies and dear sirs, he talks charmingly,
dances divinely, rides with the air of a commander-in-chief,
has the most natural grand pose possible, without ceasing for
a moment to be the young English gentleman he is. Alci-
biades, fresh from a Louis IV perruquier,[1] could not surpass
him: whatever you please; I could outdo you in sublime comparisons, were I minded to pelt him. Have you noticed that
he has a leg?'

So might it be amplified. A simple-seeming word of this
import is the triumph of the spiritual, and where it passes for
coin of value, the society has reached a high refinement:
Arcadian by the aesthetic route. Observation of Willoughby
was not, as Miss Eleanor Patterne pointed out to Lady Culmer,
drawn down to the leg, but directed to estimate him from the

leg upward. That, however, is prosaic. Dwell a short space on Mrs Mountstuart's word; and whither, into what fair region, and with how decorously voluptuous a sensation, do not we fly, who have, through mournful veneration of the Martyr Charles, a coy attachment to the Court of his Merrie Son, where the leg was ribboned with love-knots and reigned. Oh! it was a naughty Court. Yet have we dreamed of it as the period when an English cavalier was grace incarnate; far from the boor now hustling us in another sphere; beautifully mannered, every gesture dulcet. And if the ladies were . . . we will hope they have been traduced. But if they were, if they were too tender, ah! gentlemen were gentlemen then – worth perishing for! There is this dream in the English country; and it must be an aspiration after some form of melodious gentlemanliness which is imagined to have inhabited the island at one time; as among our poets the dream of the period of a circle of chivalry here is encouraged for the pleasure of the imagination.

Mrs Mountstuart touched a thrilling chord. 'In spite of men's hateful modern costume, you see he has a leg.'

That is, the leg of the born cavalier is before you: and obscure it as you will, dress degenerately, there it is for ladies who have eyes. You *see* it: or, you see *he* has it. Miss Isabel and Miss Eleanor disputed the incidence of the emphasis, but surely, though a slight difference of meaning may be heard, either will do: many, with a good show of reason, throw the accent upon *leg*. And the ladies knew for a fact that Wiloughby's leg was exquisite; he had a cavalier court-suit in his wardrobe. Mrs Mountstuart signified that the leg was to be seen because it was a burning leg. There it is, and it *will* shine through. He has the leg of Rochester, Buckingham, Dorset, Suckling; the leg that smiles, that winks, is obsequious to you, yet perforce of beauty self-satisfied; that twinkles to a tender midway between imperiousness and seductiveness, audacity and discretion; between 'you shall worship me', and 'I am devoted to you'; is your lord, your slave, alternately and in one. It is a leg of ebb and flow and high-tide ripples. Such a leg, when it has done with pretending to retire, will walk straight into the hearts of women. Nothing so fatal to them.

Self-satisfied it must be. Humbleness does not win multitudes or the sex. It must be vain to have a sheen. Captivating melodies (to prove to you the unavoidableness of self-satisfaction when you know that you have hit perfection), listen to them closely, have an inner pipe of that conceit almost ludicrous when you detect the chirp.

And you need not be reminded that he has the leg without the naughtiness. You see eminent in him what we would fain have brought about in a nation that has lost its leg in gaining a possibly cleaner morality. And that is often contested; but there is no doubt of the loss of the leg.

Well, footmen and courtiers and Scottish Highlanders, and the corps de ballet, draymen too, have legs, and staring legs, shapely enough. But what are they? not the modulated instrument we mean – simply legs for leg-work, dumb as the brutes. Our cavalier's is the poetic leg, a portent, a valiance. He has it as Cicero had a tongue. It is a lute to scatter songs to his mistress; a rapier, is she obdurate. In sooth a leg with brains in it, soul.

And its shadows are an ambush, its lights a surprise. It blushes, it pales, can whisper, exclaim. It is a peep, a part revelation, just sufferable, of the Olympian god – Jove playing carpet-knight.

For the young Sir Willoughby's family and his thoughtful admirers, it is not too much to say that Mrs Mountstuart's little word fetched an epoch of our history to colour the evening of his arrival at man's estate. He was all that Merrie Charles's court should have been, subtracting not a sparkle from what it was. Under this light he danced, and you may consider the effect of it on his company.

He had received the domestic education of a prince. Little princes abound in a land of heaped riches. Where they have not to yield military service to an Imperial master, they are necessarily here and there dainty during youth, sometimes unmanageable, and as they are bound in no personal duty to the State, each is for himself, with full present, and what is more, luxurious, prospective leisure for the practice of that allegiance. They are sometimes enervated by it: that must be in continental countries. Happily our climate and our brave blood precipitate the greater number upon the hunting-field, to do the public service of heading the chase of the fox, with benefit to their constitutions. Hence a manly as well as useful race of little princes, and Willoughby was as manly as any. He cultivated himself, he would not be outdone in popular accomplishments. Had the standard of the public taste been set in philosophy, and the national enthusiasm centred in philosophers, he would at least have worked at books. He did work at science, and had a laboratory. His admirable passion to excel, however, was chiefly directed in his youth upon sport; and so great was the passion in him, that it was commonly the presence of rivals which led him to the declaration of love.

He knew himself, nevertheless, to be the most constant of men in his attachment to the sex. He had never discouraged Laetitia Dale's devotion to him, and even when he followed in the sweeping tide of the beautiful Constantia Durham (whom Mrs Mountstuart called 'The Racing Cutter'), he thought of Laetitia, and looked at her. She was a shy violet.

Willoughby's comportment while the showers of adulation drenched him might be likened to the composure of Indian Gods undergoing worship, but unlike them he reposed upon no seat of amplitude to preserve him from a betrayal of intoxication; he had to continue tripping, dancing, exactly balancing himself, head to right, head to left, addressing his idolaters in phrases of perfect choiceness. This is only to say that it is easier to be a wooden idol than one in the flesh; yet Willoughby was equal to his task. The little prince's education teaches him that he is other than you, and by virtue of the instruction he receives, and also something, we know not what, within, he is enabled to maintain his posture where you would be tottering.

Urchins upon whose curly pates grave seniors lay their hands with conventional encomium and speculation, look older than they are immediately, and Willoughby looked older than his years, not for want of freshness, but because he felt that he had to stand eminently and correctly poised.

Hearing of Mrs Mountstuart's word on him, he smiled and said, 'It is at her service.'

The speech was communicated to her, and she proposed to attach a dedicatory strip of silk. And then they came together, and there was wit and repartee suitable to the electrical atmosphere of the dancing-room, on the march to a magical hall of supper. Willoughby conducted Mrs Mountstuart to the supper-table.

'Were I,' said she, 'twenty years younger, I think I would marry you, to cure my infatuation.'

'Then let me tell you in advance, madam,' said he, 'that I will do everything to obtain a new lease of it, except divorce you.'

They were infinitely wittier, but so much was heard and may be reported.

'It makes the business of choosing a wife for him superhumanly difficult!' Mrs Mountstuart observed, after listening to the praises she had set going again when the ladies were weeded of us, in Lady Patterne's Indian room, and could converse unhampered upon their own ethereal themes.

'Willoughby will choose a wife for himself,' said his mother.

CHAPTER 3

✠✠✠✠

Constantia Durham

THE great question for the county was debated in many
households, daughter-thronged and daughterless, long subsequent to the memorable day of Willoughby's coming of age.
Lady Busshe was for Constantia Durham. She laughed at Mrs
Mountstuart Jenkinson's notion of Laetitia Dale. She was a
little older than Mrs Mountstuart, and had known Willoughby's father, whose marriage into the wealthiest branch of
the Whitford family had been strictly sagacious. 'Patternes
marry money; they are not romantic people,' she said. Miss
Durham had money, and she had health and beauty: three
mighty qualifications for a Patterne bride. Her father, Sir John
Durham, was a large landowner in the western division of the
county; a pompous gentleman, the picture of a father-in-law
for Willoughby. The father of Miss Dale was a battered army
surgeon from India, tenant of one of Sir Willoughby's
cottages bordering Patterne Park. His girl was portionless and
a poetess. Her writing of the song in celebration of the young
baronet's birthday was thought a clever venture, bold as
only your timid creatures can be bold. She let the cat out of her
bag of verse before the multitude; she almost proposed to her
hero in her rhymes. She was pretty; her eyelashes were long
and dark, her eyes dark-blue, and her soul was ready to shoot
like a rocket out of them at a look from Willoughby. And he
looked, he certainly looked, though he did not dance with her
once that night, and danced repeatedly with Miss Durham.
He gave Laetitia to Vernon Whitford for the final dance of the
night, and he may have looked at her so much in pity of an
elegant girl allied to such a partner. The 'Phoebus Apollo
turned fasting friar' had entirely forgotten his musical gifts in

motion. He crossed himself and crossed his bewildered lady, and crossed everybody in the figure, extorting shouts of cordial laughter from his cousin Willoughby. Be it said that the hour was four in the morning, when dancers must laugh at somebody, if only to refresh their feet, and the wit of the hour administers to the wildest laughter. Vernon was likened to Theseus in the maze, entirely dependent upon his Ariadne; to a fly released from a jam-pot; to a 'salvage', or green, man caught in a web of nymphs and made to go the paces. Willoughby was inexhaustible in the happy similes he poured out to Miss Durham across the lines of Sir Roger de Coverley, and they were not forgotten, they procured him a reputation as a convivial sparkler. Rumour went the round that he intended to give Laetitia to Vernon for good, when he could decide to take Miss Durham to himself; his generosity was famous; but that decision, though the rope was in the form of a knot, seemed reluctant for the conclusive close haul; it preferred the state of slackness; and if he courted Laetitia on behalf of his cousin, his cousinly love must have been greater than his passion, one had to suppose. He was generous enough for it, or for marrying the portionless girl himself.

There was a story of a brilliant young widow of our aristocracy who had very nearly snared him. Why should he object to marry into our aristocracy? Mrs Mountstuart asked him, and he replied that the girls of that class have no money, and he doubted the quality of their blood. He had his eyes awake. His duty to his House was a foremost thought with him, and for such a reason he may have been more anxious to give the slim and not robust Laetitia to Vernon than accede to his personal inclination. The mention of the widow singularly offended him, notwithstanding the high rank of the lady named. 'A widow?' he said. 'I?' He spoke to a widow; an oldish one truly; but his wrath at the suggestion of his union with a widow led him to be for the moment oblivious of the minor shades of good taste. He desired Mrs Mountstuart to contradict the story in positive terms. He repeated his desire;

he was urgent to have it contradicted, and said again, 'A widow!' straightening his whole figure to the erectness of the letter I. She was a widow unmarried a second time, and it has been known of the stedfast women who retain the name of their first husband, or do not hamper his title with a little new squire at their skirts, that they can partially approve the objections indicated by Sir Willoughby. They are thinking of themselves when they do so, and they will rarely say, 'I might have married'; rarely within them will they avow that, with their permission, it might have been. They can catch an idea of a gentleman's view of the widow's cap. But a niceness that could feel sharply wounded by the simple rumour of his alliance with the young relict of an earl was mystifying. Sir Willoughby unbent. His military letter I took a careless glance at itself lounging idly and proudly at ease in the glass of his mind, decked with a wanton wreath, as he dropped a hint, generously vague, just to show the origin of the rumour, and the excellent basis it had for not being credited. He was chidden. Mrs Mountstuart read him a lecture. She was however able to contradict the tale of the young countess. 'There is no fear of his marrying her, my dears.'

Meanwhile there was a fear that he would lose his chance of marrying the beautiful Miss Durham.

The dilemmas of little princes are often grave. They should be dwelt on now and then for an example to poor struggling commoners, of the slings and arrows assailing fortune's most favoured men, that we may preach contentment to the wretch who cannot muster wherewithal to marry a wife, or has done it and trots the streets, pack-laden, to maintain the dame and troops of children painfully reared to fill subordinate stations. According to our reading, a moral is always welcome in a moral country, and especially so when silly envy is to be chastised by it, the restless craving for change rebuked. Young Sir Willoughby, then, stood in this dilemma: – a lady was at either hand of him; the only two that had ever, apart from metropolitan conquests, not to be recited, touched his emotions. Susceptible to beauty, he had never seen so beautiful a girl as Constantia Durham. Equally susceptible to admiration of himself, he considered Laetitia Dale a paragon of cleverness. He stood between the queenly rose and the modest violet. One he bowed to; the other bowed to him. He could not have both; it is the law governing princes and pedestrians alike. But which could he forfeit? His growing acquaintance with the world taught him to put an increasing price on the sentiments of Miss Dale. Still Constantia's beauty was of a kind to send away beholders aching. She had the glory of the racing cutter full sail on a winning breeze; and she did not court to win him, she flew. In his more reflective hour the attractiveness of that lady which held the mirror to his features was paramount. But he had passionate snatches when the magnetism of the flyer drew him in her wake. Further to add to the complexity, he loved his liberty; he was princelier free; he had more subjects, more slaves; he ruled arrogantly in the world of women; he was more himself. His metropolitan experiences did not answer to his liking the particular question, Do we bind the woman down to us idolatrously by making a wife of her?

In the midst of his deliberations, a report of the hot pursuit of Miss Durham, casually mentioned to him by Lady Busshe, drew an immediate proposal from Sir Willoughby. She accepted him, and they were engaged. She had been nibbled at, all but eaten up, while he hung dubitative; and though that was the cause of his winning her, it offended his niceness. She had not come to him out of cloistral purity, out of perfect radiancy. Spiritually, likewise, was he a little prince, a despotic prince. He wished for her to have come to him out of an eggshell, somewhat more astonished at things than a chicken, but as completely enclosed before he tapped the shell, and seeing him with her sex's eyes first of all men. She talked frankly of her cousins and friends, young males. She could have replied to his bitter wish: 'Had you asked me on the night of your twenty-first birthday, Willoughby!' Since then she had been in the dust of the world, and he conceived his peculiar antipathy, destined to be so fatal to him, from the earlier hours of his engagement. He was quaintly incapable of a jealousy of individuals. A young Captain Oxford had been foremost in the swarm pursuing Constantia. Willoughby thought as little of Captain Oxford as he did of Vernon Whitford. His enemy was the world, the mass, which confounds us in a lump, which has breathed on her whom we have selected, whom we cannot, can never, rub quite clear of her contact with the abominated crowd. The pleasure of the world is to bowl down our soldierly letter I; to encroach on our identity, soil our niceness. To begin to think is the beginning of disgust of the world.

As soon the engagement was published all the county said that there had not been a chance for Laetitia, and Mrs Mountstuart Jenkinson humbly remarked, in an attitude of penitence, 'I'm not a witch.' Lady Busshe could claim to be one; she had foretold the event. Laetitia was of the same opinion as the county. She had looked up, but not hopefully. She had only looked up to the brightest, and, as he was the highest, how could she have hoped? She was the solitary companion of a sick father, whose inveterate prognostic of her, that she would live to rule at Patterne Hall, tortured the poor girl in proportion as he seemed to derive comfort from it. The noise of the engagement merely silenced him; recluse invalids cling obstinately to their ideas. He had observed Sir Willoughby in the society of his daughter, when the young baronet revived to a sprightly boyishness immediately. Indeed, as big boy and little girl, they had played together of old. Willoughby had been a handsome, fair boy. The portrait of him at the Hall, in a hat, leaning on his pony, with crossed legs, and long flaxen curls over his shoulders, was the image of her soul's most present angel; and, as a man, he had – she did not suppose intentionally – subjected her nature to bow to him; so submissive was she, that it was fuller happiness for her to think him right in all his actions than to imagine the circumstances different. This may appear to resemble the ecstasy of the devotee of Juggernaut.[2] It is a form of the passion inspired by little princes, and we need not marvel that a conservative sex should assist to keep them in their lofty places. What were there otherwise to look up to? We should have no dazzling beacon-lights if they were levelled and treated as clod earth; and it is worth while for here and there a woman to be burned, so long as women's general adoration of an ideal young man shall be preserved. Purity is our demand of them. They may justly cry for attraction. They cannot have it brighter than in the universal bearing of the eyes of their sisters upon a little prince, one who has the ostensible virtues in his pay, and can practise them without injuring himself to make himself unsightly. Let the races of men be by-and-by astonished at their Gods, if they please. Meantime they had better continue to worship.

Laetitia did continue. She saw Miss Durham at Patterne on several occasions. She admired the pair. She had a wish to witness the bridal ceremony. She was looking forward to the day with that mixture of eagerness and withholding which we have as we draw nigh the disenchanting termination of an enchanting romance, when Sir Willoughby met her on a Sunday morning, as she crossed his park solitarily to church. They were within ten days of the appointed ceremony. He should have been away at Miss Durham's end of the county. He had, Laetitia knew, ridden over to her the day before; but there he was; and very unwontedly, quite surprisingly, he presented his arm to conduct Laetitia to the church-door, and talked and laughed in a way that reminded her of a hunting gentleman she had seen once rising to his feet, staggering from an ugly fall across hedge and fence into one of the lanes of her short winter walks. 'All's well, all sound, never better, only a scratch!' the gentleman had said, as he reeled and pressed a bleeding head. Sir Willoughby chattered of his felicity in meeting her. 'I am really wonderfully lucky,' he said, and he said that and other things over and over, incessantly talking, and telling an anecdote of county occurrences, and laughing at it with a mouth that would not widen. He went on talking in the church porch, and murmuring softly some steps up the aisle, passing the pews of Mrs Mountstuart Jenkinson and Lady Busshe. Of course he was entertaining, but what a strangeness it was to Laetitia! His face would have been half under an antique bonnet. It came very close to hers, and the scrutiny he bent on her was most solicitous.

After the service, he avoided the great ladies by sauntering up to within a yard or two of where she sat; he craved her hand on his arm to lead her forth by the park entrance to the church, all the while bending to her, discoursing rapidly, appearing radiantly interested in her quiet replies, with fits of intentness that stared itself out into dim abstraction. She hazarded the briefest replies for fear of not having understood him.

One question she asked: 'Miss Durham is well, I trust?'

And he answered 'Durham?' and said, 'There is no Miss Durham to my knowledge.'

The impression he left with her was, that he might yesterday during his ride have had an accident and fallen on his head.

She would have asked that, if she had not known him for so thorough an Englishman, in his dislike to have it thought that accidents could hurt even when they happened to him.

He called the next day to claim her for a walk. He assured her she had promised it, and he appealed to her father, who could not testify to a promise he had not heard, but begged her to leave him to have her walk. So once more she was in the park with Sir Willoughby, listening to his raptures over old days. A word of assent from her sufficed him. 'I am now myself,' was one of the remarks he repeated this day. She dilated on the beauty of the park and the Hall to gratify him.

He did not speak of Miss Durham, and Laetitia became afraid to mention her name.

At their parting, Willoughby promised Laetitia that he would call on the morrow. He did not come; and she could well excuse him, after her hearing of the tale.

It was a lamentable tale. He had ridden to Sir John Durham's mansion, a distance of thirty miles, to hear, on his arrival, that Constantia had quitted her father's house two days previously on a visit to an aunt in London, and had just sent word that she was the wife of Captain Oxford, hussar, and messmate of one of her brothers. A letter from the bride awaited Willoughby at the Hall. He had ridden back at night, not caring how he used his horse in order to get swiftly home, so forgetful of himself was he under the terrible blow. That was the night of Saturday. On the day following, being Sunday, he met Laetitia in his park, led her to church, led her out of it, and the day after that, previous to his disappearance for some weeks, was walking with her in full view of the carriages along the road.

He had, indeed, you see, been very fortunately, if not considerately, liberated by Miss Durham. He, as a man of honour, could not have taken the initiative, but the frenzy of a jealous girl might urge her to such a course; and how little he suffered from it had been shown to the world. Miss Durham, the story went, was his mother's choice for him against his heart's inclinations; which had finally subdued Lady Patterne. Consequently, there was no longer an obstacle between Sir Willoughby and Miss Dale. It was a pleasant and romantic story, and it put most people in good humour with the county's favourite, as his choice of a portionless girl of no position would not have done without the shock of astonishment at the conduct of Miss Durham, and the desire to feel that so prevailing a gentleman was not in any degree pitiable. Constantia was called 'that mad thing'. Laetitia broke forth in novel and abundant merits; and one of the chief points of requisition in relation to Patterne – a Lady Willoughby who would entertain well and animate the deadness of the Hall, became a certainty when her gentleness and liveliness and exceeding cleverness were considered. She was often a visitor at the Hall by Lady Patterne's express invitation, and sometimes on these occasions Willoughby was there too, superintending the filling up of his laboratory, though he was not at home to the county; it was not expected that he should be yet. He had taken heartily to the pursuit of science, and spoke of little else. Science, he said, was in our days the sole object worth a devoted pursuit. But the sweeping remark could hardly apply to Laetitia, of whom he was the courteous, quiet wooer you behold when a man has broken loose from an unhappy tangle to return to the lady of his first and strongest affections.

Some months of homely courtship ensued, and then, the decent interval prescribed by the situation having elapsed, Sir Willoughby Patterne left his native land on a tour of the globe.

CHAPTER 4

❌❌❌❌

Laetitia Dale

THAT was another surprise to the county.

Let us not inquire into the feelings of patiently starving women; they must obtain some sustenance of their own, since, as you perceive, they live; evidently they are not in need of a great amount of nourishment; and we may set them down for creatures with a rush-light of animal fire to warm them. They cannot have much vitality who are so little exclamatory. A corresponding sentiment of patient compassion, akin to scorn, is provoked by persons having the opportunity for pathos, and declining to use it. The public bosom was open to Laetitia for several weeks, and had she run to it to bewail herself she would have been cherished in thankfulness for a country drama. There would have been a party against her, cold people, critical of her pretensions to rise from an unrecognized sphere

to be mistress of Patterne Hall, but there would also have
been a party against Sir Willoughby, composed of the two or
three revolutionists, tired of the yoke, which are to be found
in England when there is a stir; a larger number of born sym-
pathetics, ever ready to yield the tear for the tear; and here
and there a Samaritan soul prompt to succour poor humanity
in distress. The opportunity passed undramatized. Laetitia
presented herself at church with a face mildly devout, according to her custom, and she accepted invitations to the Hall, she
assisted at the reading of Willoughby's letters to his family,
and fed on dry husks of him wherein her name was not mentioned; never one note of the summoning call for pathos did
this young lady blow.

So, very soon the public bosom closed. She had, under the
fresh interpretation of affairs, too small a spirit to be Lady
Willoughby of Patterne; she could not have entertained becomingly; he must have seen that the girl was not the match
for him in station, and off he went to conquer the remainder
of a troublesome first attachment, no longer extremely disturbing, to judge from the tenour of his letters; really
incomparable letters! Lady Busshe and Mrs Mountstuart Jenkinson enjoyed a perusal of them. Sir Willoughby appeared as
a splendid young representative island lord in these letters to
his family, despatched from the principal cities of the United
States of America. He would give them a sketch of 'our
democratic cousins', he said. Such cousins! They might all
have been in the Marines. He carried his English standard over
that continent, and by simply jotting down facts, he left an
idea of the results of the measurement to his family and
friends at home. He was an adept in the irony of incongruously grouping. The nature of the equality under the
Stars and Stripes was presented in this manner. Equality!
Reflections came occasionally: 'These cousins of ours are
highly amusing. I am among the descendants of the Round-
heads. Now and then an allusion to old domestic differences,
in perfect good temper. We go on in our way; they theirs,

in the apparent belief that Republicanism operates remarkable changes in human nature. Vernon tries hard to think it does. The upper ten of our cousins are the Infernal of Paris. The rest of them is Radical England, as far as I am acquainted with that section of my country.' – Where we compared, they were absurd; where we contrasted, they were monstrous. The contrast of Vernon's letters with Willoughby's was just as extreme. You could hardly have taken them for relatives travelling together, or Vernon Whitford for a born and bred Englishman. The same scenes furnished by these two pens might have been sketched in different hemispheres. Vernon had no irony. He had nothing of Willoughby's epistolary creative power, which, causing his family and friends to exclaim: 'How like him that is!' conjured them across the broad Atlantic to behold and clap hands at his lordliness.

They saw him distinctly, as with the naked eye; a word, a turn of the pen, or a word unsaid, offered the picture of him in America, Japan, China, Australia, nay, the continent of Europe, holding an English review of his Maker's grotesques. Vernon seemed a sheepish fellow, without stature abroad, glad of a compliment, grateful for a dinner, endeavouring sadly to digest all he saw and heard. But one was a Patterne; the other a Whitford. One had genius; the other pottered after him with the title of student. One was the English gentleman wherever he went; the other was a new kind of thing, nondescript, produced in England of late, and not likely to come to much good himself, or do much good to the country.

Vernon's dancing in America was capitally described by Willoughby. 'Adieu to our cousins!' the latter wrote on his voyage to Japan. 'I may possibly have had some vogue in their ball-rooms, and in showing them an English seat on horseback: I must resign myself if I have not been popular among them. I could not sing their national song – if a congery of States be a nation – and I must confess I listened with frigid politeness to their singing of it. A great people, no doubt. Adieu to them. I have had to tear old Vernon away. He had serious thoughts of settling, means to correspond with some of them.' On the whole, forgetting two or more 'traits of insolence' on the part of his hosts, which he cited, Willoughby escaped pretty comfortably. The president had been, consciously or not, uncivil, but one knew his origin. Upon these interjections, placable flicks of the lionly tail addressed to Britannia the Ruler, who expected him in some mildish way to lash terga cauda³ in retiring, Sir Willoughby Patterne passed from a land of alien manners; and ever after he spoke of America respectfully and pensively, with a tail tucked in, as it were. His travels were profitable to himself. The fact is, that there are cousins who come to greatness and must be pacified, or they will prove annoying. Heaven forefend a collision between cousins!

Willoughby returned to his England after an absence of three years. On a fair April morning, the last of the month, he drove along his park palings, and, by the luck of things, Laetitia was the first of his friends whom he met. She was crossing from field to field with a band of school-children, gathering wild flowers for the morrow May-day. He sprang to the ground and seized her hand. 'Laetitia Dale!' he said. He panted. 'Your name is sweet English music! And you are well?' The anxious question permitted him to read deeply in her eyes. He found the man he sought there, squeezed him passionately, and let her go, saying: 'I could not have prayed for a lovelier home-scene to welcome me than you and these children flower-gathering. I don't believe in chance. It was decreed that we should meet. Do not you think so?'

Laetitia breathed faintly of her gladness.

He begged her to distribute a gold coin among the little ones; asked for the names of some of them, and repeated: 'Mary, Susan, Charlotte – only the Christian names, pray! Well, my dears, you will bring your garlands to the Hall to-morrow morning; and mind, early! no slugabeds tomorrow; I suppose I am browned, Laetitia?' He smiled in apology for the foreign sun, and murmured, with rapture: 'The green of this English country is unsurpassed. It is wonderful. Leave England and be baked, if you would appreciate it. You can't, unless you taste exile as I have done – for how many years? How many?'

'Three,' said Laetitia.

'Thirty!' said he. 'It seems to me that length. At least, I am immensely older. But looking at you, I could think it less than three. You have not changed. You are absolutely unchanged. I am bound to hope so. I shall see you soon. I have much to talk of, much to tell you. I shall hasten to call on your father. I have specially to speak with him. I – what happiness this is, Laetitia! But I must not forget I have a mother. Adieu; for some hours – not for many!'

He pressed her hand again. He was gone.

She dismissed the children to their homes. Plucking primroses was hard labour now – a dusty business. She could have wished that her planet had not descended to earth, his presence agitated her so; but his enthusiastic patriotism was like a shower that, in the Spring season of the year, sweeps against the hard-binding East and melts the air and brings out new colours, makes life flow; and her thoughts recurred in wonderment to the behaviour of Constantia Durham. That was Laetitia's manner of taking up her weakness once more. She could almost have reviled the woman who had given this beneficent magician, this pathetic exile, of the aristocratic sunburned visage and deeply scrutinizing eyes, cause for grief. How deeply his eyes could read! The starveling of patience awoke to the idea of a feast. The sense of hunger came with it, and hope came, and patience fled. She would have rejected hope to keep patience nigh her; but surely it can not always be Winter! said her reasoning blood, and we must excuse her as best we can if she was assured by her restored warmth that Willoughby came in the order of the revolving seasons, marking a long Winter past. He had specially to speak with

her father, he had said. What could that mean? What, but –
She dared not phrase it or view it.

At their next meeting she was 'Miss Dale'.

A week later he was closeted with her father.

Mr Dale, in the evening of that pregnant day, eulogized
Sir Willoughby as a landlord. A new lease of the cottage was
to be granted him on the old terms, he said. Except that Sir
Willoughby had congratulated him in the possession of an
excellent daughter, their interview was one of landlord and
tenant, it appeared; and Laetitia said, 'So we shall not have to
leave the cottage?' in a tone of satisfaction, while she quietly
gave a wrench to the neck of the young hope in her breast. At
night her diary received the line: 'This day I was a fool.
To-morrow?'

To-morrow and many days afterwards there were dashes
instead of words.

Patience travelled back to her sullenly. As we must have
some kind of food, and she had nothing else, she took to that
and found it dryer than of yore. It is a composing but a lean
dietary. The dead are patient, and we get a certain likeness to
them in feeding on it unintermittingly overlong. Her hol-
lowed cheeks with the fallen leaf in them pleaded against herself
to justify her idol for not looking down on one like her. She
saw him when he was at the Hall. He did not notice any
change. He was exceedingly gentle and courteous. More than
once she discovered his eyes dwelling on her, and then he looked hurriedly at his mother, and Laetitia had to shut her mind
from thinking, lest thinking should be a sin and hope a guilty
spectre. But had his mother objected to her? She could not
avoid asking herself. His tour of the globe had been under-
taken at his mother's desire; she was an ambitious lady, in
failing health; and she wished to have him living with her at
Patterne, yet seemed to agree that he did wisely to reside in
London.

One day Sir Willoughby, in the quiet manner which was
his humour, informed her that he had become a country

gentleman; he had abandoned London, he loathed it as the burial-place of the individual man. He intended to sit down on his estates and have his cousin Vernon Whitford to assist him in managing them, he said; and very amusing was his description of his cousin's shifts to live by literature, and add enough to a beggarly income to get his usual two months of the year in the Alps. Previous to his great tour, Willoughby had spoken of Vernon's judgement with derision; nor was it entirely unknown that Vernon had offended his family pride by some extravagant act. But after their return he acknowledged Vernon's talents, and seemed unable to do without him.

The new arrangement gave Laetitia a companion for her walks. Pedestrianism was a sour business to Willoughby, whose exclamation of the word indicated a willingness for any amount of exercise on horseback; but she had no horse, and so, while he hunted, Laetitia and Vernon walked, and the neighbourhood speculated on the circumstances, until the ladies Eleanor and Isabel Patterne engaged her more frequently for carriage exercise, and Sir Willoughby was observed riding beside them.

A real and sunny pleasure befell Laetitia in the establishment of young Crossjay Patterne under her roof; the son of the lieutenant, now captain, of Marines; a boy of twelve with the sprights of twelve boys in him, for whose board and lodgement Vernon provided by arrangement with her father. Vernon was one of your men that have no occupation for their money, no bills to pay for repair of their property, and are insane to spend. He had heard of Captain Patterne's large family, and proposed to have his eldest boy at the Hall, to teach him; but Willoughby declined to house the son of such a father, predicting that the boy's hair would be red, his skin eruptive, and his practices detestable. So Vernon, having obtained Mr Dale's consent to accommodate this youth, stalked off to Devonport, and brought back a rosy-cheeked, round-bodied rogue of a boy, who fell upon meats and puddings, and defeated them, with a captivating simplicity in his confession that he had never had enough to eat in his life. He had gone through a training for a plentiful table. At first, after a number of helps, young Crossjay would sit and sigh heavily, in contemplation of the unfinished dish. Subsequently, he told his host and hostess that he had two sisters above his own age, and three brothers and two sisters younger than he: 'All hungry!' said the boy.

His pathos was most comical. It was a good month before he could see pudding taken away from table without a sigh of regret that he could not finish it as deputy for the Devonport household. The pranks of the little fellow, and his revel in a country life, and muddy wildness in it, amused Laetitia from morning to night. She, when she had caught him, taught him in the morning; Vernon, favoured by the chase, in the afternoon. Young Crossjay would have enlivened any household. He was not only indolent, he was opposed to the acquisition of knowledge through the medium of books, and would say: 'But I don't want to!' in a tone to make a logician thoughtful. Nature was very strong in him. He had, on each return of the hour for instruction, to be plucked out of the earth, rank of the soil, like a root, for the exercise of his big round headpiece on those tyrannous puzzles. But the habits of birds, and the place for their eggs, and the management of rabbits, and the tickling of fish, and poaching joys with combative boys of the district, and how to wheedle a cook for a luncheon for a whole day in the rain, he soon knew of his great nature. His passion for our naval service was a means of screwing his attention to lessons after he had begun to understand that the desert had to be traversed to attain midshipman's rank. He boasted ardently of his fighting father, and, chancing to be near the Hall as he was talking to Vernon and Laetitia of his father, he propounded a question close to his heart, and he put it in these words, following: 'My father's the one to lead an army!' when he paused. 'I say, Mr Whitford, Sir Willoughby's kind to me, and gives me crown-pieces, why wouldn't he see my father, and my father came here ten miles in the rain to see him, and had to walk ten miles back, and sleep at an inn?'

The only answer to be given was, that Sir Willoughby could not have been at home. 'Oh! my father saw him, and Sir Willoughby said he was no at home,' the boy replied, producing an odd ring in the ear by his repetition of 'not at home' in the same voice as the apology, plainly innocent of malice. Vernon told Laetitia, however, that the boy never asked an explanation of Sir Willoughby.

Unlike the horse of the adage, it was easier to compel young Crossjay to drink of the waters of instruction than to get him to the brink. His heart was not so antagonistic as his nature, and by degrees, owing to a proper mixture of discipline and cajolery, he imbibed. He was whistling at the cook's windows after a day of wicked truancy, on an April night, and reported adventures over the supper supplied to him. Laetitia entered the kitchen with a reproving forefinger. He jumped to kiss her, and went on chattering of a place fifteen miles distant, where he had seen Sir Willoughby riding with a young lady. The impossibility that the boy should have got so far on foot made Laetitia doubtful of his veracity, until she heard that a gentleman had taken him up on the road in a gig, and had driven him to a farm to show him strings of birds' eggs and stuffed birds of every English kind, kingfishers, yaffles, black woodpeckers, goat-sucker owls, more mouth than head, with dusty, dark-spotted wings, like moths; all very circumstantial. Still, in spite of his tea at the farm, and ride back by rail at the gentleman's expense, the tale seemed fictitious to Laetitia until Crossjay related how that he had stood to salute on the road to the railway, and taken off his cap to Sir Willoughby, and Sir Willoughby had passed him, not noticing him, though the young lady did, and looked back and nodded. The hue of truth was in that picture.

Strange eclipse, when the hue of truth comes shadowing over our bright ideal planet. It will not seem the planet's fault, but truth's. Reality is the offender; delusion our treasure that we are robbed of. Then begins with us the term of wilful delusion, and its necessary accompaniment of the disgust of reality; exhausting the heart much more than patient endurance of starvation.

Hints were dropping about the neighbourhood; the hedgeways twittered, the tree-tops cawed. Mrs Mountstuart Jenkinson was loud on the subject: 'Patterne is to have a mistress at last, you say? But there never was a doubt of his marrying – he must marry; and, so long as he does not marry a foreign woman, we have no cause to complain. He met her at Cherriton. Both were struck at the same moment. Her father is, I hear, some sort of learned man; money; no land. No house either, I believe. People who spend half their time on the Continent. They are now for a year at Upton Park. The very girl to settle down and entertain when she does think of settling. Eighteen, perfect manners; you need not ask if a beauty. Sir Willoughby will have his dues. We must teach her to make amends to him – but don't listen to Lady Busshe! He was too young at twenty-three or twenty-four. No young man is ever jilted; he is allowed to escape. A young man married is a fire-eater bound over to keep the peace; if he keeps it he worries it. At thirty-one or thirty-two he is ripe for his command, because he knows how to bend. And Sir Willoughby is a splendid creature, only wanting a wife to complete him. For a man like that to go on running about would never do. Soberly – no! It would soon be getting ridiculous. He has been no worse than other men, probably better – infinitely more excusable; but now we have him, and it was time we should. I shall see her and study her, sharply, you may be sure; though I fancy I can rely on his judgement.'

In confirmation of the swelling buzz, the Rev. Dr Middleton and his daughter paid a flying visit to the Hall, where they were seen only by the members of the Patterne family. Young Crossjay had a short conversation with Miss Middleton, and ran to the cottage full of her – she loved the navy and had a merry face. She had a smile of very pleasant humour according to Vernon. The young lady was outlined to Laetitia as tall, elegant, lively; and painted as carrying youth like a flag. With her smile of 'very pleasant humour', she could not but be winning.

Vernon spoke more of her father, a scholar of high repute; happily, a scholar of an independent fortune. His maturer recollection of Miss Middleton grew poetic, or he described her in an image to suit a poetic end: 'She gives you an idea of the Mountain Echo. Doctor Middleton has one of the grandest heads in England.'

'What is her Christian name?' said Laetitia.

He thought her Christian name was Clara.

Laetitia went to bed and walked through the day conceiving the Mountain Echo the swift, wild spirit, Clara by name, sent fleeting on a far half circle by the voice it is roused to subserve; sweeter than beautiful, high above drawing-room beauties as the colours of the sky; and if, at the same time, elegant and of loveable smiling, could a man resist her? To inspire the title of Mountain Echo in any mind, a young lady must be singularly spiritualized. Her father doated on her, Vernon said. Who would not? It seemed an additional cruelty that the grace of a poetical attractiveness should be round her, for this was robbing Laetitia of some of her own little fortune, mystical though that might be. But a man like Sir Willoughby had claims on poetry, possessing as he did every manly grace; and to think that Miss Middleton had won him by virtue of something native to her likewise, though mystically, touched Laetitia with a faint sense of relationship to the chosen girl. 'What is in me, he sees on her.' It decked her pride to think so, as a wreath on the gravestone. She encouraged her imagination to brood over Clara, and invested her designedly with romantic charms, in spite of pain; the ascetic zealot hugs his share of Heaven – most bitter, most blessed – in his hair-shirt and scourge, and Laetitia's happiness was to glorify Clara. Through that chosen rival, through her comprehension of the spirit of Sir Willoughby's choice of one such as Clara, she was linked to him yet.

Her mood of ecstatic fidelity was a dangerous exaltation; one that in a desert will distort the brain, and in the world where the idol dwells will put him, should he come nigh, to its own furnace-test, and get a clear brain out of a burnt heart. She was frequently at the Hall, helping to nurse Lady Patterne. Sir Willoughby had hitherto treated her as a dear insignificant friend, to whom it was unnecessary that he should mention the object of his rides to Upton Park.

He had, however, in the contemplation of what he was gaining, fallen into anxiety about what he might be losing. She belonged to his brilliant youth; her devotion was the bride of his youth; he was a man who lived backward almost as intensely as in the present; and, notwithstanding Laetitia's praiseworthy zeal in attending on his mother, he suspected some unfaithfulness: hardly without cause: she had not looked paler of late; her eyes had not reproached him; the secret of the old days between them had been as little concealed as it was exposed. She might have buried it, after the way of woman, whose bosoms can be tombs, if we and the world allow them to be; absolutely sepulchres, where you lie dead, ghastly. Even if not dead and horrible to think of, you may be lying cold, somewhere in a corner. Even if embalmed, you may not be much visited. And how is the world to know you are embalmed? You are no better than a rotting wretch to the world that does not have peeps of you in the woman's breast, and see lights burning and an occasional exhibition of the services of worship. There are women – tell us not of her of Ephesus!4 – that have embalmed you, and have quitted the world to keep the tapers alight, and a stranger comes, and they, who have your image before them, will suddenly blow out the vestal flames and treat you as dust to fatten the garden of their bosoms for a fresh flower of love. Sir Willoughby knew it; he had experience of it in the form of the stranger; and he knew the stranger's feelings toward his predecessor and the lady.

He waylaid Laetitia, to talk of himself and his plans: the

project of a run to Italy. Enviable? Yes, but in England you live the higher moral life. Italy boasts of sensual beauty; the spiritual is yours. 'I know Italy well; I have often wished to act as a cicerone to you there. As it is, I suppose I shall be with those who know the land as well as I do, and will not be particularly enthusiastic: – if you are what you were?' He was guilty of this perplexing twist from one person to another in a sentence more than once. While he talked exclusively of himself it seemed to her a condescension. In time he talked principally of her, beginning with her admirable care of his mother; and he wished to introduce 'a Miss Middleton' to her; he wanted her opinion of Miss Middleton; he relied on her intuition of character, had never known it err.

'If I supposed it could err, Miss Dale, I should not be so certain of myself. I am bound up in my good opinion of you, you see; and you must continue the same, or where shall I be?' Thus he was led to dwell upon friendship, and the charm of the friendship of men and women, 'Platonism', as it was called. 'I have laughed at it in the world, but not in the depth of my heart. The world's platonic attachments are laughable enough. You have taught me that the ideal of friendship *is* possible – when we find two who are capable of a disinterested esteem. The rest of life is duty; duty to parents, duty to country. But friendship is the holiday of those who can be friends. Wives are plentiful, friends are rare. I know *how* rare!'

Laetitia swallowed her thoughts as they sprang up. Why was he torturing her? – to give himself a holiday? She could bear to lose him – she was used to it – and bear his indifference, but not that he should disfigure himself; it made her poor. It was as if he required an oath of her when he said: 'Italy! But I shall never see a day in Italy to compare with the day of my return to England, or know a pleasure so exquisite as your welcome of me. Will you be true to that? May I look forward to just another such meeting?'

He pressed her for an answer. She gave the best she could. He was dissatisfied, and to her hearing it was hardly in the tone of manliness that he entreated her to reassure him; he womanized his language. She had to say: 'I am afraid I can not undertake to make it an appointment, Sir Willoughby,' before he recovered his alertness, which he did, for he was anything but obtuse, with the reply, 'You would keep it if you promised, and freeze at your post. So, as accidents happen, we must leave it to fate. The will's the thing. You know my detestation of changes. At least I have you for my tenant, and wherever I am, I see your light at the end of my park.'

'Neither my father nor I would willingly quit Ivy Cottage,' said Laetitia.

'So far, then,' he murmured. 'You will give me a long notice, and it must be with my consent if you think of quitting?'

'I could almost engage to do that,' she said.

'You love the place?'

'Yes; I am the most contented of cottagers.'

'I believe, Miss Dale, it would be well for my happiness were I a cottager.'

'That is the dream of the palace. But to be one, and not to wish to be other, is quiet sleep in comparison.'

'You paint a cottage in colours that tempt one to run from big houses and households.'

'You would run back to them faster, Sir Willoughby.'

'You may know me,' said he, bowing and passing on contentedly. He stopped. 'But I am not ambitious.'

'Perhaps you are too proud for ambition, Sir Willoughby.'

'You hit me to the life!'

He passed on regretfully. Clara Middleton did not study and know him like Laetitia Dale.

Laetitia was left to think it pleased him to play at cat and mouse. She had not 'hit him to the life', or she would have marvelled in acknowledging how sincere he was.

At her next sitting by the bedside of Lady Patterne she received a certain measure of insight that might have helped her to fathom him, if only she could have kept her feelings down.

The old lady was affectionately confidential in talking of her one subject, her son. 'And here is another dashing girl, my dear; she has money and health and beauty; and so has he; and it appears a fortunate union; I hope and pray it may be; but we begin to read the world when our eyes grow dim, because we read the plain lines, and I ask myself whether money and health and beauty on both sides have not been the mutual attraction. We tried it before; and that girl Durham was honest, whatever we may call her. I should have desired an appreciative thoughtful partner for him, a woman of mind, with another sort of wealth and beauty. She was honest, she ran away in time; there was a worse thing possible than that. And now we have the same chapter, and the same kind of person, who may not be quite as honest; and I shall not see the end of it. Promise me you will always be good to him; be my son's friend; his Egeria, he names you. Be what you were to him when that girl broke his heart, and no one, not even his mother, was allowed to see that he suffered anything. Comfort him in his sensitiveness. Willoughby has the most entire faith in you. Were that destroyed – I shudder! You are, he says, and he has often said, his image of the constant woman –'

Laetitia's hearing took in no more. She repeated to herself for days: 'His image of the constant woman!' Now, when he was a second time forsaking her, his praise of her constancy wore the painful ludicrousness of the look of a whimper on the face.

CHAPTER 5

✕✕✕✕

Clara Middleton

THE great meeting of Sir Willoughby Patterne and Miss Middleton had taken place at Cherriton Grange, the seat of a county grandee, where this young lady of eighteen was first seen rising above the horizon. She had money and health and beauty, the triune of perfect starriness, which makes all men astronomers. He looked on her, expecting her to look at him. But as soon as he looked he found that he must be in motion to win a look in return. He was one of a pack; many were ahead of him, the whole of them were eager. He had to debate within himself how best to communicate to her that he was Willoughby Patterne, before her gloves were too much soiled to flatter his niceness, for here and there, all around, she was yielding her hand to partners – obscurant males whose touch leaves a stain. Far too generally gracious was Her Starriness to please him. The effect of it, nevertheless, was to hurry him with all his might into the heat of the chase, while yet he knew no more of her than that he was competing for a prize, and Willoughby Patterne was only one of dozens to the young lady.

A deeper student of Science than his rivals, he appreciated Nature's compliment in the fair one's choice of you. We now scientifically know that in this department of the universal struggle, success is awarded to the bettermost. You spread a handsomer tail than your fellows, you dress a finer top-knot, you pipe a newer note, have a longer stride; she reviews you in competition, and selects you. The superlative is magnetic to her. She may be looking elsewhere, and you will see – the superlative will simply have to beckon, away she glides. She cannot help herself; it is her nature, and her nature is the guarantee for the noblest races of men to come of her. In complimenting you, she is a promise of superior offspring. Science thus – or it is better to say – an acquaintance with science facilitates the cultivation of aristocracy. Consequently a successful pursuit and a wresting of her from a body of competitors, tells you that you are the best man. What is more, it tells the world so.

Willoughby aired his amiable superlatives in the eye of Miss Middleton; he had a leg. He was the heir of successful competitors. He had a style, a tone, an artist tailor, an authority of manner; he had in the hopeful ardour of the chase among a multitude a freshness that gave him advantage; and together with his undeviating energy when there was a prize to be won and possessed, these were scarce resistible. He spared no pains, for he was adust and athirst for the winning-post. He courted her father, aware that men likewise, and parents preeminently, have their preference for the larger offer, the deeper pocket, the broader lands, the respectfuller consideration. Men, after their fashion, as well as women, distinguish the bettermost, and aid him to succeed, as Dr Middleton certainly did in the crisis of the memorable question proposed to his daughter within a month of Willoughby's reception at Upton Park. The young lady was astonished at his whirlwind wooing of her, and bent to it like a sapling. She begged for time; Willoughby could barely wait. She unhesitatingly owned that she liked no one better, and he consented. A calm examination of his position told him that it was unfair so long as he stood engaged, and she did not. She pleaded a desire to see a little of the world before she plighted herself. She alarmed him; he assumed the amazing god of love under the subtlest guise of the divinity. Willingly would he obey her behests, resignedly languish, were it not for his mother's desire to see the future lady of Patterne established there before she died. Love shone cunningly through the mask of filial duty, but the plea of urgency was reasonable. Dr Middleton thought it reasonable, supposing his daughter to have an inclination. She had no disinclination, though she had a maidenly desire to see a little of the world – grace for one year, she said. Willoughby reduced the year to six months, and granted that term, for which, in gratitude, she submitted to stand engaged; and that was no light whispering of a word. She was implored to enter the state of captivity by the pronunciation of vows – a private but a binding ceremonial. She had health and beauty, and money to gild these gifts; not that he stipulated for money with his bride, but it adds a lustre to dazzle the world; and, moreover, the pack of rival pursuers hung close behind, yelping and raising their dolorous throats to the moon. Captive she must be.

He made her engagement no light whispering matter. It was a solemn plighting of a troth. Why not? Having said, I am yours, she could say, I am wholly yours, I am yours forever, I swear it, I will never swerve from it, I am your wife in heart, yours utterly; our engagement is written above. To this she considerately appended, 'as far as I am concerned'; a piece of somewhat chilling generosity, and he forced her to pass him through love's catechism in turn, and came out with fervent answers that bound him to her too indissolubly to let her doubt of her being loved. And I am loved! she exclaimed to her heart's echoes, in simple faith and wonderment. Hardly had she begun to think of love ere the apparition arose in her path. She had not thought of love with any warmth, and here it was. She had only dreamed of love as one of the distant blessings of the mighty world, lying somewhere in the world's forests, across wild seas, veiled, encompassed with beautiful perils, a throbbing secrecy, but too remote to quicken her bosom's throbs. Her chief idea of it was, the enrichment of the world by love.

Thus did Miss Middleton acquiesce in the principle of selection.

And then did the best man of a host blow his triumphant horn, and loudly.

He looked the fittest; he justified the dictum of Science. The survival of the Patternes was assured. 'I would,' he said to his admirer, Mrs Mountstuart Jenkinson, 'have bargained for health above everything, but she has everything besides – lineage, beauty, breeding: is what they call an heiress, and is the most accomplished of her sex.' With a delicate art he conveyed to the lady's understanding that Miss Middleton had been snatched from a crowd, without a breath of the crowd having offended his niceness. He did it through sarcasm at your modern young women, who run about the world nibbling and nibbled at, until they know one sex as well as the other, and are not a whit less cognizant of the market than men; pure, possibly; it is not so easy to say innocent; decidedly not our feminine ideal. Miss Middleton was different: she was the true ideal, fresh-gathered morning fruit in a basket, warranted by her bloom.

Women do not defend their younger sisters for doing what they perhaps have done – lifting a veil to be seen, and peeping at a world where innocence is as poor a guarantee as a babe's caul against shipwreck. Women of the world never think of attacking the sensual stipulation for perfect bloom, silver purity, which is redolent of the Oriental origin of the love-passion of their lords. Mrs Mountstuart congratulated Sir Willoughby on the prize he had won in the fair western-eastern.

'Let me see her,' she said; and Miss Middleton was introduced and critically observed.

She had the mouth that smiles in repose. The lips met full on the centre of the bow and thinned along to a lifting dimple; the eyelids also lifted slightly at the outer corners, and seemed, like the lip into the limpid cheek, quickening up the temples, as with a run of light, or the ascension indicated off a shoot of colour. Her features were playfellows of one another, none of them pretending to rigid correctness, nor the nose to the ordinary dignity of governess among merry girls, despite which the nose was of a fair design, not acutely interrogative or inviting to gambols. Aspens imaged in water, waiting for the breeze, would offer a susceptible lover some suggestion of her face: a pure, smooth-white face, tenderly flushed in the cheeks, where the gentle dints were faintly intermelting even during quietness. Her eyes were brown, set well between mild lids, often shadowed, not unwakeful. Her hair of lighter brown, swelling above her temples on the sweep to the knot, imposed the triangle of the fabulous wild woodland visage from brow to mouth and chin, evidently in agreement with her taste; and the triangle suited her; but her face was not significant of a tameless wildness or of weakness; her equable shut mouth threw its long curve to guard the small round chin from that effect; her eyes wavered only in humour, they were steady when thoughtfulness was awakened; and at such seasons the build of her winter-beechwood hair lost the touch of nymph-like and whimsical, and strangely, by mere outline, added to her appearance of studious concentration. Observe the hawk on stretched wings over the prey he spies, for an idea of this change in the look of a young lady whom Vernon Whitford could liken to the Mountain Echo, and Mrs Mountstuart Jenkinson pronounced to be 'a dainty rogue in porcelain'.

Vernon's fancy of her must have sprung from her prompt and most musical responsiveness. He preferred the society of her learned father to that of a girl under twenty engaged to his cousin, but the charm of her ready tongue and her voice was to his intelligent understanding wit, natural wit, crystal wit, as opposed to the paste-sparkle of the wit of the town. In his encomiums he did not quote Miss Middleton's wit; neverthe-less, he ventured to speak of it to Mrs Mountstuart, causing that lady to say: 'Ah, well, I have not noticed the wit. You may have the art of drawing it out.'

No one had noticed the wit. The corrupted hearing of people required a collision of sounds, Vernon supposed. For his part, to prove their excellence, he recollected a great many of Miss Middleton's remarks; they came flying to him; and so long as he forbore to speak them aloud, they had a curious wealth of meaning. It could not be all her manner, however much his own manner might spoil them. It might be, to a certain degree, her quickness at catching the hue and shade of evanescent conversation. Possibly by remembering the whole of a conversation wherein she had her place, the wit was to be tested; only how could any one retain the heavy portion? As there was no use in being argumentative on a subject affording him personally, and apparently solitarily, refreshment and enjoyment, Vernon resolved to keep it to himself. The eulogies of her beauty, a possession in which he did not consider her so very conspicuous, irritated him in consequence. To flatter Sir Willoughby, it was the fashion to exalt her as one of the types of beauty; the one providentially selected to set off his masculine type. She was compared to those delicate flowers, the ladies of the Court of China, on rice-paper. A little French dressing would make her at home on the sward by the fountain among the lutes and whispers of the bewitching silken shepherdesses who live though they never were. Lady Busshe was reminded of the favourite lineaments of the women of Leonardo, the angels of Luini. Lady Culmer had seen crayon sketches of demoiselles of the French aristocracy resembling her. Some one mentioned an antique statue of a figure breathing into a flute: and the mouth at the flute-stop might have a distant semblance of the bend of her mouth, but this comparison was repelled as grotesque.

For once Mrs Mountstuart Jenkinson was unsuccessful. Her 'dainty rogue in porcelain' displeased Sir Willoughby. 'Why rogue?' he said. The lady's fame for hitting the mark fretted him, and the grace of his bride's fine bearing stood to support him in his objection. Clara was young, healthy, handsome; she was therefore fitted to be his wife, the mother of his children, his companion picture. Certainly they looked well side by side. In walking with her, in drooping to her, the whole man was made conscious of the female image of himself by her exquisite unlikeness. She completed him, added the softer lines wanting to his portrait before the world. He had wooed her rageingly; he courted her becomingly; with the manly self-possession enlivened by watchful tact which is pleasing to girls. He never seemed to undervalue himself in valuing her: a secret priceless in the courtship of young women that have heads; the lover doubles their sense of personal worth through not forfeiting his own. Those were proud and happy days when he rode Black Norman over to Upton Park, and his lady looked forth for him and knew him coming by the faster beating of her heart.

Her mind, too, was receptive. She took impressions of his characteristics, and supplied him a feast. She remembered his chance phrases; noted his ways, his peculiarities, as no one of her sex had done. He thanked his cousin Vernon for saying she had wit. She had it, and of so high a flavour that the more he thought of the epigram launched at her the more he grew displeased. With the wit to understand him, and the heart to worship, she had a dignity rarely seen in young ladies.

'Why rogue?' he insisted with Mrs Mountstuart.

'I said – in porcelain,' she replied.

'Rogue perplexes me.'

'Porcelain explains it.'

'She has the keenest sense of honour.'

'I am sure she is a paragon of rectitude.'

'She has a beautiful bearing.'

'The carriage of a young princess!'

'I find her perfect.'

'And still she may be a dainty rogue in porcelain.'

'Are you judging by the mind or the person, ma'am?'

'Both.'

'And which is which?'

'There's no distinction.'

'Rogue and mistress of Patterne do not go together.'

'Why not? She will be a novelty to our neighbourhood and an animation of the Hall.'

'To be frank, rogue does not rightly match with *me*.'

'Take her for a supplement.'

'You like her?'

'In love with her! I can imagine life-long amusement in her company. Attend to my advice: prize the porcelain and play with the rogue.'

Sir Willoughby nodded, unilluminated. There was nothing of rogue in himself, so there could be nothing of it in his bride. Elfishness, tricksiness, freakishness, were antipathetic to his nature; and he argued that it was impossible he should have chosen for his complement a person deserving the title. It would not have been sanctioned by his guardian genius. His closer acquaintance with Miss Middleton squared with his first impressions; you know that this is convincing; the common jury justifies the presentation of the case to them by the grand jury; and his original conclusion that she was essentially feminine, in other words, a parasite and a chalice, Clara's conduct confirmed from day to day. He began to instruct her in the knowledge of himself without reserve, and she, as she grew less timid with him, became more reflective.

'I judge by character,' he said to Mrs Mountstuart.

'If you have caught the character of a girl,' said she.

'I think I am not far off it.'

'So it was thought by the man who dived for the moon in a well.'

'How women despise their sex!'

'Not a bit. She has no character yet. You are forming it, and pray be advised and be merry; the solid is your safest guide; physiognomy and manners will give you more of a girl's character than all the divings you can do. She is a charming young woman, only she is one of that sort.'

'Of what sort?' Sir Willoughby asked, impatiently.

'Rogues in porcelain.'

'I am persuaded I shall never comprehend it.'

'I cannot help you one bit further.'

'The word rogue!'

'It was dainty rogue.'

'Brittle, would you say?'

'I am quite unable to say.'

'An innocent naughtiness?'

'Prettily moulded in a delicate substance.'

'You are thinking of some piece of Dresden you suppose her to resemble.'

'I dare say.'

'Artificial?'

'You would not have her natural?'

'I am heartily satisfied with her from head to foot, my dear Mrs Mountstuart.'

'Nothing could be better. And sometimes she will lead, and generally you will lead, and everything will go well, my dear Sir Willoughby.'

Like all rapid phrasers, Mrs Mountstuart detested the analysis of her sentence. It had an outline in vagueness, and was flung out to be apprehended, not dissected. Her directions for the reading of Miss Middleton's character were the same that she practised in reading Sir Willoughby's, whose physiognomy and manners bespoke him what she presumed him to be, a splendidly proud gentleman, with good reason.

Mrs Mountstuart's advice was wiser than her procedure, for she stopped short where he declined to begin. He dived below the surface without studying that index-page. He had won Miss Middleton's hand; he believed he had captured her heart; but he was not so certain of his possession of her soul, and he went after it. Our enamoured gentleman had therefore no tally of Nature's writing above to set beside his discoveries in the deeps. Now it is a dangerous accompaniment of this habit of driving, that where we do not light on the discoveries we anticipate, we fall to work sowing and planting; which becomes a disturbance of the gentle bosom. Miss Middleton's features were legible as to the mainspring of her character. He could have seen that she had a spirit with a natural love of liberty, and required the next thing to liberty, spaciousness, if she was to own allegiance. Those features, unhappily, instead of serving for an introduction to the within, were treated as

the mirror of himself. They were indeed of an amiable sweetness to tempt an accepted lover to angle for the first person in
the second. But he had made the discovery that their minds
differed on one or two points, and a difference of view in his
bride was obnoxious to his repose. He struck at it recurringly
to show her error under various aspects. He desired to shape
her character to the feminine of his own, and betrayed the
surprise of a slight disappointment at her advocacy of her
ideas. She said immediately: 'It is not too late, Willoughby,'
and wounded him, for he wanted her simply to be material
in his hands for him to mould her; he had no other thought.
He lectured her on the theme of the infinity of love. How was
it not too late? They were plighted; they were one eternally;
they could not be parted. She listened gravely, conceiving the
infinity as a narrow dwelling where a voice droned and
ceased not. However, she listened. She became an attentive
listener.

CHAPTER 6

✕✕✕✕

His Courtship

THE world was the principal topic of dissension between these
lovers. His opinion of the world affected her like a creature
threatened with a deprivation of air. He explained to his darling that lovers of necessity do loathe the world. They live in
the world, they accept its benefits, and assist it as well as they
can. In their hearts they must despise it, shut it out, that their
love for one another may pour in a clear channel, and with
all the force they have. They cannot enjoy the sense of security
for their love unless they fence away the world. It is, you will
allow, gross; it is a beast. Formally we thank it for the good

we get of it; only we two have an inner temple where the worship we conduct is actually, if you would but see it, an excommunication of the world. We abhor that beast to adore that divinity. This gives us our oneness, our isolation, our happiness. This is to love with the soul. Do you see, darling?

She shook her head; she could not see it. She would admit none of the notorious errors of the world; its backbiting, selfishness, coarseness, intrusiveness, infectiousness. She was young. She might, Willoughby thought, have let herself be led; she was not docile. She must be up in arms as a champion of the world; and one saw she was hugging her dream of a romantic world, nothing else. She spoilt the secret bower-song he delighted to tell over to her. And how, Powers of Love! is love-making to be pursued if we may not kick the world out of our bower and wash our hands of it? Love that does not spurn the world when lovers curtain themselves is a love – is it not so? – that seems to the unwhipped, scoffing world to go slinking into basiation's obscurity, instead of on a glorious march behind the screen. Our hero had a strong sentiment as to the policy of scorning the world for the sake of defending his personal pride and (to his honour, be it said) his lady's delicacy.

The act of scorning put them both above the world, said retro Sathanas![5] So much, as a piece of tactics; he was highly civilized: in the second instance, he knew it to be the world which must furnish the dry sticks for the bonfire of a woman's worship. He knew, too, that he was prescribing poetry to his betrothed, practicable poetry. She had a liking for poetry, and sometimes quoted the stuff in defiance of his pursed mouth and pained murmur: 'I am no poet'; but his poetry of the enclosed and fortified bower, without nonsensical rhymes to catch the ears of women, appeared incomprehensible to her, if not adverse. She would not burn the world for him; she would not, though a purer poetry is little imaginable, reduce herself to ashes, or incense, or essence, in honour of him, and so, by love's transmutation, literally be the man she was to marry. She preferred to be herself, with the egoism of women She said it: she said: 'I must be myself to be of any value to you, Willoughby.' He was indefatigable in his lectures on the aesthetics of love. Frequently, for an indemnification to her (he had no desire that she should be a loser by ceasing to admire the world), he dwelt on his own youthful ideas; and his original fancies about the world were presented to her as a substitute for the theme.

Miss Middleton bore it well, for she was sure that he meant well. Bearing so well what was distasteful to her, she became less well able to bear what she had merely noted in observation before; his view of scholarship; his manner toward Mr Vernon Whitford, of whom her father spoke warmly; the rumour concerning his treatment of a Miss Dale. And the country tale of Constantia Durham sang itself to her in a new key. He had no contempt for the world's praises. Mr Whitford wrote the letters to the county paper which gained him applause at various great houses, and he accepted it, and betrayed a tingling fright lest he should be the victim of a sneer of the world he contemned. Recollecting his remarks, her mind was afflicted by the 'something illogical' in him that we readily discover when our natures are no longer running free, and then at once we yearn for a disputation. She resolved that she would one day, one distant day, provoke it – upon what? The special point eluded her. The world is too huge a client, and too pervious, too spotty, for a girl to defend against a man. That 'something illogical' had stirred her feelings more than her intellect to revolt. She could not constitute herself the advocate of Mr Whitford. Still she marked the disputation for an event to come.

Meditating on it, she fell to picturing Sir Willoughby's face at the first accents of his bride's decided disagreement with him. The picture once conjured up would not be laid. He was handsome; so correctly handsome, that a slight unfriendly touch precipitated him into caricature. His habitual air of happy pride, of indignant contentment rather, could easily be overdone. Surprise, when he threw emphasis on it, stretched him with the tall eyebrows of a mask – limitless under the spell of caricature; and in time, whenever she was not pleased by her thoughts, she had that, and not his likeness, for the vision of him. And it was unjust, contrary to her deeper feelings; she rebuked herself, and as much as her naughty spirit permitted, she tried to look on him as the world did; an effort inducing reflections upon the blessings of ignorance. She seemed to herself beset by a circle of imps, hardly responsible for her thoughts.

He outshone Mr Whitford in his behaviour to young Crossjay. She had seen him with the boy, and he was amused, indulgent, almost frolicsome, in contradistinction to Mr Whitford's tutorly sharpness. He had the English father's tone of a liberal allowance for boys' tastes and pranks, and he ministered to the partiality of the genus for pocket-money. He did not play the schoolmaster, like bookworms who get poor little lads in their grasp.

Mr Whitford avoided her very much. He came to Upton Park on a visit to her father, and she was not particularly sorry that she saw him only at table. He treated her by fits to a level scrutiny of deep-set eyes unpleasantly penetrating. She had liked his eyes. They became unbearable; they dwelt in the memory as if they had left a phosphorescent line. She had been taken by playmate boys in her infancy to peep into hedge-leaves, where the mother-bird brooded on the nest; and the eyes of the bird in that marvellous dark thickset home, had sent her away with worlds of fancy. Mr Whitford's gaze revived her susceptibility, but not the old happy wondering. She was glad of his absence, after a certain hour that she passed with Willoughby, a wretched hour to remember. Mr Whitford had left, and Willoughby came, bringing bad news of his mother's health. Lady Patterne was fast failing. Her son spoke of the loss she would be to him; he spoke of the dreadfulness of death. He alluded to his own death to come carelessly, with a philosophical air.

'All of us must go! our time is short.'

'Very,' she assented.

It sounded like want of feeling.

'If you lose me, Clara!'

'But you are strong, Willoughby.'

'I may be cut off to-morrow.'

'Do not talk in such a manner.'

'It is as well that it should be faced.'

'I cannot see what purpose it serves.'

'Should you lose me, my love!'

'Willoughby!'

'Oh, the bitter pang of leaving you!'

'Dear Willoughby, you are distressed; your mother may recover; let us hope she will; I will help to nurse her; I have offered, you know; I am ready, most anxious. I believe I am a good nurse.'

'It is this belief – that one does not die with death!'

'That is our comfort.'

'When we love?'

'Does it not promise that we meet again?'

'To walk the world and see you perhaps – with another!'

'See me? – Where? Here?'

'Wedded . . . to another. You! my bride; whom I call mine; and you are! You would be still – in that horror! But all things are possible; women are women; they swim in infidelity, from wave to wave! I know them.'

'Willoughby, do not torment yourself and me, I beg you.'

He meditated profoundly, and asked her: 'Could you be such a saint among women?'

'I think I am a more than usually childish girl.'

'Not to forget me?'

'Oh, no.'

'Still to be mine?'

'I am yours.'

'To plight yourself?'

'It is done.'

'Be mine beyond death?'

'Married is married, I think.'

'Clara! to dedicate your life to our love! Never one touch; not one whisper! not a thought, not a dream! Could you – it agonizes me to imagine . . . be inviolate? mine above? – mine before all men, though I am gone: – true to my dust? Tell me. Give me that assurance. True to my name! – Oh, I hear them. "His relict." Buzzings about Lady Patterne. "The widow." If you knew their talk of widows! Shut your ears, my angel! But if she holds them off and keeps her path, they are forced to respect her. The dead husband is not the dishonoured wretch they fancied him, because he was out of their way. He lives in the heart of his wife. Clara! my Clara! as I live in yours, whether here or away; whether you are a wife or widow, there is no distinction for love – I am your husband – say it – eternally. I must have peace; I cannot endure the pain. Depressed, yes; I have cause to be. But it has haunted me ever since we joined hands. To have you – to lose you!'

'Is it not possible that I may be the first to die?' said Miss Middleton.

'And lose you, with the thought that you, lovely as you are, and the dogs of the world barking round you, might . . . Is it any wonder that I have my feeling for the world? This hand! – the thought is horrible. You would be surrounded; men are brutes; the scent of unfaithfulness excites them, overjoys them. And I helpless! The thought is maddening. I see a ring of monkeys grinning. There is your beauty, and man's delight in desecrating. You would be worried night and day to quit my name, to . . . I feel the blow now. You would have no rest for them, nothing to cling to without your oath.'

'An oath!' said Miss Middleton.

'It is no delusion, my love, when I tell you that with this thought upon me I see a ring of monkey faces grinning at me; they haunt me. But you do swear it! Once, and I will never trouble you on the subject again. My weakness! if you like. You will learn that it is love, a man's love, stronger than death.'

'An oath?' she said, and moved her lips to recall what she might have said and forgotten. 'To what? what oath?'

'That you will be true to me dead as well as living! Whisper it.'

'Willoughby, I shall be true to my vows at the altar.'

'To me! me!'

'It will be to you.'

'To my soul. No heaven can be for me – I see none, only torture, unless I have your word, Clara. I trust it. I will trust it implicitly. My confidence in you is absolute.'

'Then you need not be troubled.'

'It is for *you*, my love; that you may be armed and strong when I am not by to protect you.'

'Our views of the world are opposed, Willoughby.'

'Consent; gratify me; swear it. Say: "Beyond death." Whisper it. I ask for nothing more. Women think the husband's grave breaks the bond, cuts the tie, sets them loose. They wed the flesh – pah! What I call on you for is nobility; the transcendent nobility of faithfulness beyond death. "*His* widow!' let them say; a saint in widowhood.'

'My vows at the altar must suffice.'

'You will not? Clara!'

'I am plighted to you.'

'Not a word? – a simple promise? But you love me?'

'I have given you the best proof of it that I can.'

'Consider how utterly I place confidence in you.'

'I hope it is well placed.'

'I could kneel to you, to worship you, if you would, Clara!'

'Kneel to Heaven, not to me, Willoughby. I am – I wish I were able to tell what I am. I may be inconstant; I do not know myself. Think; question yourself whether I am really the person you should marry. Your wife should have great qualities of mind and soul. I will consent to hear that I do not possess them, and abide by the verdict.'

'You do; you do possess them!' Willoughby cried. 'When you know better what the world is, you will understand my

anxiety. Alive, I am strong to shield you from it; dead, helpless – that is all. You would be clad in mail, steel-proof, in-
violable, if you would ... But try to enter into my mind;
think with me, feel with me. When you have once comprehended the intensity of the love of a man like me, you will not
require asking. It is the difference of the elect and the vulgar;
of the ideal of love from the coupling of the herds. We will
let it drop. At least, I have your hand. As long as I live I have
your hand. Ought I not to be satisfied? I am; only I see
further than most men, and feel more deeply. And now I
must ride to my mother's bedside. She dies Lady Patterne! It
might have been that she ... But she is a woman of women!
With a father-in-law![6] Just heaven! Could I have stood by her
then with the same feelings of reverence? A very little, my
love, and everything gained for us by civilization crumbles;
we fall back to the first mortar-bowl we were bruised and
stirred in. My thoughts, when I take my stand to watch by her,
come to this conclusion, that, especially in women, distinction
is the thing to be aimed at. Otherwise we are a weltering
human mass. Women must teach us to venerate them, or we
may as well be bleating and barking and bellowing. So, now
enough. You have but to think a little. I must be off. It may
have happened during my absence. I will write. I shall hear
from you? Come and see me mount Black Norman. My respects to your father. I have no time to pay them in person.
One!'

He took the one – love's mystical number – from which
commonly spring multitudes; but, on the present occasion, it
was a single one, and cold. She watched him riding away on
his gallant horse, as handsome a cavalier as the world could
show, and the contrast of his recent language and his fine
figure was a riddle that froze her blood. Speech so foreign to
her ears, unnatural in tone, unmanlike even for a lover (who is
allowed a softer dialect), set her vainly sounding for the source
and drift of it. She was glad of not having to encounter eyes
like Mr Vernon Whitford's.

On behalf of Sir Willoughby, it is to be said that his mother, without infringing on the degree of respect for his decisions and sentiments exacted by him, had talked to him of Miss Middleton, suggesting a volatility of temperament in the young lady that struck him as consentaneous with Mrs Mountstuart's 'rogue in porcelain', and alarmed him as the independent observations of two world-wise women. Nor was it incumbent upon him personally to credit the volatility in order, as far as he could, to effect the soul-insurance of his bride, that he might hold the security of the policy. The desire for it was in him; his mother had merely tolled a warning bell that he had put in motion before. Clara was not a Constantia. But she was a woman, and he had been deceived by women, as a man fostering his high ideal of them will surely be. The strain he adopted was quite natural to his passion and his theme. The language of the primitive sentiments of men is of the same expression at all times, minus the primitive colours when a modern gentleman addresses his lady.

Lady Patterne died in the winter season of the new year. In April Dr Middleton had to quit Upton Park, and he had not found a place of residence, nor did he quite know what to do with himself in the prospect of his daughter's marriage and desertion of him. Sir Willoughby proposed to find him a house within a circuit of the neighbourhood of Patterne. Moreover, he invited the Rev. Doctor and his daughter to come to Patterne from Upton for a month, and make acquaintance with his aunts, the ladies Eleanor and Isabel Patterne, so that it might not be so strange to Clara to have them as her housemates after her marriage. Dr Middleton omitted to consult his daughter before accepting the invitation, and it appeared, when he did speak to her, that it should have been done. But she said, mildly, 'Very well, papa.'

Sir Willoughby had to visit the metropolis and an estate in another county, whence he wrote to his betrothed daily. He returned to Patterne in time to arrange for the welcome of his guests; too late, however, to ride over to them; and, meanwhile, during his absence, Miss Middleton had bethought herself that she ought to have given her last days of freedom to her friends. After the weeks to be passed at Patterne, very few weeks were left to her, and she had a wish to run to Switzerland or Tyrol and see the Alps; a quaint idea, her father thought. She repeated it seriously, and Dr Middleton perceived a feminine shuttle of indecision at work in her head, frightful to him, considering that they signified hesitation between the excellent library and capital wine-cellar of Patterne Hall, together with the society of that promising young scholar, Mr Vernon Whitford, on the one side, and a career of hotels – equivalent to being rammed into monster artillery with a crowd every night, and shot off on a day's journey through space every morning – on the other.

'You will have your travelling and your Alps after the ceremony,' he said.

'I think I would rather stay at home,' said she.

Dr Middleton rejoined: '*I* would.'

'But I am not married yet, papa.'

'As good, my dear.'

'A little change of scene, I thought . . .'

'We have accepted Willoughby's invitation. And he helps me to a house near you.'

'You wish to be near me, papa?'

'Proximate – at a remove: communicable.'

'Why should we separate?'

'For the reason, my dear, that you exchange a father for a husband.'

'If I do not want to exchange?'

'To purchase, you must pay, my child. Husbands are not given for nothing.'

'No. But I should have you, papa!'

'Should?'

'They have not yet parted us, dear papa.'

'What does that mean?' he asked, fussily. He was in a gentle stew already, apprehensive of a disturbance of the

serenity precious to scholars by postponements of the ceremony and a prolongation of a father's worries.

'Oh, the common meaning, papa,' she said, seeing how it
was with him.

'Ah!' said he, nodding and blinking gradually back to a
state of composure, glad to be appeased on any terms; for
mutability is but another name for the sex, and it is the enemy
of the scholar.

She suggested that two weeks of Patterne would offer
plenty of time to inspect the empty houses of the district, and
should be sufficient, considering the claims of friends, and the
necessity of going the round of London shops.

'Two or three weeks,' he agreed, hurriedly, by way of compromise with that fearful prospect.

CHAPTER 7

✖✖✖✖

The Betrothed

DURING the drive from Upton to Patterne, Miss Middleton
hoped, she partly believed, that there was to be a change in
Sir Willoughby's manner of courtship. He had been so different a wooer. She remembered with some half-conscious
desperation of fervour what she had thought of him at his first
approaches, and in accepting him. Had she seen him with the
eyes of the world, thinking they were her own? That look of
his, the look of 'indignant contentment', had then been a
most noble conquering look, splendid as a general's plume at
the gallop. It could not have altered. Was it that her eyes had
altered?

The spirit of those days rose up within her to reproach her

and whisper of their renewal: she remembered her rosy dreams and the image she had of him, her throbbing pride in him, her choking richness of happiness: and also her vain attempting to be very humble, usually ending in a carol, quaint to think of, not without charm, but quaint, puzzling.

Now men whose incomes have been restricted to the extent that they must live on their capital, soon grow relieved of the forethoughtful anguish wasting them by the hilarious comforts of the lap upon which they have sunk back, insomuch that they are apt to solace themselves for their intolerable anticipations of famine in the household by giving loose to one fit or more of reckless lavishness. Lovers in like manner live on their capital from failure of income: they, too, for the sake of stifling apprehension and piping to the present hour, are lavish of their stock, so as rapidly to attenuate it: they have their fits of intoxication in view of coming famine: they force memory into play, love retrospectively, enter the old house of the past and ravage the larder, and would gladly, even resolutely, continue in illusion if it were possible for the broadest honey-store of reminiscences to hold out for a length of time against a mortal appetite: which in good sooth stands on the alternative of a consumption of the hive or of the creature it is for nourishing. Here do lovers show that they are perishable. More than the poor clay world they need fresh supplies, right wholesome juices; as it were, life in the burst of the bud, fruits yet on the tree, rather than potted provender. The latter is excellent for by-and-by, when there will be a vast deal more to remember, and appetite shall have but one tooth remaining. Should their minds perchance have been saturated by their first impressions and have retained them, loving by the accountable light of reason, they may have fair harvests, as in the early time; but that case is rare. In other words, love is an affair of two, and is only for two that can be as quick, as constant in intercommunication as are sun and earth, through the cloud or face to face. They take their breath of life from one another in signs of affection, proofs of faithfulness, incentives to admiration. Thus it is with men and women in love's good season. But a solitary soul dragging a log must make the log a God to rejoice in the burden. That is not love.

Clara was the least fitted of all women to drag a log. Few girls would be so rapid in exhausting capital. She was feminine indeed, but she wanted comradeship, a living and frank exchange of the best in both, with the deeper feelings untroubled. To be fixed at the mouth of a mine, and to have to descend it daily, and not to discover great opulence below; on the contrary, to be chilled in subterranean sunlessness, without any substantial quality that she could grasp, only the mystery of the inefficient tallow-light in those caverns of the complacent-talking man: this appeared to her too extreme a probation for two or three weeks. How of a life-time of it!

She was compelled by her nature to hope, expect and believe that Sir Willoughby would again be the man she had known when she accepted him. Very singularly, to show her simple spirit at the time, she was unaware of any physical coldness to him; she knew of nothing but her mind at work, objecting to this and that, desiring changes. She did not dream of being on the giddy ridge of the passive or negative sentiment of love, where one step to the wrong side precipitates us into the state of repulsion.

Her eyes were lively at their meeting – so were his. She liked to see him on the steps, with young Crossjay under his arm. Sir Willoughby told her in his pleasantest humour of the boy's having got into the laboratory that morning to escape his task-master, and blown out the windows. She administered a chiding to the delinquent in the same spirit, while Sir Willoughby led her on his arm across the threshold, whispering: 'Soon for good!' In reply to the whisper, she begged for more of the story of young Crossjay. 'Come into the laboratory,' said he, a little less laughingly than softly; and Clara begged her father to come and see young Crossjay's latest pranks. Sir Willoughby whispered to her of the length of their separation, and his joy to welcome her to the house where she would reign as mistress *very* soon. He numbered the weeks. He whispered: 'Come.' In the hurry of the moment she did not examine a lightning terror that shot through her. It passed, and was no more than the shadow which bends the summer grasses, leaving a ruffle of her ideas, in wonder of her having feared herself for something. Her father was with them. She and Willoughby were not yet alone.

Young Crossjay had not accomplished so fine a piece of destruction as Sir Willoughby's humour proclaimed of him. He had connected a battery with a train of gunpowder, shattering a window-frame and unsettling some bricks. Dr Middleton asked if the youth was excluded from the library, and rejoiced to hear that it was a sealed door to him. Thither they went. Vernon Whitford was away on one of his long walks.

'There, papa, you see he is not so very faithful to you,' said Clara.

Dr Middleton stood frowning over MS notes on the table, in Vernon's handwriting. He flung up the hair from his forehead and dropped into a seat to inspect them closely. He was now immoveable. Clara was obliged to leave him there. She was led to think that Willoughby had drawn them to the library with the design to be rid of her protector, and she began to fear him. She proposed to pay her respects to the ladies Eleanor and Isabel. They were not seen, and a footman reported in the drawing-room that they were out driving. She grasped young Crossjay's hand. Sir Willoughby dispatched him to Mrs Montague, the housekeeper, for a tea of cakes and jam.

'Off!' he said, and the boy had to run.

Clara saw herself without a shield.

'And the garden!' she cried. 'I love the garden; I must go and see what flowers are up with you. In spring I care most for wild flowers, and if you will show me daffodils, and crocuses and anemones . . .'

'My dearest Clara! my bride!' said he.

'Because they are vulgar flowers?' she asked him, artlessly, to account for his detaining her.

Why would he not wait to deserve her! – no, not deserve – to reconcile her with her real position; not reconcile, but to repair the image of him in her mind, before he claimed his apparent right!

He did not wait. He pressed her to his bosom.

'You are mine, my Clara – utterly mine; every thought, every feeling. We are one: the world may do its worst. I have been longing for you, looking forward. You save me from a thousand vexations. One is perpetually crossed. That is all outside us. We two! With you I am secure! Soon! I could not tell you whether the world's alive or dead. My dearest!'

She came out of it with the sensations of the frightened child that has had its dip in sea-water, sharpened to think that after all it was not so severe a trial. Such was her idea; and she said to herself immediately: What am I that I should complain? Two minutes earlier she would not have thought it; but humiliated pride falls lower than humbleness.

She did not blame him; she fell in her own esteem; less because she was the betrothed Clara Middleton, which was now palpable as a shot in the breast of a bird, than that she was a captured woman, of whom it is absolutely expected that she must submit, and when she would rather be gazing at flowers. Clara had shame of her sex. They cannot take a step without becoming bondwomen: into what a slavery! For herself, her trial was over, she thought. As for herself, she merely complained of a prematureness and crudity best unanalyzed. In truth, she could hardly be said to complain. She did but criticize him and wonder that a man was unable to perceive, or was not arrested by perceiving, unwillingness, discordance, dull compliance; the bondwoman's due instead of the bride's consent. Oh, sharp distinction, as between two spheres!

She meted him justice; she admitted that he had spoken in a lover-like tone. Had it not been for the iteration of 'the world', she would not have objected critically to his words, though they were words of downright appropriation. He had the right to use them, since she was to be married to him. But if he had only waited before playing the privileged lover!

Sir Willoughby was enraptured with her. Even so purely coldly, statue-like, Dian-like, would he have prescribed his bride's reception of his caress. The suffusion of crimson coming over her subsequently, showing her divinely feminine in reflective bashfulness, agreed with his highest definitions of female character.

'Let me conduct you to the garden, my love,' he said.

She replied: 'I think I would rather go to my room.'

'I will send you a wild-flower posy.'

'Flowers, no; I do not like them to be gathered.'

'I will wait for you on the lawn.'

'My head is rather heavy.'

His deep concern and tenderness brought him close.

She assured him sparklingly that she was well: she was ready to accompany him to the garden and stroll over the park.

'Head*ache* it is not,' she said.

But she had to pay the fee for inviting a solicitous accepted gentleman's proximity.

This time she blamed herself and him, and the world he abused, and destiny into the bargain. And she cared less about the probation; but she craved for liberty. With a frigidity that astonished her, she marvelled at the act of kissing, and at the obligation it forced upon an inanimate person to be an accomplice. Why was she not free? By what strange right was it that she was treated as a possession?

'I will try to walk off the heaviness,' she said.

'My own girl must not fatigue herself.'

'Oh, no; I shall not.'

'Sit with me. Your Willoughby is your devoted attendant.'

'I have a desire for the air.'

'Then we will walk out.'

She was horrified to think how far she had drawn away from him, and now placed her hand on his arm to appease her self-accusations and propitiate duty. He spoke as she had wished, his manner was what she had wished; she was his bride, almost his wife; her conduct was a kind of madness; she could not understand it.

Good sense and duty counselled her to control her wayward spirit.

He fondled her hand, and to that she grew accustomed; her hand was at a distance. And what is a hand? Leaving it where it was, she treated it as a link between herself and dutiful goodness. Two months hence she was a bondwoman for life! She regretted that she had not gone to her room to strengthen herself with a review of her situation, and meet him thoroughly resigned to her fate. She fancied she would have come down to him amicably. It was his present respectfulness and easy conversation that tricked her burning nerves with the fancy. Five weeks of perfect liberty in the mountains, she thought, would have prepared her for the days of bells. All that she required was a separation offering new scenes, where she might reflect undisturbed, feel clear again.

He led her about the flower-beds; too much as if he were giving a convalescent an airing. She chafed at it, and pricked herself with remorse. In contrition she expatiated on the beauty of the garden.

'All is yours, my Clara.'

An oppressive load it seemed to her! She passively yielded to the man in his form of attentive courtier; his mansion, estate, and wealth overwhelmed her. They suggested the price to be paid. Yet she recollected that on her last departure through the park she had been proud of the rolling green and spreading trees. Poison of some sort must be operating in her. She had not come to him to-day with this feeling of sullen antagonism; she had caught it here.

'You have been well, my Clara?'

'Quite.'

'Not a hint of illness?'

'None.'

'My bride must have her health if all the doctors in the kingdom die for it! My darling!'

'And tell me: the dogs?'

'Dogs and horses are in very good condition.'

'I am glad. Do you know, I love those ancient French châteaux and farms in one, where salon windows look on poultry-yard and stalls. I like that homeliness with beasts and peasants.'

He bowed indulgently.

'I am afraid we can't do it for you in England, my Clara.'

'No.'

'And I like the farm,' said he. 'But I think our drawing-rooms have a better atmosphere off the garden. As to our peasantry, we cannot, I apprehend, modify our class demarcations without risk of disintegrating the social structure.'

'Perhaps. I proposed nothing.'

'My love, I would entreat you to propose if I were convinced that I could obey.'

'You are very good.'

'I find my merit nowhere but in your satisfaction.'

Although she was not thirsting for dulcet sayings, the peacefulness of other than invitations to the exposition of his mysteries and of their isolation in oneness, inspired her with such calm that she beat about in her brain, as if it were in the brain, for the specific injury he had committed. Sweeping from sensation to sensation, the young, whom sensations impel and distract, can rarely date their disturbance from a particular one; unless it be some great villain injury that has been done; and Clara had not felt an individual shame in his caress; the shame of her sex was but a passing protest, that left no stamp. So she conceived she had been behaving cruelly, and said, 'Willoughby'; because she was aware of the omission of his name in her previous remarks.

His whole attention was given to her.

She had to invent the sequel: 'I was going to beg you, Willoughby, do not seek to spoil me. You compliment me.

Compliments are not suited to me. You think too highly of me. It is nearly as bad as to be slighted. I am . . . I am a . . .'
But she could not follow his example; even as far as she had gone, her prim little sketch of herself, set beside her real, ugly, earnest feelings, rang of a mincing simplicity, and was a step in falseness. How could she display what she was?

'Do I not know you?' he said.

The melodious bass notes, expressive of conviction on that point, signified as well as the words that no answer was the right answer. She could not dissent without turning his music to discord, his complacency to amazement. She held her tongue, knowing that he did not know her, and speculating on the division made bare by their degrees of the knowledge, a deep cleft.

He alluded to friends in her neighbourhood and his own. The bridesmaids were mentioned.

'Miss Dale, you will hear from my aunt Eleanor, declines, on the plea of indifferent health. She is rather a morbid person, with all her really estimable qualities. It will do no harm to have none but young ladies of your own age; a bouquet of young buds: though one blowing flower among them . . . However, she has decided. My principal annoyance has been Vernon's refusal to act as my best man.'

'Mr Whitford refuses?'

'He half refuses. I do not take no from him. His pretext is a dislike to the ceremony.'

'I share it with him.'

'I sympathize with you. If we might say the words and pass from sight! There is a way of cutting off the world: I have it at times completely: I lose it again, as if it were a cabalistic phrase one had to utter. But with you! You give it me for good. It will be for ever, eternally, my Clara. Nothing can harm, nothing touch us; we are one another's. Let the world fight it out; we have nothing to do with it.'

'If Mr Whitford should persist in refusing?'

'So entirely one, that there never can be question of external influences. I am, we will say, riding home from the hunt: I see you awaiting me: I read your heart as though you were beside me. And I know that I am coming to the one who reads mine! You have me, you have me like an open book, you, and only you!'

'I am to be always at home?' Clara said, unheeded, and relieved by his not hearing.

'Have you realized it? – that we are invulnerable! The world cannot hurt us: it cannot touch us. Felicity is ours, and we are impervious in the enjoyment of it. Something divine! surely something divine on earth? Clara! – being to one another that between which the world can never interpose! What I do is right: what you do is right. Perfect to one another! Each new day we rise to study and delight in new secrets. Away with the crowd! We have not even to say it; we are in an atmosphere where the world cannot breathe.'

'Oh, the world!' Clara partly carolled on a sigh that sunk deep.

Hearing him talk as one exulting on the mountain-top, when she knew him to be in the abyss, was very strange, provocative of scorn.

'My letters?' he said, incitingly.

'I read them.'

'Circumstances have imposed a long courtship on us, my Clara; and I, perhaps lamenting the laws of decorum – I have done so! – still felt the benefit of the gradual initiation. It is not good for women to be surprised by a sudden revelation of man's character. We also have things to learn – there is matter for learning everywhere. Some day you will tell me the difference of what you think of me now, from what you thought when we first . . . ?'

An impulse of double-minded acquiescence caused Clara to stammer as on a sob:

'I – I daresay I shall.'

She added, 'If it is necessary.'

Then she cried out: 'Why do you attack the world? You always make me pity it.'

He smiled at her youthfulness. 'I have passed through that stage. It leads to my sentiment. Pity it, by all means.'

'No,' said she, 'but pity it, side with it, not consider it so bad. The world has faults; glaciers have crevices, mountains have chasms; but is not the effect of the whole sublime? Not to admire the mountain and the glacier because they can be cruel, seems to me . . . And the world is beautiful.'

'The world of nature, yes. The world of men?'

'Yes.'

'My love, I suspect you to be thinking of the world of ball-rooms.'

'I am thinking of the world that contains real and great generosity, true heroism. We see it round us.'

'We read of it. The world of the romance writer!'

'No: the living world. I am sure it is our duty to love it. I am sure we weaken ourselves if we do not. If I did not, I should be looking on mist, hearing a perpetual boom instead of music. I remember hearing Mr Whitford say that cynicism is intellectual dandyism without the coxcomb's feathers; and it seems to me that cynics are only happy in making the world as barren to others as they have made it for themselves.'

'Old Vernon!' ejaculated Sir Willoughby, with a countenance rather uneasy, as if it had been flicked with a glove. 'He strings his phrases by the dozen.'

'Papa contradicts that, and says he is very clever and very simple.'

'As to cynics, my dear Clara, oh, certainly, certainly: you are right. They are laughable, contemptible. But understand me, I mean, we cannot feel, or if we feel we cannot so intensely feel, our oneness, except by dividing ourselves from the world.'

'Is it an art?'

'If you like. It is our poetry! But does not love shun

the world? Two that love must have their sustenance in isolation.'

'No: they will be eating themselves up.'

'The purer the beauty, the more it will be out of the world.'

'But not opposed.'

'Put it in this way,' Willoughby condescended. 'Has experience the same opinion of the world as ignorance?'

'It should have more charity.'

'Does virtue feel at home in the world?'

'Where it should be an example, to my idea.'

'Is the world agreeable to holiness?'

'Then, are you in favour of monasteries?'

He poured a little runlet of half laughter over her head, of the sound assumed by genial compassion.

It is irritating to hear that when we imagine we have spoken to the point.

'Now in my letters, Clara –'

'I have no memory, Willoughby!'

'You will, however, have observed that I am not completely myself in my letters –'

'In your letters to men you may be.'

The remark threw a pause across his thoughts. He was of a sensitiveness terribly tender. A single stroke on it reverberated swellingly within the man, and most, and infuriately searching, at the spots where he had been wounded, especially where he feared the world might have guessed the wound. Did she imply that he had no hand for love-letters? Was it her meaning that women would not have much taste for his epistolary correspondence? She had spoken in the plural, with an accent on 'men'. Had she heard of Constantia? Had she formed her own judgement about the creature? The supernatural sensitiveness of Sir Willoughby shrieked a peal of affirmatives. He had often meditated on the moral obligation of his unfolding to Clara the whole truth of his conduct to Constantia; for whom, as for other suicides, there were

excuses. He at least was bound to supply them. She had behaved badly; but had he not given her some cause? If so, manliness was bound to confess it.

Supposing Clara heard the world's version first! Men whose
pride is their backbone suffer convulsions where other men are
barely aware of a shock, and Sir Willoughby was taken with
galvanic jumpings of the spirit within him, at the idea of the
world whispering to Clara that he had been jilted.

'My letters to men, you say, my love?'

'Your letters of business.'

'Completely myself in my letters of business?' He stared
indeed.

She relaxed the tension of his figure by remarking: 'You
are able to express yourself to men as your meaning dictates.
In writing to . . . to us it is, I suppose, more difficult.'

'True, my love. I will not exactly say difficult. I can
acknowledge no difficulty. Language, I should say, is not fitted
to express emotion. Passion rejects it.'

'For dumb-show and pantomime?'

'No; but the writing of it coldly.'

'Ah, coldly!'

'My letters disappoint you?'

'I have not implied that they do.'

'My feelings, dearest, are too strong for transcription. I
feel, pen in hand, like the mythological Titan at war with
Jove, strong enough to hurl mountains, and finding nothing
but pebbles. The simile is a good one. You must not judge of
me by my letters.'

'I do not; I like them,' said Clara.

She blushed, eyed him hurriedly, and seeing him complacent, resumed, 'I prefer the pebble to the mountain; but if
you read poetry you would not think human speech incapable of . . .'

'My love, I detest artifice. Poetry is a profession.'

'Our poets would prove to you . . .'

'As I have often observed, Clara, I am no poet.'

'I have not accused you, Willoughby.'

'No poet, and with no wish to be a poet. Were I one, my life would supply material, I can assure you, my love. My conscience is not entirely at rest. Perhaps the heaviest matter troubling it is that in which I was least wilfully guilty. You have heard of a Miss Durham?'

'I have heard – yes – of her.'

'She may be happy. I trust she is. If she is not, I cannot escape some blame. An instance of the difference between myself and the world, now. The world charges it upon her. I have interceded to exonerate her.'

'That was generous, Willoughby.'

'Stay. I fear I was the primary offender. But I, Clara, I, under a sense of honour, acting under a sense of honour, would have carried my engagement through.'

'What had you done?'

'The story is long, dating from an early day, in the "downy antiquity of my youth", as Vernon says.'

'Mr Whitford says that?'

'One of old Vernon's odd sayings. It's a story of an early fascination.'

'Papa tells me Mr Whitford speaks at times with wise humour.'

'Family considerations – the lady's health among other things; her position in the calculations of relatives – intervened. Still there was the fascination. I have to own it. Grounds for feminine jealousy.'

'Is it at an end?'

'Now? with you? my darling Clara! indeed at an end, or could I have opened my inmost heart to you! Could I have spoken of myself so unreservedly that in part you know me as I know myself! Oh, but would it have been possible to enclose you with myself in that intimate union? so secret, unassailable!'

'You did not speak to her as you speak to me?'

'In no degree.'

'What *could* have . . .' Clara checked the murmured exclamation.

Sir Willoughby's expoundings on his latest of texts would have poured forth, had not a footman stepped across the lawn to inform him that his builder was in the laboratory and requested permission to consult with him.

Clara's plea of a horror of the talk of bricks and joists excused her from accompanying him. He had hardly been satisfied by her manner, he knew not why. He left her, convinced that he must do and say more to reach down to her female intelligence.

She saw young Crossjay, springing with pots of jam in him, join his patron at a bound, and taking a lift of arms, fly aloft, clapping heels. Her reflections were confused. Sir Willoughby was admirable with the lad. 'Is he two men?' she thought; and the thought ensued, 'Am I unjust?' She headed a run with young Crossjay to divert her mind.

CHAPTER 8

✕✕✕✕

A Run with the Truant; a Walk with the Master

THE sight of Miss Middleton running inflamed young Crossjay with the passion of the game of hare and hounds. He shouted a view-halloo, and flung up his legs. She was fleet; she ran as though a hundred little feet were bearing her onward smooth as water over the lawn and the sweeps of grass of the park, so swiftly did the hidden pair multiply one another to speed her. So sweet was she in her flowing pace, that the boy, as became his age, translated admiration into a dogged frenzy of pursuit, and continued pounding along, when far outstripped, determined to run her down or die. Suddenly her flight wound to an end in a dozen twittering steps, and she sank. Young Crossjay attained her, with just breath enough to say: 'You are a runner!'

'I forgot you had been having your tea, my poor boy,' said she.

'And you don't pant a bit!' was his encomium.

'Dear me, no; not more than a bird. You might as well try to catch a bird.'

Young Crossjay gave a knowing nod. 'Wait till I get my second wind.'

'Now you must confess that girls run faster than boys.'

'They may at the start.'

'They do everything better.'

'They're flash-in-the-pans.'

'They learn their lessons.'

'You can't make soldiers or sailors of them, though.'

'And that is untrue. Have you never read of Mary Ambree? and Mistress Hannah Snell of Pondicherry? And there was the bride of the celebrated William Taylor. And what do you say to Joan of Arc? What do you say to Boadicea? I suppose you have never heard of the Amazons.'

'They weren't English.'

'Then it is your own countrywomen you decry, sir!'

Young Crossjay betrayed anxiety about his false position, and begged for the stories of Mary Ambree and the others who were English.

'See, you will not read for yourself, you hide and play truant with Mr Whitford, and the consequence is you are ignorant of your country's history.' Miss Middleton rebuked him, enjoying his wriggle between a perception of her fun and an acknowledgment of his peccancy. She commanded him to tell her which was the glorious Valentine's day of our naval annals;[7] the name of the hero of the day, and the name of his ship. To these questions his answers were as ready as the guns of the good ship *Captain*, for the Spanish four-decker.

'And that you owe to Mr Whitford,' said Miss Middleton.

'He bought me the books,' young Crossjay growled, and plucked at grass blades and bit them, foreseeing dimly but certainly the termination of all this.

Miss Middleton lay back on the grass and said: 'Are you going to be fond of me, Crossjay?'

The boy sat blinking. His desire was to prove to her that he was immoderately fond of her already; and he might have flown at her neck had she been sitting up, but her recumbency and eyelids half closed excited wonder in him and awe. His young heart beat fast.

'Because, my dear boy,' she said, leaning on her elbow, 'you are a very nice boy, but an ungrateful boy, and there is no telling whether you will not punish any one who cares for you. Come along with me; pluck me some of these cowslips, and the speedwells near them; I think we both love wild flowers.' She rose and took his arm. 'You shall row me on the lake while I talk to you seriously.'

It was she, however, who took the sculls at the boat-house, for she had been a playfellow with boys, and knew that one of them engaged in a manly exercise is not likely to listen to a woman.

'Now, Crossjay,' she said. Dense gloom overcame him like a cowl. She bent across her hands to laugh. 'As if I were going to lecture you, you silly boy!' He began to brighten dubiously. 'I used to be as fond of birdsnesting as you are. I like brave boys, and I like you for wanting to enter the Royal Navy. Only, how can you if you do not learn? You must get the captains to pass you, you know. Somebody spoils you: Miss Dale or Mr Whitford.'

'Do they?' sung out young Crossjay.

'Sir Willoughby does?'

'I don't know about spoil. I can come round him.'

'I am sure he is very kind to you. I dare say you think Mr Whitford rather severe. You should remember he has to teach you, so that you may pass for the navy. You must not dislike him because he makes you work. Supposing you had blown yourself up to-day! You would have thought it better to have been working with Mr Whitford.'

'Sir Willoughby says, when he's married you won't let me hide.'

'Ah! It is wrong to pet a big boy like you. Does not he what you call tip you, Crossjay?'

'Generally half-crown pieces. I've had a crown-piece. I've had sovereigns.'

'And for that you do as he bids you? And he indulges you because you . . . Well, but though Mr Whitford does not give you money, he gives you his time, he tries to get you into the navy.'

'He pays for me.'

'What do you say?'

'My keep. And, as for liking him, if he were at the bottom of the water here, I'd go down after him. I mean to learn. We're both of us here at six o'clock in the morning, when it's light, and have a swim. He taught me. Only, I never cared for schoolbooks.'

'Are you quite certain that Mr Whitford pays for you?'

'My father told me he did, and I must obey him. He heard my father was poor, with a family. He went down to see my father. My father came here once, and Sir Willoughby wouldn't see him. I know Mr Whitford does. And Miss Dale told me he did. My mother says she thinks he does it to make up to us for my father's long walk in the rain and the cold he caught coming here to Patterne.'

'So you see you should not vex him, Crossjay. He is a good friend to your father and to you. You ought to love him.'

'I like him, and I like his face.'

'Why his face?'

'It's not like those faces! Miss Dale and I talk about him. She thinks that Sir Willoughby is the best-looking man ever born.'

'Were you not speaking of Mr Whitford?'

'Yes; old Vernon. That's what Sir Willoughby calls him,' young Crossjay excused himself to her look of surprise. 'Do you know what he makes me think of? – his eyes, I mean. He makes me think of Robinson Crusoe's old goat in the cavern. I like him because he's always the same, and you're not positive about some people. Miss Middleton, if you look on at cricket, in comes a safe man for ten runs. He may get more, and he never gets less; and you should hear the old farmers talk of him in the booth. That's just my feeling.'

Miss Middleton understood that some illustration from the cricketing-field was intended to throw light on the boy's feeling for Mr Whitford. Young Crossjay was evidently warming to speak from his heart. But the sun was low, she had to dress for the dinner-table, and she landed him with regret, as at a holiday over. Before they parted, he offered to swim across the lake in his clothes, or dive to the bed for anything she pleased to throw, declaring solemnly that it should not be lost.

She walked back at a slow pace, and sung to herself above her darker-flowing thoughts, like the reed-warbler on the branch beside the night-stream; a simple song of a light-hearted sound, independent of the shifting black and grey of the flood underneath.

A step was at her heels.

'I see you have been petting my scapegrace.'

'Mr Whitford! Yes; not petting, I hope. I tried to give him a lecture. He's a dear lad, but, I fancy, trying.'

She was in fine sunset colour, unable to arrest the mounting tide. She had been rowing, she said; and, as he directed his eyes, according to his wont, penetratingly, she defended herself by fixing her mind on Robinson Crusoe's old goat in the recess of the cavern.

'I must have him away from here very soon,' said Vernon. 'Here he's quite spoiled. Speak of him to Willoughby. I can't guess at his ideas of the boy's future, but the chance of passing for the navy won't bear trifling with, and if ever there was a lad made for the navy, it's Crossjay.'

The incident of the explosion in the laboratory was new to Vernon.

'And Willoughby laughed?' he said. 'There are sea-port crammers who stuff young fellows for examination, and we shall have to pack off the boy at once to the best one of the lot we can find. I would rather have had him under me up to the last three months, and have made sure of some roots to what is knocked into his head. But he's ruined here. And I am going. So I shall not trouble him for many weeks longer. Dr Middleton is well?'

'My father is well, yes. He pounced like a falcon on your notes in the library.'

Vernon came out with a chuckle.

'They were left to attract him. I am in for a controversy.'

'Papa will not spare you, to judge from his look.'

'I know the look.'

'Have you walked far to-day?'

'Nine and a half hours. My Flibbertigibbet [8] is too much for me at times, and I had to walk off my temper.'

She cast her eyes on him, thinking of the pleasure of dealing with a temper honestly coltish, and manfully open to a specific.

'All those hours were required?'

'Not quite so long.'

'You are training for your Alpine tour.'

'It's doubtful whether I shall get to the Alps this year. I leave the Hall, and shall probably be in London with a pen to sell.'

'Willoughby knows that you leave him?'

'As much as Mont Blanc knows that he is going to be climbed by a party below. He sees a speck or two in the valley.'

'He has not spoken of it.'

'He would attribute it to changes . . .'

Vernon did not conclude the sentence.

She became breathless, without emotion, but checked by the barrier confronting an impulse to ask, what changes? She stooped to pluck a cowslip.

'I saw daffodils lower down the park,' she said. 'One or two; they're nearly over.'

'We are well off for wild flowers here,' he answered.

'Do not leave him, Mr Whitford.'

'He will not want me.'

'You are devoted to him.'

'I can't pretend that.'

'Then it is the changes you imagine you foresee . . . If any occur, why should they drive you away?'

'Well, I'm two and thirty, and have never been in the fray: a kind of nondescript, half scholar, and by nature half billman or bowman or musketeer; if I'm worth anything London's the field for me. But that's what I have to try.'

'Papa will not like your serving with your pen in London: he will say you are worth too much for that.'

'Good men are at it; I should not care to be ranked above them.'

'They are wasted, he says.'

'Error! If they have their private ambition, they may suppose they are wasted. But the value to the world of a private ambition, I do not clearly understand.'

'You have not an evil opinion of the world?' said Miss Middleton, sick at heart as she spoke, with the sensation of having invited herself to take a drop of poison.

He replied: 'One might as well have an evil opinion of a river: here it's muddy, there it's clear; one day troubled, another at rest. We have to treat it with common sense.'

'Love it?'

'In the sense of serving it.'

'Not think it beautiful?'

'Part of it is, part of it the reverse.'

'Papa would quote the "mulier formosa".'[9]

'Except that "fish" is too good for the black extremity.
"Woman" is excellent for the upper.'

'How do you say that? – not cynically, I believe. Your view
commends itself to my reason.'

She was grateful to him for not stating it in ideal contrast
with Sir Willoughby's view. If he had, so intensely did her
youthful blood desire to be enamoured of the world, that she
felt he would have lifted her off her feet. For a moment a gulf
beneath had been threatening. When she said, 'Love it?' a
little enthusiasm would have wafted her into space fierily as
wine; but the sober, 'In the sense of serving it', entered her
brain, and was matter for reflection upon it and him.

She could think of him in pleasant liberty, uncorrected by
her woman's instinct of peril. He had neither arts nor graces;
nothing of his cousin's easy social front-face. She had once
witnessed the military precision of his dancing, and had to
learn to like him before she ceased to pray that she might never
be the victim of it as his partner. He walked heroically, his
pedestrian vigour being famous, but that means one who
walks away from the sex, not excelling in the recreations
where men and women join hands. He was not much of a
horseman either. Sir Willoughby enjoyed seeing him on
horseback. And he could scarcely be said to shine in a drawing-
room, unless when seated beside a person ready for real talk.
Even more than his merits, his demerits pointed him out as a
man to be a friend to a young woman who wanted one. His
way of life pictured to her troubled spirit an enviable smoothness; and his having achieved that smooth way she considered a sign of strength; and she wished to lean in idea upon
some friendly strength. His reputation for indifference to the
frivolous charms of girls clothed him with a noble coldness,
and gave him the distinction of a far-seen solitary iceberg in
Southern waters. The popular notion of hereditary titled
aristocracy resembles her sentiment for a man that would not
flatter and could not be flattered by her sex: he appeared
superior almost to awfulness. She was young, but she had

received much flattery in her ears, and by it she had been snared; and he, disdaining to practise the fowler's arts or to cast a thought on small fowls, appeared to her to have a pride founded on natural loftiness.

They had not spoken for awhile, when Vernon said abruptly, 'The boy's future rather depends on you, Miss Middleton. I mean to leave as soon as possible, and I do not like his being here without me, though you will look after him, I have no doubt. But you may not at first see where the spoiling hurts him. He should be packed off at once to the crammer, before you are Lady Patterne. Use your influence. Willoughby will support the lad at your request. The cost cannot be great. There are strong grounds against my having him in London, even if I could manage it. May I count on you?'

'I will mention it: I will do my best,' said Miss Middleton, strangely dejected.

They were now on the lawn, where Sir Willoughby was walking with the ladies Eleanor and Isabel, his maiden aunts.

'You seem to have coursed the hare and captured the hart,' he said to his bride.

'Started the truant and run down the paedagogue,' said Vernon.

'Ay, you won't listen to me about the management of that boy,' Sir Willoughby retorted.

The ladies embraced Miss Middleton. One offered up an ejaculation in eulogy of her looks, the other of her healthfulness: then both remarked that with indulgence young Crossjay could be induced to do anything. Clara wondered whether inclination or Sir Willoughby had disciplined their individuality out of them and made them his shadows, his echoes. She gazed from them to him, and feared him. But as yet she had not experienced the power in him which could threaten and wrestle to subject the members of his household to the state of satellites. Though she had in fact been giving battle to it for several months, she had held her own too well to perceive definitely the character of the spirit opposing her.

She said to the ladies, 'Ah, no! Mr Whitford has chosen the only method for teaching a boy like Crossjay.'

'I propose to make a man of him,' said Sir Willoughby.

'What is to become of him if he learns nothing?'

'If he pleases me, he will be provided for. I have never abandoned a dependent.'

Clara let her eyes rest on his and, without turning or dropping, shut them.

The effect was discomforting to him. He was very sensitive to the intentions of eyes and tones; which was one secret of his rigid grasp of the dwellers in his household. They were taught that they had to render agreement under sharp scrutiny. Studious eyes, devoid of warmth, devoid of the shyness of sex, that suddenly closed on their look, signified a want of comprehension of some kind, it might be hostility of understanding. Was it possible he did not possess her utterly? He frowned up.

Clara saw the lift of his brows, and thought, 'My mind is my own, married or not.'

It was the point in dispute.

CHAPTER 9

✖✖✖✖

Clara and Laetitia Meet: They Are Compared

AN hour before the time for lessons next morning young Crossjay was on the lawn with a big bunch of wild flowers. He left them at the hall door for Miss Middleton, and vanished into bushes.

These vulgar weeds were about to be dismissed to the dustheap by the great officials of the household; but as it happened that Miss Middleton had seen them from the window in Crossjay's hands, the discovery was made that they were indeed his presentation-bouquet, and a footman received orders to place them before her. She was very pleased. The arrangement of the flowers bore witness to fairer fingers than the boy's own in the disposition of the rings of colour, red campion and anemone, cowslip and speedwell, primroses and wood-hyacinths; and rising out of the blue was a branch bearing thick white blossom, so thick, and of so pure a whiteness, that Miss Middleton, while praising Crossjay for soliciting the aid of Miss Dale, was at a loss to name the tree.

'It is a gardener's improvement on the Vestal of the forest, the wild cherry,' said Dr Middleton, 'and in this case we may admit the gardener's claim to be valid, though I believe that, with his gift of double blossom, he has improved away the fruit. Call this the Vestal of civilization, then; he has at least done something to vindicate the beauty of the office as well as the justness of the title.'

'It is Vernon's Holy Tree the young rascal has been despoiling,' said Sir Willoughby merrily.

Miss Middleton was informed that this double-blossom wild cherry-tree was worshipped by Mr Whitford.

Sir Willoughby promised he would conduct her to it. 'You,' he said to her, 'can bear the trial; few complexions can; it is to most ladies a crueller test than snow. Miss Dale, for example, becomes old lace within a dozen yards of it. I should like to place her under the tree beside you.'

'Dear me, though; but that is investing the hamadryad with novel and terrible functions,' exclaimed Dr Middleton.

Clara said: 'Miss Dale could drag me into a superior Court to show me fading beside her in gifts more valuable than a complexion.'

'She has a fine ability,' said Vernon.

All the world knew, so Clara knew of Miss Dale's romantic admiration of Sir Willoughby; she was curious to see Miss

Dale and study the nature of a devotion that might be, within reason, imitable – for a man who could speak with such steely coldness of the poor lady he had fascinated? Well, perhaps it was good for the hearts of women to be beneath a frost; to be schooled, restrained, turned inward on their dreams. Yes, then, his coldness was desireable; it encouraged an ideal of him. It suggested and seemed to propose to Clara's mind the divineness of separation instead of the deadly accuracy of an intimate perusal. She tried to look on him as Miss Dale might look, and while partly despising her for the dupery she envied, and more than criticizing him for the inhuman numbness of sentiment which offered up his worshipper to point a complimentary comparison, she was able to imagine a distance whence it would be possible to observe him uncritically, kindly, admiringly; as the moon a handsome mortal, for example.

In the midst of her thoughts, she surprised herself by saying: 'I certainly was difficult to instruct. I might see things clearer if I had a fine ability. I never remember to have been perfectly pleased with my immediate lesson . . .'

She stopped, wondering whither her tongue was leading her; then added, to save herself, 'And that may be why I feel for poor Crossjay.'

Mr Whitford apparently did not think it remarkable that she should have been set off gabbling of 'a fine ability', though the eulogistic phrase had been pronounced by him with an impressiveness to make his ear aware of an echo.

Sir Willoughby dispersed her vapourish confusion. 'Exactly,' he said. 'I have insisted with Vernon, I don't know how often, that you must have the lad by his affections. He won't bear driving. It had no effect on me. Boys of spirit kick at it. I think I know boys, Clara.'

He found himself addressing eyes that regarded him as though he were a small speck, a pin's head, in the circle of their remote contemplation. They were wide; they closed.

She opened them to gaze elsewhere.

He was very sensitive.

Even then, when knowingly wounding him, or because of it, she was trying to climb back to that altitude of the thin division of neutral ground, from which we see a lover's faults and are above them, pure surveyors. She climbed unsuccessfully, it is true; soon despairing and using the effort as a pretext to fall back lower.

Dr Middleton withdrew Sir Willoughby's attention from the imperceptible annoyance. 'No, sir, no: the birch! the birch! Boys of spirit commonly turn into solid men, and the solider the men the more surely do they vote for Busby.[10] For me, I pray he may be immortal in Great Britain. Sea-air nor mountain-air is half so bracing. I venture to say that the power to take a licking is better worth having than the power to administer one. Horse him and birch him if Crossjay runs from his books.'

'It is your opinion, sir?' his host bowed to him affably, shocked on behalf of the ladies.

'So positively so, sir, that I will undertake, without knowledge of their antecedents, to lay my finger on the men in public life who have not had early Busby. They are ill-balanced men. Their seat of reason is not a concrete. They won't take rough and smooth as they come. They make bad blood, can't forgive, sniff right and left for approbation, and are excited to anger if an East wind does not flatter them. Why, sir, when they have grown to be seniors, you find these men mixed up with the nonsense of their youth; you see they are unthrashed. We English beat the world because we take a licking well. I hold it for a surety of a proper sweetness of blood.'

The smile of Sir Willoughby waxed ever softer as the shakes of his head increased in contradictoriness. 'And yet,' said he, with the air of conceding a little after having answered the Rev. Doctor and convicted him of error, 'Jack requires it to keep him in order. On board ship your argument may apply. Not, I suspect, among gentlemen. No.'

'Good-night to you, gentlemen!' said Dr Middleton.

Clara heard Miss Eleanor and Miss Isabel interchange remarks:

'Willoughby would not have suffered it!'

'It would entirely have altered him!'

She sighed and put a tooth on her under-lip. The gift of humourous fancy is in women fenced round with forbidding placards; they have to choke it; if they perceive a piece of humour, for instance, the young Willoughby grasped by his master, and his horrified relatives rigid at the sight of preparations for the seed of sacrilege, they have to blindfold the mind's eye. They are society's hard-drilled soldiery. Prussians that must both march and think in step. It is for the advantage of the civilized world, if you like, since men have decreed it, or matrons have so read the decree; but here and there a younger woman, haply an uncorrected insurgent of the sex matured here and there, feels that her lot was cast with her head in a narrower pit than her limbs.

Clara speculated as to whether Miss Dale might be perchance a person of a certain liberty of mind. She asked for some little, only some little, free play of mind in a house that seemed to wear, as it were, a cap of iron. Sir Willoughby not merely ruled, he throned, he inspired: and how? She had noticed an irascible sensitiveness in him alert against a shadow of disagreement; and as he was kind when perfectly appeased, the sop was offered by him for submission. She noticed that even Mr Whitford forbore to alarm the sentiment of authority in his cousin. If he did not breathe Sir Willoughby, like the ladies Eleanor and Isabel, he would either acquiesce in a syllable or be silent. He never strongly dissented. The habit of the house, with its iron cap, was on him, as it was on the servants, and would be, oh, shudders of the shipwrecked that see their end in drowning! on the wife.

'When do I meet Miss Dale?' she inquired.

'This very evening, at dinner,' replied Sir Willoughby.

Then, thought she, there is that to look forward to.

She indulged her morbid fit, and shut up her senses that she might live in the anticipation of meeting Miss Dale; and, long before the approach of the hour, her hope of encountering any other than another dull adherent of Sir Willoughby had fled. So she was languid for two of the three minutes when she sat alone with Laetitia in the drawing-room before the rest had assembled.

'It is Miss Middleton?' Laetitia said, advancing to her. 'My jealousy tells me; for you have won my boy Crossjay's heart, and done more to bring him to obedience in a few minutes than we have been able to do in months.'

'His wild flowers were so welcome to me,' said Clara.

'He was very modest over them. And I mention it because boys of his age usually thrust their gifts in our faces fresh as they pluck them, and you were to be treated quite differently.'

'We saw his good fairy's hand.'

'She resigns her office; but I pray you not to love him too well in return; for he ought to be away reading with one of those men who get boys through their examinations. He is, we all think, a born sailor, and his place is in the navy.'

'But, Miss Dale, I love him so well that I shall consult his interests and not my own selfishness. And, if I have influence, he will not be a week with you longer. It should have been spoke of to-day; I must have been in some dream; I thought of it, I know. I will not forget to do what may be in my power.'

Clara's heart sank at the renewed engagement and plighting of herself involved in her asking a favour, urging any sort of petition. The cause was good. Besides, she was plighted already.

'Sir Willoughby is really fond of the boy,' she said.

'He is fond of exciting fondness in the boy,' said Miss Dale. 'He has not dealt much with children. I am sure he likes Crossjay; he could not otherwise be so forbearing; it is wonderful what he endures and laughs at.'

Sir Willoughby entered. The presence of Miss Dale illuminated him as the burning taper lights up consecrated plate. Deeply respecting her for her constancy, esteeming her for a model of taste, he was never in her society without that happy consciousness of shining which calls forth the treasures of the man; and these it is no exaggeration to term unbounded, when all that comes from him is taken for gold.

The effect of the evening on Clara was to render her distrustful of her later antagonism. She had unknowingly passed into the spirit of Miss Dale, Sir Willoughby aiding; for she could sympathize with the view of his constant admirer on seeing him so cordially and smoothly gay; as one may say, domestically witty, the most agreeable form of wit. Mrs Mountstuart Jenkinson discerned that he had a leg of physical perfection; Miss Dale distinguished it in him in the vital essence; and before either of these ladies he was not simply a radiant, he was a productive creature, so true it is that praise is our fructifying sun. He had even a touch of the romantic air which Clara remembered as her first impression of the favourite of the county; and strange she found it to observe this resuscitated idea confronting her experience. What if she had been captious, inconsiderate? Oh, blissful revival of the sense of peace! The happiness of pain departing was all that she looked for, and her conception of liberty was to learn to love her chains, provided that he would spare her the caress. In this mood she sternly condemned Constantia. 'We must try to do good; we must not be thinking of ourselves; we must make the best of our path in life.' She revolved these infantile precepts with humble earnestness; and not to be tardy in her striving to do good, with a remote but pleasurable glimpse of Mr Whitford hearing of it, she took the opportunity to speak to Sir Willoughby on the subject of young Crossjay, at a moment when, alighting from horseback, he had shown himself to advantage among a gallant cantering company. He showed to great advantage on horseback among men, being invariably the best mounted, and he had a cavalierly style, possibly cultivated, but effective. On foot his raised head and

half-dropped eyelids too palpably assumed superiority.
'Willoughby, I want to speak,' she said, and shrank as she
spoke, lest he should immediately grant everything in the
mood of courtship, and invade her respite; 'I want to speak of
that dear boy Crossjay. You are fond of him. He is rather an
idle boy here, and wasting time . . .'

'Now you are here, and when you are here for good, my
love for good . . .' he fluttered away in loverliness, forgetful of
Crossjay, whom he presently took up. 'The boy recognizes
his most sovereign lady, and will do your bidding, though you
should order him to learn his lessons! Who would not obey?
Your beauty alone commands. But what is there beyond? – a
grace, a hue divine, that sets you not so much above as apart,
severed from the world.'

Clara produced an active smile in duty, and pursued: 'If
Crossjay were sent at once to some house where men prepare
boys to pass for the navy, he would have his chance, and the
navy is distinctly his profession. His father is a brave man, and
he inherits bravery, and he has a passion for a sailor's life; only
he must be able to pass his examination, and he has not much
time.'

Sir Willoughby gave a slight laugh in sad amusement.

'My dear Clara, you adore the world; and I suppose you
have to learn that there is not a question in this wrangling
world about which we have not disputes and contests ad nau-
seam. I have my notions concerning Crossjay, Vernon has his.
I should wish to make a gentleman of him. Vernon marks
him for a sailor. But Vernon is the lad's protector, I am not.
Vernon took him from his father to instruct him, and he has a
right to say what shall be done with him. I do not interfere.
Only I can't prevent the lad from liking me. Old Vernon
seems to feel it. I assure you I hold entirely aloof. If I am asked,
in spite of my disapproval of Vernon's plans for the boy, to
subscribe to his departure, I can but shrug, because, as you see,
I have never opposed. Old Vernon pays for him, he is the
master, he decides, and if Crossjay is blown from the mast-

head in a gale, the blame does not fall on me. These, my dear, are matters of reason.'

'I would not venture to intrude on them,' said Clara, 'if I had not suspected that money . . .'

'Yes,' cried Willoughby; 'and it is a part. And let old Vernon surrender the boy to me, I will immediately relieve him of the burden on his purse. Can I do that, my dear, for the furtherance of a scheme I condemn? The point is thus: latterly I have invited Captain Patterne to visit me: just previous to his departure for the African Coast, where Government despatches Marines when there is no other way of killing them, I sent him a special invitation. He thanked me and curtly declined. The man, I may almost say, is my pensioner. Well, he calls himself a Patterne, he is undoubtedly a man of courage, he has elements of our blood, and the name. I think I am to be approved for desiring to make a better gentleman of the son than I behold in the father: and seeing that life from an early age on board ship has anything but made a gentleman of the father, I hold that I am right in shaping another course for the son.'

'Naval officers . . .' Clara suggested.

'Some,' said Willoughby. 'But they must be men of birth, coming out of homes of good breeding. Strip them of the halo of the title of naval officers, and I fear you would not often say gentlemen when they step into a drawing-room. I went so far as to fancy I had some claim to make young Crossjay something different. It can be done; the Patterne comes out in his behaviour to you, my love; it can be done. But if I take him, I claim undisputed sway over him. I cannot make a gentleman of the fellow if I am to compete with this person and that. In fine, he must look up to me, he must have one model.'

'Would you, then, provide for him subsequently?'

'According to his behaviour.'

'Would not that be precarious for him?'

'More so than the profession you appear inclined to choose for him?'

'But there he would be under clear regulations.'

'With me he would have to respond to affection.'

'Would you secure to him a settled income? For an idle gentleman is bad enough; a penniless gentleman . . .'

'He has only to please me, my dear, and he will be launched and protected.'

'But if he does not succeed in pleasing you?'

'Is it so difficult?'

'Oh!' Clara fretted.

'You see, my love, I answer you,' said Sir Willoughby.

He resumed: 'But let old Vernon have his trial with the lad. He has his own ideas. Let him carry them out. I shall watch the experiment.'

Clara was for abandoning her task in sheer faintness.

'Is not the question one of money?' she said, shyly, knowing Mr Whitford to be poor.

'Old Vernon chooses to spend his money that way,' replied Sir Willoughby. 'If it saves him from breaking his shins and risking his neck on his Alps, we may consider it well employed.'

'Yes,' Clara's voice occupied a pause.

She seized her languor as it were a curling snake and cast it off. 'But I understand that Mr Whitford wants your assistance. Is he not – not rich? When he leaves the Hall to try his fortune in literature in London, he may not be so well able to support Crossjay and obtain the instruction necessary for the boy: and it would be generous to help him.'

'Leaves the Hall!' exclaimed Willoughby. 'I have not heard a word of it. He made a bad start at the beginning, and I should have thought that would have tamed him: had to throw over his Fellowship; ahem! Then he received a small legacy some time back, and wanted to be off to push his luck in literature: rank gambling, as I told him. Londonizing can do him no good. I thought that nonsense of his was over years ago. What is it he has from me? – about a hundred and fifty a year: and it might be doubled for the asking: and all the books he requires: and these writers and scholars no sooner think of a book than they must have it. And do not suppose me to complain. I am a man who will not have a single shilling expended by those who serve immediately about my person. I confess to exacting that kind of dependency. Feudalism is not an objectionable thing if you can be sure of the lord. You know, Clara, and you should know me in my weakness too, I do not claim servitude, I stipulate for affection. I claim to be surrounded by persons loving me. And with one? . . . dearest! So that we two can shut out the world; we live what is the dream of others. Nothing imaginable can be sweeter. It is a veritable heaven on earth. To be the possessor of the whole of you! Your thoughts, hopes, all.'

Sir Willoughby intensified his imagination to conceive more: he could not, or could not express it, and pursued: 'But what is this talk of Vernon's leaving me? He cannot leave. He has barely a hundred a year of his own. You see, I consider him. I do not speak of the ingratitude of the wish to leave. You know, my dear, I have a deadly abhorrence of partings and such like. As far as I can, I surround myself with healthy people specially to guard myself from having my feelings wrung; and excepting Miss Dale, whom you like – my darling does like her?' – the answer satisfied him; 'with that one exception, I am not aware of a case that threatens to torment me. And here is a man, under no compulsion, talking of leaving the Hall! In the name of goodness, why? But why? Am I to imagine that the sight of perfect felicity distresses him? We are told that the world is "desperately wicked". I do not like to think it of my friends; yet otherwise their conduct is often hard to account for.'

'If it were true, you would not punish Crossjay?' Clara feebly interposed.

'I should certainly take Crossjay and make a man of him after my own model, my dear. But who spoke to you of this?'

'Mr Whitford himself. And let me give you my opinion,

Willoughby, that he will take Crossjay with him rather than leave him, if there is a fear of the boy's missing his chance of the navy.'

'Marines appear to be in the ascendant,' said Sir Willoughby, astonished at the locution and pleading in the interests of a son of one. 'Then Crossjay he must take. I cannot accept half the boy. I am,' he laughed, 'the legitimate claimant in the application for judgement before the wise king.[11] Besides, the boy has a dose of my blood in him; he has none of Vernon's, not one drop.'

'Ah!'

'You see, my love?'

'Oh, I do see; yes.'

'I put forth no pretensions to perfection,' Sir Willoughby continued. 'I can bear a considerable amount of provocation; still I can be offended, and I am unforgiving when I have been offended. Speak to Vernon, if a natural occasion should spring up. I shall, of course, have to speak to him. You may, Clara, have observed a man who passed me on the road as we were cantering home, without a hint of a touch to his hat. That man is a tenant of mine, farming six hundred acres, Hoppner by name: a man bound to remember that I have, independently of my position, obliged him frequently. His lease of my ground has five years to run. I must say I detest the churlishness of our country population, and where it comes across me I chastise it. Vernon is a different matter: he will only require to be spoken to. One would fancy the old fellow laboured now and then under a magnetic attraction to beggary. My love,' he bent to her and checked their pacing up and down, 'you are tired?'

'I am very tired to-day,' said Clara.

His arm was offered. She laid two fingers on it, and they dropped when he attempted to press them to his rib.

He did not insist. To walk beside her was to share in the stateliness of her walking.

He placed himself at a corner of the door-way for her to

pass him into the house, and doated on her cheek, her ear, and
the softly dusky nape of her neck, where this way and that the
little lighter-coloured irreclaimable curls running truant from
the comb and the knot – curls, half-curls, root-curls, vine-
ringlets, wedding-rings, fledgling feathers, tufts of down,
blown wisps – waved or fell, waved over or up or involutedly,
or strayed, loose and downward, in the form of small silken
paws, hardly any of them much thicker than a crayon shading,
cunninger than long round locks of gold to trick the heart.

Laetitia had nothing to show resembling such beauty.

CHAPTER 10

✕✕✕✕

In Which Sir Willoughby Chances to Supply the Title for Himself

NOW Vernon was useful to his cousin; he was the accomplished secretary of a man who governed his estate shrewdly
and diligently, but had been once or twice unlucky in his
judgements pronounced from the magisterial bench as a
Justice of the Peace, on which occasions a half column of
trenchant English supported by an apposite classical quotation
impressed Sir Willoughby with the value of such a secretary
in a controversy. He had no fear of that fiery dragon of scorching breath – the newspaper press – while Vernon was his right-
hand man; and as he intended to enter Parliament, he foresaw
the greater need of him. Furthermore, he liked his cousin to
date his own controversial writings, on classical subjects, from
Patterne Hall. It caused his house to shine in a foreign field;
proved the service of scholarship by giving it a flavour of a
bookish aristocracy that, though not so well worth having,
and indeed in itself contemptible, is above the material and

titular; one cannot quite say how. There, however, is the flavour. Dainty sauces are the life, the nobility, of famous dishes; taken alone, the former would be nauseating, the latter plebeian. It is thus, or somewhat so, when you have a poet, still better a scholar, attached to your household. Sir Willoughby deserved to have him, for he was above his county friends in his apprehension of the flavour bestowed by the man; and having him, he had made them conscious of their deficiency. His cook, M. Dehors, pupil of the great Godefroy, was not the only French cook in the county; but his cousin and secretary, the rising scholar, the elegant essayist, was an unparalleled decoration; of his kind, of course. Personally, we laugh at him; you had better not, unless you are fain to show that the higher world of polite literature is unknown to you. Sir Willoughby could create an abject silence at a county dinnertable by an allusion to Vernon 'at work at home upon his Etruscans or his Dorians'; and he paused a moment to let the allusion sink, laughed audibly to himself over his eccentric cousin, and let him rest.

In addition, Sir Willoughby abhorred the loss of a familiar face in his domestic circle. He thought ill of servants who could accept their dismissal without petitioning to stay with him. A servant that gave warning partook of a certain fiendishness. Vernon's project of leaving the Hall offended and alarmed the sensitive gentleman. 'I shall have to hand Letty Dale to him at last!' he thought, yielding in bitter generosity to the conditions imposed on him by the ungenerousness of another. For, since his engagement to Miss Middleton, his electrically forethoughtful mind had seen in Miss Dale, if she stayed in the neighbourhood, and remained unmarried, the governess of his infant children, often consulting with him. But here was a prospect dashed out. The two, then, may marry, and live in a cottage on the borders of his park; and Vernon can retain his post, and Laetitia her devotion. The risk of her casting it off had to be faced. Marriage has been known to have such an effect on the most faithful of women that a great passion fades to naught in their volatile bosoms when they have taken a husband. We see in women especially the triumph of the animal over the spiritual. Nevertheless, risks must be run for a purpose in view.

Having no taste for a discussion with Vernon, whom it was his habit to confound by breaking away from him abruptly when he had delivered his opinion, he left it to both the persons interesting themselves in young Crossjay to imagine that he was meditating on the question of the lad, and to imagine that it would be wise to leave him to meditate; for he could be preternaturally acute in reading any of his fellow-creatures if they crossed the current of his feelings. And, meanwhile, he instructed the ladies Eleanor and Isabel to bring Laetitia Dale on a visit to the Hall, where dinner-parties were soon to be given and a pleasing talker would be wanted, where also a woman of intellect, steeped in a splendid sentiment, hitherto a miracle of female constancy, might stir a younger woman to some emulation. Definitely to resolve to bestow Laetitia upon Vernon was more than he could do; enough that he held the card.

Regarding Clara, his genius for perusing the heart which was not in perfect harmony with him through the series of responsive movements to his own, informed him of a something in her character that might have suggested to Mrs Mountstuart Jenkinson her indefensible, absurd 'rogue in porcelain'. Idea there was none in that phrase; yet, if you looked on Clara as a delicately inimitable porcelain beauty, the suspicion of a delicately inimitable ripple over her features touched a thought of innocent roguery, wildwood roguery; the likeness to the costly and lovely substance appeared to admit a fitness in the dubious epithet. He detested but was haunted by the phrase.

She certainly had at times the look of the nymph that has gazed too long on the faun, and has unwittingly copied his lurking lip and long sliding eye. Her play with young Crossjay resembled a return of the lady to the cat; she flung herself into it as if her real vitality had been in suspense till she saw the boy. Sir Willoughby by no means disapproved of a physical liveliness that promised him health in his mate; but he began to feel in their conversations that she did not sufficiently think of making herself a nest for him. Steely points were opposed to him when he, figuratively, bared his bosom to be taken to the softest and fairest. She reasoned: in other words, armed her ignorance. She reasoned against him publicly, and lured Vernon to support her. Influence is to be counted for power, and her influence over Vernon was displayed in her persuading him to dance one evening at Lady Culmer's, after his melancholy exhibitions of himself in the art; and not only did she persuade him to stand up fronting her, she manoeuvred him through the dance like a clever boy cajoling a top to come to him without reeling, both to Vernon's contentment and to Sir Willoughby's; for he was the last man to object to a manifestation of power in his bride. Considering her influence with Vernon, he renewed the discourse upon young Crossjay; and, as he was addicted to system, he took her into his confidence, that she might be taught to look to him and act for him.

'Old Vernon has not spoken to you again of that lad?' he said.

'Yes, Mr Whitford has asked me.'

'He does not ask me, my dear!'

'He may fancy me of greater aid than I am.'

'You see, my love, if he puts Crossjay on me, he will be off. He has this craze for "enlisting" his pen in London, as he calls it; and I am accustomed to him; I don't like to think of him as a hack scribe, writing nonsense from dictation to earn a pitiful subsistence; I want him here; and, supposing he goes, he offends me; he loses a friend; and it will not be the first time that a friend has tried me too far; but if he offends me, he is extinct.'

'Is what?' cried Clara, with a look of fright.

'He becomes to me at once as if he had never been. He is extinct.'

'In spite of your affection?'

'On account of it, I might say. Our nature is mysterious, and mine as much so as any. Whatever my regrets, he goes out. This is not a language I talk to the world. I do the man no harm; I am not to be named unchristian. But . . . !'

Sir Willoughby mildly shrugged, and indicated a spreading out of the arms.

'But do, do talk to me as you talk to the world, Willoughby; give me some relief!'

'My own Clara, we are one. You should know me at my worst, we will say, if you like, as well as at my best.'

'Should I speak too?'

'What could you have to confess?'

She hung silent; the wave of an insane resolution swelled in her bosom and subsided before she said, 'Cowardice, incapacity to speak.'

'Women!' said he.

We do not expect so much of women; the heroic virtues as little as the vices. They have not to unfold the scroll of character.

He resumed, and by his tone she understood that she was now in the inner temple of him: 'I tell you these things; I quite acknowledge they do not elevate me. They help to constitute my character. I tell you most humbly that I have in me much – too much of the fallen archangel's pride.'

Clara bowed her head over a sustained in-drawn breath.

'It must be pride,' he said, in a reverie superinduced by her thoughtfulness over the revelation, and glorying in the black flames demoniacal wherewith he crowned himself.

'Can you not correct it?' said she.

He replied, profoundly vexed by disappointment: 'I am what I am. It might be demonstrated to you mathematically that it is corrected by equivalents or substitutions in my character. If it be a failing – assuming that.'

'It seems one to me: so cruelly to punish Mr Whitford for seeking to improve his fortunes.'

'He reflects on my share in his fortunes. He has had but to apply to me for his honorarium to be doubled.'

'He wishes for independence.'

'Independence of *me*!'

'Liberty!'

'At my expense!'

'Oh, Willoughby!'

'Ay, but this is the world, and I know it, my love; and beautiful as your incredulity may be, you will find it more comforting to confide in my knowledge of the selfishness of the world. My sweetest, you will? – you do! For a breath of difference between us is intolerable. Do you not feel how it breaks our magic ring? One small fissure, and we have the world with its muddy deluge! – But my subject was old Vernon. Yes, I pay for Crossjay, if Vernon consents to stay. I waive my own scheme for the lad, though I think it the better one. Now, then, to induce Vernon to stay. He has his ideas about staying under a mistress of the household; and therefore, not to contest it – he is a man of no argument; a sort of lunatic determination takes the place of it with old Vernon! – let him settle close by me, in one of my cottages; very well, and to settle him we must marry him.'

'Who is there?' said Clara, beating for the lady in her mind.

'Women,' said Willoughby, 'are born match-makers, and the most persuasive is a young bride. With a man – and a man like old Vernon! – she is irresistible. It is my wish, and that arms you. It is your wish, that subjugates him. If he goes, he goes for good. If he stays, he is my friend. I deal simply with him, as with every one. It is the secret of authority. Now Miss Dale will soon lose her father. He exists on a pension; she has the prospect of having to leave the neighbourhood of the Hall, unless she is established near us. Her whole heart is in this region; it is the poor soul's passion. Count on her agreeing. But she will require a little wooing: and old Vernon wooing! Picture the scene to yourself, my love. His notion of wooing, I suspect, will be to treat the lady like a lexicon, and turn over the leaves for the word, and fly through the leaves for another word, and so get a sentence. Don't frown at the poor old fellow, my Clara; some have the language on their tongues, and some have not. Some are very dry sticks; manly men, honest fellows, but so cut away, so polished away from the sex, that they are in absolute want of outsiders to supply the silken filaments to attach them. Actually!' Sir Willoughby laughed in Clara's face to relax the dreamy stoniness of her look. 'But I can assure you, my dearest, I have seen it. Vernon does not know how to speak – as *we* speak. He has, or he had, what is called a sneaking affection for Miss Dale. It was the most amusing thing possible; his courtship! – the air of a dog with an uneasy conscience, trying to reconcile himself with his master! We were all in fits of laughter. Of course it came to nothing.'

'Will Mr Whitford,' said Clara, 'offend you to extinction if he declines?'

Willoughby breathed an affectionate 'Tush!' to her silliness.

'We bring them together, as we best can. You see, Clara, I desire, and I will make some sacrifices to detain him.'

'But what do you sacrifice? – a cottage?' said Clara, combative at all points.

'An ideal, perhaps. I lay no stress on sacrifice. I strongly object to separations. And therefore, you will say, I prepare the ground for unions? Put your influence to good service, my love. I believe you could persuade him to give us the Highland fling on the drawing-room table.'

'There is nothing to say to him of Crossjay?'

'We hold Crossjay in reserve.'

'It is urgent.'

'Trust me. I have my ideas. I am not idle. That boy bids fair for a capital horseman. Eventualities might ...' Sir Willoughby murmured to himself, and addressing his bride, 'The cavalry? If we put him into the cavalry, we might make a gentleman of him – not be ashamed of him. Or, under certain eventualities, the Guards. Think it over, my love. De Craye, who will, I suppose, act best man for me, supposing old Vernon to pull at the collar, is a Lieutenant-Colonel in the Guards, a thorough gentleman – of the brainless class, if you like, but an elegant fellow; an Irishman; you will see him, and I should like to set a naval lieutenant beside him in a drawing-room, for you to compare them and consider the model you would choose for a boy you are interested in. Horace is grace and gallantry incarnate; fatuous, probably: I have always been too friendly with him to examine closely. He made himself one of my dogs, though my elder, and seemed to like to be at my heels. One of the few men's faces I can call admirably handsome; – with nothing behind it, perhaps. As Vernon says, "a nothing picked by the vultures and bleached by the desert". Not a bad talker, if you are satisfied with keeping up the ball. He will amuse you. Old Horace does not know how amusing he is!'

'Did Mr Whitford say that of Colonel De Craye?'

'I forget the person of whom he said it. So you have noticed old Vernon's foible? Quote him one of his epigrams, and he is in motion head and heels! It is an infallible receipt for tuning him. If I want to have him in good temper, I have only to remark, "as you said". I straighten his back instantly.'

'I,' said Clara, 'have noticed chiefly his anxiety concerning the boy; for which I admire him.'

'Creditable, if not particularly far-sighted and sagacious. Well, then, my dear, attack him at once; lead him to the subject of our fair neighbour. She is to be our guest for a week or so, and the whole affair might be concluded far enough to fix him before she leaves. She is at present awaiting the arrival of a cousin to attend on her father. A little gentle pushing will precipitate old Vernon on his knees as far as he ever can unbend them; but when a lady is made ready to expect a declaration, you know, why, she does not – does she? – demand the entire formula? – though some beautiful fortresses . . .'

He enfolded her. Clara was growing hardened to it. To this

she was fated; and not seeing any way to escape, she invoked a friendly frost to strike her blood, and passed through the minute unfeelingly. Having passed it, she reproached herself for making so much of it, thinking it a lesser endurance than to listen to him. What could she do? – she was caged; by her word of honour, as she at one time thought; by her cowardice, at another; and dimly sensible that the latter was a stronger lock than the former, she mused on the abstract question whether a woman's cowardice can be so absolute as to cast her into the jaws of her aversion. Is it to be conceived? Is there not a moment when it stands at bay? But haggard-visaged Honour then starts up claiming to be dealt with in turn; for having courage restored to her, she must have the courage to break with honour, she must dare to be faithless, and not merely say, I will be brave, but be brave enough to be dishonourable. The cage of a plighted woman hungering for her disengagement has two keepers, a noble and a vile; where on earth is creature so dreadfully enclosed? It lies with her to overcome what degrades her, that she may win to liberty by overcoming what exalts.

Contemplating her situation, this idea (or vapour of youth taking the god-like semblance of an idea) sprang, born of her present sickness, in Clara's mind; that it must be an ill-constructed tumbling world where the hour of ignorance is made the creator of our destiny by being forced to the decisive elections upon which life's main issues hang. Her teacher had brought her to contemplate his view of the world.

She thought likewise: how must a man despise women, who can expose himself as he does to me!

Miss Middleton owed it to Sir Willoughby Patterne that she ceased to think like a girl. When had the great change begun? Glancing back, she could imagine that it was near the period we call in love the first – almost from the first. And she was led to imagine it through having become barred from imagining her own emotions of that season. They were so dead as not to arise even under the form of shadows in fancy.

Without imputing blame to him, for she was reasonable so far, she deemed herself a person entrapped. In a dream somehow she had committed herself to a life-long imprisonment; and, oh terror! not in a quiet dungeon; the barren walls closed round her, talked, called for ardour, expected admiration.

She was unable to say why she could not give it; why she retreated more and more inwardly; why she invoked the frost to kill her tenderest feelings. She was in revolt, until a whisper of the day of bells reduced her to blank submission; out of which a breath of peace drew her to revolt again in gradual rapid stages, and once more the aspect of that singular day of merry blackness felled her to earth. It was alive, it advanced, it had a mouth, it had a song. She received letters of bridesmaids writing of it, and felt them as waves that hurl a log of wreck to shore. Following which afflicting sense of antagonism to the whole circle sweeping on with her, she considered the possibility of her being in a commencement of madness. Otherwise might she not be accused of a capriciousness quite as deplorable to consider? She had written to certain of these young ladies not very long since of this gentleman – how? – in what tone? And was it her madness then? – her recovery now? It seemed to her that to have written of him enthusiastically resembled madness more than to shudder away from the union; but standing alone, opposing all she has consented to set in motion, is too strange to a girl for perfect justification to be found in reason when she seeks it.

Sir Willoughby was destined himself to supply her with that key of special insight which revealed and stamped him in a title to fortify her spirit of revolt, consecrate it almost.

The popular physician of the county and famous anecdotal wit, Dr Corney, had been a guest at dinner overnight, and the next day there was talk of him, and of the resources of his art displayed by Armand Dehors on his hearing that he was to minister to the tastes of a gathering of hommes d'esprit. Sir Willoughby glanced at Dehors with his customary benevolent

irony in speaking of the persons, great in their way, who
served him. 'Why he cannot give us daily so good a dinner,
one must, I suppose, go to French nature to learn. The French
are in the habit of making up for all their deficiencies with
enthusiasm. They have no reverence; if I had said to him, "I
want something particularly excellent, Dehors", I should have
had a commonplace dinner. But they have enthusiasm on
draught, and that is what we must pull at. Know one French-
man and you know France. I have had Dehors under my eye
two years, and I can mount his enthusiasm at a word. He
took hommes d'esprit to denote men of letters. Frenchmen
have destroyed their nobility, so, for the sake of excitement,
they put up the literary man – not to worship him; that they
can't do; it's to put themselves in a state of effervescence.
They will not have real greatness above them, so they have
sham. That they may justly call it equality, perhaps! Ay, for
all your shake of the head, my good Vernon! You see, human
nature comes round again, try as we may to upset it, and the
French only differ from us in wading through blood to discover that they are at their old trick once more; "I am your
equal, sir, your born equal. Oh! you are a man of letters?
Allow me to be in a bubble about you." Yes, Vernon, and I
believe the fellow looks up to you as the head of the establishment. I am not jealous. Provided he attends to his functions!
There's a French philosopher [12] who's for naming the days of
the year after the birthdays of French men of letters. Voltaire-
day, Rousseau-day, Racine-day, so on. Perhaps Vernon will
inform us who takes April 1st.'

'A few trifling errors are of no consequence when you are in
the vein of satire,' said Vernon. 'Be satisfied with knowing a
nation in the person of a cook.'

'They may be reading us English off in a jockey!' said Dr
Middleton. 'I believe that jockeys are the exchange we make
for cooks; and our neighbours do not get the best of the
bargain.'

'No; but, my dear good Vernon, it's nonsensical,' said Sir

Willoughby; 'why be bawling every day the names of men of letters?'

'Philosophers.'

'Well, philosophers.'

'Of all countries and times. And they are the benefactors of humanity.'

'Bene –!' Sir Willoughby's derisive laugh broke the word. 'There's a pretension in all that, irreconcilable with English sound sense. Surely you see it?'

'We might,' said Vernon, 'if you like, give alternative titles to the days, or have alternating days, devoted to our great families that performed meritorious deeds upon such a day.'

The rebel Clara, delighting in his banter, was heard: 'Can we furnish sufficient?'

'A poet or two could help us.'

'Perhaps a statesman,' she suggested.

'A pugilist, if wanted.'

'For blowy days,' observed Dr Middleton, and hastily in penitence picked up the conversation he had unintentionally prostrated, with a general remark on new-fangled notions, and a word aside to Vernon; which created the blissful suspicion in Clara that her father was indisposed to second Sir Willoughby's opinions even when sharing them.

Sir Willoughby had led the conversation. Displeased that the lead should be withdrawn from him, he turned to Clara and related one of the after-dinner anecdotes of Dr Corney; and another, with a vast deal of human nature in it, concerning a valetudinarian gentleman, whose wife chanced to be desperately ill, and he went to the physicians assembled in consultation outside the sick-room, imploring them by all he valued, and in tears, to save the poor patient for him, saying: 'She is everything to me, everything; and if she dies I am compelled to run the risks of marrying again; I must marry again; for she has accustomed me so to the little attentions of a wife, that in truth I can't, I can't lose her! She must be saved!' And the loving husband of any devoted wife wrung his hands.

'Now, there, Clara, there you have the Egoist,' added Sir Willoughby. 'That is the perfect Egoist. You see what he comes to – and his wife! The man was utterly unconscious of giving vent to the grossest selfishness.'

'An Egoist!' said Clara.

'Beware of marrying an Egoist, my dear!' He bowed gallantly; and so blindly fatuous did he appear to her, that she could hardly believe him guilty of uttering the words she had heard from him, and kept her eyes on him vacantly till she came to a sudden full stop in the thoughts directing her gaze. She looked at Vernon, she looked at her father, and at the ladies Eleanor and Isabel. None of them saw the man in the word, none noticed the word; yet this word was her medical herb, her illuminating lamp, the key of him (and, alas, but she thought it by feeling her need of one), the advocate pleading in apology for her. Egoist! She beheld him – unfortunate, self-designated man that he was! – in his good qualities as well as bad under the implacable lamp, and his good were drenched in his first person singular. His generosity roared of *I* louder than the rest. Conceive him at the age of Dr Corney's hero: 'Pray, save my wife for me. I shall positively have to get another if I lose her, and one who may not love me half so well, or understand the peculiarities of my character and appreciate my attitudes.' He was in his thirty-second year, therefore a young man, strong and healthy, yet his garrulous return to his principal theme, his emphasis on I and me, lent him the seeming of an old man spotted with decaying youth.

'Beware of marrying an Egoist.'

Would he help her to escape? The idea of the scene ensuing upon her petition for release, and the being dragged round the walls of his egoism, and having her head knocked against the corners, alarmed her with sensations of sickness.

There was the example of Constantia. But that desperate young lady had been assisted by a gallant, loving gentleman; she had met a Captain Oxford.

Clara brooded on those two until they seemed heroic. She

questioned herself. Could she –? were one to come? She shut her eyes in languor, leaning the wrong way of her wishes, yet unable to say No.

Sir Willoughby had positively said beware! Marrying him would be a deed committed in spite of his express warning. She went so far as to conceive him subsequently saying: 'I warned you.' She conceived the state of marriage with him as that of a woman tied not to a man of heart, but to an obelisk lettered all over with hieroglyphics, and everlastingly hearing him expound them, relishing renewing his lectures on them.

Full surely this immovable stone-man would not release her. This petrifaction of egoism would from amazedly to austerely refuse the petition. His pride would debar him from understanding her desire to be released. And if she resolved on it, without doing it straightway in Constantia's manner, the miserable bewilderment of her father, for whom such a complication would be a tragic dilemma, had to be thought of. Her father, with all his tenderness for his child, would make a stand on the point of honour; though certain to yield to her, he would be distressed in a tempest of worry; and Dr Middleton thus afflicted threw up his arms, he shunned books, shunned speech, and resembled a castaway on the ocean, with nothing between himself and his calamity. As for the world, it would be barking at her heels. She might call the man she wrenched her hand from, Egoist; jilt, the world would call her. She dwelt bitterly on her agreement with Sir Willoughby regarding the world, laying it to his charge that her garden had become a place of nettles, her horizon an unlighted fourth side of a square.

Clara passed from person to person visiting the Hall. There was universal, and as she was compelled to see, honest admiration of the host. Not a soul had a suspicion of his cloaked nature. Her agony of hypocrisy in accepting their compliments as the bride of Sir Willoughby Patterne was poorly moderated by contempt of them for their infatuation. She tried to cheat herself with the thought that they were right and that she was the foolish and wicked inconstant. In her anxiety to strangle the rebelliousness which had been communicated from her mind to her blood, and was present with her whether her mind was in action or not, she encouraged the ladies Eleanor and Isabel to magnify the fictitious man of their idolatry, hoping that she might enter into them imaginatively, that she might to some degree subdue herself to the necessity of her position. If she partly succeeded in stupefying her antagonism, five minutes of him undid the work.

He requested her to wear the Patterne pearls for a dinner-party of grand ladies, telling her that he would commission Miss Isabel to take them to her. Clara begged leave to decline them, on the plea of having no right to wear them. He laughed at her modish modesty. 'But really it might almost be classed with affection,' said he. 'I give you the right. Virtually you are my wife.'

'No.'

'Before heaven?'

'No. We are not married.'

'As my betrothed, will you wear them, to please me?'

'I would rather not. I cannot wear borrowed jewels. These I cannot wear. Forgive me, I cannot. And, Willoughby,' she said, scorning herself for want of fortitude in not keeping to the simply blunt provocative refusal, 'does one not look like a victim decked for the sacrifice? – the garlanded heifer you see on Greek vases, in that array of jewellery?'

'My dear Clara!' exclaimed the astonished lover, 'how can you term them borrowed, when they are the Patterne jewels, our family heirloom pearls, unmatched, I venture to affirm, decidedly in my county and many others, and passing to the use of the mistress of the house in the natural course of things?'

'They are yours, they are not mine.'

'Prospectively they are yours.'

'It would be to anticipate the fact to wear them.'

'With my consent, my approval? at my request?'

'I am not yet . . . I never may be . . .'

'My wife?' He laughed triumphantly, and silenced her by manly smothering.

Her scruple was perhaps an honourable one, he said. Perhaps the jewels were safer in their iron box. He had merely intended a surprise and gratification to her.

Courage was coming to enable her to speak more plainly, when his discontinuing to insist on her wearing the jewels, under an appearance of deference of her wishes, disarmed her by touching her sympathies.

She said, however, 'I fear we do not often agree, Willoughby.'

'When you are a little older!' was the irritating answer.

'It would then be too late to make the discovery.'

'The discovery, I apprehend, is not imperative, my love.'

'It seems to me that our minds are opposed.'

'I should,' said he, 'have been awake to it at a single indication, be sure.'

'But I know,' she pursued, 'I have learned that the ideal of conduct for women is to subject their minds to the part of an accompaniment.'

'For women, my love? my wife will be in natural harmony with me.'

'Ah!' She compressed her lips. The yawn would come. 'I am sleepier here than anywhere.'

'Ours, my Clara, is the finest air of the kingdom. It has the effect of sea-air.'

'But if I am always asleep here?'

'We shall have to make a public exhibition of the Beauty.'

This dash of his liveliness defeated her.

She left him, feeling the contempt of the brain feverishly quickened and fine-pointed, for the brain chewing the cud in the happy pastures of unawakedness. So violent was the fever, so keen her introspection, that she spared few, and Vernon was not among them. Young Crossjay, whom she considered the least able of all to act as an ally, was the only one she courted with a real desire to please him, he was the one she affection-

ately envied; he was the youngest, the freest, he had the world
before him, and he did not know how horrible the world was,
or could be made to look. She loved the boy from expecting
nothing of him. Others, Vernon Whitford, for instance, could
help, and moved no hand. He read her case. A scrutiny so
penetrating under its air of abstract thoughtfulness, though his
eyes did but rest on her a second or two, signified that he read
her line by line, and to the end – excepting what she thought
of him for probing her with that sharp steel of insight without
a purpose.

She knew her mind's injustice. It was her case, her lamentable case – the impatient panic-stricken nerves of a captured
wild creature which cried for help. She exaggerated her
sufferings to get strength to throw them off, and lost it in the
recognition that they were exaggerated: and out of the conflict issued recklessness, with a cry as wild as any coming of
madness; for she did not blush in saying to herself: 'If some
one loved me!' Before hearing of Constantia, she had mused
upon liberty as a virgin Goddess – men were out of her
thoughts; even the figure of a rescuer, if one dawned in her
mind, was more angel than hero. That fair childish maidenliness had ceased. With her body straining in her dragon's
grasp, with the savour of loathing, unable to contend, unable
to speak aloud, she began to speak to herself, and all the health
of her nature made her outcry womanly: 'If I were loved!' –
not for the sake of love, but for free breathing; and her
utterance of it was to insure life and enduringness to the wish,
as the yearning of a mother on a drowning ship is to get her
infant to shore. 'If some noble gentleman could see me as I
am and not disdain to aid me! Oh! to be caught up out of this
prison of thorns and brambles. I cannot tear my own way out.
I am a coward. My cry for help confesses that. A beckoning of
a finger would change me, I believe. I could fly bleeding and
through hootings to a comrade. Oh! a comrade! I do not
want a lover. I should find another Egoist, not so bad, but
enough to make me take a breath like death. I could follow a

soldier, like poor Sally or Molly. He stakes his life for his country, and a woman may be proud of the worst of men who do that. Constantia met a soldier. Perhaps she prayed and her prayer was answered. She did ill. But, oh, how I love her for it! His name was Harry Oxford. Papa would call him her Perseus. She must have felt that there was no explaining what she suffered. She had only to act, to plunge. First she fixed her mind on Harry Oxford. To be able to speak his name and see him awaiting her, must have been relief, a reprieve. She did not waver, she cut the links, she signed herself over. Oh, brave girl! what do you think of me? But I have no Harry Whitford, I am alone. Let anything be said against women; we must be very bad to have such bad things written of us: only, say this, that to ask them to sign themselves over by oath and cere-mony, because of an ignorant promise, to the man they have been mistaken in, is – it is –' the sudden consciousness that she had put another name for Oxford, struck her a buffet, drown-ing her in crimson.

CHAPTER II

❌❌❌❌

The Double-Blossom Wild Cherry-Tree

SIR WILLOUGHBY chose a moment when Clara was with him and he had a good retreat through folding-windows to the lawn, in case of cogency on the enemy's part, to attack his cousin regarding the preposterous plot to upset the family by a scamper to London: 'By the way, Vernon, what is this you've been mumbling to everybody save me, about leaving us to pitch yourself into the stew-pot and be made broth of? London is no better, and you are fit for considerably better.

Don't, I beg you, continue to annoy me. Take a run abroad, if you are restless. Take two or three months, and join us as we are travelling home; and then think of settling, pray. Follow my example, if you like. You can have one of my cottages, or a place built for you. Anything to keep a man from destroying the sense of stability about one. In London, my dear old fellow, you lose your identity. What are you there? I ask you, what? One has the feeling of the house crumbling when a man is perpetually for shifting and cannot fix himself. Here you are known, you can study at your ease; up in London you are nobody; I tell you honestly, I feel it myself; a week of London literally drives me home to discover the individual where I left him. Be advised. You don't mean to go.'

'I have the intention,' said Vernon.

'Why?'

'I've mentioned it to you.'

'To my face?'

'Over your shoulder is generally the only chance you give me.'

'You have not mentioned it to me, to my knowledge. As to the reason, I might hear a dozen of your reasons, and I should not understand one. It's against your interests and against my wishes. Come, friend, I am not the only one you distress. Why, Vernon, you yourself have said that the English would be very perfect Jews if they could manage to live on the patriarchal system. You said it, yes, you said it! – but I recollect it clearly. Oh, as for your double-meanings, you said the thing, and you jeered at the incapacity of English families to live together, on account of bad temper; and now you are the first to break up our union! I decidedly do not profess to be a perfect Jew, but I do . . .'

Sir Willoughby caught signs of a probably smiling commerce between his bride and his cousin. He raised his face, appeared to be consulting his eyelids, and resolved to laugh: 'Well, I own it. I do like the idea of living patriarchally.' He turned to Clara. 'The Rev. Doctor one of us!'

'My father?' she said.

'Why not?'

'Papa's habits are those of a scholar.'

'That you might not be separated from him, my dear!'

Clara thanked Sir Willoughby for the kindness of thinking of her father, mentally analysing the kindness, in which at least she found no unkindness, scarcely egoism, though she knew it to be there.

'We might propose it,' said he.

'As a compliment?'

'If he would condescend to accept it as a compliment. These great scholars! . . . And if Vernon goes, our inducement for Dr Middleton to stay . . . But it is too absurd for discussion. Oh, Vernon, about Master Crossjay; I will see to it.'

He was about to give Vernon his shoulder and step into the garden, when Clara said, 'You will have Crossjay trained for the navy, Willoughby? There is not a day to lose.'

'Yes, yes; I will see to it. Depend on me for holding the young rascal in view.'

He presented his hand to her to lead her over the step to the gravel, surprised to behold how flushed she was.

She responded to the invitation by putting her hand forth from a bent elbow, with hesitating fingers. 'It should not be postponed, Willoughby.'

Her attitude suggested a stipulation before she touched him.

'It's an affair of money, as you know, Willoughby,' said Vernon. 'If I'm in London, I can't well provide for the boy for some time to come, or it's not certain that I can.'

'Why on earth should you go?'

'That's another matter. I want you to take my place with him.'

'In which case the circumstances are changed. I am responsible for him, and I have a right to bring him up according to my own prescription.'

'We are likely to have one idle lout the more.'

'I guarantee to make a gentleman of him.'

'We have too many of your gentlemen already.'

'You can't have enough, my good Vernon.'

'They're the national apology for indolence. Training a penniless boy to be one of them is nearly as bad as an education in a thieves' den; he will be just as much at war with society, if not game for the police.'

'Vernon, have you seen Crossjay's father, the now Captain of Marines? I think you have.'

'He's a good man and a very gallant officer.'

'And in spite of his qualities he's a cub, and an old cub. He is a captain now, but he takes that rank very late, you will own. There you have what you call a good man, undoubtedly a gallant officer, neutralized by the fact that he is not a gentleman. Holding intercourse with him is out of the question. No wonder Government declines to advance him rapidly. Young Crossjay does not bear your name. He bears mine, and on that point alone I should have a voice in the settlement of his career. And I say emphatically that a drawing-room approval of a young man is the best certificate for his general chances in life. I know of a City of London merchant of some sort, and I know a firm of lawyers, who will have none but University men in their office; at least, they have the preference.'

'Crossjay has a bullet head, fit neither for the University nor the drawing-room,' said Vernon; 'equal to fighting and dying for you, and that's all.'

Sir Willoughby contented himself with replying, 'The lad is a favourite of mine.'

His anxiety to escape a rejoinder caused him to step into the garden, leaving Clara behind him. 'My love!' said he, in apology, as he turned to her. She could not look stern, but she had a look without a dimple to soften it, and her eyes shone. For she had wagered in her heart that the dialogue she provoked upon Crossjay would expose the Egoist. And there were other motives, wrapped up and intertwisted, unrecognizable, sufficient to strike her with worse than the flush of her self-knowledge of wickedness when she detained him to speak of Crossjay before Vernon.

At last it had been seen that she was conscious of suffering in her association with this Egoist! Vernon stood for the world taken into her confidence. The world, then, would not think so ill of her, she thought hopefully, at the same time that she thought most evilly of herself. But self-accusations were for the day of reckoning; she would and must have the world with her, or the belief that it was coming to her, in the terrible struggle she foresaw within her horizon of self, now her utter boundary. She needed it for the inevitable conflict. Little sacrifices of her honesty might be made. Considering how weak she was, how solitary, how dismally entangled, daily disgraced beyond the power of any veiling to conceal from her fiery sensations, a little hypocrisy was a poor girl's natural weapon. She crushed her conscientious mind with the assurance that it was magnifying trifles: not entirely unaware that she was thereby preparing it for a convenient blindness in the presence of dread alternatives; but the pride of laying such stress on small sins gave her purity a blush of pleasure and overcame the inner warning. In truth she dared not think evilly of herself for long, sailing into battle as she was. Nuns and anchorites may; they have leisure. She regretted the forfeits she had to pay for self-assistance, and, if it might be won, the world's; regretted, felt the peril of the loss, and took them up and flung them.

'You see, old Vernon has no argument,' Willoughby said to her.

He drew her hand more securely on his arm, to make her sensible that she leaned on a pillar of strength.

'Whenever the little brain is in doubt, perplexed, undecided which course to adopt, she will come to me, will she not? I shall always listen,' he resumed, soothingly. 'My own! and I to you when the world vexes me. So we round our completeness. You will know me; you will know me in good time. I am not a mystery to those to whom I unfold myself.

I do not pretend to mystery: yet, I will confess, your home – your heart's – Willoughby is not exactly identical with the Willoughby before the world. One must be armed against that rough beast.'

Certain is the vengeance of the young upon monotony; nothing more certain. They do not scheme it, but sameness is a poison to their systems; and vengeance is their heartier breathing, their stretch of the limbs, run in the fields; nature avenges them.

'When does Colonel De Craye arrive?' said Clara.

'Horace? In two or three days. You wish him to be on the spot to learn his part, my love?'

She had not flown forward to the thought of Colonel De Craye's arrival; she knew not why she had mentioned him; but now she flew back, shocked, first into shadowy subterfuge, and then into the criminal's dock.

'I do not wish him to be here. I do not know that he has a part to learn. I have no wish. Willoughby, did you not say I should come to you and you would listen? – will you listen? I am so commonplace that I shall not be understood by you unless you take my words for the very meaning of the words. I am unworthy. I am volatile. I love my liberty. I want to be free . . .'

'Flitch!' he called.

It sounded necromantic.

'Pardon me, my love,' he said. 'The man you see yonder violates my express injunction that he is not to come on my grounds, and here I find him on the borders of my garden!'

Sir Willoughby waved his hand to the abject figure of a man standing to intercept him.

'Volatile, unworthy, liberty – my dearest!' he bent to her when the man had appeased him by departing, 'you are at liberty within the law, like all good women; I shall control and direct your volatility; and your sense of worthiness must be re-established when we are more intimate; it is timidity.

The sense of unworthiness is a guarantee of worthiness ensuing. I believe I am in the vein of a sermon! Whose the fault? The sight of that man was annoying. Flitch was a stable-boy, groom, and coachman, like his father before him, at the Hall thirty years; his father died in our service. Mr Flitch had not a single grievance here; only one day the demon seizes him with the notion of bettering himself, he wants his independence, and he presents himself to me with a story of a shop in our county town – Flitch! remember, if you go you go for good! – Oh, he quite comprehended – Very well; good-bye, Flitch! – the man was respectful: he looked the fool he was very soon to turn out to be. Since then, within a period of several years, I have had him, against my express injunctions, ten times on my grounds. It's curious to calculate. Of course the shop failed, and Flitch's independence consists in walking about with his hands in his empty pockets, and looking at the Hall from some elevation near.'

'Is he married? Has he children?' said Clara.

'Nine; and a wife that cannot cook or sew or wash linen.'

'You could not give him employment?'

'After his having dismissed himself?'

'It might be overlooked.'

'Here he was happy. He decided to go elsewhere, to be free – of course, of my yoke. He quitted my service against my warning. Flitch, we will say, emigrated with his wife and nine children, and the ship foundered. He returns, but his place is filled; he is a ghost here, and I object to ghosts.'

'Some work might be found for him.'

'It will be the same with old Vernon, my dear. If he goes, he goes for good. It is the vital principle of my authority to insist on that. A dead leaf might as reasonably demand to return to the tree. Once off, off for all eternity! I am sorry, but such was your decision, my friend. I have, you see, Clara, elements in me –'

'Dreadful!'

'Exert your persuasive powers with Vernon. You can do

well-nigh what you will with the old fellow. We have Miss Dale this evening for a week or two. Lead him to some ideas of her. – Elements in me, I was remarking, which will no more bear to be handled carelessly than gunpowder. At the same time, there is no reason why they should not be respected, managed with some degree of regard for me and attention to consequences. Those who have not done so have repented.'

'You do not speak to others of the elements in you,' said Clara.

'I certainly do not: I have but one bride,' was his handsome reply.

'Is it fair to me that you should show me the worst of you?'

'All myself, my own?'

His ingratiating droop and familiar smile rendered 'All myself' so affectionately meaningful in its happy reliance upon her excess of love, that at last she understood she was expected to worship him and uphold him for whatsoever he might be, without any estimation of qualities: as indeed love does, or young love does: as she perhaps did once, before he chilled her senses. That was before her 'little brain' had become active and had turned her senses to revolt.

It was on the full river of love that Sir Willoughby supposed the whole floating bulk of his personality to be securely sustained; and therefore it was that, believing himself swimming at his ease, he discoursed of himself.

She went straight away from that idea with her mental exclamation: 'Why does he not paint himself in brighter colours to me!' and the question: 'Has he no ideal of generosity and chivalry?'

But the unfortunate gentleman imagined himself to be loved, on Love's very bosom. He fancied that everything relating to himself excited maidenly curiosity, womanly reverence, ardours to know more of him, which he was ever willing to satisfy by repeating the same things. His notion of women was the primitive black and white: there are good women, bad women; and he possessed a good one. His high

opinion of himself fortified the belief that Providence, as a
matter of justice and fitness, must necessarily select a good
one for him – or what are we to think of Providence? And
this female, shaped by that informing hand, would naturally
be in harmony with him, from the centre of his profound
identity to the raying circle of his variations. Know the
centre, you know the circle, and you discover that the variations are simply characteristics, but you must travel on the
rays from the circle to get to the centre. Consequently Sir
Willoughby put Miss Middleton on one or other of these con-
verging lines from time to time. Us, too, he drags into the
deeps, but when we have harpooned a whale and are attached
to the rope, down we must go; the miracle is to see us rise
again.

   Women of mixed essences shading off the divine to the considerably lower were outside his vision of woman. His mind
could as little admit an angel in pottery as a rogue in porcelain.
For him they were what they were when fashioned at the beginning; many cracked, many stained, here and there a perfect
specimen designed for the elect of men. At a whisper of the
world he shut the prude's door on them with a slam; himself
would have branded them with the letters in the hue of fire.
Privately he did so; and he was constituted by his extreme
sensitiveness and taste for ultra-feminine refinement to be a
severe critic of them during the carnival of egoism, the love-
season. Constantia . . . can it be told? She had been, be it said, a
fair and frank young merchant with him in that season; she
was of a nature to be a mother of heroes; she met the salute,
almost half-way, ingenuously unlike the coming mothers of
the regiments of marionettes, who retire in vapours, downcast,
as by convention; ladies most flattering to the egoistical
gentleman, for they proclaim him the 'first'. Constantia's
offence had been no greater, but it was not that dramatic
performance of purity which he desired of an affianced lady,
and so the offence was great.

   The love-season is the carnival of egoism, and it brings the

touchstone to our natures. I speak of love, not the mask, and
not of the flutings upon the theme of love, but of the passion;
a flame having, like our mortality, death in it as well as life,
that may or may not be lasting. Applied to Sir Willoughby,
as to thousands of civilized males, the touchstone found him
requiring to be dealt with by his betrothed as an original
savage. She was required to play incessantly on the first re-
claiming chord which led our ancestral satyr to the measures
of the dance, the threading of the maze, and the setting con-
formably to his partner before it was accorded to him to spin
her with both hands and a chirrup of his frisky heels. To keep
him in awe and hold him enchained, there are things she must
never do, dare never say, must not think. She must be
cloistral. Now, strange and awful though it be to hear,
women perceive this requirement of them in the spirit of the
man; they perceive, too, and it may be gratefully, that they
address their performances less to the taming of the green and
prankish monsieur of the forest than to the pacification of a
voracious aesthetic gluttony, craving them insatiably, through
all the tenses, with shrieks of the lamentable letter 'I' for their
purity. Whether they see that it has its foundation in the
sensual, and distinguish the ultra-refined but lineally great-
grandson of the Hoof in this vast and dainty exacting appetite
is uncertain. They probably do not; the more the damage;
for in the appeasement of the glutton they have to practise
much simulation; they are in their way losers like their ancient
mothers. It is the palpable and material of them still which
they are tempted to flourish, wherewith to invite and allay
pursuit: a condition under which the spiritual, wherein their
hope lies, languishes. The capaciously strong in soul among
women will ultimately detect an infinite grossness in the demand for purity infinite, spotless bloom. Earlier or later they
see they have been victims of the singular Egoist, have worn a
mask of ignorance to be named innocent, have turned themselves into market produce for his delight, and have really
abandoned the commodity in ministering to the lust for it,

suffered themselves to be dragged ages back in playing upon
the fleshly innocence of happy accident to gratify his jealous
greed of possession, when it should have been their task to set
the soul above the fairest fortune and the gift of strength in
women beyond ornamental whiteness. Are they not of nature
warriors, like men? – men's mates to bear them heroes instead
of puppets? But the devouring male Egoist prefers them as
inanimate overwrought polished pure metal precious vessels,
fresh from the hands of the artificer, for him to walk away
with hugging, call all his own, drink of, and fill and drink of,
and forget that he stole them.

    This running off on a by-road is no deviation from Sir
Willoughby Patterne and Miss Clara Middleton. He, a fairly
intelligent man, and very sensitive, was blinded to what was
going on within her visibly enough, by her production of the
article he demanded of her sex. He had to leave the fair young
lady to ride to his county-town, and his design was to conduct
her through the covert of a group of laurels, there to revel in
her soft confusion. She resisted; nay, resolutely returned to
the lawn-sward. He contrasted her with Constantia in the
amorous time, and rejoiced in his disappointment. He saw the
goddess Modesty guarding Purity; and one would be bold to
say that he did not hear the Precepts, Purity's aged grannams
maternal and paternal, cawing approval of her over their
munching gums. And if you ask whether a man, sensitive and
a lover, can be so blinded, you are condemned to reperuse the
foregoing paragraph.

    Miss Middleton was not sufficiently instructed in the posi-
tion of her sex to know that she had plunged herself in the
thick of the strife of one of their great battles. Her personal
position, however, was instilling knowledge rapidly, as a
disease in the frame teaches us what we are and have to contend with. Could she marry this man? He was evidently
manageable. Could she condescend to the use of arts in
managing him to obtain a placable life? – a horror of swampy
flatness! So vividly did the sight of that dead heaven over an

unvarying level earth swim on her fancy, that she shut her eyes in angry exclusion of it as if it were outside, assailing her; and she nearly stumbled upon young Crossjay.

'Oh, have I hurt you?' he cried.

'No,' said she, 'it was my fault. Lead me somewhere away from everybody.'

The boy took her hand, and she resumed her thoughts; and, pressing his fingers and feeling warm to him both for his presence and silence, so does the blood in youth lead the mind, even cool and innocent blood, even with a touch, that she said to herself, 'And if I marry, and then . . . Where will honour be then? I marry him to be true to my word of honour, and if then . . . !' An intolerable languor caused her to sigh profoundly. It is written as she thought it; she thought in blanks, as girls do, and some women. A shadow of the male Egoist is in the chamber of their brains overawing them.

'Were I to marry, and to run!' There is the thought; she is offered up to your mercy. We are dealing with a girl feeling herself desperately situated, and not a fool.

'I'm sure you're dead tired, though,' said Crossjay.

'No, I am not; what makes you think so?' said Clara.

'I do think so.'

'But why do you think so?'

'You're so hot.'

'What makes you think that?'

'You're so red.'

'So are you, Crossjay.'

'I'm only red in the middle of the cheeks, except when I've been running. And then you talk to yourself, just as boys do when they are blown.'

'Do they?'

'They say: "I know I could have kept up longer", or, "my buckle broke", all to themselves, when they break down running.'

'And you have noticed that?'

'And, Miss Middleton, I don't wish you were a boy, but I

should like to live near you all my life and be a gentleman. I'm coming with Miss Dale this evening to stay at the Hall and be looked after, instead of stopping with her cousin who takes care of her father. Perhaps you and I'll play chess at night.'

'At night you will go to bed, Crossjay.'

'Not if I have Sir Willoughby to catch hold of. He says I'm an authority on birds' eggs. I can manage rabbits and poultry. Isn't a farmer a happy man? But he doesn't marry ladies. A cavalry officer has the best chance.'

'But you are going to be a naval officer.'

'I don't know. It's not positive. I shall bring my two dormice, and make them perform gymnastics on the dinner-table. They're such dear little things. Naval officers are not like Sir Willoughby.'

'No, they are not,' said Clara, 'they give their lives to their country.'

'And then they're dead,' said Crossjay.

Clara wished Sir Willoughby were confronting her: she could have spoken.

She asked the boy where Mr Whitford was. Crossjay pointed very secretly in the direction of the double-blossom wild-cherry. Coming within gaze of the stem, she beheld Vernon stretched at length, reading, she supposed; asleep, she discovered: his finger in the leaves of a book; and what book? She had a curiosity to know the title of the book he would read beneath these boughs, and grasping Crossjay's hand fast she craned her neck, as one timorous of a fall in peeping over chasms, for a glimpse of the page; but immediately, and still with a bent head, she turned her face to where the load of virginal blossom, whiter than summer-cloud on the sky, showered and drooped and clustered so thick as to claim colour and seem, like higher Alpine snows in noon-sunlight, a flush of white. From deep to deeper heavens of white, her eyes perched and soared. Wonder lived in her. Happiness in the beauty of the tree pressed to supplant it, and was more mortal and narrower. Reflection came, contracting her vision and weighing her to earth. Her reflection was: 'He must be good who loves to lie and sleep beneath the branches of this tree!' She would rather have clung to her first impression: wonder so divine, so unbounded, was like soaring into homes of angel-crowded space, sweeping through folded and on to folded white fountain-bow of wings, in innumerable columns; but the thought of it was no recovery of it; she might as well have striven to be a child. The sensation of happiness promised to be less short-lived in memory, and would have been had not her present disease of the longing for happiness ravaged every corner of it for the secret of its existence. The reflection took root. 'He must be good . . . !' That reflection vowed to endure. Poor by comparison with what it displaced, it presented itself to her as conferring something on him, and she would not have had it absent though it robbed her.

She looked down. Vernon was dreamily looking up.

She plucked Crossjay hurriedly away, whispering that he had better not wake Mr Whitford, and then she proposed to reverse their previous chase, and she be the hound and he the hare. Crossjay fetched a magnificent start. On his glancing behind he saw Miss Middleton walking listlessly, with a hand at her side.

'There's a regular girl!' said he in some disgust; for his theory was, that girls always have something the matter with them to spoil a game.

CHAPTER 12

✠ ✠ ✠ ✠

Miss Middleton and Mr Vernon Whitford

LOOKING upward, not quite awakened out of a transient doze, at a fair head circled in dazzling blossom, one may temporize awhile with common sense, and take it for a vision after the eyes have regained direction of the mind. Vernon did so until the plastic vision interwound with reality alarmingly. This is the embrace of a Melusine [13] who will soon have the brain if she is encouraged. Slight dalliance with her makes the very diminutive seem as big as life. He jumped to his feet, rattled his throat, planted firmness on his brows and mouth, and attacked the dream-giving earth with tremendous long strides, that his blood might be lively at the throne of understanding. Miss Middleton and young Crossjay were within hail: it was her face he had seen, and still the idea of a vision, chased from his reasonable wits, knocked hard and again for readmission. There was little for a man of humble mind toward the sex to think of in the fact of a young lady's bending rather low to peep at him asleep, except that the poise of her slender figure, between an air of spying and of listening, vividly recalled his likening of her to the Mountain Echo. Man or maid sleeping in the open air provokes your tiptoe curiosity. Men, it is known, have in that state cruelly been kissed; and no rights are bestowed on them, they are teased by a vapourish rapture; what has happened to them the poor fellows barely divine: they have a crazy step from that day. But a vision is not so distracting; it is our own, we can put it aside and return to it, play at rich and poor with it, and are not to be summoned before your laws and rules for secreting it in our treasury. Besides, it is the golden key of all the possible; new worlds expand beneath the dawn it brings us. Just outside reality, it illumines, enriches, and softens real things; – and to desire it in preference to the simple fact is a damning proof of enervation.

Such was Vernon's winding up of his brief drama of fantasy. He was aware of the fantastical element in him and soon had it under. Which of us who is of any worth is without it? He had not much vanity to trouble him, and passion was quiet, so his task was not gigantic. Especially be it remarked, that he was a man of quick pace, the sovereign remedy for the dispersing of the mental fen-mist. He had tried it and knew that nonsense is to be walked off.

Near the end of the park young Crossjay overtook him, and after acting the pumped one a trifle more than needful, cried: 'I say, Mr Whitford, there's Miss Middleton with her handkerchief out.'

'What for, my lad?' said Vernon.

'I'm sure I don't know. All of a sudden she bumped down. And, look what fellows girls are! – here she comes as if nothing had happened, and I saw her feel at her side.'

Clara was shaking her head to express a denial. 'I am not at all unwell,' she said, when she came near. 'I guessed Crossjay's business in running up to you; he's a good-for-nothing, officious boy. I was tired, and rested for a moment.'

Crossjay peered at her eyelids. Vernon looked away and said: 'Are you too tired for a stroll?'

'Not now.'

'Shall it be brisk?'

'You have the lead.'

He led at a swing of the legs that accelerated young Crossjay's to the double, but she with her short, swift, equal steps glided along easily on a line by his shoulder, and he groaned to think that of all the girls of earth this one should have been chosen for the position of fine lady.

'You won't tire me,' said she, in answer to his look.

'You remind me of the little Piedmontese Bersaglieri on the march.'

'I have seen them trotting into Como from Milan.'

'They cover a quantity of ground in a day, if the ground's flat. You want another sort of step for the mountains.'

'I should not attempt to dance up.'

'They soon tame romantic notions of them.'

'The mountains tame luxurious dreams, you mean. I see how they are conquered. I can plod. Anything to be high up!'

'Well, there you have the secret of good work: to plod on and still keep the passion fresh.'

'Yes, when we have an aim in view.'

'We always have one.'

'Captives have?'

'More than the rest of us.'

Ignorant man! What of wives miserably wedded? What aim in view have these most woeful captives? Horror shrouds it, and shame reddens through the folds to tell of innermost horror.

'Take me back to the mountains, if you please, Mr Whitford,' Miss Middleton said, fallen out of sympathy with him. 'Captives have death in view, but that is not an aim.'

'Why may not captives expect a release?'

'Hardly from a tyrant.'

'If you are thinking of tyrants, it may be so. Say the tyrant dies?'

'The prison-gates are unlocked and out comes a skeleton. But why will you talk of skeletons! The very name of mountain seems life in comparison with any other subject.'

'I assure you,' said Vernon, with the fervour of a man lighting on an actual truth in his conversation with a young lady, 'it's not the first time I have thought you would be at home in the Alps. You would walk and climb as well as you dance.'

She liked to hear Clara Middleton talked of, and of her having been thought of: and giving him friendly eyes, barely noticing that he was in a glow, she said: 'If you speak so encouragingly I shall fancy we are near an ascent.'

'I wish we were,' said he.

'We can realize it by dwelling on it, don't you think?'

'We can begin climbing.'

'Oh!' she squeezed herself shadowily.

'Which mountain shall it be?' said Vernon, in the right real earnest tone.

Miss Middleton suggested a lady's mountain first, for a trial. 'And then, if you think well enough of me – if I have not stumbled more than twice, or asked more than ten times how far it is from the top, I should like to be promoted to scale a giant.'

They went up to some of the lesser heights of Switzerland and Styria, and settled in South Tyrol, the young lady preferring this district for the strenuous exercise of her climbing powers because she loved Italian colour; and it seemed an exceedingly good reason to the genial imagination she had awakened in Mr Whitford. 'Though,' said he, abruptly, 'you are not so much Italian as French.'

She hoped she was English, she remarked.

'Of course you are English; . . . yes.' He moderated his ascent with the halting affirmative.

She inquired wonderingly why he spoke in apparent hesitation.

'Well, you have French feet, for example: French wits, French impatience,' he lowered his voice, 'and charm.'

'And love of compliments.'

'Possibly. I was not conscious of paying them.'

'And a disposition to rebel?'

'To challenge authority, at least.'

'That is a dreadful character.'

'At all events, it is a character.'

'Fit for an Alpine comrade?'

'For the best of comrades anywhere.'

'It is not a piece of drawing-room sculpture: that is the most one can say for it!' she dropped a dramatic sigh.

Had he been willing she would have continued the theme, for the pleasure a poor creature long gnawing her sensations finds in seeing herself from the outside. It fell away. After a silence, she could not renew it; and he was evidently indifferent, having to his own satisfaction dissected and stamped her a foreigner. With it passed her holiday. She had forgotten Sir Willoughby: she remembered him and said: 'You knew Miss Durham, Mr Whitford?'

He answered, briefly, 'I did.'

'Was she? . . .' some hot-faced inquiry peered forth and withdrew.

'Very handsome,' said Vernon.

'English?'

'Yes; the dashing style of English.'

'Very courageous.'

'I dare say she had a kind of courage.'

'She did very wrong.'

'I won't say no. She discovered a man more of a match with herself; luckily not too late. We're at the mercy . . .'

'Was she not unpardonable?'

'I should be sorry to think that of any one.'

'But you agree that she did wrong.'

'I suppose I do. She made a mistake and she corrected it. If she had not, she would have made a greater mistake.'

'The manner . . .'

'That was bad – as far as we know. The world has not much right to judge. A false start must now and then be made. It's better not to take notice of it, I think.'

'What is it we are at the mercy of?'

'Currents of feeling, our natures. I am the last man to preach on the subject: young ladies are enigmas to me; I fancy they must have a natural perception of the husband suitable to them, and the reverse; and if they have a certain degree of courage, it follows that they please themselves.'

'They are not to reflect on the harm they do?' said Miss Middleton.

'By all means let them reflect; they hurt nobody by doing that.'

'But a breach of faith!'

'If the faith can be kept through life, all's well.'

'And then there is the cruelty, the injury!'

'I really think that if a young lady came to me to inform me she must break our engagement – I have never been put to the proof, but to suppose it: – I should not think her cruel.'

'Then she would not be much of a loss.'

'And I should not think so for this reason, that it is impossible for a girl to come to such a resolution without previously showing signs of it to her ... the man she is engaged to. I think it unfair to engage a girl for longer than a week or two, just time enough for her preparations and publications.'

'If he is always intent on himself, signs are likely to be unheeded by him,' said Miss Middleton.

He did not answer, and she said, quickly:

'It must always be a cruelty. The world will think so. It is an act of inconstancy.'

'If they knew one another well before they were engaged.'

'Are you not singularly tolerant?' said she.

To which Vernon replied with airy cordiality:

'In some cases it is right to judge by results; we'll leave severity to the historian, who is bound to be a professional moralist and put pleas of human nature out of the scales. The lady in question may have been to blame, but no hearts were broken, and here we have four happy instead of two miserable.'

His persecuting geniality of countenance appealed to her to confirm this judgement by results, and she nodded and said: 'Four,' as the awe-stricken speak.

From that moment until young Crossjay fell into the green-rutted lane from a tree, and was got on his legs half stunned, with a hanging lip and a face like the inside of a flayed eel-skin, she might have been walking in the desert, and alone, for the pleasure she had in society.

They led the fated lad home between them, singularly

drawn together by their joint ministrations to him, in which her delicacy had to stand fire, and sweet good-nature made naught of any trial. They were hand in hand with the little fellow as physician and professional nurse.

CHAPTER 13

⋈⋈⋈⋈

The First Effort after Freedom

CROSSJAY'S accident was only another proof, as Vernon told Miss Dale, that the boy was but half monkey.

'Something fresh?' she exclaimed on seeing him brought into the Hall, where she had just arrived.

'Simply a continuation,' said Vernon. 'He is not so prehensile as he should be. He probably in extremity relies on the tail that has been docked. Are you a man, Crossjay?'

'I should think I was!' Crossjay replied, with an old man's voice, and a ghastly twitch for a smile overwhelmed the compassionate ladies.

Miss Dale took possession of him. 'You err in the other direction,' she remarked to Vernon.

'But a little bracing roughness is better than spoiling him,' said Miss Middleton.

She did not receive an answer, and she thought: 'Whatever Willoughby does is right, to this lady!'

Clara's impression was renewed when Sir Willoughby sat beside Miss Dale in the evening; and certainly she had never seen him shine so picturesquely as in his bearing with Miss Dale. The sprightly sallies of the two, their rallyings, their laughter, and her fine eyes, and his handsome gestures, won attention like a fencing match of a couple keen with the foils to display the mutual skill. And it was his design that she should admire the display; he was anything but obtuse; enjoying the match as he did and necessarily did to act so excellent a part in it, he meant the observer to see the man he was with a lady not of raw understanding. So it went on from day to day for three days.

She fancied once that she detected the agreeable stirring of the brood of jealousy, and found it neither in her heart nor in her mind, but in the book of wishes, well known to the young where they write matter which may sometimes be independent of both those volcanic albums. Jealousy would have been a relief to her, a dear devil's aid. She studied the complexion of jealousy to delude herself with the sense of the spirit being in her, and all the while she laughed, as at a vile theatre whereof the imperfection of the stage machinery rather than the performance is the wretched source of amusement.

Vernon had deeply depressed her. She was hunted by the figure 4. *Four happy instead of two miserable.* He had said it, involving her among the four; and so it must be, she considered, and she must be as happy as she could; for not only was he incapable of perceiving her state, he was unable to imagine other circumstances to surround her. How, to be just to him, were they imaginable by him or any one?

Her horrible isolation of secrecy in a world amiable in unsuspectingness frightened her. To fling away her secret, to conform, to be unrebellious, uncritical, submissive, became an impatient desire; and the task did not appear so difficult since Miss Dale's arrival. Endearments had been rare, more formal; living bodily untroubled and unashamed, and, as she phrased it, having no one to care for her, she turned insensibly in the direction where she was due; she slightly imitated Miss Dale's colloquial responsiveness. To tell truth, she felt vivacious in a moderate way with Willoughby after seeing him with Miss Dale. Liberty wore the aspect of a towering prison-wall; the desperate undertaking of climbing one side and dropping to the other was more than she, unaided, could resolve on; consequently, as no one cared for her, a worthless creature might as well cease dreaming and stipulating for the fulfilment of her dreams; she might as well yield to her fate; nay, make the best of it.

Sir Willoughby was flattered and satisfied. Clara's adopted vivacity proved his thorough knowledge of feminine nature; nor did her feebleness in sustaining it displease him. A steady look of hers had of late perplexed the man, and he was comforted by signs of her inefficiency where he excelled. The effort and the failure were both of good omen.

But she could not continue the effort. He had overweighted her too much for the mimicry of a sentiment to harden and have an apparently natural place among her impulses; and now an idea came to her that he might, it might be hoped, possibly see in Miss Dale, by present contrast, the mate he sought; by contrast with an unanswering creature like herself, he might perhaps realize in Miss Dale's greater accomplishments and her devotion to him the merit of suitability; he might be induced to do her justice. Dim as the loop-hole was, Clara fixed her mind on it till it gathered light. And as a prelude to action, she plunged herself into a state of such profound humility that to accuse it of being simulated would be venturesome, though it was not positive. The tempers of the young are liquid fires in isles of quicksand; the precious metals not yet cooled in a solid earth. Her compassion for Laetitia was less forced, but really she was almost as earnest in her self-abasement, for she had not latterly been brilliant, not even adequate to the ordinary requirements of conversation. She had no courage, no wit, no diligence, nothing that she could distinguish save discontentment like a corroding acid and she went so far in sincerity as with a curious shift of feeling to pity the man plighted to her. If it suited her purpose to pity Sir Willoughby, she was not moved by policy, be assured; her needs were her nature, her moods her mind; she had the capacity to make anything serve her by passing into it with the glance which discerned its usefulness; and this is how it is that the young, when they are in trouble, without approaching the elevation of scientific hypocrites, can teach that able class lessons in hypocrisy.

'Why should not Willoughby be happy,' she said; and the exclamation was pushed forth by the second thought: 'Then I shall be free!' Still that thought came second.

The desire for the happiness of Willoughby was fervent on his behalf, and wafted her far from friends and letters to a narrow Tyrolean valley, where a shallow river ran, with the indentations of a remotely seen army of winding ranks in column, topaz over the pebbles to hollows of ravishing emerald. There sat Liberty, after her fearful leap over the prison-wall, at peace to watch the water and the falls of sunshine on the mountain above, between descending pine-stem shadows. Clara's wish for his happiness, as soon as she had housed herself in the imagination of her freedom, was of a purity that made it seem exceedingly easy for her to speak to him.

The opportunity was offered by Sir Willoughby. Every morning after breakfast Miss Dale walked across the park to see her father, and on this occasion Sir Willoughby and Miss Middleton went with her as far as the lake, all three discoursing of the beauty of various trees, birches, aspens, poplars, beeches, then in their new green. Miss Dale loved the aspen, Miss Middleton the beech, Sir Willoughby the birch, and pretty things were said by each in praise of the favoured object, particularly by Miss Dale. So much so that when she had gone on he recalled one of her remarks, and said: 'I believe, if the whole place were swept away to-morrow, Laetitia Dale could reconstruct it and put those aspens on the north of the lake in number and situation correctly where you have them now. I would guarantee her description of it in absence correct.'

'Why should she be absent?' said Clara, palpitating.

'Well, why!' returned Sir Willoughby. 'As you say, there is no reason why. The art of life, and mine will be principally a country life – town is not life, but a tornado whirling atoms

– the art is to associate a group of sympathetic friends in our neighbourhood; and it is a fact worth noting that if ever I feel tired of the place, a short talk with Laetitia Dale refreshes it more than a month or two on the Continent. She has the well of enthusiasm. And there is a great advantage in having a cultivated person at command, with whom one can chat of any topic under the sun. I repeat, you have no need of town if you have friends like Laetitia Dale within call. My mother esteemed her highly.'

'Willoughby, she is not obliged to go.'

'I hope not. And, my love, I rejoice that you have taken to her. Her father's health is poor. She would be a young spinster to live alone in a country cottage.'

'What of your scheme?'

'Old Vernon is a very foolish fellow.'

'He has declined?'

'Not a word on the subject! I have only to propose it to be snubbed, I know.'

'You may not be aware how you throw him into the shade with her.'

'Nothing seems to teach him the art of dialogue with ladies.'

'Are not gentlemen shy when they see themselves outshone?'

'He hasn't it, my love: Vernon is deficient in the lady's tongue.'

'I respect him for that.'

'Outshone, you say? I do not know of any shining – save to one, who lights me, path and person!'

The identity of the one was conveyed to her in a bow and a soft pressure.

'Not only has he not the lady's tongue, which I hold to be a man's proper accomplishment,' continued Sir Willoughby, 'he cannot turn his advantages to account. Here has Miss Dale been with him now four days in the house. They are exactly on the same footing as when she entered it. You ask? I will tell you. It is this: it is want of warmth. Old Vernon is a scholar

– and a fish. Well, perhaps he has cause to be shy of matri-
mony; but he is a fish.'

'You are reconciled to his leaving you?'

'False alarm! The resolution to do anything unaccustomed
is quite beyond old Vernon.'

'But if Mr Oxford – Whitford ... your swans coming sailing up the lake, how beautiful they look when they are indignant! I was going to ask you, surely men witnessing a
marked admiration for some one else will naturally be discouraged?'

Sir Willoughby stiffened with sudden enlightenment.
Though the word jealousy had not been spoken, the drift of
her observations was clear. Smiling inwardly, he said, and the
sentences were not enigmas to her: 'Surely, too, young ladies
... a little? – Too far? But an old friendship! About the same as
the fitting of an old glove to a hand. Hand and glove have only
to meet. Where there is natural harmony you would not have
discord. Ay, but you have it if you check the harmony. My
dear girl! You child!'

He had actually, in this parabolic, and commendable, ob-
scureness, for which she thanked him in her soul, struck the
very point she had not named and did not wish to hear named,
but wished him to strike; he was anything but obtuse. His
exultation, of the compressed sort, was extreme, on hearing
her cry out:

'Young ladies may be. Oh! not I, not I! I can convince you.
Not that. Believe me, Willoughby. I do not know what it is to
feel that, or anything like it. I cannot conceive a claim on any
one's life – as a claim: or the continuation of an engagement
not founded on perfect, *perfect* sympathy. How should I feel it,
then? It is, as you say of Mr Ox – Whitford, beyond me.'

Sir Willoughby caught up the Ox – Whitford.

Bursting with laughter in his joyful pride, he called it a
portrait of old Vernon in society. For she thought a trifle too
highly of Vernon, as here and there a raw young lady does
think of the friends of her plighted man, which is waste of

substance properly belonging to him, as it were, in the loftier sense, an expenditure in genuflexions to way-side idols of the reverence she should bring intact to the temple. Derision instructs her.

Of the other subject – her jealousy – he had no desire to hear more. She had winced: the woman had been touched to smarting in the girl: enough. She attempted the subject once, but faintly, and his careless parrying threw her out. Clara could have bitten her tongue for that reiterated stupid slip on the name of Whitford; and because she was innocent at heart she persisted in asking herself how she could be guilty of it.

'You both know the botanic titles of these wild flowers,' she said.

'Who?' he inquired.

'You and Miss Dale.'

Sir Willoughby shrugged. He was amused.

'No woman on earth will grace a barouche so exquisitely as my Clara.'

'Where?' said she.

'During our annual two months in London. I drive a barouche there, and venture to prophesy that my equipage will create the greatest excitement of any in London. I see old Horace De Craye gazing!'

She sighed. She could not drag him to the word, or a hint of it necessary to her subject.

But there it was; she saw it. She had nearly let it go, and blushed at being obliged to name it.

'Jealousy, do you mean, Willoughby? the people in London would be jealous? – Colonel De Craye? How strange! That is a sentiment I cannot understand.'

Sir Willoughby gesticulated the 'Of course not' of an established assurance to the contrary.

'Indeed, Willoughby, I do not.'

'Certainly not.'

He was now in her trap. And he was imagining himself to be anatomizing her feminine nature.

'Can I give you a proof, Willoughby? I am so utterly incapable of it that – listen to me – were you to come to me to
tell me, as you might, how much better suited to you Miss
Dale has appeared than I am – and I fear I am not; it should be
spoken plainly; unsuited altogether, perhaps – I would, I be-
seech you to believe – you must believe me – give you . . .
give you your freedom instantly; most truly; and engage to
speak of you as I should think of you. Willoughby, you would
have no one to praise you in public and in private as I should,
for you would be to me the most honest, truthful, chivalrous
gentleman alive. And in that case I would undertake to declare
that she would not admire you more than I; Miss Dale would
not; she would not admire you more than I; not even Miss
Dale.'

This, her first direct leap for liberty, set Clara panting, and
so much had she to say that the nervous and the intellectual
halves of her clashed like cymbals, dazing and stunning her
with the appositeness of things to be said, and dividing her in
indecision as to the cunningest to move him of the many
pressing.

The condition of feminine jealousy stood revealed.

He had driven her farther than he intended.

'Come, let me allay these . . .' he soothed her with hand
and voice, while seeking for his phrase; 'these magnified pin-
points. Now, my Clara! on my honour! and when I put it forward in attestation, my honour has the most serious meaning
speech can have; ordinarily my word has to suffice for bonds,
promises, or asseverations; on my honour! not merely is
there, my poor child! no ground of suspicion, I assure you, I
declare to you, the fact of the case is the very reverse. Now,
mark me; of her sentiments I cannot pretend to speak; I did
not, to my knowledge, originate, I am not responsible for
them, and I am, before the law, as we will say, ignorant of
them; that is, I have never heard a declaration of them, and I
am, therefore, under pain of the stigma of excessive fatuity,
bound to be non-cognizant. But as to myself, I can speak for

myself, and, on my honour! Clara – to be as direct as possible, even to baldness, and you know I loathe it – I could not, I repeat, *I could not marry Laetitia Dale!* Let me impress it on you. No flatteries – we are all susceptible more or less – no conceivable condition could bring it about; no amount of admiration. She and I are excellent friends; we cannot be more. When you see us together, the natural concord of our minds is of course misleading. She is a woman of genius. I do not conceal, I profess my admiration of her. There are times when, I confess, I require a Laetitia Dale to bring me out, give and take. I am indebted to her for the enjoyment of the duet few know, few can accord with, fewer still are allowed the privilege of playing with a human being. I am indebted, I own, and I feel deep gratitude; I own to a lively friendship for Miss Dale, but if she is displeasing in the sight of my bride by . . . the breadth of an eyelash, then . . .'

Sir Willoughby's arm waved Miss Dale off away into outer darkness in the wilderness.

Clara shut her eyes and rolled her eyeballs in a frenzy of unuttered revolt from the Egoist.

But she was not engaged in the colloquy to be an advocate of Miss Dale or of common humanity.

'Ah!' she said, simply determining that the subject should not drop.

'And, ah!' he mocked her tenderly. 'True, though! And who knows better than my Clara that I require youth, health, beauty, and the other undefinable attributes fitting with mine and beseeming the station of the lady called to preside over my household and represent me? What says my other self? my fairer? But you are! my love, you are! Understand my nature rightly, and you . . .'

'I do! I do!' interposed Clara; 'if I did not by this time I should be idiotic. Let me assure you, I understand it. Oh, listen to me; one moment! Miss Dale regards me as the happiest woman on earth. Willoughby, if I possessed her good qualities, her heart and mind, no doubt I should be. It is my

wish – you must hear me, hear me out – my wish, my earnest
wish, my burning prayer, my wish to make way for her. She
appreciates you: I do not – to my shame, I do not. She worships you: I do not, I cannot. You are the rising sun to her. It
has been so for years. No one can account for love; I daresay
not for the impossibility of loving ... loving where we
should; all love bewilders me. I was not created to understand
it. But she loves you, she has pined. I believe it has destroyed
the health you demand as one item in your list. But you,
Willoughby, can restore that. Travelling, and ... and your
society, the pleasure of your society would certainly restore it.
You look so handsome together! She has unbounded devotion! as for me, I cannot idolize. I see faults: I see them daily.
They astonish and wound me. Your pride would not bear
to hear them spoken of, least of all by your wife. You
warned me to beware – that is, you said – you said something.'

Her busy brain missed the subterfuge to cover her slip of the
tongue.

Sir Willoughby struck in: 'And when I say that the entire
concatenation is based on an erroneous observation of facts,
and an erroneous deduction from that erroneous observation! – ? No, no. Have confidence in me. I propose it to you in
this instance, purely to save you from deception. You are cold,
my love? you shivered.'

'I am not cold,' said Clara. 'Some one, I suppose, was walking over my grave.'

The gulf of a caress hove in view like an enormous billow
hollowing under the curled ridge.

She stooped to a buttercup; the monster swept by.

'Your grave!' he exclaimed over her head; 'my own
girl!'

'Is not the orchis naturally a stranger in ground so far away
from the chalk, Willoughby?'

'I am incompetent to pronounce an opinion on such
important matters. My mother had a passion for every

description of flower. I fancy I have some recollection of her scattering the flower you mention over the park.'

'If she were living now!'

'We should be happy in the blessing of the most estimable of women, my Clara.'

'She would have listened to me. She would have realized what I mean.'

'Indeed, Clara – poor soul!' he murmured to himself, aloud; 'indeed you are absolutely in error. If I have seemed – but I repeat, you are deceived. The idea of "fitness" is a total hallucination. Supposing you – I do it even in play painfully – entirely out of the way, unthought of . . .'

'Extinct,' Clara said low.

'Non-existent for me,' he selected a preferable term. 'Suppose it; I should still, in spite of an admiration I have never thought it incumbent on me to conceal, still be – I speak emphatically – *utterly incapable of the offer of my hand to Miss Dale.* It may be that she is imbedded in my mind as a friend, and nothing but a friend. I received the stamp in early youth. People have noticed it – we do, it seems, bring one another out, reflecting, counter-reflecting.'

She glanced up at him with a shrewd satisfaction to see that her wicked shaft had stuck.

'You do; it is a common remark,' she said. 'The instantaneous difference when she comes near, any one might notice.'

'My love,' he opened the iron gate into the garden, 'you encourage the naughty little suspicion.'

'But it is a beautiful sight, Willoughby. I like to see you together. I like it as I like to see colours match.'

'Very well. There is no harm then. We shall often be together. I like my fair friend. But the instant! – you have only to express a sentiment of disapprobation.'

'And you dismiss her.'

'I dismiss her. That is, as to the word, I constitute myself your echo, to clear any vestige of suspicion. She goes.'

'That is a case of a person doomed to extinction without offending.'

'Not without: for whoever offends my bride, my wife, my sovereign lady, offends me: very deeply offends me.'

'Then the caprices of your wife –' Clara stamped her foot imperceptibly on the lawn-sward, which was irresponsively soft to her fretfulness. She broke from the inconsequent meaningless mild tone of irony, and said: 'Willoughby, women have their honour to swear by equally with men: – girls have: they have to swear an oath at the altar; may I to you now? Take it for uttered when I tell you that nothing would make me happier than your union with Miss Dale. I have spoken as much as I can. Tell me you release me.'

With the well-known screw-smile of duty upholding weariness worn to inanition, he rejoined: 'Allow me once more to reiterate, that it is repulsive, inconceivable, that I should *ever, under any mortal conditions, bring myself to the point of taking Miss Dale for my wife.* You reduce me to this perfectly childish protestation – pitiably childish! But, my love, have I to remind you that you and I are plighted, and that I am an honourable man?'

'I know it, I feel it – release me!' cried Clara.

Sir Willoughby severely reprehended his short-sightedness for seeing but the one proximate object in the particular attention he had bestowed on Miss Dale. He could not disavow that they had been marked, and with an object, and he was distressed by the unwonted want of wisdom through which he had been drawn to overshoot his object. His design to excite a touch of the insane emotion in Clara's bosom was too successful, and, 'I was not thinking of her,' he said to himself in his candour, contrite.

She cried again: 'Will you not, Willoughby – release me?'

He begged her to take his arm.

To consent to touch him while petitioning for a detachment, appeared discordant to Clara, but, if she expected him to accede, it was right that she should do as much as she could, and she surrendered her hand at arm's length, disdaining the imprisoned fingers. He pressed them and said: 'Dr Middleton is in the library. I see Vernon is at work with Crossjay in the West-room – the boy has had sufficient for the day. Now, is it not like old Vernon to drive his books at a cracked head before it's half mended?'

He signalled to young Crossjay, who was up and out through the folding-windows in a twinkling.

'And you will go in, and talk to Vernon of the lady in question,' Sir Willoughby whispered to Clara. 'Use your best persuasions in our joint names. You have my warrant for saying that money is no consideration; house and income are assured. You can hardly have taken me seriously when I requested you to undertake Vernon before. I was quite in earnest then as now. I prepare Miss Dale. I will not have a wedding on *our* wedding-day; but either before or after it, I gladly speed their alliance. I think now I give you the best proof possible, and though I know that with women a delusion may be seen to be groundless and still be cherished, I rely on your good sense.'

Vernon was at the window and stood aside for her to enter. Sir Willoughby used a gentle insistence with her. She bent her head as if she were stepping into a cave. So frigid was she, that a ridiculous dread of calling Mr Whitford Mr Oxford was her only present anxiety when Sir Willoughby had closed the window on them.

CHAPTER 14

✖✖✖✖

Sir Willoughby and Laetitia

'I PREPARE Miss Dale.'

Sir Willoughby thought of his promise to Clara. He trifled awhile with young Crossjay, and then sent the boy flying, and wrapped himself in meditation. So shall you see standing many a statue of statesmen who have died in harness for their country.

In the hundred and fourth chapter of the thirteenth volume of the BOOK OF EGOISM it is written: *Possession without obligation to the object possessed approaches felicity.*

It is the rarest condition of ownership. For example: the possession of land is not without obligation both to the soil and the tax-collector; the possession of fine clothing is oppressed by obligation; gold, jewelry, works of art, enviable household furniture, are positive fetters; the possession of a wife we find surcharged with obligation. In all these cases possession is a gentle term for enslavement, bestowing the sort of felicity attained to by the helot drunk. You can have the joy, the pride, the intoxication of possession; you can have no free soul.

But there is one instance of possession, and that the most perfect, which leaves us free, under not a shadow of obligation, receiving ever, never giving, or if giving, giving only of our waste; as it were (sauf votre respect), by form of perspiration, radiation, if you like; unconscious poral bountifulness; and it is a beneficent process for the system. Our possession of an adoring female's worship is this instance.

The soft cherishable Parsee is hardly at any season other than prostrate. She craves nothing save that you continue in being – her sun: which is your firm constitutional endeavour:

and thus you have a most exact alliance; she supplying spirit to your matter, while at the same time presenting matter to your spirit, verily a comfortable apposition. The Gods do bless it.

That they do so indeed is evident in the men they select for such a felicitous crown and aureole. Weak men would be rendered nervous by the flattery of a woman's worship; or they would be for returning it, at least partially, as though it could be bandied to and fro without emulgence of the poetry; or they would be pitiful, and quite spoil the thing. Some would be for transforming the beautiful solitary vestal flame by the first effort of the multiplication-table into your hearth-fire of slippered affection. So these men are not they whom the Gods have ever selected, but rather men of a pattern with themselves, very high and very solid men, who maintain the crown by holding divinely independent of the great emotion they have sown.

Even for them a pass of danger is ahead, as we shall see in our sample of one among the highest of them.

A clear approach to felicity had long been the portion of Sir Willoughby Patterne in his relations with Laetitia Dale. She belonged to him; he was quite unshackled by her. She was everything that is good in a parasite, nothing that is bad. His dedicated critic she was, reviewing him with a favour equal to perfect efficiency in her office; and whatever the world might say of him, to her the happy gentleman could constantly turn for his refreshing balsamic bath. She flew to the soul in him, pleasingly arousing sensations of that inhabitant; and he allowed her the right to fly, in the manner of kings, as we have heard, consenting to the privileges acted on by cats. These may not address their Majesties, but they may stare; nor will it be contested that the attentive circular eyes of the humble domestic creatures are an embellishment to Royal pomp and grandeur, such truly as should one day gain for them an in-weaving and figurement – in the place of bees, ermine tufts, and their various present decorations – upon the august great robes back-flowing and foaming over the gaspy page-boys.

Further to quote from the same volume of THE BOOK: *There is pain in the surrendering of that we are fain to relinquish.*

The idea is too exquisitely attenuate, as are those of the whole body-guard of the heart of Egoism, and will slip through you unless you shall have made a study of the gross of volumes of the first and second sections of THE BOOK, and that will take you up to senility; or you must make a personal entry into the pages, perchance; or an escape out of them. There was once a venerable gentleman for whom a white hair grew on the cop of his nose, laughing at removals. He resigned himself to it in the end, and lastingly contemplated the apparition. It does not concern us what effect was produced on his countenance and his mind; enough that he saw a fine thing, but not so fine as the idea cited above; which has been between the two eyes of humanity ever since women were sought in marriage. With yonder old gentleman it may have been a ghostly hair or a disease of the optic nerves; but for us it is a real growth, and humanity might profitably imitate him in his patient speculation upon it.

Sir Willoughby Patterne, though ready in the pursuit of duty and policy (an oft-united couple) to cast Miss Dale away, had to consider that he was not simply, so to speak, casting her over a hedge, he was casting her for a man to catch her; and this was a much greater trial than it had been on the previous occasion, when she went over bump to the ground. In the arms of a husband, there was no knowing how soon she might forget her soul's fidelity. It had not hurt him to sketch the project of the conjunction; benevolence assisted him; but he winced and smarted on seeing it take shape. It sullied his idea of Laetitia.

Still, if, in spite of so great a change in her fortune, her spirit could be guaranteed changeless, he, for the sake of pacifying his bride, and to keep two serviceable persons near him at command, might resolve to join them. The vision of his resolution brought with it a certain pallid contempt of the physically faithless woman; no wonder he betook himself to THE BOOK, and opened it on the scorching chapters treating of the sex, and the execrable wiles of that foremost creature of the chase, who runs for life. She is not spared in the Biggest of Books. But close it.

The writing in it having been done chiefly by men, men naturally receive their fortification from its wisdom, and half a dozen of the popular sentences for the confusion of women (cut in brass worn to a polish like sombre gold), refreshed Sir Willoughby for his undertaking.

An examination of Laetitia's faded complexion braced him very cordially.

His Clara jealous of this poor leaf!

He could have desired the transfusion of a quality or two from Laetitia to his bride; but you cannot, as in cookery, obtain a mixture of the essences of these creatures; and if, as it is possible to do, and as he had been doing recently with the pair of them at the Hall, you stew them in one pot, you are far likelier to intensify their little birth-marks of individuality. Had they a tendency to excellence it might be otherwise; they might then make the exchanges we wish for; or scientifically concocted in a harem for a sufficient length of time by a sultan anything but obtuse, they might. It is, however, fruitless to dwell on what was only a glimpse of a wild regret, like the crossing of two express trains along the rails in Sir Willoughby's head.

The ladies Eleanor and Isabel were sitting with Miss Dale, all three at work on embroideries. He had merely to look at Miss Eleanor. She rose. She looked at Miss Isabel, and rattled her châtelaine to account for her departure. After a decent interval Miss Isabel glided out. Such was the perfect discipline of the household.

Sir Willoughby played an air on the knee of his crossed leg.

Laetitia grew conscious of a meaning in the silence. She said, 'You have not been vexed by affairs to-day?'

'Affairs,' he replied, 'must be peculiarly vexatious to trouble me. Concerning the country or my personal affairs?'

'I fancy I was alluding to the country.'

'I trust I am as good a patriot as any man living,' said he; 'but I am used to the follies of my countrymen, and we are on board a stout ship. At the worst it's no worse than a rise in rates and taxes; soup at the Hall gates, perhaps; license to fell timber in one of the outer copses, or some dozen loads of coal. You hit my feudalism.'

'The knight in armour has gone,' said Laetitia, 'and the castle with the draw-bridge. Immunity for our island has gone too since we took to commerce.'

'We bartered independence for commerce. You hit our old controversy. Ay, but we do not want this overgrown population! However, we will put politics and sociology and the pack of their modern barbarous words aside. You read me intuitively. I have been, I will not say annoyed, but ruffled. I have much to do, and going into Parliament would make me almost helpless if I lose Vernon. You know of some absurd notion he has? - literary fame, and bachelor's chambers, and a chop-house, and the rest of it.'

She knew, and thinking differently in the matter of literary fame, she flushed, and, ashamed of the flush, frowned.

He bent over to her with the perusing earnestness of a gentleman about to trifle.

'You cannot intend that frown?'

'Did I frown?'

'You do.'

'Now?'

'Fiercely.'

'Oh!'

'Will you smile to reassure me?'

'Willingly, as well as I can.'

A gloom overcame him. With no woman on earth did he shine so as to recall to himself seigneur and dame of the old French Court as he did with Laetitia Dale. He did not wish the period revived, but reserved it as a garden to stray into when he was in the mood for displaying elegance and brightness in the society of a lady; and in speech Laetitia helped him to the nice delusion. She was not devoid of grace of bearing either.

Would she preserve her beautiful responsiveness to his ascendency? Hitherto she had, and for years, and quite fresh. But how of her as a married woman? Our souls are hideously subject to the conditions of our animal nature! A wife, possibly mother, it was within sober calculation that there would be great changes in her. And the hint of any change appeared a total change to one of the lofty order who, when they are called on to relinquish possession instead of aspiring to it, say, All or nothing!

Well, but if there was danger of the marriage-tie effecting the slightest alteration of her character or habit of mind, wherefore press it upon a tolerably hardened spinster!

Besides, though he did once put her hand in Vernon's for the dance, he remembered acutely that the injury then done by his generosity to his tender sensitiveness had sickened and tarnished the effulgence of two or three successive anniversaries of his coming of age. Nor had he altogether yet got over the passion of greed for the whole group of the well-favoured of the fair sex, which in his early youth had made it bitter for him to submit to the fickleness, not to say the modest fickleness, of any handsome one of them in yielding her hand to a man and suffering herself to be led away. Ladies whom he had only heard of as ladies of some beauty incurred his wrath for having lovers or taking husbands. He was of a vast embrace; and do not exclaim, in covetousness; – for well he knew that even under Moslem law he could not have them all – but as the enamoured custodian of the sex's purity, that blushes at such big spots as lovers and husbands; and it was unbearable to see it sacrificed for others. Without their purity what are they! – what are fruiterer's plums? – unsaleable. Oh, for the bloom on them!

'As I said, I lose my right hand in Vernon,' he resumed, 'and I am, it seems, inevitably to lose him, unless we contrive to fasten him down here. I think, my dear Miss Dale, you have my character. At least, I should recommend my future biographer to you – with a caution, of course. You would have to write selfishness with a dash under it. I cannot endure to lose a member of my household – not under any circumstances; and a change of feeling toward me on the part of any of my friends because of marriage, I think hard. I would ask you, how can it be for Vernon's good to quit an easy pleasant home for the wretched profession of Literature? – wretchedly paying, I mean,' he bowed to the authoress. 'Let him leave the house, if he imagines he will not harmonize with its young mistress. He is queer, though a good fellow. But he ought, in that event, to have an establishment. And my scheme for Vernon – men, Miss Dale, do not change to their old friends when they marry – my scheme, which would cause the alteration in his system of life to be barely perceptible, is to build him a poetical little cottage, large enough for a couple, on the borders of my park. I have the spot in my eye. The point is, can he live alone there? Men, I say, do not change. How is it that we cannot say the same of women?'

Laetitia remarked: 'The generic woman appears to have an extraordinary faculty for swallowing the individual.'

'As to the individual, as to a particular person, I may be wrong. Precisely because it is her case I think of, my strong friendship inspires the fear: unworthy of both, no doubt, but trace it to the source. Even pure friendship, such is the taint in us, knows a kind of jealousy; though I would gladly see her established, and near me, happy and contributing to my happiness with her incomparable social charm. Her I do not estimate generically, be sure.'

'If you do me the honour to allude to me, Sir Willoughby,' said Laetitia, 'I am my father's housemate.'

'What wooer would take that for a refusal? He would beg to be a third in the house and sharer of your affectionate burden. Honestly, why not? And I may be arguing against my own happiness; it may be the end of me!'

'The end?'

'Old friends are captious, exacting. No, not the end. Yet if my friend is not the same to me, it is the end to that form of friendship: not to the degree possibly. But when one is used to the form! And do you, in its application to friendship, scorn the word "use"? We are creatures of custom. I am, I confess, a poltroon in my affections; I dread changes. The shadow of the tenth of an inch in the customary elevation of an eyelid! – to give you an idea of my susceptibility. And, my dear Miss Dale, I throw myself on your charity, with all my weakness bare, let me add, as I could do to none but you. Consider, then, if I lose you! The fear is due to my pusillanimity entirely. High-souled women may be wives, mothers and still reserve that home for their friend. They can and will conquer the viler conditions of human life. Our states, I have always contended, our various phases have to be passed through, and there is no disgrace in it so long as they do not levy toll on the quintessential, the spiritual element. You understand me? I am no adept in these abstract elucidations.'

'You explain yourself clearly,' said Laetitia.

'I have never pretended that psychology was my forte,' said he, feeling overshadowed by her cold commendation: he was not less acutely sensitive to the fractional divisions of tones than of eyelids, being, as it were, a melody with which everything was out of tune that did not modestly or mutely accord; and to bear about a melody in your person is incomparably more searching than the best of touchstones and talismans ever invented. 'Your father's health has improved latterly?'

'He did not complain of his health when I saw him this morning. My cousin Amelia is with him, and she is an excellent nurse.'

'He has a liking for Vernon.'

'He has a great respect for Mr Whitford.'

'You have?'

'Oh, yes; I have it equally.'

'For a foundation, that is the surest. I would have the friends dearest to me begin on that. The headlong match is –! how can we describe it? By its finale I am afraid. Vernon's abilities are really to be respected. His shyness is his malady. I suppose he reflected that he was not a capitalist. He might, one would think, have addressed himself to me; my purse is not locked.'

'No, Sir Willoughby!' Laetitia said, warmly, for his donations in charity were famous.

Her eyes gave him the food he enjoyed, and basking in them, he continued:

'Vernon's income would at once have been regulated commensurately with a new position requiring an increase. This money, money, money! But the world will have it so. Happily I have inherited habits of business and personal economy. Vernon is a man who would do fifty times more with a companion appreciating his abilities and making light of his little deficiencies. They are palpable, small enough. He has always been aware of my wishes: – when perhaps the fulfilment might have sent me off on another tour of the world, home-bird though I am. When was it that our friendship commenced? In my boyhood, I know. Very many years back.'

'I am in my thirtieth year,' said Laetitia.

Surprised and pained by a baldness resembling the deeds of ladies (they have been known, either through absence of mind, or mania, to displace a wig) in the deadly intimacy which slaughters poetic admiration, Sir Willoughby punished her by deliberately reckoning that she did not look less.

'Genius,' he observed, 'is unacquainted with wrinkles'; hardly one of his prettiest speeches; but he had been wounded, and he never could recover immediately. Coming on him in a mood of sentiment, the wound was sharp. He could very well have calculated the lady's age. It was the jarring clash of her brazen declaration of it upon his low rich flute-notes that shocked him.

He glanced at the gold cathedral-clock on the mantel-piece, and proposed a stroll on the lawn before dinner. Laetitia gathered up her embroidery work.

'As a rule,' he said, 'authoresses are not needle-women.'

'I shall resign the needle or the pen if it stamps me an exception,' she replied.

He attempted a compliment on her truly exceptional character. As when the player's finger rests in distraction on the organ, it was without measure and disgusted his own hearing. Nevertheless, she had been so good as to diminish his apprehension that the marriage of a lady in her thirtieth year with his cousin Vernon would be so much of a loss to him; hence, while parading the lawn, now and then casting an eye at the window of the room where his Clara and Vernon were in council, the schemes he indulged for his prospective comfort and his feelings of the moment were in such striving harmony as that to which we hear orchestral musicians bringing their instruments under the process called tuning. It is not perfect, but it promises to be so soon. We are not angels, which have their dulcimers ever on the choral pitch. We are mortals attaining the celestial accord with effort, through a stage of pain. Some degree of pain was necessary to Sir Willoughby, otherwise he would not have seen his generosity confronting him. He grew, therefore, tenderly inclined to Laetitia once more, so far as to say within himself, 'For conversation she would be a valuable wife'. And this valuable wife he was presenting to his cousin.

Apparently, considering the duration of the conference of his Clara and Vernon, his cousin required strong persuasion to accept the present.

CHAPTER 15

✕✕✕✕

The Petition for a Release

NEITHER Clara nor Vernon appeared at the mid-day table. Dr Middleton talked with Miss Dale on classical matters, like a good-natured giant giving a child the jump from stone to stone across a brawling mountain ford, so that an unedified audience might really suppose, upon seeing her over the difficulty, she had done something for herself. Sir Willoughby was proud of her, and therefore anxious to settle her business while he was in the humour to lose her. He hoped to finish it by shooting a word or two at Vernon before dinner. Clara's petition to be set free, released from *him*, had vaguely frightened even more than it offended his pride.

Miss Isabel quitted the room.

She came back, saying: 'They decline to lunch.'

'Then we may rise,' remarked Sir Willoughby.

'She was weeping,' Miss Isabel murmured to him.

'Girlish enough,' he said.

The two elderly ladies went away together. Miss Dale, pursuing her theme with the Rev. Doctor, was invited by him to a course in the library. Sir Willoughby walked up and down the lawn, taking a glance at the West-room as he swung round on the turn of his leg. Growing impatient, he looked in at the window and found the room vacant.

Nothing was to be seen of Clara and Vernon during the afternoon. Near the dinner-hour the ladies were informed by Miss Middleton's maid that her mistress was lying down on her bed, too unwell with headache to be present. Young Crossjay brought a message from Vernon (delayed by birds' eggs in the delivery), to say that he was off over the hills, and thought of dining with Dr Corney.

Sir Willoughby despatched condolences to his bride. He was not well able to employ his mind on its customary topic, being, like the dome of a bell, a man of so pervading a ring within himself concerning himself, that the recollection of a doubtful speech or unpleasant circumstance touching him closely deranged his inward peace; and as dubious and unpleasant things will often occur, he had great need of a worshipper, and was often compelled to appeal to her for signs of antidotal idolatry. In this instance, when the need of a worshipper was sharply felt, he obtained no signs at all. The Rev. Doctor had fascinated Miss Dale; so that, both within and without, Sir Willoughby was uncomforted. His themes in public were those of an English gentleman; horses, dogs, game, sport, intrigue, scandal, politics, wines, the manly themes; with a condescension to ladies' tattle, and approbation of a racy anecdote. What interest could he possibly take in the Athenian Theatre and the girl whose flute-playing behind the scenes, imitating the nightingale, enraptured a Greek audience! He would have suspected a motive in Miss Dale's eager attentiveness, if the motive could have been conceived. Besides, the ancients were not decorous; they did not, as we make our moderns do, write for ladies. He ventured at the dinner-table to interrupt Dr Middleton once:

'Miss Dale will do wisely, I think, sir, by confining herself to your present edition of the classics.'

'That,' replied Dr Middleton, 'is the observation of a student of the dictionary of classical mythology in the English tongue.'

'The theatre is a matter of climate, sir. You will grant me that.'

'If quick wits come of climate, it is as you say, sir.'

'With us it seems a matter of painful fostering, or the need of it,' said Miss Dale, with a question to Dr Middleton, excluding Sir Willoughby, as though he had been a temporary disturbance of the flow of their dialogue.

The ladies Eleanor and Isabel, previously excellent listeners

to the learned talk, saw the necessity of coming to his rescue;
but you cannot converse with your aunts, inmates of your
house, on general subjects at table; the attempt increased his
discomposure; he considered that he had ill-chosen his father-
in-law; that scholars are an impolite race; that young or
youngish women are devotees of power in any form, and will
be absorbed by a scholar for a variation of a man; concluding
that he must have a round of dinner-parties to friends, especially ladies, appreciating him, during the Doctor's visit.
Clara's headache above, and Dr Middleton's unmannerliness
below, affected his instincts in a way to make him apprehend
that a stroke of misfortune was impending; thunder was in the
air. Still he learned something, by which he was to profit subsequently. The topic of wine withdrew the doctor from his
classics; it was magical on him. A strong fraternity of taste was
discovered in the sentiments of host and guest upon particular
wines and vintages; they kindled one another by naming great
years of the grape, and if Sir Willoughby had to sacrifice the
ladies to the topic, he much regretted a condition of things that
compelled him to sin against his habit, for the sake of being
in the conversation and probing an elderly gentleman's
foible.

Late at night he heard the house-bell, and meeting Vernon
in the hall, invited him to enter the laboratory and tell him Dr
Corney's last. Vernon was brief; Corney had not let fly a single
anecdote, he said, and lighted his candle.

'By the way, Vernon, you had a talk with Miss Middleton?'

'She will speak to you to-morrow at twelve.'

'To-morrow at twelve?'

'It gives her four-and-twenty hours.'

Sir Willoughby determined that his perplexity should be
seen; but Vernon said good-night to him, and was shooting up
the stairs before the dramatic exhibition of surprise had yielded
to speech.

Thunder was in the air and a blow coming. Sir Willoughby's

instincts were awake to the many signs, nor, though silenced, were they hushed by his harping on the frantic excesses to which women are driven by the passion of jealousy. He believed in Clara's jealousy because he really had intended to rouse it; under the form of emulation, feebly. He could not suppose she had spoken of it to Vernon. And as for the seriousness of her desire to be released from her engagement, that was little credible. Still the fixing of an hour for her to speak to him after an interval of four-and-twenty hours, left an opening for the incredible to add its weight to the suspicious mass; and who would have fancied Clara Middleton so wild a victim of the intemperate passion! He muttered to himself several assuaging observations to excuse a young lady half demented, and rejected them in a lump for their nonsensical inapplicability to Clara. In order to obtain some sleep, he consented to blame himself slightly, in the style of the enamoured historian of erring beauties alluding to their peccadilloes. He had done it to edify her. Sleep, however, failed him. That an inordinate jealousy argued an overpowering love, solved his problem until he tried to fit the proposition to Clara's character. He had discerned nothing southern in her. Latterly, with the blushing Day in prospect, she had contracted and frozen. There was no reading either of her or of the mystery.

In the morning, at the breakfast-table, a confession of sleeplessness was general. Excepting Miss Dale and Dr Middleton, none had slept a wink. 'I, sir,' the Doctor replied to Sir Willoughby, 'slept like a lexicon in your library when Mr Whitford and I are out of it.'

Vernon incidentally mentioned that he had been writing through the night.

'You fellows kill yourselves,' Sir Willoughby reproved him. 'For my part, I make it a principle to get through my work without self-slaughter.'

Clara watched her father for a symptom of ridicule. He gazed mildly on the systematic worker. She was unable to guess whether she would have in him an ally or a judge. The latter, she feared. Now that she had embraced the strife, she saw the division of the line where she stood from that one where the world places girls who are affianced wives; her father could hardly be with her; it had gone too far. He loved her, but he would certainly take her to be moved by a maddish whim; he would not try to understand her case. The scholar's detestation of a disarrangement of human affairs that had been by miracle contrived to run smoothly, would of itself rank him against her; and with the world to back his view of her, he might behave like a despotic father. How could she defend herself before him? At one thought of Sir Willoughby, her tongue made ready, and feminine craft was alert to prompt it; but to her father she could imagine herself opposing only dumbness and obstinacy.

'It is not exactly the same kind of work,' she said.

Dr Middleton rewarded her with a bushy eyebrow's beam of his revolting humour at the baronet's notion of work.

So little was needed to quicken her that she sunned herself in the beam, coaxing her father's eyes to stay with hers as long as she could, and beginning to hope he might be won to her side, if she confessed she had been more in the wrong than she felt; owned to him, that is, her error in not earlier disturbing his peace.

'I do not say it is the same,' observed Sir Willoughby, bowing to their alliance of opinion. 'My poor work is for the day, and Vernon's, no doubt, for the day to come. I contend, nevertheless, for the preservation of health as the chief implement of work.'

'Of continued work; there I agree with you,' said Dr Middleton, cordially.

Clara's heart sunk; so little was needed to deaden her.

Accuse her of an overweening antagonism to her betrothed; yet remember that though the words had not been uttered to give her good reason for it, nature reads nature; captives may be stript of everything save that power to read their tyrant; remember also that she was not, as she well knew, blameless; her rage at him was partly against herself.

The rising from table left her to Sir Willoughby. She swam away after Miss Dale, exclaiming: 'The laboratory! Will you have me for a companion on your walk to see your father? One breathes earth and heaven to-day out of doors. Isn't it Summer with a Spring Breeze? I will wander about your garden and not hurry your visit, I promise.'

'I shall be very happy indeed. But I am going immediately,' said Laetitia, seeing Sir Willoughby hovering to snap up his bride.

'Yes; and a garden-hat and I am on the march.'

'I will wait for you on the terrace.'

'You will not have to wait.'

'Five minutes at the most,' Sir Willoughby said to Laetitia, and she passed out, leaving them alone together.

'Well, and my love!' he addressed his bride almost huggingly; 'and what is the story? and how did you succeed with old Vernon yesterday? He will and he won't? He's a very woman in these affairs. I can't forgive him for giving you a headache. You were found weeping.'

'Yes, I cried,' said Clara.

'And now tell me about it. You know, my dear girl, whether he does or doesn't, our keeping him somewhere in the neighbourhood – perhaps not in the house – that is the material point. It can hardly be necessary in these days to urge marriages on. I'm sure the country is over . . . Most marriages ought to be celebrated with the funeral knell!'

'I think so,' said Clara.

'It will come to this, that marriages of consequence, and none but those, will be hailed with joyful peals.'

'Do not say such things in public, Willoughby.'

'Only to you, to you! Don't think me likely to expose myself to the world. Well, and I sounded Miss Dale, and there will be no violent obstacle. And now about Vernon?'

'I will speak to you, Willoughby, when I return from my walk with Miss Dale, soon after twelve.'

'Twelve!' said he.

'I name an hour. It seems childish. I can explain it. But it is named, I cannot deny, because I am a rather childish person perhaps, and have it prescribed to me to delay my speaking for a certain length of time. I may tell you at once that Mr Whitford is not to be persuaded by me, and the breaking of our engagement would not induce him to remain.'

'Vernon used those words?'

'It was I.'

' "The breaking of our engagement!" Come into the laboratory, my love.'

'I shall not have time.'

'Time shall stop rather than interfere with our conversation! "The breaking . . .!" But it's a sort of sacrilege to speak of it.'

'That I feel; yet it has to be spoken of.'

'Sometimes? Why? I can't conceive the occasion. You know, to me, Clara, plighted faith, the affiancing of two lovers, is a piece of religion. I rank it as holy as marriage; nay, to me it is holier; I really cannot tell you how; I can only appeal to you in your bosom to understand me. We read of divorces with comparative indifference. They occur between couples who have rubbed off all romance.'

She could have asked him in her fit of ironic iciness, on hearing him thus blindly challenge her to speak out, whether the romance might be his piece of religion.

He propitiated the more unwar-like sentiments in her by ejaculating, 'Poor souls! let them go their several ways. Married people no longer lovers are in the category of the unnameable. But the hint of the breaking of an engagement – our engagement! – between *us*? Oh!'

'Oh!' Clara came out with a swan's note swelling over mechanical imitation of him to dolorousness illimitable. 'Oh!' she breathed short, 'let it be now. Do not speak till you have heard me. My head may not be clear by-and-by. And two scenes – twice will be beyond my endurance. I am penitent for the wrong I have done you. I grieve for you. All the blame is mine. Willoughby, you must release me. Do not let me hear a word of that word; jealousy is unknown to me . . . Happy if I could call you friend and see you with a worthier than I, who might by-and-by call me friend! You have my plighted troth . . . given in ignorance of my feelings. Reprobate a weak and foolish girl's ignorance. I have thought of it, and I cannot see wickedness, though the blame is great, shameful. You have none. You are without any blame. You will not suffer as I do. You will be generous to me? I have no respect for myself when I beg you to be generous and release me.'

'But was this the . . .' Willoughby preserved his calmness, 'this, then, the subject of your interview with Vernon?'

'I have spoken to him. I did my commission, and I spoke to him.'

'Of me?'

'Of myself. I see how I hurt you; I could not avoid it. Yes, of you, as far as we are related. I said I believed you would release me. I said I could be true to my plighted word, but that you would not insist. Could a gentleman insist? But not a step beyond; not love; I have none. And, Willoughby, treat me as one perfectly worthless; I am. I should have known it a year back. I was deceived in myself. There should be love.'

'Should be!' Willoughby's tone was a pungent comment on her.

'Love, then, I find I have not. I think I am antagonistic to it. What people say of it I have not experienced. I find I was mistaken. It is lightly said, but very painful. You understand me, that my prayer is for liberty, that I may not be tied. If you can release and pardon me, or promise ultimately to pardon me, or say some kind word, I shall know it is because I am beneath you utterly that I have been unable to give you the love you should have with a wife. Only say to me, go! It is you who break the match, discovering my want of a heart. What people think of me matters little. My anxiety will be to save you annoyance.'

She waited for him; he seemed on the verge of speaking.

He perceived her expectation; he had nothing but clownish tumult within, and his dignity counselled him to disappoint her.

Swaying his head, like the Oriental palm whose shade is a blessing to the perfervid wanderer below, smiling gravely, he was indirectly asking his dignity what he could say to maintain it and deal this mad young woman a bitterly compassionate rebuke. What to think, hung remoter. The thing to do struck him first.

He squeezed both her hands, threw the door wide open, and said, with countless blinkings: 'In the laboratory we are uninterrupted. I was at a loss to guess where that most unpleasant effect on the senses came from. They are always "guessing" through the nose. I mean, the remainder of breakfast here. Perhaps I satirized them too smartly – if you know the letters. When they are not "calculating". More offensive than débris of a midnight banquet! An American tour is instructive, though not so romantic. Not so romantic as Italy, I mean. Let us escape.'

She held back from his arm. She had scattered his brains; it was pitiable: but she was in the torrent and could not suffer a pause or a change of place.

'It must be here; one minute more – I cannot go elsewhere to begin again. Speak to me here; answer my request. Once; one word. If you forgive me, it will be superhuman. But, release me.'

'Seriously,' he rejoined, 'tea-cups and coffee-cups, breadcrumbs, egg-shells, caviare, butter, beef, bacon! Can we? The room reeks.'

'Then I will go for my walk with Miss Dale. And you will speak to me when I return?'

'At all seasons. You shall go with Miss Dale. But, my dear! my love! Seriously, where are we? One hears of lovers' quarrels. Now I never quarrel. It is a characteristic of mine. And you speak of me to my cousin Vernon! Seriously, plighted faith signifies plighted faith, as much as an iron-cable is iron to hold by. Some little twist of the mind? To Vernon, of all men! Tush! she has been dreaming of a hero of perfection, and the comparison is unfavourable to her Willoughby. But, my Clara, when I say to you, that bride is bride, and you are mine, mine!'

'Willoughby, you mentioned them, – those separations of two married. You said, if they do not love – Oh! say, is it not better – instead of later?'

He took advantage of her modesty in speaking to exclaim: 'Where are we now? Bride is bride, and wife is wife, and *affianced* is, in honour, *wedded*. You cannot be released. We are united. Recognize it; united. There is no possibility of releasing a wife!'

'Not if she ran . . .?'

This was too direct to be histrionically misunderstood. He had driven her to the extremity of more distinctly imagining the circumstance she had cited, and with that cleared view the desperate creature gloried in launching such a bolt at the man's real or assumed insensibility as must, by shivering it, waken him.

But in a moment she stood in burning rose, with dimmed eyesight. She saw his horror, and, seeing, shared it; shared just then only by seeing it; which led her to rejoice with the deepest of sighs that some shame was left in her.

'Ran? ran? ran?' he said as rapidly as he blinked. 'How? where? what idea . . .?'

Close was he upon an explosion that would have sullied his conception of the purity of the younger members of the sex hauntingly.

That she, a young lady, maiden, of strictest education, should, and without his teaching, know that wives ran! – know that by running they compelled their husbands to abandon pursuit, surrender possession! – and that she should suggest it of herself as a wife! – that she should speak of running!

His ideal, the common male Egoist ideal of a waxwork sex, would have been shocked to fragments had she spoken further to fill in the outlines of these awful interjections.

She was tempted: for during the last few minutes the fire of her situation had enlightened her understanding upon a subject far from her as the ice-fields of the North a short while before; and the prospect offered to her courage if she would only outstare shame and seem at home in the doings of wickedness, was his loathing and dreading so vile a young woman. She restrained herself; chiefly, after the first bridling of maidenly timidity, because she could not bear to lower the idea of her sex even in his esteem.

The door was open. She had thoughts of flying out to breathe in an interval of truce.

She reflected on her situation hurriedly askance:

'If one must go through this, to be disentangled from an engagement, what must it be to poor women seeking to be free of a marriage?'

Had she spoken it, Sir Willoughby might have learned that she was not so iniquitously wise of the things of this world as her mere sex's instinct, roused to the intemperateness of a creature struggling with fetters, had made her appear in her dash to seize a weapon, indicated moreover by him.

Clara took up the old broken vow of women to vow it afresh: 'Never to any man will I give my hand.'

She replied to Sir Willoughby, 'I have said all. I cannot explain what I have said.'

She had heard a step in the passage. Vernon entered.

Perceiving them, he stated his mission in apology: 'Doctor Middleton left a book in this room. I see it; it's a Heinsius.'

'Ha! by the way, a book; books would not be left here if they were not brought here, with my compliments to Doctor Middleton, who may do as he pleases, though, seriously, order is order,' said Sir Willoughby. 'Come away to the laboratory,

Clara. It's a comment on human beings that wherever they
have been there's a mess, and you admirers of them,' he divided
a sickly nod between Vernon and the stale breakfast-table,
'must make what you can of it. Come, Clara.'

Clara protested that she was engaged to walk with Miss
Dale.

'Miss Dale is waiting in the hall,' said Vernon.

'Miss Dale is waiting?' said Clara.

'Walk with Miss Dale; walk with Miss Dale,' Sir Willoughby remarked, pressingly. 'I will beg her to wait another
two minutes. You shall find her in the hall when you come
down.'

He rang the bell and went out.

'Take Miss Dale into your confidence; she is quite trustworthy,' Vernon said to Clara.

'I have not advanced one step,' she replied.

'Recollect that you are in a position of your own choosing;
and if, after thinking over it, you mean to escape, you must
make up your mind to pitched battles, and not be dejected if
you are beaten in all of them; there is your only chance.'

'Not my choosing; do not say choosing, Mr Whitford. I
did not choose. I was incapable of really choosing. I consented.'

'It's the same in fact. But be sure of what you wish.'

'Yes,' she assented, taking it for her just punishment that
she should be supposed not quite to know her wishes. 'Your
advice has helped me to-day.'

'Did I advise?'

'Do you regret advising?'

'I should certainly regret a word that intruded between you
and him.'

'But you will not leave the Hall yet? You will not leave me
without a friend? If papa and I were to leave to-morrow, I
foresee endless correspondence. I have to stay at least some
days, and wear through it, and then, if I have to speak to my
poor father, you can imagine the effect on him.'

Sir Willoughby came striding in, to correct the error of his going out.

'Miss Dale awaits you, my dear. You have bonnet, hat? – No? Have you forgotten your appointment to walk with her?'

'I am ready,' said Clara, departing.

The two gentlemen behind her separated in the passage. They had not spoken.

She had read of the reproach upon women, that they divide the friendships of men. She reproached herself, but she was in action, driven by necessity, between sea and rock. Dreadful to think of! she was one of the creatures who are written about.

CHAPTER 16

✕✕✕✕

Clara and Laetitia

IN spite of his honourable caution, Vernon had said things to render Miss Middleton more angrily determined than she had been in the scene with Sir Willoughby. His counting on pitched battles and a defeat for her in all of them, made her previous feelings appear slack in comparison with the energy of combat now animating her. And she could vehemently declare that she had not chosen; she was too young, too ignorant to choose. He had wrongly used that word; it sounded malicious; and to call consenting the same in fact as choosing was wilfully unjust. Mr Whitford meant well; he was conscientious, very conscientious. But he was not the hero descending from heaven bright-sworded to smite a woman's fetters off her limbs and deliver her from the yawning mouth-abyss.

His logical coolness of expostulation with her when she cast aside the silly mission entrusted to her by Sir Willoughby and wept for herself, was unheroic in proportion to its praiseworthiness. He had left it to her to do everything she wished done, stipulating simply that there should be a pause of four-and-twenty hours for her to consider of it before she proceeded in the attempt to extricate herself. Of consolation there had not been a word. Said he, 'I am the last man to give advice in such a case'. Yet she had by no means astonished him when her confession came out. It came out, she knew not how. It was led up to by his declining the idea of marriage, and her congratulating him on his exemption from the prospect of the yoke, but memory was too dull to revive the one or two fiery minutes of broken language when she had been guilty of her dire misconduct.

This gentleman was no flatterer, scarcely a friend. He could look on her grief without soothing her. Supposing he had soothed her warmly? All her sentiments collected in her bosom to dash in reprobation of him at the thought. She nevertheless condemned him for his excessive coolness; his transparent anxiety not to be compromised by a syllable; his air of saying, 'I guessed as much, but why plead your case to me?' And his recommendation to her to be quite sure she did know what she meant, was a little insulting. She exonerated him from the intention; he treated her as a girl. By what he said of Miss Dale, he proposed that lady for imitation.

'I must be myself or I shall be playing hypocrite to dig my own pitfall,' she said to herself, while taking counsel with Laetitia as to the route for their walk, and admiring a becoming curve in her companion's hat.

Sir Willoughby, with many protestations of regret that letters of business debarred him from the pleasure of accompanying them, remarked upon the path proposed by Miss Dale, 'In that case you must have a footman.'

'Then we adopt the other,' said Clara, and they set forth.

'Sir Willoughby,' Miss Dale said to her, 'is always in alarm about our unprotectedness.'

Clara glanced up at the clouds and closed her parasol. She replied, 'It inspires timidity.'

There was that in the accent and character of the answer which warned Laetitia to expect the reverse of a quiet chatter with Miss Middleton.

'You are fond of walking?' She chose a peaceful topic.

'Walking or riding; yes, of walking,' said Clara. 'The difficulty is to find companions.'

'We shall lose Mr Whitford next week.'

'He goes?'

'He will be a great loss to me, for I do not ride,' Laetitia replied to the off-hand inquiry.

'Ah!'

Miss Middleton did not fan conversation when she simply breathed her voice.

Laetitia tried another neutral theme.

'The weather to-day suits our country,' she said.

'England, or Patterne Park? I am so devoted to mountains that I have no enthusiasm for flat land.'

'Do you call our country flat, Miss Middleton? We have undulations, hills, and we have sufficient diversity, meadows, rivers, copses, brooks, and good roads, and pretty by-paths.'

'The prettiness is overwhelming. It is very pretty to see; but to live with, I think I prefer ugliness. I can imagine learning to love ugliness. It's honest. However young you are, you cannot be deceived by it. These parks of rich people are a part of the prettiness. I would rather have fields, commons.'

'The parks give us delightful green walks, paths through beautiful woods.'

'If there is a right-of-way for the public.'

'There should be,' said Miss Dale, wondering; and Clara cried: 'I chafe at restraint: hedges and palings everywhere! I should have to travel ten years to sit down contented among these fortifications. Of course I can read of this rich kind of English country with pleasure in poetry. But it seems to me to require poetry. What would you say of human beings requiring it?'

'That they are not so companionable but that the haze of distance improves the view.'

'Then you do know that you are the wisest?'

Laetitia raised her dark eyelashes; she sought to understand. She could only fancy she did; and if she did, it meant that Miss Middleton thought her wise in remaining single.

Clara was full of a sombre preconception that her 'jealousy' had been hinted to Miss Dale.

'You knew Miss Durham?' she said.

'Not intimately.'

'As well as you know me?'

'Not so well.'

'But you saw more of her?'

'She was more reserved with me.'

'Oh! Miss Dale, I would not be reserved with you.'

The thrill of the voice caused Laetitia to steal a look. Clara's eyes were bright, and she had the readiness to run to volubility of the fever-stricken; otherwise she did not betray excitement.

'You will never allow any of these noble trees to be felled, Miss Middleton?'

'The axe is better than decay, do you not think?'

'I think your influence will be great and always used to good purpose.'

'My influence, Miss Dale? I have begged a favour this morning and can not obtain the grant.'

It was lightly said, but Clara's face was more significant, and 'What?' leaped from Laetitia's lips.

Before she could excuse herself, Clara had answered: 'My liberty.'

In another and higher tone Laetitia said, 'What?' and she looked round on her companion; she looked in the doubt that is open to conviction by a narrow aperture, and slowly and painfully yields access. Clara saw the vacancy of her expression gradually filling with woefulness.

'I have begged him to release me from my engagement, Miss Dale.'

'Sir Willoughby?'

'It is incredible to you. He refuses. You see I have no influence.'

'Miss Middleton, it is terrible!'

'To be dragged to the marriage service against one's will? Yes.'

'Oh! Miss Middleton!'

'Do you not think so?'

'That cannot be your meaning.'

'You do not suspect me of trifling? You know I would not. I am as much in earnest as a mouse in a trap.'

'No, you will not misunderstand me! Miss Middleton, such a blow to Sir Willoughby would be shocking, most cruel! He is devoted to you.'

'He was devoted to Miss Durham.'

'Not so deeply; differently.'

'Was he not very much courted at that time? He is now; not so much: he is not so young. But my reason for speaking of Miss Durham was to exclaim at the strangeness of a girl winning her freedom to plunge into wedlock. Is it comprehensible to you? She flies from one dungeon into another. These are the acts which astonish men at our conduct, and cause them to ridicule and, I dare say, despise us.'

'But, Miss Middleton, for Sir Willoughby to grant such a request, if it was made . . .'

'It was made, and by me, and will be made again. I throw it all on my unworthiness, Miss Dale. So the country will think of me, and quite justly. I would rather defend him than myself. He requires a different wife from anything I can be. That is my discovery; unhappily a late one. The blame is all mine. The world cannot be too hard on me. But I must be free if I am to be kind in my judgements even of the gentleman I have injured.'

'So noble a gentleman!' Laetitia sighed.

'I will subscribe to any eulogy of him,' said Clara, with a penetrating thought as to the possibility of a lady experienced in him like Laetitia taking him for noble. 'He has a noble air. I say it sincerely, that your appreciation of him proves his nobility.' Her feeling of opposition to Sir Willoughby pushed her to this extravagance, gravely perplexing Laetitia. 'And it is,' added Clara, as if to support what she had said, 'a withering rebuke to me; I know him less, at least have not had so long an experience of him.'

Laetitia pondered on an obscurity in these words which would have accused her thick intelligence but for a glimmer it threw on another most obscure communication. She feared it might be, strange though it seemed, jealousy, a shade of jealousy affecting Miss Middleton, as had been vaguely intimated by Sir Willoughby when they were waiting in the hall. 'A little feminine ailment, a want of comprehension of a perfect friendship'; those were his words to her: and he suggested vaguely that care must be taken in the eulogy of her friend.

She resolved to be explicit.

'I have not said that I think him beyond criticism, Miss Middleton.'

'Noble?'

'He has faults. When we have known a person for years the faults come out, but custom makes light of them; and I suppose we feel flattered by seeing what it would be difficult to be blind to! A very little flatters us! Now, do you not admire that view? It is my favourite.'

Clara gazed over rolling richness of foliage, wood and water, and a church-spire, a town and horizon hills. There sung a sky-lark.

'Not even the bird that does not fly away!' she said; meaning, she had no heart for the bird satisfied to rise and descend in this place.

Laetitia travelled to some notion, dim and immense, of Miss Middleton's fever of distaste. She shrunk from it in a kind of dread lest it might be contagious and rob her of her one ever-fresh possession of the homely picturesque; but Clara melted her by saying, 'For your sake I could love it ... in time; or some dear old English scene. Since ... since this ... this change in me, I find I cannot separate landscape from associations. Now I learn how youth goes. I have grown years older in a week. – Miss Dale, if he were to give me my freedom? if he were to cast me off? if he stood alone?'

'I should pity him.'

'Him – not me! Oh! right! I hoped you would; I knew you would.'

Laetitia's attempt to shift with Miss Middleton's shiftiness was vain; for now she seemed really listening to the language of jealousy;–jealous of the ancient Letty Dale – and immediately before the tone was quite void of it.

'Yes,' she said, 'but you make me feel myself in the dark, and when I do I have the habit of throwing myself for guidance upon such light as I have within. You shall know me, if you will, as well as I know myself. And do not think me far from the point when I say I have a feeble health. I am what the doctors call anaemic; a rather bloodless creature. The blood is life, so I have not much life. Ten years back – eleven, if I must be precise, I thought of conquering the world with a pen! The result is that I am glad of a fireside, and not sure of always having one: and that is my achievement. My days are monotonous, but if I have a dread, it is that there will be an alteration in them. My father has very little money. We subsist on what private income he has, and his pension: he was an army doctor. I may by-and-by have to live in a town for pupils. I could be grateful to any one who would save me from that. I should be astonished at his choosing to have me burden his household as well. – Have I now explained the nature of my pity? It would be the pity of common sympathy, pure lymph of pity, as nearly disembodied as can be. Last year's sheddings from the tree do not form an attractive garland. Their merit is, that they have not the ambition. I am like them. Now, Miss

Middleton, I cannot make myself more bare to you. I hope you see my sincerity.'

'I do see it,' Clara said.

With the second heaving of her heart, she cried: 'See it, and envy you that humility! proud if I could ape it! Oh, how proud if I could speak so truthfully true! – You would not have spoken so to me without some good feeling out of which friends are made. That I am sure of. To be very truthful to a person, one must have a liking. So I judge by myself. Do I presume too much?'

Kindness was on Laetitia's face.

'But now,' said Clara, swimming on the wave in her bosom, 'I tax you with the silliest suspicion ever entertained by one of your rank. Lady, you have deemed me capable of the meanest of our vices! – Hold this hand, Laetitia; my friend, will you? Something is going on in me.'

Laetitia took her hand, and saw and felt that something was going on.

Clara said, 'You are a woman.'

It was her effort to account for the something.

She swam for a brilliant instant on tears, and yielded to the overflow.

When they had fallen, she remarked upon her first long breath quite coolly: 'An encouraging picture of a rebel, is it not?'

Her companion murmured to soothe her.

'It's little, it's nothing,' said Clara, pained to keep her lips in line.

They walked forward, holding hands, deep-hearted to one another.

'I like this country better now,' the shaken girl resumed. 'I could lie down in it and ask only for sleep. I should like to think of you here. How nobly self-respecting you must be, to speak as you did! Our dreams of heroes and heroines are cold glitter beside the reality. I have been lately thinking of myself as an outcast of my sex, and to have a good woman liking me a little . . . loving? Oh, Laetitia, my friend, I should have kissed you, and not made this exhibition of myself – and if you call it hysterics, woe to you! for I bit my tongue to keep it off when I had hardly strength to bring my teeth together – if that idea of jealousy had not been in your head. You had it from him.'

'I have not alluded to it in any word that I can recollect.'

'He can imagine no other cause for my wish to be released. I have noticed, it is his instinct to reckon on women as constant by their nature. They are the needles, and he the magnet. Jealousy of you, Miss Dale! Laetitia, may I speak?'

'Say everything you please.'

'I could wish: – Do you know my baptismal name?'

'Clara.'

'At last! I could wish . . . that is, if it were your wish. Yes, I could wish that. Next to independence, my wish would be that. I risk offending you. Do not let your delicacy take arms against me. I wish him happy in the only way that he can be made happy. There is my jealousy.'

'Was it what you were going to say just now?'

'No.'

'I thought not.'

'I was going to say – and I believe the rack would not make me truthful like you, Laetitia – well, has it ever struck you: remember, I do see his merits; I speak to his faithfullest friend, and I acknowledge he is attractive, he has manly tastes and habits; but has it never struck you . . . I have no right to ask; I know that men must have faults, I do not expect them to be saints; I am not one; I wish I were.'

'Has it never struck me . . .?' Laetitia prompted her.

'That very few women are able to be straightforwardly sincere in their speech, however much they may desire to be?'

'They are differently educated. Great misfortune brings it to them.'

'I am sure your answer is correct. Have you ever known a woman who was entirely an Egoist?'

'Personally known one? We are not better than men.'

'I do not pretend that we are. I have latterly become an Egoist, thinking of no one but myself, scheming to make use of every soul I meet. But then, women are in the position of inferiors. They are hardly out of the nursery when a lasso is round their necks; and if they have beauty, no wonder they turn it to a weapon and make as many captives as they can. I do not wonder! My sense of shame at my natural weakness and the arrogance of men would urge me to make hundreds captive, if that is being a coquette. I should not have compassion for those lofty birds, the hawks. To see them with their wings clipped would amuse me. Is there any other way of punishing them?'

'Consider what you lose in punishing them.'

'I consider what they gain if we do not.'

Laetitia supposed she was listening to discursive observations upon the inequality in the relations of the sexes. A suspicion of a drift to a closer meaning had been lulled, and the colour flooded her swiftly when Clara said: 'Here is the difference I see; I see it; I am certain of it: women who are called coquettes make their conquests not of the best of men; but men who are Egoists have *good* women for their victims; women on whose devoted constancy they feed; they drink it like blood. I am sure I am not taking the merely feminine view. They punish themselves too by passing over the one suitable to them, who could really give them what they crave to have, and they go where they . . .' Clara stopped. 'I have not your power to express ideas,' she said.

'Miss Middleton, you have a dreadful power,' said Laetitia.

Clara smiled affectionately. 'I am not aware of any. Whose cottage is this?'

'My father's. Will you not come in? into the garden?'

Clara took note of ivied windows and roses in the porch. She thanked Laetitia and said: 'I will call for you in an hour.'

'Are you walking on the road alone?' said Laetitia, incredulously, with an eye to Sir Willoughby's dismay.

'I put my trust in the high-road,' Clara replied, and turned away, but turned back to Laetitia and offered her face to be kissed.

The 'dreadful power' of this young lady had fervently impressed Laetitia, and in kissing her she marvelled at her gentleness and girlishness.

Clara walked on, unconscious of her possession of power of any kind.

CHAPTER 17

✕✕✕✕

The Porcelain Vase

DURING the term of Clara's walk with Laetitia, Sir Willoughby's shrunken self-esteem, like a garment hung to the fire after exposure to tempestuous weather, recovered some of the sleekness of its velvet pile in the society of Mrs Mountstuart Jenkinson, who represented to him the world he feared and tried to keep sunny for himself by all the arts he could exercise. She expected him to be the gay Sir Willoughby, and her look being as good as an incantation summons, he produced the accustomed sprite, giving her sally for sally. Queens govern the polite. Popularity with men, serviceable as it is for winning favouritism with women, is of poor value to a sensitive gentleman, anxious even to prognostic apprehension on behalf of his pride, his comfort and his prevalence. And men are grossly purchasable; good wines have them, good cigars, a goodfellow air: they are never quite worth their salt even then; you can make head against their ill looks. But the looks of women will at one blow work on you the downright difference which is between the cock of lordly plume and the moulting. Happily they may be gained: a clever tongue will gain them, a leg. They are with you to a certainty if Nature is with you; if you are elegant and discreet: if the sun is on you, and they see you shining in it; or if they have seen you well-stationed and handsome in the sun. And once gained they are your mirrors for life, and far more constant than the glass. That tale of their caprice is absurd. Hit their imaginations once, they are your slaves, only demanding common courtier service of you. They will deny that you are ageing, they will cover you from scandal, they will refuse to see you ridiculous. Sir Willoughby's instinct, or skin, or outfloating feelers, told him of these mysteries of the influence of the sex; he had as little need to study them as a lady breathed on.

He had some need to know them in fact; and with him the need of a protection for himself called it forth; he was intuitively a conjurer in self-defence, long-sighted, wanting no directions to the herb he was to suck at when fighting a serpent. His dulness of vision into the heart of his enemy was compensated by the agile sensitiveness obscuring but rendering him miraculously active, and, without supposing his need immediate, he deemed it politic to fascinate Mrs Mountstuart and anticipate ghastly possibilities in the future by dropping a hint; not of Clara's fickleness, you may be sure; of his own, rather; or, more justly, of an altered view of Clara's character. He touched on the *rogue in porcelain.*

Set gently laughing by his relishing humour, 'I get nearer to it,' he said.

'Remember I'm in love with her,' said Mrs Mountstuart.

'That is our penalty.'

'A pleasant one for you.'

He assented. 'Is the "rogue" to be eliminated?'

'Ask when she's a mother, my dear Sir Willoughby.'

'This is how I read you: –'

'I shall accept any interpretation that is complimentary.'

'Not one will satisfy me of being sufficiently so, and so I leave it to the character to fill out the epigram.'

'Do. What hurry is there? And don't be misled by your

objection to rogue; which would be reasonable if you had not secured her.'

The door of a hollow chamber of horrible reverberation was opened within him by this remark.

He tried to say in jest, that it was not always a passionate admiration that held the rogue fast; but he muddled it in the thick of his conscious thunder, and Mrs Mountstuart smiled to see him shot from the smooth-flowing dialogue into the cataracts by one simple reminder to the lover of his luck. Necessarily, after a fall, the pitch of their conversation relaxed.

'Miss Dale is looking well,' he said.

'Fairly: she ought to marry,' said Mrs Mountstuart.

He shook his head. 'Persuade her.'

She nodded. 'Example may have some effect.'

He looked extremely abstracted. 'Yes, it is time. Where is the man you could recommend for her complement? She has now what was missing before, a ripe intelligence in addition to her happy disposition – romantic, you would say. I can't think women the worse for that.'

'A dash of it.'

'She calls it "leafage".'

'Very pretty. And have you relented about your horse Achmet?'

'I don't sell him under four hundred.'

'Poor Johnny Busshe! You forget that his wife doles him out his money. You're a hard bargainer, Sir Willoughby.'

'I mean the price to be prohibitive.'

'Very well; and "leafage" is good for hide-and-seek; especially when there is no rogue in ambush. And that's the worst I can say of Laetitia Dale. An exaggerated devotion is the scandal of our sex. They say you're the hardest man of business in the county too, and I can believe it; for at home and abroad your aim is to get the best of everybody. You see I've no leafage, I am perfectly matter-of-fact, bald.'

'Nevertheless, my dear Mrs Mountstuart, I can assure you

that conversing with you has much the same exhilarating effect on me as conversing with Miss Dale.'

'But, leafage! leafage! You hard bargainers have no compassion for devoted spinsters.'

'I tell you my sentiments absolutely.'

'And you have mine moderately expressed.'

She recollected the purpose of her morning's visit, which was to engage Dr Middleton to dine with her, and Sir Willoughby conducted her to the library-door. 'Insist,' he said.

Awaiting her reappearance, the refreshment of the talk he had sustained, not without point, assisted him to distinguish in its complete abhorrent orb the offence committed against him by his bride. And this he did through projecting it more and more away from him, so that in the outer distance it involved his personal emotions less, while observation was enabled to compass its vastness, and, as it were, perceive the whole spherical mass of the wretched girl's guilt impudently turning on its axis.

Thus to detach an injury done to us, and plant it in space, for mathematical measurement of its weight and bulk, is an art; it may also be an instinct of self-preservation; otherwise, as when mountains crumble adjacent villages are crushed, men of feeling may at any moment be killed outright by the iniquitous and the callous. But, as an art, it should be known to those who are for practising an art so beneficent, that circumstances must lend their aid. Sir Willoughby's instinct even had sat dull and crushed before his conversation with Mrs Mountstuart. She lifted him to one of his ideals of himself. Among gentlemen he was the English gentleman; with ladies his aim was the Gallican courtier of any period from Louis Treize to Louis Quinze. He could doat on those who led him to talk in that character – backed by English solidity, you understand. Roast beef stood eminent behind the soufflé and champagne. An English squire excelling his fellows at hazardous leaps in public, he was additionally a polished whisperer, a lively dia-

loguer, one for witty bouts, with something in him – capacity
for a drive and dig or two – beyond mere wit, as they soon
learned who called up his reserves, and had a bosom for pink-
ing. So much for his ideal of himself. Now, Clara not only
never evoked, never responded to it, she repelled it; there was
no flourishing of it near her. He considerately overlooked
these facts in his ordinary calculations; he was a man of
honour and she was a girl of beauty; but the accidental blooming of his ideal, with Mrs Mountstuart, on the very heels of
Clara's offence, restored him to full command of his art of detachment, and he thrust her out, quite apart from himself, to
contemplate her disgraceful revolutions.

Deeply read in the Book of Egoism that he was, he knew the
wisdom of the sentence: *An injured pride that strikes not out will
strike home.* What was he to strike with? Ten years younger,
Laetitia might have been the instrument. To think of her now
was preposterous. Beside Clara she had the hue of Winter
under the springing bough. He tossed her away, vexed to the
very soul by an ostentatious decay that shrank from comparison with the blooming creature he had to scourge in self-
defence, by some agency or other.

Mrs Mountstuart was on the step of her carriage when the
silken parasols of the young ladies were descried on a slope of
the park, where the yellow green of May-clothed beeches
flowed over the brown ground of last year's leaves.

'Who's the cavalier?' she inquired.

A gentleman escorted them.

'Vernon? No! he's pegging at Crossjay,' quoth Willoughby.

Vernon and Crossjay came out for the boy's half-hour's run
before his dinner. Crossjay spied Miss Middleton and was off
to meet her at a bound. Vernon followed him leisurely.

'The rogue has no cousin, has she?' said Mrs Mountstuart.

'It's a family of one son or one daughter for generations,'
replied Willoughby.

'And Letty Dale?'

'Cousin!' he exclaimed, as if wealth had been imputed to Miss Dale; adding: 'No male cousin.'

A railway station fly drove out of the avenue on the circle to the hall-entrance. Flitch was driver. He had no right to be there, he was doing wrong, but he was doing it under cover of an office, to support his wife and young ones, and his deprecating touches of the hat spoke of these apologies to his former master with dog-like pathos.

Sir Willoughby beckoned to him to approach.

'So you are here,' he said. 'You have luggage.'

Flitch jumped from the box and read one of the labels aloud: 'Lieutenant-Colonel H. De Craye.'

'And the colonel met the ladies? Overtook them?'

Here seemed to come dismal matter for Flitch to relate.

He began upon the abstract origin of it: he had lost his place in Sir Willoughby's establishment, and was obliged to look about for work where it was to be got, and though he knew he had no right to be where he was, he hoped to be forgiven because of the mouths he had to feed as a flyman attached to the railway station, where this gentleman, the colonel, hired him, and he believed Sir Willoughby would excuse him for driving a friend, which the colonel was, he recollected well, and the colonel recollected him, and he said, not noticing how he was rigged: 'What! Flitch! back in your old place? Am I expected?' and he told the colonel his unfortunate situation. 'Not back, colonel; no such luck for me' and Colonel De Craye was a very kind-hearted gentleman, as he always had been, and asked kindly after his family. And it might be that such poor work as he was doing now he might be deprived of, such is misfortune when it once harpoons a man; you may dive, and you may fly, but it sticks in you, once do a foolish thing. 'May I humbly beg of you, if you'll be so good, Sir Willoughby,' said Flitch, passing to evidence of the sad mishap. He opened the door of the fly, displaying fragments of broken porcelain.

'But, what, what! what's the story of this?' cried Sir Willoughby.

'What is it?' said Mrs Mountstuart, pricking up her ears.

'It was a vaws,' Flitch replied in elegy.

'A porcelain vase!' interpreted Sir Willoughby.

'China!' Mrs Mountstuart faintly shrieked.

One of the pieces was handed to her inspection.

She held it close, she held it distant. She sighed horribly.

'The man had better have hanged himself,' said she.

Flitch bestirred his misfortune-sodden features and members for a continuation of the doleful narrative.

'How did this occur?' Sir Willoughby peremptorily asked him.

Flitch appealed to his former master for testimony that he was a good and a careful driver.

Sir Willoughby thundered: 'I tell you to tell me how this occurred.'

'Not a drop, my lady! not since my supper last night, if there's any truth in me!' Flitch implored succour of Mrs Mountstuart.

'Drive straight,' she said, and braced him.

His narrative was then direct.

Near Piper's mill, where the Wicker brook crossed the Rebdon road, one of Hoppner's wagons, overloaded as usual, was forcing the horses uphill, when Flitch drove down at an easy pace, and saw himself between Hoppner's cart come to a stand and a young lady advancing: and just then the carter smacks his whip, the horses pull half mad. The young lady starts behind the cart, and up jumps the colonel, and, to save the young lady, Flitch dashed ahead and did save her, he thanked Heaven for it, and more when he came to see who the young lady was.

'She was alone?' said Sir Willoughby in tragic amazement, staring at Flitch.

'Very well, you saved her, and you upset the fly,' Mrs Mountstuart jogged him on.

'Bartlett, our old head-keeper, was a witness, my lady; I

had to drive half up the bank, and it's true – over the fly did go; and the vaws it shoots out against the twelfth mile-stone, just as though *there* was the chance for it! for nobody else was injured, and knocked against anything else, it never would have flown all to pieces, so that it took Bartlett and me ten minutes to collect every one, down to the smallest piece there was; and he said, and I can't help thinking myself, there was a Providence in it, for we all come together so as you might say we was made to do as we did.'

'So then Horace adopted the prudent course of walking on with the ladies instead of trusting his limbs again to this capsizing fly,' Sir Willoughby said to Mrs Mountstuart; and she rejoined: 'Lucky that no one was hurt.'

Both of them eyed the nose of poor Flitch, and simultaneously they delivered a verdict in 'Humph!'

Mrs Mountstuart handed the wretch a half-crown from her purse. Sir Willoughby directed the footman in attendance to unload the fly and gather up the fragments of porcelain carefully, bidding Flitch be quick in his departing.

'The colonel's wedding-present! I shall call to-morrow.' Mrs Mountstuart waved her adieu.

'Come every day! – Yes, I suppose we may guess the destination of the vase.' He bowed her off, and she cried:

'Well, now, the gift can be shared, if you're either of you for a division.' In the crash of the carriage-wheels he heard, 'At any rate there was a rogue in *that* porcelain.'

These are the slaps we get from a heedless world.

As for the vase, it was Horace De Craye's loss. Wedding-present he would have to produce, and decidedly not in chips. It had the look of a costly vase, but that was no question for the moment: – What was meant by Clara being seen walking on the high-road alone? – What snare, traceable ad inferas, had ever induced Willoughby Patterne to make her the repository and fortress of his honour?

CHAPTER 18

✖✖✖✖

Colonel De Craye

CLARA came along chatting and laughing with Colonel De Craye, young Crossjay's hand under one of her arms, and her parasol flashing; a dazzling offender; as if she wished to compel the spectator to recognize the dainty rogue in porcelain; really insufferably fair: perfect in height and grace of movement; exquisitely tressed; red-lipped, the colour striking out to a distance from her ivory skin; a sight to set the woodland dancing, and turn the heads of the town; though beautiful, a jury of art critics might pronounce her not to be. Irregular features are condemned in beauty. Beautiful figure, they could say. A description of her figure and her walking would have won her any praises: and she wore a dress cunning to embrace the shape and flutter loose about it, in the spirit of a Summer's day. Calypso-clad, Dr Middleton would have called her. See the silver birch in a breeze: here it swells, there it scatters, and it is puffed to a round and it streams like a pennon, and now gives the glimpse and shine of the white stem's line within, now hurries over it, denying that it was visible, with a chatter along the sweeping folds, while still the white peeps through. She had the wonderful art of dressing to suit the season and the sky. To-day the art was ravishingly companionable with her sweet-lighted face: too sweet, too vividly meaningful for pretty, if not of the strict severity for beautiful. Millinery would tell us that she wore a fichu of thin white muslin crossed in front on a dress of the same light stuff, trimmed with deep rose. She carried a grey-silk parasol, traced at the borders with green creepers, and across the arm devoted to Crossjay a length of trailing ivy, and in that hand a bunch of the first long grasses. These hues of red rose and pale green ruffled and pouted in the billowy white of the dress ballooning and valleying softly, like a yacht before the sail bends low; but she walked not like one blown against; resembling rather the day of the South-west driving the clouds, gallantly firm in commotion; interfusing colour and varying in her features from laugh to smile and look of settled pleasure, like the heavens above the breeze.

Sir Willoughby, as he frequently had occasion to protest to Clara, was no poet: he was a more than commonly candid English gentleman in his avowed dislike of the poet's nonsense, verbiage, verse; not one of those latterly terrorized by the noise made about the fellow into silent contempt; a sentiment that may sleep, and has not to be defended. He loathed the fellow, fought the fellow. But he was one with the poet upon that prevailing theme of verse, the charms of women. He was, to his ill-luck, intensely susceptible, and where he led men after him to admire, his admiration became a fury. He could see at a glance that Horace De Craye admired Miss Middleton. Horace was a man of taste, could hardly, could not, do other than admire; but how curious that in the setting forth of Clara and Miss Dale, to his own contemplation and comparison of them, Sir Willoughby had given but a nodding approbation of his bride's appearance! He had not attached weight to it recently.

Her conduct, and foremost, if not chiefly, her having been discovered, positively met by his friend Horace, walking on the high-road without companion or attendant, increased a sense of pain so very unusual with him that he had cause to be indignant. Coming on this condition, his admiration of the girl who wounded him was as bitter a thing as a man could feel. Resentment, fed from the main springs of his nature, turned it to wormwood, and not a whit the less was it admiration when he resolved to chastise her with a formal indication of his disdain. Her present gaiety sounded to him like laughter heard in the shadow of the pulpit.

'You have escaped!' he said to her, while shaking the hand

of his friend Horace and cordially welcoming him. 'My dear fellow! and, by the way, you had a squeak for it, I hear from Flitch.'

'I, Willoughby? not a bit,' said the colonel; 'we get into a fly to get out of it; and Flitch helped me out as well as in, good fellow; just dusting my coat as he did it. The only bit of bad management was that Miss Middleton had to step aside a trifle hurriedly.'

'You knew Miss Middleton at once?'

'Flitch did me the favour to introduce me. He first precipitated me at Miss Middleton's feet, and then he introduced me, in old oriental fashion, to my sovereign.'

Sir Willoughby's countenance was enough for his friend Horace. Quarter-wheeling to Clara, he said: ' 'Tis the place I'm to occupy for life, Miss Middleton, though one is not always fortunate to have a bright excuse for taking it at the commencement.'

Clara said: 'Happily you were not hurt, Colonel De Craye.'

'I was in the hands of the Loves. Not the Graces, I'm afraid; I've an image of myself. Dear no! My dear Willoughby, you never made such a headlong declaration as that. It would have looked like a magnificent impulse, if the posture had only been choicer. And Miss Middleton didn't laugh. At least I saw nothing but pity.'

'You did not write,' said Willoughby.

'Because it was a toss-up of a run to Ireland or here, and I came here not to go there; and, by the way, fetched a jug with me to offer up to the gods of ill-luck; and they accepted the propitiation.'

'Wasn't it packed in a box?'

'No, it was wrapped in paper, to show its elegant form. I caught sight of it in the shop yesterday and carried it off this morning, and presented it to Miss Middleton at noon, without any form at all.'

Willoughby knew his friend Horace's mood when the Irish tongue in him threatened to wag.

'You see what may happen,' he said to Clara.

'As far as I am in fault I regret it,' she answered.

'Flitch says the accident occurred through his driving up the bank to save you from the wheels.'

'Flitch may go and whisper that down the neck of his empty whisky-flask,' said Horace De Craye. 'And then let him cork it.'

'The consequence is that we have a porcelain vase broken. You should not walk on the road alone, Clara. You ought to have a companion, always. It is the rule here.'

'I had left Miss Dale at the cottage.'

'You ought to have had the dogs.'

'Would they have been any protection to the vase?'

Horace De Craye crowed cordially.

'I'm afraid not, Miss Middleton. One must go to the witches for protection to vases; and they're all in the air now, having their own way with us, which accounts for the confusion in politics and society, and the rise in the price of broomsticks, to prove it true, as they tell us, that every nook and corner wants a mighty sweeping. Miss Dale looks beaming,' said De Craye, wishing to divert Willoughby from his anger with sense as well as nonsense.

'You have not been visiting Ireland recently?' said Sir Willoughby.

'No, nor making acquaintance with an actor in an Irish part in a drama cast in the Green Island. 'Tis Flitch, my dear Willoughby, has been and stirred the native in me, and we'll present him to you for the like good office when we hear after a number of years that you've not wrinkled your forehead once at your liege lady. Take the poor old dog back home, will you? He's crazed to be at the Hall. I say, Willoughby, it would be a good bit of work to take him back. Think of it; you'll do the popular thing, I'm sure. I've a superstition that Flitch ought to drive you from the church-door. If I were in luck, I'd have him drive me.'

'The man's a drunkard, Horace.'

'He fuddles his poor nose. 'Tis merely unction to the exile. Sober struggles below. He drinks to rock his heart, because he has one. Now let me intercede for poor Flitch.'

'Not a word of him. He threw up his place.'

'To try his fortune in the world, as the best of us do, though livery runs after us to tell us there's no being an independent gentleman, and comes a cold day we haul on the metal-button coat again, with a good ha! of satisfaction. You'll do the popular thing. Miss Middleton joins in the pleading.'

'No pleading!'

'When I've vowed upon my eloquence. Willoughby, I'd bring you to pardon the poor dog?'

'Not a word of him!'

'Just one!'

Sir Willoughby battled with himself to repress a state of temper that put him to marked disadvantage beside his friend Horace in high spirits. Ordinarily he enjoyed these fits of Irish of him, which were Horace's fun and play, at times involuntary, and then they indicated a recklessness that might embrace mischief. De Craye, as Willoughby had often reminded him, was properly Norman. The blood of two or three Irish mothers in his line, however, was enough to dance him, and if his fine profile spoke of the stiffer race, his eyes and the quick run of the lip in the cheek, and a number of his qualities, were evidence of the maternal legacy.

'My word has been said about the man,' Willoughby replied.

'But I've wagered on your heart against your word, and can't afford to lose; and there's a double reason for revoking for you!'

'I don't see either of them. Here are the ladies.'

'You'll think of the poor beast, Willoughby.'

'I hope for better occupation.'

'If he drives a wheelbarrow at the Hall he'll be happier than on board a chariot at large. He's broken-hearted.'

'He's too much in the way of breakages, my dear Horace.'

'Oh, the vase! the bit of porcelain!' sung De Craye. 'Well, we'll talk him over by and by.'

'If it pleases you; but my rules are never amended.'

'Inalterable, are they? – like those of an ancient people, who might as well have worn a jacket of lead for the comfort they had of their boast. The beauty of laws for human creatures is their adaptability to new stitchings.'

Colonel De Craye walked at the heels of his leader to make his bow to the ladies Eleanor and Isabel.

Sir Willoughby had guessed the person who inspired his friend Horace to plead so pertinaciously and inopportunely for the man Flitch: and it had not improved his temper or the pose of his rejoinders; he had winced under the contrast of his friend Horace's easy, laughing, sparkling, musical air and manner with his own stiffness; and he had seen Clara's face, too, scanning the contrast – he was fatally driven to exaggerate his discontentment, which did not restore him to serenity. He would have learned more from what his abrupt swing round of the shoulder precluded his beholding. There was an interchange between Colonel De Craye and Miss Middleton; spontaneous on both sides. His was a look that said: 'You were right'; hers: 'I knew it'. Her look was calmer, and after the first instant clouded as by wearifulness of sameness; his was brilliant, astonished, speculative, and admiring, pitiful: a look that poised over a revelation, called up the hosts of wonder to question strange fact.

It had passed unseen by Sir Willoughby. The observer was the one who could also supply the key of the secret. Miss Dale had found Colonel De Craye in company with Miss Middleton at her gateway. They were laughing and talking together like friends of old standing, De Craye as Irish as he could be: and the Irish tongue and gentlemanly manner are an irresistible challenge to the opening steps of familiarity when accident has broken the ice. Flitch was their theme; and: 'Oh, but if we go up to Willoughby hand in hand; and bob a courtesy to 'm and beg his pardon for Mister Flitch, won't he melt to such a pair of suppliants? of course he will!' Miss Middleton said he would not. Colonel De Craye wagered he would; he knew Willoughby best. Miss Middleton looked simply grave; a way of asserting the contrary opinion that tells of rueful experience. 'We'll see,' said the colonel. They chatted like a couple unexpectedly discovering in one another a common dialect among strangers. Can there be an end to it when those two meet? They prattle, they fill the minutes, as though they were violently to be torn asunder at a coming signal, and must have it out while they can; it is a meeting of mountain brooks; not a colloquy, but a chasing, impossible to say which flies, which follows, or what the topic, so interlinguistic are they and rapidly counterchanging. After their conversation of an hour before, Laetitia watched Miss Middleton in surprise at her lightness of mind. Clara bathed in mirth. A boy in a summer stream shows not heartier refreshment of his whole being. Laetitia could now understand Vernon's idea of her wit. And it seemed that she also had Irish blood. Speaking of Ireland, Miss Middleton said she had cousins there, her only relatives.

'The laugh told me that,' said Colonel De Craye.

Laetitia and Vernon paced up and down the lawn. Colonel De Craye was talking with English sedateness to the ladies Eleanor and Isabel. Clara and young Crossjay strayed.

'If I might advise, I would say, do not leave the Hall immediately, not yet,' Laetitia said to Vernon.

'You know, then?'

'I cannot understand why it was that I was taken into her confidence.'

'I counselled it.'

'But it was done without an object that I can see.'

'The speaking did her good.'

'But how capricious! how changeful!'

'Better now than later.'

'Surely she has only to ask to be released? – to ask earnestly: if it is her wish.'

'You are mistaken.'

'Why does she not make a confidant of her father?'

'That she will have to do. She wished to spare him.'

'He cannot be spared if she is to break the engagement.'

'She thought of sparing him the annoyance. Now there's to be a tussle, he must share in it.'

'Or she thought he might not side with her?'

'She has not a single instinct of cunning. You judge her harshly.'

'She moved me on the walk out. Coming home I felt differently.'

Vernon glanced at Colonel De Craye.

'She wants *good* guidance,' continued Laetitia.

'She has not an idea of treachery.'

'You think so? It may be true. But she seems one born devoid of patience, easily made reckless. There is a wildness . . . I judge by her way of speaking; that at least appeared sincere. She does not practise concealment. He will naturally find it almost incredible. The change in her, so sudden, so wayward, is unintelligible to me. To me it is the conduct of a creature untamed. He may hold her to her word and be justified.'

'Let him look out if he does!'

'Is not that harsher than anything I have said of her?'

'I'm not appointed to praise her. I fancy I read the case; and it's a case of opposition of temperaments. We never can tell the person quite suited to us; it strikes us in a flash.'

'That they are *not* suited to us? Oh, no; that comes by degrees.'

'Yes, but the accumulation of evidence, or sentience, if you like, is combustible; we don't command the spark; it may be late in falling. And you argue in her favour. Consider her as a generous and impulsive girl, outwearied at last.'

'By what?'

'By anything; by his loftiness, if you like. He flies too high for her, we will say.'

'Sir Willoughby an eagle?'

'She may be tired of his eyrie.'

The sound of the word in Vernon's mouth smote on a consciousness she had of his full grasp of Sir Willoughby and her own timid knowledge, though he was not a man who played on words.

If he had eased his heart in stressing the first syllable, it was only temporary relief. He was heavy-browed enough.

'But I cannot conceive what she expects me to do by confiding her sense of her position to me,' said Laetitia.

'We none of us know what will be done. We hang on Willoughby, who hangs on whatever it is that supports him: and there we are in a swarm.'

'You see the wisdom of staying, Mr Whitford.'

'It must be over in a day or two. Yes, I stay.'

'She inclines to obey you.'

'I should be sorry to stake my authority on her obedience. We must decide something about Crossjay, and get the money for his crammer, if it is to be got. If not, I may get a man to trust me. I mean to drag the boy away. Willoughby has been at him with the tune of gentleman, and has laid hold of him by one ear. When I say "her obedience", she is not in a situation, nor in a condition to be led blindly by anybody. She must rely on herself, do everything herself. It's a knot that won't bear touching by any hand save hers.'

'I fear –' said Laetitia.

'Have no such fear.'

'If it should come to his positively refusing.'

'He faces the consequences.'

'You do not think of her.'

Vernon looked at his companion.

CHAPTER 19

✕✕✕✕

Colonel De Craye and Clara Middleton

MISS MIDDLETON finished her stroll with Crossjay by winding her trailer of ivy in a wreath round his hat and sticking her
bunch of grasses in the wreath. She then commanded him to
sit on the ground beside a big rhododendron, there to await
her return. Crossjay had informed her of a design he entertained to be off with a horde of boys nesting in high trees, and
marking spots where wasps and hornets were to be attacked in
Autumn: she thought it a dangerous business, and as the boy's
dinnerbell had very little restraint over him when he was in
the flush of a scheme of this description, she wished to make
tolerably sure of him through the charm she not unreadily believed she could fling on lads of his age. 'Promise me you will
not move from here until I come back, and when I come I will
give you a kiss.' Crossjay promised. She left him and forgot
him.

Seeing by her watch fifteen minutes to the ringing of the
bell, a sudden resolve that she would speak to her father without another minute's delay had prompted her like a super-
stitious impulse to abandon her aimless course and be direct.
She knew what was good for her; she knew it now more
clearly than in the morning. To be taken away instantly! was
her cry. There could be no further doubt. Had there been any
before? But she would not in the morning have suspected herself of a capacity for evil, and of a pressing need to be saved
from herself. She was not pure of nature: it may be that we
breed saintly souls which are: she was pure of will: fire rather
than ice. And in beginning to see the elements she was made of
she did not shuffle them to a heap with her sweet looks to
front her. She put to her account some strength, much weak-

ness; she almost dared to gaze unblinking at a perilous evil tendency. The glimpse of it drove her to her father.

'He must take me away at once; to-morrow!'

She wished to spare her father. So unsparing of herself was she, that, in her hesitation to speak to him of her change of feeling for Sir Willoughby, she would not suffer it to be attributed in her own mind to a daughter's anxious consideration about her father's loneliness; an idea she had indulged formerly. Acknowledging that it was imperative she should speak, she understood that she had refrained, even to the inflicting upon herself of such humiliation as to run dilating on her woes to others, because of the silliest of human desires to preserve her reputation for consistency. She had heard women abused for shallowness and flightiness: she had heard her father denounce them as veering weather-vanes, and his oft-repeated quid femina possit: [14] for her sex's sake, and also to appear an exception to her sex, this reasoning creature desired to be thought consistent.

Just on the instant of her addressing him, saying: 'Father,' a note of seriousness in his ear, it struck her that the occasion for saying all had not yet arrived, and she quickly interposed: 'Papa'; and helped him to look lighter. The petition to be taken away was uttered.

'To London?' said Dr Middleton. 'I don't know who'll take us in.'

'To France, papa?'

'That means hotel life.'

'Only for two or three weeks.'

'Weeks! I am under an engagement to dine with Mrs Mountstuart Jenkinson five days hence – that is, on Thursday.'

'Could we not find an excuse?'

'Break an engagement? No, my dear, not even to escape drinking a widow's wine.'

'Does a word bind us?'

'Why, what else should?'

'I think I am not very well.'

'We'll call in that man we met at dinner here: Corney: a capital doctor; an old-fashioned anecdotal doctor. How is it you are not well, my love? You look well. I cannot conceive your not being well.'

'It is only that I want change of air, papa.'

'There we are – a change! semper eadem! Women will be wanting a change of air in Paradise; a change of angels too I might surmise. A change from quarters like these to a French hotel would be a descent! – "this the seat, this mournful gloom for that celestial light?" [15] I am perfectly at home in the library here. That excellent fellow Whitford and I have real days; and I like him for showing fight to his elder and better.'

'He is going to leave.'

'I know nothing of it, and I shall append no credit to the tale until I do know. He is headstrong, but he answers to a rap.'

Clara's bosom heaved. The speechless insurrection threatened her eyes.

A South-west shower lashed the window-panes and suggested to Dr Middleton shuddering visions of the Channel passage on board a steamer.

'Corney shall see you: he is a sparkling draught in person; probably illiterate, if I may judge from one interruption of my discourse when he sat opposite me, but lettered enough to respect Learning and write out his prescription: I do not ask more of men or of physicians.' Dr Middleton said this rising, glancing at the clock and at the back of his hands. 'Quod autem secundum litteras difficillimum esse artificium? But what after letters is the more difficult practice? Ego puto medicum. The medicus next to the scholar: though I have not to my recollection required him next me, nor ever expected child of mine to be crying for that milk. Daughter she is – of the unexplained sex: we will send a messenger for Corney. Change, my dear, you will speedily have, to satisfy the most craving of women, if Willoughby, as I suppose, is in the neoteric fashion of spending a honeymoon on a railway: apt image, exposition and perpetuation of the state of mania conducting to the institution! In my time we lay by to brood on happiness; we had no thought of chasing it over a continent, mistaking hurly-burly clothed in dust for the divinity we sought. A smaller generation sacrifices to excitement. Dust and hurly-burly must perforce be the issue. And that is your modern world. Now, my dear, let us go and wash our hands. Midday-bells expect immediate attention. They know of no anteroom of assembly.'

Clara stood gathered up, despairing at opportunity lost. He had noticed her contracted shape and her eyes, and had talked magisterially to smother and overbear the something disagreeable prefigured in her appearance.

'You do not despise your girl, father?'

'I do not; I could not; I love her; I love my girl. But you need not sing to me like a gnat to propound that question, my dear.'

'Then, father, tell Willoughby to-day we have to leave to-morrow. You shall return in time for Mrs Mountstuart's dinner. Friends will take us in, the Darletons, the Erpinghams. We can go to Oxford, where you are sure of welcome. A little will recover me. Do not mention doctors. But you see I am nervous. I am quite ashamed of it; I am well enough to laugh at it, only I cannot overcome it; and I feel that a day or two will restore me. Say you will. Say it in First-Lesson-Book language; anything above a primer splits my foolish head to-day.'

Dr Middleton shrugged, spreading out his arms.

'The office of embassador from you to Willoughby, Clara? You decree me to the part of ball between two bats. The Play being assured, the prologue is a bladder of wind. I seem to be instructed in one of the mysteries of erotic esotery, yet on my word I am no wiser. If Willoughby is to hear anything from you, he will hear it from your lips.'

'Yes, father, yes. We have differences. I am not fit for contests at present; my head is giddy. I wish to avoid an illness. He and I . . . I accuse myself.'

'There is the bell!' ejaculated Dr Middleton. 'I'll debate on it with Willoughby.'

'This afternoon?'

'Somewhen, before the dinner-bell. I cannot tie myself to the minute-hand of the clock, my dear child. And let me direct you, for the next occasion when you shall bring the vowels I and A, in verbally detached letters, into collision, that you do not fill the hiatus with so pronounced a Y. It is the vulgarization of our tongue of which I y-accuse you. I do not like my girl to be guilty of it.'

He smiled to moderate the severity of the correction, and kissed her forehead.

She declared her inability to sit and eat; she went to her room, after begging him very earnestly to send her the assurance that he had spoken. She had not shed a tear, and she rejoiced in her self-control; it whispered to her of true courage when she had given herself such evidence of the reverse.

Shower and sunshine alternated through the half-hours of the afternoon, like a procession of dark and fair holding hands and passing. The shadow came, and she was chill; the light yellow in moisture, and she buried her face not to be caught up by cheerfulness. Believing that her head ached, she afflicted herself with all the heavy symptoms, and oppressed her mind so thoroughly that its occupation was to speculate on Laetitia Dale's modest enthusiasm for rural pleasures, for this place especially, with its rich foliage and peeps of scenic peace. The prospect of an escape from it inspired thoughts of a loveable round of life where the sun was not a naked ball of fire, but a friend clothed in woodland; where park and meadow swept to well-known features East and West; and distantly circling hills, and the hearts of poor cottagers too – sympathy with whom assured her of goodness – were familiar, homely to the dweller in the place, morning and night. And she had the love of wild flowers, the watchful happiness in the seasons; poets thrilled her, books absorbed. She dwelt strongly on that sincerity of feeling; it gave her root in our earth; she needed it as she pressed a hand on her eyeballs, conscious of acting the invalid, though the reasons she had for languishing under headache were so convincing that her brain refused to disbelieve in it and went some way to produce positive throbs. Otherwise she had no excuse for shutting herself in her room. Vernon Whitford would be sceptical. Headache or none, Colonel De Craye must be thinking strangely of her; she had not shown him any sign of illness. His laughter and his talk sung about her and dispersed the fiction; he was the very seawind for bracing unstrung nerves. Her ideas reverted to Sir Willoughby, and at once they had no more cohesion than the foam on a torrent-water.

But soon she was undergoing a variation of sentiment. Her maid Barclay brought her this pencilled line from her father:

'Factum est; laetus est; amantium irae, etc.' [16]

That it was done, that Willoughby had put on an air of glad acquiescence, and that her father assumed the existence of a lovers' quarrel, was wonderful to her at first sight, simple the succeeding minute. Willoughby indeed must be tired of her, glad of her going. He would know that it was not to return. She was grateful to him for perhaps hinting at the amantium irae, though she rejected the folly of the verse. And she gazed over dear homely country through her windows now. Happy the lady of the place, if happy she can be in her choice! Clara Middleton envied her the double-blossom wild cherry-tree, nothing else. One sprig of it, if it had not faded and gone to dust-colour like crusty Alpine snow in the lower hollows, and then she could depart, bearing away a memory of the best here! Her fiction of the headache pained her no longer. She changed her muslin dress for silk; she was contented with the first bonnet Barclay presented. Amicable toward every one in the house, Willoughby included, she threw up her window, breathed, blessed mankind; and she thought: 'If Willoughby would open his heart to nature, he would be relieved of his wretched opinion of the world.' Nature was then sparkling

refreshed in the last drops of a sweeping rain-curtain, favourably disposed for a background to her joyful optimism. A little
nibble of hunger within, real hunger, unknown to her of late,
added to this healthy view, without precipitating her to appease it; she was more inclined to foster it, for the sake of the
sinewy activity of mind and limb it gave her; and in the style
of young ladies very light of heart, she went downstairs like a
cascade, and like the meteor observed in its vanishing trace she
alighted close to Colonel De Craye and entered one of the
rooms off the hall.

He cocked an eye at the half-shut door.

Now you have only to be reminded that it is the habit of
the sportive gentleman of easy life, bewildered as he would
otherwise be by the tricks, twists, and windings of the
hunted sex, to parcel out fair women into classes; and some
are flyers and some are runners; these birds are wild on
the wing, those exposed their bosoms to the shot. For him
there is no individual woman. He grants her a characteristic
only to enroll her in a class. He is our immortal dunce at
learning to distinguish her as a personal variety, of a separate
growth.

Colonel De Craye's cock of the eye at the door said that he
had seen a rageing coquette go behind it. He had his excuse for
forming the judgement. She had spoken strangely of the fall of
his wedding-present, strangely of Willoughby; or there was a
sound of strangeness in an allusion to her appointed husband:
and she had treated Willoughby strangely when they met.
Above all, her word about Flitch was curious. And then that
look of hers! And subsequently she transferred her polite attentions to Willoughby's friend. After a charming colloquy,
the sweetest give and take rattle he had ever enjoyed with a
girl, she developed headache to avoid him; and next she developed blindness, for the same purpose.

He was feeling hurt, but considered it preferable to feel
challenged.

Miss Middleton came out of another door. She had seen him

when she had passed him and when it was too late to convey her recognition; and now she addressed him with an air of having bowed as she went by.

'No one?' she said. 'Am I alone in the house?'

'There is a figure naught,' said he, 'but it's as good as annihilated, and no figure at all, if you put yourself on the wrong side of it, and wish to be alone in the house.'

'Where is Willoughby?'

'Away on business.'

'Riding?'

'Achmet is the horse, and pray don't let him be sold, Miss Middleton. I am deputed to attend on you.'

'I should like a stroll.'

'Are you perfectly restored?'

'Perfectly.'

'Strong?'

'I was never better.'

'It was the answer of the ghost of the wicked old man's wife when she came to persuade him he had one chance remaining. Then, says he, I'll believe in heaven if ye'll stop that bottle, and hurls it; and the bottle broke and he committed suicide, not without suspicion of her laying a trap for him. These showers curling away and leaving sweet scents are divine, Miss Middleton. I have the privilege of the Christian name on the nuptial-day. This park of Willoughby's is one of the best things in England. There's a glimpse over the lake that smokes of a corner of Killarney; tempts the eye to dream, I mean.' De Craye wound his finger spirally upward, like a smoke-wreath. 'Are you for Irish scenery?'

'Irish, English, Scottish.'

'All's one so long as it's beautiful: yes, you speak for me. Cosmopolitanism of races is a different affair. I beg leave to doubt the true union of some; Irish and Saxon, for example, let Cupid be master of the ceremonies and the dwelling-place of the happy couple at the mouth of a Cornucopia. Yet I have seen a flower of Erin worn by a Saxon gentleman proudly;

and the Hibernian courting a Rowena! So we'll undo what I said, and consider it cancelled.'

'Are you of the rebel party, Colonel De Craye?'

'I am Protestant and Conservative, Miss Middleton.'

'I have not a head for politics.'

'The political heads I have seen would tempt me to that opinion.'

'Did Willoughby say when he would be back?'

'He named no particular time. Doctor Middleton and Mr Whitford are in the library upon a battle of the books.'

'Happy battle!'

'You are accustomed to scholars. They are rather intolerant of us poor fellows.'

'Of ignorance perhaps; not of persons.'

'Your father educated you himself, I presume?'

'He gave me as much Latin as I could take. The fault is mine that it is little.'

'Greek?'

'A little Greek.'

'Ah! And you carry it like a feather.'

'Because it is so light.'

'Miss Middleton, I could sit down to be instructed, old as I am. When women beat us, I verily believe we are the most beaten dogs in existence. You like the theatre?'

'Ours?'

'Acting, then.'

'Good acting, of course.'

'May I venture to say you would act admirably?'

'The venture is bold, for I have never tried.'

'Let me see; there is Miss Dale and Mr Whitford; you and I; sufficient for a two-act piece. THE IRISHMAN IN SPAIN would do.' He bent to touch the grass as she stepped on it. 'The lawn is wet.'

She signified that she had no dread of wet, and said: 'English women afraid of the weather might as well be shut up.'

De Craye proceeded: 'Patrick O'Neill passes over from

Hibernia to Iberia, a disinherited son of a father in the claws of the lawyers, with a letter of introduction to Don Beltran d'Arragon, a Grandee of the First Class, who has a daughter Doña Seraphina (Miss Middleton), the proudest beauty of her day, in the custody of a dueña (Miss Dale), and plighted to Don Fernan, of the Guzman family (Mr Whitford). There you have our dramatis personae.'

'You are Patrick?'

'Patrick himself. And I lose my letter, and I stand on the Prado of Madrid with the last portrait of Britannia in the palm of my hand, and crying in the purest brogue of my native land: "It's all through dropping a letter I'm here in Iberia instead of Hibernia, worse luck to the spelling!"'

'But Patrick will be sure to aspirate the initial letter of Hibernia.'

'That is clever criticism, upon my word, Miss Middleton! So he would. And there we have two letters dropped. But he'd do it in a groan, so that it wouldn't count for more than a ghost of one; and everything goes on the stage, since it's only the laugh we want on the brink of the action. Besides you are to suppose the performance before a London audience, who have a native opposite to the aspirate and wouldn't bear to hear him spoil a joke, as if he were a lord or a constable. It's an instinct of the English democracy. So with my bit of coin turning over and over in an undecided way, whether it shall commit suicide to supply me a supper, I behold a pair of Spanish eyes like violet lightning in the black heavens of that favoured clime. Won't you have violet?'

'Violet forbids my impersonation.'

'But the lustre on black is dark violet blue.'

'You remind me that I have no pretension to black.'

Colonel De Craye permitted himself to take a flitting gaze at Miss Middleton's eyes. 'Chestnut,' he said. 'Well, and Spain is the land of chestnuts.'

'Then it follows that I am a daughter of Spain.'

'Clearly.'

'Logically?'

'By positive deduction.'

'And do I behold Patrick?'

'As one looks upon a beast of burden.'

'Oh!'

Miss Middleton's exclamation was louder than the matter of the dialogue seemed to require. She caught her hands up.

In the line of the outer extremity of the rhododendron, screened from the house windows, young Crossjay lay at his length, with his head resting on a doubled arm, and his ivy-wreathed hat on his cheek, just where she had left him, commanding him to stay. Half-way toward him up the lawn, she saw the poor boy, and the spur of that pitiful sight set her gliding swiftly. Colonel De Craye followed, pulling an end of his moustache.

Crossjay jumped to his feet.

'My dear, dear Crossjay!' she addressed him and reproached him. 'And how hungry you must be! And you must be drenched! This is really too bad.'

'You told me to wait here,' said Crossjay, in shy self-defence.

'I did, and you should not have done it, foolish boy! I told him to wait for me here before luncheon, Colonel De Craye, and the foolish, foolish boy! – he has had nothing to eat, and he must have been wet through two or three times: – because I did not come to him!'

'Quite right. And the lava might overflow him and take the mould of him, like the sentinel at Pompeii, if he's of the true stuff.'

'He may have caught cold, he may have a fever.'

'He was under your orders to stay.'

'I know, and I cannot forgive myself. Run in, Crossjay, and change your clothes. Oh, run, run to Mrs Montague, and get her to give you a warm bath, and tell her from me to prepare some dinner for you. And change every garment you have. This is unpardonable of me. I said – "not for politics!" – I begin to think I have not a head for anything. But could it be imagined that Crossjay would not move for the dinner-bell! through all that rain! I forgot you, Crossjay. I am so sorry; so sorry! You shall make me pay any forfeit you like. Remember, I am deep, deep in your debt. And now let me see you run fast. You shall come in to dessert this evening.'

Crossjay did not run. He touched her hand.

'You said something?'

'What did I say, Crossjay?'

'You promised.'

'What did I promise?'

'Something.'

'Name it, my dear boy.'

He mumbled, '. . . kiss me.'

Clara plumped down on him, enveloped him and kissed him.

The affectionately remorseful impulse was too quick for a conventional note of admonition to arrest her from paying that portion of her debt. When she had sped him off to Mrs Montague, she was in a blush.

'Dear, dear Crossjay!' she said, sighing.

'Yes, he's a good lad,' remarked the colonel. 'The fellow may well be a faithful soldier and stick to his post, if he receives promise of such a solde. He is a great favourite with you.'

'He is. You will do him a service by persuading Willoughby to send him to one of those men who get boys through their naval examination. And, Colonel De Craye, will you be kind enough to ask at the dinner-table that Crossjay may come in to dessert?'

'Certainly,' said he, wondering.

'And will you look after him while you are here? See that no one spoils him. If you could get him away before you leave, it would be much to his advantage. He is born for the navy and should be preparing to enter it now.'

'Certainly, certainly,' said De Craye, wondering more.

'I thank you in advance.'

'Shall I not be usurping ...?'

'No, we leave to-morrow.'

'For a day?'

'For longer.'

'Two?'

'It will be longer.'

'A week? I shall not see you again?'

'I fear not.'

Colonel De Craye controlled his astonishment; he smother-ed a sensation of veritable pain, and amiably said: 'I feel a blow, but I am sure you would not willingly strike. We are all involved in the regrets.'

Miss Middleton spoke of having to see Mrs Montague, the housekeeper, with reference to the bath for Crossjay, and stepped off the grass. He bowed, watched her a moment, and for parallel reasons, running close enough to hit one mark, he commiserated his friend Willoughby. The winning or the losing of that young lady struck him as equally lamentable for Willoughby.

CHAPTER 20

✕✕✕✕

An Aged and a Great Wine

THE leisurely promenade up and down the lawn with ladies and deferential gentlemen, in anticipation of the dinner-bell, was Dr Middleton's evening pleasure. He walked as one who had formerly danced (in Apollo's time and the young god Cupid's), elastic on the muscles of the calf and foot, bearing his broad iron-grey head in grand elevation. The hard labour of the day approved the cooling exercise and the crowning refreshments of French cookery and wines of known vintages. He was happy at that hour in dispensing wisdom or nugae[17] to his hearers, like the Western sun whose habit it is, when he is fairly treated, to break out in quiet splendours, which by no means exhaust his treasury. Blessed indeed above his fellows, by the height of the bow-winged bird in a fair weather sunset sky above the pecking sparrow, is he that ever in the recurrent evening of his day sees the best of it ahead and soon to come. He has the rich reward of a youth and manhood of virtuous living. Dr Middleton misdoubted the future as well as the past of the man who did not, in becoming gravity, exult to dine. That man he deemed unfit for this world and the next.

An example of the good fruit of temperance, he had a comfortable pride in his digestion, and his political sentiments were attuned by his veneration of the Powers rewarding virtue. We must have a stable world where this is to be done.

The Rev. Doctor was a fine old picture; a specimen of art peculiarly English; combining in himself piety and epicurism, learning and gentlemanliness, with good room for each and a seat at one another's table: for the rest, a strong man, an athlete in his youth, a keen reader of facts and no reader of persons, genial, a giant at a task, a steady worker besides, but easily discomposed. He loved his daughter and he feared her. However much he liked her character, the dread of her sex and age was constantly present to warn him that he was not tied to perfect sanity while the damsel Clara remained unmarried. Her mother had been an amiable woman, of the poetical temperament nevertheless, too enthusiastic, imaginative, impulsive, for the repose of a sober scholar; an admirable woman, still, as you see, a woman, a fire-work. The girl resembled her. Why should she wish to run away from Patterne Hall for a single hour? Simply because she was of the sex born mutable and explosive. A husband was her proper custodian, justly relieving a father. With demagogues abroad and daughters at home, philosophy is needed for us to keep erect. Let the girl be

Cicero's Tullia: well, she dies! The choicest of them will furnish us examples of a strange perversity.

Miss Dale was beside Dr Middleton. Clara came to them and took the other side.

'I was telling Miss Dale that the signal for your subjection is my enfranchisement,' he said to her, sighing and smiling. 'We know the date. The date of an event to come certifies to it as a fact to be counted on.'

'Are you anxious to lose me?' Clara faltered.

'My dear, you have planted me on a field where I am to expect the trumpet, and when it blows I shall be quit of my nerves, no more.'

Clara found nothing to seize on for a reply in these words. She thought upon the silence of Laetitia.

Sir Willoughby advanced, appearing in a cordial mood.

'I need not ask you whether you are better,' he said to Clara, sparkled to Laetitia, and raised a key to the level of Dr Middleton's breast, remarking, 'I am going down to my inner cellar.'

'An inner cellar!' exclaimed the doctor.

'Sacred from the butler. It is interdicted to Stoneman. Shall I offer myself as guide to you? My cellars are worth a visit.'

'Cellars are not catacombs. They are, if rightly constructed, rightly considered, cloisters, where the bottle meditates on joys to bestow, not on dust misused! Have you anything great?'

'A wine aged ninety.'

'Is it associated with your pedigree that you pronounce the age with such assurance?'

'My grandfather inherited it.'

'Your grandfather, Sir Willoughby, had meritorious offspring, not to speak of generous progenitors. What would have happened had it fallen into the female line! I shall be glad to accompany you. Port? Hermitage?'

'Port.'

'Ah! We are in England!'

'There will just be time,' said Sir Willoughby, inducing Dr Middleton to step out.

A chirrup was in the reverend doctor's tone: 'Hocks, too, have compassed age. I have tasted senior Hocks. Their flavours are as a brook of many voices; they have depth also. Senatorial Port! we say. We cannot say that of any other wine. Port is deep-sea deep. It is in its flavour deep; mark the difference. It is like a classic tragedy, organic in conception. An ancient Hermitage has the light of the antique; the merit that it can grow to an extreme old age; a merit. Neither of Hermitage nor of Hock can you say that it is the blood of those long years, retaining the strength of youth with the wisdom of age. To Port for that! Port is our noblest legacy! Observe, I do not compare the wines; I distinguish the qualities. Let them live together for our enrichment; they are not rivals like the Idaean Three.[18] Were they rivals, a fourth would challenge them. Burgundy has great genius. It does wonders within its period; it does all except to keep up in the race; it is short-lived. An aged Burgundy runs with a beardless Port. I cherish the fancy that Port speaks the sentences of wisdom, Burgundy sings the inspired Ode. Or put it, that Port is the Homeric hexameter, Burgundy the pindaric dithyramb. What do you say?'

'The comparison is excellent, sir.'

'The distinction, you would remark. Pindar astounds. But his elder brings us the more sustaining cup. One is a fountain of prodigious ascent. One is the unsounded purple sea of marching billows.'

'A very fine distinction.'

'I conceive you to be now commending the similes. They pertain to the time of the first critics of those poets. Touch the Greeks, and you can nothing new; all has been said: Graiis . . . praeter, laudem nullius avaris.[19] Genius dedicated to Fame is immortal. We, sir, dedicate genius to the cloacaline floods. We do not address the unforgetting gods, but the popular stomach.'

Sir Willoughby was patient. He was about as accordantly coupled with Dr Middleton in discourse as a drum duetting with a bass-viol; and when he struck in he received correction from the paedagogue-instrument. If he thumped affirmative or negative, he was wrong. However, he knew scholars to be an unmannered species; and the doctor's learnedness would be a subject to dilate on.

In the cellar, it was the turn for the drum. Dr Middleton was tongue-tied there. Sir Willoughby gave the history of his wine in heads of chapters; whence it came to the family originally, and how it had come down to him in the quantity to be seen. 'Curiously, my grandfather, who inherited it, was a water-drinker. My father died early.'

'Indeed! Dear me!' the doctor ejaculated in astonishment and condolence. The former glanced at the contrariety of man, the latter embraced his melancholy destiny.

He was impressed with respect for the family. This cool vaulted cellar, and the central square block, or enceinte, where the thick darkness was not penetrated by the intruding lamp, but rather took it as an eye, bore witness to forethoughtful practical solidity in the man who had built the house on such foundations. A house having a great wine stored below lives in our imaginations as a joyful house, fast and splendidly rooted in the soil. And imagination has a place for the heir of the house. His grandfather a water-drinker, his father dying early, present circumstances to us arguing predestination to an illustrious heirship and career. Dr Middleton's musings were coloured by the friendly vision of glasses of the great wine; his mind was festive; it pleased him, and he chose to indulge in his whimsical, robustious, grandiose-airy style of thinking: from which the festive mind will sometimes take a certain print that we cannot obliterate immediately. Expectation is grateful, you know; in the mood of gratitude we are waxen. And he was a self-humouring gentleman.

He liked Sir Willoughby's tone in ordering the servant at his heels to take up 'those two bottles': it prescribed, without overdoing it, a proper amount of caution, and it named an agreeable number.

Watching the man's hand keenly, he said:

'But here is the misfortune of a thing super-excellent: – not more than one in twenty will do it justice.'

Sir Willoughby replied: 'Very true, sir; and I think we may pass over the nineteen.'

'Women, for example; and most men.'

'This wine would be a sealed book to them.'

'I believe it would. It would be a grievous waste.'

'Vernon is a claret man; and so is Horace De Craye. They are both below the mark of this wine. They will join the ladies. Perhaps you and I, sir, might remain together.'

'With the utmost good-will on my part.'

'I am anxious for your verdict, sir.'

'You shall have it, sir, and not out of harmony with the chorus preceding me, I can predict. Cool, not frigid.' Dr Middleton summed the attributes of the cellar on quitting it. 'North side and South. No musty damp. A pure air. Everything requisite. One might lie down one's self and keep sweet here.'

Of all our venerable British of the two Isles professing a suckling attachment to an ancient port-wine, lawyer, doctor, squire, rosy admiral, city merchant, the classic scholar is he whose blood is most nuptial to the webbed bottle. The reason must be, that he is full of the old poets. He has their spirit to sing with, and the best that Time has done on earth to feed it. He may also perceive a resemblance in the wine to the studious mind, which is the obverse of our mortality, and throws off acids and crusty particles in the piling of the years, until it is fulgent by clarity. Port hymns to his conservatism. It is magical: at one sip he is off swimming in the purple flood of the ever-youthful antique.

By comparison, then, the enjoyment of others is brutish; they have not the soul for it; but he is worthy of the wine, as are poets of Beauty. In truth, these should be severally apportioned to them, scholar and poet, as his own good thing. Let it be so.

Meanwhile Dr Middleton sipped.

After the departure of the ladies, Sir Willoughby had practised a studied curtness upon Vernon and Horace.

'You drink claret,' he remarked to them, passing it round. 'Port, I think, Doctor Middleton? The wine before you may serve for a preface. We shall have *your* wine in five minutes.'

The claret jug empty, Sir Willoughby offered to send for more. De Craye was languid over the question. Vernon rose from the table.

'We have a bottle of Doctor Middleton's port coming in,' Willoughby said to him.

'Mine, you call it?' cried the doctor.

'It's a royal wine, that won't suffer sharing,' said Vernon.

'We'll be with you, if you go into the billiard-room, Vernon.'

'I shall hurry my drinking of good wine for no man,' said the Rev. Doctor.

'Horace?'

'I'm beneath it, ephemeral, Willoughby. I am going to the ladies.'

Vernon and De Craye retired upon the arrival of the wine; and Dr Middleton sipped. He sipped and looked at the owner of it.

'Some thirty dozen?' he said.

'Fifty.'

The doctor nodded humbly.

'I shall remember, sir,' his host addressed him, 'whenever I have the honour of entertaining you, I am cellarer of that wine.'

The Rev. Doctor set down his glass. 'You have, sir, in some sense, an enviable post. It is a responsible one, if that be a blessing. On you it devolves to retard the day of the last dozen.'

'Your opinion of the wine is favourable, sir?'

'I will say this: – shallow souls run to rhapsody: – I will say, that I am consoled for not having lived ninety years back, or at any period but the present, by this one glass of your ancestral wine.'

'I am careful of it,' Sir Willoughby said, modestly; 'still its natural destination is to those who can appreciate it. You do, sir.'

'Still my good friend, still! It is a charge; it is a possession, but part in trusteeship. Though we cannot declare it an entailed estate, our consciences are in some sort pledged that it shall be a succession not too considerably diminished.'

'You will not object to drink it, sir, to the health of your grandchildren. And may you live to toast them in it on their marriage-day!'

'You colour the idea of a prolonged existence in seductive hues. Ha! It is a wine for Tithonus. This wine would speed him to the rosy Morning – aha!'

'I will undertake to sit you through it up to morning,' said Sir Willoughby, innocent of the Bacchic nuptiality of the allusion.

Dr Middleton eyed the decanter. There is a grief in gladness, for a premonition of our mortal state. The amount of wine in the decanter did not promise to sustain the starry roof of night and greet the dawn. 'Old wine, my friend, denies us the full bottle!'

'Another bottle is to follow.'

'No!'

'It is ordered.'

'I protest.'

'It is uncorked.'

'I entreat.'

'It is decanted.'

'I submit. But, mark, it must be honest partnership. You are my worthy host, sir, on that stipulation. Note the superiority of wine over Venus! – I may say, the magnanimity of wine;

our jealousy turns on him that will not share! But the corks, Willoughby. The corks excite my amazement.'

'The corking is examined at regular intervals. I remember the occurrence in my father's time. I have seen to it once.'

'It must be perilous as an operation for tracheotomy; which I should assume it to resemble in surgical skill and firmness of hand, not to mention the imminent gasp of the patient.'

A fresh decanter was placed before the doctor.

He said: 'I have but a girl to give!' He was melted.

Sir Willoughby replied: 'I take her for the highest prize this world affords.'

'I have beaten some small stock of Latin into her head, and a note of Greek. She contains a savour of the classics. I hoped once . . . But she is a girl. The nymph of the woods is in her. Still she will bring you her flower-cup of Hippocrene. She has that aristocracy – the noblest. She is fair; a Beauty, some have said, who judge not by lines. Fair to me, Willoughby! She is my sky. There were applicants. In Italy she was besought of me. She has no history. You are the first heading of the chapter. With you she will have her one tale, as it should be. "Mulier tum bene olet", you know. Most fragrant she that smells of naught. She goes to you from me, from me alone, from her father to her husband. "Ut flos in septis secretus nascitur hortis." He murmured on the lines to "Sic virgo, dum – " [20] I shall feel the parting. She goes to one who will have my pride in her, and more. I will add, who will be envied. Mr Whitford must write you a Carmen Nuptiale.'

The heart of the unfortunate gentleman listening to Dr Middleton set in for irregular leaps. His offended temper broke away from the image of Clara, revealing her as he had seen her in the morning beside Horace De Craye, distressingly sweet; sweet with the breezy radiance of an English soft-breathing day; sweet with sharpness of young sap. Her eyes, her lips, her fluttering dress that played happy mother across her bosom, giving peeps of the veiled twins; and her laughter, her slim figure, peerless carriage, all her terrible sweetness touched his wound to the smarting quick.

Her wish to be free of him was his anguish. In his pain he thought sincerely. When the pain was easier he muffled himself in the idea of her jealousy of Laetitia Dale, and deemed the wish a fiction. But she had expressed it. That was the wound he sought to comfort; for the double reason, that he could love her better after punishing her, and that to meditate on doing so masked the fear of losing her – the dread abyss she had succeeded in forcing his nature to shudder at as a giddy edge possibly near, in spite of his arts of self-defence.

'What I shall do to-morrow evening!' he exclaimed. 'I do not care to fling a bottle to Colonel De Craye and Vernon. I cannot open one for myself. To sit with the ladies will be sitting in the cold for me. When do you bring me back my bride, sir?'

'My dear Willoughby!' The Rev. Doctor puffed, composed himself, and sipped. 'The expedition is an absurdity. I am unable to see the aim of it. She had a headache, vapours. They are over, and she will show a return of good sense. I have ever maintained that nonsense is not to be encouraged in girls. I can put my foot on it. My arrangements are for staying here a further ten days, in the terms of your hospitable invitation. And I stay.'

'I applaud your resolution, sir. Will you prove firm?'

'I am never false to my engagement, Willoughby.'

'Not under pressure?'

'Under no pressure.'

'Persuasion, I should have said.'

'Certainly not. The weakness is in the yielding, either to persuasion or to pressure. The latter brings weight to bear on us; the former blows at our want of it.'

'You gratify me, Doctor Middleton, and relieve me.'

'I cordially dislike a breach in good habits, Willoughby. But I do remember – was I wrong? – informing Clara that you appeared light-hearted in regard to a departure, or gap in a visit, that was not, I must confess, to my liking.'

'Simply, my dear doctor, your pleasure was my pleasure; but make my pleasure yours, and you remain to crack many a bottle with your son-in-law.'

'Excellently said. You have a courtly speech, Willoughby. I can imagine you to conduct a lovers' quarrel with a politeness to read a lesson to well-bred damsels. Aha?'

'Spare me the futility of the quarrel.'

'All's well?'

'Clara,' replied Sir Willoughby, in dramatic epigram, 'is perfection.'

'I rejoice,' the Rev. Doctor responded; taught thus to understand that the lovers' quarrel between his daughter and his host was at an end.

He left the table a little after eleven o'clock. A short dialogue ensued upon the subject of the ladies. They must have gone to bed? Why, yes; of course they must. It is good that they should go to bed early to preserve their complexions for us. Ladies are creation's glory, but they are anti-climax, following a wine of a century old. They are anti-climax, recoil, cross-current; morally, they are repentance, penance; imagerially, the frozen North on the young brown buds bursting to green. What know they of a critic in the palate and a frame all revelry! And mark you, revelry in sobriety, containment in exultation; classic revelry. Can they, dear though they be to us, light up candelabras in the brain, to illuminate all history and solve the secret of the destiny of man? They cannot; they cannot sympathize with them that can. So therefore this division is between us; yet are we not turbaned Orientals, nor are they inmates of the harem. We are not Moslem. Be assured of it in the contemplation of the table's decanter.

Dr Middleton said: 'Then I go straight to bed.'

'I will conduct you to your door, sir,' said his host.

The piano was heard. Dr Middleton laid his hand on the balusters, and remarked: 'The ladies must have gone to bed?'

Vernon came out of the library and was hailed, 'Fellow-student!'

He waved a good-night to the Doctor, and said to Willoughby: 'The ladies are in the drawing-room.'

'I am on my way upstairs,' was the reply.

'Solitude and sleep, after such a wine as that; and forefend us human society!' the Doctor shouted. 'But, Willoughby!'

'Sir.'

'*One* to-morrow.'

'You dispose of the cellar, sir.'

'I am fitter to drive the horses of the sun. I would rigidly counsel, one, and no more. We have made a breach in the fiftieth dozen. Daily one will preserve us from having to name the fortieth quite so unseasonably. The couple of bottles per diem prognosticates disintegration, with its accompanying recklessness. Constitutionally, let me add, I bear three. I speak for posterity.'

During Dr Middleton's allocution the ladies issued from the drawing-room, Clara foremost, for she had heard her father's voice, and desired to ask him this in reference to their departure: 'Papa, will you tell me the hour to-morrow?'

She ran up the stairs to kiss him, saying again: 'When will you be ready to-morrow morning?'

Dr Middleton announced a stoutly deliberative mind in the bugle-notes of a repeated ahem. He bethought him of replying in his doctorial tongue. Clara's eager face admonished him to brevity: it began to look starved. Intruding on his vision of the houris couched in the inner cellar to be the reward of valiant men, it annoyed him. His brows joined. He said: 'I shall not be ready to-morrow morning.'

'In the afternoon?'

'Nor in the afternoon.'

'When?'

'My dear, I am ready for bed at this moment, and know of no other readiness. Ladies,' he bowed to the group in the hall below him, 'may fair dreams pay court to you this night!'

Sir Willoughby had hastily descended and shaken the hands of the ladies, directed Horace De Craye to the laboratory for a smoking-room, and returned to Dr Middleton. Vexed by the scene, uncertain of his temper if he stayed with Clara, for whom he had arranged that her disappointment should take place on the morrow, in his absence, he said: 'Good-night, good-night,' to her, with due fervour, bending over her flaccid finger-tips; then offered his arm to the Rev. Doctor.

'Ay, son Willoughby, in friendliness, if you will, though I am a man to bear my load,' the father of the stupefied girl addressed him. 'Candles, I believe, are on the first landing. Good-night, my love. Clara!'

'Papa!'

'Good-night.'

'Oh!' she lifted her breast with the interjection, standing in shame of the curtained conspiracy and herself, 'good-night'.

Her father wound up the stairs. She stepped down.

'There was an understanding that papa and I should go to London to-morrow early,' she said, unconcernedly, to the ladies, and her voice was clear, but her face too legible. De Craye was heartily unhappy at the sight.

CHAPTER 21

✕✕✕✕

Clara's Meditations

Two were sleepless that night: Miss Middleton and Colonel De Craye.

She was in a fever, lying like stone, with her brain burning. Quick natures run out to calamity in any little shadow of it

flung before. Terrors of apprehension drive them. They stop
not short of the uttermost when they are on the wings of
dread. A frown means tempest, a wind wreck; to see fire is to
be seized by it. When it is the approach of their loathing that
they fear, they are in the tragedy of the embrace at a breath;
and then is the wrestle between themselves and horror, between themselves and evil, which promises aid; themselves
and weakness, which calls on evil; themselves and the better
part of them, which whispers no beguilement.

The false course she had taken through sophistical cowardice
appalled the girl; she was lost. The advantage taken of it by
Willoughby put on the form of strength, and made her feel
abject, reptilious; she was lost, carried away on the flood of the
cataract. He had won her father for an ally. Strangely, she
knew not how, he had succeeded in swaying her father, who
had previously not more than tolerated him. 'Son Willoughby' on her father's lips meant something that scenes and scenes
would have to struggle with, to the out-wearying of her
father and herself. She revolved the 'Son Willoughby'
through moods of stupefaction, contempt, revolt, subjection.
It meant that she was vanquished. It meant that her father's
esteem for her was forfeited. She saw him a gigantic image of
discomposure.

Her recognition of her cowardly feebleness brought the
brood of fatalism. What was the right of so miserable a creature as she to excite disturbance, let her fortunes be good or
ill? It would be quieter to float, kinder to everybody. Thank
heaven for the chances of a short life! Once in a net, desperation
is graceless. We may be brutes in our earthly destinies: in our
endurance of them we need not be brutish.

She was now in the luxury of passivity, when we throw our
burden on the Powers above, and do not love them. The need
to love them drew her out of it, that she might strive with
the unbearable, and by sheer striving, even though she were
graceless, come to love them humbly. It is here that the seed
of good teaching supports a soul, for the condition might be

mapped, and where kismet whispers us to shut eyes, and instruction bids us look up, is at a well-marked cross-road of the contest.

Quick of sensation, but not courageously resolved, she perceived how blunderingly she had acted. For a punishment, it seemed to her that she who had not known her mind must learn to conquer her nature, and submit. She had accepted Willoughby; therefore she accepted him. The fact became a matter of the past, past debating.

In the abstract this contemplation of circumstances went well. A plain duty lay in her way. And then a disembodied thought flew round her, comparing her with Vernon to her discredit. He had for years borne much that was distasteful to him, for the purpose of studying, and with his poor income helping the poorer than himself. She dwelt on him in pity and envy; he had lived in this place, and so must she; and he had not been dishonoured by his modesty: he had not failed of self-control, because he had a life within. She was almost imagining she might imitate him, when the clash of a sharp physical thought, 'The difference! the difference!' told her she was woman and never could submit. Can a woman have an inner life apart from him she is yoked to? She tried to nestle deep away in herself: in some corner where the abstract view had comforted her, to flee from thinking as her feminine blood directed. It was a vain effort. The difference, the cruel fate, the defencelessness of women, pursued her, strung her to wild horses' backs, tossed her on savage wastes. In her case duty was shame: hence, it could not be broadly duty. That intolerable difference proscribed the word.

But the fire of a brain burning high and kindling everything lighted up herself against herself: – Was one so volatile as she a person with a will? – Were they not a multitude of flitting wishes that she took for a will? Was she, feather-headed that she was, a person to make a stand on physical pride? – If she could yield her hand without reflection (as she conceived she had done, from incapacity to conceive herself doing it reflectively) was she much better than purchaseable stuff that has nothing to say to the bargain?

Furthermore, said her incandescent reason, she had not suspected such art of cunning in Willoughby. Then might she not be deceived altogether – might she not have misread him? Stronger than she had fancied, might he not be likewise more estimable? The world was favourable to him; he was prized by his friends.

She reviewed him. It was all in one flash. It was not much less intentionally favourable than the world's review and that of his friends, but, beginning with the idea of them, she recollected – heard Willoughby's voice pronouncing his opinion of his friends and the world; of Vernon Whitford and Colonel De Craye for example, and of men and women. An undefined agreement to have the same regard for him as his friends and the world had, provided that he kept at the same distance from her, was the termination of this phase, occupying about a minute in time, and reached through a series of intensely vivid pictures: – his face, at her petition to be released, lowering behind them for a background and a comment.

'I cannot! I cannot!' she cried, aloud; and it struck her that her repulsion was a holy warning. Better be graceless than a loathing wife: better appear inconsistent. Why should she not appear such as she was?

Why? We answer that question usually in angry reliance on certain superb qualities, injured fine qualities of ours undiscovered by the world, not much more than suspected by ourselves, which are still our fortress, where pride sits at home, solitary and impervious as an octogenarian conservative. But it is not possible to answer it so when the brain is rageing like a pine-torch and the devouring illumination leaves not a spot of our nature covert. The aspect of her weakness was unrelieved, and frightened her back to her loathing. From her loathing, as soon as her sensations had quickened to realize it, she was hurled on her weakness. She was graceless, she was inconsistent, she was volatile, she was unprincipled, she was worse than a prey to wickedness – capable of it; she was only waiting to be misled. Nay, the idea of being misled suffused her with languor; for then the battle would be over and she a happy weed of the sea no longer suffering those tugs at the roots, but leaving it to the sea to heave and contend. She would be like Constantia then: like her in her fortunes: never so brave, she feared.

Perhaps very like Constantia in her fortunes!

Poor troubled bodies waking up in the night to behold visually the spectre cast forth from the perplexed machinery inside them, stare at it for a space, till touching consciousness they dive down under the sheets with fish-like alacrity. Clara looked at her thought, and suddenly headed downward in a crimson gulf.

She must have obtained absolution, or else it was oblivion below. Soon after the plunge her first object of meditation was Colonel De Craye. She thought of him calmly: he seemed a refuge. He was very nice, he was a holiday character. His lithe figure, neat firm footing of the stag, swift intelligent expression, and his ready frolicsomeness, pleasant humour, cordial temper, and his Irishry, whereon he was at liberty to play, as on the emblem harp of the Isle, were soothing to think of. The suspicion that she tricked herself with this calm observation of him was dismissed. Issuing out of torture, her young nature eluded the irradiating brain in search of refreshment, and she luxuriated at a feast in considering him – shower on a parched land that he was! He spread new air abroad. She had no reason to suppose he was not a good man: she could securely think of him. Besides he was bound by his prospective office in support of his friend Willoughby to be quite harmless. And besides (you are not to expect logical sequences) the showery refreshment in thinking of him lay in the sort of assurance it conveyed, that the more she thought, the less would he be likely to figure as an obnoxious official – that is, as the man to do by Willoughby at the altar what her father would, under the supposition, be doing by her. Her mind reposed on Colonel De Craye.

His name was Horace. Her father had worked with her at Horace. She knew most of the Odes and some of the Satires and Epistles of the poet. They reflected benevolent beams on the gentleman of the poet's name. He too was vivacious, had fun, common sense, elegance; loved rusticity, he said, sighed for a country life, fancied retiring to Canada to cultivate his own domain; 'modus agri non ita magnus';[21] a delight. And he, too, when in the country, sighed for town. There were strong features of resemblance. He had hinted in fun at not being rich. 'Quae virtus et quanta sit rivere parvo.'[22] But that quotation applied to and belonged to Vernon Whitford. Even so little disarranged her meditations.

She would have thought of Vernon, as her instinct of safety prompted, had not his exactions been excessive. He proposed to help her with advice only. She was to do everything for herself, do and dare everything, decide upon everything. He told her flatly that so would she learn to know her own mind; and flatly, that it was her penance. She had gained nothing by breaking down and pouring herself out to him. He would have her bring Willoughby and her father face to face, and be witness of their interview – herself the theme. What alternative was there? – obedience to the word she had pledged. He talked of patience, of self-examination and patience. But all of her – she was all marked *urgent*. This house was a cage, and the world – her brain was a cage, until she could obtain her prospect of freedom.

As for the house, she might leave it; yonder was the dawn.

She went to her window to gaze at the first colour along the grey. Small satisfaction came of gazing at that or at herself. She shunned glass and sky. One and the other stamped her as a slave in a frame. It seemed to her she had been so long in this place that she was fixed here: it was her world, and to imagine an Alp was like seeking to get back to childhood. Unless a miracle intervened here she would have to pass her days. Men are so little chivalrous now that no miracle ever intervenes. Consequently she was doomed.

She took a pen and began a letter to a dear friend, Lucy Darleton, a promised bridesmaid, bidding her countermand orders for her bridal dress, and purposing a tour in Switzerland. She wrote of the mountain country with real abandonment to imagination. It became a visioned loophole of escape. She rose and clasped a shawl over her night-dress to ward off chillness, and sitting to the table again, could not produce a word. The lines she had written were condemned: they were ludicrously inefficient. The letter was torn to pieces. She stood very clearly doomed.

After a fall of tears, upon looking at the scraps, she dressed herself, and sat by the window and watched the blackbird on the lawn as he hopped from shafts of dewy sunlight to the long-stretched dewy tree-shadows, considering in her mind that dark dews are more meaningful than bright, the beauty of the dews of woods more sweet than meadow-dews. It signified only that she was quieter. She had gone through her crisis in the anticipation of it. That is how quick natures will often be cold and hard, or not much moved, when the positive crisis arrives, and why it is that they are prepared for astonishing leaps over the gradations which should render their conduct comprehensible to us, if not excuseable. She watched the blackbird throw up his head stiff, and peck to right and left, dangling the worm on each side his orange beak. Specklebreasted thrushes were at work, and a wagtail that ran as with Clara's own rapid little steps. Thrush and blackbird flew to the nest. They had wings. The lovely morning breathed of sweet earth into her open window, and made it painful, in the dense twitter, chirp, cheep, and song of the air, to resist the innocent intoxication. O to love! was not said by her, but if she had sung, as her nature prompted, it would have been. Her war with Willoughby sprang of a desire to love repelled by distaste. Her cry for freedom was a cry to be free to love: she discovered it, half shuddering: to love, oh! no – no shape of man, nor impalpable nature either: but to love unselfishness, and helpfulness, and planted strength in something. Then, loving and being loved a little, what strength would be hers! She could utter all the words needed to Willoughby and to her father, locked in her love: walking in this world, living in that.

Previously she had cried, despairing: If I were loved! Jealousy of Constantia's happiness, envy of her escape, ruled her then: and she remembered the cry, though not perfectly her plain-speaking to herself: she chose to think she had meant: If Willoughby were capable of truly loving! For now the fire of her brain had sunk, and refuges and subterfuges were round about it. The thought of personal love was encouraged, she chose to think, for the sake of the strength it lent her to carve her way to freedom. She had just before felt rather the reverse, but she could not exist with that feeling; and it was true that freedom was not so indistinct in her fancy as the idea of love.

Were men, when they were known, like him she knew too well?

The arch-tempter's question to her was there.

She put it away. Wherever she turned it stood observing her. She knew so much of one man, nothing of the rest: naturally she was curious. Vernon might be sworn to be unlike. But he was exceptional. What of the other in the house?

Maidens are commonly reduced to read the masters of their destinies by their instincts; and when these have been edged by over-activity they must hoodwink their maidenliness to suffer themselves to read; and then they must dupe their minds, else men would soon see they were gifted to discern. Total ignorance being their pledge of purity to men, they have to expunge the writing of their perceptives on the tablets of the brain: they have to know not when they do know. The instinct of seeking to know, crossed by the task of blotting knowledge out, creates that conflict of the natural with the artificial creature to which their ultimately revealed doubleface, complained of by ever-dissatisfied men, is owing. Wonder in no degree that they indulge a craving to be fools, or that many of them act the character. Jeer at them as little for not showing growth. You have reared them to this pitch, and at this pitch they have partly civilized you. Supposing you to want it done wholly, you must yield just as many points in your requisitions as are needed to let the wits of young women reap their due harvest and be of good use to their souls. You will then have a fair battle, a braver, with better results.

Clara's inner eye traversed Colonel De Craye at a shot.

She had immediately to blot out the vision of Captain Oxford in him, the revelation of his laughing contempt for Willoughby, the view of mercurial principles, the scribbled histories of light love-passages.

She blotted it out, kept it from her mind: so she knew him, knew him to be a sweeter and a variable Willoughby, a generous kind of Willoughby, a Willoughby-butterfly, without having the free mind to summarize him and picture him for a warning. Scattered features of him, such as the instincts call up, were not sufficiently impressive. Besides, the clouded mind was opposed to her receiving impressions.

Young Crossjay's voice in the still morning air came to her ears. The dear guileless chatter of the boy's voice. Why, assuredly it was young Crossjay who was the man she loved. And he loved her. And he was going to be an unselfish, sustaining, true, strong man, the man she longed for, for anchorage. Oh, the dear voice! woodpecker and thrush in one. He never ceased to chatter to Vernon Whitford walking beside him with a swinging stride off to the lake for their morning swim. Happy couple! The morning gave them both a freshness and innocence above human. They seemed to Clara made of morning air and clear lake water. Crossjay's voice ran up and down a diatonic scale with here and there a query in semitone and a laugh on a ringing note. She wondered what he could have to talk of so incessantly, and imagined all the dialogue. He prattled of his yesterday, to-day, and to-morrow, which did not imply past and future, but his vivid present. She felt like one vainly trying to fly in hearing him; she felt old.

The consolation she arrived at was to feel maternal. She wished to hug the boy.

Trot and stride, Crossjay and Vernon entered the park, careless about wet grass, not once looking at the house. Crossjay ranged ahead and picked flowers, bounding back to show them. Clara's heart beat at a fancy that her name was mentioned. If those flowers were for her she would prize them.

The two bathers dipped over an undulation.

Her loss of them rattled her chains.

Deeply dwelling on their troubles has the effect upon the young of helping to forgetfulness; for they cannot think without imagining, their imaginations are saturated with their pleasures, and the collision, though they are unable to exchange sad for sweet, distills an opiate.

'Am I solemnly engaged?' she asked herself. She seemed to be awakening.

She glanced at her bed, where she had passed the night of ineffectual moaning, and out on the high wave of grass, where Crossjay and his good friend had vanished.

Was the struggle all to be gone over again?

Little by little her intelligence of her actual position crept up to submerge her heart.

'I am in his house!' she said. It resembled a discovery, so strangely had her opiate and power of dreaming wrought through her tortures. She said it gasping. She was in his house, his guest, his betrothed, sworn to him. The fact stood out cut in steel on the pitiless daylight.

That consideration drove her to be an early wanderer in the wake of Crossjay.

Her station was among the beeches on the flank of the boy's return; and while waiting there the novelty of her waiting to waylay anyone – she who had played the contrary part! – told her more than it pleased her to think. Yet she could admit that she did desire to speak with Vernon, as with a counsellor, harsh and curt, but wholesome.

The bathers reappeared on the grass-ridge, racing and flapping wet towels.

Some one hailed them. A sound of the galloping hoof drew her attention to the avenue. She saw Willoughby dash across the park level, and dropping a word to Vernon, ride away. Then she allowed herself to be seen.

Crossjay shouted. Willoughby turned his head, but not his horse's head. The boy sprang up to Clara. He had swum across the lake and back; he had raced Mr Whitford – and beaten him! How he wished Miss Middleton had been able to be one of them!

Clara listened to him enviously. Her thought was: We women are nailed to our sex!

She said: 'And you have just been talking to Sir Willoughby.'

Crossjay drew himself up to give an imitation of the baronet's hand-moving in adieu.

He would not have done that had he not smelled sympathy with the performance.

She declined to smile. Crossjay repeated it, and laughed. He made a broader exhibition of it to Vernon approaching: 'I say, Mr Whitford, who's this?'

Vernon doubled to catch him. Crossjay fled and resumed his magnificent air in the distance.

'Good-morning, Miss Middleton; you are out early,' said Vernon, rather pale and stringy from his cold swim, and rather hard-eyed with the sharp exercise following it.

She had expected some of the kindness she wanted to reject, for he could speak very kindly, and she regarded him as her doctor of medicine, who would at least present the futile drug.

'Good-morning,' she replied.

'Willoughby will not be home till the evening.'

'You could not have had a finer morning for your bath.'

'No.'

'I will walk as fast as you like.'

'I'm perfectly warm.'

'But you prefer fast walking.'

'Out.'

'Ah! yes, that I understand. The walk back! Why is Willoughby away to-day?'

'He has business.'

After several steps she said: 'He makes very sure of papa.'

'Not without reason, you will find,' said Vernon.

'Can it be? I am bewildered. I had papa's promise.'

'To leave the Hall for a day or two.'

'It would have been . . .'

'Possibly. But other heads are at work as well as yours. If you had been in earnest about it you would have taken your father into your confidence at once. That was the course I ventured to propose, on the supposition.'

'In earnest! I cannot imagine that you doubt it. I wished to spare him.'

'This is a case in which he can't be spared.'

'If I had been bound to any other. I did not know then *who* held me a prisoner. I thought I had only to speak to him sincerely.'

'Not many men would give up their prize for a word, Willoughby the last of any.'

'Prize' rang through her thrillingly from Vernon's mouth, and soothed her degradation.

She would have liked to protest that she was very little of a prize; a poor prize; not one at all in general estimation; only one to a man reckoning his property; no prize in the true sense.

The importunity of pain saved her.

'Does he think I can change again? Am I treated as something won in a lottery? To stay here is indeed more than I can bear. And if he is calculating – Mr Whitford, if he calculates on another change, his plotting to keep me here is inconsiderate, not very wise. Changes *may* occur in absence.'

'Wise or not, he has the right to scheme his best to keep you.'

She looked on Vernon with a shade of wondering reproach.

'Why? What right?'

'The right you admit when you ask him to release you. He has the right to think you deluded; and to think you may come to a better mood if you remain – a mood more agreeable to him, I mean. He has that right absolutely. You are bound to remember also that you stand in the wrong. You confess it when you appeal to his generosity. And every man has the right to retain a treasure in his hand if he can. Look straight at these facts.'

'You expect me to be all reason!'

'Try to be. It's the way to learn whether you are really in earnest.'

'I will try. It will drive me to worse!'

'Try honestly. What is wisest now is, in my opinion, for you to resolve to stay. I speak in the character of the person you sketched for yourself as requiring. Well, then, a friend repeats the same advice. You might have gone with your father: now you will only disturb him and annoy him. The chances are he will refuse to go.'

'Are women ever so changeable as men, then! Papa consented; he agreed; he had some of my feeling; I saw it. That was yesterday. And at night. He spoke to each of us at night in a different tone from usual. With me he was hardly affectionate. But when you advise me to stay, Mr Whitford, you do not perhaps reflect that it would be at the sacrifice of all candour.'

'Regard it as a probational term.'

'It has gone too far with me.'

'Take the matter into the head: try the case there.'

'Are you not counselling me as if I were a woman of intellect?'

The crystal ring in her voice told him that tears were near to flowing.

He shuddered slightly. 'You have intellect,' he said, nodded, and crossed the lawn, leaving her. He had to dress.

She was not permitted to feel lonely, for she was immediately joined by Colonel De Craye.

CHAPTER 22

✗✗✗✗

The Ride

CROSSJAY darted up to her a nose ahead of the colonel.

'I say, Miss Middleton, we're to have the whole day to ourselves, after morning lessons. Will you come and fish with me and see me bird's-nest?'

'Not for the satisfaction of beholding another cracked crown, my son,' the colonel interposed: and bowing to Clara: 'Miss Middleton is handed over to my exclusive charge for the day, with her consent?'

'I scarcely know,' said she, consulting a sensation of languor that seemed to contain some reminiscence. 'If I am here. My father's plans are uncertain. I will speak to him. If I am here, perhaps Crossjay would like a ride in the afternoon.'

'Oh, yes,' cried the boy; 'out over Bournden, through Mewsey up to Closham Beacon, and down on Aspenwell, where there's a common for racing. And ford the stream!'

'An inducement for you,' De Craye said to her.

She smiled and squeezed the boy's hand.

'We won't go without you, Crossjay.'

'You don't carry a comb, my man, when you bathe?'

At this remark of the colonel's young Crossjay conceived the appearance of his matted locks in the eyes of his adorable lady. He gave her one dear look through his redness, and fled.

'I like that boy,' said De Craye.

'I love him,' said Clara.

Crossjay's troubled eyelids in his honest young face became a picture for her.

'After all, Miss Middleton, Willoughby's notions about him are not so bad, if we consider that you will be in the place of a mother to him.'

'I think them bad.'

'You are disinclined to calculate the good fortune of the boy in having more of you on land than he would have in crown and anchor buttons!'

'You have talked of him with Willoughby.'

'We had a talk last night.'

Of how much? thought she.

'Willoughby returns?' she said.

'He dines here, I know; for he holds the key of the inner cellar, and Doctor Middleton does him the honour to applaud his wine. Willoughby was good enough to tell me that he thought I might contribute to amuse you.'

She was brooding in stupefaction on her father and the wine as she requested Colonel De Craye to persuade Willoughby to take the general view of Crossjay's future and act on it.

'He seems fond of the boy, too,' said De Craye, musingly.

'You speak in doubt?'

'Not at all. But is he not – men are queer fish! – make allowance for us – a trifle tyrannical, pleasantly, with those he is fond of?'

'If they look right and left?'

It was meant for an interrogation; it was not with the sound of one that the words dropped. 'My dear Crossjay!' she sighed. 'I would willingly pay for him out of my own purse, and I will do so rather than have him miss his chance. I have not mustered resolution to propose it.'

'I may be mistaken, Miss Middleton. He talked of the boy's fondness of him.'

'He would.'

'I suppose he is hardly peculiar in liking to play Pole-star.'

'He may not be.'

'For the rest, your influence should be all-powerful.'

'It is not.'

De Craye looked with a wandering eye at the heavens.

'We are having a spell of weather perfectly superb. And the odd thing is, that whenever we have splendid weather at home we're all for rushing abroad. I'm booked for a Mediterranean cruise – postponed to give place to your ceremony.'

'That?' she could not control her accent.

'What worthier?'

She was guilty of a pause.

De Craye saved it from an awkward length. 'I have written half an essay on Honeymoons, Miss Middleton.'

'Is that the same as a half-written essay, Colonel De Craye?'

'Just the same, with the difference that it's a whole essay written all on one side.'

'On which side?'

'The bachelor's.'

'Why does he trouble himself with such topics?'

'To warm himself for being left out in the cold.'

'Does he feel envy?'

'He has to confess it.'

'He has liberty.'

'A commodity he can't tell the value of if there's no one to buy.'

'Why should he wish to sell?'

'He's bent on completing his essay.'

'To make the reading dull.'

'There we touch the key of the subject. For what is to rescue the pair from a monotony multiplied by two? And so a bachelor's recommendation, when each has discovered the right sort of person to be dull with, pushes them from the church-door on a round of adventures containing a spice of peril, if

'tis to be had. Let them be in danger of their lives the first or
second day. A bachelor's loneliness is a private affair of his
own; he hasn't to look into a face to be ashamed of feeling it
and inflicting it at the same time; 'tis his pillow; he can punch
it an he pleases, and turn it over t'other side, if he's for a
mighty variation; there's a dream in it. But our poor couple
are staring wide awake. All their dreaming's done. They've
emptied their bottle of elixir, or broken it; and she has a
thirst for the use of the tongue, and he to yawn with a crony;
and they may converse, they're not aware of it, more than the
desert that has drunk a shower. So as soon as possible she's
away to the ladies, and he puts on his Club. That's what your
bachelor sees and would like to spare them; and if he didn't
see something of the sort he'd be off with a noose round his
neck, on his knees in the dew to the morning milkmaid.'

'The bachelor is happily warned and on his guard,' said
Clara, diverted, as he wished her to be. 'Sketch me a few of
the adventures you propose.'

'I have a friend who rowed his bride from the Houses of
Parliament up the Thames to the Severn on into North Wales.
They shot some pretty weirs and rapids.'

'That was nice.'

'They had an infinity of adventures, and the best proof of
the benefit they derived is, that they forgot everything about
them except that the adventures occurred.'

'Those two must have returned bright enough to please
you.'

'They returned, and shone like a wrecker's beacon to the
mariner. You see, Miss Middleton, there was the landscape,
and the exercise, and the occasional bit of danger. I think it's to
be recommended. The scene is always changing, and not too
fast; and 'tis not too sublime, like big mountains, to tire them
of their everlasting big Ohs. There's the difference between
going into a howling wind and launching among zephyrs.
They have fresh air and movement, and not in a railway
carriage; they can take in what they look on. And she has the

steering ropes, and that's a wise commencement. And my lord
is all day making an exhibition of his manly strength, bowing
before her some sixty to the minute; and she, to help him, just
inclines when she's in the mood. And they're face to face in
the nature of things, and are not under the obligation of looking the unutterable, because, you see, there's business in hand;
and the boat's just the right sort of third party, who never
interferes, but must be attended to. And they feel they're
labouring together to get along, all in the proper proportion;
and whether he has to labour in life or not, he proves his
ability. What do you think of it, Miss Middleton?'

'I think you have only to propose it, Colonel De
Craye.'

'And if they capsize, why, 'tis a natural ducking!'

'You forgot the lady's dressing-bag.'

'The stain on the metal for a constant reminder of his
prowess in saving it! Well, and there's an alternative to that
scheme, and a finer: – This, then: they read dramatic pieces
during courtship, to stop the saying of things over again till
the drum of the ear becomes nothing but a drum to the poor
head, and a little before they affix their signatures to the fatal
Registry-book of the vestry, they enter into an engagement
with a body of provincial actors to join the troop on the day of
their nuptials, and away they go in their coach and four, and
she is Lady Kitty Caper for a month, and he Sir Harry High-
flyer. See the honeymoon spinning! The marvel to me is that
none of the young couples do it. They could enjoy the world,
see life, amuse the company, and come back fresh to their own
characters, instead of giving themselves a dose of Africa without a savage to diversify it: an impression they never get over,
I'm told. Many a character of the happiest auspices has irreparable mischief done it by the ordinary honeymoon. For my
part, I rather lean to the second plan of campaign.'

Clara was expected to reply, and she said: 'Probably because
you are fond of acting. It would require capacity on both
sides.'

'Miss Middleton, *I* would undertake to breathe the enthusiasm for the stage and the adventure.'

'You are recommending it generally.'

'Let my gentleman only have a fund of enthusiasm. The lady will kindle. She always does at a spark.'

'If he has not any?'

'Then I'm afraid they must be mortally dull.'

She allowed her silence to speak; she knew that it did so too eloquently, and could not control the personal adumbration she gave to the one point of light revealed in, 'if he has not any'. Her figure seemed immediately to wear a cap and cloak of dulness.

She was full of revolt and anger, she was burning with her situation; if sensible of shame now at anything that she did, it turned to wrath and threw the burden on the author of her desperate distress. The hour for blaming herself had gone by, to be renewed ultimately perhaps in a season of freedom. She was bereft of her insight within at present, so blind to herself that, while conscious of an accurate reading of Willoughby's friend, she thanked him in her heart for seeking simply to amuse her and slightly succeeding. The afternoon's ride with him and Crossjay was an agreeable beguilement to her in prospect.

Laetitia came to divide her from Colonel De Craye. Dr Middleton was not seen before his appearance at the breakfast-table, where a certain air of anxiety in his daughter's presence produced the semblance of a raised map at intervals on his forehead. Few sights on earth are more deserving of our sympathy than a good man who has a troubled conscience thrust on him.

The Rev. Doctor's perturbation was observed. The ladies Eleanor and Isabel, seeing his daughter to be the cause of it, blamed her, and would have assisted him to escape, but Miss Dale, whom he courted with that object, was of the opposite faction. She made way for Clara to lead her father out. He called to Vernon, who merely nodded while leaving the room by the window with Crossjay.

Half an eye on Dr Middleton's pathetic exit in captivity sufficed to tell Colonel De Craye that parties divided the house. At first he thought how deplorable it would be to lose Miss Middleton for two days or three: and it struck him that Vernon Whitford and Laetitia Dale were acting oddly in seconding her, their aim not being discernible. For he was of the order of gentlemen of the obscurely-clear in mind who have a predetermined acuteness in their watch upon the human play, and mark men and women as pieces of a bad game of chess, each pursuing an interested course. His experience of a section of the world had educated him – as gallant, frank, and manly a comrade as one could wish for – up to this point. But he soon abandoned speculations, which may be compared to a shaking anemometer that will not let the troubled indicator take station. Reposing on his perceptions and his instincts, he fixed his attention on the chief persons, only glancing at the others to establish a postulate, that where there are parties in a house the most bewitching person present is the origin of them. It is ever Helen's achievement. Miss Middleton appeared to him bewitching beyond mortal; sunny in her laughter, shadowy in her smiling; a young lady shaped for perfect music with a lover.

She was that, and no less, to every man's eye on earth. High breeding did not freeze her lovely girlishness. – But Willoughby did. This reflection intervened to blot luxurious picturings of her, and made itself acceptable by leading him back to several instances of an evident want of harmony of the pair.

And now (for purely undirected impulse all within us is not, though we may be eye-bandaged agents under direction) it became necessary for an honourable gentleman to cast vehement rebukes at the fellow who did not comprehend the jewel he had won. How could Willoughby behave like so complete a donkey! De Craye knew him to be in his interior stiff, strange, exacting: women had talked of him; he had been too much for one woman – the dashing Constantia: he had worn one woman, sacrificing far more for him than Constantia, to death. Still, with such a prize as Clara Middleton, Willoughby's behaviour was past calculating in its contemptible absurdity. And during courtship! And courtship of that girl! It was the way of a man ten years after marriage.

The idea drew him to picture her doatingly in her young matronly bloom ten years after marriage: without a touch of age, matronly wise, womanly sweet: perhaps with a couple of little ones to love, never having known the love of a man.

To think of a girl like Clara Middleton never having at nine-and-twenty, and with two fair children! known the love of a man or the loving of a man, possibly, became torture to the Colonel.

For a pacification he had to reconsider that she was as yet only nineteen and unmarried.

But she was engaged, and she was unloved. One might swear to it, that she was unloved. And she was not a girl to be satisfied with a big house and a high-nosed husband.

There was a rapid alteration of the sad history of Clara the unloved matron solaced by two little ones. A childless Clara tragically loving and beloved flashed across the dark glass of the future.

Either way her fate was cruel.

Some astonishment moved De Craye in the contemplation of the distance he had stepped in this morass of fancy. He distinguished the choice open to him of forward or back, and he selected forward. But fancy was dead: the poetry hovering about her grew invisible to him: he stood in the morass; that was all he knew; and momently he plunged deeper; and he was aware of an intense desire to see her face, that he might study her features again: he understood no more.

It was the clouding of the brain by the man's heart, which had come to the knowledge that it was caught.

A certain measure of astonishment moved him still. It had hitherto been his portion to do mischief to women and avoid the vengeance of the sex. What was there in Miss Middleton's face and air to ensnare a veteran handsome man of society numbering six-and-thirty years, nearly as many conquests? 'Each bullet has got its commission.' He was hit at last. That accident effected by Mr Flitch had fired the shot. Clean through the heart, does not tell us of our misfortune, till the heart is asked to renew its natural beating. It fell into the condition of the porcelain vase over a thought of Miss Middleton standing above his prostrate form on the road, and walking beside him to the Hall. Her words? What have they been? She had not uttered words, she had shed meanings. He did not for an instant conceive that he had charmed her: the charm she had cast on him was too thrilling for coxcombry to lift a head; still she had enjoyed his prattle. In return for her touch upon the Irish fountain in him, he had manifestly given her relief. And could not one see that so sprightly a girl would soon be deadened by a man like Willoughby? Deadened she was: she had not responded to a compliment on her approaching marriage. An allusion to it killed her smiling. The case of Mr Flitch, with the half wager about his reinstation in the sevice of the Hall, was conclusive evidence of her opinion of Willoughby.

It became again necessary that he should abuse Willoughby for his folly. Why was the man worrying her? In some way he was worrying her.

What if Willoughby as well as Miss Middleton wished to be quit of the engagement? . . .

For just a second, the handsome, woman-flattered officer proved his man's heart more whole than he supposed it. That great organ, instead of leaping at the thought, suffered a check.

Bear in mind that his heart was not merely man's, it was a conqueror's. He was of the race of amorous heroes who glory in pursuing, overtaking, subduing: wresting the prize from a rival, having her ripe from exquisitely feminine inward conflicts, plucking her out of resistance in good old primitive fashion. You win the creature in her delicious flutterings. He liked her thus, in cooler blood, because of society's admiration of the capturer, and somewhat because of the strife, which always enhances the value of a prize, and refreshes our vanity in recollection.

Moreover, he had been matched against Willoughby: the circumstance had occurred two or three times. He could name a lady he had won, a lady he had lost. Willoughby's large fortune and grandeur of style had given him advantages at the start. But the start often means the race – with women, and a bit of luck.

The gentle check upon the galloping heart of Colonel De Craye endured no longer than a second – a simple side-glance in a headlong pace. Clara's enchantingness for a temperament like his, which is to say, for him specially, in part through the testimony her conquest of himself presented as to her power of sway over the universal heart known as man's, assured him she was worth winning even from a hand that dropped her.

He had now a double reason for exclaiming at the folly of Willoughby. Willoughby's treatment of her showed either temper or weariness. Vanity and judgement led De Craye to guess the former. Regarding her sentiments for Willoughby, he had come to his own conclusion. The certainty of it caused him to assume that he possessed an absolute knowledge of her character: she was an angel, born supple; she was a heavenly soul, with half a dozen of the tricks of earth. Skittish filly was among his phrases; but she had a bearing and a gaze that forbade the dip in the common gutter for wherewithal to paint the creature she was.

Now, then, to see whether he was wrong for the first time in his life! If not wrong, he had a chance.

There could be nothing dishonourable in rescuing a girl from an engagement she detested. An attempt to think it a service to Willoughby failed midway. De Craye dismissed that chicanery. It would be a service to Willoughby in the end, without question. There was that to soothe his manly honour. Meanwhile he had to face the thought of Willoughby as an antagonist, and the world looking heavy on his honour as a friend.

Such considerations drew him tenderly close to Miss Middleton. It must, however, be confessed that the mental ardour of Colonel De Craye had been a little sobered by his glance at the possibility of both of the couple being of one mind on the subject of their betrothal. Desirable as it was that they should be united in disagreeing, it reduced the romance to platitude, and the third person in the drama to the appearance of a stick. No man likes to play that part. Memoirs of the favourites of Goddesses, if we had them, would confirm it of men's tastes in this respect, though the divinest be the prize. We behold what part they played.

De Craye chanced to be crossing the hall from the laboratory to the stables when Clara shut the library-door behind her. He said something whimsical, and did not stop, nor did he look twice at the face he had been longing for.

What he had seen made him fear there would be no ride out with her that day. Their next meeting reassured him; she was dressed in her riding-habit, and wore a countenance resolutely cheerful. He gave himself the word of command to take his tone from her.

He was of a nature as quick as Clara's. Experience pushed him further than she could go in fancy; but experience laid a sobering finger on his practical steps, and bade them hang upon her initiative. She talked little. Young Crossjay cantering ahead was her favourite subject. She was very much changed since the early morning: his liveliness, essayed by him at a hazard, was unsuccessful; grave English pleased her best. The descent from that was naturally to melancholy. She mentioned a regret she had that the Veil was interdicted to women in Protestant countries. De Craye was fortunately silent; he could think of no other veil than the Moslem, and when her meaning struck his witless head, he admitted to himself that devout attendance on a young lady's mind stupefies man's intelligence. Half an hour later, he was as foolish in supposing it a confidence. He was again saved by silence.

In Aspenwell village she drew a letter from her bosom and called to Crossjay to post it. The boy sung out, 'Miss Lucy Darleton! What a nice name!'

Clara did not show that the name betrayed anything.

She said to De Craye, 'It proves he should not be here thinking of nice names.'

Her companion replied, 'You may be right.' He added, to avoid feeling too subservient: 'Boys will.'

'Not if they have stern masters to teach them their daily lessons, and some of the lessons of existence.'

'Vernon Whitford is not stern enough?'

'Mr Whitford has to contend with other influences here.'

'With Willoughby?'

'Not with Willoughby.'

He understood her. She touched the delicate indication firmly. The man's heart respected her for it; not many girls could be so thoughtful or dare to be so direct; he saw that she had become deeply serious, and he felt her love of the boy to be maternal, past maiden sentiment.

By this light of her seriousness, the posting of her letter in a distant village, not entrusting it to the Hall post-box, might have import; not that she would apprehend the violation of her private correspondence, but we like to see our letter of weighty meaning pass into the mouth of the public box.

Consequently this letter was important. It was to suppose a sequency in the conduct of a variable damsel. Coupled with her remark about the Veil, and with other things, not words, breathing from her (which were the breath of her condition), it was not unreasonably to be supposed. She might even be a very consistent person. If one only had the key of her!

She spoke once of an immediate visit to London, supposing that she could induce her father to go. De Craye remembered the occurrence in the Hall at night, and her aspect of distress.

They raced along Aspenwell Common to the ford; shallow,

to the chagrin of young Crossjay, between whom and themselves they left a fitting space for his rapture in leading his
pony to splash up and down, lord of the stream.

Swiftness of motion so strikes the blood on the brain that
our thoughts are lightnings, the heart is master of them.

De Craye was heated by his gallop to venture on the angling
question: 'Am I to hear the names of the bridesmaids?'

The pace had nerved Clara to speak to it sharply: 'There is
no need.'

'Have I no claim?'

She was mute.

'Miss Lucy Darleton, for instance; whose name I am almost
as much in love with as Crossjay.'

'She will not be bridesmaid to me.'

'She declines? Add my petition, I beg.'

'To all? or to her?'

'Do all the bridesmaids decline?'

'The scene is too ghastly.'

'A marriage?'

'Girls have grown sick of it.'

'Of weddings? We'll overcome the sickness.'

'With some.'

'Not with Miss Darleton? You tempt my eloquence.'

'You wish it?'

'To win her consent? Certainly.'

'The scene?'

'Do I wish that?'

'Marriage!' exclaimed Clara, dashing into the ford, fearful
of her ungovernable wildness and of what it might have
kindled. – You, father! you have driven me to unmaidenli-
ness! – She forgot Willoughby, in her father, who would not
quit a comfortable house for her all but prostrate beseeching;
would not bend his mind to her explanations, answered her
with the horrid iteration of such deaf misunderstanding as
may be associated with a tolling bell.

De Craye allowed her to catch Crossjay by herself. They

entered a narrow lane, mysterious with possible birds' eggs in the May-green hedges. As there was not room for three abreast, the colonel made up the rear-guard, and was consoled by having Miss Middleton's figure to contemplate; but the readiness of her joining in Crossjay's pastime of the nest-hunt was not so pleasing to a man that she had wound to a pitch of excitement. Her scornful accent on 'Marriage' rang through him. Apparently she was beginning to do with him just as she liked, herself entirely unconcerned.

She kept Crossjay beside her till she dismounted, and the colonel was left to the procession of elephantine ideas in his head, whose ponderousness he took for natural weight. We do not with impunity abandon the initiative. Men who have yielded it are like cavalry put on the defensive; a very small force with an ictus will scatter them.

Anxiety to recover lost ground reduced the dimensions of his ideas to a practical standard.

Two ideas were opposed like duellists bent on the slaughter of one another. Either she amazed him by confirming the suspicions he had gathered of her sentiments for Willoughby in the moments of his introduction to her; or she amazed him as a model for coquettes – the married and the widow might apply to her for lessons.

These combatants exchanged shots, but remained standing; the encounter was undecided. Whatever the result, no person so seductive as Clara Middleton had he ever met. Her cry of loathing, 'Marriage!' coming from a girl, rang faintly clear of an ancient virginal aspiration of the sex to escape from their coil, and bespoke a pure, cold, savage pride that transplanted his thirst for her to higher fields.

CHAPTER 23

✗✗✗✗

Treats of the Union of Temper and Policy

SIR WILLOUGHBY meanwhile was on a line of conduct suiting his appreciation of his duty to himself. He had deluded himself with the simple notion that good fruit would come of the union of temper and policy.

No delusion is older, none apparently so promising, both parties being eager for the alliance. Yet the theorist upon human nature will say, they are obviously of adverse disposition. And this is true, inasmuch as neither of them will submit to the yoke of an established union; as soon as they have done their mischief, they set to work tugging for a divorce. But they have attractions, the one for the other, which precipitate them to embrace whenever they meet in a breast; each is earnest with the owner of it to get him to officiate forthwith as wedding-priest. And here is the reason: temper, to warrant its appearance, desires to be thought as deliberative as policy, and policy, the sooner to prove its shrewdness, is impatient for the quick blood of temper.

It will be well for men to resolve at the first approaches of the amorous but fickle pair upon interdicting even an accidental temporary junction: for the astonishing sweetness of the couple when no more than the ghosts of them have come together in a projecting mind is an intoxication beyond fermented grapejuice or a witch's brewage; and under the guise of active wits they will lead us to the parental meditation of antics compared with which a Pagan Saturnalia were less impious in the sight of sanity. This is full-mouthed language; but on our studious way through any human career we are subject to fits of moral elevation; the theme inspires it, and the sage residing in every civilized bosom approves it.

Decide at the outset, that temper is fatal to policy: hold them with both hands in division. One might add, be doubtful of your policy and repress your temper: it would be to suppose you wise. You can, however, by incorporating two or three captains of the great army of truisms bequeathed to us by ancient wisdom, fix in your service those veteran old standfasts to check you. They will not be serviceless in their admonitions to your understanding, and they will so contrive to reconcile with it the natural caperings of the wayward young sprig Conduct, that the latter, who commonly learns to walk upright and straight from nothing softer than raps of a bludgeon on his crown, shall foot soberly, appearing at least wary of dangerous corners.

Now Willoughby had not to be taught that temper is fatal to policy; he was beginning to see in addition that the temper he encouraged was particularly obnoxious to the policy he adopted; and although his purpose in mounting horse after yesterday frowning on his bride was definite, and might be deemed sagacious, he bemoaned already the fatality pushing him ever farther from her in chase of a satisfaction impossible to grasp.

But the bare fact that her behaviour demanded a line of policy crossed the grain of his temper: it was very offensive.

Considering that she wounded him severely, her reversal of their proper parts, by taking the part belonging to him, and requiring his watchfulness, and the careful dealings he was accustomed to expect from others, and had a right to exact of her, was injuriously unjust. The feelings of a man hereditarily sensitive to property accused her of a trespassing imprudence, and knowing himself, by testimony of his household, his tenants, and the neighbourhood, and the world was well, amiable when he received his dues, he contemplated her with an air of stiff-backed ill-treatment, not devoid of a certain sanctification of martyrdom.

His bitterest enemy would hardly declare that it was he who was in the wrong.

Clara herself had never been audacious enough to say that. Distaste of his person was inconceivable to the favourite of society. The capricious creature probably wanted a whipping to bring her to the understanding of the principle called mastery, which is in man.

But was he administering it? If he retained a hold on her, he could undoubtedly apply the scourge at leisure; any kind of scourge; he could shun her, look on her frigidly, unbend to her to find a warmer place for sarcasm, pityingly smile, ridicule, pay court elsewhere. He could do these things if he retained a hold on her; and he could do them well because of the faith he had in his renowned amiability; for in doing them, he could feel that he was other than he seemed, and his own cordial nature was there to comfort him while he bestowed punishment. Cordial indeed, the chills he endured were flung from the world. His heart was in that fiction: half the hearts now beating have a mild form of it to keep them merry: and the chastisement he desired to inflict was really no more than righteous vengeance for an offended goodness of heart. Clara figuratively, absolutely perhaps, on her knees, he would raise her and forgive her. He yearned for the situation. To let her understand how little she had known him! It would be worth the pain she had dealt, to pour forth the stream of re-established confidences, to paint himself to her as he was; as he was in the spirit, not as he was to the world: though the world had reason to do him honour.

First, however, she would have to be humbled.

Something whispered that his hold on her was lost.

In such a case, every blow he struck would set her flying farther, till the breach between them would be past bridging.

Determination not to let her go was the best finish to this perpetually revolving round which went like the same old wheel-planks of a water mill in his head at a review of the injury he sustained. He had come to it before, and he came to it again. There was his vengeance. It melted him, she was so sweet! She shone for him like the sunny breeze on water. Thinking of her caused a catch of his breath.

The dreadful young woman had a keener edge for the senses of men than sovereign beauty.

It would be madness to let her go.

She affected him like an outlook on the great Patterne estate after an absence, when his welcoming flag wept for pride above Patterne Hall!

It would be treason to let her go.

It would be cruelty to her.

He was bound to reflect that she was of tender age, and the foolishness of the wretch was excusable to extreme youth.

We toss away a flower that we are tired of smelling and do not wish to carry. But the rose – young woman – is not cast off with impunity. A fiend in shape of man is always behind us to appropriate her. He that touches that rejected thing is larcenous. Willoughby had been sensible of it in the person of Laetitia: and by all the more that Clara's charms exceeded the faded creature's, he felt it now. Ten thousand Furies thickened about him at a thought of her lying by the road-side without his having crushed all bloom and odour out of her which might tempt even the curiosity of the fiend, man.

On the other hand, supposing her to lie there untouched, universally declined by the sniffling, sagacious dog-fiend, a miserable spinster for years, he could conceive notions of his remorse. A soft remorse may be adopted as an agreeable sensation within view of the wasted penitent whom we have struck a trifle too hard. Seeing her penitent, he certainly would be willing to surround her with little offices of compromising kindness. It would depend on her age. Supposing her still youngish, there might be captivating passages between them, as thus, in a style not unfamiliar:

'And was it my fault, my poor girl? Am I to blame, that you have passed a lonely, unloved youth?'

'No, Willoughby! The irreparable error was mine, the blame is mine, mine only. I live to repent it. I do not seek, for

I have not deserved, your pardon. Had I it, I should need my own self-esteem to presume to clasp it to a bosom ever unworthy of you.'

'I may have been impatient, Clara: we are human!'

'Never be it mine to accuse one on whom I laid so heavy a weight of forbearance!'

'Still, my old love! – for I am merely quoting history in naming you so – I cannot have been perfectly blameless.'

'To me you were, and are.'

'Clara!'

'Willoughby!'

'Must I recognize the bitter truth that we two, once nearly one! so nearly one! are eternally separated?'

'I have envisaged it. My friend – I may call you friend; you have ever been my friend, my best friend! Oh, that eyes had been mine to know the friend I had! – Willoughby, in the darkness of night, and during days that were as night to my soul, I have seen the inexorable finger pointing my solitary way through the wilderness from a Paradise forfeited by my most wilful, my wanton, sin. We have met. It is more than I have merited. We part. In mercy let it be for ever. Oh, terrible word! Coined by the passions of our youth, it comes to us for our sole riches when we are bankrupt of earthly treasures, and is the passport given by Abnegation unto Woe that prays to quit this probationary sphere. Willoughby, we part. It is better so.'

'Clara! one – one only – one last – one holy kiss!'

'If these poor lips, that once were sweet to you . . .'

The kiss, to continue the language of the imaginative composition of his time, favourite readings in which had inspired Sir Willoughby with a colloquy so pathetic, was imprinted.

Ay, she had the kiss, and no mean one. It was intended to swallow every vestige of dwindling attractiveness out of her, and there was a bit of scandal springing of it in the background that satisfactorily settled her business, and left her 'enshrined in memory, a divine recollection to him', as his popular romances would say, and have said for years.

Unhappily, the fancied salute of her lips encircled him with the breathing Clara. She rushed up from vacancy like a wind summoned to wreck a stately vessel.

His reverie had thrown him into severe commotion. The slave of a passion thinks in a ring, as hares run: he will cease where he began. Her sweetness had set him off, and he whirled back to her sweetness: and that being incalculable and he insatiable, you have the picture of his torments when you consider that her behaviour made her as a cloud to him.

Riding slack, horse and man, in the likeness of those two ajog homeward from the miry hunt, the horse pricked his ears, and Willoughby looked down from his road along the hills on the race headed by young Crossjay with a short start over Aspenwell Common to the ford. There was no mistaking who they were, though they were well-nigh a mile distant below. He noticed that they did not overtake the boy. They drew rein at the ford, talking not simply face to face, but face in face. Willoughby's novel feeling of he knew not what drew them up to him, enabling him to fancy them bathing in one another's eyes. Then she sprang through the ford, De Craye following, but not close after – and why not close? She had flicked him with one of her peremptorily saucy speeches when she was bold with the gallop. They were not unknown to Willoughby. They signified intimacy.

Last night he had proposed to De Craye to take Miss Middleton for a ride the next afternoon. It never came to his mind then that he and his friend had formerly been rivals. He wished Clara to be amused. Policy dictated that every thread should be used to attach her to her residence at the Hall until he could command his temper to talk to her calmly and overwhelm her, as any man in earnest, with command of temper and a point of vantage, may be sure to whelm a young woman. Policy, adulterated by temper, yet policy it was that had sent him on his errand in the early morning to beat about

for a house and garden suitable to Dr Middleton within a
circuit of five, six, or seven miles of Patterne Hall. If the Rev.
Doctor liked the house and took it (and Willoughby had
seen the place to suit him), the neighbourhood would be a
chain upon Clara: and if the house did not please a gentleman
rather hard to please (except in a venerable wine), an excuse
would have been started for his visiting other houses, and he
had that response to his importunate daughter, that he
believed an excellent house was on view. Dr Middleton had
been prepared by numerous hints to meet Clara's black
misreading of a lovers' quarrel, so that everything looked
full of promise as far as Willoughby's exercise of policy
went.

But the strange pang traversing him now convicted him of
a large adulteration of profitless temper with it. The loyalty of
De Craye to a friend, where a woman walked in the drama,
was notorious. It was there, and a most flexible thing it was:
and it soon resembled reason manipulated by the sophists.
Not to have reckoned on his peculiar loyalty was proof of the
blindness cast on us by temper.

And De Craye had an Irish tongue; and he had it under control, so that he could talk good sense and airy nonsense at
discretion. The strongest overboiling of English Puritan contempt of a gabbler, would not stop women from liking it.
Evidently Clara did like it, and Willoughby thundered on her
sex. Unto such brainless things as these do we, under the irony
of circumstances, confide our honour!

For he was no gabbler. He remembered having rattled in
earlier days; he had rattled with an object to gain, desiring to
be taken for an easy, careless, vivacious, charming fellow, as
any young gentleman may be who gaily wears the golden
dish of Fifty thousand pounds per annum nailed to the back
of his very saintly young pate. The growth of the critical
spirit in him, however, had informed him that slang had been
a principal component of his rattling; and as he justly supposed
it a betraying art for his race and for him, he passed through

the prim and the yawning phases of affected indifference, to the pure Puritanism of a leaden contempt of gabblers.

They snare women, you see – girls! How despicable the host of girls! – at least, that girl below there!

Married women understood him: widows did. He placed an exceedingly handsome and flattering young widow of his acquaintance, Lady Mary Lewison, beside Clara for a comparison, involuntarily; and at once, in a flash, in despite of him (he would rather it had been otherwise), and in despite of Lady Mary's high birth and connections as well, the silver lustre of the maid sicklied the poor widow.

The effect of the luckless comparison was to produce an image of surpassingness in the features of Clara that gave him the final, or mace-blow. Jealousy invaded him.

He had hitherto been free of it, regarding jealousy as a foreign devil, the accursed familiar of the vulgar. Luckless fellows might be victims of the disease; he was not; and neither Captain Oxford, nor Vernon, nor De Craye, nor any of his compeers, had given him one shrewd pinch: the woman had, not the man; and she in quite a different fashion from his present wallowing anguish: she had never pulled him to earth's level, where jealousy gnaws the grasses. He had boasted himself above the humiliating visitation.

If that had been the case, we should not have needed to trouble ourselves much about him. A run or two with the pack of imps would have satisfied us. But he desired Clara Middleton manfully enough, at an intimation of rivalry to be jealous; in a minute the foreign devil had him, he was flame: flaming verdigris, one might almost dare to say, for an exact illustration; such was actually the colour; but accept it as unsaid.

Remember the poets upon jealousy. It is to be haunted in the heaven of two by a Third; preceded or succeeded, therefore surrounded, embraced, hugged by this infernal Third: it is Love's bed of burning marl; to see and taste the withering Third in the bosom of sweetness; to be dragged through the past and find the fair Eden of it sulphurous; to be dragged to the gates of the future and glory to behold them blood: to adore the bitter creature trebly and with treble power to clutch her by the windpipe: it is to be cheated, derided, shamed, and abject and supplicating, and consciously demoniacal in treacherousness, and victoriously self-justified in revenge.

And still there is no change in what men feel, though in what they do the modern may be judicious.

You know the many paintings of man transformed to rage-ing beast by the curse: and this, the fieriest trial of our egoism, worked in the Egoist to produce division of himself from himself, a concentration of his thoughts upon another object, still himself, but in another breast, which had to be looked at and into for the discovery of him. By the gaping jaw-chasm of his greed we may gather comprehension of his insatiate force of jealousy. Let her go? Not though he were to become a mark of public scorn in strangling her with the yoke! His concentration was marvellous. Unused to the exercise of imaginative powers, he nevertheless conjured her before him visually till his eyeballs ached. He saw none but Clara, hated none, loved none, save the intolerable woman. What logic was in him de-duced her to be individual and most distinctive from the cir-cumstance that only she had ever wrought these pangs. She had made him ready for them, as we know. An idea of De Craye being no stranger to her when he arrived at the Hall, dashed him at De Craye for a second: it might be or might not be that they had a secret; – Clara was the spell. So prodigiously did he love and hate, that he had no permanent sense except for her. The soul of him writhed under her eyes at one mo-ment, and the next it closed on her without mercy. She was his possession escaping; his own gliding away to the Third.

There would be pangs for him too, that Third! Standing at the altar to see her fast-bound, soul and body, to another, would be good roasting fire.

It would be good roasting fire for her too, should she be averse. To conceive her aversion was to burn her and devour her. She would then be his! – what say you? Burned and devoured! Rivals would vanish then. Her reluctance to espouse the man she was plighted to would cease to be uttered, cease to be felt.

At last he believed in her reluctance. All that had been wanted to bring him to the belief was the scene on the common; such a mere spark, or an imagined spark! But the presence of the Third was necessary; otherwise he would have had to suppose himself personally distasteful.

Women have us back to the conditions of primitive man, or they shoot us higher than the topmost star. But it is as we please. Let them tell us what we are to them: for us, they are our back and front of life: the poet's Lesbia, the poet's Beatrice; ours is the choice. And were it proved that some of the bright things are in the pay of Darkness, with the stamp of his coin on their palms, and that some are the very angels we hear sung of, not the less might we say that they find us out; they have us by our leanings. They are to us what we hold of best or worst within. By their state is our civilization judged: and if it is hugely animal still, that is because primitive men abound and will have their pasture. Since the lead is ours, the leaders must bow their heads to the sentence. Jealousy of a woman is the primitive egoism seeking to refine in a blood gone to savagery under apprehension of an invasion of rights; it is in action the tiger threatened by a rifle when his paw is rigid on quick flesh; he tears the flesh for rage at the intruder. The Egoist, who is our original male in giant form, had no bleeding victim beneath his paw, but there was the sex to mangle. Much as he prefers the well-behaved among women, who can worship and fawn, and in whom terror can be inspired, in his wrath he would make of Beatrice a Lesbia Quadrantaria.[23]

Let women tell us of their side of the battle. We are not so much the test of the Egoist in them as they to us. Movements of similarity shown in crowned and undiademed ladies of intrepid independence, suggest their occasional capacity to be like men when it is given to them to hunt. At present they fly, and there is the difference. Our manner of the chase informs them of the creature we are.

Dimly as young women are informed, they have a youthful ardour of detestation that renders them less tolerant of the Egoist than their perceptive elder sisters. What they do perceive, however, they have a redoubtable grasp of, and Clara's behaviour would be indefensible if her detective feminine vision might not sanction her acting on its direction. Seeing him as she did, she turned from him and shunned his house as the antre of an ogre. She had posted her letter to Lucy Darleton. Otherwise, if it had been open to her to dismiss Colonel De Craye, she might, with a warm kiss to Vernon's pupil, have seriously thought of the next shrill steam-whistle across yonder hills for a travelling companion on the way to her friend Lucy; so abhorrent was to her the putting of her horse's head toward the Hall. Oh, the breaking of bread there! It had to be gone through for another day and more; that is to say, forty hours, it might be six-and-forty hours; and no prospect of sleep to speed any of them on wings!

Such were Clara's inward interjections while poor Willoughby burned himself out with verdigris flame having the savour of bad metal, till the hollow of his breast was not unlike to a corroded old cuirass, found, we will assume, by criminal lantern-beams in a digging beside green-mantled pools of the sullen soil, lumped with a strange adhesive concrete. How else picture the sad man? — the cavity felt empty to him, and heavy; sick of an ancient and mortal combat, and burning; deeply dinted too:

> With the starry hole
> Whence fled the soul:

very sore; important for aught save sluggish agony; a specimen and the issue of strife.

Measurelessly to loathe was not sufficient to save him from pain: he tried it: nor to despise; he went to a depth there also.

The fact that she was a healthy young woman returned to the surface of his thoughts like the murdered body pitched into the river, which will not drown, and calls upon the elements of dissolution to float it. His grand hereditary desire to transmit his estates, wealth and name to a solid posterity, while it prompted him in his loathing and contempt of a nature mean and ephemeral compared with his, attached him desperately to her splendid healthiness. The council of elders, whose descendant he was, pointed to this young woman for his mate. He had wooed her with the idea that they consented. O she was healthy! And he likewise: but, as if it had been a duel between two clearly designated by quality of blood to bid a House endure, she was the first who taught him what it was to have sensations of his mortality.

He could not forgive her. It seemed to him consequently politic to continue frigid and let her have a further taste of his shadow, when it was his burning wish to strain her in his arms to a flatness provoking his compassion.

'You have had your ride?' he addressed her politely in the general assembly on the lawn.

'I have had my ride, yes,' Clara replied.

'Agreeable, I trust?'

'Very agreeable.'

So it appeared. Oh, blushless!

The next instant he was in conversation with Laetitia, questioning her upon a dejected droop of her eyelashes.

'I am, I think,' said she, 'constitutionally melancholy.'

He murmured to her: 'I believe in the existence of specifics, and not far to seek, for all our ailments except those we bear at the hands of others.'

She did not dissent.

De Craye, whose humour for being convinced that Willoughby cared about as little for Miss Middleton as she for him was nourished by his immediate observation of them, dilated on the beauty of the ride and his fair companion's equestrian skill.

'You should start a travelling circus,' Willoughby rejoined.

'But the idea's a worthy one! – There's another alternative to the expedition I proposed, Miss Middleton,' said De Craye. 'And I be clown? I haven't a scruple of objection. I must read up books of jokes.'

'Don't,' said Willoughby.

'I'd spoil my part! But a natural clown won't keep up an artificial performance for an entire month, you see; which is the length of time we propose. He'll exhaust his nature in a day and be bowled over by the dullest regular donkey-engine with paint on his cheeks and a nodding topknot.'

'What is this expedition "we" propose?'

De Craye was advised in his heart to spare Miss Middleton any allusion to honeymoons.

'Merely a game to cure dulness.'

'Ah!' Willoughby acquiesced. 'A month, you said?'

'One'd like it to last for years.'

'Ah! You are driving one of Mr Merriman's witticisms at me, Horace; I am dense.'

Willoughby bowed to Dr Middleton, and drew him from Vernon, filially taking his turn to talk with him closely.

De Craye saw Clara's look as her father and Willoughby went aside thus linked.

It lifted him over anxieties and casuistries concerning loyalty. Powder was in the look to make a warhorse breathe high and shiver for the signal.

CHAPTER 24

✕✕✕✕

Contains an Instance of the Generosity of Willoughby

OBSERVERS of a gathering complication and a character in
action commonly resemble gleaners who are intent only on
picking up the ears of grain and huddling their store. Disin-
terestedly or interestedly they wax over-eager for the little
trifles, and make too much of them. Observers should begin
upon the precept that not all we see is worth hoarding, and
that the things we see are to be weighed in the scale with what
we know of the situation, before we commit ourselves to a
measurement. And they may be accurate observers without
being good judges. They do not think so, and their bent is to
glean hurriedly and form conclusions as hasty, when their
business should be sift at each step, and question.

Miss Dale seconded Vernon Whitford in the occupation of
counting looks and tones, and noting scraps of dialogue. She
was quite disinterested; he quite believed that he was; to this
degree they were competent for their post; and neither of
them imagined they could be personally involved in the
dubious result of the scenes they witnessed. They were but
anxious observers, diligently collecting. She fancied Clara
susceptible to his advice: he had fancied it, and was considering it one of his vanities. Each mentally compared Clara's
abruptness in taking them into her confidence with her
abstention from any secret word since the arrival of Colonel
De Craye. Sir Willoughby requested Laetitia to give Miss
Middleton as much of her company as she could; showing that
he was on the alert. Another Constantia Durham seemed
beating her wings for flight. The suddenness of the evident
intimacy between Clara and Colonel De Craye shocked
Laetitia; their acquaintance could be computed by hours. Yet

at their first interview she had suspected the possibility of worse than she now supposed to be; and she had begged Vernon not immediately to quit the Hall, in consequence of that faint suspicion. She had been led to it by meeting Clara and De Craye at her cottage-gate, and finding them as fluent and laughter-breathing in conversation as friends. Unable to realize the rapid advance to a familiarity, more ostensible than actual, of two lively natures, after such an introduction as they had undergone: and one of the two pining in a drought of liveliness: Laetitia listened to their wager of nothing at all – a *no* against a *yes* – in the case of poor Flitch; and Clara's, 'Willoughby will not forgive'; and De Craye's 'Oh, he's human': and the silence of Clara and De Craye's hearty cry, 'Flitch shall be a gentleman's coachman in his old seat again, or I haven't a tongue!' to which there was a negative of Clara's head: and it then struck Laetitia that this young betrothed lady, whose alienated heart acknowledged no lord an hour earlier, had met her match, and, as the observer would have said, her destiny. She judged of the alarming possibility by the recent revelation to herself of Miss Middleton's character, and by Clara's having spoken to a man as well (to Vernon), and previously. That a young lady should speak on the subject of the inner holies to a man, though he were Vernon Whitford, was incredible to Laetitia; but it had to be accepted as one of the dread facts of our inexplicable life, which drag our bodies at their wheels and leave our minds exclaiming. Then, if Clara could speak to Vernon, which Laetitia would not have done for a mighty bribe, she could speak to De Craye, Laetitia thought deductively: this being the logic of untrained heads opposed to the proceeding whereby their condemnatory deduction hangs. – Clara must have spoken to De Craye!

Laetitia remembered how winning and prevailing Miss Middleton could be in her confidences. A gentleman hearing her might forget his duty to his friend, she thought, for she had been strangely swayed by Clara: ideas of Sir Willoughby that she had never before imagined herself to entertain had been sown in her, she thought; not asking herself whether the searchingness of the young lady had struck them and bidden them rise from where they lay imbedded. Very gentle women take in that manner impressions of persons, especially of the worshipped person, wounding them; like the new fortifications with embankments of soft earth, where explosive missiles bury themselves harmlessly until they are plucked out; and it may be a reason why those injured ladies outlive a Clara Middleton similarly battered.

Vernon less than Laetitia took into account that Clara was in a state of fever, scarcely reasonable. Her confidences to him he had excused, as a piece of conduct, in sympathy with her position. He had not been greatly astonished by the circumstances confided; and, on the whole, as she was excited and unhappy, he excused her thoroughly; he could have extolled her: it was natural that she should come to him, brave in her to speak so frankly, a compliment that she should condescend to treat him as a friend. Her position excused her widely. But she was not excused for making a confidential friend of De Craye. There was a difference.

Well, the difference was, that De Craye had not the smarting sense of honour with women which our meditator had: an impartial judiciary, it will be seen: and he discriminated between himself and the other justly: but sensation surging to his brain at the same instant, he reproached Miss Middleton for not perceiving that difference as clearly, before she betrayed her position to De Craye, which Vernon assumed that she had done. Of course he did. She had been guilty of it once: why, then, in the mind of an offended friend, she would be guilty of it twice. There was evidence. Ladies, fatally predestined to appeal to that from which they have to be guarded, must expect severity when they run off their railed highroad: justice is out of the question: man's brains might, his blood cannot administer it to them. By chilling him to the bone they may get what they cry for. But that is a method deadening to their point of appeal.

In the evening, Miss Middleton and the colonel sang a duet. She had of late declined to sing. Her voice was noticeably firm. Sir Willoughby said to her, 'You have recovered your richness of tone, Clara.' She smiled and appeared happy in pleasing him. He named a French ballad. She went to the music-rack and gave the song unasked. He should have been satisfied, for she said to him at the finish, 'Is that as you like it?' He broke from a murmur to Miss Dale, 'Admirable.' Some one mentioned a Tuscan popular canzone. She waited for Willoughby's approval, and took his nod for a mandate.

Traitress! he could have bellowed.

He had read of this characteristic of caressing obedience of the women about to deceive. He had in his time profited by it.

'Is it intuitively or by their experience that our neighbours across Channel surpass us in the knowledge of your sex?' he said to Miss Dale, and talked through Clara's apostrophe to the "Santissima Virgine Maria", still treating temper as a part of policy, without any effect on Clara; and that was matter for sickly green reflections. The lover who cannot wound has indeed lost anchorage; he is woefully adrift: he stabs air, which is to stab himself. Her complacent proof-armour bids him know himself supplanted.

During the short conversational period before the ladies retired for the night, Miss Eleanor alluded to the wedding by chance. Miss Isabel replied to her, and addressed an interrogation to Clara. De Craye foiled it adroitly. Clara did not utter a syllable. Her bosom lifted to a wavering height and sank. Subsequently she looked at De Craye vacantly, like a person awakened, but she looked. She was astonished by his readiness, and thankful for the succour. Her look was cold, wide, unfixed, with nothing of gratitude or of personal in it. The look, however, stood too long for Willoughby's endurance. Ejaculating 'Porcelain!' he uncrossed his legs; a signal for the ladies Eleanor and Isabel to retire. Vernon bowed to Clara as she was rising. He had not been once in her eyes, and he expected a partial recognition at the good-night. She said, it turning her head to Miss Isabel, who was condoling once more with Colonel De Craye over the ruins of his wedding-present, the porcelain vase, which she supposed to have been in Willoughby's mind when he displayed the signal. Vernon walked off to his room, dark as one smitten blind: bile tumet jecur:[24] her stroke of neglect hit him there where a blow sends thick obscuration upon eyeballs and brain alike.

Clara saw that she was paining him and regretted it when they were separated. That was her real friend! But he prescribed too hard a task. Besides, she had done everything he demanded of her, except the consenting to stay where she was and wear out Willoughby, whose dexterity wearied her small stock of patience. She had vainly tried remonstrance and supplication with her father hoodwinked by his host, she refused to consider how; through wine? – the thought was repulsive.

Nevertheless, she was drawn to the edge of it by the contemplation of her scheme of release. If Lucy Darleton was at home; if Lucy invited her to come: if she flew to Lucy: oh! then her father would have cause for anger. He would not remember that but for hateful wine! . . .

What was there in this wine of great age which expelled reasonableness, fatherliness? He was her dear father: she was his beloved child: yet something divided them; something closed her father's ears to her: and could it be that incomprehensible seduction of the wine? Her dutifulness cried violently no. She bowed, stupefied, to his arguments for remaining awhile, and rose clear-headed and rebellious with the reminiscence of the many strong reasons she had urged against them.

The strangeness of men, young and old, the little things (she regarded a grand wine as a little thing) twisting and changing them, amazed her. And these are they by whom women are abused for variability! Only the most imperious reasons, never mean trifles, move women, thought she. Would women do an injury to one they loved for oceans of that – ah, pah!

And women must respect men. They necessarily respect a

father. 'My dear, dear father!' Clara said in the solitude of her chamber, musing on all his goodness, and she endeavoured to reconcile the desperate sentiments of the position he forced her to sustain, with those of a venerating daughter. The blow which was to fall on him beat on her heavily in advance. 'I have not one excuse!' she said, glancing at numbers and a mighty one. But the idea of her father suffering at her hands cast her down lower than self-justification. She sought to imagine herself sparing him. It was too fictitious.

The sanctuary of her chamber, the pure white room so homely to her maidenly feelings, whispered peace, only to follow the whisper with another that went through her swelling to a roar, and leaving her as a string of music unkindly smitten. If she stayed in this house her chamber would no longer be a sanctuary. Dolorous bondage! Insolent death is not worse. Death's worm we cannot keep away, but when he has us we are numb to dishonour, happily senseless.

Youth weighed her eyelids to sleep, though she was quivering, and quivering she awoke to the sound of her name beneath her window. 'I can love still, for I love him,' she said, as she luxuriated in young Crossjay's boy's voice, again envying him his bath in the lake waters, which seemed to her to have the power to wash away grief and chains. Then it was that she resolved to let Crossjay see the last of her in this place. He should be made gleeful by doing her a piece of service; he should escort her on her walk to the railway station next morning, thence be sent flying for a long day's truancy, with a little note of apology on his behalf that she would write for him to deliver to Vernon at night.

Crossjay came running to her after his breakfast with Mrs Montague, the housekeeper, to tell her he had called her up.

'You won't to-morrow: I shall be up far ahead of you,' said she; and musing on her father, while Crossjay vowed to be up the first, she thought it her duty to plunge into another expostulation.

Willoughby had need of Vernon on private affairs. Dr

Middleton betook himself as usual to the library, after answering 'I will ruin you yet,' to Willoughby's liberal offer to despatch an order to London for any books he might want.

His fine unruffled air, as of a mountain in still morning beams, made Clara not indisposed to a preliminary scene with Willoughby that might save her from distressing him, but she could not stop Willoughby; as little could she look an invitation. He stood in the Hall, holding Vernon by the arm. She passed him; he did not speak, and she entered the library.

'What now, my dear? what is it?' said Dr Middleton, seeing that the door was shut on them.

'Nothing, papa,' she replied, calmly.

'You've not locked the door, my child? You turned something there: try the handle.'

'I assure you, papa, the door is not locked.'

'Mr Whitford will be here instantly. We are engaged on tough matter. Women have not, and opinion is universal that they never will have, a conception of the value of time.'

'We are vain and shallow, my dear papa.'

'No, no, not you, Clara. But I suspect you to require to learn by having work in progress how important is . . . is a quiet commencement of the day's task. There is not a scholar who will not tell you so. We must have a retreat. These invasions! – So you intend to have another ride to-day? They do you good. To-morrow we dine with Mrs Mountstuart Jenkinson, an estimable person indeed, though I do not perfectly understand our accepting. – You have not to accuse me of sitting over wine last night, my Clara! I never do it, unless I am appealed to for my judgement upon a wine.'

'I have come to entreat you to take me away, papa.'

In the midst of the storm aroused by this renewal of perplexity, Dr Middleton replaced a book his elbow had knocked over in his haste to dash the hair off his forehead, crying: 'Whither? To what spot? That reading of guide-books, and idle people's notes of Travel, and picturesque correspondence in the newspapers, unsettles man and maid. My objection to the living in hotels is known. I do not hesitate to say that I do cordially abhor it. I have had penitentially to submit to it in your dear mother's time, καὶ τρισκακοδαίμων²⁵ up to the full ten thousand times. But will you not comprehend that to the older man his miseries are multiplied by his years? But is it utterly useless to solicit your sympathy with an old man, Clara?'

'General Darleton will take us in, papa.'

'His table is detestable. I say nothing of that; but his wine is poison. Let that pass – I should rather say, let it not pass! – but our political views are not in accord. True, we are not under the obligation to propound them in presence, but we are destitute of an opinion in common. We have no discourse. Military men *have* produced, or diverged in, noteworthy epicures; they are often devout; they have blossomed in lettered men: they are gentlemen; the country rightly holds them in honour; but, in fine, I reject the proposal to go to General Darleton – Tears?'

'No, papa.'

'I do hope not. Here we have everything man can desire; without contest, an excellent host. You have your transitory tea-cup tempests, which you magnify to hurricanes, in the approved historic manner of the book of Cupid. And all the better; I repeat, it is the better that you should have them over in the infancy of the alliance. Come in!' Dr Middleton shouted cheerily in response to a knock at the door.

He feared the door was locked: he had a fear that his daughter intended to keep it locked.

'Clara!' he cried.

She reluctantly turned the handle, and the ladies Eleanor and Isabel came in, apologizing with as much coherence as Dr Middleton ever expected from their sex. They wished to speak to Clara, but they declined to take her away. In vain the Rev. Doctor assured them she was at their service; they protested that they had very few words to say, and would not intrude one moment further than to speak them.

Like a shy deputation of young scholars before the master, these very words to come were preceded by none at all; a dismal and trying cause; refreshing however to Dr Middleton, who joyfully anticipated that the ladies could be induced to take away Clara when they had finished.

'We may appear to you a little formal,' Miss Isabel began, and turned to her sister.

'We have no intention to lay undue weight on our mission, if mission it can be called,' said Miss Eleanor.

'Is it intrusted to you by Willoughby?' said Clara.

'Dear child, that you may know it all the more earnest with us, and our personal desire to contribute to your happiness: therefore does Willoughby intrust the speaking of it to us.'

Hereupon the sisters alternated in addressing Clara, and she gazed from one to the other, piecing fragments of empty signification to get the full meaning when she might.

'— And in saying, your happiness, dear Clara, we have our Willoughby's in view, which is dependent on yours.'

'— And we never could sanction that our own inclinations should stand in the way.'

'— No. We love the old place; and if it were only our punishment for loving it too idolatrously, we should deem it ground enough for our departure.'

'— Without, really, an idea of unkindness; none, not any.'

'— Young wives naturally prefer to be undisputed queens of their own establishment.'

'— Youth and age!'

'But I,' said Clara, 'have never mentioned, never had a thought . . .'

'— You have, dear child, a lover who in his solicitude for your happiness both sees what you desire and what is due to you.'

'— And for us, Clara, to recognize what is due to you is to act on it.'

'— Besides, dear, a sea-side cottage has always been one of our dreams.'

'– We have not to learn that we are a couple of old maids, incongruous associates for a young wife in the government of a great house.'

'– With our antiquated notions, questions of domestic management might arise, and with the best will in the world to be harmonious!'

'– So, dear Clara, consider it settled.'

'– From time to time gladly shall we be your guests.'

'– Your guests, dear, not censorious critics.'

'And you think me such an Egoist! – dear ladies! The suggestion of so cruel a piece of selfishness wounds me. I would not have had you leave the Hall. I like your society; I respect you. My complaint, if I had one, would be, that you do not sufficiently assert yourselves. I could have wished you to be here for an example to me. I would not have allowed you to go. What can he think of me! Did Willoughby speak of it this morning?'

It was hard to distinguish which was the completer dupe of these two echoes of one another in worship of a family idol.

'Willoughby,' Miss Eleanor presented herself to be stamped with the title hanging ready for the first that should open her lips, 'our Willoughby is observant – he is ever generous – and he is not less forethoughtful. His arrangement is for our good on all sides.'

'An index is enough,' said Miss Isabel, appearing in her turn the monster dupe.

'You will not have to leave, dear ladies. Were I mistress here I should oppose it.'

'Willoughby blames himself for not reassuring you before.'

'Indeed we blame ourselves for not undertaking to go.'

'Did he speak of it first this morning?' said Clara; but she could draw no reply to that from them. They resumed the duet, and she resigned herself to have her ears boxed with nonsense.

'So, it is understood?' said Miss Eleanor.

'I see your kindness, ladies.'

'And I am to be Aunt Eleanor again?'

'And I Aunt Isabel?'

Clara could have wrung her hands at the impediment which prohibited her delicacy from telling them why she could not name them so as she had done in the earlier days of Willoughby's courtship. She kissed them warmly, ashamed of kissing, though the warmth was real.

They retired with a flow of excuses to Dr Middleton for disturbing him. He stood at the door to bow them out, and holding the door for Clara to wind up the procession, discovered her at a far corner of the room.

He was debating upon the advisability of leaving her there, when Vernon Whitford crossed the hall from the laboratory door, a mirror of himself in his companion air of discomposure.

That was not important, so long as Vernon was a check on Clara, but the moment Clara, thus baffled, moved to quit the library, Dr Middleton felt the horror of having an uncomfortable face opposite.

'No botheration, I hope? It's the worst thing possible to work on. Where have you been? I suspect your weak point is not to arm yourself in triple brass against bother and worry, and no good work can you do unless you do. You have come out of that laboratory.'

'I have, sir. – Can I get you any book?' Vernon said to Clara.

She thanked him, promising to depart immediately.

'Now you are at the section of Italian literature, my love,' said Dr Middleton. 'Well, Mr Whitford, the laboratory – ah! – where the amount of labour done within the space of a year would not stretch an electric current between this Hall and the railway station: say, four miles, which I presume the distance to be. Well, sir, and a dilettantism costly in time and machinery is as ornamental as foxes' tails and deer's horns to an independent gentleman whose fellows are contented with the latter decorations for their civic wreath. Willoughby, let me remark, has recently shown himself most considerate for my girl. As far as I could gather – I have been listening to a dialogue of ladies – he is as generous as he is discreet. There are certain combats in which to be the one to succumb is to claim the honours; – and that is what women will not learn. I doubt their seeing the glory of it.'

'I have heard of it; I have been with Willoughby,' Vernon said, hastily, to shield Clara from her father's allusive attacks. He wished to convey to her that his interview with Willoughby had not been profitable in her interests, and that she had better at once, having him present to support her, pour out her whole heart to her father. But how was it to be conveyed? She would not meet his eyes, and he was too poor an intriguer to be ready on the instant to deal out the verbal obscurities which are transparencies to one.

'I shall regret it, if Willoughby has annoyed you, for he stands high in my favour,' said Dr Middleton.

Clara dropped a book. Her father started higher than the nervous impulse warranted in his chair. Vernon tried to win a glance, and she was conscious of his effort, but her angry and guilty feelings, prompting her resolution to follow her own counsel, kept her eyelids on the defensive.

'I don't say he annoys me, sir. I am here to give him my advice, and if he does not accept it I have no right to be annoyed. Willoughby seems annoyed that Colonel De Craye should talk of going to-morrow or next day.'

'He likes his friends about him. Upon my word, a man of a more genial heart you might march a day without finding. But you have it on the forehead, Mr Whitford.'

'Oh, no, sir.'

'There,' Dr Middleton drew his finger along his brows.

Vernon felt along his own, and coined an excuse for their blackness; not aware that the direction of his mind toward Clara pushed him to a kind of clumsy double meaning, while he satisfied an inward and craving wrath, as he said: 'By the way, I have been racking my head; I must apply to you, sir. I have a line, and I am uncertain of the run of the line. Will this pass, do you think?

      ' "In Asination's tongue he asinates";

signifying that he excels any man of us at donkey-dialect.'

After a decent interval for the genius of criticism to seem to have been sitting under his frown, Dr Middleton rejoined with sober jocularity:'No, sir, it will not pass; and your uncertainty in regard to the run of the line would only be extended were the line centipedal. Our recommendation is, that you erase it before the arrival of the ferule. This might do:

      ' "In Assignation's name he assignats";

signifying that he pre-eminently flourishes hypothetical promises to pay by appointment. That might pass. But you will forbear to cite me for your authority.'

'The line would be acceptable if I could get it to apply,' said Vernon.

'Or this . . .' Dr Middleton was offering a second suggestion, but Clara fled, astonished at men as she never yet had been. Why, in a burning world they would be exercising their minds in absurdities! And those two were scholars, learned men! And both knew they were in the presence of a soul in a tragic fever!

A minute after she had closed the door they were deep in their work. Dr Middleton forgot his alternative line.

'Nothing serious?' he said in reproof of the want of honourable clearness on Vernon's brows.

'I trust not, sir; it's a case for common sense.'

'And you call that not serious?'

'I take Hermann's praise of the versus dochmiachus to be not only serious but unexaggerated,' said Vernon.

Dr Middleton assented and entered on the voiceful ground of Greek metres, shoving your dry dusty world from his elbows.

CHAPTER 25

☒☒☒☒

The Flight in Wild Weather

THE morning of Lucy Darleton's letter of reply to her friend Clara was fair before sunrise, with luminous colours that are an omen to the husbandman. Clara had no weather-eye for the rich Eastern crimson, nor a quiet space within her for the beauty. She looked on it as her gate of promise, and it set her throbbing with a revived belief in radiant things which she had once dreamed of to surround her life, but her accelerated pulses narrowed her thoughts upon the machinery of her project. She herself was metal, pointing all to her one aim when in motion. Nothing came amiss to it, everything was fuel; fibs, evasions, the serene battalions of white lies parallel on the march with dainty rogue falsehoods. She had delivered herself of many yesterday in her engagements for to-day. Pressure was put on her to engage herself, and she did so liberally, throwing the burden of deceitfulness on the extraordinary pressure. 'I want the early part of the morning; the rest of the day I shall be at liberty.' She said it to Willoughby, Miss Dale, Colonel De Craye, and only the third time was she aware of the delicious double meaning. Hence she associated it with the colonel.

Your loudest outcry against the wretch who breaks your rules is in asking how a tolerably conscientious person could have done this and the other besides the main offence, which you vow you could overlook but for the minor objections pertaining to conscience, the incomprehensible and abominable lies, for example, or the brazen coolness of the lying. Yet you know that we live in an undisciplined world, where in our seasons of activity we are servants of our design, and that this comes of our passions, and those of our position. Our design shapes us for the work in hand, the passions man the ship, the position is their apology: and now should conscience be a passenger on board, a merely seeming swiftness of our vessel will keep him dumb as the unwilling guest of a pirate captain scudding from the cruiser half in cloven brine through rocks and shoals to save his black flag. Beware the false position.

That is easy to say: sometimes the tangle descends on us like a net of blight on a rose-bush. There is then an instant choice for us between courage to cut loose, and desperation if we do not. But not many men are trained to courage; young women are trained to cowardice. For them to front an evil with plain speech is to be guilty of effrontery and forfeit the waxen polish of purity, and therewith their commanding place in the market. They are trained to please man's taste, for which purpose they soon learn to live out of themselves, and look on themselves as he looks, almost as little disturbed as he by the undiscovered. Without courage, conscience is a sorry guest; and if all goes well with the pirate captain, conscience will be made to walk the plank for being of no service to either party.

Clara's fibs and evasions disturbed her not in the least that morning. She had chosen desperation, and she thought herself very brave because she was just brave enough to fly from her abhorrence. She was light-hearted, or, more truly, drunken-hearted. Her quick nature realized the out of prison as vividly and suddenly as it had sunk suddenly and leadenly under the sense of imprisonment. Vernon crossed her mind: that was a friend! Yes, and there was a guide; but he would disapprove, and even he, thwarting her way to sacred liberty, must be thrust aside.

What would he think? They might never meet, for her to know. Or one day in the Alps they might meet, a middle-aged couple, he famous, she regretful only to have fallen below his lofty standard. 'For, Mr Whitford,' says she, very earnestly, 'I did wish at that time, believe me or not, to merit your approbation.' The brows of the phantom Vernon whom she conjured up were stern, as she had seen them yesterday in the library.

She gave herself a chiding for thinking of him when her mind should be intent on that which he was opposed to.

It was a livelier relaxation to think of young Crossjay's shame-faced confession presently, that he had been a laggard in bed while she swept the dews. She laughed at him, and immediately Crossjay popped out on her from behind a tree, causing her to clap hand to heart and stand fast. A conspirator is not of the stuff to bear surprises. He feared he had hurt her, and was manly in his efforts to soothe: he had been up 'hours', he said, and had watched her coming along the avenue, and did not mean to startle her: it was the kind of fun he played with fellows, and if he had hurt her, she might do anything to him she liked, and she would see if he could not stand to be punished. He was urgent with her to inflict corporal punishment on him.

'I shall leave it to the boatswain to do that when you're in the navy,' said Clara.

'The boatswain daren't strike an officer! so now you see what you know of the navy,' said Crossjay.

'But you could not have been out before me, you naughty boy, for I found all the locks and bolts when I went to the door.'

'But you didn't go to the back door, and Sir Willoughby's private door: you came out by the hall door; and I know what you want, Miss Middleton, you want not to pay what you've lost.'

'What have I lost, Crossjay?'

'Your wager.'

'What was that?'

'You know.'

'Speak.'

'A kiss.'

'Nothing of the sort. But, dear boy, I don't love you less for not kissing you. All that is nonsense: you have to think only of learning, and to be truthful. Never tell a story: suffer anything rather than be dishonest.' She was particularly impressive upon the silliness and wickedness of falsehood, and added: 'Do you hear?'

'Yes: but you kissed me when I had been out in the rain that day.'

'Because I promised.'

'And, Miss Middleton, you betted a kiss yesterday.'

'I am sure, Crossjay – no, I will not say I am sure: but can you say you are sure you were out first this morning? Well, will you say you are sure that when you left the house you did not see me in the avenue? You can't: ah!'

'Miss Middleton, I do really believe I was dressed first.'

'Always be truthful, my dear boy, and then you may feel that Clara Middleton will always love you.'

'But, Miss Middleton, when you're married you won't be Clara Middleton.'

'I certainly shall, Crossjay.'

'No, you won't, because I'm so fond of your name!'

She considered, and said: 'You have warned me, Crossjay, and I shall not marry. I shall wait,' she was going to say, 'for you,' but turned the hesitation to a period. 'Is the village where I posted my letter the day before yesterday too far for you?'

Crossjay howled in contempt. 'Next to Clara, my favourite's Lucy,' he said.

'I thought Clara came next to Nelson,' said she; 'and a long way off too, if you're not going to be a landlubber.'

'I'm not going to be a landlubber, Miss Middleton, you may be absolutely positive on your solemn word.'

'You're getting to talk like one a little now and then, Crossjay.'

'Then I won't talk at all.'

He stuck to his resolution for one whole minute.

Clara hoped that on this morning of a doubtful though imperative venture she had done some good.

They walked fast to cover the distance to the village post-office, and back before the breakfast hour: and they had plenty of time, arriving too early for the opening of the door, so that Crossjay began to dance with an appetite, and was despatched to besiege a bakery. Clara felt lonely without him, apprehensively timid in the shuttered, unmoving village street. She was glad of his return. When at last her letter was handed to her, on the testimony of the postman that she was the lawful applicant, Crossjay and she put out on a sharp trot to be back at the Hall in good time. She took a swallowing glance of the first page of Lucy's writing:

'Telegraph, and I will meet you. I will supply you with everything you can want for the two nights, if you cannot stop longer.'

That was the gist of the letter. A second, less voracious, glance at it along the road brought sweetness: – Lucy wrote:

'Do I love you as I did? my best friend, you must fall into unhappiness to have the answer to that.'

Clara broke a silence.

'Yes, dear Crossjay, and if you like you shall have another walk with me after breakfast. But, remember, you must not say where you have gone with me. I shall give you twenty shillings to go and buy those birds' eggs and the butterflies you want for your collection; and mind, promise me, to-day is your last day of truancy. Tell Mr Whitford how ungrateful you know you have been, that he may have some hope of you. You know the way across the fields to the railway station?'

'You save a mile; you drop on the road by Combline's mill, and then there's another five-minutes' cut, and the rest's road.'

'Then, Crossjay, immediately after breakfast run round behind the pheasantry, and there I'll find you. And if any one comes to you before I come, say you are admiring the plumage of the Himalaya – the beautiful Indian bird; and if we're found together, we run a race, and of course you can catch me, but you mustn't until we're out of sight. Tell Mr Vernon at night – tell Mr Whitford at night you had the money from me as part of my allowance to you for pocket-money. I used to like to have pocket-money, Crossjay. And you may tell him I gave you the holiday, and I may write to him for his excuse, if he is not too harsh to grant it. He can be very harsh.'

'You look right into his eyes next time, Miss Middleton. I used to think him awful till he made me look at him. He says men ought to look straight at one another, just as we do when he gives me my boxing-lesson, and then we won't have quarrelling half so much. I can't recollect everything he says.'

'You are not bound to, Crossjay.'

'No, but you like to hear.'

'Really, dear boy. I can't accuse myself of having told you that.'

'No, but, Miss Middleton, you do. And he's fond of your singing and playing on the piano, and watches you.'

'We shall be late if we don't mind,' said Clara, starting to a pace close on a run.

They were in time for a circuit in the park to the wild double cherry-blossom, no longer all white. Clara gazed up from under it, where she had imagined a fairer visible heavenliness than any other sight of earth had ever given her. That was when Vernon lay beneath. But she had certainly looked above, not at him. The tree seemed sorrowful in its withering flowers of the colour of trodden snow.

Crossjay resumed the conversation.

'He says ladies don't like him much.'

'Who says that?'

'Mr Whitford.'

'Were those his words?'

'I forget the words: but he said they wouldn't be taught by him, like me, ever since you came; and since you came I've liked him ten times more.'

'The more you like him the more I shall like you, Crossjay.'

The boy raised a shout and scampered away to Sir Willoughby, at the appearance of whom Clara felt herself nipped and curling inward. Crossjay ran up to him with every sign of pleasure. Yet he had not mentioned him during the walk; and Clara took it for a sign that the boy understood the entire satisfaction Willoughby had in mere shows of affection, and acted up to it. Hardly blaming Crossjay, she was a critic of the scene, for the reason that youthful creatures who have ceased to love a person, hunger for evidence against him to confirm their hard animus, which will seem to them sometimes, when he is not immediately irritating them, brutish, because they can not analyze it and reduce it to the multitude of just antagonisms whereof it came. It has passed by large accumulation into a sombre and speechless load upon the senses, and fresh evidence, the smallest item, is a champion to speak for it. Being about to do wrong, she grasped at this eagerly, and brooded on the little of vital and truthful that there was in the man and how he corrupted the boy. Nevertheless, she instinctively imitated Crossjay in an almost sparkling salute to him.

'Good-morning, Willoughby; it was not a morning to lose: have you been out long?'

He retained her hand. 'My dear Clara! and you, have you not overfatigued yourself? Where have you been?'

'Round – everywhere! And I am certainly not tired.'

'Only you and Crossjay? You should have loosened the dogs.'

'Their barking would have annoyed the house.'

'Less than I am annoyed to think of you without protection.'

He kissed her fingers: it was a loving speech.

'The household . . .' said Clara, but would not insist to convict him of what he could not have perceived.

'If you outstrip me another morning, Clara, promise me to take the dogs; will you?'

'Yes.'

'To-day I am altogether yours.'

'Are you?'

'From the first to the last hour of it! – So you fall in with Horace's humour pleasantly?'

'He is very amusing.'

'As good as though one had hired him!'

'Here comes Colonel De Craye.'

'He must think we *have* hired him!'

She noticed the bitterness of Willoughby's tone. He sang out a good-morning to De Craye, and remarked that he must go to the stables.

'Darleton? Darleton, Miss Middleton?' said the colonel, rising from his bow to her: 'a daughter of General Darleton? If so, I have had the honour to dance with her. And have not you? – practised with her, I mean; or gone off in a triumph to dance it out as young ladies do? So you know what a delightful partner she is.'

'She is!' cried Clara, enthusiastic for her succouring friend, whose letter was the treasure in her bosom.

'Oddly, the name did not strike me yesterday, Miss Middleton. In the middle of the night it rang a little silver bell in my ear, and I remembered the lady I was half in love with, if only for her dancing. She is dark, of your height, as light on her feet; a sister in another colour. Now that I know her to be your friend . . .!'

'Why, you may meet her, Colonel De Craye.'

'It'll be to offer her a castaway. And one only meets a charming girl to hear that she's engaged! 'Tis not a line of a ballad, Miss Middleton, but out of the heart.'

'Lucy Darleton . . . You were leading me to talk seriously to you, Colonel De Craye.'

'Will you one day? – and not think me a perpetual tumbler! You have heard of melancholy clowns. You will find the face not so laughable behind my paint. When I was thirteen years younger I was loved, and my dearest sank to the grave. Since then I have not been quite at home in life; probably because of finding no one so charitable as she. 'Tis easy to win smiles and hands, but not so easy to win a woman whose faith you would trust as your own heart before the enemy. I was poor then. She said: "The day after my twenty-first birthday"; and that day I went for her, and I wondered they did not refuse me at the door. I was shown upstairs, and I saw her, and saw death. She wished to marry me, to leave me her fortune!'

'Then, never marry,' said Clara, in an underbreath.

She glanced behind.

Sir Willoughby was close, walking on turf.

'I must be cunning to escape him after breakfast,' she thought.

He had discarded his foolishness of the previous days, and the thought in him could have replied: 'I am a dolt if I let you out of my sight.'

Vernon appeared, formal as usual of late. Clara begged his excuse for withdrawing Crossjay from his morning swim. He nodded.

De Craye called to Willoughby for a book of the trains.

'There's a card in the smoking-room; eleven, one, and four are the hours, if you must go,' said Willoughby.

'You leave the Hall, Colonel De Craye?'

'In two or three days, Miss Middleton.'

She did not request him to stay: his announcement produced no effect on her. Consequently, thought he – well, what? nothing: well, then, she might not be minded to stay herself. Otherwise she would have regretted the loss of an amusing companion: that is the modest way of putting it. There is a modest and a vain for the same sentiment; and both may be simultaneously in the same breast; and each one as honest as the other; so shy is man's vanity in the presence of here and there a lady. She liked him: she did not care a pin for him – how could she? yet she liked him: O, to be able to do her some kindling bit of service! These were his consecutive fancies, resolving naturally to the exclamation, and built on the conviction that she did not love Willoughby, and waited for a spirited lift from circumstances. His call for a book of the

trains had been a sheer piece of impromptu, in the mind as
well as on the mouth. It sprang, unknown to him, of conjectures he had indulged yesterday and the day before. This
morning she would have an answer to her letter to her friend,
Miss Lucy Darleton, the pretty dark girl, whom De Craye
was astonished not to have noticed more when he danced
with her. She, pretty as she was, had come to his recollection
through the name and rank of her father, a famous general of
cavalry, and tactician in that arm. The colonel despised himself for not having been devoted to Clara Middleton's friend.

The morning's letters were on the bronze plate in the hall.
Clara passed on her way to her room without inspecting
them. De Craye opened an envelope and went upstairs to
scribble a line. Sir Willoughby observed their absence at the
solemn reading to the domestic servants in advance of breakfast. Three chairs were unoccupied. Vernon had his own
notions of a mechanical service – and a precious profit he derived from them! but the other two seats returned the stare
Willoughby cast at their backs with an impudence that reminded him of his friend Horace's calling for a book of the
trains, when a minute afterward he admitted he was going to
stay at the Hall another two days, or three. The man possessed
by jealousy is never in need of matter for it: he magnifies;
grass is jungle, hillocks are mountains. Willoughby's legs
crossing and uncrossing audibly, and his tight-folded arms
and clearing of the throat, were faint indications of his condition.

'Are you in fair health this morning, Willoughby?' Dr
Middleton said to him after he had closed his volumes.

'The thing is not much questioned by those who know me
intimately,' he replied.

'Willoughby unwell!' and, 'He is health incarnate!' exclaimed the ladies Eleanor and Isabel.

Laetitia grieved for him. Sun-rays on a pest-stricken city,
she thought, were like the smile of his face. She believed that
he deeply loved Clara, and had learned more of her alienation.

He went into the hall to look into the well for the pair of malefactors; on fire with what he could not reveal to a soul.

De Craye was in the housekeeper's room, talking to young Crossjay, and Mrs Montague just come up to breakfast. He had heard the boy chattering, and as the door was ajar he peeped in, and was invited to enter. Mrs Montague was very fond of hearing him talk: he paid her the familiar respect which a lady of fallen fortunes, at a certain period after the fall, enjoys as a befittingly sad souvenir, and the respectfulness of the lord of the house was more chilling.

She bewailed the boy's trying his constitution with long walks before he had anything in him to walk on.

'And where did you go this morning, my lad?' said De Craye.

'Ah, you know the ground, colonel,' said Crossjay. 'I am hungry! I shall eat three eggs and some bacon, and buttered cakes, and jam, then begin again, on my second cup of coffee.'

'It's not braggadocio,' remarked Mrs Montague. 'He waits empty from five in the morning till nine, and then he comes famished to my table, and eats too much.'

'Oh! Mrs Montague, that is what the country people call roemancing. For, Colonel De Craye, I had a bun at seven o'clock. Miss Middleton forced me to go and buy it.'

'A stale bun, my boy?'

'Yesterday's: there wasn't much of a stopper to you in it, like a new bun.'

'And where did you leave Miss Middleton when you went to buy the bun? You should never leave a lady; and the street of a country town is lonely at that early hour. Crossjay, you surprise me.'

'She forced me to go, colonel. Indeed she did. What do I care for a bun! And she was quite safe. We could hear the people stirring in the post-office, and I met our postman going for his letter-bag. I didn't want to go: bother the bun! – but you can't disobey Miss Middleton. I never want to, and wouldn't.'

'There we're of the same mind,' said the colonel, and Crossjay shouted, for the lady whom they exalted was at the door.

'You will be too tired for a ride this morning,' De Craye said to her, descending the stairs.

She swung a bonnet by the ribands. 'I don't think of riding to-day.'

'Why did you not depute your mission to me?'

'I like to bear my own burdens, as far as I can.'

'Miss Darleton is well?'

'I presume so.'

'Will you try her recollection for me?'

'It will probably be quite as lively as yours was.'

'Shall you see her soon?'

'I hope so.'

Sir Willoughby met her at the foot of the stairs, but refrained from giving her a hand that shook.

'We shall have the day together,' he said.

Clara bowed.

At the breakfast-table she faced a clock.

De Craye took out his watch. 'You are five and a half minutes too slow by that clock, Willoughby.'

'The man omitted to come from Rendon to set it last week, Horace. He will find the hour too late here for him when he does come.'

One of the ladies compared the time of her watch with De Craye's, and Clara looked at hers and gratefully noted that she was four minutes in arrear.

She left the breakfast-room at a quarter to ten, after kissing her father. Willoughby was behind her. He had been soothed by thinking of his personal advantages over De Craye, and he felt assured that if he could be solitary with his eccentric bride and fold her in himself, he would, cutting temper adrift, be the man he had been to her not so many days back. Considering how few days back, his temper was roused, but he controlled it.

They were slightly dissenting as De Craye stepped into the hall.

'A present worth examining,' Willoughby said to her: 'and I do not dwell on the costliness. Come presently, then. I am at your disposal all day. I will drive you in the afternoon to call on Lady Busshe to offer your thanks: but you must see it first. It is laid out in the laboratory.'

'There is time before the afternoon,' said Clara.

'Wedding-presents?' interposed De Craye.

'A porcelain service from Lady Busshe, Horace.'

'Not in fragments? Let me have a look at it. I'm haunted by an idea that porcelain always goes to pieces. I'll have a look and take a hint. We're in the laboratory, Miss Middleton.'

He put his arm under Willoughby's. The resistance to him was momentary: Willoughby had the satisfaction of the thought that De Craye being with him was not with Clara; and seeing her giving orders to her maid Barclay, he deferred his claim on her company for some short period.

De Craye detained him in the laboratory, first over the China cups and saucers, and then with the latest of London – tales of youngest Cupid upon subterranean adventures, having high titles to light him. Willoughby liked the tale thus illuminated, for without the title there was no special savour in such affairs, and it pulled down his betters in rank. He was of a morality to reprobate the erring dame while he enjoyed the incidents. He could not help interrupting De Craye to point at Vernon through the window, striding this way and that, evidently on the hunt for young Crossjay. 'No one here knows how to manage the boy except myself. But go on, Horace,' he said, checking his contemptuous laugh; and Vernon did look ridiculous, out there half-drenched already in a white rain, again shuffled off by the little rascal. It seemed that he was determined to have his runaway: he struck up the avenue at full pedestrian racing pace.

'A man looks a fool cutting after a cricket-ball; but putting on steam in a storm of rain to catch a young villain out of sight, beats anything I've witnessed,' Willoughby resumed, in his amusement.

'Aiha!' said De Craye, waving a hand to accompany the melodious accent, 'there are things to beat that for fun.'

He had smoked in the laboratory, so Willoughby directed a servant to transfer the porcelain service to one of the sitting-rooms for Clara's inspection of it.

'You're a bold man,' De Craye remarked. 'The luck may be with you, though. I wouldn't handle the fragile treasure for a trifle.'

'I believe in my luck,' said Willoughby.

Clara was now sought for. The lord of the house desired her presence impatiently, and had to wait. She was in none of the lower rooms. Barclay, her maid, upon interrogation, declared she was in none of the upper. Willoughby turned sharp on De Craye: he was there.

The ladies Eleanor and Isabel and Miss Dale were consulted. They had nothing to say about Clara's movements, more than that they could not understand her exceeding restlessness. The idea of her being out of doors grew serious; heaven was black, hard thunder rolled, and lightning flushed the battering rain. Men bearing umbrellas, shawls, and cloaks were dispatched on a circuit of the park. De Craye said: 'I'll be one.'

'No,' cried Willoughby, starting to interrupt him, 'I can't allow it.'

'I've the scent of a hound, Willoughby; I'll soon be on the track.'

'My dear Horace, I won't let you go.'

'Adieu, dear boy! and if the lady's discoverable, I'm the one to find her.'

He stepped to the umbrella-stand. There was then a general question whether Clara had taken her umbrella. Barclay said she had. The fact indicated a wider stroll than round inside the park: Crossjay was likewise absent. De Craye nodded to himself.

Willoughby struck a rattling blow on the barometer.

'Where's Pollington?' he called, and sent word for his man Pollington to bring big fishing-boots and waterproof wrappers.

An urgent debate within him was in progress.

Should he go forth alone on his chance of discovering Clara and forgiving her under his umbrella and cloak? or should he prevent De Craye from going forth alone on the chance he vaunted so impudently?

'You will offend me, Horace, if you insist,' he said.

'Regard me as an instrument of destiny, Willoughby,' replied De Craye.

'Then we go in company.'

'But that's an addition of one that cancels the other by conjunction, and's worse than simple division: for I can't trust my wits unless I rely on them alone, you see.'

'Upon my word, you talk at times most unintelligible stuff, to be frank with you, Horace. Give it in English.'

''Tis not suited, perhaps, to the genius of the language, for I thought I talked English.'

'Oh, there's English gibberish as well as Irish, we know!'

'And a deal foolisher when they do go at it; for it won't bear squeezing, we think, like Irish.'

'Where,' exclaimed the ladies, 'where can she be! The storm is terrible.'

Laetitia suggested the boathouse.

'For Crossjay hadn't a swim this morning!' said De Craye.

No one reflected on the absurdity that Clara should think of taking Crossjay for a swim in the lake, and immediately after his breakfast: it was accepted as a suggestion, at least that she and Crossjay had gone to the lake for a row.

In the hopefulness of the idea, Willoughby suffered De Craye to go on his chance unaccompanied. He was near chuckling. He projected a plan for dismissing Crossjay and remaining in the boathouse with Clara, luxuriating in the prestige which would attach to him for seeking and finding her.

Deadly sentiments intervened. Still he might expect to be alone with her where she could not slip from him.

The throwing open of the hall-doors for the gentlemen presented a framed picture of a deluge. All the young-leaved trees were steely black, without a gradation of green, drooping and pouring, and the song of rain had become an inveterate hiss.

The ladies beholding it exclaimed against Clara, even apostrophized her, so dark are trivial errors when circumstances frown. She must be mad to tempt such weather: she was very giddy; she was never at rest. Clara! Clara! how could you be so wild! Ought we not to tell Dr Middleton?

Laetitia induced them to spare him.

'Which way do you take?' said Willoughby, rather fearful that his companion was not to be got rid of now.

'Any way,' said De Craye. 'I chuck up my head like a half-penny, and go by the toss.'

This enrageing nonsense drove off Willoughby. De Craye saw him cast a furtive eye at his heels to make sure he was not followed, and thought, 'Jove! he may be fond of her. But he's not on the track. She's a determined girl, if I'm correct. She's a girl of a hundred thousand. Girls like that make the right sort of wives for the right men. They're the girls to make men think of marrying. To-morrow! only give me a chance. They stick to you fast when they do stick.'

Then a thought of her flower-like drapery and face caused him fervently to hope she had escaped the storm.

Calling at the West park-lodge he heard that Miss Middleton had been seen passing through the gate with Master Crossjay; but she had not been seen coming back. Mr Vernon Whitford had passed through half an hour later.

'After his young man!' said the colonel.

The lodge-keeper's wife and daughter knew of Master Crossjay's pranks; Mr Whitford, they said, had made inquiries about him, and must have caught him and sent him home to change his dripping things; for Master Crossjay had come back, and had declined shelter in the lodge; he seemed to be crying; he went away soaking over the wet grass, hanging his head. The opinion at the lodge was that Master Crossjay was unhappy.

'He very properly received a wigging from Mr Whitford, I have no doubt,' said Colonel De Craye.

Mother and daughter supposed it to be the case, and considered Crossjay very wilful for not going straight home to the Hall to change his wet clothes; he was drenched.

De Craye drew out his watch. The time was ten minutes past eleven. If the surmise he had distantly spied was correct, Miss Middleton would have been caught in the storm midway to her destination. By his guess at her character (knowledge of it, he would have said), he judged that no storm would daunt her on a predetermined expedition. He deduced in consequence that she was at the present moment flying to her friend, the charming brunette Lucy Darleton.

Still, as there was a possibility of the rain having been too much for her, and as he had no other speculation concerning the route she had taken, he decided upon keeping along the road to Rendon, with a keen eye at cottage and farmhouse windows.

CHAPTER 26

✖✖✖✖

Vernon in Pursuit

THE lodgekeeper had a son, who was a chum of Master Crossjay's, and errant-fellow with him upon many adventures; for this boy's passion was to become a gamekeeper, and accompanied by one of the head-gamekeeper's youngsters, he and

Crossjay were in the habit of rangeing over the country, preparing for a profession delightful to the tastes of all three. Crossjay's prospective connection with the mysterious ocean bestowed the title of captain on him by common consent; he led them, and when missing for lessons he was generally in the society of Jacob Croom or Jonathan Fernaway. Vernon made sure of Crossjay when he perceived Jacob Croom sitting on a stool in the little lodge-parlour. Jacob's appearance of a diligent perusal of a book he had presented to the lad, he took for a decent piece of trickery. It was with amazement that he heard from the mother and daughter, as well as Jacob, of Miss Middleton's going through the gate before ten o'clock with Crossjay beside her, the latter too hurried to spare a nod to Jacob. That she, of all on earth, should be encouraging Crossjay to truancy was incredible. Vernon had to fall back upon Greek and Latin aphoristic shots at the sex to believe it.

Rain was universal; a thick robe of it swept from hill to hill; thunder rumbled remote, and between the ruffled roars the downpour pressed on the land with a great noise of eager gobbling, much like that of the swine's trough fresh filled, as though a vast assembly of the hungered had seated themselves clamorously and fallen to on meats and drinks in a silence, save of the chaps. A rapid walker poetically and humourously minded gathers multitudes of images on his way. And rain, the heaviest you can meet, is a lively companion when the resolute pacer scorns discomfort of wet clothes and squealing boots. South-western rain-clouds, too, are never long sullen: they enfold and will have the earth in a good strong glut of the kissing overflow; then, as a hawk with feathers on his beak of the bird in his claw lifts head, they rise and take veiled feature in long climbing watery lines: at any moment they may break the veil and show soft upper cloud, show sun on it, show sky, green near the verge they spring from, of the green of grass in early dew; or, along a travelling sweep that rolls asunder overhead, heaven's laughter of purest blue among titanic white shoulders: it may mean fair smiling for awhile,

or be the lightest interlude; but the water lines, and the drifting, the chasing, the upsoaring, all in a shadowy fingering of
form, and the animation of the leaves of the trees pointing
them on, the bending of the tree-tops, the snapping of
branches, and the hurrahings of the stubborn hedge at wrestle
with the flaws, yielding but a leaf at most, and that on a fling,
make a glory of contest and wildness without aid of colour to
inflame the man who is at home in them from old association
on road, heath, and mountain. Let him be drenched, his heart
will sing. And thou, trim cockney, that jeerest, consider thy-
self, to whom it may occur to be out in such a scene, and with
what steps of a nervous dancing-master it would be thine to
play the hunted rat of the elements, for the preservation of the
one imagined dry spot about thee, somewhere on thy luckless
person! The taking of rain and sun alike befits men of our
climate, and he who would have the secret of a strengthening
intoxication must court the clouds of the South-west with a
lover's blood.

Vernon's happy recklessness was dashed by fears for Miss
Middleton. Apart from those fears, he had the pleasure of a
gull wheeling among foam-streaks of the wave. He supposed
the Swiss and Tyrol Alps to have hidden their heads from him
for many a day to come, and the springing and chiming
South-west was the next best thing. A milder rain descended;
the country expanded darkly defined underneath the moving
curtain; the clouds were as he liked to see them, scaling; but
their skirts dragged. Torrents were in store, for they coursed
streamingly still and had not the higher lift, or eagle ascent,
which he knew for one of the signs of fairness, nor had the
hills any belt of mist-like vapour.

On a step of the stile leading to the short-cut to Rendon
young Crossjay was espied. A man-tramp sat on the top-bar.

'There you are; what are you doing there? Where's Miss
Middleton?' said Vernon. 'Now, take care before you open
your mouth.'

Crossjay shut the mouth he had opened.

'The lady has gone away over to a station, sir,' said the tramp.

'You fool!' roared Crossjay, ready to fly at him.

'But ain't it now, young gentleman? Can you say it ain't?'

'I gave you a shilling, you ass!'

'You give me that sum, young gentleman, to stop here and take care of you, and here I stopped.'

'Mr Whitford!' Crossjay appealed to his master, and broke off in disgust. 'Take care of me! As if anybody who knows me would think I wanted taking care of! Why, what a beast you must be, you fellow!'

'Just as you like, young gentleman. I chaunted you all I know, to keep up your downcast spirits. You did want comforting. You wanted it rarely. You cried like an infant.'

'I let you "chaunt", as you call it, to keep you from swearing.'

'And why did I swear, young gentleman? because I've got an itchy coat in the wet, and no shirt for a lining. And no breakfast to give me a stomach for this kind of weather. That's what I've come to in this world! I'm a walking moral. No wonder I swears, when I don't strike up a chaunt.'

'But why are you sitting here wet through, Crossjay! Be off home at once, and change, and get ready for me.'

'Mr Whitford, I promised, and I tossed this fellow a shilling not to go bothering Miss Middleton.'

'The lady wouldn't have none o' the young gentleman, sir, and I offered to go pioneer for her to the station, behind her, at a respectful distance.'

'As if! – you treacherous cur!' Crossjay ground his teeth at the betrayer. 'Well, Mr Whitford, and I didn't trust him, and I stuck to him, or he'd have been after her whining about his coat and stomach, and talking of his being a moral. He repeats that to everybody.'

'She has gone to the station?' said Vernon.

Not a word on that subject was to be won from Crossjay.

'How long since?' Vernon partly addressed Mr Tramp.

The latter became seized with shivers as he supplied the information that it might be a quarter of an hour or twenty minutes. 'But what's time to me, sir? If I had reg'lar meals, I should carry a clock in my inside. I got the rheumatics instead.'

'Way there!' Vernon cried, and took the stile at a vault.

'That's what gentlemen can do, who sleeps in their beds warm,' moaned the tramp. 'They've no joints.'

Vernon handed him a half-crown piece, for he had been of use for once.

'Mr Whitford, let me come. If you tell me to come I may. Do let me come,' Crossjay begged with great entreaty. 'I sha'n't see her for . . .'

'Be off, quick!' Vernon cut him short and pushed on.

The tramp and Crossjay were audible to him; Crossjay spurning the consolations of the professional sad man.

Vernon spun across the fields, timing himself by his watch to reach Rendon station ten minutes before eleven, though without clearly questioning the nature of the resolution which precipitated him. Dropping to the road, he had better foothold than on the slippery field-path, and he ran. His principal hope was that Clara would have missed her way. Another pelting of rain agitated him on her behalf. Might she not as well be suffered to go? – and sit three hours and more in a railway-carriage with wet feet!

He clasped the visionary little feet to warm them on his breast. – But Willoughby's obstinate fatuity deserved the blow! – But neither she nor her father deserved the scandal. But she was desperate. Could reasoning touch her? If not, what would? He knew of nothing. Yesterday he had spoken strongly to Willoughby, to plead with him to favour her departure and give her leisure to sound her mind, and he had left his cousin, convinced that Clara's best measure was flight: a man so cunning in a pretended obtuseness backed by senseless pride, and in petty tricks that sprang of a grovelling tyranny, could only be taught by facts.

Her recent treatment of him, however, was very strange; so strange that he might have known himself better if he had reflected on the bound with which it shot him to a hard suspicion. De Craye had prepared the world to hear that he was leaving the Hall. Were they in concert? The idea struck at his heart colder than if her damp little feet had been there.

Vernon's full exoneration of her for making a confidant of himself, did not extend its leniency to the young lady's character when there was question of her doing the same with a second gentleman. He could suspect much: he could even expect to find De Craye at the station.

That idea drew him up in his run, to meditate on the part he should play; and by drove little Dr Corney on the way to Rendon, and hailed him, and gave his cheerless figure the nearest approach to an Irish hug in the form of a dry seat under an umbrella and water-proof covering.

'Though it is the worst I can do for you, if you decline to supplement it with a dose of hot brandy and water at the Dolphin,' said he: 'and I'll see you take it, if you please. I'm bound to ease a Rendon patient out of the world. Medicine's one of their superstitions, which they cling to the harder the more useless it gets. Pill and priest launch him happy between them. – "And what's on your conscience, Pat?" – "It's whether your blessing, your Riverence, would disagree with another drop." "Then put the horse before the cart, my son, and you shall have the two in harmony, and God speed ye!" – Rendon station, did you say, Vernon? You shall have my prescription at the Railway Arms, if you're hurried. You have the look. What is it? Can I help?'

'No. And don't ask.'

'You're like the Irish Grenadier who had a bullet in a humiliating situation. Here's Rendon, and through it we go with a spanking clatter. Here's Doctor Corney's dog-cart post-haste again. For there's no dying without him now, and Repentance is on the death-bed for not calling him in before. Half a charge of humbug hurts no son of a gun, friend Vernon, if he'd have his firing take effect. Be tender to't in man or woman, particularly woman. So, by goes the meteoric doctor, and I'll bring noses to window-panes, you'll see, which reminds me of the sweetest young lady *I* ever saw, and the luckiest man. When is she off for her bridal trousseau? And when are they spliced? I'll not call her perfection, for that's a post, afraid to move. But she's a dancing sprig of the tree next it. Poetry's wanted to speak of her. I'm Irish and inflammable, I suppose, but I never looked on a girl to make a man comprehend the entire holy meaning of the word rapturous, like that one. And away she goes! We'll not say another word. But you're a Grecian, friend Vernon. Now, couldn't you think her just a whiff of an idea of a daughter of a peccadillo-Goddess?'

'Deuce take you, Corney, drop me here; I shall be late for the train,' said Vernon, laying hand on the doctor's arm to check him on the way to the station in view.

Dr Corney had a Celtic intelligence for a meaning behind an illogical tongue. He drew up, observing: 'Two minutes run won't hurt you.'

He slightly fancied he might have given offence, though he was well acquainted with Vernon and had a cordial grasp at the parting.

The truth must be told that Vernon could not at the moment bear any more talk from an Irishman. Dr Corney had succeeded in persuading him not to wonder at Clara Middleton's liking for Colonel de Craye.

CHAPTER 27

✕✕✕✕

At the Railway Station

CLARA stood in the waiting-room contemplating the white rails of the rain-swept line. Her lips parted at the sight of Vernon.

'You have your ticket?' said he.

She nodded, and breathed more freely; the matter-of-fact question was reassuring.

'You are wet,' he resumed; and it could not be denied.

'A little. I do not feel it.'

'I must beg you to come to the inn hard by – half a dozen steps. We shall see your train signalled. Come.'

She thought him startlingly authoritative, but he had good sense to back him; and depressed as she was by the dampness, she was disposed to yield to reason if he continued to respect her independence. So she submitted outwardly, resisted inwardly, on the watch to stop him from taking any decisive lead.

'Shall we be sure to see the signal, Mr Whitford?'

'I'll provide for that.'

He spoke to the station-clerk, and conducted her across the road.

'You are quite alone, Miss Middleton?'

'I am: I have not brought my maid.'

'You must take off boots and stockings at once, and have them dried. I'll put you in the hands of the landlady.'

'But my train!'

'You have full fifteen minutes, besides fair chances of delay.'

He seemed reasonable, the reverse of hostile, in spite of his commanding air, and that was not unpleasant in one friendly to her adventure. She controlled her alert mistrustfulness, and passed from him to the landlady, for her feet were wet and cold, the skirts of her dress were soiled; generally inspecting herself, she was an object to be shuddered at, and she was grateful to Vernon for his inattention to her appearance.

Vernon ordered Dr Corney's dose, and was ushered upstairs to a room of portraits, where the publican's ancestors and family sat against the walls, flat on their canvas as weeds of the botanist's portfolio, although corpulency was pretty generally insisted on, and there were formidable battalions of bust among the females. All of them had the aspect of the national energy which has vanquished obstacles to subside on its ideal. They all gazed straight at the guest. 'Drink, and come to this!' they might have been labelled to say to him. He was in the private Walhalla of a large class of his countrymen. The existing host had taken forethought to be of the party in his prime, and in the central place, looking fresh-fattened there and sanguine from the performance. By and by a son would shove him aside; meanwhile he shelved his parent, according to the manners of energy.

One should not be a critic of our works of Art in uncomfortable garments. Vernon turned from the portraits to a stuffed pike in a glass case, and plunged into sympathy with the fish for a refuge.

Clara soon rejoined him, saying: 'But you, you must be very wet. You were without an umbrella. You must be wet through, Mr Whitford.'

'We're all wet through, to-day,' said Vernon. 'Crossjay's wet through, and a tramp he met.'

'The horrid man! But Crossjay should have turned back when I told him. Cannot the landlord assist you? You are not tied to time. I begged Crossjay to turn back when it began to rain: when it became heavy I compelled him. So you met my poor Crossjay?'

'You have not to blame him for betraying you. The tramp did that. I was thrown on your track quite by accident. Now pardon me for using authority, and don't be alarmed, Miss Middleton; you are perfectly free for me; but you must not run a risk to your health. I met Doctor Corney coming along, and he prescribed hot brandy and water for a wet skin, especially for sitting in it. There's the stuff on the table; I see you have been aware of a singular odour; you must consent to sip some, as medicine; merely to give you warmth.'

'Impossible, Mr Whitford: I could not taste it. But pray, obey Dr Corney, if he ordered it for you.'

'I can't, unless you do.'

'I will, then: I will try.'

She held the glass, attempted, and was baffled by the reek of it.

'Try: you can do anything,' said Vernon.

'Now that you find me here, Mr Whitford! Anything for myself, it would seem, and nothing to save a friend. But I will really try.'

'It must be a good mouthful.'

'I will try. And you will finish the glass?'

'With your permission, if you do not leave too much.'

They were to drink out of the same glass; and she was to drink some of this infamous mixture: and she was in a kind of hotel alone with him: and he was drenched in running after her: — all this came of breaking loose for an hour.

'Oh, what a misfortune that it should be such a day, Mr Whitford!'

'Did you not choose the day?'

'Not the weather.'

'And the worst of it is, that Willoughby will come upon Crossjay wet to the bone, and pump him and get nothing but shufflings, blank lies, and then find him out and chase him from the house.'

Clara drank immediately, and more than she intended. She held the glass as an enemy to be delivered from, gasping, uncertain of her breath.

'Never let me be asked to endure such a thing again.'

'You are unlikely to be running away from father and friends again.'

She panted still with the fiery liquid she had gulped: and she wondered that it should belie its reputation in not fortifying her, but rendering her painfully susceptible to his remarks.

'Mr Whitford, I need not seek to know what you think of me.'

'What I think? I don't think at all; I wish to serve you if I can.'

'Am I right in supposing you a little afraid of me? You should not be. I have deceived no one. I have opened my heart to you, and am not ashamed of having done so.'

'It is an excellent habit, they say.'

'It is not a habit with me.'

He was touched, and for that reason, in his dissatisfaction with himself, not unwilling to hurt. 'We take our turn, Miss Middleton. I'm no hero, and a bad conspirator, so I am not of much avail.'

'You have been reserved – but I am going, and I leave my character behind. You condemned me to the poison-bowl; you have not touched it yourself.'

'In vino veritas: if I do I shall be speaking my mind.'

'Then do, for the sake of mind and body.'

'It won't be complimentary.'

'You can be harsh. Only say everything.'

'Have we time?'

They looked at their watches.

'Six minutes,' Clara said.

Vernon's had stopped, penetrated by his total drenching.

She reproached herself. He laughed to quiet her. 'My dies solemnes are sure to give me duckings; I'm used to them. As for the watch, it will remind me that it stopped when you went.'

She raised the glass to him. She was happier and hoped for some little harshness and kindness mixed that she might carry away to travel with and think over.

He turned the glass as she had given it, turned it round in putting it to his lips: a scarce perceptible manœuvre, but that she had given it expressly on one side.

It may be hoped that it was not done by design. Done even accidentally, without a taint of contrivance, it was an affliction to see, and coiled through her, causing her to shrink and redden.

Fugitives are subject to strange incidents; they are not vessels lying safe in harbour. She shut her lips tight, as if they had stung. The realizing sensitiveness of her quick nature accused them of a loss of bloom. And the man who made her smart like this was formal as a railway official on a platform.

'Now we are both pledged in the poison-bowl,' said he. 'And it has the taste of rank poison, I confess. But the doctor prescribed it, and at sea we must be sailors. Now, Miss Middleton, time presses: will you return with me?'

'No! no!'

'Where do you propose to go?'

'To London; to a friend – Miss Darleton.'

'What message is there for your father?'

'Say I have left a letter for him in a letter to be delivered to you.'

'To me! And what message for Willoughby?'

'My maid Barclay will hand him a letter at noon.'

'You have sealed Crossjay's fate.'

'How?'

'He is probably at this instant undergoing an interrogation. You may guess at his replies. The letter will expose him, and Willoughby does not pardon.'

'I regret it. I cannot avoid it. Poor boy! My dear Crossjay! I did not think of how Willoughby might punish him. I was very thoughtless. Mr Whitford, my pin-money shall go for his education. Later, when I am a little older, I shall be able to support him.'

'That's an encumbrance; you should not tie yourself to drag it about. You are unalterable, of course, but circumstances are

not, and as it happens, women are more subject to them than
we are.'

'But I will not be!'

'Your command of them is shown at the present moment.'

'Because I determine to be free?'

'No: because you do the contrary; you don't determine:
you run away from the difficulty, and leave it to your father
and friends to bear. As for Crossjay, you see you destroy one
of his chances. I should have carried him off before this, if I
had not thought it prudent to keep him on terms with Willoughby. We'll let Crossjay stand aside. He'll behave like a
man of honour, imitating others who have had to do the
same for ladies.'

'Have spoken falsely to shelter cowards, you mean, Mr
Whitford. Oh, I know. – I have but two minutes. The die is
cast. I cannot go back. I must get ready. Will you see me to
the station? I would rather you should hurry home.'

'I will see the last of you. I will wait for you here. An express
runs ahead of your train, and I have arranged with the clerk
for a signal; I have an eye on the window.'

'You are still my best friend, Mr Whitford.'

'Though?'

'Well, though you do not perfectly understand what torments have driven me to this.'

'Carried on tides and blown by winds?'

'Ah! you do not understand.'

'Mysteries?'

'Sufferings are not mysteries, they are very simple facts.'

'Well, then, I don't understand. But decide at once. I wish
you to have your free will.'

She left the room.

Dry stockings and boots are better for travelling in than
wet ones, but in spite of her direct resolve, she felt when drawing them on like one that has been tripped. The goal was desirable, the ardour was damped. Vernon's wish that she should
have her free will compelled her to sound it: and it was of

course to go, to be liberated, to cast off incubus and hurt her father? injure Crossjay? distress her friends? No, and ten times no!

She returned to Vernon in haste, to shun the reflex of her mind.

He was looking at a closed carriage drawn up at the station door.

'Shall we run over now, Mr Whitford?'

'There's no signal. Here it's not so chilly.'

'I ventured to enclose my letter to papa in yours, trusting you would attend to my request to you to break the news to him gently and plead for me.'

'We will all do the utmost we can.'

'I am doomed to vex those who care for me. I tried to follow your counsel.'

'First you spoke to me, and then you spoke to Miss Dale; and at least you have a clear conscience.'

'No.'

'What burdens it?'

'I have done nothing to burden it.'

'Then it's a clear conscience.'

'No.'

Vernon's shoulders jerked. Our patience with an innocent duplicity in women is measured by the place it assigns to us and another. If he had liked he could have thought: 'You have not done but meditated something to trouble conscience.' That was evident, and her speaking of it was proof too of the willingness to be clear. He would not help her. Man's blood, which is the link with women and responsive to them on the instant for or against, obscured him. He shrugged anew when she said: 'My character would have been degraded utterly by my staying there. Could you advise it?'

'Certainly not the degradation of your character,' he said, black on the subject of De Craye, and not lightened by feelings which made him sharply sensible of the beggarly dependant that he was, or poor adventuring scribbler that he was to become.

'Why did you pursue me and wish to stop me, Mr Whitford?' said Clara, on the spur of a wound from his tone.

He replied: 'I suppose I'm a busybody; I was never aware of it till now.'

'You are my friend. Only you speak in irony so much. That was irony, about my clear conscience. I spoke to you and to Miss Dale: and then I rested and drifted. Can you not feel for me, that to mention it is like a scorching furnace? Willoughby has entangled papa. He schemes incessantly to keep me entangled. I fly from his cunning as much as from anything. I dread it. I have told you that I am more to blame than he, but I must accuse him. And wedding-presents! and congratulations! And to be his guest!'

'All that makes up a plea in mitigation,' said Vernon.

'Is it not sufficient for you?' she asked him, timidly.

'You have a masculine good sense that tells you you won't be respected if you run. Three more days there might cover a retreat with your father.'

'He will not listen to me. He confuses me; Willoughby has bewitched him.'

'Commission me: I will see that he listens.'

'And go back? Oh, no! To London! Besides, there is the dining with Mrs Mountstuart this evening; and I like her very well, but I must avoid her. She has a kind of idolatry . . . And what answers can I give? I supplicate her with looks. She observes them, my efforts to divert them from being painful produce a comic expression to her, and I am a charming "rogue", and I am entertained on the topic she assumes to be principally interesting me. I must avoid her. The thought of her leaves me no choice. She is clever. She could tattoo me with epigrams.'

'Stay: there you can hold your own.'

'She has told me you give me credit for a spice of wit. I have not discovered my possession. We have spoken of it; we call it your delusion. She grants me some beauty; that must be hers.'

'There's no delusion in one case or the other, Miss Middleton. You have beauty and wit; public opinion will say, wildness: indifference to your reputation will be charged on you, and your friends will have to admit it. But you will be out of *this* difficulty.'

'Ah – to weave a second?'

'Impossible to judge until we see how you escape the first. And I have no more to say. I love your father. His humour of sententiousness and doctorial stilts is a mask he delights in, but you ought to know him and not be frightened by it. If you sat with him an hour at a Latin task, and if you took his hand and told him you could not leave him, and no tears! – he would answer you at once. It would involve a day or two further; disagreeable to you, no doubt: preferable to the present mode of escape, as I think. But I have no power whatever to persuade. I have not the "lady's tongue". My appeal is always to reason.'

'It is a compliment. I loathe the "lady's tongue".'

'It's a distinctly good gift, and I wish I had it. I might have succeeded instead of failing, and appearing to pay a compliment.'

'Surely the express train is very late, Mr Whitford?'

'The express has gone by.'

'Then we will cross over.'

'You would rather not be seen by Mrs Mountstuart. That is her carriage drawn up at the station, and she is in it.'

Clara looked, and with the sinking of her heart said: 'I must brave her!'

'In that case I will take my leave of you here, Miss Middleton.'

She gave him her hand. 'Why is Mrs Mountstuart at the station to-day?'

'I suppose she has driven to meet one of the guests for her

dinner-party. Professor Crooklyn was promised to your father, and he may be coming by the down-train.'

'Go back to the Hall!' exclaimed Clara. 'How can I? I have no more endurance left in me. If I had some support! – if it were the sense of secretly doing wrong, it might help me through. I am in a web. I cannot do right, whatever I do. There is only the thought of saving Crossjay. Yes, and sparing papa. – Good-bye, Mr Whitford. I shall remember your kindness gratefully. I cannot go back.'

'You will not?' said he, tempting her to hesitate.

'No.'

'But if you are seen by Mrs Mountstuart, you must go back. I'll do my best to take her away. Should she see you you must patch up a story and apply to her for a lift. That, I think, is imperative.'

'Not to my mind,' said Clara.

He bowed hurriedly, and withdrew. After her confession, peculiar to her, of possibly finding sustainment in secretly doing wrong, her flying or remaining seemed to him a choice of evils: and whilst she stood in bewildered speculation on his reason for pursuing her – which was not evident – he remembered the special fear inciting him, and so far did her justice as to have at himself on that subject. He had done something perhaps to save her from a cold: such was his only consolatory thought. He had also behaved like a man of honour, taking no personal advantage of her situation; but to reflect on it recalled his astonishing dryness. The strict man of honour plays a part that he should not reflect on till about the fall of the curtain, otherwise he will be likely sometimes to feel the shiver of foolishness at his good conduct.

CHAPTER 28

❌❌❌❌

The Return

POSTED in observation at a corner of the window Clara saw
Vernon cross the road to Mrs Mountstuart Jenkinson's carriage, transformed to the leanest pattern of himself by narrowed shoulders and raised coat-collar. He had such an air
of saying, 'Tom's a-cold', that her skin crept in sympathy.

Presently he left the carriage and went into the station: a
bell had rung. Was it her train? He approved her going, for
he was employed in assisting her to go: a proceeding at
variance with many things he had said, but he was as full of
contradiction to-day as women are accused of being. The
train came up. She trembled: no signal had appeared, and
Vernon must have deceived her.

He returned; he entered the carriage, and the wheels were
soon in motion. Immediately thereupon, Flitch's fly drove
past, containing Colonel De Craye.

Vernon could not but have perceived him.

But what was it that had brought the colonel to this place?
The pressure of Vernon's mind was on her and foiled her
efforts to assert her perfect innocence, though she knew she
had done nothing to allure the colonel hither. Excepting
Willoughby, Colonel De Craye was the last person she would
have wished to encounter.

She had now a dread of hearing the bell which would tell
her that Vernon had not deceived her, and that she was out of
his hands, in the hands of some one else.

She bit at her glove; she glanced at the concentrated eyes of
the publican's family portraits, all looking as one; she noticed
the empty tumbler, and went round to it and touched it, and
the silly spoon in it.

A little yielding to desperation shoots us to strange distances! Vernon had asked her whether she was alone. Connecting that inquiry, singular in itself, and singular in his manner of putting it, with the glass of burning liquid, she repeated: 'He must have seen Colonel De Craye!' and she stared at the empty glass, as at something that witnessed to something: for Vernon was not your supple cavalier assiduously on the smirk to pin a gallantry to commonplaces. But all the doors are not open in a young lady's consciousness, quick of nature though she may be: some are locked and keyless, some will not open to the key, some are defended by ghosts inside. She could not have said what the something witnessed to. If we by chance know more, we have still no right to make it more prominent than it was with her. And the smell of the glass was odious; it disgraced her. She had an impulse to pocket the spoon for a memento, to show it to grandchildren for a warning. Even the prelude to the morality to be uttered on the occasion sprang to her lips: 'Here, my dears, is a spoon you would be ashamed to use in your teacups, yet it was of more value to me at one period of my life than silver and gold in pointing out, etc.': the conclusion was hazy, like the conception; she had her idea.

And in this mood she ran down-stairs and met Colonel De Craye on the station steps.

The bright illumination of his face was that of the confident man confirmed in a risky guess in the crisis of doubt and dispute.

'Miss Middleton!' his joyful surprise predominated; the pride of an accurate forecast, adding: 'I am not too late to be of service?'

She thanked him for the offer.

'Have you dismissed the fly, Colonel De Craye?'

'I have just been getting change to pay Mr Flitch. He passed me on the road. He is interwound with our fates to a certainty. I had only to jump in; I knew it, and rolled along like a magician commanding a genie.'

'Have I been . . .'

'Not seriously, nobody doubts you being under shelter. You will allow me to protect you? My time is yours.'

'I was thinking of a running visit to my friend Miss Darleton.'

'May I venture? I had the fancy that you wished to see Miss Darleton to-day. You cannot make the journey unescorted.'

'Please retain the fly. Where is Willoughby?'

'He is in jack-boots. But may I not, Miss Middleton? I shall never be forgiven if you refuse me.'

'There has been searching for me?'

'Some hallooing. But why am I rejected? Besides, I don't require the fly; I shall walk if I am banished. Flitch is a wonderful conjurer, but the virtue is out of him for the next four-and-twenty hours. And it will be an opportunity to me to make my bow to Miss Darleton!'

'She is rigorous on the conventionalities, Colonel De Craye.'

'I'll appear before her as an ignoramus or a rebel, whichever she likes best to take in leading-strings. I remember her. I was greatly struck by her.'

'Upon recollection!'

'Memory didn't happen to be handy at the first mention of the lady's name. As the general said of his ammunition and transport, there's the army! – but it was leagues in the rear. Like the footman who went to sleep after smelling fire in the house, I was thinking of other things. It will serve me right to be forgotten – if I am. I've a curiosity to know: a remainder of my coxcombry. Not that exactly: a wish to see the impression I made on your friend. – None at all? But any pebble casts a ripple.'

'That is hardly an impression,' said Clara, pacifying her irresoluteness with this light talk.

'The utmost to be hoped for by men like me! I have your permission? – one minute – I will get my ticket.'

'Do not,' said Clara.

'Your man-servant entreats you!'

She signified a decided negative with the head, but her eyes were dreamy. She breathed deep: this thing done would cut the cord. Her sensation of languor swept over her.

De Craye took a stride. He was accosted by one of the railway-porters. Flitch's fly was in request for a gentleman. A portly old gentleman bothered about luggage appeared on the landing.

'The gentleman can have it,' said De Craye, handing Flitch his money.

'Open the door,' Clara said to Flitch.

He tugged at the handle with enthusiasm. The door was open: she stepped in.

'Then mount the box and I'll jump up beside you,' De Craye called out, after the passion of regretful astonishment had melted from his features.

Clara directed him to the seat fronting her; he protested indifference to the wet; she kept the door unshut. His temper would have preferred to buffet the angry weather. The invitation was too sweet.

She heard now the bell of her own train. Driving beside the railway embankment she met the train: it was eighteen minutes late, by her watch. And why, when it flung up its whale-spouts of steam, she was not journeying in it, she could not tell. She had acted of her free will: that she could say. Vernon had not induced her to remain; assuredly her present companion had not; and her whole heart was for flight: yet she was driving back to the Hall, not devoid of calmness. She speculated on the circumstance enough to think herself incomprehensible, and there left it, intent on the scene to come with Willoughby.

'I must choose a better day for London,' she remarked.

De Craye bowed, but did not remove his eyes from her.

'Miss Middleton, you do not trust me.'

She answered: 'Say in what way. It seems to me that I do.'

THE EGOIST

'I may speak?'

'If it depends on my authority.'

'Fully?'

'Whatever you have to say. Let me stipulate, be not very grave. I want cheering in wet weather.'

'Miss Middleton, Flitch is charioteer once more. Think of it. There's a tide that carries him perpetually to the place where he was cast forth, and a thread that ties us to him in continuity. I have not the honour to be a friend of long standing: one ventures on one's devotion: it dates from the first moment of my seeing you. Flitch is to blame, if any one. Perhaps the spell would be broken, were he reinstated in his ancient office.'

'Perhaps it would,' said Clara, not with her best of smiles. Willoughby's pride of relentlessness appeared to her to be receiving a blow by rebound, and that seemed high justice.

'I am afraid you were right; the poor fellow has no chance,' De Craye pursued. He paused, as for decorum in the presence of misfortune, and laughed sparklingly: 'Unless I engage him, or pretend to! I verily believe that Flitch's melancholy person on the skirts of the Hall completes the picture of the Eden within. – Why will you not put some trust in me, Miss Middleton?'

'But why should you not pretend to engage him then, Colonel De Craye?'

'We'll plot it, if you like. Can you trust me for that?'

'For any act of disinterested kindness, I am sure.'

'You mean it?'

'Without reserve. You could talk publicly of taking him to London.'

'Miss Middleton, just now you were going. My arrival changed your mind. You distrust me: and ought I to wonder? The wonder would be all the other way. You have not had the sort of report of me which would persuade you to confide, even in a case of extremity. I guessed you were going. Do you ask me how? I cannot say. Through what they call sympathy, and that's inexplicable. There's natural sympathy, natural antipathy. People have to live together to discover how deep it is!'

Clara breathed her dumb admission of his truth.

The fly jolted and threatened to lurch.

'Flitch, my dear man!' the colonel gave a murmuring remonstrance; 'for,' said he to Clara, whom his apostrophe to Flitch had set smiling, 'we're not safe with him, however we make believe, and he'll be jerking the heart out of me before he has done. – But if two of us have not the misfortune to be united when they come to the discovery, there's hope. That is, if one has courage and the other has wisdom. Otherwise they may go to the yoke in spite of themselves. The great enemy is Pride, who has them both in a coach and drives them to the fatal door, and the only thing to do is to knock him off his box while there's a minute to spare. And as there's no pride like the pride of possession, the deadliest wound to him is to make that doubtful. Pride won't be taught wisdom in any other fashion. But one must have the courage to do it!'

De Craye trifled with the window-sash, to give his words time to sink in solution.

Who but Willoughby stood for Pride? And who, swayed by languor, had dreamed of a method that would be surest and swiftest to teach him the wisdom of surrendering her?

'You know, Miss Middleton, I study character,' said the colonel.

'I see that you do,' she answered.

'You intend to return?'

'Oh, decidedly.'

'The day is unfavourable for travelling, I must say.'

'It is.'

'You may count on my discretion in the fullest degree. I throw myself on your generosity when I assure you that it was not my design to surprise a secret. I guessed the station, and went there, to put myself at your disposal.'

'Did you,' said Clara, reddening slightly, 'chance to see

Mrs Mountstuart Jenkinson's carriage pass you when you drove up to the station?'

De Craye had passed a carriage. 'I did not see the lady. She was in it?'

'Yes. And therefore it is better to put discretion on one side: we may be certain she saw you.'

'But not you, Miss Middleton.'

'I prefer to think that I am seen. I have a description of courage, Colonel De Craye, when it is forced on me.'

'I have not suspected the reverse. Courage wants training, as well as other fine capacities. Mine is often rusty and rheumatic.'

'I cannot hear of concealment or plotting.'

'Except, pray, to advance the cause of poor Flitch!'

'He shall be excepted.'

The colonel screwed his head round for a glance at his coachman's back.

'Perfectly guaranteed to-day!' he said of Flitch's look of solidity. 'The convulsion of the elements appears to sober our friend; he is only dangerous in calms. Five minutes will bring us to the park-gates.'

Clara leaned forward to gaze at the hedgeways in the neighbourhood of the Hall strangely renewing their familiarity with her. Both in thought and sensation she was like a flower beaten to earth, and she thanked her feminine mask for not showing how nerveless and languid she was. She could have accused Vernon of a treacherous cunning for imposing it on her free will to decide her fate.

Involuntarily she sighed.

'There is a train at three,' said De Craye, with splendid promptitude.

'Yes, and one at five. We dine with Mrs Mountstuart to-night. And I have a passion for solitude! I think I was never intended for obligations. The moment I am bound I begin to brood on freedom.'

'Ladies who say that, Miss Middleton . . .!'

'What of them?'

'They're feeling too much alone.'

She could not combat the remark: by her self-assurance that she had the principle of faithfulness, she acknowledged to herself the truth of it: – there is no freedom for the weak. Vernon had said that once. She tried to resist the weight of it, and her sheer inability precipitated her into a sense of pitiful dependence.

Half an hour earlier it would have been a perilous condition to be traversing in the society of a closely scanning reader of fair faces. Circumstances had changed. They were at the gates of the park.

'Shall I leave you?' said De Craye.

'Why should you?' she replied.

He bent to her gracefully.

The mild subservience flattered Clara's languor. He had not compelled her to be watchful on her guard, and she was unaware that he passed it when she acquiesced to his observation, 'An anticipatory story is a trap to the teller.'

'It is,' she said. She had been thinking as much.

He threw up his head to consult the brain comically with a dozen little blinks.

'No, you are right, Miss Middleton, inventing beforehand never prospers: 'tis a way to trip our own cleverness. Truth and mother-wit are the best counsellors: and as you are the former, I'll try to act up to the character you assign me.'

Some tangle, more prospective than present, seemed to be about her as she reflected. But her intention being to speak to Willoughby without subterfuge, she was grateful to her companion for not tempting her to swerve. No one could doubt his talent for elegant fibbing, and she was in the humour both to admire and adopt the art, so she was glad to be rescued from herself. How mother-wit was to second truth she did not inquire, and as she did not happen to be thinking of Crossjay, she was not troubled by having to consider how truth and his tale of the morning would be likely to harmonize.

Driving down the park, she had full occupation in questioning whether her return would be pleasing to Vernon, who was the virtual cause of it, though he had done so little to promote it: so little that she really doubted his pleasure in seeing her return.

CHAPTER 29

✖✖✖✖

In Which the Sensitiveness of Sir Willoughby Is Explained: and He Receives Much Instruction

THE Hall-clock over the stables was then striking twelve. It was the hour for her flight to be made known, and Clara sat in a turmoil of dim apprehension that prepared her nervous frame for a painful blush on her being asked by Colonel De Craye whether she had set her watch correctly. He must, she understood, have seen through her at the breakfast-table: and was she not cruelly indebted to him for her evasion of Willoughby? Such perspicacity of vision distressed and frightened her; at the same time she was obliged to acknowledge that he had not presumed on it. Her dignity was in no way the worse for him. But it had been at a man's mercy, and there was the affliction.

She jumped from the fly as if she were leaving danger behind. She could at the moment have greeted Willoughby with a conventionally friendly smile. The doors were thrown open and young Crossjay flew out to her. He hung and danced on her hand, pressed the hand to his mouth, hardly believing that he saw and touched her, and in a lingo of dashes and asterisks related how Sir Willoughby had found him under the boathouse eaves and pumped him, and had been sent off to Hoppner's farm, where there was a sick child, and on along the road to a labourer's cottage: 'For I said you're so kind to poor people, Miss Middleton; that's true, now that *is* true. And I said you wouldn't have me with you for fear of contagion!' This was what she had feared.

'Every crack and bang in a boy's vocabulary,' remarked the colonel, listening to him after he had paid Flitch.

The latter touched his hat till he had drawn attention to himself, when he exclaimed, with rosy melancholy: 'Ah! my lady, ah! colonel, if ever I lives to drink some of the old port wine in the old Hall at Christmastide!' Their healths would on that occasion be drunk, it was implied. He threw up his eyes at the windows, humped his body and drove away.

'Then Mr Whitford has not come back?' said Clara to Crossjay.

'No, Miss Middleton. Sir Willoughby has, and he's upstairs in his room dressing.'

'Have you seen Barclay?'

'She has just gone into the laboratory. I told her Sir Willoughby wasn't there.'

'Tell me, Crossjay, had she a letter?'

'She had something.'

'Run: say I am here; I want the letter, it is mine.'

Crossjay sprang away and plunged into the arms of Sir Willoughby.

'One has to catch the fellow like a foot-ball,' exclaimed the injured gentleman, doubled across the boy and holding him fast, that he might have an object to trifle with, to give himself countenance: he needed it. 'Clara, you have not been exposed to the weather?'

'Hardly at all.'

'I rejoice. You found shelter?'

'Yes.'

'In one of the cottages?'

'Not in a cottage; but I was perfectly sheltered. Colonel De Craye passed a fly before he met me . . .'

'Flitch again!' ejaculated the colonel.

'Yes, you have luck, you have luck,' Willoughby addressed him, still clutching Crossjay and treating his tugs to get loose as an invitation to caresses. But the foil barely concealed his livid perturbation.

'Stay by me, sir,' he said at last sharply to Crossjay, and Clara touched the boy's shoulder in admonishment of him.

She turned to the colonel as they stepped into the hall: 'I have not thanked you, Colonel De Craye.' She dropped her voice to its lowest: 'A letter in my handwriting in the laboratory.'

Crossjay cried aloud with pain.

'I have you!' Willoughby rallied him with a laugh not unlike the squeak of his victim.

'You squeeze awfully hard, sir.'

'Why, you milksop!'

'Am I! But I want to get a book.'

'Where is the book?'

'In the laboratory.'

Colonel De Craye, sauntering by the laboratory door, sung out: 'I'll fetch you your book. What is it? EARLY NAVIGATORS? INFANT HYMNS? I think my cigar-case is in here.'

'Barclay speaks of a letter for me,' Willoughby said to Clara, 'marked to be delivered to me at noon!'

'In case of my not being back earlier; it was written to avert anxiety,' she replied.

'You are very good.'

'Oh, good! Call me anything but good. Here are the ladies. Dear ladies!' Clara swam to meet them as they issued from a morning-room into the hall, and interjections reigned' for a couple of minutes.

Willoughby relinquished his grasp of Crossjay, who darted instantaneously at an angle to the laboratory, whither he followed, and he encountered De Craye coming out, but passed him in silence.

Crossjay was rangeing and peering all over the room. Willoughby went to his desk and the battery-table and the mantelpiece. He found no letter. Barclay had undoubtedly informed him that she had left a letter for him in the laboratory, by order of her mistress after breakfast.

He hurried out and ran upstairs in time to see De Craye and Barclay breaking a conference.

He beckoned to her. The maid lengthened her upper lip and beat her dress down smooth: signs of the apprehension of a crisis and of the getting ready for action.

'My mistress's bell has just rung, Sir Willoughby.'

'You had a letter for me.'

'I said . . .'

'You said when I met you at the foot of the stairs that you had left a letter for me in the laboratory.'

'It is lying on my mistress's toilet-table.'

'Get it.'

Barclay swept round with another of her demure grimaces. It was apparently necessary with her that she should talk to herself in this public manner.

Willoughby waited for her; but there was no reappearance of the maid.

Struck by the ridicule of his posture of expectation, and of his whole behaviour, he went to his bedroom suite, shut himself in, and paced the chambers, amazed at the creature he had become. Agitated like the commonest of wretches, destitute of self-control, not able to preserve a decent mask, he, accustomed to inflict these emotions and tremours upon others, was at once the puppet and dupe of an intriguing girl. His very stature seemed lessened. The glass did not say so, but the shrunken heart within him did, and wailfully too. Her compunction – 'Call me anything but good' – coming after her return to the Hall beside De Craye, and after the visible passage of a secret between them in his presence, was a confession: it blew at him with the fury of a furnace-blast in his face. Egoist agony wrung the outcry from him that dupery is a more blessed condition. He desired to be deceived.

He could desire such a thing only in a temporary transport;

for above all he desired that no one should know of his being deceived; and were he a dupe the deceiver would know it, and her accomplice would know it, and the world would soon know of it: that world against whose tongue he stood defenceless. Within the shadow of his presence he compressed opinion, as a strong frost binds the springs of earth, but beyond it his shivering sensitiveness ran about in dread of a stripping in a wintry atmosphere. This was the ground of his hatred of the world: it was an appalling fear on behalf of his naked eidolon, the tender infant Self swaddled in his name before the world, for which he felt as the most highly civilized of men alone can feel, and which it was impossible for him to stretch out hands to protect. There the poor little loveable creature ran for any mouth to blow on; and frost-nipped and bruised, it cried to him, and he was of no avail! Must we not detest a world that so treats us? We loathe it the more, by the measure of our contempt for them, when we have made the people within the shadow-circle of our person slavish.

And he had been once a young prince in popularity: the world had been his possession. Clara's treatment of him was a robbery of land and subjects. His grander dream had been a marriage with a lady of so glowing a fame for beauty and attachment to her lord that the world perforce must take her for witness to merits which would silence detraction and almost, not quite (it was undesireable), extinguish envy. But for the nature of women his dream would have been realized. He could not bring himself to denounce Fortune. It had cost him a grievous pang to tell Horace De Craye he was lucky; he had been educated in the belief that Fortune specially prized and cherished little Willoughby: hence of necessity his maledictions fell upon women, or he would have forfeited the last blanket of a dream warm as poets revel in.

But if Clara deceived him, he inspired her with timidity. There was matter in that to make him wish to be deceived. She had not looked him much in the face: she had not crossed his eyes: she had looked deliberately downward, keeping her head up, to preserve an exterior pride. The attitude had its bewitchingness: the girl's physical pride of stature scorning to bend under a load of conscious guilt, had a certain blackangel beauty for which he felt a hugging hatred: and according to his policy when these fits of amorous meditation seized him, he burst from the present one in the mood of his more favourable conception of Clara, and sought her out.

The quality of the mood of hugging hatred is, that if you are disallowed the hug, you do not hate the fiercer.

Contrariwise the prescription of a decorous distance of two feet ten inches, which is by measurement the delimitation exacted of a rightly respectful deportment, has this miraculous effect on the great creature man, or often it has: that his peculiar hatred returns to the reluctant admiration begetting it, and his passion for the hug falls prostrate as one of the Faithful before the shrine; he is reduced to worship by fasting.

(For these mysteries, consult the sublime chapter in the GREAT BOOK, the Seventy-first on LOVE, wherein nothing is written, but the Reader receives a Lanthorn, a Powder-cask, and a Pick-axe, and therewith pursues his yellow-dusking path across the rubble of preceding excavators in the solitary quarry: a yet more instructive passage than the overscrawled Seventieth, or French Section, whence the chapter opens, and where hitherto the polite world has halted.)

The hurry of the hero is on us, we have no time to spare for mining works: he hurried to catch her alone, to wreak his tortures on her in a bitter semblance of bodily worship, and satiated, then comfortably to spurn. He found her protected by Barclay on the stairs.

'That letter for me?' he said.

'I think I told you, Willoughby, there was a letter I left with Barclay to reassure you in case of my not returning early,' said Clara. 'It was unnecessary for her to deliver it.'

'Indeed? But any letter, any writing of yours, and from you to me! You have it still?'

'No, I have destroyed it.'

'That was wrong,'

'It could not have given you pleasure.'

'My dear Clara, one line from you!'

'There were but three.'

Barclay stood sucking her lips. A maid in the secrets of her mistress is a purchaseable maid, for if she will take a bribe with her right hand she will with her left; all that has to be calculated is the nature and amount of the bribe: such was the speculation indulged by Sir Willoughby, and he shrank from the thought and declined to know more than that he was on a volcanic hillside where a thin crust quaked over lava. This was a new condition with him, representing Clara's gain in their combat. Clara did not fear his questioning so much as he feared her candour.

Mutually timid, they were of course formally polite, and no plain speaking could have told one another more distinctly that each was defensive. Clara stood pledged to the fib; packed, sealed and posted; and he had only to ask to have it, supposing that he asked with a voice not exactly peremptory. She said in her heart, 'It is your fault: you are relentless and you would ruin Crossjay to punish him for devoting himself to me, like the poor thoughtless boy he is! and so I am bound in honour to do my utmost for him.'

The reciprocal devotedness, moreover, served two purposes: it preserved her from brooding on the humiliation of her lame flight, and flutter back, and it quieted her mind in regard to the precipitate intimacy of her relations with Colonel De Craye. Willoughby's boast of his implacable character was to blame. She was at war with him, and she was compelled to put the case in that light. Crossjay must be shielded from one who could not spare an offender, so Colonel De Craye quite naturally was called on for his help, and the colonel's dexterous aid appeared to her more admirable than alarming.

Nevertheless, she would not have answered a direct

question falsely. She was for the fib, but not the lie; at a word she could be disdainful of subterfuges. Her look said that. Willoughby perceived it. She had written him a letter of three lines: 'There were but three': and she had destroyed the letter. Something perchance was repented by her? Then she had done him an injury! Between his wrath at the suspicion of an injury, and the prudence enjoined by his abject coveting of her, he consented to be fooled for the sake of vengeance, and something besides.

'Well! here you are, safe; I have you!' said he, with courtly exultation: 'and that is better than your handwriting. I have been all over the country after you.'

'Why did you? We are not in a barbarous land,' said Clara.

'Crossjay talks of your visiting a sick child, my love: – you have changed your dress?'

'You see.'

'The boy declared you were going to that farm of Hoppner's, and some cottage. I met at my gates a tramping vagabond who swore to seeing you and the boy in a totally contrary direction.'

'Did you give him money?'

'I fancy so.'

'Then he was paid for having seen me.'

Willoughby tossed his head: it might be as she suggested; beggars are liars.

'But who sheltered you, my dear Clara? You had not been heard of at Hoppner's.'

'The people have been indemnified for their pains. To pay them more would be to spoil them. You disperse money too liberally. There was no fever in the place. Who could have anticipated such a downpour! I want to consult Miss Dale on the important theme of a dress I think of wearing at Mrs Mountstuart's to-night.'

'Do. She is unerring.'

'She has excellent taste.'

'She dresses very simply herself.'

'But it becomes her. She is one of the few women whom I feel I could not improve with a touch.'

'She has judgement.'

He reflected and repeated his encomium.

The shadow of a dimple in Clara's cheek awakened him to the idea that she had struck him somewhere: and certainly he would never again be able to put up the fiction of her jealousy of Laetitia. What, then, could be this girl's motive for praying to be released? The interrogation humbled him: he fled from the answer.

Willoughby went in search of De Craye. That sprightly intriguer had no intention to let himself be caught solus. He was undiscoverable until the assembly sounded, when Clara dropped a public word or two, and he spoke in perfect harmony with her. After that, he gave his company to Willoughby for an hour at billiards, and was well beaten.

The announcement of a visit of Mrs Mountstuart Jenkinson took the gentlemen to the drawing-room, rather suspecting that something stood in the way of her dinner-party. As it happened, she was lamenting only the loss of one of the jewels of the party: to wit, the great Professor Crooklyn, invited to meet Dr Middleton at her table; and she related how she had driven to the station by appointment, the professor being notoriously a bother-headed traveller: as was shown by the fact that he had missed his train in town, for he had not arrived; nothing had been seen of him. She cited Vernon Whitford for her authority that the train had been inspected, and the platform scoured to find the professor.

'And so,' said she, 'I drove home your Green Man to dry him; he was wet through and chattering; the man was exactly like a skeleton wrapped in a sponge, and if he escapes a cold he must be as invulnerable as he boasts himself. These athletes are terrible boasters.'

'They climb their Alps to crow,' said Clara, excited by her apprehension that Mrs Mountstuart would speak of having seen the colonel near the station.

There was a laugh, and Colonel De Craye laughed loudly as it flashed through him that a quick-witted impressionable girl like Miss Middleton must, before his arrival at the Hall, have speculated on such obdurate clay as Vernon Whitford was, with humourous despair at his uselessness to her. Glancing round, he saw Vernon standing fixed in a stare at the young lady.

'You heard that, Whitford?' he said, and Clara's face betokening an extremer contrition than he thought was demanded, the colonel rallied the Alpine climber for striving to be the tallest of them – Signor Excelsior! – and described these conquerors of mountains pancaked on the rocks in desperate embraces, bleached here, burned there, barked all over, all to be able to say they had been up 'so high' – had conquered another mountain! He was extravagantly funny and self-satisfied: a conqueror of the sex having such different rewards of enterprise.

Vernon recovered in time to accept the absurdities heaped on him.

'Climbing peaks won't compare with hunting a wriggler,' said he.

His allusion to the incessant pursuit of young Crossjay to pin him to lessons was appreciated.

Clara felt the thread of the look he cast from herself to Colonel De Craye. She was helpless, if he chose to misjudge her. Colonel De Craye did not!

Crossjay had the misfortune to enter the drawing-room while Mrs Mountstuart was compassionating Vernon for his ducking in pursuit of the wriggler; which De Craye likened to 'going through the river after his eel:' and immediately there was a cross-questioning of the boy between De Craye and Willoughby on the subject of his latest truancy, each gentleman trying to run him down in a palpable fib. They were succeeding brilliantly when Vernon put a stop to it by marching him off to hard labour. Mrs Mountstuart was led away to inspect the beautiful porcelain service, the present of Lady Busshe. 'Porcelain again!' she said to Willoughby, and would have signalled to the 'dainty rogue' to come with them, had not Clara been leaning over to Laetitia, talking to her in an attitude too graceful to be disturbed. She called his attention to it, slightly wondering at his impatience. She departed to meet an afternoon train on the chance that it would land the professor. 'But tell Dr Middleton,' said she, 'I fear I shall have no one worthy of him! And,' she added to Willoughby, as she walked out to her carriage, 'I shall expect you to do the great-gunnery talk at table.'

'Miss Dale keeps it up with him best,' said Willoughby.

'She does everything best! But my dinner-table is involved, and I cannot count on a young woman to talk across it. I would hire a lion of a menagerie, if one were handy, rather than have a famous scholar at my table, unsupported by another famous scholar. Doctor Middleton would ride down a duke when the wine is in him. He will terrify my poor flock. The truth is, we can't leaven him: I foresee undigested lumps of conversation, unless you devote yourself.'

'I will devote myself,' said Willoughby.

'I can calculate on Colonel De Craye and our porcelain beauty for any quantity of sparkles, if you promise that. They play well together. You are not to be one of the gods to-night, but a kind of Jupiter's cup-bearer; – Juno's, if you like; and Lady Busshe and Lady Culmer, and all your admirers shall know subsequently what you have done. You see my alarm. I certainly did not rank Professor Crooklyn among the possibly faithless, or I never would have ventured on Doctor Middleton at my table. My dinner-parties have hitherto been all successes. Naturally I feel the greater anxiety about this one. For a single failure is all the more conspicuous. The exception is everlastingly cited! It is not so much what people say, but my own sentiments. I hate to fail. However, if you are true, we may do.'

'Whenever the great gun goes off I will fall on my face, madam!'

'Something of that sort,' said the dame, smiling, and leaving him to reflect on the egoism of women. For the sake of her dinner-party he was to be a cipher in attendance on Dr Middleton, and Clara and De Craye were to be encouraged in sparkling together! And it happened that he particularly wished to shine. The admiration of his county made him believe he had a flavour in general society that was not yet distinguished by his bride, and he was to relinquish his opportunity in order to please Mrs Mountstuart! Had she been in the pay of his rival, she could not have stipulated for more.

He remembered young Crossjay's instant quietude, after struggling in his grasp, when Clara laid her hand on the boy: and from that infinitesimal circumstance he deduced the boy's perception of a differing between himself and his bride, and a transfer of Crossjay's allegiance from him to her. She shone; she had the gift of female beauty; the boy was attracted to it. That boy must be made to feel his treason. But the point of the cogitation was, that similarly were Clara to see her affianced shining, as shine he could when lighted up by admirers, there was the probability that the sensation of her littleness would animate her to take aim at him once more. And then was the time for her chastisement.

A visit to Dr Middleton in the library satisfied him that she had not been renewing her entreaties to leave Patterne. No, the miserable coquette had now her pastime, and was content to stay. Deceit was in the air: he heard the sound of the shuttle of deceit without seeing it; but, on the whole, mindful of what he had dreaded during the hours of her absence, he was rather flattered, witheringly flattered. What was it that he had dreaded? Nothing less than news of her running away. Indeed a silly fancy, a lover's fancy! yet it had led him so far as to suspect, after parting with De Craye in the rain, that his friend and his bride were in collusion, and that he should not see them again. He had actually shouted on the rainy road the theatric call 'Fooled!' – one of the stage-cries which are cries of nature! particularly the cry of nature with men who have driven other men to the cry.

Constantia Durham had taught him to believe women capable of explosions of treason at half a minute's notice. And strangely, to prove that women are all of a pack, she had worn exactly the same placidity of countenance just before she fled, as Clara yesterday and to-day; no nervousness, no flushes, no twitches of the brows, but smoothness, ease of manner – an elegant sisterliness, one might almost say: as if the creature had found a midway and borderline to walk on between cruelty and kindness, and between repulsion and attraction; so that up to the verge of her breath she did forcefully attract, repelling at one foot's length with her armour of chill serenity. Not with any disdain, with no passion: such a line as she herself pursued she indicated to him on a neighbouring parallel. The passion in her was like a place of waves evaporated to a crust of salt. Clara's resemblance to Constantia in this instance was ominous. For him whose tragic privilege it had been to fold each of them in his arms, and weigh on their eyelids, and see the dissolving mist-deeps in their eyes, it was horrible. Once more the comparison overcame him. Constantia he could condemn for revealing too much to his manly sight: she had met him almost half-way: well, that was complimentary and sanguine: but her frankness was a baldness often rendering it doubtful which of the two, lady or gentleman, was the object of the chase – an extreme perplexity to his manly soul. Now Clara's inner spirit was shyer, shy as a doe down those rose-tinged abysses; she allured both the lover and the hunter; forests of heavenliness were in her flitting eyes. Here the difference of these fair women made his present fate an intolerable anguish. For if Constantia was like certain of the ladies whom he had rendered unhappy, triumphed over, as it is queerly called, Clara was not. Her individuality as a woman was a thing he had to bow to. It was impossible to roll her up in the sex and bestow a kick on the travelling bundle. Hence he loved her, though she hurt him. Hence his wretchedness, and but for the hearty sincerity of his faith in the Self he loved likewise and more, he would have been hangdog abject.

As for De Craye, Willoughby recollected his own exploits too proudly to put his trust in a man. That fatal conjunction of temper and policy had utterly thrown him off his guard, or he would not have trusted the fellow even in the first hour of his acquaintance with Clara. But he had wished her to be amused while he wove his plans to retain her at the Hall: – partly imagining that she would weary of his neglect: vile delusion! In truth he should have given festivities, he should have been the sun of a circle, and have revealed himself to her in his more dazzling form. He went near to calling himself foolish after the tremendous reverberation of 'Fooled!' had ceased to shake him.

How behave? It slapped the poor gentleman's pride in the face to ask. A private talk with her would rouse her to renew her supplications. He saw them flickering behind the girl's transparent calmness. That calmness really drew its dead ivory hue from the suppression of them: something as much he guessed; and he was not sure either of his temper or his policy if he should hear her repeat her profane request.

An impulse to address himself to Vernon and discourse with him jocularly on the childish whim of a young lady, moved perhaps by some whiff of jealousy, to shun the yoke, was checked. He had always taken so superior a pose with Vernon that he could not abandon it for a moment: on such a subject too! Besides, Vernon was one of your men who entertain the ideas about women of fellows that have never conquered one: or only one, we will say in his case, knowing his secret history; and that one no flag to boast of. Densely ignorant of the sex, his nincompoopish idealizations, at other times preposterous, would now be annoying. He would probably presume on Clara's inconceivable lapse of dignity to read his master a lecture: he was quite equal to a philippic upon woman's rights. This man had not been afraid to say that he talked common sense to women. He was an example of the consequence!

Another result was that Vernon did not talk sense to men. Willoughby's wrath at Clara's exposure of him to his cousin dismissed the proposal of a colloquy so likely to sting his temper, and so certain to diminish his loftiness. Unwilling to speak to anybody, he was isolated, yet consciously begirt by the mysterious action going on all over the house, from Clara and De Craye to Laetitia and young Crossjay, down to Barclay the maid. His blind sensitiveness felt as we may suppose a spider to feel when plucked from his own web and set in the centre of another's. Laetitia looked her share in the mystery. A burden was on her eyelashes. How she could have come to any suspicion of the circumstances, he was unable to imagine. Her intense personal sympathy, it might be; he thought so with some gentle pity for her – of the paternal pat-back order of pity. She adored him, by decree of Venus; and the Goddess had not decreed that he should find consolation in adoring her. Nor could the temptings of prudent counsel in his head induce him to run the risk of such a total turnover as the incurring of Laetitia's pity of himself by confiding in her. He checked that impulse also, and more sovereignly. For him to be pitied by Laetitia seemed an upsetting of the scheme of Providence. Providence, otherwise the discriminating dispensation of the good things of life, had made him the beacon, her the bird: she was really the last person to whom he could unbosom. The idea of his being in a position that suggested his doing so, thrilled him with fits of rage; and it appalled him. There appeared to be another Power. The same which had humiliated him once was menacing him anew. For it could not be Providence, whose favourite he had ever been. We must have a couple of Powers to account for discomfort when Egoism is the kernel of our religion. Benevolence had singled him for uncommon benefits: malignancy was at work to rob him of them. And you think well of the world, do you!

Of necessity he associated Clara with the darker Power pointing the knife at the quick of his pride. Still, he would have raised her weeping: he would have stanched her wounds bleeding: he had an infinite thirst for her misery, that he might ease his heart of its charitable love. Or let her commit herself, and be cast off. Only she must commit herself glaringly, and be cast off by the world as well. Contemplating her in the form of a discarded weed, he had a catch of the breath: she was fair. He implored his Power that Horace De Craye might not be the man! Why any man? An illness, fever, fire, runaway horses, personal disfigurement, a laming, were sufficient. And then a formal and noble offer on his part to keep to the engagement with the unhappy wreck: yes, and to lead the limping thing to the altar, if she insisted. His imagination conceived it, and the world's applause besides.

Nausea, together with a sense of duty to his line, extinguished that loathsome prospect of a mate, though without obscuring his chivalrous devotion to his gentleman's word of honour, which remained in his mind to compliment him permanently.

On the whole, he could reasonably hope to subdue her to admiration. He drank a glass of champagne at his dressing; an unaccustomed act, but, as he remarked casually to his man Pollington, for whom the rest of the bottle was left, he had taken no horse-exercise that day.

Having to speak to Vernon on business, he went to the schoolroom, where he discovered Clara, beautiful in full evening attire, with her arm on young Crossjay's shoulder, and heard that the hard task-master had abjured Mrs Mountstuart's party, and had already excused himself, intending to keep Crossjay to the grindstone. Willoughby was for the boy, as usual, and more sparklingly than usual. Clara looked at him in some surprise. He rallied Vernon with great zest, quite silencing him when he said: 'I bear witness that the fellow was here at his regular hour for lessons, and were you?' He laid his hand on Crossjay, touching Clara's.

'You will remember what I told you, Crossjay,' said she, rising from the seat gracefully to escape the touch. 'It is my command.'

Crossjay frowned and puffed.

'But only if I'm questioned,' he said.

'Certainly,' she replied.

'Then I question the rascal,' said Willoughby, causing a start. 'What, sir, is your opinion of Miss Middleton in her robe of state this evening?'

'Now, the truth, Crossjay!' Clara held up a finger; and the boy could see she was playing at archness, but for Willoughby it was earnest. 'The truth is not likely to offend you or me either,' he murmured to her.

'I wish him never, never, on any excuse, to speak anything else.'

'I always did think her a Beauty,' Crossjay growled. He hated the having to say it.

'There!' exclaimed Sir Willoughby, and bent, extending an arm to her. 'You have not suffered from the truth, my Clara!'

Her answer was: 'I was thinking how he might suffer if he were taught to tell the reverse.'

'Oh, for a fair lady!'

'That is the worst of teaching, Willoughby.'

'We'll leave it to the fellow's instinct; he has our blood in him. I could convince you, though, if I might cite circumstances. Yes! But yes! And yes again! The entire truth cannot invariably be told. I venture to say it should not.'

'You would pardon it for the "fair lady"?'

'Applaud, my love.'

He squeezed the hand within his arm, contemplating her.

She was arrayed in a voluminous robe of pale blue silk vapourous with trimmings of light gauze of the same hue, gaze de Chambéry, matching her fair hair and clear skin for the complete overthrow of less inflammable men than Willoughby.

'Clara!' sighed he.

'If so, it would really be generous,' she said, 'though the teaching is bad.'

'I fancy I can be generous.'

'Do we ever know?'

He turned his head to Vernon, issuing brief succinct instructions for letters to be written, and drew her into the hall, saying: 'Know? There are people who do *not* know themselves and as they are the majority they manufacture the axioms. And it is assumed that we have to swallow them. I may observe that I think I know. I decline to be engulphed in those majorities. "Among them, but not of them." I know this, that my aim in life is to be generous.'

'Is it not an impulse or disposition rather than an aim?'

'So much I know,' pursued Willoughby, refusing to be tripped. But she rang discordantly in his ear. His 'fancy that he could be generous' and his 'aim at being generous' had met with no response. 'I have given proofs,' he said, briefly, to drop a subject upon which he was not permitted to dilate; and he murmured, 'People acquainted with me . . .!' She was asked if she expected him to boast of generous deeds. 'From childhood!' she heard him mutter; and she said to herself, 'Release me, and you shall be everything!'

The unhappy gentleman ached as he talked: for with men and with hosts of women to whom he was indifferent, never did he converse in this shambling, third-rate, sheepish manner, devoid of all highness of tone and the proper precision of an authority. He was unable to fathom the cause of it, but Clara imposed it on him, and only in anger could he throw it off. The temptation to an outburst that would flatter him with the sound of his authoritative voice had to be resisted on a night when he must be composed if he intended to shine, so he merely mentioned Lady Busshe's present, to gratify spleen by preparing the ground for dissension, and prudently acquiesced in her anticipated slipperiness. She would rather not look at it now, she said.

'Not now; very well,' said he.

His immediate deference made her regretful. 'There is hardly time, Willoughby.'

'My dear, we shall have to express our thanks to her.'

'I cannot.'

His arm contracted sharply. He was obliged to be silent.

Dr Middleton, Laetitia, and the ladies Eleanor and Isabel joining them in the hall, found two figures linked together in a shadowy indication of halves that have fallen apart and hang on the last thread of junction. Willoughby retained her hand on his arm; he held to it as the symbol of their alliance, and oppressed the girl's nerves by contact, with a frame labouring for breath. De Craye looked on them from overhead. The carriages were at the door, and Willoughby said, 'Where's Horace? I suppose he's taking a final shot at his Book of Anecdotes and neat collection of Irishisms.'

'No,' replied the colonel, descending. 'That's a spring works of itself and has discovered the secret of continuous motion, more's the pity! – unless you'll be pleased to make it of use to Science.'

He gave a laugh of good-humour.

'Your laughter, Horace, is a capital comment on your wit.'

Willoughby said it with the air of one who has flicked a whip.

''Tis a genial advertisement of a vacancy,' said De Craye.

'Precisely: three parts auctioneer to one for the property.'

'Oh, if you have a musical quack, score it a point in his favour, Willoughby, though you don't swallow his drug.'

'If he means to be musical, let him keep time.'

'Am I late?' said De Craye to the ladies, proving himself an adept in the art of being gracefully vanquished, and so winning tender hearts.

Willoughby had refreshed himself. At the back of his mind there was a suspicion that his adversary would not have yielded so flatly without an assurance of practically triumphing, secretly getting the better of him; and it filled him with venom for a further bout at the next opportunity: but as he had been sarcastic and mordant, he had shown Clara what he could do in a way of speaking different from the lamentable cooing stuff, gasps and feeble protestations to which, he knew not how, she reduced him. Sharing the opinion of his race, that blunt personalities, or the pugilistic form, administered directly on the salient features, are exhibitions of mastery in such encounters, he felt strong and solid, eager for the successes of the evening. De Craye was in the first carriage as escort to the ladies Eleanor and Isabel. Willoughby, with Clara, Laetitia, and Dr Middleton, followed, all silent, for the Rev. Doctor was ostensibly pondering; and Willoughby was damped a little when he unlocked his mouth to say:

'And yet I have not observed that Colonel de Craye is anything of a Celtiberian Egnatius meriting fustigation for an untimely display of well-whitened teeth, sir: "quicquid est, ubicunque est, quodcunque agit, renidet:" 26 – ha? a morbus neither charming nor urbane to the general eye, however consolatory to the actor. But this gentleman does not offend so, or I am so strangely prepossessed in his favour as to be an incompetent witness.'

Dr Middleton's persistent ha? eh? upon an honest frown of inquiry plucked an answer out of Willoughby that was meant to be humourously scornful, and soon became apologetic under the Doctor's interrogatively grasping gaze.

'These Irishmen,' Willoughby said, 'will play the professional jester as if it were an office they were born to. We must play critic now and then, otherwise we should have them deluging us with their Joe Millerisms.'

'With their O'Millerisms you would say, perhaps?'

Willoughby did his duty to the joke, but the Rev. Doctor, though he wore the paternal smile of a man that has begotten hilarity, was not perfectly propitiated, and pursued: 'Nor to my apprehension is "the man's laugh the comment on his wit" unchallengeably new: instances of cousinship germane to the phrase will recur to you. But it has to be noted that it was a phrase of assault; it was ostentatiously battery;

and I would venture to remind you, friend, that among the elect, considering that it is as fatally facile to spring the laugh upon a man as to deprive him of his life, considering that we have only to condescend to the weapon, and that the more popular necessarily the more murderous that weapon is, – among the elect, to which it is your distinction to aspire to belong, the rule holds to abstain from any employment of the obvious, the percoct, and likewise, for your own sake, from the epitonic, the overstrained; for if the former, by readily assimilating with the understandings of your audience, are empowered to commit assassination on your victim, the latter come under the charge of unseemliness, inasmuch as they are a description of public suicide. Assuming, then, manslaughter to be your pastime, and hari-kari not to be your bent, the phrase, to escape criminality, must rise in you as you would have it fall on him, ex improviso. Am I right?'

'I am in the habit of thinking it impossible, sir, that you can be in error,' said Willoughby.

Dr Middleton left it the more emphatic by saying nothing further.

Both his daughter and Miss Dale, who had disapproved the waspish snap at Colonel De Craye, were in wonderment of the art of speech which could so soothingly inform a gentleman that his behaviour had not been gentlemanly.

Willoughby was damped by what he comprehended of it for a few minutes. In proportion as he realized an evening with his ancient admirers he was restored, and he began to marvel greatly at his folly in not giving banquets and Balls, instead of making a solitude about himself and his bride. For solitude, thought he, is good for the man, the man being a creature consumed by passion; woman's love, on the contrary, will only be nourished by the reflex light she catches of you in the eyes of others, she having no passion of her own, but simply an instinct driving her to attach herself to whatsoever is most largely admired, most shining. So thinking, he determined to change his course of conduct, and he was happier. In the first gush of our wisdom drawn directly from experience there is a mental intoxication that cancels the old world and establishes a new one, not allowing us to ask whether it is too late.

CHAPTER 30

✕✕✕✕

Treating of the Dinner-Party at Mrs Mountstuart Jenkinson's

VERNON and young Crossjay had tolerably steady work together for a couple of hours, varied by the arrival of a plate of meat on a tray for the master, and some interrogations put to him from time to time by the boy in reference to Miss Middleton. Crossjay made the discovery that if he abstained from alluding to Miss Middleton's beauty he might water his dusty path with her name nearly as much as he liked. Mention of her beauty incurred a reprimand. On the first occasion his master was wistful. 'Isn't she glorious!' Crossjay fancied he had started a sovereign receipt for blessed deviations. He tried it again, but paedagogue-thunder broke over his head.

'Yes, only I can't understand what she means, Mr Whitford,' he excused himself. 'First I was not to tell; I know I wasn't, because she said so; she quite as good as said so. Her last words were: "Mind, Crossjay, you know nothing about me", when I stuck to that beast of a tramp, who's a "walking moral", and gets money out of people by snuffling it.'

'Attend to your lesson, or you'll be one,' said Vernon.

'Yes, but, Mr Whitford, now I *am* to tell. I'm to answer straight out to every question.'

'Miss Middleton is anxious that you should be truthful.'

'Yes; but in the morning she told me not to tell.'

'She was in a hurry. She has it on her conscience that you may have misunderstood her, and she wishes you never to be guilty of an untruth, least of all on her account.'

Crossjay committed an unspoken resolution to the air in a violent sigh: 'Ah!' and said: 'If I were sure!'

'Do as she bids you, my boy.'

'But I don't know what it is she wants.'

'Hold to her last words to you.'

'So I do. If she told me to run till I dropped, on I'd go.'

'She told you to study your lessons; do that.'

Crossjay buckled to his book, invigorated by an imagination of his liege lady on the page.

After a studious interval, until the impression of his lady had subsided, he resumed: 'She's so funny. She's just like a girl, and then she's a lady, too. She's my idea of a princess. And Colonel De Craye! Wasn't he taught dancing! When he says something funny he ducks and seems to be setting to his partner. I should like to be as clever as her father. That is a clever man. I dare say Colonel De Craye will dance with her to-night. I wish I was there.'

'It's a dinner-party, not a dance,' Vernon forced himself to say, to dispel that ugly vision.

'Isn't it, sir? I thought they danced after dinner-parties, Mr Whitford, have you ever seen her run?'

Vernon pointed him to his task.

They were silent for a lengthened period.

'But does Miss Middleton mean me to speak out if Sir Willoughby asks me?' said Crossjay.

'Certainly. You needn't make much of it. All's plain and simple.'

'But I'm positive, Mr Whitford, he wasn't to hear of her going to the post-office with me before breakfast. And how did Colonel De Craye find her and bring her back, with that old Flitch? He's a man and can go where he pleases, and I'd have found her, too, give me the chance. You know, I'm fond

of Miss Dale, but she – I'm very fond of her – but you can't
think she's a girl as well. And about Miss Dale, when she says
a thing, there it is, clear. But Miss Middleton has a lot of
meanings. Never mind; I go by what's inside, and I'm pretty
sure to please her.'

'Take your chin off your hand and your elbow off the book,
and fix yourself,' said Vernon, wrestling with the seduction of
Crossjay's idolatry, for Miss Middleton's appearance had been
preternaturally sweet on her departure, and the next pleasure
to seeing her was hearing of her from the lips of this passionate young poet.

'Remember that you please her by speaking truth,' Vernon
added, and laid himself open to questions upon the truth, by
which he learnt, with a perplexed sense of envy and sympathy,
that the boy's idea of truth strongly approximated to his conception of what should be agreeable to Miss Middleton.

He was lonely, bereft of the bard, when he had tucked
Crossjay up in his bed and left him. Books he could not read;
thoughts were disturbing. A seat in the library and a stupid
stare helped to pass the hours, and but for the spot of sadness
moving meditation in spite of his effort to stun himself, he
would have borne a happy resemblance to an idiot in the sun.
He had verily no command of his reason. She was too beautiful! Whatever she did was best. That was the refrain of the
fountain-song in him; the burden being her whims, variations,
inconsistencies, wiles; her tremblings between good and
naughty, that might be stamped to noble or to terrible; her
sincereness, her duplicity, her courage, cowardice, possibilities
for heroism and for treachery. By dint of dwelling on the
theme, he magnified the young lady to extraordinary stature.
And he had sense enough to own that her character was yet
liquid in the mould, and that she was a creature of only
naturally youthful wildness provoked to freakishness by the
ordeal of a situation shrewd as any that can happen to her sex
in civilized life. But he was compelled to think of her extravagantly, and he leaned a little to the discrediting of her,

because her actual image unmanned him and was unbearable; and to say at the end of it: 'She is too beautiful! whatever she does is best,' smoothed away the wrong he did her. Had it been in his power he would have thought of her in the abstract – the stage contiguous to that which he adopted: but the attempt was luckless; the Stagyrite [27] would have failed in it. What philosopher could have set down that face of sun and breeze and nymph in shadow as a point in a problem?

The library door was opened at midnight by Miss Dale. She closed it quietly. 'You are not working, Mr Whitford? I fancied you would wish to hear of the evening. Professor Crooklyn arrived after all! Mrs Mountstuart is bewildered: she says she expected you, and that you did not excuse yourself to her, and she cannot comprehend, et caetera. That is to say, she chooses bewilderment to indulge in the exclamatory. She must be very much annoyed. The professor did come by the train she drove to meet!'

'I thought it probable,' said Vernon.

'He had to remain a couple of hours at the Railway Inn; no conveyance was to be found for him. He thinks he has caught a cold, and cannot stifle his fretfulness about it. He may be as learned as Doctor Middleton; he has not the same happy constitution. Nothing more unfortunate could have occurred; he spoilt the party. Mrs Mountstuart tried petting him, which drew attention to him, and put us all in his key for several awkward minutes, more than once. She lost her head; she was unlike herself. I may be presumptuous in criticizing her, but should not the president of a dinner-table treat it like a battlefield, and let the guest that sinks descend, and not allow the voice of a discordant, however illustrious, to rule it? Of course, it is when I see failures that I fancy I could manage so well: comparison is prudently reserved in the other cases. I am a daring critic, no doubt, because I know I shall never be tried by experiment. I have no ambition to be tried.'

She did not notice a smile of Vernon's, and continued: 'Mrs Mountstuart gave him the lead upon any subject he chose. I thought the professor never would have ceased talking of a young lady who had been at the inn before him drinking hot brandy and water with a gentleman!'

'How did he hear of that?' cried Vernon, roused by the malignity of the Fates.

'From the landlady, trying to comfort him. And a story of her lending shoes and stockings while those of the young lady were drying. He has the dreadful snappish humourous way of recounting which impresses it; the table took up the subject of this remarkable young lady, and whether she was a lady of the neighbourhood, and who she could be that went abroad on foot in heavy rain. It was painful to me; I knew enough to be sure of who she was.'

'Did she betray it?'

'No.'

'Did Willoughby look at her?'

'Without suspicion then.'

'Then?'

'Colonel De Craye was diverting us, and he was very amusing. Mrs Mountstuart told him afterward that he ought to be paid salvage for saving the wreck of her party. Sir Willoughby was a little too cynical; he talked well; what he said was good, but it was not good-humoured; he has not the reckless indifference of Colonel De Craye to uttering nonsense that amusement may come of it. And in the drawing-room he lost such gaiety as he had. I was close to Mrs Mountstuart when Professor Crooklyn approached her and spoke in my hearing of *that* gentleman and *that* young lady. They were, you could see by his nods, Colonel De Craye and Miss Middleton.'

'And she at once mentioned it to Willoughby?'

'Colonel De Craye gave her no chance, if she sought it. He courted her profusely. Behind his rattle he must have brains. It ran in all directions to entertain her and her circle.'

'Willoughby knows nothing?'

'I cannot judge. He stood with Mrs Mountstuart a minute as we were taking leave. She looked strange. I heard her say:

"The rogue." He laughed. She lifted her shoulders. He scarcely opened his mouth on the way home.'

'The thing must run its course,' Vernon said, with the philosophical air which is desperation rendered decorous. 'Willoughby deserves it. A man of full growth ought to know that nothing on earth tempts Providence so much as the binding of a young woman against her will. Those two are mutually attracted: they're both . . . They meet, and the mischief's done: both are bright. He can persuade with a word. Another might discourse like an angel and it would be useless. I said everything I could think of, to no purpose. And so it is: there are those attractions! – just as, with her, Willoughby is the reverse, he repels. I'm in about the same predicament – or should be if she were plighted to me. That is, for the length of five minutes; about the space of time I should require for the formality of handing her back her freedom. How a sane man can imagine a girl like that . . .! But if she has changed she has changed! You can't conciliate a withered affection. This detaining her, and tricking, and not listening, only increases her aversion; she learns the art in turn. Here she is, detained by fresh plots to keep Dr Middleton at the Hall. That's true, is it not?' He saw that it was. 'No, she's not to blame! She has told him her mind; he won't listen. The question then is, whether she keeps to her word, or breaks it. It's a dispute between a conventional idea of obligation and an injury to her nature. Which is the more dishonourable thing to do? Why, you and I see in a moment that her feelings guide her best. It's one of the few cases in which nature may be consulted like an oracle.'

'Is she so sure of her nature?' said Miss Dale.

'You may doubt it; I do not. I am surprised at her coming back. De Craye is a man of the world, and advised it, I suppose. He – well, I never had the persuasive tongue, and my failing doesn't count for much.'

'But the suddenness of the intimacy!'

'The disaster is rather famous "at first sight". He came in a fortunate hour . . . for him. A pigmy's a giant if he can manage to arrive in season. The à propos puffs us to the heroic size. Did you not notice that there was danger, at their second or third glance? You counselled me to hang on here, where the amount of good I do in proportion to what I have to endure is microscopic.'

'It was against your wishes, I know,' said Laetitia, and when the words were out she feared that they were tentative. Her delicacy shrank from even seeming to sound him in relation to a situation so delicate as Miss Middleton's.

The same sentiment guarded him from betraying himself, and he said: 'Partly against. We both foresaw the possible – because, like most prophets, we knew a little more of circumstances enabling us to see the fatal. A pigmy would have served, but De Craye is a handsome, intelligent, pleasant fellow.'

'Sir Willoughby's friend!'

'Well, in these affairs! A great deal must be charged on the goddess.'

'That is really Pagan fatalism!'

'Our modern word for it is Nature. Science condescends to speak of natural selection. Look at these! They are both graceful and winning and witty, bright to mind and eye, made for one another, as country people say. I can't blame him. Besides, we don't know that he's guilty. We're quite in the dark, except that we're certain how it must end. If the chance should occur to you of giving Willoughby a word of counsel – it may – you might, without irritating him as my knowledge of his plight does, hint at your eyes being open. His insane dread of a detective world makes him artificially blind. As soon as he fancies himself seen, he sets to work spinning a web, and he discerns nothing else. It's generally a clever kind of web; but if it's a tangle to others it's the same to him, and a veil as well. He is preparing the catastrophe, he forces the issue. Tell him of her extreme desire to depart. Treat her as mad, to soothe him. Otherwise one morning he will wake a second time . . .! It is perfectly certain. And the second time it will be entirely his own fault. Inspire him with some philosophy.'

'I have none.'

'If I thought so, I would say you have better. There are two kinds of philosophy, mine and yours. Mine comes of coldness, yours of devotion.'

'He is unlikely to choose me for his confidante.'

Vernon meditated. 'One can never quite guess what he will do, from never knowing the heat of the centre in him which precipitates his actions: he has a great art of concealment. As to me, as you perceive, my views are too philosophical to let me be of use to any of them. I blame only the one who holds to the bond. The sooner I am gone! – in fact, I cannot stay on. So Dr Middleton and the Professor did not strike fire together?'

'Doctor Middleton was ready, and pursued him, but Professor Crooklyn insisted on shivering. His line of blank verse, "A Railway platform and a Railway inn!" became pathetic in repetition. He must have suffered.'

'Somebody has to!'

'Why the innocent?'

'He arrives à propos. But remember that Fridolin [28] sometimes contrives to escape and have the guilty scorched. The Professor would not have suffered if he had missed his train, as he appears to be in the habit of doing. Thus his unaccustomed good-fortune was the cause of his bad.'

'You saw him on the platform?'

'I am unacquainted with the professor. I had to get Mrs Mountstuart out of the way.'

'She says she described him to you. "Complexion of a sweetbread, consistency of a quenelle, grey, and like a Saint without his dish."'

'Her descriptions are strikingly accurate, but she forgot to sketch his back, and all that I saw was a narrow sloping back and a broad hat resting the brim on it. My report to her spoke of an old gentleman of dark complexion, as the only traveller on the platform. She has faith in the efficiency of her descriptive powers, and so she was willing to drive off immediately. The intention was a start to London. Colonel De Craye came up and effected in five minutes what I could not compass in thirty.'

'But you saw Colonel De Craye pass you?'

'My work was done; I should have been an intruder. Besides I was acting wet jacket with Mrs Mountstuart to get her to drive off fast, or she might have jumped out in search of her Professor herself.'

'She says you were lean as a fork, with the wind whistling through the prongs.'

'You see how easy it is to deceive one who is an artist in phrases. Avoid them, Miss Dale; they dazzle the penetration of the composer. That is why people of ability like Mrs Mountstuart see so little; they are so bent on describing brilliantly. However, she is kind and charitable at heart. I have been considering to-night that, to cut this knot as it is now, Miss Middleton might do worse than speak straight out to Mrs Mountstuart. No one else would have such influence with Willoughby. The simple fact of Mrs Mountstuart's knowing of it would be almost enough. But courage would be required for that. Good-night, Miss Dale.'

'Good-night, Mr Whitford. You pardon me for disturbing you?'

Vernon pressed her hand reassuringly. He had but to look at her and review her history to think his cousin Willoughby punished by just retribution. Indeed, for any maltreatment of the dear boy Love by man or by woman, coming under your cognizance, you, if you be of common soundness, shall behold the retributive blow struck in your time.

Miss Dale retired thinking how like she and Vernon were to one another in the toneless condition they had achieved through sorrow. He succeeded in masking himself from her, owing to her awe of the circumstances. She reproached herself for not having the same devotion to the cold idea of duty as he had; and though it provoked inquiry, she would not stop to ask why he had left Miss Middleton a prey to the sparkling colonel. It seemed a proof of the philosophy he preached.

As she was passing by young Crossjay's bedroom door a face appeared. Sir Willoughby slowly emerged and presented himself in his full length, beseeching her to banish alarm.

He said it in a hushed voice, with a face qualified to create sentiment.

'Are you tired? sleepy?' said he.

She protested that she was not: she intended to read for an hour.

He begged to have the hour dedicated to him. 'I shall be relieved by conversing with a friend.'

No subterfuge crossed her mind; she thought his midnight visit to the boy's bedside a pretty feature in him; she was full of pity, too; she yielded to the strange request, feeling that it did not become 'an old woman' to attach importance even to the public discovery of midnight interviews involving herself as one, and feeling also that she was being treated as an old friend in the form of a very old woman. Her mind was bent on arresting any recurrence to the project she had so frequently outlined in the tongue of innuendo, of which, because of her repeated tremblings under it, she thought him a master.

He conducted her along the corridor to the private sitting-room of the ladies Eleanor and Isabel.

'Deceit!' he said, while lighting the candles on the mantel-piece.

She was earnestly compassionate, and a word that could not relate to her personal destinies refreshed her by displacing her apprehensive antagonism and giving pity free play.

CHAPTER 31

✖✖✖✖

Sir Willoughby Attempts and Achieves Pathos

BOTH were seated. Apparently he would have preferred to watch her dark downcast eyelashes in silence under sanction of his air of abstract meditation and the melancholy superinducing it. Blood-colour was in her cheeks; the party had inspirited her features. Might it be that lively company, an absence of economical solicitudes, and a flourishing home were all she required to make her bloom again? The supposition was not hazardous in presence of her heightened complexion.

She raised her eyes. He could not meet her look without speaking.

'Can *you* forgive deceit?'

'It would be to boast of more charity than I know myself to possess, were I to say that I can, Sir Willoughby. I hope I am able to forgive. I cannot tell. I should like to say yes.'

'Could you live with the deceiver?'

'No.'

'No. I could have given that answer for you. No semblance of union should be maintained between the deceiver and ourselves. Laetitia!'

'Sir Willoughby?'

'Have I no right to your name?'

'If it pleases you to . . .'

'I speak as my thoughts run, and they did not know a Miss Dale so well as a dear Laetitia: my truest friend! You have talked with Clara Middleton?'

'We had a conversation.'

Her brevity affrighted him. He flew off in a cloud.

'Reverting to that question of deceivers: is it not your opinion that to pardon, to condone, is to corrupt society by passing off as pure what is false? Do we not,' he wore the smile of haggard playfulness of a convalescent child the first day back to its toys, 'Laetitia, do we not impose a counterfeit on the currency?'

'Supposing it to be really deception.'

'Apart from my loathing of deception, of falseness in any shape, upon any grounds, I hold it an imperious duty to expose, punish, off with it. I take it to be one of the forms of noxiousness which a good citizen is bound to extirpate. I am not myself good citizen enough, I confess, for much more than passive abhorrence. I do not forgive: I am at heart serious and I cannot forgive: – there is no possible reconciliation, there can be only an ostensible truce, between the two hostile powers dividing this world.'

She glanced at him quickly.

'Good and evil!' he said.

Her face expressed a surprise relapsing on the heart.

He spelt the puckers of her forehead to mean that she feared he might be speaking unchristianly.

'You will find it so in all religions, my dear Laetitia: the Hindoo, the Persian, ours. It is universal; an experience of our humanity. Deceit and sincerity cannot live together. Truth must kill the lie, or the lie will kill truth. I do not forgive. All I say to the person is, go!'

'But that is right! that is generous!' exclaimed Laetitia, glad to approve him for the sake of escaping her critical soul, and relieved by the idea of Clara's difficulty solved.

'*Capable* of generosity, perhaps,' he mused, aloud.

She wounded him by not supplying the expected enthusiastic asseveration of her belief in his general tendency to magnanimity.

He said, after a pause: 'But the world is not likely to be impressed by anything not immediately gratifying it. People change, I find: as we increase in years we cease to be the heroes we were. I myself am insensible to change: I do not admit the charge. Except in this we will say: personal ambition. I have it no more. And what is it when we have it? Decidedly a confession of inferiority! That is, the desire to be distinguished is an acknowledgement of insufficiency. But I have still the craving for my dearest friends to think well of me. A weakness? Call it so. Not a dishonourable weakness!'

Laetitia racked her brain for the connection of his present speech with the preceding dialogue. She was baffled, from not knowing 'the heat of the centre in him', as Vernon opaquely phrased it, in charity to the object of her worship.

'Well,' said he, unappeased, 'and besides the passion to excel, I have changed somewhat in the heartiness of my thirst for the amusements incident to my station. I do not care to keep a stud – I was once tempted: nor hounds. And I can remember the day when I determined to have the best kennels and the best breed of horses in the kingdom. Puerile! What is distinction of that sort, or of any acquisition and accomplishment? We ask! One's *self* is not the greater. To seek it, owns to our smallness, in real fact; and when it is attained, what then? My horses are good, they are admired, I challenge the county to surpass them: well? These are but my horses; the praise is of the animals, not of me. I decline to share in it. Yet I know men content to swallow the praise of their beasts and be semi-equine. The littleness of one's fellows in the mob of life is a very strange experience! One may regret to have lost the simplicity of one's forefathers, which could accept those and other distinctions with a cordial pleasure, not to say pride. As, for instance, I am, as it is called, a dead shot. "Give your acclamations, gentlemen, to my ancestors, from whom I inherited a steady hand and quick sight." They do not touch *me.* Where I do not find myself – and *I* am *essentially* I – no applause can move me. To speak to you as I would speak to none, admiration – you know that in my early youth I swam in flattery – I had to swim to avoid drowning! – admiration of my personal gifts has grown tasteless. Changed, therefore, inasmuch as there has been a growth of spirituality. We are all in submission to mortal laws, and so far I have indeed changed. I may add that it is unusual for country gentlemen to apply themselves to scientific researches. These are, however, in the spirit of the time. I apprehended that instinctively when at College. I forsook the classics for science. And thereby escaped the vice of domineering self-sufficiency peculiar to classical men, of which you had an amusing example in the carriage, on the way to Mrs Mountstuart's this evening. Science is modest; slow, if you like; it deals with facts, and having mastered them, it masters men; of necessity, not with a stupid, loud-mouthed arrogance: words big and oddly garbed as the Pope's body-guard. Of course, one bows to the Infallible; we must, when his giant mercenaries level bayonets.'

Sir Willoughby offered Miss Dale half a minute that she might in gentle feminine fashion acquiesce in the implied re-proof of Dr Middleton's behaviour to him during the drive to Mrs Mountstuart's. She did not.

Her heart was accusing Clara of having done it a wrong and a hurt. For while he talked he seemed to her to justify Clara's feelings and her conduct: and her own reawakened sensations of injury came to the surface a moment to look at him, affirming that they pardoned him, and pitied, but hardly wondered.

The heat of the centre in him had administered the comfort he wanted, though the conclusive accordant notes he loved on woman's lips, that subservient harmony of another instrument desired of musicians when they have done their solo-playing, came not to wind up the performance: not a single bar. She did not speak. Probably his Laetitia was overcome, as he had long known her to be when they conversed; nerve-subdued, unable to deploy her mental resources or her musical. Yet ordinarily she had command of the latter. – Was she too con-doling? Did a reason exist for it? Had the impulsive and des-perate girl spoken out to Laetitia to the fullest? – shameless daughter of a domineering sire that she was! Ghastlier in-quiry (it struck the centre of him with a sounding ring), was Laetitia pitying him overmuch for worse than the pain of a little difference between lovers – for treason on the part of his bride? Did she know of a rival? know more than he?

When the centre of him was violently struck he was a genius in penetration. He guessed that she did know: and by this was he presently helped to achieve pathos.

'So my election was for Science,' he continued; 'and if it makes me, as I fear, a rara avis among country gentlemen, it unites me, puts me in the main, I may say, in the only current of progress – a word sufficiently despicable in their political jargon. – You enjoyed your evening at Mrs Mountstuart's?'

'Very greatly.'

'She brings her Professor to dine here the day after tomorrow. Does it astonish you? You started.'

'I did not hear the invitation.'

'It was arranged at the table: you and I were separated – cruelly, I told her: she declared that we see enough of one another, and that it was good for me that we should be separated; neither of which is true. I may not have known what is the best for me: I do know what is good. If in my younger days I egregiously erred, that, taken of itself alone, is, assuming me to have sense and feeling, the surer proof of present wisdom. I can testify in person that wisdom is pain. If pain is to add to wisdom, let me suffer! Do you approve of that, Laetitia?'

'It is well said.'

'It is felt. Those who themselves have suffered should know the benefit of the resolution.'

'One may have suffered so much as to wish only for peace.'

'True: but you! have you?'

'It would be for peace, if I prayed for any earthly gift.'

Sir Willoughby dropped a smile on her. 'I mentioned the Pope's parti-coloured body-guard just now. In my youth their singular attire impressed me. People tell me they have been re-uniformed: I am sorry. They remain one of my liveliest recollections of the Eternal City. They affected my sense of

humour, always alert in me, as you are aware. We English
have humour. It is the first thing struck in us when we land
on the Continent: our risible faculties are generally active all
through the tour. Humour, or the clash of sense with novel
examples of the absurd, is our characteristic. I do not condescend to boisterous displays of it. I observe, and note the
people's comicalities for my correspondence. But you have
read my letters – most of them, if not all?'

'Many of them.'

'I was with you then! – I was about to say – that Swiss-
guard reminded me – you have not been in Italy. I have constantly regretted it. You are the very woman, you have the
soul for Italy. I know no other of whom I could say it, with
whom I should not feel that she was out of place, discordant
with me. Italy and Laetitia! often have I joined you together.
We shall see. I begin to have hopes. Here you have literally
stagnated. Why, a dinner-party refreshes you! What would
not travel do, and that heavenly climate! You are a reader of
history and poetry. Well, poetry! I never yet saw the poetry
that expressed the tenth part of what I feel in the presence of
beauty and magnificence, and when I really meditate – profoundly. Call me a positive mind. I feel: only I feel too
intensely for poetry. By the nature of it, poetry cannot be
sincere. I will have sincerity. Whatever touches our emotions
should be spontaneous, not a craft. I know you are in favour of
poetry. You would win me, if any one could. But history!
there I am with you. Walking over ruins: at night: the arches
of the solemn black amphitheatre pouring moonlight on us –
the moonlight of Italy!'

'You would not laugh there, Sir Willoughby?' said
Lactitia, rousing herself from a stupor of apprehensive amazement, to utter something and realize actual circumstances.

'Besides, you, I think, or I am mistaken in you' – he devi-
ated from his projected speech – 'you are not a victim of the
sense of association and the ludicrous.'

'I can understand the influence of it: I have at least a conception of the humourous, but ridicule would not strike me in the Coliseum of Rome. I could not bear it, no, Sir Willoughby!'

She appeared to be taking him in very strong earnest, by thus petitioning him not to laugh in the Coliseum, and now he said: 'Besides, you are one who could accommodate yourself to the society of the ladies, my aunts. Good women, Laetitia! I cannot imagine them de trop in Italy, or in a household. I have of course reason to be partial in my judgement.'

'They are excellent and most amiable ladies; I love them,' said Laetitia, fervently; the more strongly excited to fervour by her enlightenment as to his drift.

She read it that he designed to take her to Italy with the ladies: – after giving Miss Middleton her liberty; that was necessarily implied. And that was truly generous. In his boyhood he had been famous for his bountifulness in scattering silver and gold. Might he not have caused himself to be misperused in later life?

Clara had spoken to her of the visit and mission of the ladies to the library: and Laetitia daringly conceived herself to be on the certain track of his meaning, she being able to enjoy their society as she supposed him to consider that Miss Middleton did not, and would not either abroad or at home.

Sir Willoughby asked her: 'You could travel with them?'
'Indeed I could!'
'Honestly?'
'As affirmatively as one may protest. Delightedly.'
'Agreed. It is an undertaking.' He put his hand out. 'Whether I be of the party or not! To Italy, Laetitia! It would give me pleasure to be with you, and it will, if I must be excluded, to think of you in Italy.'

His hand was out. She had to feign inattention or yield her own. She had not the effrontery to pretend not to see, and she yielded it. He pressed it, and whenever it shrunk a quarter inch to withdraw, he shook it up and down, as an instrument that had been lent him for due emphasis to his remarks. And very emphatic an amorous orator can make it upon a captive lady.

'I am unable to speak decisively on that or any subject. I am, I think you once quoted, "tossed like a weed on the ocean." Of myself I can speak: I cannot speak for a second person. I am infinitely harassed. If I could cry, "To Italy tomorrow!" Ah! . . . Do not set me down for complaining. I know the lot of man. But, Laetitia, deceit! deceit! It is a bad taste in the mouth. It sickens us of humanity. I compare it to an earthquake: we lose all our reliance on the solidity of the world. It is a betrayal not simply of the person; it is a betrayal of humankind. My friend! Constant friend! No, I will not despair. Yes, I have faults; I will remember them. Only, forgiveness is another question. Yes, the injury I *can* forgive; the falseness never. In the interests of humanity, no. So young, and such deceit!'

Laetitia's bosom rose: her hand was detained: a lady who has yielded it cannot wrestle to have it back; those outworks which protect her treacherously shelter the enemy aiming at the citadel when he has taken them. In return for the silken armour bestowed on her by our civilization, it is exacted that she be soft and civil nigh up to perishing-point. She breathed tremulously high, saying on her top-breath: 'If it – it may not be so; it can scarcely . . .' A deep sigh intervened. It saddened her that she knew so much.

'For when I love I love,' said Sir Willoughby; 'my friends and my servants know that. There can be no medium: not with me. I give all, I claim all. As I am absorbed, so must I absorb. We both cancel and create, we extinguish and we illumine one another. The error may be in the choice of an object: it is not in the passion. Perfect confidence, perfect abandonment. I repeat, I claim it because I give it. The selfishness of love may be denounced: it is a part of us. My answer would be, it is an element only of the noblest of us! Love, Laetitia! I speak of love. But one who breaks faith to drag us through the mire, who betrays, betrays and hands us over to the world, whose prey we become identically because of virtues we were educated to think it a blessing to possess: tell me the name for that! – Again, it has ever been a principle with me to respect the sex. But if we see women false, treacherous . . . Why indulge in these abstract views, you would ask! The world presses them on us, full as it is of the vilest specimens. They seek to pluck up every rooted principle: they sneer at our worship: they rob us of our religion. This bitter experience of the world drives us back to the antidote of what we knew before we plunged into it: of one . . . of something we esteemed and still esteem. Is that antidote strong enough to expel the poison? I hope so! I believe so! To lose faith in womankind is terrible.'

He studied her. She looked distressed: she was not moved.

She was thinking that, with the exception of a strain of haughtiness, he talked excellently to men, at least in the tone of the things he meant to say; but that his manner of talking to women went to an excess in the artificial tongue – the tutored tongue of sentimental deference of the towering male: he fluted exceedingly; and she wondered whether it was this which had wrecked him with Miss Middleton.

His intuitive sagacity counselled him to strive for pathos to move her. It was a task; for while he perceived her to be not ignorant of his plight, he doubted her knowing the extent of it, and as his desire was merely to move her without an exposure of himself, he had to compass being pathetic as it were under the impediments of a mailed and gauntletted knight, who cannot easily heave the bosom, or show it heaving.

Moreover, pathos is a tide: often it carries the awakener of it off his feet, and whirls him over and over armour and all in ignominious attitudes of helpless prostration, whereof he may well be ashamed in the retrospect. We cannot quite preserve our dignity when we stoop to the work of calling forth tears. Moses had probably to take a nimble jump away from the rock after that venerable Law-giver had knocked the water out of it.

However, it was imperative in his mind that he should be sure he had the power to move her.

He began; clumsily at first, as yonder gauntletted knight attempting the briny handkerchief.

'What are we! We last but a very short time. Why not live to gratify our appetites? I might really ask myself why. All the means of satiating them are at my disposal. But no: I must aim at the highest: – at that which in my blindness I took for the highest. You know the sportsman's instinct, Laetitia; he is not tempted by the stationary object. Such are we in youth, toying with happiness, leaving it, to aim at the dazzling and attractive.'

'We gain knowledge,' said Laetitia.

'At what a cost!'

The exclamation summoned self-pity to his aid, and pathos was handy.

'By paying half our lives for it and all our hopes! Yes, we gain knowledge, we are the wiser; very probably my value surpasses now what it was when I was happier. But the loss! That youthful bloom of the soul is like health to the body; once gone, it leaves cripples behind. Nay, my friend and precious friend, these four fingers I must retain. They seem to me the residue of a wreck: you shall be released shortly: absolutely, Laetitia, I have nothing else remaining – We have spoken of deception; what of being undeceived? – when one whom we adored is laid bare, and the wretched consolation of a worthy object is denied to us. No misfortune can be like that. Were it death, we could worship still. Death would be preferable. But may you be spared to know a situation in which the comparison with your inferior is forced on you to your disadvantage and your loss because of your generously giving up your whole heart to the custody of some shallow, light-minded, self – ! . . . We will not deal in epithets. If I were to find as many bad names for the serpent as there are spots on his body, it would be serpent still, neither better nor worse. The loneliness! And the darkness! Our luminary is extinguished. Self-respect refuses to continue worshipping, but the affection will not be turned aside. We are literally in the dust, we grovel, we would fling away self-respect if we could; we would adopt for a model the creature preferred to us; we would humiliate, degrade ourselves; we cry for justice as if it were for pardon . . .'

'For pardon! when we are straining to grant it!' Laetitia murmured, and it was as much as she could do. She remembered how in her old misery her efforts after charity had twisted her round to feel herself the sinner, and beg forgiveness in prayer: a noble sentiment, that filled her with pity of the bosom in which it had sprung. There was no similarity between his idea and hers, but her idea had certainly been roused by his word 'pardon', and he had the benefit of it in the moisture of her eyes. Her lips trembled, tears fell.

He had heard something; he had not caught the words, but they were manifestly favourable; her sign of emotion assured him of it and of the success he had sought. There was one woman who bowed to him to all eternity! He had inspired one woman with the mysterious, man-desired passion of self-abandonment, self-immolation! The evidence was before him. At any instant he could, if he pleased, fly to her and command her enthusiasm.

He had, in fact, perhaps by sympathetic action, succeeded in striking the same springs of pathos in her which animated his lively endeavour to produce it in himself.

He kissed her hand; then released it, quitting his chair to bend above her soothingly.

'Do not weep, Laetitia, you see that I do not; I can smile. Help me to bear it; you must not unman me.'

She tried to stop her crying, but self-pity threatened to rain all her long years of grief on her head, and she said: 'I must go . . . I am unfit . . . good-night, Sir Willoughby.'

Fearing seriously that he had sunk his pride too low in her consideration, and had been carried farther than he intended on the tide of pathos, he remarked: 'We will speak about

Crossjay to-morrow. His deceitfulness has been gross. As I said, I am grievously offended by deception. But you are tired. Good-night, my dear friend.'

'Good-night, Sir Willoughby.'

She was allowed to go forth.

Colonel De Craye coming up from the smoking-room, met her and noticed the state of her eyelids, as he wished her good-night. He saw Willoughby in the room she had quitted, but considerately passed without speaking, and without reflecting why he was considerate.

Our hero's review of the scene made him, on the whole, satisfied with his part in it. Of his power upon one woman he was now perfectly sure: – Clara had agonized him with a doubt of his personal mastery of any. One was a poor feast, but the pangs of his flesh during the last few days and the latest hours caused him to snatch at it, hungrily if contemptuously. A poor feast, she was yet a fortress, a point of succour, both shield and lance; a cover and an impetus. He could now encounter Clara boldly. Should she resist and defy him, he would not be naked and alone; he foresaw that he might win honour in the world's eye from his position – a matter to be thought of only in most urgent need. The effect on him of his recent exercise in pathos was to compose him to slumber. He was for the period well satisfied.

His attendant imps were well satisfied likewise, and danced around about his bed after the vigilant gentleman had ceased to debate on the question of his unveiling of himself past forgiveness of her to Laetitia, and had surrendered to sleep the present direction of his affairs.

CHAPTER 32

✗✗✗✗

Laetitia Dale Discovers a Spiritual Change and Dr Middleton a Physical

CLARA tripped over the lawn in the early morning to Laetitia to greet her. She broke away from a colloquy with Colonel De Craye under Sir Willoughby's windows. The colonel had been one of the bathers, and he stood like a circus-driver flicking a wet towel at Crossjay capering.

'My dear, I am very unhappy!' said Clara.

'My dear, I bring you news,' Laetitia replied.

'Tell me. But the poor boy is to be expelled! He burst into Crossjay's bedroom last night and dragged the sleeping boy out of bed to question him, and he had the truth. That is one comfort: only Crossjay is to be driven from the Hall, because he was untruthful previously – for me; to serve me; really, I feel it was at my command. Crossjay will be out of the way to-day, and has promised to come back at night to try to be forgiven. You must help me, Laetitia.'

'You are free, Clara! If you desire it, you have but to ask for your freedom.'

'You mean . . .'

'He will release you.'

'You are sure?'

'We had a long conversation last night.'

'I owe it to you?'

'Nothing is owing to me. He volunteered it.'

Clara made as if to lift her eyes in apostrophe. 'Professor Crooklyn! Professor Crooklyn! I see. I did not guess that.'

'Give credit for some generosity, Clara; you are unjust.'

'By and by: I will be more than just by and by. I will prac-tise on the trumpet: I will lecture on the greatness of the souls of men when we know them thoroughly. At present we do but half know them, and we are unjust. You are not deceived, Laetitia? There is to be no speaking to papa? no delusions? You have agitated me. I feel myself a very small person indeed. I feel I can understand those who admire him. He gives me back my word simply? clearly? without – Oh, that long wrangle in scenes and letters? And it will be arranged for papa and me to go not later than to-morrow? Never shall I be able to explain to any one how I fell into this! I am frightened at myself when I think of it. I take the whole blame: I have been scandalous. And, dear Laetitia! you came out so early in order to tell me?'

'I wished you to hear it.'

'Take my heart.'

'Present me with a part – but for good!'

'Fie! But you have a right to say it.'

'I mean no unkindness; but is not the heart you allude to an alarmingly searching one?'

'Selfish it is, for I have been forgetting Crossjay. If we are going to be generous, is not Crossjay to be forgiven? If it were only that the boy's father is away fighting for his country, en-dangering his life day by day, and for a stipend not enough to support his family, we are bound to think of the boy! Poor dear silly lad! with his "I say, Miss Middleton, why wouldn't (some one) see my father when he came here to call on him, and had to walk back ten miles in the rain?" – I could almost fancy that did me mischief . . . But we have a splendid morn-ing after yesterday's rain. And we will be generous. Own, Laetitia, that it is possible to gild the most glorious day of creation.'

'Doubtless the spirit may do it and make its hues perma-nent,' said Laetitia.

'You to me, I to you, he to us. Well, then, if he does, it shall be one of my heavenly days. Which is for the probation of experience. We are not yet at sunset.'

'Have you seen Mr Whitford this morning?'

'He passed me.'

'Do not imagine him ever ill-tempered.'

'I had a governess, a learned lady, who taught me in person the picturesqueness of grumpiness. Her temper was ever perfect, because she was never in the wrong, but I being so, she was grumpy. She carried my iniquity under her brows, and looked out on me through it. I was a trying child.'

Laetitia said, laughing: 'I can believe it!'

'Yet I liked her and she liked me: we were a kind of foreground and background: she threw me into relief, and I was an apology for her existence.'

'You picture her to me.'

'She says of me now that I am the only creature she has loved. Who knows that I may not come to say the same of her?'

'You would plague her and puzzle her still.'

'Have I plagued and puzzled Mr Whitford?'

'He reminds you of her?'

'You said you had her picture.'

'Ah, do not laugh at him. He is a true friend.'

'The man who can be a friend is the man who will presume to be a censor.'

'A mild one.'

'As to the sentence he pronounces, I am unable to speak, but his forehead is Rhadamanthine condemnation.'

'Dr Middleton!'

Clara looked round. 'Who? I? Did you hear an echo of papa? He would never have put Rhadamanthus over European souls, because it appears that Rhadamanthus judged only the Asiatic; so you are wrong, Miss Dale. My father is infatuated with Mr Whitford. What can it be? We women cannot sound the depths of scholars, probably because their pearls have no value in our market; except when they deign to chasten an impertinent; and Mr Whitford stands aloof from any notice of small fry. He is deep, studious, excellent; and does it not strike you that if he descended among us he would be like a Triton ashore?'

Laetitia's habit of wholly subservient sweetness, which was her ideal of the feminine, not yet conciliated with her acuter character, owing to the absence of full pleasure from her life – the unhealed wound she had sustained and the cramp of a bondage of such old date as to seem iron – induced her to say, as if consenting: 'You think he is not quite at home in society?' But she wished to defend him strenuously, and as a consequence she had to quit the self-imposed ideal of her daily acting, whereby – the case being unwonted, very novel to her – the lady's intelligence became confused through the process that quickened it; so sovereign a method of hoodwinking our bright selves is the acting of a part, however naturally it may come to us! and to this will each honest autobiographical member of the animated world bear witness.

She added: 'You have not found him sympathetic? He is. You fancy him brooding, gloomy? He is the reverse, he is cheerful, he is indifferent to personal misfortune. Dr Corney says there is no laugh like Vernon Whitford's, and no humour like his. Latterly he certainly . . . But it has not been your cruel word grumpiness. The truth is, he is anxious about Crossjay: and about other things; and he wants to leave. He is at a disadvantage beside very lively and careless gentlemen at present, but your "Triton ashore" is unfair, it is ugly. He is, I can say, the truest man I know.'

'I did not question his goodness, Laetitia.'

'You throw an accent on it.'

'Did I? I must be like Crossjay, who declares he likes fun best.'

'Crossjay ought to know him, if anybody should. Mr Whitford has defended you against me, Clara, even since I took to calling you Clara. Perhaps when you supposed him so like your ancient governess, he was meditating how he could aid you. Last night he gave me reasons for thinking you would do wisely to confide in Mrs Mountstuart. It is no longer necessary. I merely mention it. He is a devoted friend.'

'He is an untiring pedestrian.'

'Oh!'

Colonel De Craye, after hovering near the ladies in the hope of seeing them divide, now adopted the system of making three that two may come of it.

As he joined them with his glittering chatter, Laetitia looked at Clara to consult her, and saw the face rosy as a bride's.

The suspicion she had nursed sprung out of her arms a muscular fact on the spot.

'Where is my dear boy?' Clara said.

'Out for a holiday,' the colonel answered in her tone.

'Advise Mr Whitford not to waste his time in searching for Crossjay, Laetitia. Crossjay is better out of the way to-day. At least, I thought so just now. Has he pocket-money, Colonel De Craye?'

'My lord can command his inn.'

'How thoughtful you are!'

Laetitia's bosom swelled upon a mute exclamation, equivalent to: 'Woman! woman! snared ever by the sparkling and frivolous! undiscerning of the faithful, the modest and beneficent!'

In the secret musings of moralists this dramatic rhetoric survives.

The comparison was all of her own making, and she was indignant at the contrast, though to what end she was indignant she could not have said, for she had no idea of Vernon as a rival of De Craye in the favour of a plighted lady. But she was jealous on behalf of her sex: her sex's reputation seemed at stake, and the purity of it was menaced by Clara's idle preference of the shallower man. When the young lady spoke so carelessly of being like Crossjay, she did not perhaps know that a likeness, based on a similarity of their enthusiasms, loves, and appetites, had been established between women and boys. Laetitia had formerly chafed at it, rejecting it utterly, save when now and then in a season of bitterness she handed here and there a volatile young lady (none but the young) to be stamped with the degrading brand. Vernon might be as philosophical as he pleased. To her the gaiety of these two, Colonel

De Craye and Clara Middleton, was distressingly musical: they harmonized painfully. The representative of her sex was hurt by it.

She had to stay beside them: Clara held her arm. The colonel's voice dropped at times to something very like a whisper. He was answered audibly and smoothly. The quick-witted gentleman accepted the correction: but in immediately paying assiduous attentions to Miss Dale, in the approved intriguer's fashion, he showed himself in need of another amounting to a reproof. Clara said: 'We have been consulting, Laetitia, what is to be done to cure Professor Crooklyn of his cold.' De Craye perceived that he had taken a wrong step, and he was mightily surprised that a lesson in intrigue should be read to him of all men. Miss Middleton's audacity was not so astonishing: he recognized grand capabilities in the young lady. Fearing lest she should proceed further and cut away from him his vantage-ground of secrecy with her, he turned the subject and was adroitly submissive.

Clara's manner of meeting Sir Willoughby expressed a timid disposition to friendliness upon a veiled inquiry, understood by none save Laetitia, whose brain was racked to convey assurances to herself of her not having misinterpreted him. Could there be any doubt? She resolved that there could not be; and it was upon this basis of reason that she fancied she had led him to it. Legitimate or not, the fancy sprang from a solid foundation. Yesterday morning she could not have conceived it. Now she was endowed to feel that she had power to influence him, because now, since the midnight, she felt some emancipation from the spell of his physical mastery. He did not appear to her as a different man, but she had grown sensible of being a stronger woman. He was no more the cloud over her, nor the magnet; the cloud once heaven-suffused, the magnet fatally compelling her to sway round to him. She admired him still: his handsome air, his fine proportions, the courtesy of his bending to Clara and touching of her hand, excused a fanatical excess of admiration on the part of a woman in her youth, who is never the anatomist of the hero's lordly graces. But now she admired him piecemeal. When it came to the putting of him together, she did it coldly. To compassionate him was her utmost warmth. Without conceiving in him anything of the strange old monster of earth which had struck the awakened girl's mind of Miss Middleton, Laetitia classed him with other men; he was 'one of them'. And she did not bring her disenchantment as a charge against him. She accused herself, acknowledged the secret of the change to be, and her youthfulness was dead: – otherwise could she have given him compassion, and not herself have been carried on the flood of it? The compassion was fervent, and pure too. She supposed he would supplicate; she saw that Clara Middleton was pleasant with him only for what she expected of his generosity. She grieved. Sir Willoughby was fortified by her sorrowful gaze as he and Clara passed out together to the laboratory arm in arm.

Laetitia had to tell Vernon of the uselessness of his beating the house and grounds for Crossjay. Dr Middleton held him fast in discussion upon an overnight's classical wrangle with Professor Crooklyn, which was to be renewed that day. The Professor had appointed to call expressly to renew it. 'A fine scholar,' said the Rev. Doctor, 'but crotchety, like all men who cannot stand their Port.'

'I hear that he had a cold,' Vernon remarked. 'I hope the wine was good, sir.'

As when the foreman of a sentimental jury is commissioned to inform an awful Bench exact in perspicuous English, of a verdict that must of necessity be pronounced in favour of the hanging of the culprit, yet would fain attenuate the crime of a palpable villain by a recommendation to mercy, such foreman, standing in the attentive eye of a master of grammatical construction, and feeling the weight of at least three sentences on his brain, together with a prospect of judicial interrogation for the discovery of his precise meaning, is oppressed, himself is put on trial in turn, and he hesitates, he recapitulates, the fear of involution leads him to be involved; as far as a man so posted may, he on his own behalf appeals for mercy; entreats that his indistinct statement of preposterous reasons may be taken for understood, and would gladly, were permission to do it credible, throw in an imploring word that he may sink back among the crowd without for the one imperishable moment publicly swinging in his lordship's estimation: – much so, moved by chivalry toward a lady, courtesy to the recollection of a hostess, and particularly by the knowledge that his hearer would expect with a certain frigid rigour charity of him, Dr Middleton paused, spoke and paused: he stammered. Ladies, he said, were famous poisoners in the Middle Ages. His opinion was, that we had a class of manufacturing wine merchants on the watch for widows in this country. But he was bound to state the fact of his waking at his usual hour to the minute unassailed by headache. On the other hand, this was a condition of blessedness unanticipated when he went to bed. Mr Whitford, however, was not to think that he entertained rancour toward the wine. It was no doubt dispensed with the honourable intention of cheering. In point of flavour execrable, judging by results it was innocuous.

'The test of it shall be the effect of it upon Professor Crooklyn, and his appearance in the forenoon according to promise,' Dr Middleton came to an end with his perturbed balancings. 'If I hear more of the eight or twelve winds discharged at once upon a railway platform, and the young lady who dries herself of a drenching by drinking brandy and water with a gentleman at a railway inn, I shall solicit your sanction to my condemnation of the wine as anti-Bacchic and a counterfeit presentment. Do not misjudge me. Our hostess is not responsible. But widows should marry.'

'You must contrive to stop the Professor, sir, if he should attack his hostess in that manner,' said Vernon.

'Widows should marry!' Dr Middleton repeated.

He murmured of objecting to be at the discretion of a

butler; unless, he was careful to add, the aforesaid functionary could boast of an University education; and even then, said he, it requires a line of ancestry to train a man's taste.

The Rev. Doctor smothered a yawn. The repression of it caused a second one, a real monster, to come, big as our old friend of the sea advancing on the chained-up Beauty.

Disconcerted by this damning evidence of indigestion, his countenance showed that he considered himself to have been too lenient to the wine of an unhusbanded hostess. He frowned terribly.

In the interval Laetitia told Vernon of Crossjay's flight for the day, hastily bidding the master to excuse him: she had no time to hint the grounds of excuse. Vernon mentally made a guess.

Dr Middleton took his arm and discharged a volley at the crotchetty scholarship of Professor Crooklyn, whom to confute by book, he directed his march to the library. Having persuaded himself that he was dyspeptic, he had grown irascible. He denounced all dining out, eulogized Patterne Hall as if it were his home, and remembered he had dreamed in the night – a most humiliating sign of physical disturbance. 'But let me find a house in proximity to Patterne, as I am induced to suppose I shall,' he said, 'and here only am I to be met when I stir abroad.'

Laetitia went to her room. She was complacently anxious enough to prefer solitude and be willing to read. She was more seriously anxious about Crossjay than about any of the others. For Clara would be certain to speak very definitely, and how then could a gentleman oppose her? He would supplicate, and could she be brought to yield? It was not to be expected of a young lady who had turned from Sir Willoughby. His inferiors would have had a better chance. Whatever his faults, he had that element of greatness which excludes the intercession of pity. Supplication would be with him a form of condescension. It would be seen to be such. His was a monumental pride that could not stoop. She had preserved this image of the gentleman for a relic in the shipwreck of her idolatry. So she mused between the lines of her book, and finishing her reading and marking the page, she glanced down on the lawn. Dr Middleton was there, and alone; his hands behind his back, his head bent. His meditative pace and unwonted perusal of the turf proclaimed that a non-sentimental jury within had delivered an unmitigated verdict upon the widow's wine. Laetitia hurried to find Vernon.

He was in the hall. As she drew near him, the laboratory door opened and shut.

'It is being decided,' said Laetitia.

Vernon was paler than the hue of perfect calmness.

'I want to know whether I ought to take to my heels like Crossjay, and shun the Professor,' he said.

They spoke in under-tones, furtively watching the door.

'I wish what she wishes, I am sure; but it will go badly with the boy,' said Laetitia.

'Oh, well, then I'll take him,' said Vernon, 'I would rather. I think I can manage it.'

Again the laboratory door opened. This time it shut behind Miss Middleton. She was highly flushed. Seeing them, she shook the storm from her brows, with a dead smile; the best piece of serenity she could put on for public wear.

She took a breath before she moved.

Vernon strode out of the house.

Clara swept up to Laetitia.

'You were deceived!'

The hard sob of anger barred her voice.

Laetitia begged her to come to her room with her.

'I want air: I must be by myself,' said Clara, catching at her garden-hat.

She walked swiftly to the portico steps and turned to the right, to avoid the laboratory windows.

CHAPTER 33

✠✠✠✠

In Which the Comic Muse Has an Eye on Two Good Souls

CLARA met Vernon on the bowling-green among the laurels. She asked him where her father was.

'Don't speak to him now,' said Vernon.

'Mr Whitford, will you?'

'It is not advisable just now. Wait.'

'Wait? Why not now?'

'He is not in the right humour.'

She choked. There are times when there is no medicine for us in sages, we want slaves; we scorn to temporize, we must overbear. On she sped, as if she had made the mistake of exchanging words with a post.

The scene between herself and Willoughby was a thick mist in her head, except the burden and result of it, that he held to her fast, would neither assist her to depart nor disengage her.

Oh, men! men! They astounded the girl; she could not define them to her understanding. Their motives, their tastes, their vanity, their tyranny, and the domino on their vanity, the baldness of their tyranny, clinched her in feminine antagonism to brute power. She was not the less disposed to rebellion by a very present sense of the justice of what could be said to reprove her. She had but one answer: 'Anything but marry him!' It threw her on her nature, our last and headlong advocate, who is quick as the flood to hurry us from the heights to our level, and lower, if there be accidental gaps in the channel. For say we have been guilty of misconduct: can we redeem it by violating that which we are and live by? The question sinks us back to the luxuriousness of a sunny relinquishment of effort in the direction against tide. Our nature, becomes ingenious in devices, penetrative of the enemy, confidently citing its cause for being frankly elfish or worse. Clara saw a particular way of forcing herself to be surrendered. She shut her eyes from it: the sight carried her too violently to her escape; but her heart caught it up and huzzaed. To press the points of her fingers at her bosom, looking up to the sky as she did, and cry: 'I am not my own; I am his!' was instigation sufficient to make her heart leap up with all her body's blush to urge it to recklessness. A despairing creature then may say she has addressed the heavens and has had no answer to restrain her.

Happily for Miss Middleton, she had walked some minutes in her chafing fit before the falcon eye of Colonel De Craye spied her away on one of the beech-knots.

Vernon stood irresolute. It was decidedly not a moment for disturbing Dr Middleton's composure. He meditated upon a conversation, as friendly as possible, with Willoughby. Round on the front-lawn, he beheld Willoughby and Dr Middleton together, the latter having halted to lend attentive ear to his excellent host. Unnoticed by them or disregarded, Vernon turned back to Laetitia, and sauntered, talking with her of things current for as long as he could endure to listen to praise of his pure self-abnegation; proof of how well he had disguised himself, but it smacked unpleasantly to him. His humourous intimacy with men's minds likened the source of this distaste to the gallant all-or-nothing of the gambler, who hates the little when he cannot have the much, and would rather stalk from the tables clean-picked than suffer ruin to be tickled by driblets of the glorious fortune he has played for and lost. If we are not to be beloved, spare us the small coin of compliments on character; especially when they compliment only our acting. It is partly endurable to win eulogy for our stately fortitude in losing, but Laetitia was unaware that he flung away a stake; so she could not praise him for his merits.

'Willoughby makes the pardoning of Crossjay conditional,'

he said, 'and the person pleading for him has to grant the terms. How could you imagine Willoughby would give her up! How could he! Who! . . . He should, is easily said. I was no witness of the scene between them just now, but I could have foretold the end of it; I could almost recount the passages. The consequence is, that everything depends upon the amount of courage she possesses. Dr Middleton won't leave Patterne yet. And it is of no use to speak to him to-day. And she is by nature impatient, and is rendered desperate.'

'Why is it of no use to speak to Dr Middleton today?' cried Laetitia.

'He drank wine yesterday that did not agree with him; he can't work. To-day he is looking forward to Patterne Port. He is not likely to listen to any proposals to leave to-day.'

'Goodness!'

'I know the depth of that cry!'

'*You* are excluded, Mr Whitford.'

'Not a bit of it; I am in with the rest. Say that men are to be exclaimed at. Men have a right to expect you to know your own minds when you close on a bargain. You don't know the world or yourselves very well, it's true; still the original error is on your side, and upon that you should fix your attention. She brought her father here, and no sooner was he very comfortably established than she wished to dislocate him.'

'I cannot explain it; I cannot comprehend it,' said Laetitia.

'You are Constancy.'

'No.' She coloured. 'I am "in with rest". I do not say I should have done the same. But I have the knowledge that I must not sit in judgement on her. I can waver.'

She coloured again. She was anxious that he should know her to be not that stupid statue of Constancy in a corner doating on the antic Deception. Reminiscences of the interview overnight made it oppressive to her to hear herself praised for always pointing like the needle. Her newly enfranchised individuality pressed to assert its existence. Vernon, however, not seeing this novelty, continued, to her excessive discomfort, to baste her old abandoned image with his praises. They checked hers; and, moreover, he had suddenly conceived an envy of her life-long, uncomplaining, almost unaspiring, constancy of sentiment. If you know lovers when they have not reason to be blissful, you will remember that in this mood of admiring envy they are given to fits of uncontrollable maundering. Praise of constancy, moreover, smote shadowily a certain inconstant, enough to seem to ruffle her smoothness and do no hurt. He found his consolation in it, and poor Laetitia writhed. Without designing to retort, she instinctively grasped at a weapon of defence in further exalting his devotedness; which reduced him to cast his head to the heavens and implore them to partially enlighten her. Nevertheless, maunder he must; and he recurred to it in a way so utterly unlike himself that Laetitia stared in his face. She wondered whether there could be anything secreted behind this everlasting theme of constancy. He took her awakened gaze for a summons to asseverations of sincerity, and out they came. She would have fled from him, but to think of flying was to think how little it was that urged her to fly, and yet the thought of remaining and listening to praises undeserved and no longer flattering, was a torture.

'Mr Whitford, I bear no comparison with you.'

'I do and must set you for my example, Miss Dale.'

'Indeed, you do wrongly; you do not know me.'

'I could say that. For years . . .!'

'Pray, Mr Whitford!'

'Well, I have admired it. You show us how self can be smothered.'

'An echo would be a retort on you!'

'On me? I am never thinking of anything else.'

'I could say that.'

'You are necessarily conscious of not swerving.'

'But I do; I waver dreadfully; I am not the same two days running.'

'You are the same, with "ravishing divisions" upon the same.'

'And you without the "divisions". I draw such support as I have from you.'

'From some simulacrum of me, then. And that will show you how little you require support.'

'I do not speak my own opinion only.'

'Whose?'

'I am not alone.'

'Again let me say, I wish I were like you!'

'Then let me add, I would willingly make the exchange!'

'You would be amazed at your bargain.'

'Others would be!'

'Your exchange would give me the qualities I'm in want of, Miss Dale.'

'Negative, passive, at the best, Mr Whitford. But *I* should have . . .'

'Oh! – pardon me. But you inflict the sensations of a boy, with a dose of honesty in him, called up to receive a prize he has won by the dexterous use of a crib.'

'And how do you suppose she feels who has a crown of Queen o' the May forced on her head when she is verging on November?'

He rejected her analogy, and she his. They could neither of them bring to light the circumstances which made one another's admiration so unbearable. The more he exalted her for constancy, the more did her mind become bent upon critically examining the object of that imagined virtue; and the more she praised him for possessing the spirit of perfect friendliness, the fiercer grew the passion in him which disdained the imputation, hissing like a heated iron-bar that flings the water-drops to steam. He would none of it; would rather have stood exposed in his profound foolishness.

Amiable though they were, and mutually affectionate, they came to a stop in their walk, longing to separate, and not seeing how it was to be done, they had so knit themselves together with the pelting of their interlaudation.

'I think it is time for me to run home to my father for an hour,' said Laetitia.

'I ought to be working,' said Vernon.

Good progress was made to the disgarlanding of themselves thus far; yet, an acutely civilized pair, the abruptness of the transition from floweriness to commonplace affected them both, Laetitia chiefly, as she had broken the pause, and she remarked: 'I am really Constancy in my opinions.'

'Another title is customary where stiff opinions are concerned. Perhaps by and by you will learn your mistake, and then you will acknowledge the name for it.'

'How?' said she. 'What shall I learn?'

'If you learn that I am a grisly Egoist?'

'You? And it would not be egoism,' added Laetitia, revealing to him at the same instant as to herself that she swung suspended on a scarce credible guess.

'– Will nothing pierce your ears, Mr Whitford?'

He heard the intruding voice, but he was bent on rubbing out the cloudy letters Laetitia had begun to spell, and he stammered, in a tone of matter-of-fact: 'Just that and no better'; then turned to Mrs Mountstuart Jenkinson.

'– Or are you resolved you will never see Professor Crooklyn when you look on him?' said the great lady.

Vernon bowed to the Professor and apologized to him shufflingly and rapidly, incoherently, and with a red face; which induced Mrs Mountstuart to scan Laetitia's.

After lecturing Vernon for his abandonment of her yesterday evening, and flouting his protestations, she returned to the business of the day. 'We walked from the lodge-gates to see the park and prepare ourselves for Dr Middleton. We parted last night in the middle of a controversy and are rageing to resume it. Where is our redoubtable antagonist?'

Mrs Mountstuart wheeled Professor Crooklyn round to accompany Vernon.

'We,' she said, 'are for modern English scholarship, opposed to the champion of German.'

'The contrary,' observed Professor Crooklyn.

'Oh! We,' she corrected the error serenely, 'are for German scholarship opposed to English.'

'Certain editions.'

'We defend certain editions.'

'Defend is a term of imperfect application to my position, ma'am.'

'My dear Professor, you have in Dr Middleton a match for you in conscientious pugnacity, and you will not waste it upon me. There, there they are; there he is. Mr Whitford will conduct you. I stand away from the first shock.'

Mrs Mountstuart fell back to Laetitia, saying: 'He pores over a little inexactitude in phrases, and pecks at it like a domestic fowl.'

Professor Crooklyn's attitude and air were so well described that Laetitia could have laughed.

'These mighty scholars have their flavour,' the great lady hastened to add, lest her younger companion should be misled to suppose that they were not valuable to a governing hostess: 'their shadow-fights are ridiculous, but they have their flavour at a table. Last night, no: I discard all mention of last night. We failed: as none else in this neighbourhood could fail, but we failed. If we have among us a cormorant-devouring young lady who drinks up all the – ha! – brandy and water – of our inns and occupies all our flys, why, our condition is abnormal, and we must expect to fail: we are deprived of accommodation for accidental circumstances. How Mr Whitford could have missed seeing Professor Crooklyn! And what was *he* doing at the station, Miss Dale?'

'Your portrait of Professor Crooklyn was too striking, Mrs Mountstuart, and deceived him by its excellence. He appears to have seen only the blank side of the slate.'

'Ah! He is a faithful friend of his cousin, do you not think?'

'He is the truest of friends.'

'As for Dr Middleton,' Mrs Mountstuart diverged from her inquiry, 'he will swell the letters of my vocabulary to gigantic proportions if I see much of him: he is contagious.'

'I believe it is a form of his humour.'

'I caught it of him yesterday at my dinner-table in my distress, and must pass it off as a form of mine, while it lasts. I talked Dr Middleton half the dreary night through to my pillow. Your candid opinion, my dear, come! As for me, I don't hesitate. We seemed to have sat down to a solitary performance on the bass-viol. We were positively an assembly of insects during thunder. My very soul thanked Colonel De Craye for his diversions, but I heard nothing but Dr Middleton. It struck me that my table was petrified, and every one sat listening to bowls played overhead.'

'I was amused.'

'Really? You delight me. Who knows but that my guests were sincere in their congratulations on a thoroughly successful evening? I have fallen to this, you see! And I know wretched people! that as often as not it is their way of condolling with one. I do it myself: but only where there have been amiable efforts. But imagine *my* being congratulated for that! – Good-morning, Sir Willoughby. – The worst offender! and I am in no pleasant mood with him,' Mrs Mountstuart said aside to Laetitia, who drew back, retiring.

Sir Willoughby came on a step or two. He stopped to watch Laetitia's figure swimming to the house.

So, as, for instance, beside a stream, when a flower on the surface extends its petals drowning to subside in the clear still water, we exercise our privilege to be absent in the charmed contemplation of a beautiful natural incident.

A smile of pleased abstraction melted on his features.

CHAPTER 34

�֎✖✖✖

Mrs Mountstuart and Sir Willoughby

'GOOD-MORNING, my dear Mrs Mountstuart,' Sir Willoughby wakened himself to address the great lady. 'Why has she fled?'

'Has any one fled?'

'Laetitia Dale.'

'Letty Dale? Oh, if you call that flying. Possibly to renew a close conversation with Vernon Whitford, that I cut short. You frightened me with your "Shepherds-tell-me" air and tone. Lead me to one of your garden-seats: out of hearing to Dr Middleton, I beg. He mesmerizes me, he makes me talk Latin. I was curiously susceptible last night. I know I shall everlastingly associate him with an abortive entertainment and solos on big instruments. We were flat.'

'Horace was in good vein.'

'You were not.'

'And Laetitia – Miss Dale talked well, I thought.'

'She talked with you, and no doubt she talked well. We did not mix. The yeast was bad. You shot darts at Colonel De Craye: you tried to sting. You brought Dr Middleton down on you. Dear me, that man is a reverberation in my head. Where is your lady and love?'

'Who?'

'Am I to name her?'

'Clara? I have not seen her for the last hour. Wandering, I suppose.'

'A very pretty summer bower,' said Mrs Mountstuart, seating herself. 'Well, my dear Sir Willoughby, preferences, preferences are not to be accounted for, and one never knows whether to pity or congratulate, whatever may occur. I want to see Miss Middleton.'

'Your "dainty rogue in porcelain" will be at your beck – you lunch with us? – before you leave.'

'So now you have taken to quoting me, have you?'

'But "a romantic tale on her eyelashes" is hardly descriptive any longer.'

'Descriptive of whom? Now you are upon Laetitia Dale!'

'I quote you generally. She has now a graver look.'

'And well may have!'

'Not that the romance has entirely disappeared.'

'No; it looks as if it were in print.'

'You have hit it perfectly, as usual, ma'am.'

Sir Willoughby mused.

Like one resuming his instrument to take up the melody in a concerted piece, he said: 'I thought Laetitia Dale had a singularly animated air last night.'

'Why – !' Mrs Mountstuart mildly gaped.

'I want a new description of her. You know, I collect your mottoes and sentences.'

'It seems to me she is coming three parts out of her shell, and wearing it as a hood for convenience.'

'Ready to issue forth at an invitation? Admirable! exact!'

'Ay, my good Sir Willoughby, but are we so very admirable and exact? Are we never to know our own minds?'

He produced a polysyllabic sigh, like those many-jointed compounds of poets in happy languages, which are copious in a single expression: 'Mine is known to me. It always has been. Cleverness in women is not uncommon. Intellect is the pearl. A woman of intellect is as good as a Greek statue; she is divinely wrought, and she is divinely rare.'

'Proceed,' said the lady, confiding a cough to the air.

'The rarity of it: and it is not mere intellect, it is a sympathetic intellect; or else it is an intellect in perfect accord with an intensely sympathetic disposition; – the rarity of it makes it too precious to be parted with when once we have met it. I prize it the more the older I grow.'

'Are we on the feminine or the neuter?'

'I beg pardon?'

'The universal or the individual?'

He shrugged. 'For the rest, psychological affinities may exist coincident with and entirely independent of material or moral prepossessions, relations, engagements, ties.'

'Well, that is not the raving of passion, certainly,' said Mrs Mountstuart, 'and it sounds as if it were a comfortable doctrine for men. On that plea, you might all of you be having Aspasia and a wife. We saw your fair Middleton and Colonel de Craye at a distance as we entered the park. Professor Crooklyn is under some hallucination.'

'What more likely?'

The readiness and the double-bearing of the reply struck her comic sense with awe.

'The Professor must hear that. He insists on the fly, and the inn, and the wet boots, and the warming mixture, and the testimony of the landlady and the railway porter.'

'I say, what more likely?'

'Than that he should insist?'

'If he is under the hallucination!'

'He may convince others.'

'I have only to repeat . . .'

'"What more likely?" It's extremely philosophical. Coincident with a pursuit of the psychological affinities.'

'Professor Crooklyn will hardly descend, I suppose, from his classical altitudes to lay his hallucinations before Dr Middleton?'

'Sir Willoughby, you are the pink of chivalry!'

By harping on Laetitia, he had emboldened Mrs Mountstuart to lift the curtain upon Clara. It was offensive to him, but the injury done to his pride had to be endured for the sake of his general plan of self-protection.

'Simply desirous to save my guests from annoyance of any

kind,' he said, 'Dr Middleton can look "Olympus and thunder", as Vernon calls it.'

'Don't. I see him. That look! It is Dictionary-bitten! Angry, horned Dictionary! – an apparition of Dictionary in the night – to a dunce!'

'One would undergo a good deal to avoid the sight.'

'What the man must be in a storm! Speak as you please of yourself: you are a true and chivalrous knight to dread it for her. But now, candidly, how is it you cannot condescend to a little management? Listen to an old friend. You are too lordly. No lover can afford to be incomprehensible for half an hour. Stoop a little. Sermonizings are not to be thought of. You can govern unseen. You are to know that I am one who disbelieves in philosophy in love. I admire the look of it, I give no credit to the assumption. I rather like lovers to be out at times: it makes them picturesque, and it enlivens their monotony. I perceived she had a spot of wildness. It's proper that she should wear it off before marriage.'

'Clara? The wildness of an infant!' said Willoughby, paternally, musing over an inward shiver. 'You saw her at a distance just now, or you might have heard her laughing. Horace diverts her excessively.'

'I owe him my eternal gratitude for his behaviour last night. She was one of my bright faces. Her laughter was delicious; rain in the desert! It will tell you what the load on me was, when I assure you those two were merely a spectacle to me – points I scored in a lost game. And I know they were witty.'

'They both have wit; a kind of wit,' Willoughby assented.

'They struck together like a pair of cymbals.'

'Not the highest description of instrument. However, they amuse me. I like to hear them when I am in the vein.'

'That vein should be more at command with you, my friend. You can be perfect, if you like.'

'Under your tuition.'

Willoughby leaned to her, bowing languidly. He was easier in his pain for having hoodwinked the lady. She was the outer world to him; she could tune the world's voice; prescribe which of the two was to be pitied, himself or Clara; and he did not intend it to be himself, if it came to the worst.

They were far away from that at present, and he continued: 'Probably a man's power of putting on a face is not equal to a girl's. I detest petty dissensions. Probably I show it when all is not quite smooth. Little fits of suspicion vex me. It is a weakness, not to play them off, I know. Men have to learn the arts which come to women by nature. I don't sympathize with suspicion, from having none myself.'

His eyebrows shot up. That ill-omened man Flitch had sidled round by the bushes to within a few feet of him.

Flitch primarily defended himself against the accusation of drunkenness, which was hurled at him to account for his audacity in trespassing against the interdict; but he admitted that he had taken 'something short' for a fortification in visiting scenes where he had once been happy – at Christmastide, when all the servants, and the butler at head, grey old Mr Chessington, sat in rows, toasting the young heir of the old Hall in the old port wine! Happy had he been then, before ambition for a shop, to be his own master and an independent gentleman, had led him into his quagmire: – to look back envying a dog on the old estate, and sigh for the smell of Patterne stables: sweeter than Arabia, his drooping nose appeared to say.

He held up close against it something that imposed silence on Sir Willoughby as effectively as a cunning exordium in oratory will enchain mobs to swallow what is not complimenting them; and this he displayed secure in its being his licence to drivel his abominable pathos. Sir Willoughby recognized Clara's purse. He understood at once how the man must have come by it: he was not so quick in devising a means of stopping the tale. Flitch foiled him. 'Intact,' he replied to the question: 'What have you there?' He repeated this grand word. And then he turned to Mrs Mountstuart to speak of Paradise and Adam, in whom he saw the prototype of himself; also the Hebrew people in the bondage of Egypt, discoursed of by the clergymen, not without a likeness to him.

'Sorrows have done me one good, to send me attentive to church, my lady,' said Flitch, 'when I might have gone to London, the coachman's home, and been driving some honourable family, with no great advantage to my morals, according to what I hear of. And a purse found under the seat of a fly in London would have a poor chance of returning *intact* to the young lady losing it.'

'Put it down on that chair; inquiries will be made, and you will see Sir Willoughby,' said Mrs Mountstuart. 'Intact, no doubt; it is not disputed.'

With one motion of a finger she set the man rounding. Flitch halted; he was very regretful of the termination of his feast of pathos, and he wished to relate the finding of the purse, but he could not encounter Mrs Mountstuart's look; he slouched away in very close resemblance to the ejected Adam of illustrated books.

'It's my belief that naturalness among the common people has died out of the kingdom,' she said.

Willoughby charitably apologized for him. 'He has been fuddling himself.'

Her vigilant considerateness had dealt the sensitive gentleman a shock, plainly telling him she had her ideas of his actual posture. Nor was he unhurt by her superior acuteness and her display of authority on his grounds.

He said, boldly, as he weighed the purse, half tossing it: 'It's not unlike Clara's.'

He feared that his lips and cheeks were twitching, and as he grew aware of a glassiness of aspect that would reflect any suspicion of a keen-eyed woman, he became bolder still! 'Laetitia's, I know it is not. Hers is an ancient purse.'

'A present from you!'

'How do you hit on that, my dear lady?'

'Deductively.'

'Well, the purse looks as good as new in quality, like the owner.'

'The poor dear has not much occasion for using it.'

'You are mistaken: she uses it daily.'

'If it were better filled, Sir Willoughby, your old scheme might be arranged. The parties do not appear so unwilling. Professor Crooklyn and I came on them just now rather by surprise, and I assure you their heads were close, faces meeting, eyes musing.'

'Impossible.'

'Because when they approach the point, you won't allow it! Selfish!'

'Now,' said Willoughby, very animatedly, 'question Clara. Now, do, my dear Mrs Mountstuart, do speak to Clara on that head; she will convince you I have striven quite recently: – against myself, if you like. I have instructed her to aid me, given her the fullest instructions, carte blanche. *She* cannot possibly have a doubt. I may look to her to remove any you may entertain from your mind on the subject. I have proposed, seconded, and chorussed it, and it will *not* be arranged. If you expect me to deplore that fact, I can only answer that my actions are under my control, my feelings are not. I will do everything consistent with the duties of a man of honour – perpetually running into fatal errors because he did not properly consult the dictates of those feelings at the right season. I can violate them: but I can no more command them than I can my destiny. They were crushed of old, and so let them be now. Sentiments we won't discuss; though you know that sentiments have a bearing on social life: are factors, as they say in their later jargon. I never speak of mine. To you I could. It is not necessary. If old Vernon, instead of flattening his chest at a desk, had any manly ambition to take part in public affairs, she would be the woman for him. I have called her my Egeria. She would be his Cornelia. One could swear of her that she would have noble off-spring! – But old Vernon has had his disappointment, and will moan over it up to the end. And she? So it appears. I have tried; yes, personally: without effect. In other matters I may have influence with her: not in that one. She declines. She will live and die Laetitia Dale. We are alone: I confess to you, I love the name. It's an old song in my ears. Do not be too ready with a name for *me*. Believe me – I speak from my experience hitherto – there is a fatality in these things. I cannot conceal from my poor girl that this fatality exists . . .'

'Which is the poor girl at present?' said Mrs Mountstuart, cool in a mystification.

'And though she will tell you that I have authorized and – Clara Middleton – done as much as man can to institute the union you suggest, she will own that she is conscious of the presence of this – fatality, I call it for want of a better title – between us. It drives her in one direction, me in another – or would, if I submitted to the pressure. She is not the first who has been conscious of it.'

'Are we laying hold of a third poor girl?' said Mrs Mountstuart. 'Ah! I remember. And I remember we used to call it playing fast and loose in those days, not fatality. It is very strange. It may be that you were unblushingly courted in those days, and excusable; and we all supposed . . . but away you went for your tour.'

'My mother's medical receipt for me. Partially it succeeded. She was for grand marriages: not I. I could make, I could not be, a sacrifice. And then I went in due time to Doctor Cupid on my own account. She has the kind of attraction . . . But one changes! On revient toujours. First we begin with a liking; then we give ourselves up to the passion of beauty: then comes the serious question of suitableness of the mate to match us; and perhaps we discover that we were wiser in early youth than somewhat later. However, she has beauty. Now, Mrs Mountstuart, you do admire her. Chase the idea of the "dainty rogue" out of your view of her: you admire her: she is captivating; she has a particular charm of her own, nay, she has real beauty.'

Mrs Mountstuart fronted him to say: 'Upon my word, my dear Sir Willoughby, I think she has it to such a degree that I don't know the man who could hold out against her if she took the field. She is one of the women who are dead shots with men. Whether it's in their tongues or their eyes, or it's an effusion and an atmosphere – whatever it is, it's a spell, another fatality for you!'

'Animal; not spiritual!'

'Oh, she hasn't the head of Letty Dale.'

Sir Willoughby allowed Mrs. Mountstuart to pause and follow her thoughts.

'Dear me!' she exclaimed. 'I noticed a change in Letty Dale last night; and to-day. She looked fresher and younger; extremely well: which is not what I can say for you, my friend. Fatalizing is not good for the complexion.'

'Don't take away my health, pray,' cried Willoughby, with a snapping laugh.

'Be careful,' said Mrs Mountstuart. 'You have got a sentimental tone. You talk of "feelings crushed of old". It is to a woman, not to a man that you speak, but that sort of talk is a way of making the ground slippery. I listen in vain for a natural tongue; and when I don't hear it, I suspect plotting in men. You show your under-teeth too at times when you draw in a breath, like a condemned high-caste Hindoo my husband took me to see in a jail in Calcutta, to give me some excitement when I was pining for England. The creature did it regularly as he breathed; you did it last night, and you have been doing it to-day, as if the air cut you to the quick. You have been spoilt. You have been too much anointed. What I've just mentioned is a sign with me of a settled something on the brain of a man.'

'The brain?' said Sir Willoughby, frowning.

'Yes, you laugh sourly, to look at,' said she. 'Mountstuart told me that the muscles of the mouth betray men sooner than the eyes, when they have cause to be uneasy in their minds.'

'But, ma'am, I shall not break my word; I shall not, not;

I intend, I have resolved to keep it. I do *not* fatalize, let my complexion be black or white. Despite my resemblance to a high-caste malefactor of the Calcutta prison-wards . . .'

'Friend! friend! you know how I chatter.'

He saluted her finger-ends. 'Despite the extraordinary display of teeth, you will find me go to execution with perfect calmness; with a resignation as good as happiness.'

'Like a Jacobite lord under the Georges.'

'You have told me that you wept to read of one: like him, then. My principles have not changed, if I have. When I was younger, I had an idea of a wife who would be with me in my thoughts as well as aims: a woman with a spirit of romance, and a brain of solid sense. I shall sooner or later dedicate myself to a public life; and shall, I suppose, want the counsellor or comforter who ought always to be found at home. It may be unfortunate that I have the ideal in my head. But I would never make rigorous demands for specific qualities. The cruellest thing in the world is to set up a living model before a wife, and compel her to copy it. In any case, here we are upon the road: the die is cast. I shall not reprieve myself. I cannot release her. Marriage represents facts, courtship fancies. She will be cured by-and-by of that coveting of everything that I do, feel, think, dream, imagine . . . ta-ta-ta-ta ad infinitum. Laetitia was invited here to show her the example of a fixed character – solid as any concrete substance you would choose to build on, and not a whit the less feminine.'

'Ta-ta-ta-ta ad infinitum. You need not tell me you have a design in all that you do, Willoughby Patterne.'

'You smell the autocrat? Yes, he can mould and govern the creatures about him. His toughest rebel is himself! If you see Clara . . . You wish to see her, I think you said?'

'Her behaviour to Lady Busshe last night was queer.'

'If you will. She makes a mouth at porcelain. Toujours la porcelaine! For me, her pettishness is one of her charms, I confess it. Ten years younger, I could not have compared them.'

'Whom?'

'Laetitia and Clara.'

'Sir Willoughby, in any case, to quote you, here we are all upon the road, and we must act as if events were going to happen; and I must ask her to help me on the subject of my wedding-present, for I don't want to have her making mouths at mine, however pretty – and she does it prettily.'

'"Another dedicatory offering to the *rogue* in me!" she says of porcelain.'

'Then porcelain it shall not be. I mean to consult her; I have come determined upon a chat with her. I think I understand. But she produces false impressions on those who don't know you both. "I shall have that porcelain back", says Lady Busshe to me, when we were shaking hands last night: "I think," says she, "it should have been the Willow Pattern." And she really said: "He's in for being jilted a second time!"'

Sir Willoughby restrained a bound of his body that would have sent him up some feet into the air. He felt his skull thundered at within.

'Rather than that it should fall upon her!' ejaculated he, correcting his resemblance to the high-caste culprit as soon as it recurred to him.

'But you know Lady Busshe,' said Mrs Mountstuart, genuinely solicitous to ease the proud man of his pain. She could see through him to the depth of the skin, which his fencing sensitiveness vainly attempted to cover as it did the heart of him. 'Lady Busshe is nothing without her flights, fads, and fancies. She has always insisted that you have an unfortunate nose. I remember her saying on the day of your majority, it was the nose of a monarch destined to lose a throne.'

'Have I ever offended Lady Busshe?'

'She trumpets you. She carries Lady Culmer with her too, and you may expect a visit of nods and hints and pots of alabaster. They worship you: you are the hope of England in their eyes, and no woman is worthy of you: but they are a pair of fatalists, and if you begin upon Letty Dale with them, you might as well forbid your banns. They will be all over the country exclaiming on predestination and marriages made in heaven.'

'Clara and her father!' cried Sir Willoughby.

Dr Middleton and his daughter appeared in the circle of shrubs and flowers.

'Bring her to me, and save me from the polyglot,' said Mrs Mountstuart, in affright at Dr Middleton's manner of pouring forth into the ears of the downcast girl.

The leisure he loved that he might debate with his genius upon any next step was denied to Willoughby: he had to place his trust in the skill with which he had sown and prepared Mrs Mountstuart's understanding to meet the girl – beautiful abhorred that she was! detested darling! thing to squeeze to death and throw to the dust, and mourn over!

He had to risk it; and at an hour when Lady Busshe's prognostic grievously impressed his intense apprehensiveness of nature.

As it happened that Dr Middleton's notion of a disagreeable duty in colloquy was to deliver all that he contained, and escape the listening to a syllable of reply, Willoughby withdrew his daughter from him opportunely.

'Mrs Mountstuart wants you, Clara.'

'I shall be very happy,' Clara replied, and put on a new face.

An imperceptible nervous shrinking was met by another force in her bosom, that pushed her to advance without a sign of reluctance. She seemed to glitter.

She was handed to Mrs Mountstuart.

Dr Middleton laid his hand over Willoughby's shoulder, retiring on a bow before the great lady of the district. He blew and said: 'An opposition of female instincts to masculine intellect necessarily creates a corresponding antagonism of intellect to instinct.'

'Her answer, sir? Her reasons? Has she named any?'

'The cat,' said Dr Middleton, taking breath for a sentence, 'that humps her back in the figure of the letter H, or a Chinese bridge has given the dog her answer and her reasons, we may presume: but he that undertakes to translate them into human speech might likewise venture to propose an addition to the alphabet and a continuation of Homer. The one performance would be not more wonderful than the other. Daughters, Willoughby, daughters! Above most human peccancies, I do abhor a breach of faith. She will not be guilty of that. I demand a cheerful fulfilment of a pledge: and I sigh to think that I cannot count on it without administering a lecture.'

'She will soon be my care, sir.'

'She shall be. Why, she is as good as married. She is at the altar. She is in her house. She is – why, where is she not? She has entered the sanctuary. She is out of the market. This maenad shriek for freedom would happily entitle her to the Republican cap – the Phrygian – in a revolutionary Parisian procession. To me it has no meaning; and but that I cannot credit child of mine with mania, I should be in trepidation of her wits.'

Sir Willoughby's livelier fears were pacified by the information that Clara had simply emitted a cry. Clara had once or twice given him cause for starting and considering whether to think of her sex differently or condemningly of her, yet he could not deem her capable of fully unbosoming herself even to him, and under excitement. His idea of the cowardice of girls combined with his ideal of a waxwork sex to persuade him that though they are often (he had experienced it) wantonly desperate in their acts, their tongues are curbed by rosy prudency. And this was in his favour. For if she proved speechless and stupid with Mrs Mountstuart, the lady would turn her over, and beat her flat, beat her angular, in fine, turn her to any shape, despising her, and cordially believe him to be the model gentleman of Christendom. She would fill in the outlines he had sketched to her of a picture that he had small pride in by comparison with his early vision of a fortune-favoured, triumphing squire, whose career is like the sun's intelligibly lordly to all comprehensions. Not like your model gentleman, that has to be expounded – a thing for abstract esteem! However, it was the choice left to him. And an alternative was enfolded in that. Mrs Mountstuart's model gentleman could marry either one of two women, throwing the other overboard. He was bound to marry: he was bound to take to himself one of them: and whichever one he selected would cast a lustre on his reputation. At least she would rescue him from from the claws of Lady Busshe, and her owl's hoot of 'Willow Pattern', and her hag's shriek of 'twice jilted'. That flying infant Willoughby – his unprotected little incorporeal omnipresent Self (not thought of so much as passionately felt for) – would not be scoffed at as the luckless with women. A fall indeed from his original conception of his name of fame abroad! But Willoughby had the high consolation of knowing that others have fallen lower. There is the fate of the devils to comfort us, if we are driven hard. *For one of your pangs another bosom is racked by ten*, we read in the solacing Book.

With all these nice calculations at work, Willoughby stood above himself, contemplating his active machinery, which he could partly criticize but could not stop, in a singular wonderment at the aims and schemes and tremours of one who was handsome, manly, acceptable in the world's eyes: and had he not loved himself most heartily he would have been divided to the extent of repudiating that urgent and excited half of his being, whose motions appeared as those of a body of insects perpetually erecting and repairing a structure of extraordinary pettiness. He loved himself too seriously to dwell on the division for more than a minute or so. But having seen it, and for the first time, as he believed, his passion for the woman causing it became surcharged with bitterness, atrabiliar.

A glance behind him, as he walked away with Dr Middleton, showed Clara, cunning creature that she was, airily executing her malicious graces in the preliminary courtesies with Mrs Mountstuart.

CHAPTER 35

✠✠✠✠

Miss Middleton and Mrs Mountstuart

'SIT beside me, fair Middleton,' said the great lady.

'Gladly,' said Clara, bowing to her title.

'I want to sound you, my dear.'

Clara presented an open countenance with a dim interrogation on the forehead. 'Yes?' she said, submissively.

'You were one of my bright faces last night. I was in love with you. Delicate vessels ring sweetly to a finger-nail, and if the wit is true, you answer to it; that I can see, and that is what I like. Most of the people one has at a table are drums. A rub-a-dub-dub on them is the only way to get a sound. When they can be persuaded to do it upon one another, they call it conversation.'

'Colonel De Craye was very funny.'

'Funny, and witty too.'

'But never spiteful.'

'These Irish or half Irishmen are my taste. If they're not politicians, mind; I mean Irish gentlemen. I will never have another dinner-party without one. Our men's tempers are uncertain. You can't get them to forget themselves. And when the wine is in them the nature comes out, and they must be buffeting, and upstart politics, and good-bye to harmony! My husband, I am sorry to say, was one of those who have a long account of ruined dinners against them. I have seen him and his friends red as the roast and white as the boiled with wrath on a popular topic they had excited themselves over, intrinsically not worth a snap of the fingers. In London!' exclaimed Mrs Mountstuart, to aggravate the charge against her lord in the Shades. 'But town or country, the table should be sacred. I have heard women say it is a plot on the side of the men to teach us our littleness. I don't believe they have a plot. It would be to compliment them on a talent. I believe they fall upon one another blindly, simply because they are full: which is, we are told, the preparation for the fighting Englishman. They cannot eat and keep a truce. Did you notice that dreadful Mr Capes?'

'The gentleman who frequently contradicted papa? But Colonel De Craye was good enough to relieve us.'

'How, my dear?'

'You did not hear him? He took advantage of an interval when Mr Capes was breathing after a paean to his friend, the Governor – I think – of one of the Presidencies, to say to the lady beside him: "He was a wonderful administrator and great logician; he married an Anglo-Indian widow, and soon after published a pamphlet in favour of Suttee."'

'And what did the lady say?'

'She said: "Oh!"'

'Hark at her! And was it heard?'

'Mr Capes granted the widow, but declared he had never seen the pamphlet in favour of Suttee, and disbelieved in it. He insisted that it was to be named Sati. He was vehement.'

'Now I do remember: – which must have delighted the colonel. And Mr Capes retired from the front upon a repetition of "in toto, in toto". As if "in toto" were the language of a dinner-table! But what will ever teach these men? Must we import Frenchmen to give them an example in the art of conversation, as their grandfathers brought over marquises to instruct them in salads? And our young men too! Women have to take to the hunting-field to be able to talk with them, and be on a par with their grooms. Now, there was Willoughby Patterne, a prince among them formerly. Now, did you observe him last night? did you notice how, instead of conversing, instead of assisting me – as he was bound to do doubly owing to the defection of Vernon Whitford: a thing I don't yet comprehend – there he sat sharpening his lower lip for cutting remarks. And at my best man! at Colonel De

Craye! If he had attacked Mr Capes, with his Governor of
Bomby, as the man pronounces it, or Colonel Wildjohn and
his Protestant Church in Danger, or Sir Wilson Pettifer harping on his Monarchical Republic, or any other! No, he preferred to be sarcastic upon friend Horace, and he had the
worst of it. Sarcasm is so silly! What is the gain if he has been
smart? People forget the epigram and remember the other's
good temper. On that field, my dear, you must make up your
mind to be beaten by "friend Horace". I have my prejudices
and I have my prepossessions, but I love good temper, and I
love wit, and when I see a man possessed of both, I set my cap
at him, and there's my flat confession, and highly unfeminine
it is.'

'Not at all!' cried Clara.

'We are one, then.'

Clara put up a mouth empty of words: she was quite one
with her. Mrs Mountstuart pressed her hand. 'When one does
get intimate with a dainty rogue!' she said. 'You forgive me
all that, for I could vow that Willoughby has betrayed me.'

Clara looked soft, kind, bright, in turns, and clouded instantly when the lady resumed: 'A friend of my own sex, and
young, and a close neighbour, is just what I would have
prayed for. And I'll excuse you, my dear, for not being so
anxious about the friendship of an old woman. But I shall be
of use to you, you will find. In the first place, I never tap for
secrets. In the second, I keep them. Thirdly, I have some
power. And fourth, every young married woman has need
of a friend like me. Yes, and Lady Patterne heading all the
county will be the stronger for my backing. You don't look
so mighty well pleased, my dear. Speak out.'

'Dear Mrs Mountstuart!'

'I tell you, I am very fond of Willoughby, but I saw the
faults of the boy and see the man's. He has the pride of a king,
and it's a pity if you offend it. He is prodigal in generosity, but
he can't forgive. As to his own errors, you must be blind
to them as a Saint. The secret of him is, that he is one of those

excessively civilized creatures who aim at perfection: and I
think he ought to be supported in his conceit of having attained it; for the more men of that class, the greater our
influence. He excels in manly sports, because he won't be excelled in anything, but as men don't comprehend his fineness,
he comes to us; and his wife must manage him by that key.
You look down at the idea of managing. It has to be done.
One thing you may be assured of, he will be proud of you.
His wife won't be very much enamoured of herself if she is
not the happiest woman in the world. You will have the best
horses, the best dresses, the finest jewels in England; and an
incomparable cook. The house will be changed the moment
you enter it as Lady Patterne. And, my dear, just where he is,
with all his graces, deficient of attraction, yours will tell. The
sort of Othello he would make, or Leontes, I don't know,
and none of us ever needs to know. My impression is, that
if even a shadow of a suspicion flitted across him, he is a sort
of man to double-dye himself in guilt by way of vengeance in
anticipation of an imagined offence. Not uncommon with
men. I have heard strange stories of them: and so will you in
your time to come, but not from me. No young woman shall
ever be the sourer for having been my friend. One word of
advice now we are on the topic: never play at counter-strokes
with him. He will be certain to out-stroke you, and you will
be driven further than you meant to go. They say we beat
men at that game; and so we do, at the cost of beating ourselves. And if once we are started, it is a race-course ending
on a precipice – over goes the winner. We must be moderately slavish to keep our place; which is given us in appearance; but appearances make up a remarkably large part of
life, and far the most comfortable, so long as we are discreet
at the right moment. He is a man whose pride, when hurt,
would run his wife to perdition to solace it. If he married a
troublesome widow, his pamphlet on Suttee would be out
within the year. Vernon Whitford would receive instructions
about it the first frosty moon. You like Miss Dale?'

'I think I like her better than she likes me,' said Clara.

'Have you never warmed together?'

'I have tried it. She is not one bit to blame. I can see how it is that she misunderstands me: or justly condemns me, perhaps I should say.'

'The hero of two women must die and be wept over in common before they can appreciate one another. You are not cold?'

'No.'

'You shuddered, my dear.'

'Did I?'

'I do sometimes. Feet will be walking over one's grave, wherever it lies. Be sure of this: Willoughby Patterne is a man of unimpeachable honour.'

'I do not doubt it.'

'He means to be devoted to you. He has been accustomed to have women hanging around him like votive offerings.'

'I . . .'

'You cannot: of course not: any one could see that at a glance. You are all the sweeter to me for not being tame. Marriage cures a multitude of indispositions.'

'Oh! Mrs Mountstuart, will you listen to me?'

'Presently. Don't threaten me with confidences. Eloquence is a terrible thing in woman. I suspect, my dear, that we both know as much as could be spoken.'

'You hardly suspect the truth, I fear.'

'Let me tell you one thing about jealous men – when they are not blackamoors married to disobedient daughters. I speak of our civil creature of the drawing-rooms: and lovers, mind, not husbands: two distinct species, married or not: – they're rarely given to jealousy unless they are flighty themselves. The jealousy fixes them. They have only to imagine that we are for some fun likewise and they grow as deferential as my footman, as harmless as the sportsman whose gun has burst. Ah! my fair Middleton, am I pretending to teach you? You have read him his lesson, and my table suffered for it last night, but I bear no rancour.'

'You bewilder me, Mrs Mountstuart.'

'Not if I tell you that you have driven the poor man to try whether it would be possible for him to give you up.'

'I have?'

'Well, and you are successful.'

'I am?'

'Jump, my dear!'

'He will?'

'When men love stale instead of fresh, withered better than blooming, excellence in the abstract rather than the palpable. With their idle prate of feminine intellect, and a grotto nymph, and a mother of Gracchi! Why, he must think me dazed with admiration of him to talk to me! One listens, you know. And he is one of the men who cast a kind of physical spell on you while he has you by the ear, until you begin to think of it by talking to somebody else. I suppose there are clever people who do see deep into the breast while dialogue is in progress. One reads of them. No, my dear, you have very cleverly managed to show him that it isn't at all possible: he can't. And the real cause for alarm, in my humble opinion, is lest your amiable foil should have been a trifle, as he would say, deceived, too much in earnest, led too far. One may reprove him for not being wiser, but men won't learn without groaning that they are simply weapons taken up to be put down when done with. Leave it to me to compose him. – Willoughby can't give you up. I'm certain he has tried; his pride has been horridly wounded. You were shrewd, and he has had his lesson. If these little rufflings don't come before marriage they come after; so it's not time lost; and it's good to be able to look back on them. You are very white, my child.'

'Can you, Mrs Mountstuart, can you think I would be so heartlessly treacherous?'

'Be honest, fair Middleton, and answer me: Can you say

you had not a corner of an idea of producing an effect on Willoughby?'

Clara checked the instinct of her tongue to defend her reddening cheeks, with a sense that she was disintegrating and crumbling, but she wanted this lady for a friend, and she had to submit to the conditions, and be red and silent.

Mrs Mountstuart examined her leisurely.

'That will do. Conscience blushes. One knows it by the conflagration. Don't be hard on yourself: there you are in the other extreme. That blush of yours would count with me against any quantity of evidence – all the Crooklyns in the kingdom. You lost your purse.'

'I discovered that it was lost this morning.'

'Flitch has been here with it. Willoughby has it. You will ask him for it; he will demand payment: you will be a couple of yards' length or so of cramoisy: and there ends the episode, nobody killed, only a poor man melancholy-wounded, and I must offer him my hand to mend him, vowing to prove to him that Suttee was properly abolished. Well, and now to business. I said I wanted to sound you. You have been overdone with porcelain. Poor Lady Busshe is in despair at your disappointment. Now, I mean my wedding-present to be to your taste.'

'Madam!'

'Who is the madam you are imploring?'

'Dear Mrs Mountstuart!'

'Well?'

'I shall fall in your esteem. Perhaps you will help me. No one else can. I am a prisoner: I am compelled to continue this imposture. Oh, I shun speaking much: you object to it and I dislike it: but I must endeavour to explain to you that I am unworthy of the position you think a proud one.'

'Tut-tut; we are all unworthy, cross our arms, bow our heads, and accept the honours. Are you playing humble handmaid? What an old organ-tune that is! Well? Give me reasons.'

'I do not wish to marry.'

'He's the great match of the county!'

'I cannot marry him.'

'Why, you are at the church door with him! Cannot marry him?'

'It does not bind me.'

'The church door is as binding as the altar to an honourable girl. What have you been about? Since I am in for confidences, half ones won't do. We must have honourable young women as well as men of honour. You can't imagine he is to be thrown over now, at this hour? What have you against him? come!'

'I have found that I do not . . .'

'What?'

'Love him.'

Mrs Mountstuart grimaced transiently. 'That is no answer. The cause!' she said. 'What has he done?'

'Nothing.'

'And when did you discover this nothing?'

'By degrees: unknown to myself; suddenly.'

'Suddenly and by degrees? I suppose it's useless to ask for a head. But if all this is true, you ought not to be here.'

'I wish to go; I am unable.'

'Have you had a scene together?'

'I have expressed my wish.'

'In roundabout? – girl's English?'

'Quite clearly. Oh, very clearly.'

'Have you spoken to your father?'

'I have.'

'And what does Dr Middleton say?'

'It is incredible to him.'

'To me too! I can understand little differences, little whims, caprices: we don't settle into harness for a tap on the shoulder as a man becomes a knight: but to break and bounce away from an unhappy gentleman at the church door is either mad-

ness or it's one of the things without a name. You think you
are quite sure of yourself?'

'I am so sure, that I look back with regret on the time when
I was not.'

'But you were in love with him.'

'I was mistaken.'

'No love?'

'I have none to give.'

'Dear me! – Yes, yes, but that tone of sorrowful conviction
is often a trick, it's not new: and I know that assumption of
plain sense to pass off a monstrosity.' Mrs Mountstuart struck
her lap. 'Soh! but I've had to rack my brain for it: feminine
disgust? You have been hearing imputations of his past life?
moral character? No? Circumstances might make him behave
unkindly, not unhandsomely: and we have no claim over a
man's past, or it's too late to assert it. What is the case?'

'We are quite divided.'

'Nothing in the way of . . . nothing green-eyed?'

'Far from that!'

'Then name it.'

'We disagree.'

'Many a very good agreement is founded on disagreeing.
It's to be regretted that you are not portionless. If you had
been, you would have made very little of disagreeing. You are
just as much bound in honour as if you had the ring on your
finger.'

'In honour! But I appeal to his, I am no wife for him.'

'But if he insists, you consent?'

'I appeal to reason. Is it, madame . . .'

'But, I say, if he insists, you consent?'

'He will insist upon his own misery as well as mine.'

Mrs Mountstuart rocked herself. 'My poor Sir Willoughby! What a fate! – And I took you for a clever girl!
Why, I have been admiring your management of him! And
here am I bound to take a lesson from Lady Busshe. My dear
good Middleton, don't let it be said that Lady Busshe saw

deeper than I! I put some little vanity in it, I own: I won't conceal it. She declares that when she sent her present – I don't believe her – she had a premonition that it would come back. Surely you won't justify the extravagances of a woman without common reverence: – for anatomize him as we please to ourselves, he is a splendid man (and I did it chiefly to encourage and come at you). We don't often behold such a lordly-looking man: so conversable too when he feels at home; a picture of an English gentleman! The very man we want married for our neighbourhood! A woman who can openly talk of expecting him to be twice jilted! You shrink. It is repulsive. It would be incomprehensible: except, of course, to Lady Busshe, who rushed to one of her violent conclusions, and became a prophetess. Conceive a woman's imagining it could happen twice to the same man! I am not sure she did not send the identical present that arrived and returned once before: you know, the Durham engagement. She told me last night she had it back. I watched her listening very suspiciously to Professor Crooklyn. My dear, it is her passion to foretell disasters – her passion! And when they are confirmed, she triumphs, of course. We shall have her domineering over us with sapient nods at every trifle occurring. The county will be unendurable. Unsay it, my Middleton! And don't answer like an oracle because I do all the talking. Pour out to me. You'll soon come to a stop and find the want of reason in the want of words. I assure you that's true. – Let me have a good gaze at you. No,' said Mrs Mountstuart, after posturing herself to peruse Clara's features, 'brains you have; one can see it by the nose and the mouth. I could vow you are the girl I thought you; you have your wits on tiptoe. How of the heart?'

'None,' Clara sighed.

The sigh was partly voluntary, though unforced; as one may with ready sincerity act a character that is our own only through sympathy.

Mrs Mountstuart felt the extra weight in the young lady's

falling breath. There was no necessity for a deep sigh over an absence of heart or confession of it. If Clara did not love the man to whom she was betrothed, sighing about it signified – what? some pretence; and a pretence is the cloak of a secret. Girls do not sigh in that way with compassion for the man they have no heart for, unless at the same time they should be oppressed by the knowledge or dread of having a heart for some one else. As a rule, they have no compassion to bestow on him: you might as reasonably expect a soldier to bewail the enemy he strikes in action: they must be very disengaged to have it. And supposing a show of the thing to be exhibited, when it has not been worried out of them, there is a reserve in the background: they are pitying themselves under a mask of decent pity of their wretch.

So ran Mrs Mountstuart's calculations, which were like her suspicion, coarse and broad, not absolutely incorrect, but not of an exact measure with the truth. That pin's head of the truth is rarely hit by design. The search after it of the professionally penetrative in the dark of a bosom may bring it forth by the heavy knocking all about the neighbourhood that we call good guessing, but it does not come out clean; other matter adheres to it; and being more it is less than truth. The unadulterate is to be had only by faith in it or by waiting for it.

A lover! thought the sagacious dame. There was no lover: some love there was: or, rather, there was a preparation of the chamber, with no lamp yet lighted.

'Do you positively tell me you have no heart for the position of first lady of the county?' said Mrs Mountstuart.

Clara's reply was firm: 'None whatever.'

'My dear, I will believe you on one condition. Look at me. You have eyes. If you are for mischief, you are armed for it. But how much better, when you have won a prize, to settle down and wear it! Lady Patterne will have entire occupation for her flights and whimsies in leading the county. And the man, surely the man – he behaved badly last night: but a

beauty like this –' she pushed a finger at Clara's cheek, and
doated a half instant, 'you have the very beauty to break in an
ogre's temper. And the man is as governable as he is present-
able. You have the beauty the French call – no, it's the beauty
of a queen of elves: one sees them lurking about you, one
here, one there. Smile – they dance: be doleful – they hang
themselves. No, there's not a trace of satanic; at least, not yet.
And come, come, my Middleton, the man is a man to be
proud of. You can send him into Parliament to wear off his
humours. To my thinking, he has a fine style: conscious? I
never thought so before last night. I can't guess what has happened to him recently. He was once a young Grand Mon-
arque. He was really a superb young English gentleman. Have
you been wounding him?'

'It is my misfortune to be obliged to wound him,' said
Clara.

'Quite needlessly, my child, for marry him you must.'

Clara's bosom rose: her shoulders rose too, narrowing, and
her head fell slight back.

Mrs Mountstuart exclaimed: 'But the scandal! You would
never, never think of following the example of that Durham
girl? – whether she was provoked to it by jealousy or not. It
seems to have gone so astonishingly far with you in a very
short time, that one is alarmed as to where you will stop.
Your look just now was downright revulsion.'

'I fear it is. It is. I am past my own control. Dear madam,
you have my assurance that I will not behave scandalously or
dishonourably. What I would entreat of you is to help me. I
know this of myself: I am not the best of women. I am impatient, wickedly. I should be no good wife. Feelings like mine
teach me unhappy things of myself.'

'Rich, handsome, lordly, influential, brilliant health, fine
estates,' Mrs Mountstuart enumerated in petulant accents as
there started across her mind some of Sir Willoughby's attributes for the attraction of the soul of woman. 'I suppose you
wish me to take you in earnest?'

'I appeal to you for help.'

'What help?'

'Persuade him of the folly of pressing me to keep my word.'

'I will believe you, my dear Middleton, on one condition: – your talk of no heart is nonsense. A change like this, if one is to believe in the change, occurs through the heart, not because there is none. Don't you see that? But if you want me for a friend, you must not sham stupid. It's bad enough in itself: the imitation's horrid. You have to be honest with me, and answer me right out. You came here on this visit intending to marry Willoughby Patterne.'

'Yes.'

'And *gradually* you *suddenly* discovered, since you came here, that you did not intend it, if you could find a means of avoiding it.'

'Oh, madam, yes, it is true.'

'Now comes the test. And, my lovely Middleton, your flaming cheeks won't suffice for me this time. The old serpent can blush like an innocent maid on occasion. You are to speak, and you are to tell me in six words why that was: and don't waste one on "madam", or "Oh! Mrs Mountstuart!" Why did you change?'

'I came – When I came I was in some doubt. Indeed I speak the truth. I found I could not give him the admiration he has, I dare say, a right to expect. I turned – it surprised me; it surprises me now. But so completely! So that to think of marrying him is . . .'

'Defer the simile,' Mrs Mountstuart interposed. 'If you hit on a clever one, you will never get the better of it. Now, by just as much as you have outstripped my limitation of words to you, you show me you are dishonest.'

'I could make a vow.'

'You would forswear yourself.'

'Will you help me?'

'If you are perfectly ingenuous, I may try.'

'Dear lady, what more can I say?'

'It may be difficult. You can reply to a catechism.'

'I shall have your help?'

'Well, yes; though I don't like stipulations between friends. There is no man living to whom you could willingly give your hand? That is my question. I cannot possibly take a step unless I know. Reply briefly: there is or there is not.'

Clara sat back with bated breath, mentally taking the leap into the abyss, realizing it, and the cold prudence of abstention, and the delirium of the confession. Was there such a man? It resembled freedom to think there was: to avow it promised freedom.

'Oh, Mrs Mountstuart!'

'Well?'

'You will help me?'

'Upon my word, I shall begin to doubt your desire for it.'

'*Willingly* give my hand, madam?'

'For shame! And with wits like yours, can't you perceive where hesitation in answering such a question lands you?'

'Dearest lady, will you give me your hand? may I whisper?'

'You need not whisper; I won't look.'

Clara's voice trembled on a tense chord.

'There is one . . . compared with him I feel my insignificance. If I could aid him!'

'What necessity have you to tell me more than that there is one?'

'Ah, madam, it is different: not as you imagine. You bid me be scrupulously truthful: I am: I wish you to know the different kind of feeling it is from what might be suspected from . . . a confession. To give my hand, is beyond any thought I have ever encouraged. If you had asked me whether there is one whom I admire – yes, I do. I cannot help admiring a beautiful and brave self-denying nature. It is one whom you must pity, and to pity casts you beneath him: for you pity him because it is his nobleness that has been the enemy of his fortunes. He lives for others.'

Her voice was musically thrilling in that low muted tone of the very heart, impossible to deride or disbelieve.

Mrs Mountstuart set her head nodding on springs.

'Is he clever?'

'Very.'

'He talks well?'

'Yes.'

'Handsome?'

'He might be thought so.'

'Witty?'

'I think he is.'

'Gay, cheerful?'

'In his manner.'

'Why, the man would be a mountebank if he adopted any other. And poor?'

'He is not wealthy.'

Mrs Mountstuart preserved a lengthened silence, but nipped Clara's fingers once or twice to reassure her without approving. 'Of course he's poor,' she said at last; 'directly the reverse of what you *could* have, it *must* be. Well, my fair Middleton, I can't say you have been dishonest. I'll help you as far as I'm able. How, it is quite impossible to tell. We're in the mire. The best way seems to me to get this pitiable angel to cut some ridiculous capers and present you another view of him. I don't believe in his innocence. He knew you to be a plighted woman.'

'He has not once by word or sign hinted a disloyalty.'

'Then how do you know . . .'

'I do not know.'

'He is not the cause of your wish to break your engagement?'

'No.'

'Then you have succeeded in just telling me nothing. What is?'

'Ah! madam!'

'You would break your engagement purely because the admirable creature is in existence?'

Clara shook her head: she could not say she was dizzy. She had spoken out more than she had ever spoken to herself: and in doing so she had cast herself a step beyond the line she dared to contemplate.

'I won't detain you any longer,' said Mrs Mountstuart. 'The more we learn, the more we are taught that we are not so wise as we thought we were. I have to go to school to Lady Busshe! I really took you for a very clever girl. If you change again, you will notify the important circumstance to me, I trust.'

'I will,' said Clara, and no violent declaration of the impossibility of her changeing again would have had such an effect on her hearer.

Mrs Mountstuart scanned her face for a new reading of it to match with her later impressions.

'I am to do as I please with the knowledge I have gained?'

'I am utterly in your hands, madam.'

'I have not meant to be unkind.'

'You have not been unkind; I could embrace you.'

'I am rather too shattered, and kissing won't put me together. I laughed at Lady Busshe! No wonder you went off like a rocket with a disappointing bouquet when I told you you had been successful with poor Sir Willoughby and he could not give you up. I noticed that. A woman like Lady Busshe, always prying for the lamentable, would have required no further enlightenment. Has he a temper?'

Clara did not ask her to signalize the person thus abruptly obtruded.

'He has faults,' she said.

'There's an end to Sir Willoughby, then! Though I don't say he will give you up even when he hears the worst, if he must hear it, as for his own sake he should. And I won't say he ought to give you up. He'll be the pitiable angel if he does. For you – but you don't deserve compliments; they would be immoral. You have behaved badly, badly, badly. I have never had such a right-about-face in my life. You will deserve the stigma: you will be notorious: you will be called Number Two. Think of that! Not even original! We will break the conference, or I shall twaddle to extinction. I think I heard the luncheon bell.'

'It rang.'

'You don't look fit for company, but you had better come.'

'Oh, yes; every day it's the same.'

'Whether you're in my hands or I'm in yours, we're a couple of arch-conspirators against the peace of the family whose table we're sitting at, and the more we rattle the viler we are, but we must do it to ease our minds.'

Mrs Mountstuart spread the skirts of her voluminous dress, remarking further: 'At a certain age our teachers are young people: we learn by looking backward. It speaks highly for me that I have not called you mad. — Full of faults, goodish-looking, not a bad talker, cheerful, poorish; — and she prefers that to this!' the great lady exclaimed in her reverie while emerging from the circle of shrubs upon a view of the Hall.

Colonel De Craye advanced to her; certainly good-looking, certainly cheerful, by no means a bad talker, nothing of a Croesus, and variegated with faults.

His laughing smile attacked the irresolute hostility of her mien, confident as the sparkle of sunlight in a breeze. The effect of it on herself angered her on behalf of Sir Willoughby's bride.

'Good-morning, Mrs Mountstuart; I believe I am the last to greet you.'

'And how long do you remain here, Colonel De Craye?'

'I kissed earth when I arrived, like the Norman William, and consequently I've an attachment to the soil, ma'am.'

'You're not going to take possession of it, I suppose?'

'A handful would satisfy me.'

'You play the Conqueror pretty much, I have heard. But property is held more sacred than in the times of the Norman William.'

'And speaking of property, Miss Middleton, your purse is found,' he said.

'I know it is,' she replied as unaffectedly as Mrs Mountstuart could have desired, though the ingenuous air of the girl incensed her somewhat.

Clara passed on.

'You restore purses,' observed Mrs Mountstuart.

Her stress on the word and her look thrilled De Craye; for there had been a long conversation between the young lady and the dame.

'It was an article that dropped and was not stolen,' said he.

'Barely sweet enough to keep, then!'

'I think I could have felt to it like poor Flitch, the flyman, who was the finder.'

'If you are conscious of these temptations to appropriate what is not your own, you should quit the neighbourhood.'

'And do it elsewhere? But that's not virtuous counsel.'

'And I'm not counselling in the interests of your virtue, Colonel De Craye.'

'And I dared for a moment to hope that you were, ma'am,' he said, ruefully drooping.

They were close to the dining-room window, and Mrs Mountstuart preferred the terminating of a dialogue that did not promise to leave her features the austerely iron cast with which she had commenced it. She was under the spell of gratitude for his behaviour yesterday evening at her dinnertable; she could not be very severe.

CHAPTER 36

❈ ❈ ❈ ❈

Animated Conversation at a Luncheon-Table

VERNON was crossing the hall to the dining-room as Mrs Mountstuart stepped in. She called to him: 'Are the champions reconciled?'

He replied: 'Hardly that, but they have consented to meet at an altar to offer up a victim to the gods in the shape of modern poetic imitations of the classical.'

'That seems innocent enough. The Professor has not been anxious about his chest?'

'He recollects his cough now and then.'

'You must help him to forget it.'

'Lady Busshe and Lady Culmer are here,' said Vernon, not supposing it to be a grave announcement until the effect of it on Mrs Mountstuart admonished him.

She dropped her voice: 'Engage my fair friend for one of your walks the moment we rise from table. You may have to rescue her; but do. I mean it.'

'She's a capital walker,' Vernon remarked in simpleton style.

'There's no necessity for any of your pedestrian feats,' Mrs Mountstuart said, and let him go, turning to Colonel De Craye to pronounce an encomium on him: 'The most open-minded man I know! Warranted to do perpetual service, and no mischief. If you were all . . . instead of catching at every prize you covet! Yes, you would have your reward for un-selfishness, I assure you. Yes, and where you seek it! That is what none of you men will believe.'

'When you behold me in your own livery!' cried the colonel.

'Do I?' said she, dallying with a half-formed design to be

confidential. 'How is it one is always tempted to address you in the language of innuendo? I can't guess.'

'Except that as a dog doesn't comprehend good English we naturally talk bad to him.'

The great lady was tickled. Who could help being amused by this man? And after all, if her fair Middleton chose to be a fool there could be no gainsaying her, sorry though poor Sir Willoughby's friends must feel for him.

She tried not to smile.

'You are too absurd. Or a baby, you might have added.'

'I hadn't the daring.'

'I'll tell you what, Colonel De Craye, I shall end by falling in love with you; and without esteeming you, I fear.'

'The second follows as surely as the flavour upon a draught of Bacchus, if you'll but toss off the glass, ma'am.'

'We women, sir, think it should be first.'

' 'Tis to transpose the seasons, and give October the blossom and April the apple, and no sweet one! Esteem's a mellow thing that comes after bloom and fire, like an evening at home; because if it went before it would have no father and couldn't hope for progeny; for there'd be no nature in the business. So please, ma'am, keep to the original order, and you'll be nature's child, and I the most blessed of mankind.'

'Really, were I fifteen years younger. I am not so certain . . . I might try and make you harmless.'

'Draw the teeth of the lamb so long as you pet him!'

'I challenged you, colonel, and I won't complain of your pitch. But now lay your wit down beside your candour, and descend to an every-day level with me for a minute.'

'Is it innuendo?'

'No; though I daresay it would be easier for you to respond to if it were.'

'I'm the straightforwardest of men at a word of command.'

'This is a whisper. Be alert, as you were last night. Shuffle the table well. A little liveliness will do it. I don't imagine malice, but there's curiosity, which is often as bad, and not so lightly foiled. We have Lady Busshe and Lady Culmer here.'

'To sweep the cobwebs out of the sky!'

'Well, then, can you fence with broomsticks?'

'I have had a bout with them in my time.'

'They are terribly direct.'

'They "give point", as Napoleon commanded his cavalry to do.'

'You must help me to ward it.'

'They will require variety in the conversation.'

'Constant. You are an angel of intelligence, and if I have the judgeing of you, I'm afraid you'll be allowed to pass, in spite of the scandal above. Open the door; I don't unbonnet.'

De Craye threw the door open.

Lady Busshe was at that moment saying, 'And are we indeed to have you for a neighbour, Dr Middleton?'

The Rev. Doctor's reply was drowned by the new arrivals.

'I thought you had forsaken us,' observed Sir Willoughby to Mrs Mountstuart.

'And run away with Colonel De Craye? I'm too weighty, my dear friend. Besides, I have not looked at the wedding-presents yet.'

'The very object of our call!' exclaimed Lady Culmer.

'I have to confess I am in dire alarm about mine,' Lady Busshe nodded across the table at Clara. 'Oh! you may shake your head, but I would rather hear a rough truth than the most complimentary evasion.'

'How would you define a rough truth, Dr Middleton?' said Mrs Mountstuart.

Like the trained warrior who is ready at all hours for the trumpet to arms, Dr Middleton waked up for judicial allocution in a trice.

'A rough truth, madam, I should define to be that description of truth which is not imparted to mankind without a powerful impregnation of the roughness of the teller.'

'It is a rough truth, ma'am, that the world is composed of

fools, and that the exceptions are knaves,' Professor Crooklyn furnished that example avoided by the Rev. Doctor.

'Not to precipitate myself into the jaws of the foregone definition, which strikes me as being as happy as Jonah's whale, that could carry probably the most learned man of his time inside without the necessity of digesting him,' said De Craye, 'a rough truth is a rather strong charge of universal nature for the firing off of a modicum of personal fact.'

'It is a rough truth that Plato is Moses atticizing,' said Vernon to Dr Middleton, to keep the diversion alive.

'And that Aristotle had the globe under his cranium,' rejoined the Rev. Doctor.

'And that the Moderns live on the Ancients.'

'And that not one in ten thousand can refer to the particular treasury he filches.'

'The Art of our days is a revel of rough truth,' remarked Professor Crooklyn.

'And the literature has laboriously mastered the adjective, wherever it may be in relation to the noun,' Dr Middleton added.

'Orson's first appearance at court was in the figure of a rough truth, causing the Maids of Honour, accustomed to Tapestry Adams, astonishment and terror,' said De Craye.

That he might not be left out of the sprightly play, Sir Willoughby levelled a lance at the quintain, smiling on Laetitia. 'In fine, caricature is rough truth.'

She said, 'Is one end of it, and realistic directness is the other.'

He bowed. 'The palm is yours.'

Mrs Mountstuart admired herself as each one trotted forth in turn characteristically, with one exception unaware of the aid which was being rendered to a distressed damsel wretchedly incapable of decent hypocrisy. Her intrepid lead had shown her hand to the colonel and drawn the enemy at a blow.

Sir Willoughby's 'in fine', however, did not please her:

still less did his lackadaisical Lothario-like bowing and smiling
to Miss Dale: and he perceived it and was hurt. For how,
carrying his tremendous load, was he to compete with these
unhandicapped men in the game of nonsense she had such a
fondness for starting at a table? He was further annoyed to
hear Miss Eleanor and Miss Isabel Patterne agree together that
'caricature' was the final word of the definition. Relatives
should know better than to deliver these awards to us in
public.

'Well?' quoth Lady Busshe, expressive of stupefaction at
the strange dust she had raised.

'Are they on view, Miss Middleton?' inquired Lady
Culmer.

'There's a regiment of us on view and ready for inspection.'
Colonel De Craye bowed to her, but she would not be foiled.
'Miss Middleton's admirers are always on view,' said he.

'Are they to be seen?' said Lady Busshe.

Clara made her face a question, with a laudable smoothness.

'The wedding-presents,' Lady Culmer explained.

'No.'

'Otherwise, my dear, we are in danger of duplicating and
triplicating and quadruplicating, not at all to the satisfaction
of the bride.'

'But there's a worse danger to encounter in the "on view",
my lady,' said De Craye; 'and that's the magnetic attraction
a display of wedding-presents is sure to have for the ineffable
burglar, who must have a nuptial soul in him, for wherever
there's that collection on view, he's never a league off. And 'tis
said he knows a lady's dressing-case presented to her on the
occasion fifteen years after the event.'

'As many as fifteen?' said Mrs Mountstuart.

'By computation of the police. And if the presents are on
view, dogs are of no use, nor bolts, nor bars: – he's worse than
Cupid. The only protection to be found, singular as it may be
thought, is in a couple of bottles of the oldest Jamaica rum in
the British Isles.'

'Rum?' cried Lady Busshe.

'The liquor of the Royal Navy, my lady. And with your permission, I'll relate the tale in proof of it. I had a friend engaged to a young lady, niece of an old sea-captain of the old school, the Benbow school, the wooden leg and pigtail school; a perfectly salt old gentleman with a pickled tongue, and a dash of brine in every deed he committed. He looked rolled over to you by the last wave on the shore, sparkling: he was Neptune's own for humour. And when his present to the bride was opened, sure enough there lay a couple of bottles of the oldest Jamaica rum in the British Isles, born before himself, and his father to boot. 'Tis a fabulous spirit I beg you to believe in, my lady, the sole merit of the story being its portentous veracity. The bottles were tied to make them appear twins, as they both had the same claim to seniority. And there was a label on them, telling their great age, to maintain their identity. They were in truth a pair of patriarchal bottles rivalling many of the biggest houses in the kingdom for antiquity. They would have made the donkey that stood between the two bundles of hay look at them with obliquity: supposing him to have, for an animal, a rum taste, and a turn for hilarity. Wonderful old bottles! So, on the label, just over the date, was written large: UNCLE BENJAMIN'S WEDDING PRESENT TO HIS NIECE BESSY. Poor Bessy shed tears of disappointment and indignation enough to float the old gentleman on his native element, ship and all. She vowed it was done curmudgeonly to vex her, because her uncle hated wedding-presents and had grunted at the exhibition of cups and saucers, and this and that beautiful service, and épergnes and inkstands, mirrors, knives and forks, dressing-cases, and the whole mighty category. She protested, she flung herself about, she declared those two ugly bottles should not join the exhibition in the dining-room, where it was laid out for days, and the family ate their meals where they could, on the walls, like flies. But there was also Uncle Benjamin's legacy on view, in the distance, so it was ruled against her that the bottles should have their place. And one fine morning down came the family after a fearful row of the domestics; shouting, screaming, cries for the police, and murder topping all. What did they see? They saw two prodigious burglars extended along the floor, each with one of the twin bottles in his hand, and a remainder of the horror of the midnight hanging about his person like a blown fog, sufficient to frighten them while they kicked him entirely intoxicated. Never was wilder disorder of wedding-presents, and not one lost! – owing, you'll own, to Uncle Benjy's two bottles of ancient Jamaica rum.'

Colonel De Craye concluded with an asseveration of the truth of the story.

'A most provident, far-sighted old sea-captain!' exclaimed Mrs Mountstuart, laughing at Lady Busshe and Lady Culmer.

These ladies chimed in with her gingerly.

'And have you many more clever stories, Colonel De Craye?' said Lady Busshe.

'Ah! my lady, when the tree begins to count its gold 'tis nigh upon bankruptcy.'

'Poetic!' ejaculated Lady Culmer, spying at Miss Middleton's rippled countenance, and noting that she and Sir Willoughby had not interchanged word or look.

'But that in the case of your Patterne Port a bottle of it would outvalue the catalogue of nuptial presents, Willoughby, I would recommend your stationing some such constabulary to keep watch and ward,' said Dr Middleton, as he filled his glass, taking Bordeaux in the middle of the day, under a consciousness of virtue and its reward to come at half-past seven in the evening.

'The rascals would require a dozen of that, sir,' said De Craye.

'Then it is not to be thought of. Indeed one!' Dr Middleton negatived the idea.

'We are no further advanced than when we began,' observed Lady Busshe.

'If we are marked to go by stages,' Mrs Mountstuart assented.

'Why, then, we shall be called old coaches,' remarked the colonel.

'You,' said Lady Culmer, 'have the advantage of us in a closer acquaintance with Miss Middleton. You know her tastes, and how far they have been consulted in the little souvenirs already grouped somewhere, although not yet for inspection. I am at sea. And here is Lady Busshe in deadly alarm. There is plenty of time to effect a change – though we are drawing on rapidly to the fatal day, Miss Middleton. We are, we are very near it. Oh! yes. I am one who thinks that these little affairs should be spoken of openly, without that ridiculous bourgeois affectation, so that we may be sure of giving satisfaction. It is a transaction like everything else in life. I, for my part, wish to be remembered favourably. I put it as a test of breeding to speak of these things as plain matter-of-fact. You marry; I wish you to have something by you to remind you of me. What shall it be? – useful or ornamental. For an ordinary household the choice is not difficult. But where wealth abounds we are in a dilemma.'

'And with persons of decided tastes,' added Lady Busshe. 'I am really very unhappy,' she protested to Clara.

Sir Willoughby dropped Laetitia; Clara's look of a sedate resolution to preserve silence on the topic of the nuptial gifts made a diversion imperative.

'Your porcelain was exquisitely chosen, and I profess to be a connoisseur,' he said. 'I am poor in Old Saxony, as you know; I can match the country in Sèvres, and my inheritance of China will not easily be matched in the country.'

'You may consider your Dragon vases a present from young Crossjay,' said De Craye.

'How?'

'Hasn't he abstained from breaking them? the capital boy! Porcelain and a boy in the house together is a case of prospective disaster fully equal to Flitch and a fly.'

'You thould understand that my friend Horace – whose wit is in this instance founded on another tale of a boy – brought us a magnificent piece of porcelain, destroyed by the capsizing of his conveyance from the station,' said Sir Willoughby to Lady Busshe.

She and Lady Culmer gave out lamentable Ohs, while Miss Eleanor and Miss Isabel Patterne sketched the incident. Then the lady visitors fixed their eyes in united sympathy upon Clara: recovering from which, after a contemplation of marble, Lady Busshe emphasized, 'No, you do not love porcelain, it is evident, Miss Middleton.'

'I am glad to be assured of it,' said Lady Culmer.

'Oh, I know that face: I know that look,' Lady Busshe affected to remark rallyingly: 'it is not the first time I have seen it.'

Sir Willoughby smarted to his marrow. 'We will rout these fancies of an overscrupulous generosity, my dear Lady Busshe.'

Her unwonted breach of delicacy in speaking publicly of her present, and the vulgar persistency of her sticking to the theme, very much perplexed him. And if he mistook her not, she had just alluded to the demoniacal Constantia Durham. It might be that he had mistaken her: he was on guard against his terrible sensitiveness. Nevertheless it was hard to account for this behaviour of a lady greatly his friend and admirer, a lady of birth. And Lady Culmer as well! – likewise a lady of birth. Were they in collusion? had they a suspicion? He turned to Laetitia's face for the antidote to his pain.

'Oh, but you are not one yet, and I shall require two voices to convince me,' Lady Busshe rejoined, after another stare at the marble.

'Lady Busshe, I beg you not to think me ungrateful,' said Clara.

'Fiddle! – gratitude! it is to please your taste, to satisfy *you*. I care for gratitude as little as for flattery.'

'But gratitude is flattering,' said Vernon.

'Now, no metaphysics, Mr Whitford.'

'But do care a bit for flattery, my lady,' said De Craye. ' 'Tis the finest of the Arts; we might call it moral sculpture. Adepts in it can cut their friends to any shape they like by practising it with the requisite skill. I myself, poor hand as I am, have made a man act Solomon by constantly praising his wisdom. He took a sagacious turn at an early period of the dose. He weighed the smallest question of his daily occasions with a deliberation truly oriental. Had I pushed it, he'd have hired a baby and a couple of mothers to squabble over the undivided morsel.'

'I shall hope for a day in London with you,' said Lady Culmer to Clara.

'You did not forget the Queen of Sheba?' said Mrs Mountstuart to De Craye.

'With her appearance, the game has to be resigned to her entirely,' he rejoined.

'That is,' Lady Culmer continued, 'if you do not despise an old woman for your comrade on a shopping excursion.'

'Despise whom we fleece!' exclaimed Dr Middleton. 'Oh, no, Lady Culmer, the sheep is sacred.'

'I am not so sure,' said Vernon.

'In what way, and to what extent, are you not so sure?' said Dr Middleton.

'The natural tendency is to scorn the fleeced.'

'I stand for the contrary. Pity, if you like: particularly when they bleat.'

'This is to assume that makers of gifts are a fleeced people: I demur,' said Mrs Mountstuart.

'Madam, we are expected to give; we are incited to give; you have dubbed it the fashion to give; and the person refusing to give, or incapable of giving, may anticipate that he will be regarded as benignly as a sheep of a drooping and flaccid wool by the farmer, who is reminded by the poor beast's appearance of a strange dog that worried the flock. Even Captain Benjamin, as you have seen, was unable to withstand the demand on him. The hymeneal pair are licensed freebooters levying blackmail on us; survivors of an uncivilized period. But in taking without mercy, I venture to trust that the manners of a happier era instruct them not to scorn us. I apprehend that Mr Whitford has a lower order of latrons in his mind.'

'Permit me to say, sir, that you have not considered the ignoble aspect of the fleeced,' said Vernon. 'I appeal to the ladies: would they not, if they beheld an ostrich walking down a Queen's Drawing Room, clean-plucked, despise him though they were wearing his plumes?'

'An extreme supposition, indeed,' said Dr Middleton, frowning over it; 'scarcely legitimately to be suggested.'

'I think it fair, sir, as an instance.'

'Has the circumstance occurred, I would ask?'

'In life? a thousand times.'

'I fear so,' said Mrs Mountstuart.

Lady Busshe showed symptoms of a desire to leave a profitless table.

Vernon started up, glancing at the window.

'Did you see Crossjay?' he said to Clara.

'No; I must, if he is there,' said she.

She made her way out, Vernon after her. They both had the excuse.

'Which way did the poor boy go?' she asked him.

'I have not the slightest idea,' he replied. 'But put on your bonnet, if you would escape that pair of inquisitors.'

'Mr Whitford, what humiliation!'

'I suspect you do not feel it the most, and the end of it can't be remote,' said he.

Thus it happened that when Lady Busshe and Lady Culmer quitted the dining-room, Miss Middleton had spirited herself away from summoning voice and messenger.

Sir Willoughby apologized for her absence. 'If I could be jealous, it would be of that boy Crossjay.'

'You are an excellent man, and the best of cousins,' was Lady Busshe's enigmatical answer.

The exceedingly lively conversation at his table was lauded by Lady Culmer.

'Though,' said she, 'what it all meant, and what was the drift of it, I couldn't tell to save my life. Is it every day the same with you here?'

'Very much.'

'How you must enjoy a spell of dulness!'

'If you said simplicity and not talking for effect! I generally cast anchor by Laetitia Dale.'

'Ah!' Lady Busshe coughed. 'But the fact is, Mrs Mountstuart is made for cleverness!'

'I think, my lady, Laetitia Dale is to the full as clever as any of the stars Mrs Mountstuart assembles, or I.'

'Talkative cleverness, I mean.'

'In conversation as well. Perhaps you have not yet given her a chance.'

'Yes, yes, she is clever, of course, poor dear. She is looking better too.'

'Handsome, I thought,' said Lady Culmer.

'She varies,' observed Sir Willoughby.

The ladies took seat in their carriage and fell at once into a close-bonnet colloquy. Not a single allusion had they made to the wedding-presents after leaving the luncheon-table. The cause of their visit was obvious.

CHAPTER 37

※※※※

*Contains Clever Fencing and Intimations of the
Need for It*

THAT woman, Lady Busshe, had predicted, after the event,
Constantia Durham's defection. She had also, subsequent to
Willoughby's departure on his travels, uttered sceptical things
concerning his rooted attachment to Laetitia Dale. In her
bitter vulgarity, that beaten rival of Mrs Mountstuart Jenkinson for the leadership of the county had taken his nose for a
melancholy prognostic of his fortunes; she had recently played
on his name: she had spoken the hideous English of his fate.
Little as she knew, she was alive to the worst interpretation of
appearances. No other eulogy occurred to her now than to
call him the best of cousins, because Vernon Whitford was
housed and clothed and fed by him. She had nothing else to
say for a man she thought luckless! She was a woman barren
of wit, stripped of style, but she was wealthy and a gossip – a
forge of showering sparks – and she carried Lady Culmer with
her. The two had driven from his house to spread the malignant rumour abroad; already they blew the biting world on
his raw wound. Neither of them was like Mrs Mountstuart, a
witty woman, who could be hoodwinked; they were dull
women, who steadily kept on their own scent of the fact, and
the only way to confound such inveterate forces was to be
ahead of them, and seize and transform the expected fact,
and astonish them, when they came up to him, with a totally
unanticipated fact.

'You see, you were in error, ladies.'

'And so we were, Sir Willoughby, and we acknowledge it.
We never could have guessed *that*!'

Thus the phantom couple in the future delivered

themselves, as well they might at the revelation. He could run far ahead.

Ay, but to combat these dolts, facts had to be encountered, deeds done, in groaning earnest. These representatives of the pig-sconces of the population judged by circumstances: airy shows and seems had no effect on them. Dexterity of fence was thrown away.

A flying peep at the remorseless might of dulness in compelling us to a concrete performance counter to our inclinations, if we would deceive its terrible instinct, gave Willoughby for a moment the survey of a sage. His intensity of personal feeling struck so vivid an illumination of mankind at intervals that he would have been individually wise, had he not been moved by the source of his accurate perceptions to a personal feeling of opposition to his own sagacity. He loathed and he despised the vision, so his mind had no benefit of it, though he himself was whipped along. He chose rather (and the choice is open to us all) to be flattered by the distinction it revealed between himself and mankind.

But if he was not as others were, why was he discomfited, solicitous, miserable? To think that it should be so, ran dead against his conqueror's theories wherein he had been trained, which, so long as he gained success awarded success to native merit, grandeur to the grand in soul, as light kindles light: nature presents the example. His early training, his bright beginning of life, had taught him to look to earth's principal fruits as his natural portion, and it was owing to a girl that he stood a mark for tongues, naked, wincing at the possible malignity of a pair of harridans. Why not whistle the girl away?

Why, then he would be free to enjoy, careless, younger than his youth in the rebound to happiness!

And then would his nostrils begin to lift and sniff at the creeping up of a thick pestiferous vapour. Then in that volume of stench would he discern the sullen yellow eye of malice. A malarious earth would hunt him all over it. The breath of the world, the world's view of him, was partly his vital breath, his view of himself. The ancestry of the tortured man had bequeathed him this condition of high civilization among their other bequests. Your withered contracted Egoists of the hut and the grot reck not of public opinion; they crave but for liberty and leisure to scratch themselves and soothe an excessive scratch. Willoughby was expansive, a blooming one, born to look down upon a tributary world, and to exult in being looked to. Do we wonder at his consternation in the prospect of that world's blowing foul on him? Princes have their obligations to teach them they are mortal, and the brilliant heir of a tributary world is equally enchained by the homage it brings him; – more, inasmuch as it is immaterial, elusive, not gathered by the tax, and he cannot capitally punish the treasonable recusants. Still must he be brilliant; he must court his people. He must ever, both in his reputation and his person, aching though he be, show them a face and a leg.

The wounded gentleman shut himself up in his laboratory, where he could stride to and fro, and stretch out his arms for physical relief, secure from observation of his fantastical shapes, under the idea that he was meditating. There was perhaps enough to make him fancy it in the heavy fire of shots exchanged between his nerves and the situation; there were notable flashes. He would not avow that he was in an agony: it was merely a desire for exercise.

Quintessence of worldliness, Mrs Mountstuart appeared through his farthest window, swinging her skirts on a turn at the end of the lawn, with Horace De Craye smirking beside her. And the woman's vaunted penetration was unable to detect the histrionic Irishism of the fellow. Or she liked him for his acting and nonsense; nor she only. The voluble beast was created to snare women. Willoughby became smitten with an adoration of stedfastness in women. The incarnation of that divine quality crossed his eyes. She was clad in beauty.

A horrible nondescript convulsion composed of yawn and groan drove him to his instruments, to avert a renewal of the

shock; and while arranging and fixing them for their unwonted task, he compared himself advantageously with men
like Vernon and De Craye, and others of the county, his
fellows in the hunting-field and on the Magistrate's bench,
who neither understood nor cared for solid work, beneficial
practical work, the work of Science.

He was obliged to relinquish it: his hand shook.

'Experiments will not advance much at this rate,' he said,
casting the noxious retardation on his enemies.

It was not to be contested that he must speak with Mrs
Mountstuart, however he might shrink from the trial of his
facial muscles. Her not coming to him seemed ominous: nor
was her behaviour at the luncheon-table quite obscure. She
had evidently instigated the gentlemen to cross and counter-
chatter Lady Busshe and Lady Culmer. For what purpose?

Clara's features gave the answer.

They were implacable. And he could be the same.

In the solitude of his room he cried right out: 'I swear it,
I will never yield her to Horace De Craye! She shall feel some
of my torments, and try to get the better of them by knowing
she deserves them.' He had spoken it, and it was an oath upon
the record.

Desire to do her intolerable hurt became an ecstasy in his
veins, and produced another stretching fit that terminated in
a violent shake of the body and limbs; during which he was a
spectacle for Mrs Mountstuart at one of the windows. He
laughed as he went to her, saying: 'No, no work to-day; it
won't be done, positively refuses.'

'I am taking the Professor away,' said she; 'he is fidgety
about the cold he caught.'

Sir Willoughby stepped out to her. 'I was trying at a bit of
work for an hour, not to be idle all day.'

'You work in that den of yours every day?'

'Never less than an hour, if I can snatch it.'

'It is a wonderful resource!'

The remark set him throbbing and thinking that a prolongation of his crisis exposed him to the approaches of some organic malady, possibly heart-disease.

'A habit,' he said. 'In there I throw off the world.'

'We shall see some results in due time.'

'I promise none: I like to be abreast of the real knowledge of my day, that is all.'

'And a pearl among country gentlemen!'

'In your gracious consideration, my dear lady. Generally speaking, it would be more advisable to become a chatterer and keep an anecdotal note-book. I could not do it, simply because I could not live with my own emptiness for the sake of making an occasional display of fireworks. I aim at solidity. It is a narrow aim, no doubt; not much appreciated.'

'Laetitia Dale appreciates it.'

A smile of enforced ruefulness, like a leaf curling in heat, wrinkled his mouth.

Why did she not speak of her conversation with Clara?

'Have they caught Crossjay?' he said.

'Apparently they are giving chase to him.'

The likelihood was, that Clara had been overcome by timidity.

'Must you leave us?'

'I think it prudent to take Professor Crooklyn away.'

'He still . . .'

'The extraordinary resemblance!'

'A word aside to Dr Middleton will dispel that.'

'You are thoroughly good.'

This hateful encomium of commiseration transfixed him. Then she knew of his calamity!

'Philosophical,' he said, 'would be the proper term, I think.'

'Colonel De Craye, by the way, promises me a visit when he leaves you.'

'To-morrow?'

'The earlier the better. He is too captivating; he is delightful. He won me in five minutes. I don't accuse him.

Nature gifted him to cast the spell. We are weak women, Sir Willoughby.'

She knew!

'Like to like: the witty to the witty, ma'am.'

'You won't compliment me with a little bit of jealousy?'

'I forbear from complimenting *him*.'

'Be philosophical, of course, if you have the philosophy.'

'I pretend to it. Probably I suppose myself to succeed because I have no great requirement of it; I cannot say. We are riddles to ourselves.'

Mrs Mountstuart pricked the turf with the point of her parasol. She looked down and she looked up.

'Well?' said he to her eyes.

'Well, and where is Laetitia Dale?'

He turned about to show his face elsewhere.

When he fronted her again, she looked very fixedly, and set her head shaking.

'It will not do, my dear Sir Willoughby!'

'What?'

'It.'

'I never could solve enigmas.'

'Playing ta-ta-ta-ta ad infinitum, then. Things have gone far. All parties would be happier for an excursion. Send her home.'

'Laetitia? I can't part with her.'

Mrs Mountstuart put a tooth on her under lip as her head renewed its brushing negative.

'In what way can it be hurtful that she should be here, ma'am?' he ventured to persist.

'Think.'

'She is proof.'

'Twice!'

The word was big artillery. He tried the affectation of a staring stupidity. She might have seen his heart thump, and he quitted the mask for an agreeable grimace.

'She is inaccessible. She is my friend. I guarantee her, on

my honour. Have no fear for her. I beg you to have confidence
in me. I would perish rather. No soul on earth is to be compared with her.'

Mrs Mountstuart repeated 'Twice!'

The low monosyllable, musically spoken in the same tone of
warning of a gentle ghost, rolled a thunder that maddened
him, but he dared not take it up to fight against it on plain
terms.

'Is it for my sake?' he said.

'It will not do, Sir Willoughby.'

She spurred him to a frenzy.

'My dear Mrs Mountstuart, you have been listening to tales.
I am not a tyrant. I am one of the most easy-going of men.
Let us preserve the forms due to society: I say no more. As
for poor old Vernon, people call me a good sort of cousin; I
should like to see him comfortably married; decently married
this time. I have proposed to contribute to his establishment.
I mention it to show that the case has been practically considered. He has had a tolerably souring experience of the state;
he might be inclined if, say, you took him in hand, for another
venture. It's a demoralizing lottery. However, government
sanctions it.'

'But, Sir Willoughby, what is the use of my taking him in
hand when, as you tell me, Laetitia Dale holds back?'

'She certainly does.'

'Then we are talking to no purpose, unless you undertake
to melt her.'

He suffered a lurking smile to kindle to some strength of
meaning.

'You are not over-considerate in committing me to such an
office.'

'You are afraid of the danger?' she all but sneered.

Sharpened by her tone, he said, 'I have such a love of sted-
fastness of character, that I should be a poor advocate in the
endeavour to break it. And frankly, I know the danger. I saved
my honour when I made the attempt: that is all I can say.'

'Upon my word,' Mrs Mountstuart threw back her head to let her eyes behold him summarily over their fine aquiline bridge, 'you have the art of mystification, my good friend.'

'Abandon the idea of Laetitia Dale.'

'And marry your cousin Vernon to whom? Where are we?'

'As I said, ma'am, I am an easy-going man. I really have not a spice of the tyrant in me. An intemperate creature held by the collar may have that notion of me, while pulling to be released as promptly as it entered the noose. But I do strictly and sternly object to the scandal of violent separations, open breaches of solemn engagements, a public rupture. Put it that I am the cause, I will not consent to a violation of decorum. Is that clear? It is just possible for things to be arranged so that all parties may be happy in their way without much hubbub. Mind, it is not I who have willed it so. I am, and I am forced to be, passive. But I will not be obstructive.'

He paused, waving his hand to signify the vanity of the more that might be said.

Some conception of him, dashed by incredulity, excited the lady's intelligence.

'Well!' she exclaimed, 'you have planted me in the land of conjecture. As my husband used to say, I don't see light, but I think I see the lynx that does. We won't discuss it at present. I certainly must be a younger woman than I supposed, for I am learning hard. – Here comes the Professor, buttoned up to the ears, and Dr Middleton flapping in the breeze. There will be a cough, and a footnote referring to the young lady at the station, if we stand together, so please order my carriage.'

'You found Clara complacent? roguish?'

'I will call to-morrow. You have simplified my task, Sir Willoughby, very much; that is, assuming that I have not entirely mistaken you. I am so far in the dark that I have to help myself by recollecting how Lady Busshe opposed my view of a certain matter formerly. Scepticism is her forte.

It will be the very oddest thing if after all . . . No, I shall own, romance has not departed. Are you fond of dupes?'

'I detest the race.'

'An excellent answer. I could pardon you for it.' She refrained from adding, 'If you are making one of me.'

Sir Willoughby went to ring for her carriage.

She knew. That was palpable: Clara had betrayed him. 'The earlier Colonel De Craye leaves Patterne Hall the better': she had said that: and, 'all parties would be happier for an excursion'. She knew the position of things and she guessed the remainder. But what she did not know, and could not divine, was the man who fenced her. He speculated further on the witty and the dull. These latter are the redoubt-able body. They will have facts to convince them: they had, he confessed it to himself, precipitated him into the novel sphere of his dark hints to Mrs Mountstuart; from which the utter darkness might allow him to escape, yet it embraced him singularly, and even pleasantly, with the sense of a fact established.

It embraced him even very pleasantly. There was an end to his tortures. He sailed on a tranquil sea, the husband of a stedfast woman – no rogue. The exceeding beauty of sted-fastness in women clothed Laetitia in graces Clara could not match. A tried stedfast woman is the one jewel of the sex. She points to her husband like the sunflower; her love illumi-nates him; she lives in him, for him; she testifies to his worth; she drags the world to his feet; she leads the chorus of his praises; she justifies him in his own esteem. Surely there is not on earth such beauty!

If we have to pass through anguish to discover it and cherish the peace it gives to clasp it, calling it ours, is a full reward.

Deep in his reverie, he said his adieus to Mrs Mountstuart, and strolled up the avenue behind the carriage-wheels, unwill-ing to meet Laetitia till he had exhausted the fresh savour of the cud of fancy.

Supposing it done! –

It would be generous on his part. It would redound to his credit.

His home would be a fortress, impregnable to tongues. He would have divine security in his home.

One who read and knew and worshipped him would be sitting there star-like: sitting there, awaiting him, his fixed star.

It would be marriage with a mirror, with an echo; marriage with a shining mirror, a choric echo.

It would be marriage with an intellect, with a fine understanding; to make his home a fountain of repeatable wit: to make his dear old Patterne Hall the luminary of the county.

He revolved it as a chant: with anon and anon involuntarily a discordant animadversion on Lady Busshe. His attendant imps heard the angry inward cry.

Forthwith he set about painting Laetitia in delectable human colours, like a miniature of the past century, reserving her ideal figure for his private satisfaction. The world was to bow to her visible beauty, and he gave her enamel and glow, a taller stature, a swimming air, a transcendency that exorcized the image of the old witch who had driven him to this.

The result in him was, that Laetitia became humanly and avowedly beautiful. Her dark eyelashes on the pallor of her cheeks lent their aid to the transformation, which was a necessity to him, so it was performed. He received the waxen impression.

His retinue of imps had a revel. We hear wonders of men, and we see a lifting up of hands in the world. The wonders would be explained, and never a hand need to interject, if the mystifying man were but accompanied by that monkey-eyed confraternity. They spy the heart and its twists.

The heart is the magical gentleman. None of them would follow where there was no heart. The twists of the heart are the comedy.

‘ *The secret of the heart is its pressing love of self* ’, says the Book. By that secret the mystery of the organ is legible: and a comparison of the heart to the mountain rillet is taken up to show us the unbaffled force of the little channel in seeking to swell its volume, strenuously, sinuously, ever in pursuit of self; the busiest as it is the most single-aiming of forces on our earth. And we are directed to the sinuosities for posts of observation chiefly instructive.

Few maintain a stand there. People see, and they rush away to interchange liftings of hands at the sight, instead of patiently studying the phenomenon of energy.

Consequently a man in love with one woman, and in all but absolute consciousness, behind the thinnest of veils, preparing his mind to love another, will be barely credible. The particular hunger of the forceful but adaptable heart is the key of him. Behold the mountain rillet, become a brook, become a torrent, how it inarms a handsome boulder: yet if the stone will not go with it, on it hurries, pursuing self in extension, down to where perchance a dam has been raised of a sufficient depth to enfold and keep it from inordinate restlessness. Laetitia represented this peaceful restraining space in prospect.

But she was a faded young woman. He was aware of it; and systematically looking at himself with her upturned orbs, he accepted her benevolently as a God grateful for worship, and used the divinity she imparted to paint and renovate her. His heart required her so. The heart works the springs of imagination; imagination received its commission from the heart, and was a cunning artist.

Cunning to such a degree of seductive genius that the masterpiece it offered to his contemplation enabled him simultaneously to gaze on Clara and think of Laetitia. Clara came through the park-gates with Vernon, a brilliant girl indeed, and a shallow one: a healthy creature, and an animal; attractive, but capricious, impatient, treacherous, foul; a woman to drag men through the mud. She approached.

CHAPTER 38

※※※

In Which We Take a Step to the Centre
of Egoism

THEY met; Vernon soon left them.

'You have not seen Crossjay?' Willoughby inquired.

'No,' said Clara. 'Once more I beg you to pardon him. He spoke falsely, owing to his poor boy's idea of chivalry.'

'The chivalry to the sex which commences in lies ends by creating the woman's hero, whom we see about the world and in certain courts of law.'

His ability to silence her was great: she could not reply to speech like that.

'You have,' said he, 'made a confidante of Mrs Mountstuart.'

'Yes.'

'This is your purse.'

'I thank you.'

'Professor Crooklyn has managed to make your father acquainted with your project. That, I suppose, is the railway-ticket in the fold of the purse. He was assured at the station that you had taken a ticket to London, and would not want the fly.'

'It is true. I was foolish.'

'You have had a pleasant walk with Vernon – turning me in and out?'

'We did not speak of you. You allude to what he would never consent to.'

'He's an honest fellow, in his old-fashioned way. He's a secret old fellow. Does he ever talk about his wife to you?'

Clara dropped her purse, and stooped and picked it up.

'I know nothing of Mr Whitford's affairs,' she said, and she opened the purse and tore to pieces the railway ticket.

'The story's a proof that romantic spirits do not furnish the most romantic history. You have the word "chivalry" frequently on your lips. He chivalrously married the daughter of the lodging-house where he resided before I took him. We obtained information of the auspicious union in a newspaper report of Mrs Whitford's drunkenness and rioting at a London railway terminus – probably the one whither your ticket would have taken you yesterday, for I heard the lady was on her way to us for supplies, the connubial larder being empty.'

'I am sorry; I am ignorant; I have heard nothing; I know nothing,' said Clara.

'You are disgusted. But half the students and authors you hear of marry in that way. And very few have Vernon's luck.'

'She had good qualities?' asked Clara.

Her under lip hung.

It looked like disgust; he begged her not indulge the feeling.

'Literary men, it is notorious, even with the entry to society, have no taste in women. The housewife is their object. Ladies frighten and would, no doubt, be an annoyance and hindrance to them at home.'

'You said he was fortunate.'

'You have a kindness for him.'

'I respect him.'

'He is a friendly old fellow in his awkward fashion; honourable, and so forth. But a disreputable alliance of that sort sticks to a man. The world will talk. Yes, he was fortunate so far; he fell into the mire and got out of it. Were he to marry again . . .'

'She . . .'

'Died. Do not be startled; it was a natural death. She responded to the sole wishes left to his family. He buried the woman, and I received him. I took him on my tour. A second marriage might cover the first: there would be a buzz about the old business: the woman's relatives write to him still, try to bleed him, I dare say. However, now you understand his gloominess. I don't imagine he regrets his loss. He probably sentimentalizes, like most men when they are well rid of a burden. You must not think the worse of him.'

'I do not,' said Clara.

'I defend him whenever the matter's discussed.'

'I hope you do.'

'Without approving his folly. I can't wash him clean.'

They were at the Hall-doors. She waited for any personal communications he might be pleased to make, and as there was none, she ran upstairs to her room.

He had tossed her to Vernon in his mind, not only pain-lessly, but with a keen acid of satisfaction. The heart is the wizard.

Next he bent his deliberate steps to Laetitia.

The mind was guilty of some hesitation; the feet went forward.

She was working at an embroidery by an open window. Colonel De Craye leaned outside, and Willoughby pardoned her air of demure amusement, on hearing him say: 'No, I have had one of the pleasantest half-hours of my life, and would rather idle here, if idle you will have it, than employ my faculties on horse-back,'

'Time is not lost in conversing with Miss Dale,' said Willoughby.

The light was tender to her complexion where she sat in partial shadow.

De Craye asked whether Crossjay had been caught. Laetitia murmured a kind word for the boy. Willoughby examined her embroidery.

The ladies Eleanor and Isabel appeared.

They invited her to take carriage exercise with them.

Laetitia did not immediately answer, and Willoughby remarked: 'Miss Dale has been reproving Horace for idleness, and I recommend you to enlist him to do duty, while I relieve him here.'

The ladies had but to look at the colonel. He was at their disposal, if they would have him. He was marched to the carriage.

Laetitia plied her threads.

'Colonel De Craye spoke of Crossjay,' she said. 'May I hope you have forgiven the poor boy, Sir Willoughby?'

He replied: 'Plead for him.'

'I wish I had eloquence.'

'In my opinion you have it.'

'If he offends, it is never from meanness. At school, among comrades, he would shine. He is in too strong a light; his feelings and his moral nature are over-excited.'

'That was not the case when he was at home with you.'

'I am severe; I am stern.'

'A Spartan mother!'

'My system of managing a boy would be after that model: except in this: he should always feel that he could obtain forgiveness.'

'Not at the expense of justice?'

'Ah! young creatures are not to be arraigned before the higher Courts. It seems to me perilous to terrify their imaginations. If we do so, are we not likely to produce the very evil we are combating? The alternations for the young should be school and home: and it should be in their hearts to have confidence that forgiveness alternates with discipline. They are of too tender an age for the rigours of the world; we are in danger of hardening them. I prove to you that I am not possessed of eloquence. You encouraged me to speak, Sir Willoughby.'

'You speak wisely, Laetitia.'

'I think it true. Will not you reflect on it? You have only to do so to forgive him. I am growing bold indeed, and shall have to beg forgiveness for myself.'

'You still write? you continue to work with your pen?' said Willoughby.

'A little; a very little.'

'I do not like you to squander yourself, waste yourself, on the public. You are too precious to feed the beast. Giving out incessantly must end by attenuating. Reserve yourself for your friends. Why should they be robbed of so much of you? Is it not reasonable to assume that by lying fallow you would be more enriched for domestic life? Candidly, had I authority I would confiscate your pen: I would "away with that bauble". You will not often find me quoting Cromwell, but his words apply in this instance. I would say rather, that lancet. Perhaps it is the more correct term. It bleeds you, it wastes you. For what? For a breath of fame!'

'I write for money.'

'And there – I would say of another – you subject yourself to the risk of mental degradation. Who knows? – moral! Trafficking the brains for money must bring them to the level of the purchasers in time. I confiscate your pen, Laetitia.'

'It will be to confiscate your own gift, Sir Willoughby.'

'Then that proves – will you tell me the date?'

'You sent me a gold pen-holder on my sixteenth birthday.'

'It proves my utter thoughtlessness then, and later. And later!'

He rested an elbow on his knee, and covered his eyes, murmuring in that profound hollow which is haunted by the voice of a contrite past: 'And later!'

The deed could be done. He had come to the conclusion that it could be done, though the effort to harmonize the figure sitting near him, with the artistic figure of his purest pigments, had cost him labour and a blinking of the eyelids. That also could be done. Her pleasant tone, sensible talk, and the light favouring her complexion, helped him in his effort. She was a sober cup; sober and wholesome. Deliriousness is for adolescence. The men who seek intoxicating cups are men who invite their fates.

Curiously, yet as positively as things can be affirmed, the husband of this woman would be able to boast of her virtues and treasures abroad, as he could not – impossible to say why not – boast of a beautiful wife or a blue-stocking wife. One of her merits as a wife would be this extraordinary neutral merit of a character that demanded colour from the marital hand, and would take it.

Laetitia had not to learn that he had much to distress him. Her wonder at his exposure of his grief counteracted a fluttering of vague alarm. She was nervous; she sat in expectation of some burst of regrets or of passion.

'I may hope that you have pardoned Crossjay?' she said.

'My friend,' said he, uncovering his face, 'I am governed by principles. Convince me of an error, I shall not obstinately pursue a premeditated course. But you know me. Men who have not principles to rule their conduct are – well, they are unworthy of a half hour of companionship with you. I will speak to you to-night. I have letters to dispatch. To-night: at twelve: in the room where we spoke last. Or await me in the drawing-room. I have to attend to my guests till late.'

He bowed; he was in a hurry to go.

The deed could be done. It must be done; it was his destiny.

CHAPTER 39

✕✕✕✕

In the Heart of the Egoist

But already he had begun to regard the deed as his executioner. He dreaded meeting Clara. The folly of having retained her stood before him. How now to look on her and keep a sane resolution unwavering? She tempted to the insane. Had

she been away, he could have walked through the performance composed by the sense of doing a duty to himself;
perhaps faintly hating the poor wretch he made happy at last,
kind to her in a manner, polite. Clara's presence in the house
previous to the deed, and, oh, heaven! after it, threatened his
wits. Pride? He had none; he cast it down for her to trample
it; he caught it back ere it was trodden on. Yes; he had pride:
he had it as a dagger in his breast: his pride was his misery.
But he was too proud to submit to misery. 'What I do is
right.' He said the words, and rectitude smoothed his path,
till the question clamoured for answer: Would the world
countenance and endorse his pride in Laetitia? At one time,
yes. And now? Clara's beauty ascended, laid a beam on him.

We are on board the labouring vessel of humanity in a
storm, when cries and countercries ring out, disorderliness
mixes the crew, and the fury of self-preservation divides:
this one is for the ship, that one for his life. Clara was the
former to him, Laetitia the latter. But what if there might not
be greater safety in holding tenaciously to Clara than in
casting her off for Laetitia? No, she had done things to set his
pride throbbing in the quick. She had gone bleeding about
first to one, then to another; she had betrayed him to Vernon,
and to Mrs Mountstuart; a look in the eyes of Horace De
Craye said, to him as well: to whom not? He might hold to
her for vengeance; but that appetite was short-lived in him
if it ministered nothing to his purposes. 'I discard all idea of
vengeance,' he said, and thrilled burningly to a smart in his
admiration of the man who could be so magnanimous under
mortal injury; for the more admirable he, the more pitiable.
He drank a drop or two of self-pity like a poison, repelling
the assaults of public pity. Clara must be given up. It must
be seen by the world that, as he felt, the thing he did was right.
Laocoon of his own serpents, he struggled to a certain magnificence of attitude in the muscular net of constrictions he flung
around himself. Clara must be given up. Oh, bright Abominable! She must be given up: but not to one whose touch of

her would be darts in the blood of the yielder, snakes in his bed: she must be given up to an extinguisher; to be the second wife of an old-fashioned semi-recluse, disgraced in his first. And were it publicly known that she had been cast off, and had fallen on old Vernon for a refuge, and part in spite, part in shame, part in desperation, part in a fit of good sense under the circumstances, espoused him, her beauty would not influence the world in its judgement. The world would know what to think. As the instinct of self-preservation whispered to Willoughby, the world, were it requisite, might be taught to think what it assuredly would not think if she should be seen tripping to the altar with Horace De Craye. Self-preservation, not vengeance, breathed that whisper. He glanced at her iniquity for a justification of it, without any desire to do her a permanent hurt: he was highly civilized: but with a strong intention to give her all the benefit of a scandal, supposing a scandal, or ordinary tattle.

'And so he handed her to his cousin and secretary, Vernon Whitford, who opened his mouth and shut his eyes.'

You hear the world? How are we to stop it from chattering? Enough that he had no desire to harm her. Some gentle anticipations of her being tarnished were imperative; they came spontaneously to him; otherwise the radiance of that bright Abominable in loss would have been insufferable; he could not have borne it; he could never have surrendered her.

Moreover, a happy present effect was the result. He conjured up the anticipated chatter and shrug of the world so vividly that her beauty grew hectic with the stain, bereft of its formidable magnetism. He could meet her calmly; he had steeled himself. Purity in women was his principal stipulation, and a woman puffed at, was not the person to cause him tremours.

Consider him indulgently; the Egoist is the Son of Himself. He is likewise the Father. And the son loves the father, the father the son; they reciprocate affection, through the closest of ties; and shall they view behaviour unkindly wounding either of them, not for each other's dear sake abhorring the criminal? They would not injure you, but they cannot consent to see one another suffer or crave in vain. The two rub together in sympathy besides relationship to an intenser one. Are you, without much offending, sacrificed by them, it is on the altar of their mutual love, to filial piety or paternal tenderness: the younger has offered a dainty morsel to the elder, or the elder to the younger. Absorbed in their great example of devotion do they not think of you. They are beautiful.

Yet is it most true that the younger has the passions of youth: whereof will come division between them; and this is a tragic state. They are then pathetic. This was the state of Sir Willoughby lending ear to his elder, until he submitted to bite at the fruit proposed to him – with how wry a mouth the venerable senior chose not to mark. At least, as we perceive, a half of him was ripe of wisdom in his own interests. The cruder half had but to be obedient to the leadership of sagacity for his interests to be secured, and a filial disposition assisted him; painfully indeed; but the same rare quality directed the good gentleman to swallow his pain. That the son should bewail his fate were a dishonour to the sire. He reverenced, and submitted. Thus, to say, consider him indulgently, is too much an appeal for charity on behalf of one requiring but initial anatomy – a slicing in halves – to exonerate, perchance exalt him. The Egoist is our fountain-head, primeval man: the primitive is born again, the elemental reconstituted. Born again, into new conditions, the primitive may be highly polished of men, and forfeit nothing save the roughness of his original nature. He is not only his own father, he is ours; and he is also our son. We have produced him, he us. Such were we, to such are we returning: not other, sings the poet, than one who toilfully works his shallop against the tide, 'si brachia forte remisit': – let him haply relax the labour of his arms, however high up the stream, and back he goes, 'in pejus', to the early principle of our being, with seeds and plants, that are as carelessly weighed in the hand and as indiscriminately husbanded as our humanity. [29]

Poets on the other side may be cited for an assurance that the primitive is not the degenerate: rather is he a sign of the indestructibility of the race, of the ancient energy in removing obstacles to individual growth; a sample of what we would be, had we his concentrated power. He is the original innocent, the pure simple. It is we who have fallen; we have melted into Society, diluted our essence, dissolved. He stands in the midst monumentally, a land-mark of the tough and honest old Ages, with the symbolic alphabet of striking arms and running legs, our early language, scrawled over his person, and the glorious first flint and arrow-head for his crest: at once the spectre of the Kitchen-midden and our ripest issue.

But Society is about him. The occasional spectacle of the primitive dangling on a rope has impressed his mind with the strength of his natural enemy: from which uncongenial sight he has turned shuddering hardly less to behold the blast that is blown upon a reputation where one has been disrespectful of the many. By these means, through meditation on the contrast of circumstances in life, a pulse of imagination has begun to stir, and he has entered the upper sphere or circle of spiritual Egoism: he has become the civilized Egoist; primitive still, as sure as man has teeth, but developed in his manner of using them.

Degenerate or not (and there is no just reason to suppose it) Sir Willoughby was a social Egoist, fiercely imaginative in whatsoever concerned him. He had discovered a greater realm than that of the sensual appetites, and he rushed across and around it in his conquering period with an Alexander's pride. On these wind-like journeys he had carried Constantia, subsequently Clara; and however it may have been in the case of Miss Durham, in that of Miss Middleton it is almost certain she caught a glimpse of his interior from sheer fatigue in hearing him discourse of it. What he revealed was not the cause of her sickness: women can bear revelations – they are exciting: but the monotonousness. He slew imagination. There is no direr disaster in love than the death of imagination. He dragged her through the labyrinths of his penetralia, in his hungry coveting to be loved more and still more, more still, until imagination gave up the ghost, and he talked to her plain hearing like a monster. It must have been that; for the spell of the primitive upon women is masterful up to the time of contact.

'And so he handed her to his cousin and secretary, Vernon Whitford, who opened his mouth and shut his eyes.'

The urgent question was, how it was to be accomplished. Willoughby worked at the subject with all his power of concentration: a power that had often led him to feel and say, that as a barrister, a diplomatist, or a general, he would have won his grades: and granting him a personal interest in the business, he might have achieved eminence: he schemed and fenced remarkably well.

He projected a scene, following expressions of anxiety on account of old Vernon and his future settlement: and then – Clara maintaining her doggedness, to which he was now so accustomed that he could not conceive a change in it – says he: 'If you determine on breaking I give you back your word *on one condition*.' Whereupon she starts: he insists on her promise: she declines: affairs resume their former footing; she frets: she begs for the disclosure: he flatters her by telling her his desire to keep her in the family: she is unilluminated, but strongly moved by curiosity: he philosophizes on marriage – 'What are we? poor creatures! we must get through life as we can, doing as much good as we can to those we love; and think as you please, I love old Vernon. Am I not giving you the greatest possible proof of it?' She will not see. Then flatly out comes the one condition. That and no other. 'Take Vernon and I release you.' She refuses. Now ensues the debate, all the oratory being with him. 'Is it because of his unfortunate first marriage? You assured me you thought no worse of him,' etc. She declares the proposal revolting. He can distinguish nothing that should offend her in a proposal to make his cousin happy if she will not him. Irony and sarcasm relieve his emotions, but he convinces her he is dealing plainly and intends generosity. She is confused; she speaks in maiden fashion.

He touches again on Vernon's early escapade. She does not enjoy it. The scene closes with his bidding her reflect on it, and remember the one condition of her release. Mrs Mountstuart Jenkinson, now reduced to believe that he burns to be free, is then called in for an interview with Clara. His aunts Eleanor and Isabel besiege her. Laetitia in passionate earnest besieges her. Her father is wrought on to besiege her. Finally Vernon is attacked by Willoughby and Mrs Mountstuart: – and here, Willoughby chose to think, was the main difficulty. But the girl has money; she is agreeable; Vernon likes her; she is fond of his 'Alps', they have tastes in common, he likes her father, and in the end he besieges her. Will she yield? De Craye is absent. There is no other way of shunning a marriage she is incomprehensibly but frantically averse to. She is in the toils. Her father will stay at Patterne Hall as long as his host desires it. She hesitates, she is overcome; in spite of a certain nausea due to Vernon's preceding alliance, she yields.

Willoughby revolved the entire drama in Clara's presence. It helped him to look on her coolly. Conducting her to the dinner-table, he spoke of Crossjay, not unkindly; and at table, he revolved the set of scenes with a heated animation that took fire from the wine and the face of his friend Horace, while he encouraged Horace to be flowingly Irish. He nipped the fellow good-humouredly once or twice, having never felt so friendly to him since the day of his arrival; but the position of critic is instinctively taken by men who do not flow: and Patterne Port kept Dr Middleton in a benevolent reserve when Willoughby decided that something said by De Craye was not new, and laughingly accused him of failing to consult his anecdotal notebook for the double-cross to his last sprightly sally. 'Your sallies are excellent, Horace, but spare us your Aunt Sallies!' De Craye had no repartee, nor did Dr Middleton challenge a pun. We have only to sharpen our wits to trip your seductive rattler whenever we may choose to think proper; and evidently, if we condescended to it, we could do better than he. The critic who has hatched a witticism is impelled to this opinion. Judging by the smiles of the ladies, they thought so, too.

Shortly before eleven o'clock Dr Middleton made a Spartan stand against the offer of another bottle of Port. The regulation couple of bottles had been consumed in equal partnership, and the Rev. Doctor and his host were free to pay a ceremonial visit to the drawing-room, where they were not expected. A piece of work of the elder ladies, a silken boudoir sofa-rug, was being examined, with high approval of the two younger. Vernon and Colonel De Craye had gone out in search of Crossjay, one to Mr Dale's cottage, the other to call at the head and under-gamekeeper's. They were said to be strolling and smoking, for the night was fine. Willoughby left the room and came back with the key of Crossjay's door in his pocket. He foresaw that the delinquent might be of service to him.

Laetitia and Clara sang together. Laetitia was flushed, Clara pale. At eleven they saluted the ladies Eleanor and Isabel. Willoughby said 'Good-night' to each of them, contrasting as he did so the downcast look of Laetitia with Clara's frigid directness. He divined that they were off to talk over their one object of common interest, Crossjay. Saluting his aunts, he took up the rug, to celebrate their diligence and taste; and that he might make Dr Middleton impatient for bed, he provoked him to admire it, held it out and laid it out, and caused the courteous old gentleman some confusion in hitting on fresh terms of commendation.

Before midnight the room was empty. Ten minutes later Willoughby paid it a visit, and found it untenanted by the person he had engaged to be there. Vexed by his disappointment, he paced up and down, and chanced abstractedly to catch the rug in his hand; for what purpose, he might well ask himself; admiration of ladies' work, in their absence, was unlikely to occur to him. Nevertheless, the touch of the warm, soft silk was meltingly feminine. A glance at the mantel-piece clock told him Laetitia was twenty minutes behind the hour.

Her remissness might endanger all his plans, alter the whole course of his life. The colours in which he painted her were too lively to last; the madness in his head threatened to subside. Certain it was that he could not be ready a second night for the sacrifice he had been about to perform.

The clock was at the half hour after twelve. He flung the silken thing on the central ottoman, extinguished the lamps, and walked out of the room, charging the absent Laetitia to bear her misfortune with a consciousness of deserving it.

CHAPTER 40

✕✕✕✕

Midnight: Sir Willoughby and Laetitia: with Young Crossjay under a Coverlet

YOUNG Crossjay was a glutton at holidays and never thought of home till it was dark. The close of the day saw him several miles away from the Hall, dubious whether he would not round his numerous adventures by sleeping at an inn; for he had lots of money, and the idea of jumping up in the morning in a strange place was thrilling. Besides, when he was shaken out of sleep by Sir Willoughby, he had been told that he was to go, and not to show his face at Patterne again. On the other hand, Miss Middleton had bidden him come back. There was little question with him which person he should obey: he followed his heart.

Supper at an inn, where he found a company to listen to his adventures, delayed him, and a short cut, intended to make up for it, lost him his road. He reached the Hall very late, ready to be in love with the horrible pleasure of a night's rest under the stars, if necessary. But a candle burned at one of the back windows. He knocked, and a kitchen-maid let him in. She had a bowl of hot soup prepared for him. Crossjay tried a mouthful to please her. His head dropped over it. She roused him to his feet, and he pitched against her shoulder. The dry air of the kitchen department had proved too much for the tired youngster. Mary, the maid, got him to step as firmly as he was able, and led him by the back-way to the hall, bidding him creep noiselessly to bed. He understood his position in the house, and though he could have gone fast to sleep on the stairs, he took a steady aim at his room and gained the door cat-like. The door resisted. He was appalled and unstrung in a minute. The door was locked. Crossjay felt as if he were in the presence of Sir Willoughby. He fled on ricketty legs, and had a fall and bumps down half a dozen stairs. A door opened above. He rushed across the hall to the drawing-room, invitingly open, and there staggered in darkness to the ottoman and rolled himself in something sleek and warm, soft as hands of ladies, and redolent of them; so delicious that he hugged the folds about his head and heels. While he was endeavouring to think where he was his legs curled, his eyelids shut, and he was in the thick of the day's adventures, doing yet more wonderful things.

He heard his own name: that was quite certain. He knew that he heard it with his ears, as he pursued the fleetest dreams ever accorded to mortal. It did not mix: it was outside him, and like the danger-pole in the ice, which the skater shooting hither and yonder comes on again, it recurred; and now it marked a point in his career, now it caused him to relax his pace; he began to circle, and whirled closer round it, until, as at a blow, his heart knocked, he tightened himself, thought of bolting, and lay dead-still to throb and hearken.

'Oh! Sir Willoughby,' a voice had said.

The accents were sharp with alarm.

'My friend! my dearest!' was the answer.

'I came to speak of Crossjay.'

'Will you sit here on the ottoman?'

'No, I cannot wait. I hoped I had heard Crossjay return. I would rather not sit down. May I entreat you to pardon him when he comes home?'

'You, and you only, may do so. I permit none else. Of Crossjay to-morrow.'

'He may be lying in the fields. We are anxious.'

'The rascal can take pretty good care of himself.'

'Crossjay is perpetually meeting accidents.'

'He shall be indemnified if he has had excess of punishment.'

'I think I will say good-night, Sir Willoughby.'

'When freely and unreservedly you have given me your hand.'

There was hesitation.

'To say good-night?'

'I ask you for your hand.'

'Good-night, Sir Willoughby.'

'You do not give it. You are in doubt? Still? What language must I use to convince you? And yet you know me. Who knows me but you? You have always known me. You are my home and my temple. Have you forgotten your verses of the day of my majority?

> "The dawn-star has arisen
> In plenitude of light . . ."

'Do not repeat them, pray!' cried Laetitia, with a gasp.

'I have repeated them to myself a thousand times: in India, America, Japan: they were like our English skylark, carolling to me.

> "My heart, now burst thy prison
> With proud aërial flight!"

'Oh, I beg you will not force me to listen to nonsense that I wrote when I was a child. No more of those most foolish lines!

If you knew what it is to write and despise one's writing, you would not distress me. And since you will not speak of Cross-jay to-night allow me to retire.'

'You know me, and therefore you know my contempt for verses, as a rule, Laetitia. But not for yours to me. Why should you call them foolish? They expressed your feelings – hold them sacred. They are something religious to me, not mere poetry. Perhaps the third verse is my favourite . . .'

'It will be more than I can bear!'

'You were in earnest when you wrote them?'

'I was very young, very enthusiastic, very silly.'

'You were and are my image of constancy!'

'It is an error, Sir Willoughby; I am far from being the same.'

'We are all older, I trust wiser. I am, I will own; much wiser. Wise at last! I offer you my hand.'

She did not reply. 'I offer you my hand and name, Laetitia.' No response.

'You think me bound in honour to another?'

She was mute.

'I am free. Thank Heaven! I am free to choose my mate – the woman I have always loved! Freely and unreservedly, as I ask you to give your hand, I offer mine. You are the mistress of Patterne Hall; my wife.'

She had not a word.

'My dearest! do you not rightly understand? The hand I am offering you is disengaged. It is offered to the lady I respect above all others. I have made the discovery that I cannot love without respecting; and as I will not marry without loving, it ensues that I am free – I am yours. At last? – your lips move: tell me the words. *Have always loved*, I said. You carry in your bosom the magnet of constancy, and I, in spite of apparent deviations, declare to you that I have never ceased to be sensible of the attraction. And now there is not an impediment. We two against the world! we are one. Let me confess to an old foible – perfectly youthful, and you will ascribe it to youth:

once I desired to absorb. I mistrusted; that was the reason: I perceive it. You teach me the difference of an alliance with a lady of intellect. The pride I have in you, Laetitia, definitely cures me of that insane passion – call it an insatiable hunger. I recognize it as a folly of youth. I have, as it were, gone the tour, to come home to you – at last? – and live our manly life of comparative equals. At last, then! But remember that in the younger man you would have had a despot – perhaps a jealous despot. Young men, I assure you, are orientally inclined in their ideas of love. Love gets a bad name from them. We, my Laetitia, do not regard love as a selfishness. If it is, it is the essence of life. At least it is our selfishness rendered beautiful. I talk to you like a man who has found a compatriot in a foreign land. It seems to me that I have not opened my mouth for an age. I certainly have not unlocked my heart. Those who sing for joy are not unintelligible to me. If I had not something in me worth saying I think I should sing. In every sense you reconcile me to men and the world, Laetitia. Why press you to speak? I will be the speaker. As surely as you know me, I know you: and – '

Laetitia burst forth with: 'No!'

'I do not know you?' said he, searchingly mellifluous.

'Hardly.'

'How not?'

'I am changed.'

'In what way?'

'Deeply.'

'Sedater?'

'Materially.'

'Colour will come back: have no fear; I promise it. If you imagine you want renewing *I* have the specific, I, my love, I!'

'Forgive me – will you tell me, Sir Willoughby, whether you have broken with Miss Middleton?'

'Rest satisfied, my dear Laetitia. She is as free as I am. I can do no more than a man of honour should do. She releases me. To-morrow or next day she departs. We, Laetitia, you

and I, my love, are home birds. It does not do for the home
bird to couple with the migratory. The little imperceptible
change you allude to, is nothing. Italy will restore you. I am
ready to stake my own health – never yet shaken by a doctor
of medicine: – I say medicine advisedly, for there are doctors
of divinity who would shake giants: – that an Italian trip
will send you back – that I shall bring you home from
Italy a blooming bride. You shake your head – despondently?
My love, I guarantee it. Cannot I give you colour? Behold!
Come to the light, look in the glass.'

'I may redden,' said Laetitia. 'I suppose that is due to the
action of the heart. I am changed. Heart, for any other purpose, I have not. I am like you, Sir Willoughby, in this: I
could not marry without loving, and I do not know what love
is, except that it is an empty dream.'

'Marriage, my dearest . . .'

'You are mistaken.'

'I will cure you, my Laetitia. Look to me, I am the tonic. It
is not common confidence, but conviction. I, my love, I!'

'There is no cure for what I feel, Sir Willoughby.'

'Spare me the formal prefix, I beg. You place your hand
in mine, relying on me. I am pledge for the remainder. We
end as we began: my request is for your hand – your hand in
marriage.'

'I cannot give it.'

'To be my wife!'

'It is an honour; I must decline it.'

'Are you quite well, Laetitia? I propose in the plainest terms
I can employ, to make you Lady Patterne – mine.'

'I am compelled to refuse.'

'Why? Refuse? Your reason!'

'The reason has been named.'

He took a stride to inspirit his wits.

'There's a madness comes over women at times, I know.
Answer me, Laetitia: – by all the evidence a man can have, I
could swear it: – but answer me; you loved me once?'

'I was an exceedingly foolish, romantic girl.'

'You evade my question: I am serious. Oh!' he walked away from her booming a sound of utter repudiation of her present imbecility, and hurrying to her side, said: 'But it was manifest to the whole world! It was a legend. To love like Laetitia Dale, was a current phrase. You were an example, a light to women: no one was your match for devotion. You were a precious cameo, still gazing! And I was the object. You loved me. You loved me, you belonged to me, you were mine, my possession, my jewel; I was prouder of your constancy than of anything else that I had on earth. It was a part of the order of the universe to me. A doubt of it would have disturbed my creed. Why, good heaven! where are we? Is nothing solid on earth? You loved me!'

'I was childish, indeed.'

'You loved me passionately!'

'Do you insist on shaming me through and through, Sir Willoughby? I have been exposed enough.'

'You cannot blot out the past: it is written, it is recorded. You loved me devotedly, silence is no escape. You loved me.'

'I did.'

'You never loved me, you shallow woman! "I did!" As if there could be a cessation of a love! What are we to reckon on as ours? We prize a woman's love; we guard it jealously, we trust to it, dream of it; *there* is our wealth; there is our talisman! And when we open the casket it has flown! – barren vacuity! – we are poorer than dogs. As well think of keeping a costly wine in potter's clay as love in the heart of a woman! There are women – women! Oh, they are all of a stamp – coin! Coin for any hand! It's a fiction, an imposture – they cannot love. They are the shadows of men. Compared with men, they have as much heart in them as the shadow beside the body. Laetitia!'

'Sir Willoughby.'

'You refuse my offer?'

'I must.'

'You refuse to take me for your husband?'

'I cannot be your wife.'

'You have changed? . . . you have set your heart? . . . you could marry? . . . there is a man? . . . you could marry one! I will have an answer, I am sick of evasions. What was in the mind of Heaven when women were created, will be the riddle to the end of the world! Every good man in turn has made the inquiry. I have a right to know who robs me – We may try as we like to solve it. – Satan is painted laughing! – I say I have a right to know who robs me. Answer me.'

'I shall not marry.'

'That is not an answer.'

'I love no one.'

'You loved me. – You are silent? – but you confessed it. Then you confess it was a love that could die! Are you unable to perceive how that redounds to my discredit? You loved me, you have ceased to love me. In other words you charge me with incapacity to sustain a woman's love. You accuse me of inspiring a miserable passion that cannot last a lifetime! You let the world see that I am a man to be aimed at for a temporary mark! And simply because I happen to be in your neighbourhood at an age when a young woman is impressionable! You make a public example of me as a man for whom women may have a caprice, but that is all; he cannot enchain them; he fascinates passingly; they fall off. Is it just, for me to be taken up and cast down at your will? Reflect on, that scandal! Shadows? Why, a man's shadow is faithful to him at least. What are women? There is not a comparison in nature that does not tower above them! not one that does not hoot at them! I, throughout my life, guided by absolute deference to their weakness – paying them politeness, courtesy – whatever I touch I am happy in, except when I touch women! How is it? What is the mystery? Some monstrous explanation must exist. What can it be? I am favoured by fortune from my birth until I enter into relations with women. But will you be so good as to account for it in your

defence of them? Oh! were the relations dishonourable, it
would be quite another matter. *Then* they ... I could recount ... I disdain to chronicle such victories. Quite another
matter. But they are flies, and I am something more stable.
They are flies. I look beyond the day; I owe a duty to my line.
They are flies. I foresee it, I shall be crossed in my fate so long
as I fail to shun them – flies! Not merely born for the day, I
maintain that they are spiritually ephemeral – Well, my
opinion of your sex is directly traceable to you. You may
alter it, or fling another of us men out on the world with the
old bitter experience. Consider this, that it is on your head if
my ideal of women is wrecked. It rests with you to restore it.
I love you. I discover that you are the one woman I have
always loved. I come to you, I sue you, and suddenly – you
have changed! "I have changed: I am not the same." What
can it mean? "I cannot marry: I love no one." And you say
you do not know what love is – avowing in the same breath
that you did love me! Am I the empty dream? My hand,
heart, fortune, name, are yours, at your feet; you kick them
hence. I am here – you reject me. But why, for what mortal
reason am I here other than my faith in your love? You drew
me to you, to repel me, and have a wretched revenge.'

'You know it is not that, Sir Willoughby.'

'Have you any possible suspicion that I am still entangled,
not, as I assure you I am, perfectly free in fact and in honour?'

'It is not that.'

'Name it; for you see your power. Would you have me
kneel to you, madam?'

'Oh, no; it would complete my grief.'

'You feel grief? Then you believe in my affection, and you
hurl it away. I have no doubt that as a poetess you would say,
love is eternal. And you have loved me. And you tell me you
love me no more. You are not very logical, Laetitia Dale.'

'Poetesses rarely are: if I am one, which I little pretend to
be for writing silly verses. I have passed out of that delusion,
with the rest.'

'You shall not wrong those dear old days, Laetitia. I see them now; when I rode by your cottage and you were at your window, pen in hand, your hair straying over your forehead. Romantic, yes; not foolish. Why were you foolish in thinking of me? Some day I will commission an artist to paint me that portrait of you from my description. And I remember when we first whispered . . . I remember your trembling. You have forgotten – I remember. I remember our meeting in the park on the path to church. I remember the heavenly morning of my return from my travels, and the same Laetitia meeting me, stedfast and unchangeable. Could I ever forget? Those are ineradicable scenes; pictures of my youth, interwound with me. I may say, that as I recede from them, I dwell on them the more. Tell me, Laetitia, was there not a certain prophecy of your father's concerning us two? I fancy I heard of one. There was one.'

'He was an invalid. Elderly people nurse illusions.'

'Ask yourself, Laetitia, who is the obstacle to the fulfilment of his prediction? – truth, if ever a truth was foreseen on earth. You have not changed so far that you would feel *no* pleasure in gratifying him? I go to him to-morrow morning with the first light.'

'You will compel me to follow, and undeceive him.'

'Do so, and I denounce an unworthy affection you are ashamed to avow.'

'That would be idle, though it would be base.'

'Proof of love, then! For no one but you should it be done, and no one but you dare accuse me of a baseness.'

'Sir Willoughby, you will let my father die in peace.'

'He and I together will contrive to persuade you.'

'You tempt me to imagine that you want a wife at any cost.'

'You, Laetitia, you.'

'I am tired,' she said. 'It is late, I would rather not hear more. I am sorry if I have caused you pain. I suppose you to have spoken with candour. I defend neither my sex nor myself. I can only say I am a woman as good as dead: happy to be made happy in my way, but so little alive that I can not realize any other way. As for love, I am thankful to have broken a spell. You have a younger woman in your mind; I am an old one: I have no ambition and no warmth. My utmost prayer is to float on the stream – a purely physical desire of life: I have no strength to swim. Such a woman is not the wife for you, Sir Willoughby. Good night.'

'One final word. Weigh it. Express no conventional regrets. Resolutely you refuse?'

'Resolutely I do.'

'You refuse?'

'Yes.'

'I have sacrificed my pride for nothing! You refuse?'

'Yes.'

'Humbled myself! And this is the answer! You do refuse?'

'I do.'

'Good night, Laetitia Dale.'

He gave her passage.

'Good night, Sir Willoughby.'

'I am in your power,' he said, in a voice between supplication and menace that laid a claw on her, and she turned and replied:

'You will not be betrayed.'

'I can trust you . . .?'

'I go home to-morrow before breakfast.'

'Permit me to escort you upstairs.'

'If you please: but I see no one here either to-night or to-morrow.'

'It is for the privilege of seeing the last of you.'

They withdrew.

Young Crossjay listened to the drumming of his head. Somewhere in or over the cavity a drummer rattled tremendously.

Sir Willoughby's laboratory door shut with a slam.

Crossjay tumbled himself off the ottoman. He stole up to the unclosed drawing-room door, and peeped. Never was a boy more thoroughly awakened. His object was to get out of the house and go through the night avoiding everything human, for he was big with information of a character that he knew to be of the nature of gunpowder, and he feared to explode. He crossed the hall. In the passage to the scullery he ran against Colonel De Craye.

'So there you are,' said the colonel, 'I've been hunting you.'

Crossjay related that his bedroom door was locked and the key gone, and Sir Willoughby sitting up in the laboratory.

Colonel De Craye took the boy to his own room, where Crossjay lay on a sofa, comfortably covered over and snug in a swelling pillow; but he was restless; he wanted to speak, to bellow, to cry; and he bounced round to his left side, and bounced to his right, not knowing what to think, except that there was treason to his adored Miss Middleton.

'Why, my lad, you're not half a campaigner,' the colonel called out to him; attributing his uneasiness to the material discomfort of the sofa: and Crossjay had to swallow the taunt, bitter though it was. A dim sentiment of impropriety in unburdening his overcharged mind on the subject of Miss Middleton to Colonel De Craye restrained him from defending himself; and so he heaved and tossed about till daybreak. At an early hour, while his hospitable friend, who looked very handsome in profile half breast and head above the sheets, continued to slumber, Crossjay was on his legs and away.

'He says I'm not half a campaigner, and a couple of hours of bed are enough for me,' the boy thought proudly, and snuffed the springing air of the young sun on the fields. A glance back at Patterne Hall dismayed him, for he knew not how to act, and he was immoderately combustible, too full of knowledge for self-containment; much too zealously excited on behalf of his dear Miss Middleton to keep silent for many hours of the day.

CHAPTER 41

✕✕✕✕

The Rev. Dr Middleton, Clara, and Sir Willoughby

WHEN Master Crossjay tumbled down the stairs Laetitia was in Clara's room, speculating on the various mishaps which might have befallen that battered youngster; and Clara listened anxiously after Laetitia had run out, until she heard Sir Willoughby's voice; which in some way satisfied her that the boy was not in the house.

She waited, expecting Miss Dale to return; then undressed, went to bed, tried to sleep. She was tired of strife. Strange thoughts for a young head shot through her: as, that it is possible for the sense of duty to counteract distaste; and that one may live a life apart from one's admirations and dislikes: she owned the singular strength of Sir Willoughby in outwearying; she asked herself how much she had gained by struggling: – every effort seemed to expend her spirit's force, and rendered her less able to get the clear vision of her prospects, as though it had sunk her deeper: the contrary of her intention to make each further step confirm her liberty. Looking back, she marvelled at the things she had done. Looking round, how ineffectual they appeared! She had still the great scene of positive rebellion to go through with her father.

The anticipation of that was the cause of her extreme discouragement. He had not spoken to her since he became aware of her attempted flight: but the scene was coming; and besides the wish not to inflict it on him, as well as to escape it herself, the girl's peculiar unhappiness lay in her knowledge that they were alienated and stood opposed, owing to one among the more perplexing masculine weaknesses, which she could not hint at, dared barely think of, and would not name in her meditations. Diverting to other subjects, she allowed herself to exclaim, 'Wine, wine!' in renewed wonder of what there could be in wine to entrap venerable men and obscure their judgements. She was too young to consider that her being very much in the wrong gave all the importance to the cordial glass in a venerable gentleman's appreciation of his dues. Why should he fly from a priceless wine to gratify the caprices of a fantastical child guilty of seeking to commit a breach of faith? He harped on those words. Her fault was grave. No doubt the wine coloured it to him, as a drop or two will do in any cup: still her fault was grave.

She was too young for such considerations. She was ready to expatiate on the gravity of her fault, so long as the humiliation assisted to her disentanglement: her snared nature in the toils would not permit her to reflect on it further. She had never accurately perceived it: for the reason perhaps that Willoughby had not been moving in his appeals: but, admitting the charge of waywardness, she had come to terms with conscience, upon the understanding that she was to perceive it and regret it and do penance for it by-and-by: – by renouncing marriage altogether? How light a penance!

In the morning, she went to Laetitia's room, knocked, and had no answer.

She was informed at the breakfast-table of Miss Dale's departure. The ladies Eleanor and Isabel feared it to be a case of urgency at the cottage. No one had seen Vernon, and Clara requested Colonel De Craye to walk over to the cottage for news of Crossjay. He accepted the commission, simply to obey and be in her service: assuring her, however, that there was no need to be disturbed about the boy. He would have told her more, had not Dr Middleton led her out.

Sir Willoughby marked a lapse of ten minutes by his watch. His excellent aunts had ventured a comment on his appearance that frightened him lest he himself should be the person to betray his astounding discomfiture. He regarded his conduct as an act of madness, and Laetitia's as no less that of a madwoman – happily mad! Very happily mad indeed! Her rejection of his ridiculously generous proposal seemed to show an intervening hand in his favour, that sent her distraught at the right moment. He entirely trusted her to be discreet; but she was a miserable creature, who had lost the one last chance offered her by Providence, and furnished him with a signal instance of the mediocrity of woman's love.

Time was flying. In a little while Mrs Mountstuart would arrive. He could not fence her without a design in his head; he was destitute of an armoury if he had no scheme: he racked the brain only to succeed in rousing phantasmal vapours. Her infernal 'Twice!' would cease now to apply to Laetitia; it would be an echo of Lady Busshe. Nay, were all in the secret, *Thrice* jilted! might become the universal roar. And this, he reflected bitterly, of a man whom nothing but duty to his line had arrested from being the most mischievous of his class with women! Such is our reward for uprightness!

At the expiration of fifteen minutes by his watch, he struck a knuckle on the library door. Dr Middleton held it open to him.

'You are disengaged, sir?'

'The sermon is upon the paragraph which is toned to awaken the clerk,' replied the Rev. Doctor.

Clara was weeping.

Sir Willoughby drew near her solicitously.

Dr Middleton's mane of silvery hair was in a state bearing witness to the vehemence of the sermon, and Willoughby said: 'I hope, sir, you have not made too much of a trifle.'

'I believe, sir, that I have produced an effect, and that was the point in contemplation.'

'Clara! my dear Clara!' Willoughby touched her.

'She sincerely repents her conduct, I may inform you,' said Dr Middleton.

'My love!' Willoughby whispered. 'We have had a misunderstanding. I am at a loss to discover where I have been guilty, but I take the blame, all the blame. I implore you not to weep. Do me the favour to look at me. I would not have had you subjected to any interrogation whatever.'

'You are not to blame,' Clara said on a sob.

'Undoubtedly Willoughby is not to blame. It was not he who was bound on a runaway errand in flagrant breach of duty and decorum, nor he who inflicted a catarrh on a brother of my craft and cloth,' said her father.

'The clerk, sir, has pronounced Amen,' observed Willoughby.

'And no man is happier to hear an ejaculation that he has laboured for with so much sweat of his brow than the parson, I can assure you,' Dr Middleton mildly groaned. 'I have notions of the trouble of Abraham. A sermon of that description is an immolation of the parent, however it may go with the child.'

Willoughby soothed his Clara.

'I wish I had been here to share it. I might have saved you some tears. I may have been hasty in our little dissensions. I will acknowledge that I have been. My temper is often irascible.'

'And so is mine!' exclaimed Dr Middleton. 'And yet I am not aware that I made the worse husband for it. Nor do I rightly comprehend how a probably justly excitable temper can stand for a plea in mitigation of an attempt at an outrageous breach of faith.'

'The sermon is over, sir.'

'Reverberations!' the Rev. Doctor waved his arm placably. 'Take it for thunder heard remote.'

'Your hand, my love,' Willoughby murmured.

The hand was not put forth.

Dr Middleton remarked the fact. He walked to the window, and perceiving the pair in the same position when he faced about, he delivered a cough of admonition.

'It is cruel!' said Clara.

'That the owner of your hand should petition you for it?' inquired her father.

She sought refuge in a fit of tears.

Willoughby bent above her, mute.

'Is a scene that is hardly conceivable as a parent's obligation once in a lustrum, to be repeated within the half hour?' shouted her father.

She drew up her shoulders and shook; let them fall and dropped her head.

'My dearest! your hand!' fluted Willoughby.

The hand surrendered; it was much like the icicle of a sudden thaw.

Willoughby squeezed it to his ribs.

Dr Middleton marched up and down the room with his arms locked behind him. The silence between the young people seemed to denounce his presence.

He said, cordially: 'Old Hiems has but to withdraw for buds to burst. "Jam ver egelidos refert tepores." The equinoctial fury departs. 30 I will leave you for a term.'

Clara and Willoughby simultaneously raised their faces with opposing expressions.

'My girl!' Her father stood by her, laying gentle hand on her.

'Yes, papa, I will come out to you,' she replied to his apology for the rather heavy weight of his vocabulary, and smiled.

'No, sir, I beg you will remain,' said Willoughby.

'I keep you frost-bound.'

Clara did not deny it.

Willoughby emphatically did.

Then which of them was the more lover-like? Dr Middleton would for the moment have supposed his daughter.

Clara said: 'Shall you be on the lawn, papa?'

Willoughby interposed. 'Stay, sir; give us your blessing.'

'That you have.' Dr Middleton hastily motioned the paternal ceremony in outline.

'A few minutes, papa,' said Clara.

'Will she name the day?' came eagerly from Willoughby.

'I cannot!' Clara cried in extremity.

'The day is important on its arrival,' said her father; 'but apprehend the decision to be of the chief importance at present. First prime your piece of artillery, my friend.'

'The decision is taken, sir.'

'Then I will be out of the way of the firing. Hit what day you please.'

Clara checked herself on an impetuous exclamation. It was done that her father might not be detained.

Her astute self-compression sharpened Willoughby as much as it mortified and terrified him. He understood how he would stand in an instant were Dr Middleton absent. Her father was the tribunal she dreaded, and affairs must be settled and made irrevocable while he was with them. To sting the blood of the girl, he called her his darling, and half enwound her, shadowing forth a salute.

She strung her body to submit, seeing her father take it as a signal for his immediate retirement.

Willoughby was upon him before he reached the door.

'Hear us out, sir. Do not go. Stay, at my entreaty. I fear we have not come to a perfect reconcilement.'

'If that is your opinion,' said Clara, 'it is good reason for not distressing my father.'

'Dr Middleton, I love your daughter. I wooed her and won her; I had your consent to our union, and I was the happiest of mankind. In some way, since her coming to my house, I know not how – she will not tell me, or cannot – I offended. One may be innocent and offend. I have never pretended to impeccability, which is an admission that I may very naturally offend. My appeal to her is for an explanation or for pardon. I obtain neither. Had our positions been reversed, oh, not for any real offence – not for the worst that can be imagined – I think not – I hope not – could I have been tempted to propose the dissolution of our engagement. To love is to love, with me; an engagement a solemn bond. With all my errors I have that merit of utter fidelity – to the world laughable! I confess to a multitude of errors; I have that single merit, and am not the more estimable in your daughter's eyes on account of it, I fear. In plain words, I am, I do not doubt, one of the fools among men; of the description of human dog commonly known as faithful – whose destiny is that of a tribe. A man who cries out when he is hurt is absurd, and I am not asking for sympathy. Call me luckless. But I abhor a breach of faith. A broken pledge is hateful to me. I should regard it myself as a form of suicide. There are principles which civilized men must contend for. Our social fabric is based on them. As my word stands for me, I hold others to theirs. If that is not done, the world is more or less a carnival of counterfeits. In this instance – Ah! Clara, my love! and you have principles: you have inherited, you have been indoctrinated with them: have I, then, in my ignorance, offended past penitence, that you, of all women? . . . And without being able to name my sin! – Not only for what I lose by it, but in the abstract, judicially – apart from the sentiment of personal interest, grief, pain, and the possibility of my having to endure that which no temptation would induce me to commit: – judicially; – I fear, sir, I am a poor forensic orator . . .'

'The situation, sir, does not demand a Cicero: proceed,' said Dr Middleton, balked in his approving nods at the right true things delivered.

'Judicially, I am bold to say, though it may appear a presumption in one suffering acutely, I abhor a breach of faith.'

Dr Middleton brought his nod down low upon the phrase he had anticipated. 'And I,' said he, 'personally, and presently, abhor a breach of faith. Judicially? Judicially to examine, judicially to condemn: but does the judicial mind detest? I think, sir, we are not on the bench when we say that we abhor: we have unseated ourselves. Yet our abhorrence of bad conduct is very certain. You would signify, impersonally: which suffices for this exposition of your feelings.'

He peered at the gentleman under his brows, and resumed: 'She has had it, Willoughby; she has had it in plain Saxon and in uncompromising Olympian. There is, I conceive, no necessity to revert to it.'

'Pardon me, sir, but I am still unforgiven.'

'You must babble out the rest between you. I am about as much at home as a turkey with a pair of pigeons.'

'Leave us, father,' said Clara.

'First join our hands, and let me give you that title, sir.'

'Reach the good man your hand, my girl; forthright, from the shoulder, like a brave boxer. Humour a lover. He asks for his own.'

'It is more than I can do, father.'

'How, it is more than you can do? You are engaged to him, a plighted woman.'

'I do not wish to marry.'

'The apology is inadequate.'

'I am unworthy . . .'

'Chatter! chatter!'

'I beg him to release me.'

'Lunacy!'

'I have no love to give him.'

'Have you gone back to your cradle, Clara Middleton?'

'Oh, leave us, dear father!'

'My offence, Clara, my offence! What is it? Will you only name it?'

'Father, will you leave us? We can better speak together . . .'

'We have spoken, Clara, how often!' Willoughby resumed, 'with what result? – that you loved me, that you have ceased to love me: that your heart was mine, that you have withdrawn it, plucked it from me: that you request me to consent to a sacrifice involving my reputation, my life. And what have I done? I am the same, unchangeable. I loved and love you: my heart was yours, and is, and will be yours forever. You are my affianced – that is, my wife. What have I done?'

'It is indeed useless,' Clara sighed.

'Not useless, my girl, that you should inform this gentleman, your affianced husband, of the ground of the objection you conceived against him.'

'I cannot say.'

'Do you know?'

'If I could name it, I could hope to overcome it.'

Dr Middleton addressed Sir Willoughby.

'I verily believe we are directing the girl to dissect a caprice. Such things are seen large by these young people, but as they have neither organs, nor arteries, nor brains, nor membranes, dissection and inspection will be alike profitlessly practised. Your inquiry is natural for a lover, whose passion to enter into relations with the sex is ordinarily in proportion to his ignorance of the stuff composing them. At a particular age they traffic in whims: which are, I presume, the spiritual of hysterics; and are indubitably preferable, so long as they are not pushed too far. Examples are not wanting to prove that a flighty initiative on the part of the male is a handsome corrective. In that case, we should probably have had the roof off the house, and the girl now at your feet. Ha!'

'Despise me, father. I am punished for ever thinking myself the superior of any woman,' said Clara.

'Your hand out to him, my dear, since he is for a formal reconciliation; and I can't wonder.'

'Father! I have said I do not . . . I have said I cannot . . .'

'By the most merciful! what? what? the name for it, words for it!'

'Do not frown on me, father. I wish him happiness. I cannot marry him. I do not love him.'

'You will remember that you informed me aforetime that you did love him.'

'I was ignorant . . . I did not know myself. I wish him to be happy.'

'You deny him the happiness you wish him!'

'It would not be for his happiness were I to wed him.'

'Oh!' burst from Willoughby.

'You hear him. He rejects your prediction, Clara Middleton.'

She caught her clasped hands up to her throat. 'Wretched, wretched, both!'

'And you have not a word against him, miserable girl.'

'Miserable! I am.'

'It is the cry of an animal!'

'Yes, father.'

'You feel like one? Your behaviour is of that shape. You have not a word?'

'Against myself: not against him.'

'And I, when you speak so generously, am to yield you? give you up?' cried Willoughby. 'Ah! my love, my Clara, impose what you will on me; not that. It is too much for man. It is, I swear it, beyond my strength.'

'Pursue, continue the strain; 'tis in the right key,' said Dr Middleton, departing.

Willoughby wheeled and waylaid him with a bound.

'Plead for me, sir; you are all-powerful. Let her be mine, she shall be happy, or I will perish for it. I will call it on my head. – Impossible! I cannot lose her. Lose you, my love? It would be to strip myself of every blessing of body and soul. It would be to deny myself possession of grace, beauty, wit, all the incomparable charms of loveliness of mind and person in woman, and plant myself in a desert. You are my mate, the sum of everything I call mine. Clara, I should be less than man to submit to such a loss. Consent to it? But I love you! I worship you! How can I consent to lose you . . .?'

He saw the eyes of the desperately wily young woman slink sideways. Dr Middleton was pacing at ever shorter lengths closer by the door.

'You hate me?' Willoughby sunk his voice.

'If it should turn to hate!' she murmured.

'Hatred of your husband?'

'I could not promise,' she murmured, more softly in her wiliness.

'Hatred?' he cried aloud, and Dr Middleton stopped in his walk and flung up his head: 'Hatred of your husband? of the man you have vowed to love and honour? Oh, no! Once mine, it is not to be feared. I trust to my knowledge of your nature; I trust in your blood, I trust in your education. Had I nothing else to inspire confidence, I could trust in your eyes. And, Clara, take the confession: I would rather be hated than lose you. For if I lose you, you are in another world, out of this one holding me in its death-like cold; but if you hate me we are together, we are still together. Any alliance, any, in preference to separation!'

Clara listened with critical ear. His language and tone were new; and comprehending that they were in part addressed to her father, whose phrase: 'A breach of faith': he had so cunningly used, disdain of the actor prompted the extreme blunder of her saying – frigidly though she said it:

'You have not talked to me in this way before.'

'Finally,' remarked her father, summing up the situation to settle it from that little speech, 'he talks to you in this way now; and you are under my injunction to stretch your hand out to him for a symbol of union, or to state your objection to that course. He, by your admission, is at the terminus, and there, failing the why not, must you join him.'

Her head whirled. She had been severely flagellated and weakened previous to Willoughby's entrance. Language to express her peculiar repulsion eluded her. She formed the words, and perceived that they would not stand to bear a breath from her father. She perceived too that Willoughby was as ready with his agony of supplication as she with hers. If she had tears for a resource, he had gestures quite as eloquent; and a cry of her loathing of the union would fetch a countervailing torrent of the man's love. – What could she say? he is an Egoist? The epithet has no meaning in such a scene. *Invent!* shrieked the hundred-voiced instinct of dislike within her, and alone with her father, alone with Willoughby, she could have invented some equivalent, to do her heart justice for the injury it sustained in her being unable to name the true and immense objection: but the pair in presence paralyzed her. She dramatized them each springing forward by turns, with crushing rejoinders. The activity of her mind revelled in giving them a tongue, but would not do it for herself. Then ensued the inevitable consequence of an incapacity to speak at the heart's urgent dictate: heart and mind became divided. One throbbed hotly, the other hung aloof; and mentally, while the sick inarticulate heart kept clamouring, she answered it with all that she imagined for those two men to say. And she dropped poison on it to still its reproaches: bidding herself remember her fatal postponements in order to preserve the seeming of consistency before her father; calling it hypocrite; asking herself, what was she! who loved her! And thus beating down her heart, she completed the mischief with a piercing view of the foundation of her father's advocacy of Willoughby, and more lamentably asked herself what her value was, if she stood bereft of respect for her father.

Reason, on the other hand, was animated by her better nature to plead his case against her: she clung to her respect for him, and felt herself drowning with it: and she echoed Willoughby consciously, doubling her horror with the consciousness, in crying out on a world where the most sacred feelings are subject to such lapses. It doubled her horror, that she should echo the man: but it proved that she was no better than he: only some years younger. Those years would soon be outlived: after which, he and she would be of a pattern. She was unloved: she did no harm to any one by keeping her word to this man; she had pledged it, and it would be a breach of faith not to keep it. No one loved her. Behold the quality of her father's love! To give him happiness was now the principal aim for her, her own happiness being decently buried; and here he was happy: why should she be the cause of his going and losing the poor pleasure he so much enjoyed?

The idea of her devotedness flattered her feebleness. She betrayed signs of hesitation; and in hesitating, she looked away from a look at Willoughby, thinking (so much against her nature was it to resign herself to him) that it would not have been so difficult with an ill-favoured man. With one horribly ugly, it would have been a horrible exultation to cast off her youth and take the fiendish leap.

Unfortunately for Sir Willoughby, he had his reasons for pressing impatience; and seeing her deliberate, seeing her hasty look at his fine figure, his opinion of himself combined with his recollection of a particular maxim of the Great Book to assure him that her resistance was over: chiefly owing, as he supposed, to his physical perfections.

Frequently indeed, in the contest between gentlemen and ladies, have the maxims of the Book stimulated the assailant to victory. They are rosy with blood of victims. To hear them is to hear a horn that blows the mort: has blown it a thousand times. It is good to remember how often they have succeeded, when, for the benefit of some future Lady Vauban,[31] who may bestir her wits to gather maxims for the inspiriting of the Defence, the circumstance of a failure has to be recorded.

Willoughby could not wait for the melting of the snows. He saw full surely the dissolving process; and sincerely admiring and coveting her as he did, rashly this ill-fated gentleman attempted to precipitate it, and so doing arrested.

Whence might we draw a note upon yonder maxim, in words akin to these: Make certain ere a breath come from thee that thou be not a frost.

'Mine! She is mine!' he cried: 'mine once more! mine utterly! mine eternally!' and he followed up his devouring exclamations in person as she, less decidedly, retreated. She retreated as young ladies should ever do, two or three steps, and he would not notice that she had become an angry Dian, all arrows: her maidenliness in surrendering pleased him. Grasping one fair hand, he just allowed her to edge on the outer circle of his embrace, crying: 'Not a syllable of what I have gone through! You shall not have to explain it, my Clara. I will study you more diligently, to be guided by you, my darling. If I offend again, my wife will not find it hard to speak what my bride withheld – I do not ask why: perhaps not able to weigh the effect of her reticence: not at that time, when she was younger and less experienced, estimating the sacredness of a plighted engagement. It is past, we are one, my dear sir and father. You may leave us now.'

'I profoundly rejoice to hear that I may,' said Dr Middleton.

Clara writhed her captured hand.

'No, papa, stay. It is an error, an error. You must not leave me. Do not think me utterly, eternally, belonging to any one but you. No one shall say I am his but you.'

'Are you quicksands, Clara Middleton, that nothing can be built on you? Whither is a flighty head and a shifty will carrying the girl?'

'Clara and I, sir,' said Willoughby.

'And so you shall,' said the Doctor, turning about.

'Not yet, papa.' Clara sprang to him.

'Why, you, you, you, it was you who craved to be alone with Willoughby!' her father shouted; 'and here we are rounded to our starting-point, with the solitary difference that now you do not want to be alone with Willoughby. First I am bidden go; next I am pulled back; and judging by collar and coat-tail, I suspect you to be a young woman to wear an angel's temper threadbare before you determine upon which one of the tides driving him to and fro you intend to launch on yourself. Where is your mind?'

Clara smoothed her forehead.

'I wish to please you, papa.'

'I request you to please the gentleman who is your appointed husband.'

'I am anxious to perform my duty.'

'That should be a satisfactory basis for you, Willoughby; – as girls go!'

'Let me, sir, simply entreat to have her hand in mine before you.'

'Why not, Clara?'

'Why an empty ceremony, papa?'

'The implication is, that she is prepared for the important one, friend Willoughby.'

'Her hand, sir; the reassurance of her hand in mine under your eyes: – after all that I have suffered, I claim it, I think I claim it reasonably, to restore me to confidence.'

'Quite reasonably; which is not to say, necessarily; but, I will add, justifiably; and it may be, sagaciously, when dealing with the volatile.'

'And here,' said Willoughby, 'is my hand.'

Clara recoiled.

He stepped on. Her father frowned. She lifted both her hands from the shrinking elbows, darted a look of repulsion at her pursuer, and ran to her father, crying: 'Call it my mood! I am volatile, capricious, flighty, very foolish. But you see that I attach a real meaning to it, and feel it to be binding: I cannot think it an empty ceremony, if it is before you. Yes, only be a little considerate to your moody girl. She will be in a fitter state in a few hours. Spare me this moment; I must collect myself. I thought I was free; I thought he would not press me. If I give my hand hurriedly now, I shall, I know, immediately repent it. There is the picture of me! But, papa, I mean to try to be above that, and if I go and walk by myself, I shall grow calm to perceive where my duty lies . . .'

'In which direction shall you walk?' said Willoughby.

'Wisdom is not upon a particular road,' said Dr Middleton.

'I have a dread, sir, of that one which leads to the railway-station.'

'With some justice!' Dr Middleton sighed over his daughter.

Clara coloured to deep crimson: but she was beyond anger, and was rather gratified by an offence coming from Willoughby.

'I will promise not to leave his grounds, papa.'

'My child, you have threatened to be a breaker of promises.'

'Oh!' she wailed. 'But I will make it a vow to you.'

'Why not make it a vow to me this moment, for this gentleman's contentment, that he shall be your husband within a given period?'

'I will come to you voluntarily. I burn to be alone.'

'I shall lose her,' exclaimed Willoughby, in heartfelt earnest.

'How so?' said Dr Middleton. 'I have her, sir, if you will favour me by continuing in abeyance. – You will come within an hour voluntarily, Clara; and you will either at once yield your hand to him or you will furnish reasons, and they must be good ones, for withholding it.'

'Yes, papa.'

'You will?'

'I will.'

'Mind, I say *reasons.*'

'Reasons, papa. If I have none . . .'

'If you have none that are to my satisfaction, you implicitly and instantly, and cordially obey my command.'

'I will obey.'

'What more would you require?' Dr Middleton bowed to Sir Willoughby in triumph.

'Will she . . .'

'Sir! sir!'

'She is your daughter, sir. I am satisfied.'

'She has perchance wrestled with her engagement, as the aboriginals of a land newly discovered by a crew of adventurous colonists do battle with the garments imposed on them by our considerate civilization; – ultimately to rejoice with excessive dignity in the wearing of a battered cocked-hat and trowsers not extending to the shanks: but she did not break her engagement, sir; and we will anticipate that, moderating a young woman's native wildness, she may, after the manner of my comparison, take a similar pride in her fortune in good season.'

Willoughby had not leisure to sound the depth of Dr Middleton's compliment. He had seen Clara gliding out of the room during the delivery; and his fear returned on him that, not being won, she was lost.

'She has gone.' Her father noticed her absence. 'She does not waste time in her mission to procure that astonishing product of a shallow soil, her reasons; if such be the object of her search. But no: it signifies that she deems herself to have need of composure – nothing more. No one likes to be turned about; we like to turn ourselves about; and in the question of an act to be committed, we stipulate that it shall be our act – girls and others. After the lapse of an hour, it will appear to her as her act. Happily, Willoughby, we do not dine away from Patterne to-night.'

'No, sir.'

'It may be attributable to a sense of deserving, but I could plead guilty to a weakness for old Port to-day.'

'There shall be an extra bottle, sir.'

'All going favourably with you, as I have no cause to doubt,' said Dr Middleton, with the motion of wafting his host out of the library.

CHAPTER 42

※※※※

Shows the Divining Arts of a Perceptive Mind

STARTING from the Hall a few minutes before Dr Middleton and Sir Willoughby had entered the drawing-room overnight, Vernon parted company with Colonel De Craye at the park-gates, and betook himself to the cottage of the Dales, where nothing had been heard of his wanderer; and he received the same disappointing reply from Dr Corney, out of the bed-room window of the genial physician, whose astonishment at his covering so long a stretch of road at night for news of a boy like Crossjay – gifted with the lives of a cat – became violent and rapped Punch-like blows on the window-sill at Vernon's refusal to take shelter and rest. Vernon's excuse was that he had 'no one but that fellow to care for', and he strode off, naming a farm five miles distant. Dr Corney howled an invitation to early breakfast to him, in the event of his passing on his way back, and retired to bed to think of him. The result of a variety of conjectures caused him to set Vernon down as Miss Middleton's knight, and he felt a strong compassion for his poor friend. 'Though,' thought he, 'a hopeless attachment is as pretty an accompaniment to the tune of life as a gentleman might wish to have, for it's one of those big doses of discord which make all the minor ones fit in like an agreeable harmony, and so he shuffles along as pleasantly as the fortune-favoured, when they come to compute!'

Sir Willoughby was the fortune-favoured in the little doctor's mind; that high-stepping gentleman having wealth, and public consideration, and the most ravishing young lady in the world for a bride. Still, though he reckoned all these advantages enjoyed by Sir Willoughby at their full value, he could imagine the ultimate balance of good fortune to be in favour of Vernon. But to do so, he had to reduce the whole calculation to the extreme abstract, and feed his lean friend, as it were, on dew and roots; and the happy effect for Vernon lay in a distant future, on the borders of old age, where he was to be blessed with his lady's regretful preference, and rejoice in the fruits of good constitutional habits. The reviewing mind was Irish. Sir Willoughby was a character of man profoundly opposed to Dr Corney's nature; the latter's instincts bristled with antagonism – not to his race, for Vernon was of the same race, partly of the same blood, and Corney loved him: the type of person was the annoyance. And the circumstance of its prevailing successfulness in the country where he was placed, while it held him silent as if under a law, heaped stores of insurgency in the Celtic bosom. Corney contemplating Sir Willoughby, and a trotting kern governed by Strongbow, have a point of likeness between them; with the point of difference that Corney was enlightened to know of a friend better adapted for eminent station, and especially better adapted to please a lovely lady – could these high-bred Englishwomen but be taught to conceive another idea of manliness than the formal carved-in-wood idol of their national worship!

Dr Corney breakfasted very early, without seeing Vernon. He was off to a patient while the first lark of the morning carolled above, and the business of the day, not yet fallen upon men in the shape of cloud, was happily intermixed with nature's hues and pipings. Turning off the high-road up a green lane, an hour later, he beheld a youngster prying into a hedge head and arms, by the peculiar strenuous twist of whose hinder parts, indicative of a frame plunged on the pursuit in hand, he clearly distinguished young Crossjay. Out came eggs. The doctor pulled up.

'What bird?' he bellowed.

'Yellowhammer,' Crossjay yelled back.

'Now, sir, you'll drop a couple of those eggs in the nest.'

'Don't order me,' Crossjay was retorting. 'Oh, it's you, Doctor Corney. Good-morning. I said that, because I always do drop a couple back. I promised Mr Whitford I would, and Miss Middleton too.'

'Had breakfast?'

'Not yet.'

'Not hungry?'

'I should be if I thought about it.'

'Jump up.'

'I think I'd rather not, Doctor Corney.'

'And you'll just do what Doctor Corney tells you; and set your mind on rashers of curly fat bacon and sweetly smoking coffee, toast, hot cakes, marmalade, and damson-jam. Wide go the fellow's nostrils, and there's water at the dimples of his mouth! Up, my man.'

Crossjay jumped up beside the doctor, who remarked, as he touched his horse: 'I don't want a man this morning, though I'll enlist you in my service if I do. You're fond of Miss Middleton?'

Instead of answering, Crossjay heaved the sigh of love that bears a burden.

'And so am I,' pursued the doctor: 'You'll have to put up with a rival. It's worse than fond: I'm in love with her. How do you like that?'

'I don't mind how many *love* her,' said Crossjay.

'You're worthy of a gratuitous breakfast in the front parlour of the best hotel of the place they call Arcadia. And how about your bed last night?'

'Pretty middling.'

'Hard, was it, where the bones haven't cushion?'

'I don't care for bed. A couple of hours, and that's enough for me.'

'But you're fond of Miss Middleton anyhow, and that's a virtue.'

To his great surprise, Dr Corney beheld two big round tears force their way out of this tough youngster's eyes, and all the while the boy's face was proud.

Crossjay said, when he could trust himself to disjoin his lips: 'I want to see Mr Whitford.'

'Have you got news for him?'

'I've something to ask him. It's about what I ought to do.'

'Then, my boy, you have the right name addressed in the wrong direction: for I found you turning your shoulders on Mr Whitford. And he has been out of his bed hunting you all the unholy night you've made it for him. That's melancholy. What do you say to asking my advice?'

Crossjay sighed. 'I can't speak to anybody but Mr Whitford.'

'And you're hot to speak to him?'

'I want to.'

'And I found you running away from him. You're a curiosity, Mr Crossjay Patterne.'

'Ah! so'd anybody be who knew as much as I do,' said Crossjay, with a sober sadness that caused the doctor to treat him seriously.

'The fact is,' he said, 'Mr Whitford is beating the country for you. My best plan will be to drive you to the Hall.'

'I'd rather not go to the Hall,' Crossjay spoke resolutely.

'You won't see Miss Middleton anywhere but at the Hall.'

'I don't want to see Miss Middleton, if I can't be a bit of use to her.'

'No danger threatening the lady, is there?'

Crossjay treated the question as if it had not been put.

'Now, tell me,' said Dr Corney, 'would there be a chance for me, supposing Miss Middleton were disengaged?'

The answer was easy. 'I'm sure she wouldn't.'

'And why, sir, are you so cock sure?'

There was no saying; but the doctor pressed for it, and at last Crossjay gave his opinion that she would take Mr Whitford.

The doctor asked why; and Crossjay said it was because Mr Whitford was the best man in the world. To which, with a lusty 'Amen to that,' Dr Corney remarked: 'I should have fancied Colonel De Craye would have had the first chance: he's more of a lady's man.'

Crossjay surprised him again by petulantly saying: 'Don't.'

The boy added: 'I don't want to talk, except about birds and things. What a jolly morning it is! I saw the sun rise. No rain to-day. You're right about hungry, Doctor Corney!'

The kindly little man swung his whip. Crossjay informed him of his disgrace at the Hall, and of every incident connected with it, from the tramp to the baronet, save Miss Middleton's adventure and the night scene in the drawing-room. A strong smell of something left out struck Dr Corney, and he said: 'You'll not let Miss Middleton know of my affection. After all, it's only a little bit of love. But, as Patrick said to Kathleen, when she owned to such a little bit, "that's the best bit of all!" and he was as right as I am about hungry.'

Crossjay scorned to talk of loving, he declared. 'I never tell Miss Middleton what I feel. Why, there's Miss Dale's cottage!'

'It's nearer to your empty inside than my mansion,' said the doctor, 'and we'll stop just to inquire whether a bed's to be had for you there to-night, and if not, I'll have you with me, and bottle you, and exhibit you, for you're a rare specimen. Breakfast you may count on from Mr Dale. I spy a gentleman.'

'It's Colonel De Craye.'

'Come after news of you.'

'I wonder!'

'Miss Middleton sends him; of course she does.'

Crossjay turned his full face to the doctor. 'I haven't seen her for such a long time! But he saw me last night, and he might have told her that, if she's anxious. – Good-morning, colonel. I've had a good walk, and a capital drive, and I'm as hungry as the boat's crew of Captain Bligh.'

He jumped down.

The colonel and the doctor saluted, smiling.

'I've rung the bell,' said De Craye.

A maid came to the gate, and upon her steps appeared Miss Dale, who flung herself at Crossjay, mingling kisses and reproaches. She scarcely raised her face to the colonel more than to reply to his greeting, and excuse the hungry boy for hurrying indoors to breakfast.

'I'll wait,' said De Craye. He had seen that she was paler than usual. So had Dr Corney; and the doctor called to her concerning her father's health. She reported that he had not yet risen, and took Crossjay to herself.

'That's well,' said the doctor, 'if the invalid sleeps long. The lady is not looking so well, though. But ladies vary; they show the mind on the countenance, for want of the punching we meet with to conceal it; they're like military flags for a funeral or a gala; one day furled, and next day streaming. Men are ships' figure-heads, about the same for a storm or a calm, and not too handsome, thanks to the ocean. It's an age since we encountered last, colonel: on board the Dublin boat, I recollect, and a night it was.'

'I recollect that you set me on my legs, doctor.'

'Ah! and you'll please to notify that Corney's no quack at sea, by favour of the monks of the Chartreuse, whose elixir has power to still the waves. And we hear that miracles are done with!'

'Roll a physician and a monk together, doctor!'

'True: it'll be a miracle if they combine. Though the cure of the soul is often the entire and total cure of the body: and it's maliciously said that the body given over to our treatment is a signal to set the soul flying. By the way, colonel, that boy has a trifle on his mind.'

'I suppose he has been worrying a farmer or a game-keeper.'

'Try him. You'll find him tight. He's got Miss Middleton on the brain. There's a bit of a secret; and he's not so cheerful about it.'

'We'll see,' said the colonel.

Dr Corney nodded. 'I have to visit my patient here presently. I'm too early for him: so I'll make a call or two on the lame birds that are up,' he remarked, and drove away.

De Craye strolled through the garden. He was a gentleman of those actively perceptive wits which, if ever they reflect, do so by hops and jumps: upon some dancing mirror within, we may fancy. He penetrated a plot in a flash; and in a flash he formed one; but in both cases, it was after long hovering and not over-eager deliberation, by the patient exercise of his quick perceptives. The fact that Crossjay was considered to have Miss Middleton on the brain, threw a series of images of everything relating to Crossjay for the last forty hours into relief before him: and as he did not in the slightest degree speculate on any one of them, but merely shifted and surveyed them, the falcon that he was in spirit as well as in his handsome face leisurely allowed his instinct to direct him where to strike. A reflective disposition has this danger in action, that it commonly precipitates conjecture for the purpose of working upon probabilities with the methods and in the tracks to which it is accustomed: and to conjecture rashly is to play into the puzzles of the maze. He who can watch circling above it awhile, quietly viewing, and collecting in his eye, gathers matter that makes the secret thing discourse to the brain by weight and balance; he will get either the right clue or none; more frequently none; but he will escape the entanglement of his own cleverness, he will always be nearer to the enigma than the guesser or the calculator, and he will retain a breadth of vision forfeited by them. He must, however, to have his chance of success, be acutely besides calmly perceptive, a reader of features, audacious at the proper moment.

De Craye wished to look at Miss Dale. She had returned home very suddenly, not, as it appeared, owing to her father's illness; and he remembered a redness of her eyelids when he passed her on the corridor one night. She sent Crossjay out to him as soon as the boy was well filled. He sent Crossjay back with a request. She did not yield to it immediately. She stepped to the front door reluctantly, and seemed disconcerted. De Craye begged for a message to Miss Middleton. There was none to give. He persisted. But there was really none at present, she said.

'You won't entrust me with the smallest word?' said he, and set her visibly thinking whether she could dispatch a word. She could not; she had no heart for messages.

'I shall see her in a day or two, Colonel De Craye.'

'She will miss you severely.'

'We shall soon meet.'

'And poor Willoughby!'

Laetitia coloured and stood silent.

A butterfly of some rarity allured Crossjay.

'I fear he has been doing mischief,' she said. 'I cannot get him to look at me.'

'His appetite is good?'

'Very good indeed.'

De Craye nodded. A boy with a noble appetite is never a hopeless lock.

The colonel and Crossjay lounged over the garden.

'And now,' said the colonel, 'we'll see if we can't arrange a meeting between you and Miss Middleton. You're a lucky fellow, for she's always thinking of you.'

'I know I'm always thinking of her,' said Crossjay.

'If ever you're in a scrape, she's the person you must go to.'

'Yes, if I know where she is!'

'Why, generally she'll be at the Hall.'

There was no reply: Crossjay's dreadful secret jumped to his throat. He certainly was a weaker lock for being full of breakfast.

'I want to see Mr Whitford so much,' he said.

'Something to tell him?'

'I don't know what to do: I don't understand it!' The secret wriggled to his mouth. He swallowed it down. 'Yes, I want to talk to Mr Whitford.'

'He's another of Miss Middleton's friends.'

'I know he is. He's true steel.'

'We're all her friends, Crossjay. I flatter myself I'm a Toledo when I'm wanted. How long had you been in the house last night before you ran into me?'

'I don't know, sir; I fell asleep for some time, and then I woke . . .'

'Where did you find yourself?'

'I was in the drawing-room.'

'Come, Crossjay, you're not a fellow to be scared by ghosts? You looked it when you made a dash at my midriff.'

'I don't believe there are such things. Do you, colonel? You can't!'

'There's no saying. We'll hope not; for it wouldn't be fair fighting. A man with a ghost to back him'd beat any ten. We couldn't box him or play cards, or stand a chance with him as a rival in love. Did you, now, catch a sight of a ghost?'

'They weren't ghosts!' Crossjay said what he was sure of, and his voice pronounced his conviction.

'I doubt whether Miss Middleton is particularly happy,'

remarked the colonel. 'Why? Why, you upset her, you know, now and then.'

The boy swelled. 'I'd do . . . I'd go . . . I wouldn't have her unhappy . . . It's that! that's it! And I don't know what I ought to do. I wish I could see Mr Whitford.'

'You get into such headlong scrapes, my lad.'

'I wasn't in any scrape yesterday.'

'So you made yourself up a comfortable bed in the drawing-room? Luckily Sir Willoughby didn't see you.'

'He didn't, though!'

'A close shave, was it?'

'I was under a covering of something silk.'

'He woke you?'

'I suppose he did. I heard him.'

'Talking?'

'He was talking.'

'What! talking to himself?'

'No.'

The secret threatened Crossjay to be out or suffocate him. De Craye gave him a respite.

'You like Sir Willoughby, don't you?'

Crossjay produced a still-born affirmative.

'He's kind to you,' said the colonel; 'he'll set you up and look after your interests.'

'Yes, I like him,' said Crossjay, with his customary rapidity in touching the subject; 'I like him; he's kind and all that, and tips and plays with you, and all that; but I never can make out why he wouldn't see my father when my father came here to see him ten miles, and had to walk back ten miles in the rain, to go by rail a long way, down home, as far as Devonport, because Sir Willoughby wouldn't see him, though he was at home, my father saw. We all thought it so odd: and my father wouldn't let us talk much about it. My father's a very brave man.'

'Captain Patterne is as brave a man as ever lived,' said De Craye.

'I'm positive you'd like him, colonel.'

'I know of his deeds, and I admire him, and that's a good step to liking.'

He warmed the boy's thoughts of his father.

'Because, what they say at home is, a little bread and cheese, and a glass of ale, and a rest, to a poor man – lots of great houses will give you that, and we wouldn't have asked for more than that. My sisters say they think Sir Willoughby must be selfish. He's awfully proud; and perhaps it was because my father wasn't dressed well enough. But what can we do? We're very poor at home, and lots of us, and all hungry. My father says he isn't paid very well for his services to the Government. He's only a marine.'

'He's a hero!' said De Craye.

'He came home very tired, with a cold, and had a doctor. But Sir Willoughby did send him money, and mother wished to send it back, and my father said she was not like a woman – with our big family. He said he thought Sir Willoughby an extraordinary man.'

'Not at all; very common; indigenous,' said De Craye. 'The art of cutting is one of the branches of a polite education in this country, and you'll have to learn it, if you expect to be looked on as a gentleman and a Patterne, my boy. I begin to see how it is Miss Middleton takes to you so. Follow her directions. But I hope you did not listen to a private conversation. Miss Middleton would not approve of that.'

'Colonel De Craye, how could I help myself? I heard a lot before I knew what it was. There was poetry!'

'Still, Crossjay, if it was important – was it?'

The boy swelled again, and the colonel asked him, 'Does Miss Dale know of your having played listener?'

'She!' said Crossjay. 'Oh, I couldn't tell *her*.'

He breathed thick; then came a threat of tears. 'She wouldn't do anything to hurt Miss Middleton. I'm sure of that. It wasn't her fault. She – There goes Mr Whitford!' Crossjay bounded away.

The colonel had no inclination to wait for his return. He walked fast up the road, not perspicuously conscious that his motive was to be well in advance of Vernon Whitford: to whom, after all, the knowledge imparted by Crossjay would be of small advantage. That fellow would probably trot off to Willoughby to row him for breaking his word to Miss Middleton! There are men, thought De Craye, who see nothing, feel nothing.

He crossed a stile into the wood above the lake, where, as he was in the humour to think himself signally lucky, espying her, he took it as a matter of course that the lady who taught his heart to leap should be posted by the Fates. And he wondered little at her power, for rarely had the world seen such union of princess and sylph as in that lady's figure. She stood holding by a beech-branch, gazing down on the water.

She had not heard him. When she looked she flushed at the spectacle of one of her thousand thoughts, but she was not startled; the colour overflowed a grave face.

'And 'tis not quite the first time that Willoughby has played this trick!' De Craye said to her, keenly smiling with a parted mouth.

Clara moved her lips to recall remarks introductory to so abrupt and strange a plunge.

He smiled in that peculiar manner of an illuminated comic perception: for the moment he was all falcon; and he surprised himself more than Clara, who was not in the mood to take surprises. It was the sight of her which had animated him to strike his game; he was down on it.

Another instinct at work (they spring up in twenties oftener than in twos when the heart is the hunter) prompted him to directness and quickness, to carry her on the flood of the discovery.

She regained something of her mental self-possession as soon as she was on a level with a meaning she had not yet inspected; but she had to submit to his lead, distinctly perceiving where its drift divided to the forked currents of what might be in his mind and what was in hers.

'Miss Middleton, I bear a bit of a likeness to the messenger to the glorious despot – my head is off if I speak not true! Everything I have is on the die. Did I guess wrong your wish? – I read it in the dark, by the heart. But here's a certainty: Willoughby sets you free.'

'You have come from him?' she could imagine nothing else, and she was unable to preserve a disguise; she trembled.

'From Miss Dale.'

'Ah!' Clara drooped. 'She told me that once.'

''Tis the fact that tells it now.'

'You have not seen him since you left the house?'

'Darkly: clear enough: not unlike the hand of destiny – through a veil. He offered himself to Miss Dale last night, about between the witching hours of twelve and one.'

'Miss Dale . . .'

'Would she other? Could she? The poor lady has languished beyond a decade. She's love in the feminine person.'

'Are you speaking seriously, Colonel De Craye?'

'Would I dare to trifle with you, Miss Middleton?'

'I have reason to know it cannot be.'

'If I have a head, it is a fresh and blooming truth. And more – I stake my vanity on it!'

'Let me go to her.' She stepped.

'Consider,' said he.

'Miss Dale and I are excellent friends. It would not seem indelicate to her. She has a kind of regard for me, through Crossjay. – Oh, can it be? There must be some delusion. You have seen – you wish to be of service to me; you may too easily be deceived. Last night? – he last night . . .? And this morning!'

''Tis not the first time our friend has played the trick, Miss Middleton.'

'But this is incredible, that last night . . . and this morning, in my father's presence, he presses! . . . You have seen Miss

Dale? Everything is possible of him: they were together, I know. Colonel De Craye, I have not the slightest chance of concealment with you. I think I felt that when I first saw you. Will you let me hear why you are so certain?'

'Miss Middleton, when I first had the honour of looking on you, it was in a posture that necessitated my looking up, and morally so it has been since. I conceived that Willoughby had won the greatest prize of earth. And next I was led to the conclusion that he had won it to lose it. Whether he much cares, is the mystery I haven't leisure to fathom. Himself is the principal consideration with himself, and ever was.'

'You discovered it!' said Clara.

'He uncovered it,' said De Craye. 'The miracle was, that the world wouldn't see. But the world is a piggy-wiggy world for the wealthy fellow who fills a trough for it, and that he has always very sagaciously done. Only women besides myself have detected him. I have never exposed him; I have been an observer pure and simple; and because I apprehended another catastrophe – making something like the fourth, to my knowledge, one being public . . .'

'You knew Miss Durham?'

'And Harry Oxford too. And they're a pair as happy as blackbirds in a cherry-tree, in a summer sunrise, with the owner of the garden asleep. Because of that apprehension of mine, I refused the office of best man till Willoughby had sent me a third letter. He insisted on my coming. I came, saw, and was conquered. I trust with all my soul I did not betray myself. I owed that duty to my position of concealing it. As for entirely hiding that I had used my eyes, I can't say: they must answer for it.'

The colonel was using his eyes with an increasing suavity that threatened more than sweetness.

'I believe you have been sincerely kind,' said Clara. 'We will descend to the path round the lake.'

She did not refuse her hand on the descent, and he let it escape the moment the service was done. As he was performing the admirable character of the man of honour, he had to attend to the observance of details; and sure of her though he was beginning to feel, there was a touch of the unknown in Clara Middleton which made him fear to stamp assurance; despite a barely resistible impulse, coming of his emotions and approved by his maxims. He looked at the hand, now a free lady's hand. Willoughby settled, his chance was great. Who else was in the way? No one. He counselled himself to wait for her; she might have ideas of delicacy. Her face was troubled, speculative; the brows clouded, the lips compressed.

'You have not heard this from Miss Dale?' she said.

'Last night they were together: this morning she fled. I saw her this morning distressed. She is unwilling to send you a message: she talks vaguely of meeting you some days hence. And it is not the first time he has gone to her for his consolation.'

'That is not a proposal,' Clara reflected. 'He is too prudent. He did not propose to her at the time you mention. Have you not been hasty, Colonel De Craye?'

Shadows crossed her forehead. She glanced in the direction of the house and stopped her walk.

'Last night, Miss Middleton, there was a listener.'

'Who?'

'Crossjay was under that pretty silk coverlet worked by the Miss Patternes. He came home late, found his door locked, and dashed downstairs into the drawing-room, where he snuggled up and dropped asleep. The two speakers woke him; they frightened the poor dear lad in his love for you, and after they had gone, he wanted to run out of the house, and I met him just after I had come back from my search, bursting, and took him to my room, and laid him on the sofa, and abused him for not lying quiet. He was restless as a fish on a bank. When I woke in the morning he was off. Doctor Corney came across him somewhere on the road and drove him to the cottage. I was ringing the bell. Corney told me the boy had you on his brain, and was miserable, so Crossjay and I had a talk.'

'Crossjay did not repeat to you the conversation he had heard?' said Clara.

'No.'

She smiled rejoicingly, proud of the boy, as she walked on. 'But you'll pardon me, Miss Middleton – and I'm for him as much as you are – if I was guilty of a little angling.'

'My sympathies are with the fish.'

'The poor fellow had a secret that hurt him. It rose to the surface crying to be hooked, and I spared him twice or thrice, because he had a sort of holy sentiment I respected, that none but Mr Whitford ought to be his father confessor.'

'Crossjay!' she cried, hugging her love of the boy.

'The secret was one not to be communicated to Miss Dale of all people.'

'He said that?'

'As good as the very words. She informed me, too, that she couldn't induce him to face her straight.'

'Oh, that looks like it. And Crossjay was unhappy? Very unhappy?'

'He was just where tears are on the brim, and would have been over, if he were not such a manly youngster.'

'It looks . . .' She reverted in thought to Willoughby, and doubted, and blindly stretched hands to her recollection of the strange old monster she had discovered in him. Such a man could do anything.

That conclusion fortified her to pursue her walk to the house and give battle for freedom. Willoughby appeared to her scarce human, unreadable, save by the key that she could supply. She determined to put faith in Colonel De Craye's marvellous divination of circumstances in the dark. Marvels are solid weapons when we are attacked by real prodigies of nature. Her countenance cleared. She conversed with De Craye of the polite and the political world, throwing off her personal burden completely, and charming him.

At the edge of the garden, on the bridge that crossed the ha-ha from the park, he had a second impulse, almost a warning within, to seize his heavenly opportunity to ask for thanks and move her tender lowered eyelids to hint at his reward. He repressed it, doubtful of the wisdom.

Something like 'heaven forgive me' was in Clara's mind, though she would have declared herself innocent before the scrutator.

CHAPTER 43

✖✖✖✖

In Which Sir Willoughby Is Led to Think That the Elements Have Conspired Against Him

CLARA had not taken many steps in the garden before she learned how great was her debt of gratitude to Colonel De Craye. Willoughby and her father were awaiting her. De Craye, with his ready comprehension of circumstances, turned aside unseen among the shrubs. She advanced slowly.

'The vapours, we may trust, have dispersed?' her father hailed her.

'One word, and these discussions are over, we dislike them equally,' said Willoughby.

'No scenes,' Dr Middleton added. 'Speak your decision, my girl, pro forma, seeing that he who has the right demands it, and pray release me.'

Clara looked at Willoughby.

'I have decided to go to Miss Dale for her advice.'

There was no appearance in him of a man that has been shot.

'To Miss Dale? – for advice?'

Dr Middleton invoked the Furies. 'What is the signification of this new freak?'

'Miss Dale must be consulted, papa.'

'Consulted with reference to the disposal of your hand in marriage?'

'She must be.'

'Miss Dale, do you say?'

'I do, Papa.'

Dr Middleton regained his natural elevation from the bend of body habitual with men of an established sanity, paedagogues and others, who are called on at odd intervals to inspect the magnitude of the infinitesimally absurd in human nature: small, that is, under the light of reason, immense in the realms of madness.

His daughter profoundly confused him. He swelled out his chest, remarking to Willoughby: 'I do not wonder at your scared expression of countenance, my friend. To discover yourself engaged to a girl mad as Cassandra, without a boast of the distinction of her being sun-struck, can be no specially comfortable an enlightenment. I am opposed to delays, and I will not have a breach of faith committed by daughter of mine.'

'Do not repeat those words,' Clara said to Willoughby.

He started. She had evidently come armed. But how, within so short a space? What could have instructed her? And in his bewilderment he gazed hurriedly above, gulped air, and cried: 'Scared, sir? I am not aware that my countenance can show a scare. I am not accustomed to sue for long: I am unable to sustain the part of humble supplicant. She puts me out of harmony with creation – We are plighted, Clara. It is pure waste of time to speak of soliciting advice on the subject.'

'Would it be a breach of faith for me to break my engagement?' she said.

'You ask?'

'It is a breach of sanity to propound the interrogation,' said her father.

She looked at Willoughby. 'Now?'

He shrugged haughtily.

'Since last night?' she said.

'Last night?'

'Am I not released?'

'Not by me.'

'By your act.'

'My dear Clara!'

'Have you not virtually disengaged me?'

'I who claim you as mine?'

'Can you?'

'I do and must.'

'After last night?'

'Tricks! shufflings! Jabber of a barbarian woman upon the evolutions of a serpent!' exclaimed Dr Middleton. 'You were to capitulate, or to furnish reasons for your refusal. You have none. Give him your hand, girl, according to the compact. I praised you to him for returning within the allotted term, and now forbear to disgrace yourself and me.'

'Is he perfectly free to offer his? Ask him, papa.'

'Perform your duty. Do let us have peace!'

'Perfectly free! as on the day when I offered it first,' Willoughby frankly waved his honourable hand.

His face was blanched: enemies in the air seemed to have whispered things to her: he doubted the fidelity of the Powers above.

'Since last night?' said she.

'Oh, if you insist, I reply, since last night.'

'You know what I mean, Sir Willoughby.'

'Oh, certainly.'

'You speak the truth?'

'"*Sir* Willoughby!"' her father ejaculated in wrath. 'But will you explain what you mean, epitome that you are of all the contradictions and mutabilities ascribed to women from the beginning! "Certainly", he says, and knows no more than I. She begs grace for an hour, and returns with a fresh store of evasions, to insult the man she has injured. It is my humiliation to confess that our share in this contract is rescued from public ignominy by his generosity. Nor can I congratulate him on his fortune, should he condescend to bear with you to the utmost; for instead of the young woman I supposed myself to be bestowing on him, I see a fantastical planguncula [32] enlivened by the wanton tempers of a nursery chit. If one may conceive a meaning in her, in miserable apology for such behaviour, some spirit of jealousy informs the girl.'

'I can only remark that there is no foundation for it,' said Willoughby. 'I am willing to satisfy you, Clara. Name the person who discomposes you. I can scarcely imagine one to exist: but who can tell?'

She could name no person. The detestable imputation of jealousy would be confirmed if she mentioned a name: and indeed Laetitia was not to be named.

He pursued his advantage: 'Jealousy is one of the fits I am a stranger to, – I fancy, sir, that gentlemen have dismissed it. I speak for myself. – But I can make allowances. In some cases, it is considered a compliment; and often a word will soothe it. The whole affair is so senseless! However, I will enter the witness-box, or stand at the prisoner's bar! Anything to quiet a distempered mind.'

'Of you, sir,' said Dr Middleton, 'might a parent be justly proud.'

'It is not jealousy; I could not be jealous!' Clara cried, stung by the very passion; and she ran through her brain for a suggestion to win a sign of meltingness if not esteem from her father. She was not an iron maiden, but one among the nervous natures which live largely in the moment, though she was then sacrificing it to her nature's deep dislike. 'You may be proud of me again, papa.'

She could hardly have uttered anything more impolitic.

'Optume; but deliver yourself ad rem,' he rejoined, alarmingly pacified. 'Firmavit fidem. [33] Do you likewise, and double on us no more like puss in the field.'

'I wish to see Miss Dale,' she said.

Up flew the Rev. Doctor's arms in wrathful despair resembling an imprecation.

'She is at the cottage. You could have seen her,' said Willoughby.

Evidently she had not.

'Is it untrue that last night, between twelve o'clock and one, in the drawing-room, you proposed marriage to Miss Dale?'

He became convinced that she must have stolen down-stairs during his colloquy with Laetitia, and listened at the door.

'On behalf of old Vernon?' he said, lightly laughing. 'The idea is not novel, as you know. They are suited, if they could see it. – Laetitia Dale and my cousin Vernon Whitford, sir.'

'Fairly schemed, my friend, and I will say for you, you have the patience, Willoughby, of a husband!'

Willoughby bowed to the encomium, and allowed some fatigue to be visible. He half yawned: 'I claim no happier title, sir,' and made light of the weariful discussion.

Clara was shaken: she feared that Crossjay had heard incorrectly, or that Colonel De Craye had guessed erroneously. It was too likely that Willoughby should have proposed Vernon to Laetitia.

There was nothing to reassure her save the vision of the panic amazement of his face at her persistency in speaking of Miss Dale. She could have declared on oath that she was right, while admitting all the suppositions to be against her. And unhappily all the Delicacies (a doughty battalion for the defence of ladies until they enter into difficulties and are shorn of them at a blow, bare as dairy-maids), all the body-guard of a young gentlewoman, the drawing-room sylphides, which bear her train, which wreathe her hair, which modulate her voice and tone her complexion, which are arrows and shield to awe the creature man, forbade her utterance of what she felt, on pain of instant fulfilment of their oft-repeated threat of late to leave her to the last remnant of a protecting sprite. She could not, as in a dear melodrama, from the aim of a pointed finger denounce him, on the testimony of her instincts, false of speech, false in deed. She could not even declare that she doubted his truthfulness. The refuge of a sullen fit, the refuge of tears, the pretext of a mood, were denied her now by the rigour of those laws of decency which are a garment to ladies of pure breeding.

'One more respite, papa,' she implored him, bitterly conscious of the closer tangle her petition involved, and, if it must be betrayed of her, perceiving in an illumination how the knot might become so woefully Gordian that haply in a cloud of wild events the intervention of a gallant gentleman out of heaven, albeit in the likeness of one of earth, would have to cut it: her cry within, as she succumbed to weakness, being fervider, 'Anything but marry this one!' She was faint with strife and dejected, a condition in the young when their imaginative energies hold revel uncontrolled and are projectively desperate.

'No respite!' said Willoughby, genially.

'And I say, no respite!' observed her father. 'You have assumed a position that has not been granted you, Clara Middleton.'

'I cannot bear to offend you, father.'

'Him! Your duty is not to offend him. Address your excuses to him. I refuse to be dragged over the same ground, to reiterate the same command perpetually.'

'If authority is deputed to me, I claim you,' said Willoughby.

'You have not broken faith with me?'

'Assuredly not, or would it be possible for me to press my claim?'

'And join the right hand to the right,' said Dr Middleton; 'no, it would not be possible. What insane root she has been nibbling, I know not, but she must consign herself to the guidance of those whom the gods have not abandoned, until her intellect is liberated. She was once . . . there: I look not back – if she it was, and no simulacrum of a reasonable daughter. I welcome the appearance of my friend Mr Whitford. He is my sea-bath and supper on the beach of Troy, after the day's battle and dust.'

Vernon walked straight up to them: an act unusual with with him, for he was shy of committing an intrusion.

Clara guessed by that, and more by the dancing frown of speculative humour he turned on Willoughby, that he had come charged in support of her. His forehead was curiously lively, as of one who has got a surprise well under, to feed on its amusing contents.

'Have you seen Crossjay, Mr Whitford?' she said.

'I've pounced on Crossjay; his bones are sound.'

'Where did he sleep?'

'On a sofa, it seems.'

She smiled, with good hope – Vernon had the story.

Willoughby thought it just to himself that he should defend his measure of severity.

'The boy lied; he played a double game.'

'For which he should have been reasoned with at the Grecian portico of a boy,' said the Rev. Doctor.

'My system is different, sir. I could not inflict what I would not endure myself.'

'So is Greek excluded from the later generations; and you leave a field, the most fertile in the moralities in youth, unplowed and unsown. Ah! well. This growing too fine is our way of relapsing upon barbarism. Beware of over-sensitiveness, where nature has plainly indicated her alternative gateway of knowledge. And now, I presume, I am at liberty.'

'Vernon will excuse us for a minute or two.'

'I hold by Mr Whitford now I have him.'

'I'll join you in the laboratory, Vernon,' Willoughby nodded bluntly.

'We will leave them, Mr Whitford. They are at the time-honoured dissension upon a particular day, that, for the sake of dignity, blushes to be named.'

'What day?' said Vernon, like a rustic.

'*The* day, these people call it.'

Vernon sent one of his vivid eyeshots from one to the other. His eyes fixed on Willoughby's with a quivering glow, beyond amazement, as if his humour stood at furnace-heat, and absorbed all that came.

Willoughby motioned to him to go.

'Have you seen Miss Dale, Mr Whitford?' said Clara.

He answered, 'No. Something has shocked her.'

'Is it her feeling for Crossjay?'

'Ah!' Vernon said to Willoughby, 'your pocketing of the key of Crossjay's bedroom door was a master-stroke!'

The celestial irony suffused her, and she bathed and swam in it, on hearing its dupe reply: 'My methods of discipline are short. I was not aware that she had been to his door.'

'But I may hope that Miss Dale will see me,' said Clara. 'We are in sympathy about the boy.'

'Mr Dale might be seen. He seems to be of a divided mind with his daughter,' Vernon rejoined. 'She has locked herself up in her room.'

'He is not the only father in that unwholesome predicament,' said Dr Middleton.

'He talks of coming to you, Willoughby.'

'Why to me?' Willoughby chastened his irritation: 'He will be welcome, of course. It would be better that the boy should come.'

'If there is a chance of your forgiving him,' said Clara.

'Let the Dales know I am prepared to listen to the boy, Vernon. There can be no necessity for Mr Dale to drag himself here.'

'How are Mr Dale and his daughter of a divided mind, Mr Whitford?' said Clara.

Vernon simulated an uneasiness. With a vacant gaze that enlarged around Willoughby and was more discomforting than intentness, he replied: 'Perhaps she is unwilling to give him her entire confidence, Miss Middleton.'

'In which respect, then, our situations present their solitary point of unlikeness in resemblance, for I have it in excess,' observed Dr Middleton.

Clara dropped her eyelids for the wave to pass over. 'It

struck me that Miss Dale was a person of the extremest candour.'

'Why should we be prying into the domestic affairs of the Dales?' Willoughby interjected, and drew out his watch, merely for a diversion; he was on tiptoe to learn whether Vernon was as well instructed as Clara, and hung to the view that he could not be, while drenching in the sensation that he was: – and if so, what were the Powers above but a body of conspirators? He paid Laetitia that compliment. He could not conceive the human betrayal of the secret. Clara's discovery of it had set his common sense adrift.

'The domestic affairs of the Dales do not concern me,' said Vernon.

'And yet, my friend,' Dr Middleton balanced himself, and with an air of benevolent slyness the import of which did not awaken Willoughby, until too late, remarked: 'They might concern you. I will even add, that there is a probability of your being not less than the fount and origin of this division of father and daughter, though Willoughby in the drawing-room last night stands accusably the agent.'

'Favour me, sir, with an explanation,' said Vernon, seeking to gather it from Clara.

Dr Middleton threw the explanation upon Willoughby.

Clara communicated as much as she was able in one of those looks of still depth which say, Think! and without causing a thought to stir, takes us into the pellucid mind.

Vernon was enlightened before Willoughby had spoken. His mouth shut rigidly, and there was a springing increase of the luminous wavering of his eyes. Some star that Clara had watched at night was like them in the vivid wink and over-flow of its light. Yet, as he was perfectly sedate, none could have suspected his blood to be chasing wild with laughter, and his frame strung to the utmost to keep it from volleying. So happy was she in his aspect, that her chief anxiety was to re-cover the name of the star whose shining beckons and speaks, and is in the quick of spirit-fire. It is the sole star which on a

night of frost and strong moonlight preserves an indomitable
fervency: that she remembered, and the picture of a hoar earth
and a lean Orion in flooded heavens, and the star beneath
Eastward of him: but the name! the name! – She heard Willoughby indistinctly.

'Oh, the old story; another effort; you know my wish; a
failure, of course, and no thanks on either side, I suppose I
must ask your excuse. – They neither of them see what's good
for them, sir.'

'Manifestly, however,' said Dr Middleton, 'if one may
opine from the division we have heard of, the father is disposed to back your nominee.'

'I can't say; as far as I am concerned, I made a mess of it.'

Vernon withstood the incitement to acquiesce, but he
sparkled with his recognition of the fact.

'You meant well, Willoughby.'

'I hope so, Vernon.'

'Only you have driven her away.'

'We must resign ourselves.'

'It won't affect me, for I'm off to-morrow.'

'You see, sir, the thanks I get.'

'Mr Whitford,' said Dr Middleton, 'you have a tower of
strength in the lady's father.'

'Would you have me bring it to bear upon the lady, sir?'

'Wherefore not?'

'To make her marriage a matter of obedience to her
father?'

'Ay, my friend, a lusty lover would have her gladly on those
terms, well knowing it to be for the lady's good. What do you
say, Willoughby?'

'Sir! Say? What can I say? Miss Dale has not plighted her
faith. Had she done so, she is a lady who would never dishonour it.'

'She is an ideal of constancy, who would keep to it though
it had been broken on the other side,' said Vernon, and Clara
thrilled.

'I take that, sir, to be a statue of constancy, modelled upon which a lady of our flesh may be proclaimed as graduating for the condition of idiocy,' said Dr Middleton.

'But faith is faith, sir.'

'But the broken is the broken, sir, whether in porcelain or in human engagements; and all that one of the two continuing faithful, I should rather say, regretful, can do, is to devote the remainder of life to the picking up of the fragments; an occupation properly to be pursued, for the comfort of mankind, within the enclosure of an appointed asylum.'

'You destroy the poetry of sentiment, Dr Middleton.'

'To invigorate the poetry of nature, Mr Whitford.'

'Then you maintain, sir, that when faith is broken by one, the engagement ceases, and the other is absolutely free?'

'I do; I am the champion of that platitude, and sound that knell to the sentimental world; and since you have chosen to defend it, I will appeal to Willoughby, and ask him if he would not side with the world of good sense in applauding the nuptials of man or maid married within a month of a jilting?'

Clara slipped her arm under her father's.

'Poetry, sir,' said Willoughby, 'I never have been hypocrite enough to pretend to understand or care for.'

Dr Middleton laughed. Vernon too seemed to admire his cousin for a reply that rung in Clara's ears as the dullest ever spoken. Her arm grew cold on her father's. She began to fear Willoughby again.

He depended entirely on his agility to elude the thrusts that assailed him. Had he been able to believe in the treachery of the Powers above, he would at once have seen design in these deadly strokes, for his feelings had rarely been more acute than at the present crisis; and he would then have led away Clara, to wrangle it out with her, relying on Vernon's friendliness not to betray him to her father: but a wrangle with Clara promised no immediate fruits, nothing agreeable; and the lifelong trust he had reposed in his protecting genii obscured his intelligence to evidence he would otherwise have accepted on the spot, on the faith of his delicate susceptibility to the mildest impressions which wounded him. Clara might have stooped to listen at the door: she might have heard sufficient to create a suspicion. But Vernon was not in the house last night; she could not have communicated it to him, and he had not seen Laetitia, who was, besides trustworthy, an admirable if a foolish and ill-fated woman.

Preferring to consider Vernon a pragmatical moralist played upon by a sententious drone, he thought it politic to detach them, and vanquish Clara while she was in the beaten mood, as she had appeared before Vernon's vexatious arrival.

'I'm afraid, my dear fellow, you are rather too dainty and fussy for a very successful wooer,' he said. 'It's beautiful on paper, and absurd in life. We have a bit of private business to discuss. We will go inside, sir, I think. I will soon release you.'

Clara pressed her father's arm.

'More?' said he.

'Five minutes. There's a slight delusion to clear, sir. My dear Clara, you will see with different eyes.'

'Papa wishes to work with Mr Whitford.'

Her heart sunk to hear her father say: 'No,'tis a lost morning. I must consent to pay tax of it for giving another young woman to the world. I have a daughter! You will, I hope, compensate me, Mr Whitford, in the afternoon. Be not downcast. I have observed you meditative of late. You will have no clear brain so long as that stuff is on the mind. I could venture to propose to do some pleading for you, should it be needed for the prompter expedition of the affair.'

Vernon briefly thanked him, and said:

'Willoughby has exerted all his eloquence, and you see the result: you have lost Miss Dale and I have not won her. He did everything that one man can do for another in so delicate a case: even to the repeating of her famous birthday verses to him, to flatter the poetess. His best efforts were foiled by the lady's indisposition for me.'

'Behold,' said Dr Middleton, as Willoughby, electrified by

the mention of the verses, took a sharp stride or two, 'you have in him an advocate who will not be rebuffed by one refusal, and I can affirm that he is tenacious, pertinacious as are few. Justly so. Not to believe in a lady's No is the approved method of carrying that fortress built to yield. Although unquestionably to have a young man pleading in our interests with a lady counts its objections. Yet Willoughby being notoriously engaged, may be held to enjoy the privileges of his elders.'

'As an engaged man, sir, he was on a level with his elders in pleading on my behalf with Miss Dale,' said Vernon.

Willoughby strode and muttered. Providence had grown mythical in his thoughts, if not malicious: and it is the peril of this worship that the object will wear such an alternative aspect when it appears no longer subservient.

'Are we coming, sir?' he said, and was unheeded. The Rev. Doctor would not be defrauded of rolling his billow.

'As an honourable gentleman faithful to his own engagement and desirous of establishing his relatives, he deserves, in my judgement, the lady's esteem as well as your cordial thanks; nor should a temporary failure dishearten either of you, notwithstanding the precipitate retreat of the lady from Patterne, and her seclusion in her sanctum on the occasion of your recent visit.'

'Supposing he had succeeded,' said Vernon, driving Willoughby to frenzy, 'should I have been bound to marry?'

Matter for cogitation was offered to Dr Middleton.

'The proposal was without your sanction?'

'Entirely.'

'You admire the lady?'

'Respectfully.'

'You do not incline to the state?'

'An inch of an angle would exaggerate my inclination.'

'How long are we to stand and hear this insufferable nonsense you talk?' cried Willoughby.

'But if Mr Whitford was not consulted . . .' Dr Middleton

said, and was overborne by Willoughby's hurried, 'Oblige
me, sir. – Oblige me, my good fellow!' He swept his arm to
Vernon, and gestured a conducting hand to Clara.

'Here is Mrs Mountstuart!' she exclaimed.

Willoughby stared. Was it an irruption of a friend or a foe?
He doubted, and stood petrified between the double question.

Clara had seen Mrs Mountstuart and Colonel De Craye
separating: and now the great lady sailed along the sward like
a royal barge in festival trim.

She looked friendly, but friendly to everybody, which was
always a frost on Willoughby, and terribly friendly to Clara.

Coming up to her she whispered: 'News, indeed! Wonderful! I could not credit his hint of it yesterday. Are you satisfied?'

'Pray, Mrs Mountstuart, take an opportunity to speak to
papa,' Clara whispered in return.

Mrs Mountstuart bowed to Dr Middleton, nodded to Vernon, and swam upon Willoughby, with, 'Is it? But *is* it? Am
I really to believe? You have? My dear Sir Willoughby?
Really?'

The confounded gentleman heaved on a bare plank of
wreck in mid sea.

He could oppose only a paralyzed smile to the assault.

His intuitive discretion taught him to fall back a step while
she said, 'So!' the plummet word of our mysterious deep
fathoms; and he fell back further saying, 'Madam?' in a tone
advising her to speak low.

She recovered her volubility, followed his partial retreat,
and dropped her voice,—

'Impossible to have imagined it as an actual fact! You were
always full of surprises, but this! this! Nothing manlier, nothing more gentlemanly has ever been done: nothing: nothing
that so completely changes an untenable situation into a comfortable and proper footing for everybody. It is what I like:
it is what I love: – sound sense! Men are so selfish: one cannot
persuade them to be reasonable in such positions. But you,

Sir Willoughby, have shown wisdom and sentiment: the rarest of all combinations in men.'

'Where have you –' Willoughby contrived to say.

'Heard? The hedges, the housetops, everywhere. All the neighbourhood will have it before nightfall. Lady Busshe and Lady Culmer will soon be rushing here, and declaring they never expected anything else, I do not doubt. I am not so pretentious. I beg your excuse for that "twice" of mine yesterday. Even if it hurt my vanity, I should be happy to confess my error: I was utterly out. But then I did not reckon on a fatal attachment, I thought men were incapable of it. I thought we women were the only poor creatures persecuted by a fatality. It *is* a fatality! You tried hard to escape, indeed you did. And she will do honour to your final surrender, my dear friend. She is gentle, and very clever, very: she is devoted to you: she will entertain excellently. I see her like a flower in sunshine. She will expand to a perfect hostess. Patterne will shine under her reign; you have my warrant for that. And so will you. Yes, you flourish best when adored. It must be adoration. You have been under a cloud of late. Years ago I said it was a match, when no one supposed you could stoop. Lady Busshe would have it was a screen, and she was deemed high wisdom. The world will be with you. All the women will be: excepting, of course, Lady Busshe, whose pride is in prophecy; and she will soon be too glad to swell the host. There, my friend, your sincerest and oldest admirer congratulates you. I could not contain myself; I was compelled to pour forth. And now I must go and be talked to by Dr Middleton. How does he take it? They leave?'

'He is perfectly well,' said Willoughby, aloud, quite distraught.

She acknowledged his just correction of her for running on to an extreme in low-toned converse, though they stood sufficiently isolated from the others. These had by this time been joined by Colonel De Craye, and were all chatting in a group – of himself, Willoughby horribly suspected.

Clara was gone from him! Gone! but he remembered his oath and vowed it again: not to Horace de Craye! She was gone, lost, sunk into the world of waters of rival men, and he determined that his whole force should be used to keep her from that man, the false friend who had supplanted him in her shallow heart, and might, if he succeeded, boast of having done it by simply appearing on the scene.

Willoughby intercepted Mrs Mountstuart as she was passing over to Dr Middleton. 'My dear lady! spare me a minute.'

De Craye sauntered up, with a face of the friendliest humour: 'Never was man like you, Willoughby, for shaking new patterns in a kaleidoscope.'

'Have you turned punster, Horace?' Willoughby replied, smarting to find yet another in the demon secret, and he draw Dr Middleton two or three steps aside, and hurriedly begged him to abstain from prosecuting the subject with Clara. 'We must try to make her happy as we best can, sir. She may have her reasons – a young lady's reasons!' He laughed, and left the Rev. Doctor considering within himself under the arch of his lofty frown of stupefaction.

De Craye smiled slyly and winningly as he shadowed a deep droop on the bend of his head before Clara, signifying his absolute devotion to her service, and this present good fruit for witness of his merits.

She smiled sweetly though vaguely. There was no concealment of their intimacy.

'The battle is over,' Vernon said quietly, when Willoughby had walked some paces beside Mrs Mountstuart, adding: 'You may expect to see Mr Dale here. He knows.'

Vernon and Clara exchanged one look, hard on his part, in contrast with her softness, and he proceeded to the house.

De Craye waited for a word or a promising look. He was patient, being self-assured, and passed on.

Clara linked her arm with her father's once more, and said, on a sudden brightness: 'Sirius, papa!'

He repeated it in the profoundest manner: 'Sirius! And is there,' he asked, 'a feminine scintilla of sense in that?'

'It is the name of the star I was thinking of, dear papa.'

'It was the star observed by King Agamemnon before the sacrifice in Aulis. You were thinking of that? But, my love, my Iphigenia, you have not a father who will insist on sacrificing you.'

'Did I hear him tell you to humour me, papa?'

Dr Middleton humphed.

'Verily the dog-star rages in many heads,' he responded.

CHAPTER 44

✕✕✕✕

Dr Middleton: the Ladies Eleanor and Isabel: and Mr Dale

CLARA looked up at the flying clouds. She travelled with them now, and tasted freedom, but she prudently forbore to vex her father; she held herself in reserve.

They were summoned by the midday bell.

Few were speakers at the meal, few were eaters. Clara was impelled to join it by her desire to study Mrs Mountstuart's face. Willoughby was obliged to preside. It was a meal of an assembly of mutes and plates, that struck the ear like the well-known sound of a collection of offerings in church after an impressive exhortation from the pulpit. A sally of Colonel De Craye's met the reception given to a charity-boy's muffled burst of animal spirits in the silence of the sacred edifice. Willoughby tried politics with Dr Middleton, whose regular appetite preserved him from uncongenial speculations when the hour for appeasing it had come; and he alone did honour to the dishes, replying to his host:

'Times are bad, you say, and we have a Ministry doing with us what they will. Well, sir, and that being so, and opposition a manner of kicking them into greater stability, it is the time for wise men to retire within themselves, with the steady determination of the seed in the earth to grow. Repose upon nature, sleep in firm faith, and abide the seasons. That is my counsel to the weaker party.'

The counsel was excellent, but it killed the topic.

Dr Middleton's appetite was watched for the signal to rise and breathe freely; and such is the grace accorded to a good man of an untroubled conscience engaged in doing his duty to himself, that he perceived nothing of the general restlessness; he went through the dishes calmly, and as calmly he quoted Milton to the ladies Eleanor and Isabel, when the company sprung up all at once upon his closing his repast. Vernon was taken away from him by Willoughby. Mrs Mountstuart beckoned covertly to Clara. Willoughby should have had something to say to him, Dr Middleton thought: the position was not clear. But the situation was not disagreeable; and he was in no serious hurry, though he wished to be enlightened.

'This,' Dr Middleton said to the spinster aunts, as he accompanied them to the drawing-room, 'shall be no lost day for me if I may devote the remainder of it to you.'

'The thunder, we fear, is not remote,' murmured one.

'We fear it is imminent,' sighed the other.

They took to chanting in alternation.

'– We are accustomed to peruse our Willoughby, and we know him by a shadow.'

'– From his infancy to his glorious youth and his established manhood.'

'– He was ever the soul of chivalry.'

'– Duty: duty first. The happiness of his family. The well-being of his dependants.'

'– If proud of his name it was not an overweening pride; it was founded in the conscious possession of exalted qualities.'

'– He could be humble when occasion called for it.'

Dr Middleton bowed to the litany, feeling that occasion called for humbleness from him.

'Let us hope . . .!' he said, with unassumed penitence on behalf of his inscrutable daughter.

The ladies resumed:

'– Vernon Whitford, not of his blood, is his brother!'

'– A thousand instances! Laetitia Dale remembers them better than we.'

'– That any blow should strike him!'

'– That another should be in store for him!'

'– It seems impossible he can be quite misunderstood!'

'Let us hope . . .!' said Dr Middleton.

'– One would not deem it too much for the dispenser of goodness to expect to be a little looked up to!'

'– When he was a child he one day mounted a chair, and there he stood in danger, would not let us touch him, because he was taller than we, and we were to gaze. Do you remember him, Eleanor? "I am the sun of the house!" It was inimitable!'

'– Your feelings; he would have your feelings! He was fourteen when his cousin Grace Whitford married, and we lost him. They had been the greatest friends; and it was long before he appeared among us. He has never cared to see her since.'

'–But he has befriended her husband. Never has he failed in generosity. His only fault is –'

'– His sensitiveness. And that is –'

'– His secret. And that –'

'– You are not to discover! It is the same with him in manhood. No one will accuse Willoughby Patterne of a deficiency of manlinesss: but what is it? – he suffers as none suffer if he is not loved. He himself is unalterably constant in affection.'

'– What it is no one can say. We have lived with him all his life, and we know him ready to make any sacrifice; only, he does demand the whole heart in return. And if he doubts, he looks as we have seen him to-day.'

'– Shattered: as we have never seen him look before.'

'We will hope,' said Dr Middleton, this time hastily. He tingled to say, 'what it was': he had it in him to solve perplexity in their inquiry. He did say, adopting familiar speech to suit the theme, 'You know, ladies, we English come of a rough stock. A dose of rough dealing in our youth does us no harm, braces us. Otherwise we are likely to feel chilly: we grow too fine where tenuity of stature is necessarily buffeted by gales, namely, in our self-esteem. We are barbarians, on a forcing soil of wealth, in a conservatory of comfortable security; but still barbarians. So, you see, we shine at our best when we are plucked out of that, to where hard blows are given, in a state of war. In a state of war we are at home, our men are high-minded fellows, Scipios and good legionaries. In the state of peace we do not live in peace: our native roughness breaks out in unexpected places, under extraordinary aspects – tyrannies, extravagances, domestic exactions: and if we have not had sharp early training . . . within and without . . . the old-fashioned island-instrument to drill into us the civilization of our masters, the ancients, we show it by running here and there to some excess. Ahem. Yet,' added the Rev. Doctor, abandoning his effort to deliver a weighty truth obscurely for the comprehension of dainty spinster ladies, the superabundance of whom in England was in his opinion largely the cause of our decay as a people, 'Yet I have not observed this ultra-sensitiveness in Willoughby. He has borne to hear more than I, certainly no example of the frailty, could have endured.'

'He concealed it,' said the ladies. 'It is intense.'

'Then is it a disease?'

'It bears no explanation; it is mystic.'

'It is a cultus, then, a form of self-worship.'

'Self!' they ejaculated. 'But is not Self indifferent to others? Is it Self that craves for sympathy, love, and devotion?'

'He is an admirable host, ladies.'

'He is admirable in all respects.'

'Admirable must he be who can impress discerning women,

his life-long housemates, so favourably. He is, I repeat, a perfect host.'

'He will be a perfect husband.'

'In all probability.'

'It is a certainty. Let him be loved and obeyed, he will be guided. That is the secret for her whom he so fatally loves. That, if we had dared, we would have hinted to her. She will rule him through her love of him, and through him all about her. And it will not be a rule he submits to, but a love he accepts. If she could see it!'

'– If she were a metaphysician!' sighed Dr Middleton.

'– But a sensitiveness so keen as his might –'

'– Fretted by an unsympathizing mate –'

'– In the end become, for the best of us is mortal –'

'– Callous!'

'– He would feel perhaps as much –'

'– Or more –'

'– He would still be tender –'

'–, But he might grow outwardly hard!'

Both ladies looked up at Dr Middleton, as they revealed the dreadful prospect.

'It is the story told of corns!' he said, sad as they.

The three stood drooping: the ladies with an attempt to digest his remark; the Rev. Doctor in dejection lest his gallantry should no longer continue to wrestle with his good sense.

He was rescued.

The door opened and a footman announced:

'Mr Dale.'

Miss Eleanor and Miss Isabel made a sign to one another of raising their hands.

They advanced to him, and welcomed him.

'Pray be seated, Mr Dale. You have not brought us bad news of our Laetitia?'

'So rare is the pleasure of welcoming you here, Mr Dale, that we are in some alarm, when, as we trust, it should be matter for unmixed congratulation.'

'Has Doctor Corney been doing wonders?'

'I am indebted to him for the drive to your house, ladies,' said Mr Dale, a spare, close-buttoned gentleman, with an Indian complexion deadened in the sick-chamber. 'It is unusual for me to stir from my precincts.'

'The Rev. Dr Middleton.'

Mr Dale bowed. He seemed surprised.

'You live in a splendid air, sir,' observed the Rev. doctor.

'I can profit little by it, sir,' replied Mr Dale. He asked the ladies: 'Will Sir Willoughby be disengaged?'

They consulted. 'He is with Vernon. We will send to him.'

The bell was rung.

'I have had the gratification of making the acquaintance of your daughter, Mr Dale, a most estimable lady,' said Dr Middleton.

Mr Dale bowed. 'She is honoured by your praises, sir. To the best of my belief – I speak as a father – she merits them. Hitherto I have had no doubts.'

'Of Laetitia?' exclaimed the ladies; and spoke of her as gentleness and goodness incarnate.

'Hitherto I have devoutly thought so,' said Mr Dale.

'Surely she is the very sweetest nurse, the most devoted of daughters.'

'As far as concerns her duty to her father, I can say she is that, ladies.'

'In all her relations, Mr Dale!'

'It is my prayer,' he said.

The footman appeared. He announced that Sir Willoughby was in the laboratory with Mr Whitford, and the door locked.

'Domestic business,' the ladies remarked. 'You know Willoughby's diligent attention to affairs, Mr Dale.'

'He is well?' Mr Dale inquired.

'In excellent health.'

'Body and mind?'

'But, dear Mr Dale, he is never ill.'

'Ah! for one to hear that who is never well! And Mr Whitford is quite sound?'

'Sound? The question alarms me for myself,' said Dr Middleton. 'Sound as our Constitution, the Credit of the country, the reputation of our Prince of poets. I pray you to have no fears for him.'

Mr Dale gave the mild little sniff of a man thrown deeper into perplexity.

He said: 'Mr Whitford works his head; he is a hard student; he may not be always, if I may so put it, at home on worldly affairs.'

'Dismiss that defamatory legend of the student, Mr Dale; and take my word for it, that he who persistently works his head has the strongest for all affairs.'

'Ah! Your daughter, sir, is here?'

'My daughter is here, sir, and will be most happy to present her respects to the father of her friend, Miss Dale.'

'They are friends?'

'Very cordial friends.'

Mr Dale administered another feebly pacifying sniff to himself.

'Laetitia!' he sighed, in apostrophe, and swept his forehead with a hand seen to shake.

The ladies asked him anxiously whether he felt the heat of the room; and one offered him a smelling-bottle.

He thanked them. 'I can hold out until Sir Willoughby comes.'

'We fear to disturb him when his door is locked, Mr Dale; but, if you wish it, we will venture on a message. You have really no bad news of our Laetitia? She left us hurriedly this morning, without any leave-taking, except a word to one of the maids, that your condition required her immediate presence.'

'My condition! And now her door is locked to me! We have spoken through the door, and that is all. I stand sick and stupefied between two locked doors, neither of which will open, it appears, to give me the enlightenment I need more than medicine.'

'Dear me!' cried Dr Middleton, 'I am struck by your description of your position, Mr Dale. It would aptly apply to our humanity of the present generation; and were these the days when I sermonized, I could propose that it should afford me an illustration for the pulpit. For my part, when doors are' closed I try not their locks; and I attribute my perfect equanimity, health even, to an uninquiring acceptation of the fact that they are closed to me. I read my page by the light I have. On the contrary, the world of this day, if I may presume to quote you for my purpose, is heard knocking at those two locked doors of the secret of things on each side of us, and is beheld standing sick and stupefied because it has got no response to its knocking. Why, sir, let the world compare the diverse fortunes of the beggar and the postman: knock to give, and it is opened unto you: knock to crave, and it continues, shut. I say, carry a letter to your locked door, and you shall have a good reception: but there is none that is handed out. For which reason . . .'

Mr Dale swept a perspiring forehead, and extended his hand in supplication. 'I am an invalid, Dr Middleton,' he said. 'I am unable to cope with analogies. I have but strength for the slow digestion of facts.'

'For facts, we are bradypeptics to a man, sir. We know not yet if nature be a fact or an effort to master one. The world has not yet assimilated the first fact it stepped on. We are still in the endeavour to make good blood of the fact of our being.'

Pressing his hands at his temples, Mr Dale moaned: 'My head twirls; I did unwisely to come out. I came on an impulse; I trust, honourable. I am unfit – I cannot follow you, Dr Middleton. Pardon me.'

'Nay, sir, let me say, from my experience of my countrymen, that if you do not follow me and can abstain from abusing me in consequence, you are magnanimous,' the Rev. Doctor replied, hardly consenting to let go the man he had

found to indemnify him for his gallant service of acquiescing
as a mute to the ladies, though he knew his breathing robust-
fulness to be as an East wind to weak nerves, and himself an
engine of punishment when he had been torn for a day from
his books.

Miss Eleanor said: 'The enlightenment you need, Mr Dale?
Can we enlighten you?'

'I think not,' he answered, faintly. 'I think I will wait for
Sir Willoughby ... or Mr Whitford. If I can keep my strength.
Or could I exchange – I fear to break down – two words with
the young lady who is, was ... '

'Miss Middleton, my daughter, sir? She shall be at your
disposition; I will bring her to you.' Dr Middleton stopped at
the window. 'She, it is true, may better know the mind of Miss
Dale than I. But I flatter myself I know the gentleman better.
I think, Mr Dale, addressing you as the lady's father, you will
find me a persuasive, I could be an impassioned, advocate in
his interests.'

Mr Dale was confounded; the weakly sapling caught in a
gust falls back as he did.

'Advocate?' he said. He had little breath.

'His impassioned advocate, I repeat; for I have the highest
opinion of him. You see, sir, I am acquainted with the circumstances. I believe,' Dr Middleton half turned to the ladies, 'we
must, until your potent inducements, Mr Dale, have been
joined to my instances, and we overcome what feminine
scruples there may be, treat the circumstances as not generally
public. Our Strephon may be chargeable with shyness. But
if for the present it is incumbent on us, in proper consideration for the parties, not to be nominally precise, it is hardly
requisite in this household that we should be. He is now for
protesting indifference to the state. I fancy we understand
that phase of amatory frigidity. Frankly, Mr Dale, I was once
in my life myself refused by a lady, and I was not indignant,
merely indifferent to the marriage-tie.'

'My daughter *has* refused him, sir?'

'Temporarily it would appear that she has declined the proposal.'

'He was at liberty . . .? he could honourably . . .?'

'His best friend and nearest relative is your guarantee.'

'I know it; I hear so; I am informed of that: I have heard of the proposal, and that he could honourably make it. Still, I am helpless, I cannot move, until I am assured that my daughter's reasons are such as a father need not underline.'

'Does the lady, perchance, equivocate?'

'I have not seen her this morning; I rise late. I hear an astounding account of the cause for her departure from Patterne, and I find her door locked to me – no answer.'

'It is that she had no reasons to give, and she feared the demand for them.'

'Ladies!' dolorously exclaimed Mr Dale.

'We guess the secret, we guess it!' they exclaimed in reply; and they looked smilingly, as Dr Middleton looked.

'She had no reasons to give?' Mr Dale spelled these words to his understanding. 'Then, sir, she knew you not adverse?'

'Undoubtedly, by my high esteem for the gentleman, she must have known me not adverse. But she would not consider me a principal. She could hardly have conceived me an obstacle. I am simply the gentleman's friend. A zealous friend, let me add.'

Mr Dale put out an imploring hand; it was too much for him.

'Pardon me; I have a poor head. And your daughter the same, sir?'

'We will not measure it too closely, but I may say, my daughter the same, sir. And likewise – may I not add – these ladies.'

Mr Dale made sign that he was overfilled. 'Where am I! And Laetitia refused him?'

'Temporarily, let us assume. Will it not partly depend on you, Mr Dale?'

'But what strange things have been happening during my

daughter's absence from the cottage!' cried Mr Dale, betraying an elixir in his veins. 'I feel that I could laugh if I did not dread to be thought insane. She refused his hand, and he was at liberty to offer it? My girl! We are all on our heads. The fairy-tales were right and the lesson-books were wrong. But it is really, it is really very demoralizing. An invalid – and I am one, and no momentary exhilaration will be taken for the contrary – clings to the idea of stability, order. The slightest disturbance of the wonted course of things unsettles him. Why, for years I have been prophesying it! and for years I have had everything against me, and now when it is confirmed, I am wondering that I must not call myself a fool!'

'And for years, dear Mr Dale, this union, in spite of counter-currents and human arrangements, has been our Willoughby's constant preoccupation,' said Miss Eleanor.

'His most cherished aim,' said Miss Isabel.

'The name was not spoken by me,' said Dr Middleton. 'But it is out, and perhaps better out, if we would avoid the chance of mystifications. I do not suppose we are seriously committing a breach of confidence, though he might have wished to mention it to you first himself. I have it from Willoughby that last night he appealed to your daughter, Mr Dale – not for the first time, if I apprehend him correctly; and unsuccessfully. He despairs. I do not: supposing, that is, your assistance vouchsafed to us. And I do not despair, because the gentleman is a gentleman of worth, of acknowledged worth. You know him well enough to grant me that. I will bring you my daughter to help me in sounding his praises.'

Dr Middleton stepped through the window to the lawn on an elastic foot, beaming with the happiness he felt charged to confer on his friend Mr Whitford.

'Ladies! it passes all wonders,' Mr Dale gasped.

'Willoughby's generosity does pass all wonders,' they said in chorus.

The door opened; Lady Busshe and Lady Culmer were announced.

CHAPTER 45

✖✖✖✖

The Patterne Ladies: Mr Dale: Lady Busshe and Lady Culmer: with Mrs Mountstuart Jenkinson

LADY BUSSHE and Lady Culmer entered spying to right and left. At the sight of Mr Dale in the room Lady Busshe murmured to her friend: 'Confirmation!'

Lady Culmer murmured: 'Corney is quite reliable.'

'The man is his own best tonic.'

'He is invaluable for the country.'

Miss Eleanor and Miss Isabel greeted them.

The amiability of the Patterne ladies combined with their total eclipse behind their illustrious nephew invited enterprising women of the world to take liberties, and they were not backward.

Lady Busshe said: 'Well? the news! we have the outlines. Don't be astonished: we know the points: we have heard the gun. I could have told you as much yesterday. I *saw* it. And I guessed it the day before. Oh, I do believe in fatalities now. Lady Culmer and I agree to take that view: it is the simplest. Well, and are you satisfied, my dears?'

The ladies grimaced interrogatively: 'With what?'

'With it? with all! with her! with him!'

'Our Willoughby?'

'Can it be possible that they require a dose of Corney?' Lady Busshe remarked to Lady Culmer.

'They play discretion to perfection,' said Lady Culmer. 'But, my dears, we are in the secret.'

'How did she behave?' whispered Lady Busshe. 'No high flights and flutters, I do hope. She was well-connected, they say; though I don't comprehend what they mean by a line of scholars – one thinks of a row of pinafores: and she was pretty.'

That is well enough at the start. It never will stand against brains. He had the two in the house to contrast them, and . . . the result! A young woman with brains – in a house – beats all your beauties. Lady Culmer and I have determined on that view. He thought her a delightful partner for a dance, and found her rather tiresome at the end of the gallopade. I saw it yesterday, clear as daylight. She did not understand him, and he did understand her. That will be our report.'

'She is young: she will learn,' said the ladies uneasily, but in total ignorance of her meaning.

'And you are charitable, and always were. I remember you had a good word for that girl Durham.'

Lady Busshe crossed the room to Mr Dale, who was turning over leaves of a grand book of the heraldic devices of our great Families.

'Study it,' she said, 'study it, my dear Mr Dale; you are in it, by right of possessing a clever and accomplished daughter. At page 300 you will find the Patterne crest. And mark me, she will drag you into the peerage before she has done – relatively, you know. Sir Willoughby and wife will not be contented to sit down and manage the estates. Has not Laetitia immense ambition? And very creditable, I say.'

Mr Dale tried to protest something. He shut the book, examining the binding, flapped the cover with a finger, hoped her ladyship was in good health, alluded to his own and the strangeness of the bird out of the cage.

'You will probably take up your residence here, in a larger and handsomer cage, Mr Dale.'

He shook his head. 'Do I apprehend . . .' he said.

'I *know*,' said she.

'Dear me, can it be?'

Mr Dale gazed upward, with the feelings of one awakened late to see a world alive in broad daylight.

Lady Busshe dropped her voice. She took the liberty permitted to her with an inferior in station, while treating him to a tone of familiarity in acknowledgment of his expected rise;

which is high breeding, or the exact measurement of social dues.

'Laetitia will be happy, you may be sure. I love to see a long and faithful attachment rewarded – love it! Her tale is the triumph of patience. Far above Grizzel! No woman will be ashamed of pointing to Lady Patterne. You are uncertain? You are in doubt? Let me hear – as low as you like. But there is no doubt of the new shifting of the scene? – no doubt of the proposal? Dear Mr Dale! a very little louder. You are here because –? of course you wish to see Sir Willoughby. She? I did not catch you quite. She? . . . it seems, you say . . .?'

Lady Culmer said to the Patterne ladies:

'You must have had a distressing time. These affairs always mount up to a climax, unless people are very wellbred. We saw it coming. Naturally we did not expect such a transformation of brides: who could? If I had laid myself down on my back to think, I should have had it. I am unerring when I set to speculating on my back. One is cooler: ideas come; they have not to be forced. That is why I am brighter on a dull winter afternoon, on the sofa, beside my tea-service, than at any other season. However, your trouble is over. When did the Middletons leave?'

'The Middletons leave?' said the ladies.

'Dr Middleton and his daughter.'

'They have not left us.'

'The Middletons are here?'

'They are here, yes. Why should they have left Patterne?'

'Why?'

'Yes. They are likely to stay some days longer.'

'Goodness!'

'There is no ground for any report to the contrary, Lady Culmer.'

'No ground!'

Lady Culmer called out to Lady Busshe.

A cry came back from that startled dame.

'She has refused him!'

'Who?'

'*She* has.'

'She? – Sir Willoughby?'

'Refused! – declines the honour.'

'Oh, never! No, that carries the incredible beyond romance. But is he perfectly at . . .'

'Quite, it seems. And she was asked in due form and refused.'

'No, and no again!'

'My dear, I have it from Mr Dale.'

'Mr Dale, what can be the signification of her conduct?'

'Indeed, Lady Culmer,' said Mr Dale, not unpleasantly agitated by the interest he excited, in spite of his astonishment at a public discussion of the matter in this house, 'I am in the dark. Her father should know, but I do not. Her door is locked to me; I have not seen her. I am absolutely in the dark. I am a recluse. I have forgotten the ways of the world. I should have supposed her father would first have been addressed.'

'Tut-tut. Modern gentlemen are not so formal; they are creatures of impulse and take a pride in it. He spoke. We settle that. But where did you get this tale of a refusal?'

'I have it from Dr Middleton.'

'From Dr Middleton?' shouted Lady Busshe.

'The Middletons are here,' said Lady Culmer.

'What whirl are we in?' Lady Busshe got up, ran two or three steps and seated herself in another chair. 'Oh! do let us proceed upon system. If not we shall presently be rageing; we shall be dangerous. The Middletons are here, and Dr Middleton himself communicates to Mr Dale that Laetitia Dale has refused the hand of Sir Willoughby, who is ostensibly engaged to his own daughter! And pray, Mr Dale, how did Dr Middleton speak of it? Compose yourself; there is no violent hurry, though our sympathy with you and our interest in all the parties does perhaps agitate us a little. Quite at your leisure – speak!'

'Madam . . . Lady Busshe.' Mr Dale gulped a ball in his

throat. 'I see no reason why I should not speak. I do not see how I can have been deluded. The Miss Patternes heard him. Dr Middleton began upon it, not I. I was unaware, when I came, that it was a refusal. I had been informed that there was a proposal. My authority for the tale was positive. The object of my visit was to assure myself of the integrity of my daughter's conduct. She had always the highest sense of honour. But passion is known to mislead, and there was this most strange report. I feared that our humblest apologies were due to Dr Middleton and his daughter. I know the charm Laetitia can exercise. Madam, in the plainest language, without a possibility of my misapprehending him, Dr Middleton spoke of himself as the advocate of the suitor for my daughter's hand. I have a poor head. I supposed at once an amicable rupture between Sir Willoughby and Miss Middleton, or that the version which had reached me of their engagement was not strictly accurate. My head is weak. Dr. Middleton's language is trying to a head like mine; but I can speak positively on the essential points: he spoke of himself as ready to be the impassioned advocate of the suitor for my daughter's hand. Those were his words. I understood him to entreat me to intercede with her. Nay, the name was mentioned. There was no concealment. I am certain there could not be a misapprehension. And my feelings were touched by his anxiety for Sir Willoughby's happiness. I attributed it to a sentiment upon which I need not dwell. Impassioned advocate, he said.'

'We are in a perfect maelstrom!' cried Lady Busshe, turning to everybody.

'It is a complete hurricane!' cried Lady Culmer.

A light broke over the faces of the Patterne ladies. They exchanged it with one another.

They had been so shocked as to be almost offended by Lady Busshe, but their natural gentleness and habitual submission rendered them unequal to the task of checking her.

'Is it not,' said Miss Eleanor, 'a misunderstanding that a change of names will rectify?'

'This is by no means the first occasion,' said Miss Isabel, 'that Willoughby has pleaded for his cousin Vernon.'

'We deplore extremely the painful error into which Mr Dale has fallen.'

'It springs, we now perceive, from an entire misapprehension of Dr Middleton.'

'Vernon was in his mind. It was clear to us.'

'Impossible that it could have been Willoughby!'

'You see the impossibility, the error!'

'And the Middletons here!' said Lady Busshe. 'Oh, if we leave unilluminated we shall be the laughing-stock of the county. Mr Dale, please, wake up. Do you see? You may have been mistaken.'

'Lady Busshe,' he woke up; 'I may have mistaken Dr Middleton; he has a language that I can compare only to a review-day of the field forces. But I have the story on authority that I cannot question: it is confirmed by my daughter's unexampled behaviour. And if I live through this day I shall look about me as a ghost to-morrow.'

'Dear Mr Dale!' said the Patterne ladies, compassionately.

Lady Busshe murmured to them: 'You know the two did not agree; they did not get on: I saw it; I predicted it.'

'She will understand him in time,' said they.

'Never. And my belief is, they have parted by consent, and Letty Dale wins the day at last. Yes, now I do believe it.'

The ladies maintained a decided negative, but they knew too much not to feel perplexed, and they betrayed it, though they said: 'Dear Lady Busshe! is it credible, in decency?'

'Dear Mrs Mountstuart!' Lady Busshe invoked her great rival appearing among them: 'You come most opportunely; we are in a state of inextricable confusion: we are bordering on frenzy. You, and none but you, can help us. You know, you always know; we hang on you. Is there any truth in it? a particle?'

Mrs Mountstuart seated herself regally. 'Ah, Mr Dale!'

she said, inclining to him. 'Yes, dear Lady Busshe, there is a particle.'

'Now, do not roast us. You can; you have the art. I have the whole story. That is, I have a part. I mean, I have the outlines, I cannot be deceived, but you can fill them in, I know you can. I saw it yesterday. Now, tell us, tell us. It must be quite true or utterly false. Which is it?'

'Be precise.'

'His fatality! you called her. Yes, I was sceptical. But here we have it all come round again, and if the tale is true, I shall own you infallible. Has he? – and she?'

'Both.'

'And the Middletons here? They have not gone; they keep the field. And more astounding, she refuses him. And to add to it, Dr Middleton intercedes with Mr Dale for Sir Willoughby.'

'Dr. Middleton intercedes!' This was rather astonishing to Mrs Mountstuart.

'For Vernon,' Miss Eleanor emphasized.

'For Vernon Whitford, his cousin,' said Miss Isabel, still more emphatically.

'Who,' said Mrs Mountstuart, with a sovereign lift and turn of her head, 'speaks of a refusal?'

'I have it from Mr Dale,' said Lady Busshe.

'I had it, I thought, distinctly from Dr Middleton,' said Mr Dale.

'That Willoughby proposed to Laetitia for his cousin Vernon, Doctor Middleton meant,' said Miss Eleanor.

Her sister followed: 'Hence this really ridiculous misconception! – sad, indeed,' she added, for balm to Mr Dale. 'Willoughby was Vernon's proxy. His cousin, if not his first, is ever the second thought with him.'

'But can we continue . . .?'

'Such a discussion!'

Mrs Mountstuart gave them a judicial hearing. They were regarded in the county as the most indulgent of nonentities, and she as little as Lady Busshe was restrained from the burning topic in their presence. She pronounced:

'Each party is right, and each is wrong.'

A dry: 'I shall shriek!' came from Lady Busshe.

'Cruel!' groaned Lady Culmer.

'Mixed, you are all wrong. Disentangled, you are each of you right. Sir Willoughby does think of his cousin Vernon; he is anxious to establish him; he is the author of a proposal to that effect.'

'We know it!' the Patterne ladies exclaimed. 'And Laetitia rejected poor Vernon once more!'

'Who spoke of Miss Dale's rejection of Mr Whitford?'

'Is he not rejected?' Lady Culmer inquired.

'It is in debate, and at this moment being decided.'

'Oh, do be seated, Mr Dale,' Lady Busshe implored him, rising to thrust him back to his chair if necessary. 'Any dislocation, and we are thrown out again! We must hold together if this riddle is ever to be read. Then, dear Mrs Mountstuart, we are to say that there is no truth in the other story?'

'You are to say nothing of the sort, dear Lady Busshe.'

'Be merciful! And what of the fatality?'

'As positive as the Pole to the needle.'

'She has not refused him?'

'Ask your own sagacity.'

'Accepted?'

'Wait.'

'And all the world's ahead of me! Now, Mrs Mountstuart, you are oracle. Riddles, if you like, only speak. If we can't have corn, why, give us husks.'

'Is any one of us able to anticipate events, Lady Busshe?'

'Yes, I believe that you are. I bow to you. I do sincerely. So it's another person for Mr Whitford? You nod. And it is our Laetitia for Sir Willoughby? You smile. You would not deceive me? A very little, and I run about crazed and howl at your doors. And Dr Middleton is made to play blind man in the midst? And the other person is – now I see day! An amicable

rupture, and a smooth new arrangement. She has money;
she was never the match for our hero; never; I saw it yesterday, and before, often; and so he hands her over – tuthe-rum-
tum-tum, tuthe-rum-tum-tum,' Lady Busshe struck a quick
march on her knee. 'Now isn't that clever guessing? The
shadow of a clue for me. And because I know human nature.
One peep, and I see the combination in a minute. So he keeps
the money in the family, becomes a benefactor to his cousin
by getting rid of the girl, and succumbs to his fatality. Rather
a pity he let it ebb and flow so long. Time counts the tides,
you know. But it improves the story. I defy any other county
in the kingdom to produce one fresh and living to equal it.
Let me tell you I suspected Mr Whitford, and I hinted it
yesterday.'

'Did you indeed!' said Mrs Mountstuart, humouring her
excessive acuteness.

'I really did. There is that dear good man on his feet again.
And looks agitated again.'

Mr Dale had been compelled both by the lady's voice and
his interest in the subject to listen. He had listened more than
enough; he was exceedingly nervous. He held on by his chair,
afraid to quit his moorings, and 'Manners!' he said to himself
unconsciously aloud, as he cogitated on the libertine way with
which these chartered great ladies of the district discussed his
daughter. He was heard and unnoticed. The supposition, if
any, would have been that he was admonishing himself.

At this juncture Sir Willoughby entered the drawing-room
by the garden window, and simultaneously Dr Middleton by
the door.

CHAPTER 46

❈❈❈❈

The Scene of Sir Willoughby's Generalship

HISTORY, we may fear, will never know the qualities of leadership inherent in Sir Willoughby Patterne to fit him for the post of Commander of an army, seeing that he avoided the fatigues of the service and preferred the honours bestowed in his country upon the quiet administrators of their own estates: but his possession of particular gifts, which are military, and especially of the proleptic mind, which is the stamp and sign-warrant of the heaven-sent General, was displayed on every urgent occasion when, in the midst of difficulties likely to have extinguished one less alert than he to the threatening aspect of disaster, he had to manoeuvre himself.

He had received no intimation of Mr Dale's presence in his house, nor of the arrival of the dreaded women Lady Busshe and Lady Culmer: his locked door was too great a terror to his domestics. Having finished with Vernon, after a tedious endeavour to bring the fellow to a sense of the policy of the step urged on him, he walked out on the lawn with the desire to behold the opening of an interview not promising to lead to much, and possibly to profit by its failure. Clara had been prepared, according to his directions, by Mrs Mountstuart Jenkinson, as Vernon had been prepared by him. His wishes, candidly and kindly expressed both to Vernon and Mrs Mountstuart, were, that since the girl appeared disinclined to make him a happy man, she would make one of his cousin. Intimating to Mrs Mountstuart that he would be happier without her, he alluded to the benefit of the girl's money to poor old Vernon, the general escape from a scandal if old Vernon could manage to catch her as she dropped, the harmonious arrangement it would be for all parties. And only on the condition of her taking Vernon would he consent to give her up. This he said imperatively, adding that such was the meaning of the news she had received relating to Laetitia Dale. From what quarter had she received it? he asked. She shuffled in her reply, made a gesture to signify that it was in the air, universal, and fell upon the proposed arrangement. He would listen to none of Mrs Mountstuart's woman-of-the-world instances of the folly of pressing it upon a girl who had shown herself a girl of spirit. She foretold the failure. He would not be advised; he said: 'It is my scheme'; and perhaps the look of mad benevolence about it induced the lady to try whether there was a chance that it would hit the madness in our nature, and somehow succeed or lead to a pacification. Sir Willoughby condescended to arrange things thus for Clara's good; he would then proceed to realize his own. Such was the face he put upon it. We can wear what appearance we please before the world until we are found out, nor is the world's praise knocking upon hollowness always hollow music; but Mrs Mountstuart's laudation of his kindness and simplicity disturbed him; for though he had recovered from his rebuff enough to imagine that Laetitia could not refuse him under reiterated pressure, he had let it be supposed that she was a submissive handmaiden throbbing for her elevation; and Mrs Mountstuart's belief in it afflicted his recent bitter experience; his footing was not perfectly secure. Besides, assuming it to be so, he considered the sort of prize he had won; and a spasm of downright hatred of a world for which we make mighty sacrifices to be repaid in a worn, thin, comparatively valueless coin, troubled his counting of his gains. Laetitia, it was true, had not passed through other hands in coming to him, as Vernon would know it to be Clara's case: time only had worn her: but the comfort of the reflection was annoyed by the physical contrast of the two. Hence an unusual melancholy in his tone that Mrs Mountstuart thought touching. It had the scenic effect on her which greatly contributes to delude the wits. She talked of him to Clara as being a man who had revealed an unsuspected depth.

Vernon took the communication curiously. He seemed readier to be in love with his benevolent relative than with the lady. He was confused, undisguisedly moved, said the plan was impossible, out of the question, but thanked Willoughby for the best of intentions, thanked him warmly. After saying that the plan was impossible, the comical fellow allowed himself to be pushed forth on the lawn to see how Miss Middleton might have come out of her interview with Mrs Mountstuart. Willoughby observed Mrs Mountstuart meet him, usher him to the place she had quitted among the shrubs, and return to the open turf-spaces. He sprang to her.

'She will listen,' Mrs Mountstuart said: 'She likes him, respects him, thinks he is a very sincere friend, clever, a scholar, and a good mountaineer; and thinks you mean very kindly. So much I have impressed on her, but I have not done much for Mr Whitford.'

'She consents to listen,' said Willoughby, snatching at that as the death-blow to his friend Horace.

'She consents to listen, because you have arranged it so that if she declined she would be rather a savage.'

'You think it will have no result?'

'None at all.'

'Her listening will do.'

'And you must be satisfied with it.'

'We shall see.'

' "Anything for peace", she says: and I don't say that a gentleman with a tongue would not have a chance. She wishes to please you.'

'Old Vernon has no tongue for women, poor fellow! You will have us be spider or fly, and if a man can't spin a web all he can hope is not to be caught in one. She knows his history, too, and that won't be in his favour. How did she look when you left them?'

'Not so bright: like a bit of china that wants dusting. She

looked a trifle *gauche*, it struck me; more like a country girl with the hoyden taming in her than the well-bred creature she is. I did not suspect her to have feeling. You must remember, Sir Willoughby, that she has obeyed your wishes, done her utmost: I do think we may say she has made some amends; and if she is to blame she repents, and you will not insist too far.'

'I do insist,' said he.

'Beneficent, but a tyrant!'

'Well, well.' He did not dislike the character.

They perceived Dr Middleton wandering over the lawn, and Willoughby went to him to put him on the wrong track: Mrs Mountstuart swept into the drawing-room. Willoughby quitted the Rev. Doctor, and hung about the bower where he supposed his pair of dupes had by this time ceased to stutter mutually: – or what if they had found the word of harmony? He could bear that, just bear it. He rounded the shrubs, and, behold, both had vanished. The trellis decorated emptiness. His idea was, that they had soon discovered their inability to be turtles: and desiring not to lose a moment while Clara was fretted by the scene, he rushed to the drawing-room with the hope of lighting on her there, getting her to himself, and finally, urgently, passionately offering her the sole alternative of what she had immediately rejected. Why had he not used passion before, instead of limping crippled between temper and policy? He was capable of it: as soon as imagination in him conceived his personal feelings unwounded and unimperiled, the might of it inspired him with heroical confidence, and Clara grateful, Clara softly moved, led him to think of Clara melted. Thus anticipating her he burst into the room.

One step there warned him that he was in the jaws of the world. We have the phrase, that a man is himself under certain trying circumstances. There is no need to say it of Sir Willoughby: he was thrice himself when danger menaced, himself inspired him. He could read at a single glance the Polyphemus eye in the general head of a company. Lady

Busshe, Lady Culmer, Mrs Mountstuart, Mr Dale, had a similarity in the variety of their expressions that made up one giant eye for him perfectly, if awfully, legible. He discerned the fact that his demon secret was abroad, universal. He ascribed it to fate. He was in the jaws of the world, on the world's teeth. This time he thought Laetitia must have betrayed him, and bowing to Lady Busshe and Lady Culmer, gallantly pressing their fingers and responding to their becks and archnesses, he ruminated on his defences before he should accost her father. He did not want to be alone with the man, and he considered how his presence might be made useful.

'I am glad to see you, Mr Dale. Pray, be seated. Is it nature asserting her strength? or the efficacy of medicine? I fancy it can't be both. You have brought us back your daughter?'

Mr Dale sank into a chair, unable to resist the hand forcing him.

'No, Sir Willoughby, no. I have not; I have not seen her since she came home this morning from Patterne.'

'Indeed? She is unwell?'

'I cannot say. She secludes herself.'

'Has locked herself in,' said Lady Busshe.

Willoughby threw her a smile. It made them intimate. This was an advantage against the world, but an exposure of himself to the abominable woman.

Dr Middleton came up to Mr Dale to apologize for not presenting his daughter Clara, whom he could find neither in nor out of the house.

'We have in Mr Dale, as I suspected,' he said to Willoughby, 'a stout ally.'

'If I may beg two minutes with you, Sir Willoughby,' said Mr Dale.

'Your visits are too rare for me to allow of your numbering the minutes,' Willoughby replied. 'We cannot let Mr Dale escape us now that we have him, I think, Dr Middleton.'

'Not without ransom,' said the Rev. Doctor.

Mr Dale shook his head. 'My strength, Sir Willoughby, will not sustain me long.'

'You are at home, Mr Dale.'

'Not far from home, in truth, but too far for an invalid beginning to grow sensible of weakness.'

'You will regard Patterne as your home, Mr Dale,' Willoughby repeated for the world to hear.

'Unconditionally?' Dr Middleton inquired, with a humourous air of dissenting.

Willoughby gave him a look that was coldly courteous, and then he looked at Lady Busshe. She nodded imperceptibly. Her eyebrows rose, and Willoughby returned a similar nod.

Translated, the signs ran thus:

'— Pestered by the Rev. gentleman: — I see you are. Is the story I have heard correct? Possibly it may err in a few details.'

This was fettering himself in loose manacles.

But Lady Busshe would not be satisfied with the compliment of the intimate looks and nods. She thought she might still be behind Mrs Mountstuart; and she was a bold woman, and anxious about him, half-crazed by the riddle of the pot she was boiling in, and having very few minutes to spare.

Not extremely reticent by nature, privileged by station, and made intimate with him by his covert looks, she stood up to him. 'One word to an old friend. Which is the father of the fortunate creature? I don't know how to behave to them.'

No time was afforded him to be disgusted with her vulgarity and audacity.

He replied, feeling her rivet his gyves: 'The house will be empty to-morrow.'

'I see. A decent withdrawal, and very well cloaked. We had a tale here of her running off to decline the honour, afraid, or on her dignity or something.'

How was it that the woman was ready to accept the altered posture of affairs in his house — if she had received a hint of them? He forgot that he had prepared her in self-defence.

'From whom did you have that?' he asked.

'Her father. And the lady aunts declare it was the cousin she refused!'

Willoughby's brain turned over. He righted it for action, and crossed the room to the ladies Eleanor and Isabel. His ears tingled. He and his whole story discussed in public! Himself unroofed! And the marvel that he of all men should be in such a tangle, naked and blown on, condemned to use his cunningest arts to unwind and cover himself, struck him as though the lord of his kind were running the gantlet of a legion of imps. He felt their lashes.

The ladies were talking to Mrs Mountstuart and Lady Culmer of Vernon and the suitableness of Laetitia to a scholar. He made sign to them, and both rose.

'It is the hour for your drive. To the cottage! Mr Dale is ill. She must come. Her sick father! No delay, going or returning. Bring her here at once.'

'Poor man!' they sighed; and 'Willoughby,' said one, and the other said: 'There is a strange misconception you will do well to correct.'

They were about to murmur what it was. He swept his hand round, and excusing themselves to their guests, obediently they retired.

Lady Busshe at his entreaty remained, and took a seat beside Lady Culmer and Mrs Mountstuart.

She said to the latter: 'You have tried scholars. What do you think?'

'Excellent, but hard to mix,' was the reply.

'I never make experiments,' said Lady Culmer.

'Some one must!' Mrs Mountstuart groaned over her dull dinner-party.

Lady Busshe consoled her. 'At any rate, the loss of a scholar is no loss to the county.'

'They are well enough in towns,' Lady Culmer said.

'And then I am sure you must have them by themselves.'

'We have nothing to regret.'

'My opinion.'

The voice of Dr Middleton in colloquy with Mr Dale swelled on a melodious thunder: 'For whom else should I plead as the passionate advocate I proclaimed myself to you, sir? There is but one man known to me who would move me to back him upon such an adventure. Willoughby, join me. I am informing Mr Dale . . .'

Willoughby stretched his hands out to Mr Dale to support him on his legs, though he had shown no sign of a wish to rise.

'You are feeling unwell, Mr Dale.'

'Do I look very ill, Sir Willoughby?'

'It will pass. Laetitia will be with us in twenty minutes.'

Mr Dale struck his hands in a clasp. He looked alarmingly ill, and satisfactorily revealed to his host how he could be made to look so.

'I was informing Mr Dale that the petitioner enjoys our concurrent good wishes: and mine in no degree less than yours, Willoughby,' observed Dr Middleton, whose billows grew the bigger for a check. He supposed himself speaking confidentially. 'Ladies have the trick, they have, I may say, the natural disposition for playing enigma now and again. Pressure is often a sovereign specific. Let it be tried upon her all round from every radiating line of the circle. You she refuses. Then I venture to propose myself to appeal to her. My daughter has assuredly an esteem for the applicant that will animate a woman's tongue in such a case. The ladies of the house will not be backward. Lastly, if necessary, we trust the lady's father to add his instances. My prescription is, to fatigue her negatives; and where no rooted objection exists, I maintain it to be the unfailing receipt for the conduct of the siege. No woman can say No forever. The defence has not such resources against even a single assailant, and we shall have solved the problem of continuous motion before she will have learned to deny in perpetuity. That I stand on.'

Willoughby glanced at Mrs Mountstuart.

'What is that?' she said. 'Treason to our sex, Dr Middleton?'

'I think I heard that no woman can say No forever!' remarked Lady Busshe.

'To a loyal gentleman, ma'am: assuming the field of the recurring request to be not unholy ground; consecrated to affirmatives rather.'

Dr Middleton was attacked by three angry bees. They made him say yes and no alternately so many times that he had to admit in men a shiftier yieldingness than women were charged with.

Willoughby gesticulated, as mute chorus on the side of the ladies; and a little show of party spirit like that, coming upon their excitement under the topic, inclined them to him genially.

He drew Mr Dale away while the conflict subsided in sharp snaps of rifles and an interval rejoinder of a cannon.

Mr Dale had shown by signs that he was growing fretfully restive under his burden of doubt.

'Sir Willoughby, I have a question. I beg you to lead me where I may ask it. I know my head is weak.'

'Mr Dale, it is answered when I say that my house is your home, and that Laetitia will soon be with us.'

'Then this report is true?'

'I know nothing of reports. You are answered.'

'Can my daughter be accused of any shadow of falseness, dishonourable dealing?'

'As little as I.'

Mr Dale scanned his face. He saw no shadow.

'For I should go to my grave bankrupt if that could be said of her; and I have never yet felt poor, though you know the extent of a pensioner's income. Then this tale of a refusal . . . ?'

'Is nonsense.'

'She has accepted?'

'There are situations, Mr Dale, too delicate to be clothed in positive definitions.'

'Ah, Sir Willoughby, but it becomes a father to see that his daughter is not forced into delicate situations. I hope all is well. I am confused. It may be my head. She puzzles me. You are not . . . Can I ask it here? You are quite . . . ? Will you moderate my anxiety? My infirmities must excuse me.'

Sir Willoughby conveyed by a shake of the head and a pressure of Mr Dale's hand, that he was not, and that he was quite.

'Dr Middleton?' said Mr Dale.

'He leaves us to-morrow.'

'Really!' The invalid wore a look as if wine had been poured into him. He routed his host's calculations by calling to the Rev. Doctor. 'We are to lose you, sir?'

Willoughby attempted an interposition, but Dr Middleton crashed through it like the lordly organ swallowing a flute.

'Not before I score my victory, Mr Dale, and establish my friend upon his rightful throne.'

'You do not leave to-morrow, sir?'

'Have you heard, sir, that I leave to-morrow?'

Mr Dale turned to Sir Willoughby.

The latter said: 'Clara named to-day. To-morrow I thought preferable.'

'Ah!' Dr Middleton towered on the swelling exclamation, but with no dark light. He radiated splendidly. 'Yes, then, to-morrow. That is, if we subdue the lady.'

He advanced to Willoughby, seized his hand, squeezed it, thanked him, praised him. He spoke under his breath, for a wonder; but: 'We are in your debt lastingly, my friend', was heard, and he was impressive, he seemed subdued, and saying aloud: 'Though I should wish to aid in the reduction of that fortress', he let it be seen that his mind was rid of a load.

Dr Middleton partly stupefied Willoughby by his way of taking it, but his conduct was too serviceable to allow of speculation on his readiness to break the match. It was the turning-point of the engagement.

Lady Busshe made a stir.

'I cannot keep my horses waiting any longer,' she said, and beckoned. Sir Willoughby was beside her immediately. 'You are admirable! perfect! Don't ask me to hold my tongue.

I retract, I recant. It *is* a fatality. I have resolved upon that view. You could stand the shot of beauty, not of brains. That is our report. There! And it's delicious to feel that the county wins you. No tea. I cannot possibly wait. And, oh! here she is. I must have a look at her. My dear Laetitia Dale!'

Willoughby hurried to Mr Dale!

'You are not to be excited, sir: compose yourself. You will recover and be strong to-morrow: you are at home; you are in your own house; you are in Laetitia's drawing-room. All will be clear to-morrow. Till to-morrow we talk riddles by consent. Sit, I beg. You stay with us.'

He met Laetitia and rescued her from Lady Busshe, murmuring, with the air of a lover who says, 'my love! my sweet!' that she had done rightly to come and come at once.

Her father had been thrown into the proper condition of clammy nervousness to create the impression. Laetitia's anxiety sat prettily on her long eyelashes as she bent over him in his chair.

Hereupon Dr Corney appeared; and his name had a bracing effect on Mr Dale. 'Corney has come to drive me to the cottage,' he said. 'I am ashamed of this public exhibition of myself, my dear. Let us go. My head is a poor one.'

Dr Corney had been intercepted. He broke from Sir Willoughby with a dozen little nods of accurate understanding of him, even to beyond the mark of the communications. He touched his patient's pulse lightly, briefly sighed with professional composure, and pronounced: 'Rest. Must not be moved. No, no, nothing serious,' he quieted Laetitia's fears, 'but rest, rest. A change of residence for a night will tone him. I will bring him a draught in the course of the evening. Yes, yes, I'll fetch everything wanted from the cottage for you and for him. Repose on Corney's forethought.'

'You are sure, Dr Corney?' said Laetitia, frightened on her father's account and on her own.

'Which aspect will be the best for Mr Dale's bedroom?' the hospitable ladies Eleanor and Isabel inquired.

'South east, decidedly: let him have the morning sun: a warm air, a vigorous air, and a bright air, and the patient wakes and sings in his bed.'

Still doubtful whether she was in a trap, Laetitia whispered to her father of the privacy and comforts of his home.

He replied to her that he thought he would rather be in his own home.

Dr Corney positively pronounced No to it.

Laetitia breathed again of home, but with the sigh of one overborne.

The ladies Eleanor and Isabel took the word from Willoughby, and said: 'But you are at home, my dear. This is your home. Your father will be at least as well attended here as at the cottage.'

She raised her eyelids on them mournfully, and by chance diverted her look to Dr Middleton, quite by chance.

It spoke eloquently to the assembly of all that Willoughby desired to be imagined.

'But there is Crossjay,' she cried. 'My cousin has gone, and the boy is left alone. I cannot have him left alone. If we, if, if, Dr Corney, you are sure it is unsafe for papa to be moved to-day, Crossjay must . . . he cannot be left.'

'Bring him with you, Corney,' said Sir Willoughby; and the little doctor heartily promised that he would, in the event of his finding Crossjay at the cottage, which he thought a distant probability.

'He gave me his word he would not go out till my return,' said Laetitia.

'And if Crossjay gave you his word,' the accents of a new voice vibrated close by, 'be certain that he will not come back with Dr Corney unless he has authority in your handwriting.'

Clara Middleton stepped gently to Laetitia, and with a manner that was an embrace, as much as kissed her for what she was doing on behalf of Crossjay. She put her lips in a pouting form to simulate saying: 'Press it.'

'He is to come,' said Laetitia.

'Then write him his permit.'

There was a chatter about Crossjay and the sentinel true to his post that he could be, during which Laetitia distressfully scribbled a line for Dr Corney to deliver to him. Clara stood near. She had rebuked herself for want of reserve in the presence of Lady Busshe and Lady Culmer, and she was guilty of a slightly excessive containment when she next addressed Laetitia. It was, like Laetitia's look at Dr Middleton, opportune: enough to make a man who watched as Willoughby did a fatalist for life: the shadow of a difference in her bearing toward Laetitia sufficed to impute acting either to her present coolness or her previous warmth. Better still, when Dr Middleton said: 'So we leave to-morrow, my dear, and I hope you have written to the Darletons', Clara flushed and beamed, and repressed her animation on a sudden, with one grave look, that might be thought regretful, to where Willoughby stood.

Chance works for us when we are good captains.

Willoughby's pride was high, though he knew himself to be keeping it up like a fearfully dexterous juggler, and for an empty reward: but he was in the toils of the world.

'Have you written? The post-bag leaves in half an hour,' he addressed her.

'We are expected, but I will write,' she replied: and her not having yet written counted in his favour.

She went to write the letter. Dr Corney had departed on his mission to fetch Crossjay and medicine. Lady Busshe was impatient to be gone. 'Corney,' she said to Lady Culmer, 'is a deadly gossip.'

'Inveterate,' was the answer.

'My poor horses!'

'Not the young pair of bays?'

'Luckily they are, my dear. And don't let me hear of dining to-night!'

Sir Willoughby was leading out Mr Dale to a quiet room,

contiguous to the invalid gentleman's bedchamber. He resigned him to Laetitia in the hall, that he might have the pleasure of conducting the ladies to their carriage.

'As little agitation as possible. Corney will soon be back,' he said, bitterly admiring the graceful subservience of Laetitia's figure to her father's weight on her arm.

He had won a desperate battle, but what had he won? What had the world given him in return for his efforts to gain it? Just a shirt, it might be said: simple scanty clothing, no warmth. Lady Busshe was unbearable; she gabbled; she was ill-bred, permitted herself to speak of Dr Middleton as ineligible, no loss to the county. And Mrs Mountstuart was hardly much above her, with her inevitable stroke of caricature: — 'You see Doctor Middleton's pulpit scampering after him with legs!' Perhaps the Rev. Doctor did punish the world for his having forsaken his pulpit, and might be conceived as haunted by it at his heels, but Willoughby was in the mood to abhor comic images; he hated the perpetrators of them and the grinners. Contempt of this laughing empty world, for which he had performed a monstrous immolation, led him to associate Dr Middleton in his mind, and Clara too, with the desireable things he had sacrificed — a shape of youth and health; a sparkling companion; a face of innumerable charms; and his own veracity; his inner sense of his dignity; and his temper, and the limpid frankness of his air of scorn, that was to him a visage of candid happiness in the dim retrospect. Haply also he had sacrificed more: he looked scientifically into the future: he might have sacrificed a nameless more. And for what? he asked again. For the favourable looks and tongues of these women whose looks and tongues he detested!

'Dr Middleton says he is indebted to me: I am deeply in *his* debt,' he remarked.

'It is we who are in *your* debt for a lovely romance, my dear Sir Willoughby,' said Lady Busshe, incapable of taking a correction, so thoroughly had he imbued her with his fiction, or with the belief that she had a good story to circulate.

Away she drove, rattling her tongue to Lady Culmer.

'A hat and horn, and she would be in the old figure of a post-boy on a hue-and-cry sheet,' said Mrs Mountstuart.

Willoughby thanked the great lady for her services, and she complimented the polished gentleman on his noble self-possession. But she complained at the same time of being defrauded of her 'charmer', Colonel De Craye, since luncheon. An absence of warmth in her compliment caused Willoughby to shrink and think the wretched shirt he had got from the world no covering after all: a breath flapped it.

'He comes to me to-morrow, I believe,' she said, reflecting on her superior knowledge of facts in comparison with Lady Busshe, who would presently be hearing of something novel, and exclaiming: 'So, *that* is why you patronized the colonel!' And it was nothing of the sort, for Mrs Mountstuart could honestly say she was not the woman to make a business of her pleasure.

'Horace is an enviable fellow,' said Willoughby, wise in The Book which bids us ever for an assuagement to fancy our friend's condition worse than our own, and recommends the deglutition of irony as the most balsamic for wounds in the whole moral pharmacopoeia.

'I don't know,' she replied, with a marked accent of deliberation.

'The colonel is to have you to himself to-morrow!'

'I can't be sure of what I shall have in the colonel!'

'Your perpetual sparkler?'

Mrs Mountstuart set her head in motion. She left the matter silent.

'I'll come for him in the morning,' she said, and her carriage whirled her off.

Either she had guessed it, or Clara had confided to her the treacherous passion of Horace De Craye.

However, the world was shut away from Patterne for the night.

CHAPTER 47

❉❉❉❉

Sir Willoughby and His Friend Horace De Craye

WILLOUGHBY shut himself up in his laboratory to brood awhile after the conflict. Sounding through himself, as it was habitual with him to do, for the plan most agreeable to his taste, he came on a strange discovery among the lower circles of that microcosm. He was no longer guided in his choice by liking and appetite: he had to put it on the edge of a sharp discrimination, and try it by his acutest judgement before it was acceptable to his heart: and knowing well the direction of his desire, he was nevertheless unable to run two strides on a wish. He had learned to read the world: his partial capacity for reading persons had fled. The mysteries of his own bosom were bare to him; but he could comprehend them only in their immediate relation to the world outside. This hateful world had caught him and transformed him to a machine. The discovery he made was, that in the gratification of the egoistic instinct we may so beset ourselves as to deal a slaughtering wound upon Self to whatsoever quarter we turn.

Surely there is nothing stranger in mortal experience. The man was confounded. At the game of Chess it is the dishonour of our adversary when we are stale-mated: but in life, combatting the world, such a winning of the game questions our sentiments.

Willoughby's interpretation of his discovery was directed by pity: he had no other strong emotion left in him. He pitied himself, and he reached the conclusion that he suffered because he was active; he could not be quiescent. Had it not been for his devotion to his house and name, never would he have stood twice the victim of womankind. Had he been selfish, he would have been the happiest of men! He said it aloud. He schemed benevolently for his unborn young, and for the persons about him: hence he was in a position forbidding a step under pain of injury to his feelings. He was generous: otherwise would he not in scorn of soul, at the outset, straight off have pitched Clara Middleton to the wanton winds? He was faithful in his affection: Laetitia Dale was beneath his roof to prove it. Both these women were examples of his power of forgiveness, and now a tender word to Clara might fasten shame on him – such was her gratitude! And if he did not marry Laetitia, laughter would be devilish all around him – such was the world's! Probably Vernon would not long be thankful for the chance which varied the monotony of his days. What of Horace? Willoughby stripped to enter the ring with Horace: he cast away disguise. That man had been the first to divide him in the all but equal slices of his egoistic from his amatory self: murder of his individuality was the crime of Horace De Craye. And further, suspicion fixed on Horace (he knew not how, except that The Book bids us be suspicious of those we hate) as the man who had betrayed his recent dealings with Laetitia.

Willoughby walked the thoroughfares of the house to meet Clara and make certain of her either for himself, or, if it must be, for Vernon, before he took another step with Laetitia Dale. Clara could reunite him, turn him once more into a whole and an animated man; and she might be willing. Her willingness to listen to Vernon promised it. 'A gentleman with a tongue would have a chance', Mrs Mountstuart had said. How much greater the chance of a lover! For he had not yet supplicated her: he had shown pride and temper. He could woo, he was a torrential wooer. And it would be glorious to swing round on Lady Busshe and the world, with Clara nestling under an arm, and protest astonishment at the erroneous and utterly unfounded anticipations of any other development. And it would righteously punish Laetitia.

Clara came downstairs, bearing her letter to Miss Darleton.

'*Must* it be posted?' Willoughby said, meeting her in the hall.

'They expect us any day, but it will be more comfortable for papa,' was her answer. She looked kindly in her new shyness.

She did not seem to think he had treated her contemptuously in flinging her to his cousin, which was odd!

'You have seen Vernon?'

'It was your wish.'

'You had a talk?'

'We conversed.'

'A long one?'

'We walked some distance.'

'Clara, I tried to make the best arrangement I could.'

'Your intention was generous.'

'He took no advantage of it?'

'It could not be treated seriously.'

'It was meant seriously.'

'There I see the generosity.'

Willoughby thought this encomium, and her consent to speak on the subject, and her scarcely embarrassed air and richness of tone in speaking, very strange: and strange was her taking him quite in earnest. Apparently she had no feminine sensation of the unwontedness and the absurdity of the matter!

'But, Clara, am I to understand that he did not speak out?'

'We are excellent friends.'

'To miss it, though his chance were the smallest!'

'You forget that it may not wear that appearance to him.'

'He spoke not one word of himself?'

'No.'

'Ah! the poor old fellow was taught to see it was hopeless – chilled. May I plead? Will you step into the laboratory for a minute? We are two sensible persons . . .'

'Pardon me, I must go to papa.'

'Vernon's personal history, perhaps . . .'

'I think it honourable to him.'

'Honourable! – 'hem!'

'By comparison.'

'Comparison with what?'

'With others.'

He drew up to relieve himself of a critical and condemnatory expiration of a certain length. This young lady knew too
much. But how physically exquisite she was!

'Could you, Clara, could you promise me – I hold to it. I
must have it, I know his shy tricks – promise me to give him
ultimately another chance? Is the idea repulsive to you?'

'It is one not to be thought of.'

'It is not repulsive?'

'Nothing could be repulsive in Mr Whitford.'

'I have no wish to annoy you, Clara.'

'I feel bound to listen to you, Willoughby. Whatever I can
do to please you, I will. It is my life-long duty.'

'Could you, Clara, could you conceive it, could you simply
conceive it – give him your hand?'

'As a friend. Oh, yes.'

'In marriage.'

She paused. She, so penetrative of him when he opposed
her, was hoodwinked when he softened her feelings: for the
heart, though the clearest, is not the most constant instructor
of the head; the heart, unlike the often obtuser head, works for
itself and not for the commonwealth.

'You are so kind . . . I would do much . . .' she said.

'Would you accept him – marry him? He is poor.'

'I am not ambitious of wealth.'

'*Would* you marry him?'

'Marriage is not in my thoughts.'

'But could you marry him?'

Willoughby expected no. In his expectation of it he hung
inflated.

She said these words: 'I could engage to marry no one else.'

His amazement breathed without a syllable.

He flapped his arms, resembling for the moment those birds

of enormous body which attempt a rise upon their wings and achieve a hop.

'Would you engage it?' he said, content to see himself stepped on as an insect if he could but feel the agony of his false friend Horace – their common pretensions to win her were now of that comparative size.

'Oh, there can be no necessity. And an oath – no!' said Clara, inwardly shivering at a recollection.

'But you could?'

'My wish is to please you.'

'You could?'

'I said so.'

It has been known to the patriotic mountaineer of a hoary pile of winters, with little life remaining in him, but that little on fire for his country, that by the brink of the precipice he has flung himself on a young and lusty invader, dedicating himself exultingly to death if only he may score a point for his country by extinguishing in his country's enemy the stronger man. So likewise did Willoughby, in the blow that deprived him of hope, exult in the toppling over of Horace De Craye. They perished together, but which one sublimely relished the headlong descent? And Vernon taken by Clara would be Vernon simply tolerated. And Clara taken by Vernon would be Clara previously touched, smirched. Altogether he could enjoy his fall.

It was at least upon a comfortable bed, where his pride would be dressed daily and would never be disagreeably treated.

He was henceforth Laetitia's own. The bell telling of Dr Corney's return was a welcome sound to Willoughby, and he said good-humouredly: 'Wait, Clara, you will see your hero Crossjay.'

Crossjay and Dr Corney tumbled into the hall. Willoughby caught Crossjay under the arms to give him a lift in the old fashion pleasing to Clara to see. The boy was heavy as lead.

'I had work to hook him and worse to net him,' said Dr Corney. 'I had to make him believe he was to nurse every soul in the house, you among them, Miss Middleton.'

Willoughby pulled the boy aside.

Crossjay came back to Clara heavier in looks than his limbs had been. She dropped her letter in the hall-box, and took his hand to have a private hug of him. When they were alone, she said: 'Crossjay, my dear, my dear! you look unhappy.'

'Yes, and who wouldn't be, and you're not to marry Sir Willoughby!' his voice threatened a cry. 'I know you're not, for Dr Corney says you are going to leave.'

'Did you so very much wish it, Crossjay?'

'I should have seen a lot of you, and I sha'n't see you at all, and I'm sure if I'd known I wouldn't have – And he has been and tipped me this.'

Crossjay opened his fist in which lay three gold pieces.

'That was very kind of him,' said Clara.

'Yes, but how can I keep it?'

'By handing it to Mr Whitford to keep for you.'

'Yes, but, Miss Middleton, oughtn't I to tell him? I mean Sir Willoughby.'

'What?'

'Why, that I' – Crossjay got close to her – 'why, that I, that I – you know what you used to say. I wouldn't tell a lie, but oughtn't I, without his asking . . . and this money! I don't mind being turned out again.'

'Consult Mr Whitford,' said Clara.

'I know what you think, though.'

'Perhaps you had better not say anything at present, dear boy.'

'But what am I to do with this money?'

Crossjay held the gold pieces out as things that had not yet mingled with his ideas of possession.

'I listened, and I told of him,' he said. 'I couldn't help listening, but I went and told; and I don't like being here, and his money, and he not knowing what I did. Haven't you heard? I'm certain I know what you think, and so do I, and I must take my luck. I'm always in mischief, getting into a mess or getting out of it. I don't mind, I really don't, Miss Middleton, I can sleep in a tree quite comfortably. If you're not going to be here, I'd just as soon be anywhere. I must try to earn my living some day. And why not a cabin-boy? Sir Cloudesley Shovel [34] was no better. And I don't mind his being wrecked at last, if you're drowned an admiral. So I shall go and ask him to take his money back, and if he asks me I shall tell him, and there. You know what it is: I guessed that from what Dr Corney said. I'm sure I know you're thinking what's manly. Fancy me keeping his money, and you not marrying him! I wouldn't mind driving a plough. I shouldn't make a bad gamekeeper. Of course I love boats best, but you can't have everything.'

'Speak to Mr Whitford first,' said Clara, too proud of the boy for growing as she had trained him, to advise a course of conduct opposed to his notions of manliness, though now that her battle was over she would gladly have acquiesced in little casuistic compromises for the sake of the general peace.

Some time later Vernon and Dr Corney were arguing upon the question. Corney was dead against the sentimental view of the morality of the case propounded by Vernon as coming from Miss Middleton and partly shared by him. 'If it's on the boy's mind,' Vernon said, 'I can't prohibit his going to Willoughby and making a clean breast of it, especially as it involves me, and sooner or later I should have to tell him myself.'

Dr Corney said no at all points. 'Now hear me,' he said, finally. 'This is between ourselves, and no breach of confidence, which I'd not be guilty of for forty friends, though I'd give my hand from the wrist-joint for one – my left, that's to say. Sir Willoughby puts me one or two searching interrogations on a point of interest to him, his house and name. Very well, and good night to that, and I wish Miss Dale had been ten years younger, or had passed the ten with no heart-risings and sinkings wearing to the tissues of the frame and the moral fibre to boot. She'll have a fairish health, with a little occasional doctoring; taking her rank and wealth in right earnest, and shying her pen back to Mother Goose. She'll do. And, by the way, I think it's to the credit of my sagacity that I fetched Mr Dale here fully primed, and roused the neighbourhood, which I did, and so fixed our gentleman, neat as a prodded eel on a pair of prongs – namely, the positive fact and the general knowledge of it. But, mark me, my friend. We understand one another at a nod. This boy, young Squire Crossjay, is a good stiff hearty kind of a Saxon boy, out of whom you may cut as gallant a fellow as ever wore epaulettes. I like him, you like him, Miss Dale and Miss Middleton like him; and Sir Willoughby Patterne, of Patterne Hall and other places, won't be indisposed to like him mightily in the event of the sun being seen to shine upon him with a particular determination to make him appear a prominent object, because a solitary, and a Patterne.' Dr Corney lifted his chest and his finger: 'Now mark me, and verbum sap: Crossjay must not offend Sir Willoughby. I say no more. Look ahead. Miracles happen, but it's best to reckon that they won't. Well, now, and Miss Dale. She'll not be cruel.'

'It appears as if she would,' said Vernon, meditating on the cloudy sketch Dr Corney had drawn.

'She can't, my friend. Her position's precarious; her father has little besides a pension. And her writing damages her health. She can't. And she likes the baronet. Oh, it's only a little fit of proud blood. She's the woman for him. She'll manage him – give him an idea he's got a lot of ideas. It'd kill her father if she were obstinate. He talked to me, when I told him of the business, about his dream fulfilled, and if the dream turns to vapour, he'll be another example that we hang more upon dreams than realities for nourishment, and medicine too. Last week I couldn't have got him out of his house with all my art and science. Oh, she'll come round.

Her father prophesied this, and I'll prophesy that. She's fond of him.'

'She was.'

'She sees through him?'

'Without quite doing justice to him now,' said Vernon. 'He can be generous – in his way.'

'How?' Corney inquired, and was informed that he should hear in time to come.

Meanwhile Colonel De Craye, after hovering over the park and about the cottage for the opportunity of pouncing on Miss Middleton alone, had returned crest-fallen for once, and plumped into Willoughby's hands.

'My dear Horace,' Willoughby said, 'I've been looking for you all the afternoon. The fact is – I fancy you'll think yourself lured down here on false pretences: but the truth is, I am not so much to blame as the world will suppose. In point of fact, to be brief, Miss Dale and I . . . I never consult other men how they would have acted. The fact of the matter is, Miss Middleton . . . I fancy you have partly guessed it.'

'Partly,' said De Craye.

'Well, she has a liking that way, and if it should turn out strong enough, it's the best arrangement I can think of.'

The lively play of the colonel's features fixed in a blank inquiry.

'One can back a good friend for making a good husband,' said Willoughby. 'I could not break with her in the present stage of affairs without seeing to that. And I can speak of her highly, though she and I have seen in time that we do not suit one another. My wife must have brains.'

'I have always thought it,' said Colonel De Craye, glistening, and looking hungry as a wolf through his wonderment.

'There will not be a word against her, you understand. You know my dislike of tattle and gossip. However, let it fall on me; my shoulders are broad. I have done my utmost to persuade her, and there seems a likelihood of her consenting. She tells me her wish is to please me, and this will please me.'

'Certainly. Who's the gentleman?'

'My best friend, I tell you. I could hardly have proposed another. Allow this business to go on smoothly just now.'

There was an uproar within the colonel to blind his wits, and Willoughby looked so friendly that it was possible to suppose the man of projects had mentioned his best friend to Miss Middleton.

And who was the best friend?

Not having accused himself of treachery, the quick-eyed colonel was duped.

'Have you his name handy, Willoughby?'

'That would be unfair to him at present, Horace – ask yourself – and to her. Things are in a ticklish posture at present. Don't be hasty.'

'Certainly. I don't ask. Initials'll do.'

'You have a remarkable aptitude for guessing, Horace, and this case offers you no tough problem – if ever you acknowledged toughness. I have a regard for her and for him – for both pretty equally; you know I have, and I should be thoroughly thankful to bring the matter about.'

'Lordly!' said De Craye.

'I don't see it. I call it sensible.'

'Oh, undoubtedly. The style, I mean. Tolerably antique?'

'Novel, I should say, and not the worse for that. We want plain practical dealings between men and women. Usually we go the wrong way to work. And I loathe sentimental rubbish.'

De Craye hummed an air. 'But the lady?' said he.

'I told you, there seems a likelihood of her consenting.'

Willoughby's fish gave a perceptible little leap now that he had been taught to exercise his aptitude for guessing.

'Without any of the customary preliminaries on the side of the gentleman?' he said.

'We must put him through his paces, friend Horace. He's a notorious blunderer with women; hasn't a word for them, never marked a conquest.'

De Craye crested his plumes under the agreeable banter. He presented a face humourously sceptical.

'The lady is positively not indisposed to give the poor fellow a hearing?'

'I have cause to think she is not,' said Willoughby, glad of acting the indifference to her which could talk of her inclinations.

'Cause?'

'Good cause.'

'Bless us!'

'As good as one can have with a woman.'

'Ah!'

'I assure you.'

'Ah! Does it seem like her, though?'

'Well, she wouldn't engage herself to accept him.'

'Well, that seems more like her.'

'But she said she could engage to marry no one else.'

The colonel sprang up, crying: 'Clara Middleton said it?' He curbed himself. 'That's a bit of wonderful compliancy.'

'She wishes to please me. We separate on those terms. And I wish her happiness. I've developed a heart lately and taken to think of others.'

'Nothing better. You appear to make cock sure of the other party – our friend?'

'You know him too well, Horace, to doubt his readiness.'

'Do *you*, Willoughby?'

'She has money and good looks. Yes, I can say I do.'

'It wouldn't be much of a man who'd want hard pulling to that lighted altar!'

'And if he requires persuasion, you and I, Horace, might bring him to his senses.'

'Kicking, 'twould be!'

'I like to see everybody happy about me,' said Willoughby, naming the hour as time to dress for dinner.

The sentiment he had delivered was De Craye's excuse for grasping his hand and complimenting him; but the colonel betrayed himself by doing it with an extreme fervour almost tremulous.

'When shall we hear more?' he said.

'Oh, probably to-morrow,' said Willoughby. 'Don't be in such a hurry.'

'I'm an infant asleep!' the colonel replied, departing.

He resembled one, to Willoughby's mind: or a traitor drugged.

'There is a fellow I thought had some brains!'

Who are not fools to be set spinning if we choose to whip them with their vanity! It is the consolation of the great to watch them spin. But the pleasure is loftier, and may comfort our un-merited misfortune for a while, in making a false friend drunk.

Willoughby, among his many preoccupations, had the satisfaction of seeing the effect of drunkenness on Horace De Craye when the latter was in Clara's presence. He could have laughed. Cut in keen epigram were the marginal notes added by him to that chapter of The Book which treats of friends and a woman; and had he not been profoundly preoccupied, troubled by recent intelligence communicated by the ladies, his aunts, he would have played the two together for the royal amusement afforded him by his friend Horace.

CHAPTER 48

✕✕✕✕

The Lovers

THE hour was close upon eleven at night. Laetitia sat in the room adjoining her father's bedchamber. Her elbow was on the table beside her chair, and two fingers pressed her temples. The state between thinking and feeling, when both are molten and flow by us, is one of our nature's intermissions, coming after thought has quieted the fiery nerves, and can do no more. She seemed to be meditating. She was conscious only of a struggle past.

She answered a tap at the door, and raised her eyes on Clara. Clara stepped softly. 'Mr Dale is asleep?'

'I hope so.'

'Ah! dear friend.'

Laetitia let her hand be pressed.

'Have you had a pleasant evening?'

'Mr Whitford and papa have gone to the library.'

'Colonel De Craye has been singing?'

'Yes – with a voice! I thought of you upstairs, but could not ask him to sing piano.'

'He is probably exhilarated.'

'One would suppose it: he sang well.'

'You are not aware of any reason?'

'It cannot concern me.'

Clara was in rosy colour, but could meet a steady gaze.

'And Crossjay has gone to bed?'

'Long since. He was at dessert. He would not touch anything.'

'He is a strange boy.'

'Not very strange, Laetitia.'

'He did not come to me to wish me good-night.'

'That is not strange.'

'It is his habit at the cottage and here; and he professes to like me.'

'Oh, he does. I may have wakened his enthusiasm, but you he loves.'

'Why do you say it is not strange, Clara?'

'He fears you a little.'

'And why should Crossjay fear me?'

'Dear, I will tell you. Last night – You will forgive him, for it was by accident: his own bed-room door was locked and he ran down to the drawing-room and curled himself up on the

ottoman, and fell asleep, under that padded silken coverlet of
the ladies – boots and all, I am afraid!'

Laetitia profited by this absurd allusion, thanking Clara in
her heart for the refuge.

'He should have taken off his boots,' she said.

'He slept there, and woke up. Dear, he meant no harm.
Next day he repeated what he had heard. You will blame
him. He meant well in his poor boy's head. And now it is
over the county. Ah! do not frown.'

'That explains Lady Busshe!' exclaimed Laetitia.

'Dear, dear friend,' said Clara. 'Why – I presume on your
tenderness for me; but let me: to-morrow I go – why will you
reject your happiness? Those kind good ladies are deeply
troubled. They say your resolution is inflexible; you resist
their entreaties and your father's. Can it be that you have any
doubt of the strength of this attachment? I have none. I have
never had a doubt that it was the strongest of his feelings. If
before I go I could see you ... both happy, I should be
relieved, I should rejoice.'

Laetitia said, quietly: 'Do you remember a walk we had one
day together to the cottage?'

Clara put up her hands with the motion of intending to stop
her ears.

'Before I go!' said she. 'If I might know this was to be,
which all desire, before I leave, I should not feel as I do now.
I long to see you happy ... him, yes, him too. Is it like asking
you to pay my debt? Then, please! But, no; I am not more
than partly selfish on this occasion. He has won my gratitude.
He can be really generous.'

'An Egoist?'

'Who is?'

'You have forgotten our conversation on the day of our
walk to the cottage?'

'Help me to forget it – that day, and those days, and all
those days! I should be glad to think I passed a time beneath
the earth, and have risen again. I was the Egoist. I am sure, if I

had been buried, I should not have stood up seeing myself more vilely stained, soiled, disfigured – oh! Help me to forget my conduct, Laetitia. He and I were unsuited – and I remember I blamed myself then. You and he are not: and now I can perceive the pride that can be felt in him. The worst that can be said is that he schemes too much.'

'Is there any fresh scheme?' said Laetitia.

The rose came over Clara's face.

'You have not heard? It was impossible, but it was kindly intended. Judging by my own feeling at this moment, I can understand his. We love to see our friends established.'

Laetitia bowed. 'My curiosity is piqued, of course.'

'Dear friend, to-morrow we shall be parted. I trust to be thought of by you as a little better in grain than I have appeared, and my reason for trusting it is that I know I have been always honest – a boorish young woman in my stupid mad impatience: but not insincere. It is no lofty ambition to desire to be remembered in that character, but such is your Clara, she discovers. I will tell you. It is his wish . . . his wish that I should promise to give my hand to Mr Whitford. You see the kindness.'

Laetitia's eyes widened and fixed:

'You think it kindness?'

'The intention. He sent Mr Whitford to me, and I was taught to expect him.'

'Was that quite kind to Mr Whitford?'

'What an impression I must have made on you during that walk to the cottage, Laetitia! I do not wonder; I was in a fever.'

'You consented to listen?'

'I really did. It astonishes me now, but I thought I could not refuse.'

'My poor friend Vernon Whitford tried a love speech?'

'He? no: Oh! no.'

'You discouraged him?'

'I? No.'

'Gently, I mean.'

'No.'

'Surely you did not dream of trifling? He has a deep heart.'

'Has he?'

'You ask that: and you know something of him.'

'He did not expose it to me, dear; not even the surface of the mighty deep.'

Laetitia knitted her brows.

'No,' said Clara, 'not a coquette: she is not a coquette, I assure you.'

With a laugh, Laetitia replied: 'You have still the "dreadful power" you made me feel that day.'

'I wish I could use it to good purpose!'

'He did not speak?'

'Of Switzerland, Tyrol, the Iliad, Antigone.'

'That was all?'

'No, Political Economy. Our situation, you will own, was unexampled: or mine was. Are you interested in me?'

'I should be if I knew your sentiments.'

'I was grateful to Sir Willoughby: grieved for Mr Whitford.'

'Real grief?'

'Because the task imposed on him of showing me politely that he did not enter into his cousin's ideas was evidently very great, extremely burdensome.'

'You, so quick-eyed in some things, Clara!'

'He felt for me. I saw that in his avoidance of . . . And he was, as he always is, pleasant. We rambled over the park for I know not how long, though it did not seem long.'

'Never touching that subject?'

'Not ever neighbouring it, dear. A gentleman should esteem the girl he would ask . . . certain questions. I fancy he has a liking for me as a volatile friend.'

'If he had offered himself?'

'Despising me?'

'You can be childish, Clara. Probably you delight to tease. He had his time of it, and it is now my turn.'

'But he must despise me a little.'

'Are you blind?'

'Perhaps, dear, we both are, a little.'

The ladies looked deeper into one another.

'Will you answer me?' said Laetitia.

'Your if? If he had, it would have been an act of condescension.'

'You are too slippery.'

'Stay, dear Laetitia. He was considerate in forbearing to pain me.'

'That is an answer. You allowed him to perceive that it would have pained you.'

'Dearest, if I may convey to you what I was, in a simile for comparison: I think I was like a fisherman's float on the water, perfectly still, and ready to go down at any instant, or up. So much for my behaviour.'

'Similes have the merit of satisfying the finder of them, and cheating the hearer,' said Laetitia. 'You admit that your feelings would have been painful.'

'I was a fisherman's float: please admire my simile; any way you like, this way or that, or so quiet as to tempt the eyes to go to sleep. And suddenly I might have disappeared in the depths, or flown in the air. But no fish bit.'

'Well, then, to follow you, supposing the fish or the fisherman, for I don't know which is which . . . Oh, no, no: this is too serious for imagery. I am to understand that you thanked him at least for his reserve.'

'Yes.'

'Without the slightest encouragement to him to break it?'

'A fisherman's float, Laetitia!'

Baffled and sighing, Laetitia kept silence for a space.

The simile chafed her wits with a suspicion of a meaning hidden in it.

'If he had spoken?' she said.

'He is too truthful a man.'

'And the railings of men at pussy women who wind about and will not be brought to a mark, become intelligible to me.'

'Then Laetitia, if he had spoken, if, and one could have imagined him sincere . . .'

'So truthful a man?'

'I am looking at myself. If! – why, then, I should have burnt to death with shame. Where have I read? – some story – of an inextinguishable spark. That would have been shot into my heart.'

'Shame, Clara? You are free.'

'As much as remains of me.'

'I could imagine a certain shame, in such a position, where there was no feeling but pride.'

'I could not imagine it where there was no feeling but pride.'

Laetitia mused. 'And you dwell on the kindness of a proposition so extraordinary!' Gaining some light, impatiently she cried: 'Vernon loves you.'

'Do not say it!'

'I have seen it.'

'I have never had a sign of it.'

'There is the proof.'

'When it might have been shown again and again!'

'The greater proof!'

'Why did he not speak when he was privileged? – strangely, but privileged.'

'He feared.'

'Me?'

'Feared to wound you – and himself as well, possibly. Men may be pardoned for thinking of themselves in these cases.'

'But why should he fear?'

'That another was dearer to you?'

'What cause had I given . . . Ah! see! He could fear that; suspect it! See his opinion of me! Can he care for such a girl? Abuse me, Laetitia. I should like a good round of abuse. I need

purification by fire. What have I been in this house? I have a
sense of whirling through it like a madwoman. And to be
loved, after it all! – No! we must be hearing a tale of an anti-
quary prizing a battered relic of the battle-field that no one
else would look at. To be loved, I see, is to feel our littleness,
hollowness – feel shame. We come out in all our spots. Never
to have given me one sign, when a lover would have been so
tempted! Let me be incredulous, my own dear Laetitia.
Because he is a man of honour, you would say! But are you
unconscious of the torture you inflict? For if I am – you say
it – loved by this gentleman, what an object it is he loves –
that has gone clamouring about more immodestly than
women will bear to hear of, and she herself to think of! Oh,
I have seen my own heart. It is a frightful spectre. I have seen a
weakness in me that would have carried me anywhere. And
truly I shall be charitable to women – I have gained that. But
loved! by Vernon Whitford! The miserable little me to be
taken up and loved after tearing myself to pieces! Have you
been simply speculating? You have no positive knowledge of
it! Why do you kiss me?'

'Why do you tremble and blush so?'

Clara looked at her as clearly as she could. She bowed her
head. 'It makes my conduct worse!'

She received a tenderer kiss for that. It was her avowal, and
it was understood: to know that she had loved or had been
ready to love him, shadowed her in the retrospect.

'Ah! you read me through and through,' said Clara, sliding
to her for a whole embrace.

'Then there never was cause for him to fear?' Laetitia
whispered.

Clara slid her head more out of sight. 'Not that my heart
. . . But I said I have seen it; and it is unworthy of him. And if,
as I think now, I could have been so rash, so weak, wicked, unpardonable – such thoughts were in me! – then to hear him
speak would make it necessary for me to uncover myself and
tell him – incredible to you, yes! – that while . . . yes, Laetitia,

all this is true: and thinking of him as the noblest of men, I could have welcomed any help to cut my knot. So there,' said Clara, issuing from her nest with winking eyelids, 'you see the pain I mentioned.'

'Why did you not explain it to me at once?'

'Dearest, I wanted a century to pass.'

'And you feel that it has passed?'

'Yes; in Purgatory – with an angel by me. My report of the place will be favourable. Good angel, I have yet to say something.'

'Say it, and expiate.'

'I think I did fancy once or twice, very dimly, and especially to-day . . . properly I ought not to have had any idea: but his coming to me, and his not doing as another would have done, seemed . . . A gentleman of real nobleness does not carry the common light for us to read him by. I wanted his voice; but silence, I think, did tell me more: if a nature like mine could only have had faith without hearing the rattle of a tongue.'

A knock at the door caused the ladies to exchange looks.

Laetitia rose as Vernon entered.

'I am just going to my father for a few minutes,' she said.

'And I have just come from yours,' Vernon said to Clara.

She observed a very threatening expression in him.

The sprite of contrariety mounted to her brain to indemnify her for her recent self-abasement. Seeing the bedroom door shut on Laetitia, she said: 'And of course papa has gone to bed'; implying, 'otherwise –'

'Yes, he has gone. He wished me well.'

'His formula of good-night would embrace that wish.'

'And failing, it will be good-night for good to me!'

Clara's breathing gave a little leap. 'We leave early to-morrow.'

'I know. I have an appointment at Bregenz for June.'

'So soon? With papa?'

'And from there we break into Tyrol, and round away to the right, Southward.'

'To the Italian Alps! And was it assumed that I should be of this expedition?'

'Your father speaks dubiously.'

'You have spoken of me, then?'

'I ventured to speak of you. I am not over-bold, as you know.'

Her lovely eyes troubled the lids to hide their softness.

'Papa should not think of my presence with him dubiously.'

'He leaves it to you to decide.'

'Yes, then: many times: all that can be uttered.'

'Do you consider what you are saying?'

'Mr Whitford, I shut my eyes and say Yes.'

'Beware. I give you one warning. If you shut your eyes –'

'Of course,' she flew from him, 'big mountains must be satisfied with my admiration at their feet.'

'That will do for a beginning.'

'They speak encouragingly.'

'One of them.' Vernon's breast heaved high.

'To be at your feet makes a mountain of you?' said she.

'With the heart of a mouse if that satisfies me!'

'You tower too high; you are inaccessible.'

'I give you a second warning. You may be seized and lifted.'

'Some one would stoop, then.'

'To plant you like the flag on the conquered peak!'

'You have indeed been talking to papa, Mr Whitford.'

Vernon changed his tone.

'Shall I tell you what he said?'

'I know his language so well.'

'He said –'

'But you have acted on it?'

'Only partly. He said –'

'You will teach me nothing.'

'He said . . .'

'Vernon, no! oh! not in this house!'

That supplication coupled with his name confessed the end to which her quick vision perceived she was being led, where she would succumb.

She revived the same shrinking in him from a breath of their great word yet: not here; somewhere in the shadow of the mountains.

But he was sure of her. And their hands might join. The two hands thought so, or did not think, behaved like innocents.

The spirit of Dr Middleton, as Clara felt, had been blown into Vernon, rewarding him for forthright outspeaking. Over their books, Vernon had abruptly shut up a volume and related the tale of the house. 'Has this man a spice of religion in him?' the Rev. Doctor asked midway. Vernon made out a fair general case for his cousin in that respect. 'The complemental dot on his i of a commonly civilized human creature!' said Dr Middleton, looking at his watch and finding it too late to leave the house before morning. The risky communication was to come. Vernon was proceeding with the narrative of Willoughby's generous plan when Dr Middleton electrified him by calling out: 'He whom of all men living I should desire my daughter to espouse!' and Willoughby rose in the Rev. Doctor's esteem: he praised that sensibly minded gentleman, who could acquiesce in the turn of mood of a little maid, albeit Fortune had withheld from him a taste of the switch at school. The father of the little maid's appreciation of her volatility was exhibited in his exhortation to Vernon to be off to her at once with his authority to finish her moods and assure him of peace in the morning. Vernon hesitated. Dr Middleton remarked upon being not so sure that it was not he who had done the mischief. Thereupon Vernon, to prove his honesty, made his own story bare. 'Go to her,' said Dr Middleton. Vernon proposed a meeting in Switzerland, to which Dr Middleton assented, adding: 'Go to her': and as he appeared a total stranger to the decorum of the situation, Vernon put his delicacy aside, and taking his heart up, obeyed. He too had pondered on Clara's consent to meet him after she knew of Willoughby's terms, and her grave sweet manner during the ramble over the park. Her father's breath had been blown into him; so now, with nothing but the faith lying in sensation to convince him of his happy fortune (and how unconvincing that may be until the mind has grasped and stamped it, we experience even then when we acknowledge that we are most blessed), he held her hand. And if it was hard for him, for both, but harder for the man, to restrain their particular word from a flight to heaven when the cage stood open and nature beckoned, he was practised in self-mastery, and she loved him the more.

Laetitia was a witness of their union of hands on her coming back to the room.

They promised to visit her very early in the morning, neither of them conceiving that they left her to a night of storm and tears.

She sat meditating on Clara's present appreciation of Sir Willoughby's generosity.

CHAPTER 49

✗✗✗✗

Laetitia and Sir Willoughby

WE cannot be abettors of the tribes of imps whose revelry is in the frailties of our poor human constitution. They have their place and their service, and so long as we continue to be what we are now, they will hang on to us, restlessly plucking at the garments which cover our nakedness, nor ever ceasing to twitch them and strain at them until they have fairly stripped us for one of their horrible Walpurgis nights: when the laughter heard is of a character to render laughter frightful to the ears of men throughout the remainder of their days. But if in these festival hours under the beams of Hecate they are uncontrollable by the Comic Muse, she will not flatter them with her presence during the course of their insane and impious hilarities, whereof a description would out-Brocken Brockens and make Graymalkin and Paddock too intimately our familiars.

It shall suffice to say that from hour to hour of the midnight to the grey-eyed morn, assisted at intervals by the ladies Eleanor and Isabel, and by Mr Dale awakened and re-awakened – hearing the vehemence of his petitioning outcry to soften her obduracy – Sir Willoughby pursued Laetitia with solicitations to espouse him, until the inveteracy of his wooing wore the aspect of the life-long love he raved of aroused to a state of mania. He appeared, he departed, he returned; and all the while his imps were about him and upon him, riding him, prompting, driving, inspiring him with outrageous pathos, an eloquence to move any one but the dead, which its object seemed to be in her torpid attention. He heard them, he talked to them, caressed them; he flung them off, and ran from them, and stood vanquished for them to mount him again and swarm on him. There are men thus imp-haunted. Men who, setting their minds upon an object, must have it, breed imps. They are noted for their singularities, as their converse with the invisible and amazing distractions, are called. Willoughby became aware of them that night. He said to himself, upon one of his dashes into solitude: I believed I am possessed! And if he did not actually believe it, but only suspected it, or framed speech to account for the transformation he had undergone into a desperately beseeching creature, having lost acquaintance with his habitual personality, the operations of an impish host had undoubtedly smitten his consciousness.

He had them in his brain: for while burning with an ardour for Laetitia, that incited him to frantic excesses of language and comportment, he was aware of shouts of the names of

Lady Busshe and Mrs Mountstuart Jenkinson, the which, freezing him as they did, were directly the cause of his hurrying to a wilder extravagance and more headlong determination to subdue before break of day the woman he almost dreaded to behold by daylight, though he had now passionately persuaded himself of his love of her. He could not, he felt, stand in the daylight without her. She was his morning. She was, he raved, his predestinated wife. He cried, 'Darling!' both to her and to solitude. Every prescription of his ideal of demeanour as an example to his class and country, was abandoned by the enamoured gentleman. He had lost command of his countenance. He stooped so far as to kneel, and not gracefully. Nay, it is in the chronicles of the invisible host around him, that in a fit of supplication, upon a cry of 'Laetitia!' twice repeated, he whimpered.

Let so much suffice. And indeed not without reason do the multitudes of the servants of the Muse in this land of social policy avoid scenes of an inordinate wantonness, which detract from the dignity of our leaders and menace human nature with confusion. Sagacious are they who conduct the individual on broad lines, over familiar tracks, under well-known characteristics. What men will do, and amorously minded men will do, is less the question than what it is politic they should be shown to do.

The night wore through. Laetitia was bent, but had not yielded. She had been obliged to say – and how many times she could not bear to recollect: 'I do not love you; I have no love to give'; and issuing from such a night to look again upon the face of day, she scarcely felt that she was alive.

The contest was renewed by her father with the singing of the birds. Mr Dale then produced the first serious impression she had received. He spoke of their circumstances, of his being taken from her and leaving her to poverty, in weak health; of the injury done to her health by writing for bread; and of the oppressive weight he would be relieved of by her consenting.

He no longer implored her; he put the case on common ground.

And he wound up: 'Pray do not be ruthless, my girl.'

The practical statement, and this adjuration incongruously to conclude it, harmonized with her disordered understanding, her loss of all sentiment, and her desire to be kind. She sighed to herself: 'Happily, it is over!'

Her father was too weak to rise. He fell asleep. She was bound down to the house for hours; and she walked round her room, here at the door, there at the windows, thinking of Clara's remark of a century passing. She had not wished it, but a light had come on her to show her what she would have supposed a century could not have effected: she saw the impossible of overnight a possible thing: not desireable, yet possible, wearing the features of the possible. Happily, she had resisted too firmly to be again besought.

Those features of the possible once beheld allured the mind to reconsider them. Wealth gives us the power to do good on earth. Wealth enables us to see the world, the beautiful scenes of the earth. Laetitia had long thirsted both for a dowering money-bag at her girdle, and the wings to fly abroad over lands which had begun to seem fabulous in her starved imagination. Then, moreover, if her sentiment for this gentleman was gone, it was only a delusion gone; accurate sight and knowledge of him would not make a woman the less helpful mate. That was the mate he required: and he could be led. A sentimental attachment would have been serviceless to him. Not so the woman allied by a purely rational bond: and he wanted guiding. Happily, she had told him too much of her feeble health and her lovelessness to be reduced to submit to another attack.

She busied herself in her room, arranging for her departure, so that no minutes might be lost after her father had breakfasted and dressed.

Clara was her earliest visitor, and each asked the other whether she had slept, and took the answer from the face presented to her. The rings of Laetitia's eyes were very dark. Clara was her mirror, and she said: 'A singular object to be persecuted through a night for her hand! I know these two damp dead leaves I wear on my cheeks to remind me of midnight vigils. But you have slept well, Clara.'

'I have slept well, and yet I could say I have not slept at all, Laetitia. I was with you, dear, part in dream and part in thought: hoping to find you sensible before I go.'

'Sensible. That is the word for me.'

Laetitia briefly sketched the history of the night; and Clara said, with a manifest sincerity that testified of her gratitude to Sir Willoughby: 'Could you resist him, so earnest as he is?'

Laetitia saw the human nature, without sourness: and replied, 'I hope, Clara, you will not begin with a large stock of sentiment, for there is nothing like it for making you hard, matter-of-fact, worldly, calculating.'

The next visitor was Vernon, exceedingly anxious for news of Mr Dale. Laetitia went into her father's room to obtain it for him. Returning, she found them both with sad visages, and she ventured, in alarm for them, to ask the cause.

'It's this,' Vernon said: 'Willoughby will everlastingly tease that boy to be loved by him. Perhaps, poor fellow, he had an excuse last night. Anyhow, he went into Crossjay's room this morning, woke him up and talked to him, and set the lad crying, and what with one thing and another Crossjay got a berry in his throat, as he calls it, and poured out everything he knew and all he had done. I needn't tell you the consequence. He has ruined himself here for good, so I must take him.'

Vernon glanced at Clara. 'You must indeed,' said she. 'He is my boy as well as yours. No chance of pardon?'

'It's not likely.'

'Laetitia!'

'What can I do?'

'Oh! what can you not do?'

'I do *not* know.'

'Teach him to forgive!'

Laetitia's brows were heavy and Clara forbore to torment her.

She would not descend to the family breakfast-table. Clara would fain have stayed to drink tea with her in her own room, but a last act of conformity was demanded of the liberated young lady. She promised to run up the moment breakfast was over. Not unnaturally, therefore, Laetitia supposed it to be she to whom she gave admission, half an hour later, with a glad cry of, 'Come in, dear.'

The knock had sounded like Clara's.

Sir Willoughby entered.

He stepped forward. He seized her hands. 'Dear!' he said. 'You cannot withdraw that. You call me dear. I am, I must be dear to you. The word is out, by accident or not, but, by heaven, I have it and I give it up to no one. And love me or not – marry me, and my love will bring it back to you. You have taught me I am not so strong. I must have you by my side. You have powers I did not credit you with.'

'You are mistaken in me, Sir Willoughby,' Laetitia said feebly, outworn as she was.

'A woman who can resist me by declining to be my wife, through a whole night of entreaty, has the quality I need for my house, and I will batter at her ears for months, with as little rest as I had last night, before I surrender my chance of her. But I told you last night I want you within the twelve hours. I have staked my pride on it. By noon you are mine: you are introduced to Mrs Mountstuart as mine, as the lady of my life and house. And to the world! I shall not let you go.'

'You will not detain me here, Sir Willoughby?'

'I will detain you. I will use force and guile. I will spare nothing.'

He raved for a term, as he had done overnight.

On his growing rather breathless, Laetitia said: 'You do not ask me for love?'

'I do not. I pay you the higher compliment of asking for *you*, love or no love. My love shall be enough. Reward me or not. I am not used to be denied.'

'But do you know what you ask for? Do you remember what I told you of myself? I am hard, materialistic; I have lost faith in romance, the skeleton is present with me all over life. And my health is not good. I crave for money. I should marry to be rich. I should not worship you. I should be a burden, barely a living one, irresponsive and cold. Conceive such a wife, Sir Willoughby!'

'It will be you!'

She tried to recall how this would have sung in her ears long back. Her bosom rose and fell in absolute dejection. Her ammunition of arguments against him had been expended overnight.

'You are so unforgiving,' she said.

'Is it I who am?'

'You do not know me.'

'But you are the woman of all the world who knows *me*, Laetitia.'

'Can you think it better for you to be known?'

He was about to say other words: he checked them. 'I believe I do not know myself. Anything you will, only give me your hand; give it; trust to me; you shall direct me. If I have faults, help me to obliterate them.'

'Will you not expect me to regard them as the virtues of meaner men?'

'You will be my wife!'

Laetitia broke from him, crying: 'Your wife, your critic! Oh, I cannot think it possible. Send for the ladies. Let them hear me.'

'They are at hand,' said Willoughby, opening the door.

They were in one of the upper rooms anxiously on the watch.

'Dear ladies,' Laetitia said to them, as they entered. 'I am going to wound you, and I grieve to do it: but rather now than later, if I am to be your housemate. He asks me for a hand that cannot carry a heart, because mine is dead. I repeat it. I used to think the heart a woman's marriage portion for her husband. I see now that she may consent, and he accept her, without one. But it is right that you should know what I am when I consent. I was once a foolish, romantic girl; now I am a sickly woman, all illusions vanished. Privation has made me what an abounding fortune usually makes of others – I am an Egoist. I am not deceiving you. That is my real character. My girl's view of him has entirely changed; and I am almost indifferent to the change. I can endeavour to respect him, I cannot venerate.'

'Dear child!' the ladies gently remonstrated.

Willoughby motioned to them.

'If we are to live together, and I could very happily live with you,' Laetitia continued to address them, 'you must not be ignorant of me. And if you, as I imagine, worship him blindly, I do not know how we are to live together. And never shall you quit this house to make way for me. I have a hard detective eye. I see many faults.'

'Have we not all of us faults, dear child?'

'Not such as he has; though the excuses of a gentleman nurtured in idolatry may be pleaded. But he should know that they are seen, and seen by her he asks to be his wife, that no misunderstanding may exist, and while it is yet time he may consult his feelings. He worships himself.'

'Willoughby?'

'He is vindictive.'

'Our Willoughby?'

'That is not your opinion, ladies. It is firmly mine. Time has taught it me. So, if you and I are at such variance, how can we live together? It is an impossibility.'

They looked at Willoughby. He nodded imperiously.

'We have never affirmed that our dear nephew is devoid of faults. If he is offended . . . And supposing he claims to be foremost, is it not his rightful claim, made good by much generosity? Reflect, dear Laetitia. We are your friends too.'

She could not chastise the kind ladies any further.

'You have always been my good friends.'

'And you have no other charge against him?'

Laetitia was milder in saying, 'He is unpardoning.'

'Name one instance, Laetitia.'

'He has turned Crossjay out of his house, interdicting the poor boy ever to enter it again.'

'Crossjay,' said Willoughby, 'was guilty of a piece of infamous treachery.'

'Which is the cause of your persecuting me to become your wife!'

There was a cry of 'Persecuting!'

'No young fellow behaving so basely can come to good,' said Willoughby, stained about the face with flecks of redness at the lashings he received.

'Honestly,' she retorted. 'He told of himself: and he must have anticipated the punishment he would meet. He should have been studying with a master for his profession. He has been kept here in comparative idleness to be alternately petted and discarded: no one but Vernon Whitford, a poor gentleman doomed to struggle for a livelihood by literature – I know something of that struggle – too much for me! – no one but Mr Whitford for his friend.'

'Crossjay is forgiven,' said Willoughby.

'You promise me that?'

'He shall be packed off to a crammer at once.'

'But my home must be Crossjay's home.'

'You are mistress of my house, Laetitia.'

She hesitated. Her eyelashes grew moist. 'You can be generous.'

'He is, dear child!' the ladies cried. 'He is. Forget his errors, in his generosity, as we do.'

'There is that wretched man Flitch.'

'That sot has gone about the county for years to get me a bad character,' said Willoughby.

'It would have been generous in you to have offered him another chance. He has children.'

'Nine. And I am responsible for them?'

'I speak of being generous.'

'Dictate.' Willoughby spread out his arms.

'Surely now you should be satisfied, Laetitia?' said the ladies.

'Is *he*?'

Willoughby perceived Mrs Mountstuart's carriage coming down the avenue.

'To the full.' He presented his hand.

She raised hers with the fingers catching back before she ceased to speak and dropped it: –

'Ladies. You are witnesses that there is no concealment, there has been no reserve, on my part. May Heaven grant me kinder eyes than I have now. I would not have you change your opinion of him; only that you should see how I read him. For the rest, I vow to do my duty by him. Whatever is of worth in me is at his service. I am very tired. I feel I must yield or break. This is his wish, and I submit.'

'And I salute my wife,' said Willoughby, making her hand his own, and warming to his possession as he performed the act.

Mrs Mountstuart's indecent hurry to be at the Hall before the departure of Dr Middleton and his daughter, afflicted him with visions of the physical contrast which would be sharply perceptible to her this morning of his Laetitia beside Clara.

But he had the lady with brains! He had: and he was to learn the nature of that possession in the woman who is our wife.

CHAPTER 50

✕✕✕✕

Upon Which the Curtain Falls

'PLAIN sense upon the marriage question is my demand upon man and woman, for the stopping of many a tragedy.'

These were Dr Middleton's words in reply to Willoughby's brief explanation.

He did not say that he had shown it parentally while the tragedy was threatening, or at least there was danger of a precipitate descent from the levels of comedy. The parents of hymeneal men and women he was indisposed to consider as dramatis personae. Nor did he mention certain sympathetic regrets he entertained in contemplation of the health of Mr Dale, for whom, poor gentleman, the proffer of a bottle of the Patterne Port would be an egregious mockery. He paced about, anxious for his departure, and seeming better pleased with the society of Colonel De Craye than with that of any of the others. Colonel De Craye assiduously courted him, was anecdotal, deferential, charmingly vivacious, the very man the Rev. Doctor liked for company when plunged in the bustle of the preliminaries to a journey.

'You would be a cheerful travelling comrade, sir,' he remarked, and spoke of his doom to lead his daughter over the Alps and Alpine lakes for the Summer months.

Strange to tell, the Alps, for the Summer months, was a settled project of the colonel's.

And thence Dr. Middleton was to be hauled along to the habitable quarters of North Italy in high Summer-tide.

That also had been traced for a route on the map of Colonel De Craye.

'We are started in June, I am informed,' said Dr Middleton.

June, by miracle, was the month the colonel had fixed upon.

'I trust we shall meet, sir,' said he.

'I would gladly reckon it in my catalogue of pleasures,' the Rev. Doctor responded; 'for in good sooth it is conjecturable that I shall be left very much alone.'

'Paris, Strasburg, Basle?' the colonel inquired.

'The Lake of Constance, I am told,' said Dr Middleton.

Colonel De Craye spied eagerly for an opportunity of exchanging a pair of syllables with the third and fairest party of this glorious expedition to come.

Willoughby met him, and rewarded the colonel's frankness in stating that he was on the lookout for Miss Middleton to take his leave of her, by furnishing him the occasion. He conducted his friend Horace to the Blue Room, where Clara and Laetitia were seated circling a half embrace with a brook of chatter, and contrived an excuse for leading Laetitia forth. Some minutes later Mrs Mountstuart called aloud for the colonel, to drive him away. Willoughby, whose good offices were unabated by the services he performed to each in rotation, ushered her into the Blue Room, hearing her say, as she stood at the entrance: 'Is the man coming to spend a day with me with a face like that?'

She was met and detained by Clara.

De Craye came out.

'What are you thinking of?' said Willoughby.

'I was thinking,' said the colonel, 'of developing a heart, like you, and taking to think of others.'

'At last!'

'Ay, you're a true friend, Willoughby, a true friend. And a cousin to boot!'

'What! has Clara been communicative?'

'The itinerary of a voyage Miss Middleton is going to make.'

'Do you join them?'

'Why, it would be delightful, Willoughby, but it happens

I've got a lot of powder I want to let off, and so I've an idea of shouldering my gun along the sea-coast and shooting gulls: which'll be a harmless form of committing patricide and matricide and fratricide – for there's my family, and I come of it! – the gull! And I've to talk lively to Mrs Mountstuart for something like a matter of twelve hours, calculating that she goes to bed at midnight: and I wouldn't bet on it; such is the energy of ladies of that age!'

Willoughby scorned the man who could not conceal a blow, even though he joked over his discomfiture.

'Gull!' he muttered.

'A bird that's easy to be had, and better for stuffing than for eating,' said De Craye. 'You'll miss your cousin.'

'I have,' replied Willoughby, 'one fully equal to supplying his place.'

There was confusion in the hall for a time, and an assembly of the household to witness the departure of Dr Middleton and his daughter. Vernon had been driven off by Dr Corney, who further recommended rest for Mr Dale, and promised to keep an eye for Crossjay along the road.

'I think you will find him at the station, and if you do, command him to come straight back here,' Laetitia said to Clara.

The answer was an affectionate squeeze, and Clara's hand was extended to Willoughby, who bowed over it with perfect courtesy, bidding her adieu.

So the knot was cut. And the next carriage to Dr Middleton's was Mrs Mountstuart's, conveying the great lady and Colonel De Craye.

'I beg you not to wear that face with me,' she said to him. 'I have had to dissemble, which I hate, and I have quite enough to endure, and I must be amused, or I shall run away from you and enlist that little countryman of yours, and him I can count on to be professionally restorative. Who can fathom the heart of a girl! Here is Lady Busshe right once more! And I was wrong. She must be a gambler by nature. I never should have risked such a guess as that. Colonel De

Craye, you lengthen your face preternaturally, you distort it purposely.'

'Ma'am,' returned De Craye, 'the boast of our army is never to know when we are beaten, and that tells of a great-hearted soldiery. But there's a field where the Briton must own his defeat, whether smiling or crying, and I'm not so sure that a short howl doesn't do him honour.'

'She was, I am certain, in love with Vernon Whitford all along, Colonel De Craye!'

'Ah!' the colonel drank it in. 'I have learnt that it was not the gentleman in whom I am chiefly interested. So it was not so hard for the lady to vow to friend Willoughby she would marry no one else?'

'Girls are unfathomable! And Lady Busshe – I know she did not go by character – shot one of her random guesses, and she triumphs. We shall never hear the last of it. And I had all the opportunities. I'm bound to confess I had.'

'Did you by chance, ma'am,' De Craye said, with a twinkle, 'drop a hint to Willoughby of her turn for Vernon Whitford?'

'No,' said Mrs Mountstuart, 'I'm not a mischief-maker; and the policy of the county is to keep him in love with himself, or Patterne will be likely to be as dull as it was without a lady enthroned. When his pride is at ease he is a prince. I can read men. Now, Colonel De Craye, pray, be lively.'

'I should have been livelier, I'm afraid, if you had dropped a bit of a hint to Willoughby. But you're the magnanimous person, ma'am, and revenge for a stroke in the game of love shows us unworthy to win.'

Mrs Mountstuart menaced him with her parasol. 'I forbid sentiments, Colonel De Craye. They are always followed by sighs.'

'Grant me five minutes of inward retirement, and I'll come out formed for your commands, ma'am,' said he.

Before the termination of that space De Craye was enchanting Mrs Mountstuart, and she in consequence was restored to her natural wit.

So, and much so universally, the world of his dread and his unconscious worship wagged over Sir Willoughby Patterne and his change of brides, until the preparations for the festivities of the marriage flushed him in his county's eyes to something of the splendid glow he had worn on the great day of his majority. That was upon the season when two lovers met between the Swiss and Tyrol Alps over the Lake of Constance. Sitting beside them the Comic Muse is grave and sisterly. But taking a glance at the others of her late company of actors, she compresses her lips.

Notes

✕✕✕✕

1. (p. 43). *fresh from a Louis IV perruquier:* Though the phrase appears thus in all the editions authorized by Meredith, it seems clear that he means a 'Louis XIV perruquier'.

2. (p. 53). *the devotee of Juggernaut.* Here Meredith appears to be confusing Indian customs and, if we relate this to the later reference in the same paragraph to *a woman to be burned*, to be assuming that the rite of sati or suttee, the self-immolation of widows, was in some way connected with the worship of the deity Jagganath in his temple of Puri. There was no such connexion.

3. (p. 59). *lash terga cauda:* Lash his tail from side to side.

4. (p. 67). *her of Ephesus:* A reference to the celebrated tale told by Petronius, in the *Satyricon*, of the newly widowed Ephesian lady who was consoled by a sentry ordered to guard the crucified bodies of three criminals; during his amatory absence from duty, one of the bodies was taken away, and the widow obligingly gave the corpse of her husband to hang in its place and so save her lover from punishment.

5. (p. 81). *retro Sathanas:* Get thee behind me, Satan.

6. (p. 87). *father-in-law:* Stepfather; this usage continued throughout the nineteenth century, and in some districts survives colloquially.

7. (p. 105). *the glorious Valentine's day of our naval annals:* 14 February 1797, when Sir John Jarvis, in his flagship the *Captain*, defeated the Spanish fleet at the Battle of Cape St Vincent.

8. (p.) 109. *Flibbertigibbet:* An attendant fiend.

9. (p. 110). *Papa would quote the 'mulier formosa':* The reference is to the opening passage of the *Ars Poetica*, where Horace talks of 'a woman, beautiful to the waist, ending in the black tail of an ugly fish'.

10. (p. 116). *Busby:* Dr Richard Busby, a seventeenth-century headmaster of Westminster School and a notorious flogger.

11. (p. 124). *the wise king:* Solomon who, when two women disputed the parenthood of a child, proposed to cut the infant in two,

whereupon the real mother revealed herself by pleading for its life at the risk of losing it.

12. (p. 135). *a French philosopher:* Auguste Comte, the nineteenth-century founder of the philosophy of Positivism; Sir Willoughby is parodying his suggestion that the birthdays of benefactors of the human race (not necessarily French men of letters) should be celebrated in the calendar of his new humanitarian religion. At this time Meredith was closely associated with the English Positivists, including Frederic Harrison and especially Leslie Stephen, who gave some of his characteristics to the shaping of Vernon Whitford.

13. (p. 156). *Melusine:* A fairy or water-nymph of French legend, in nature half-woman and half-fish. She married Count Raymond de Poitiers who built Lusignan Castle for her; her condition was that Raymond should never visit her on a Saturday, but he broke his promise, Melusine turned into a serpent, and ever since that day her eerie cries are supposed to prelude the deaths of the lords of Lusignan.

14. (p. 225). *quid femina possit:* What a woman can do. From Virgil's *Aeneid*, Book V: 'Knowledge of what a woman can do in the madness of dishonoured love aroused uneasy forebodings in the Trojans' hearts.'

15. (p. 226). '*this the seat, this mournful gloom for that celestial light*': *Paradise Lost*, Book I, lines 242–5, which Dr Middleton somewhat condenses. The full version runs:

'Is this the region, this the soil, the clime,'
Said then the lost Archangel, 'this the seat
That we must change for Heaven? this mournful gloom
For that celestial light? . . .'

16. (p. 229). '*Factum est; laetus est; amantium irae, etc.*': 'It is done; he is happy; the quarrelling of lovers, etc.' The quotation from Terence which Dr Middleton leaves uncompleted continues '*amoris integratio est*' – 'is the renewal of love', and it is this unsaid passage that of course gives point to his remark.

17. (p. 237). *nugae:* Trifling jests.

18. (p. 239). *the Idaean Three:* The goddesses Aphrodite, Hera and Athene, who on Mount Ida submitted to the judgement of the

mortal Paris as to who was the most beautiful and hence worthy to receive at his hands the golden apple.

19. (p. 239). *Graiis ... praeter, laudem nullius avaris:* Horace, in the *Ars Poetica*, tells us that 'The Greeks ... coveted nothing beyond renown.' It is appropriate to Dr Middleton's ensuing remarks that Horace goes on to suggest the relative unworthiness of the Romans with their 'slavish love of money'.

20. (p. 244). '*Ut flos in septis secretus nascitur hortis ... Sic virgo, dum ...*': From Song LXII of the *Carmina* of Catullus: 'Like a flower springing secretly in an enclosed garden ... So a virgin ...' The whole passage, of which Meredith allows Dr Middleton to murmur five lines unreproduced, likens the Virgin to the flower protected and unplucked, and the last line, which the Doctor never completes, clearly mirrors his preoccupations at this time. '*Sic virgo, dum intacta manet, dum cara suis est ...*' 'So a virgin, while she is whole, while she is the darling of her kinsfolk ...'

21. (p. 253). *modus agri non ita magnus:* A piece of land, not very large. (Horace, *Satires,* II.vi.1.)

22. (p. 253). *Quae virtus et quanta sit rivere parvo:* How virtuous and how greatly so it is to live on little. (Horace, *Satires,* II.ii.1.)

23. (p. 284). *Lesbia Quadrantaria:* Lesbia was the name under which Catullus wrote his love poems to the profligate Clodia, a Roman lady whom Cicero called Quadrantaria, meaning roughly 'worth a farthing'; she is said to have sold herself for a quarter of the then much-debased Roman copper coin, the *as.*

24. (p. 292). *bile tumet jecur.* [My] liver swells with bile. (Horace, *Odes,* I.xiii.4.)

25. (p. 295). καὶ τρισκακοδαίμων: Triply unfortunate.

26. (p. 361). *Celtiberian Egnatius:* Catullus dedicates one of his Songs to the baiting of the Roman Egnatius. 'Egnatius, who has dazzlingly white teeth,' begins the poem, 'grins always and everywhere'. Lines 6 and 7, quoted by Dr Middleton, tell us that 'whatever happens, no matter where, no matter what he is doing, he always grins'. The Celtiberians were a native Spanish people with whom the Romans were often in conflict, and Catullus tells in vivid detail, which Meredith dared not reproduce for his Victorian readers, how they had white teeth and bright pink gums because each morning they vigorously scrubbed their teeth with their own urine.

27. (p. 366). *the Stagyrite:* Aristotle.

28. (p. 370). *Fridolin:* Countess Cunigond's page in Schiller's *Der Gang nach der Eisenhammer;* unjustly accused of making love to her, he incurs the enmity of the count, who orders that he be thrown into the furnace in a foundry, but, by a lucky chain of circumstance, his accuser is burnt instead.

29. (p. 467). *si brachia forte remisit:* If he has by chance relaxed his arms. *in pejus:* For the worse. The two fragments come from a passage in Virgil's *Georgics* (Book 1, lines 199–203), which run as follows:

> Sic omnia fatis
> In peius ruere ac retro sublapsa referri
> Non aliter quam qui adverso vix flumine lembum
> Remigiis subigit, si bracchia forte remisit,
> Atque illum in praeceps prono rapit alveus amni.

Dr Middleton roughly paraphrases the last three lines.

30. (p. 487). *Jam ver egelidos renfert repores. The equinoctial fury departs:* These are the first lines of the song in which Catullus celebrates his departure from Bithynia (*Carmina*, xlvi)

> Iam ver egelidos renfert repores,
> Iam caeli furor aequinoctialis
> Iocundis Zephyri silescit aureis.

'Now the spring brings back to us its mild airs, now the equinoctial fury of the heavens is calmed by the happy Zephyrs.'

31. (p. 495). *Lady Vauban:* The Seigneur de Vauban was the military engineer to Louis XIV, and one of the great fortification builders of all time; many of his works still stand in France.

32. (p. 518). *plangulcula:* The wax effigy used by a sorcerer.

33. (p. 518). *Optume:* Excellent. *ad rem:* To the point. *Firmavit fidem:* He has plighted his troth.

34. (p. 572). *Sir Cloudesley Shovel:* Sir Clowdesley Shovell (1650–1707) was long held up as one of the rare examples of high naval officers rising up from the ranks. A shoemaker's apprentice, he ran away to sea, took part in many of the great naval battles of the 1690s, assisted in the storming of Gibraltar in 1704, and in 1707 died when his ship foundered and sank with all hands off the Scilly Isles.

FOR THE BEST IN PAPERBACKS, LOOK FOR THE 🐧

In every corner of the world, on every subject under the sun, Penguin represents quality and variety – the very best in publishing today.

For complete information about books available from Penguin – including Puffins, Penguin Classics and Arkana – and how to order them, write to us at the appropriate address below. Please note that for copyright reasons the selection of books varies from country to country.

In the United Kingdom: Please write to *Dept E.P., Penguin Books Ltd, Harmondsworth, Middlesex, UB7 0DA.*

If you have any difficulty in obtaining a title, please send your order with the correct money, plus ten per cent for postage and packaging, to *PO Box No 11, West Drayton, Middlesex*

In the United States: Please write to *Dept BA, Penguin, 299 Murray Hill Parkway, East Rutherford, New Jersey 07073*

In Canada: Please write to *Penguin Books Canada Ltd, 2801 John Street, Markham, Ontario L3R 1B4*

In Australia: Please write to the *Marketing Department, Penguin Books Australia Ltd, P.O. Box 257, Ringwood, Victoria 3134*

In New Zealand: Please write to the *Marketing Department, Penguin Books (NZ) Ltd, Private Bag, Takapuna, Auckland 9*

In India: Please write to *Penguin Overseas Ltd, 706 Eros Apartments, 56 Nehru Place, New Delhi, 110019*

In the Netherlands: Please write to *Penguin Books Netherlands B.V., Postbus 195, NL–1380AD Weesp*

In West Germany: Please write to *Penguin Books Ltd, Friedrichstrasse 10–12, D–6000 Frankfurt/Main 1*

In Spain: Please write to *Longman Penguin España, Calle San Nicolas 15, E–28013 Madrid*

In Italy: Please write to *Penguin Italia s.r.l., Via Como 4, I-20096 Pioltello (Milano)*

In France: Please write to *Penguin Books Ltd, 39 Rue de Montmorency, F-75003 Paris*

In Japan: Please write to *Longman Penguin Japan Co Ltd, Yamaguchi Building, 2–12–9 Kanda Jimbocho, Chiyoda-Ku, Tokyo 101*